FORTRESS I[N

C.J. Cherryh is the aut[hor of
Rimrunners, among nu[merous] winner of the Hugo Award, she makes her home in Oklahoma, USA.

Voyager

C. J. CHERRYH

Fortress in the Eye of Time

HarperCollins*Publishers*

Voyager
An Imprint of HarperCollins*Publishers*
77–85 Fulham Palace Road,
Hammersmith, London W6 8JB

This paperback edition 1995
1 3 5 7 9 8 6 4 2

First published in Great Britain by
HarperCollins*Publishers* 1995

ISBN 0 00 648220 1

Set in Sabon

Printed in Great Britain by
HarperCollinsManufacturing Glasgow

For Lynn and Jane for a lot of hours ...
through the lightning strikes
and the rest of it

CHAPTER 1

~

Its name had been Galasien once, a city of broad streets and thriving markets, of docks crowded with bright-sailed river craft. The shrines of its gods and heroes, their altars asmoke with incense offerings, had watched over commerce and statecraft, lords and ladies, workmen and peasant farmers alike, in long and pleasant prosperity.

Its name under the Sihhë lords had been Ynefel. For nine centuries four towers reigned here under that name as the forest crept closer. The one-time citadel of the Galasieni in those years stood no longer as the heart of a city, but as a ruin-girt keep, stronghold of the foreign Sihhë kings, under whom the river Lenúalim's shores had known a rule of unprecedented and far-reaching power, a darker reign from its beginning, and darker still in its calamity.

Now forest thrust up the stones of old streets. Whin and blackberry choked the standing walls of the old Galasieni ruins, blackberry that fed the birds that haunted the high towers. Old forest, dark forest, of oaks long grown and sapped by mistletoe and vines, ringed the last standing towers of Ynefel on every side but riverward.

Through that forest now came only the memory of a road, which crossed a broken-down, often-patched ghost of a bridge. The Lenúalim, which ran murkily about the mossy, eroded stonework of the one-time wharves, carried only flotsam from its occasional floods. Kingdoms of a third and younger age thrived on the northern and southern reaches of the Lenúalim, but rarely did the men of those young lands find cause to venture into this haunted place. South of those lands lay the sea, while northward at the source of the Lenúalim, lay the oldest lands of all, lands of legendary origin for the vanished Galasieni as well as for the Sihhë: the

1

Shadow Hills, the brooding peaks of the Hafsandyr, the lands of the legendary Arachim and the wide wastes where ice never gave up its hold.

Such places still existed, perhaps. But no black-sailed ships from the north came in this third age, and the docks of Ynefel had long since gone to tumbled stone, stones slick with moss, buried in mud, overgrown with trees, indistinguishable at last from the forest.

Call it Galasien, or Ynefel, it had become a shadow-place from a shadow-age, its crumbling, weathered towers poised on the rock that had once been the base of a great citadel. The seat of power for two ages of wizardry had become, in the present reign of men, a place of curious, disturbing fancies. Ynefel, tree-drowned in its sea of forest, was the last or the first outpost of the Old Lands . . . first, as one stood with his face to the West, where the sea lords of old had fallen and new kings ruled, so soon forgetful that they had been servants of the Sihhë; or the last edge of an older world, as one might look out north and east toward Elwynor and Amefel, which lay across the Lenúalim's windings and beyond Marna Wood.

In those two districts alone of the East the crumbling hills retained their old Galasieni names. In those lands of upstart men, there remained, however few and remote in the hills, country shrines to the Nineteen gods Galasien had known – while in Elwynor the rulers still called themselves Regents, remembering the Sihhë kings.

Nowadays in Ynefel birds stole blackberries, and built their nests haphazardly in the eaves and in the loft. A colony of swifts lodged in one great chimney and another in the vaulted hall of Sihhë kings. Rain and years eroded the strange faces that looked out of the remaining walls. Gargoyle faces – faces of heroes, faces of the common and the mighty of lost Galasien – they adorned its crazily joined towers, its ramshackle gates, fragments of statues seeming by curious whimsy to gaze out of the walls of the present fortress: some that smiled, some that seemed to smirk in malice, and some, the faces of Galasien's vanished kings, serene and blind.

2

This was the view as one looked up from the walls of Ynefel.

This was the view over which an old man gazed: this was the state of affairs in which he lived, bearded and bent, and solitary.

And, judging the portent of the season and the clouds, leaden-gray at twilight, the old man frowned and took his way in some haste down the rickety steps, well aware of danger in the later hours, in the creeping of Shadows across the many gables and roofs. He did not further tempt them. Age was on him. His power, which had held the years and the Shadows at bay, was fading, and would fade more swiftly still when this night's work was done: such strength as he had, he held close within himself, and guarded, and hoarded with a miser's single purpose.

Until now.

He reached the door and shut it with a Word, a tap of his staff, a touch of his gnarled hand. Thus secure, he caught a calmer breath, and descended the steeply winding stairs with a limp and a tapping that echoed through the creaking maze of stairs and balconies, down and down into the wooden hollowness of Ynefel.

He lived alone here. He had lived alone for – he ceased to count the years, except tonight, when death seemed so close, so . . . seductive in the face of his preparations.

Better, he had long thought, to fade quietly.

Better, he had determined unto himself, to deal no more with the Shadows and to stay to the sunlight. Better to listen no more to the sifting of time through the wood and stone of this old ruin. He owed nothing to the future. He owed far less to the past.

We deserved our fate, he thought bitterly. We were too self-confident. And not virtuous, no, none of us virtuous. So it was fit that, in the end of everything, we killed each other.

Fit, as well, that we were neither thorough nor resolute, even in that extreme moment. To every truth we found exception; to every answer, another question. We doubted everything. We abhorred the demon in ourselves and doubted our own abhorrence.

3

And, inappropriate to the end, we linger. We cannot believe even in our own calamity.

Tapping of a knobbed and crooked staff, creaking of age-hollowed wooden steps – brought echoes, down and down to the foot of those steps, to the cluttered study in the heart of the fortress. There was sound in Ynefel, until he stopped, in the heart of his preparations.

There was living breath in this room, until he held his.

Always the gnawing doubt. Never peace. Never certainty.

There was even yet a chance for him to fare northward on the Road, to evade Elwynor and seek the Old Kingdoms that might, remotely might, remain alive in Hafsandyr. To walk so long and so far his aging strength might still suffice, or if it failed, in what innocence remained to an old wizard, he might lie down by that Road in the rains and the wind and sleep until life faded.

It would be a way to his own peace, perhaps, the ending his kind had never found the courage to make.

But he was Galasieni. He had not the resolve to believe even in his own death – and this was both the bane and the source of his power. He was of the Old Magic, and had no use for nowadays' healers and wisewomen and petty warlocks with their small, illusory magics, least of all for the diviners and the searchers into old lore who wanted to lay hold of magics they could not imagine. Oh, illusions he could make. Illusions and glamors he could cast. But no illusions, now, would he work, as he squatted by the fire. He needed no books, no grammaries, nothing but the essence of his power.

He needed no fire. The air would have done as well.

But his hands reached into the substance of the heat, tugged at the very fabric of the flame and drew out strands that spun and rose in the remaining light. The strands drew upon the air, and drew on the stone of the walls and the age of the trees that made the dusty timbers of Ynefel: they built themselves, and wove themselves, and became . . . a possibility.

Only one man had reached this skill, only one, in the age of the Old Kingdoms.

4

A second had reached for it, at the dawn of the Sihhë.

A third attempted it, this night. His name was Mauryl Gestaurien. And the magic he wrought was not a way to peace.

That, too, was characteristic of his kind.

He spoke a Word. He stared into a point in the charged insubstance of the air, tinier than a mote of dust. He was at that moment aware of the whole mass of stone around the room, aware of the Shadows among the gables, that insinuated threads into cracks and crevices of shutters, that crept among the rafters, seeking toward his study. He drew the light in Ynefel inward, until it was only in this room.

In that moment, Shadows edged under the doors and ran along the masonry joints of the walls. Shadows found their way down the chimney hole, and the fire shrank.

In that moment a wind began to blow, and Shadows jumped and capered about the rafters above the study, and seeped down the chimney like soot.

Came a mote of dust, catching the light, just that small, just that substantial, and no more.

Came a sparkle in that mote, that became a light like the uncertain moon, like the reflection of a star.

Came a creaking of all the ill-set timbers of the keep at once, and a fast fluttering of shadows that made the faces set into the walls seem to shift expression and open their mouths in dread.

Came a sifting of dust of the walls and dust from the wooden ceiling and the stone vault; and the dust fell on that point of light, and sparkled.

A gust of wind blasted down the chimney throat, blew fire and cinders into the room. Shadows clawed at the stones and reached for the spark in the whirl of dust.

But the spark became a sudden crack of lightning, whitening the gray stone of the walls, drinking the feeble glow of the fire into shocked remembrance of bright threads weaving, turning and knotting and coming apart again.

Mauryl groaned as the scattered elements resisted. He

doubted. At the last moment – he attempted exception, equivocation, revision of what he reached for.

On the brink of failure – snatched, desperately, instead, after simple life.

A shadow grew in the heart of the twisting threads, the shadow of a man, as the light faded . . . shadow that grew substantial and became living flesh and bone, the form of a young man naked and beautiful in the ordinary grayness of an untidy room.

The young man's nostrils drew in a breath. His eyes opened. They were gray as the stone, serene as the silence.

Mauryl shook with his effort, with the triumph of his magic . . .

Trembled, in doubt of all his work, all his skill, all his wisdom . . . now that done was done and it stood before him.

The light was gone, except the fire tamely burning in the hearth, amid a blasted scatter of chimney ash across the stones. Mauryl stretched out his hand, leaning on his staff with the other, the room gone close and breathless to him, light leaping in ordinary shadow about the clutter of parchments and birds' wings, alembics and herb-bundles.

Mauryl beckoned, crooked a finger, the one hand trembling violently, the other clenched on his staff. He beckoned a second time, impatiently, angrily, fearing catastrophe, commanding obedience.

Slowly the youth moved, a tentative step, a second, a third.

Alarmed, Mauryl raised the knobbed staff like a barrier, and the advance ceased. He stared into gray, quiet eyes and judged carefully, conservatively, before he lowered that ward and leaned on his staff with both arthritic hands, out of strength, out of resources.

The Shadows lurked still in the corners of the study, moving quietly in the gusting of wind down the chimney. Thunder muttered from an outraged and ominous heaven.

The young man stood still and, absent the focus offered him by the lifted staff, gazed about his surroundings: the hall, the cobwebby labyrinth of beams and wooden stairs and balconies above balconies above balconies . . . the cabinets and tables and disarray of parchments and oddments of dead animals and leaves. Nothing in particular seemed to stay his eye or beg his attention: all things perhaps were inconsequential to him, or all things were equally important and amazing; his expression gave no hint which. He put a hand to his own heart and looked down at his naked body, which still seemed to glow with light like candleflame through wax. He flexed the fingers of that hand and watched, seemingly entranced, the movement of the tendons under his flesh, as if that was the greatest, the most inexplicable magic of all.

Dazed, Mauryl said to himself, and took courage then, though shakily, to proceed on his judgment. He came close enough to touch, to meet the gray, wonder-filled stare of a fearsome innocence. "Come," he said to the Shaping, offering his hand. "Come," he ordered the second time, and prepared to say again, sternly, in the case, as with some things dreadful and unruly, three callings might prove the charm.

But the youth moved another step, and, feeling increasingly the weakness in his own knees, Mauryl led the Shaping over to sit on the bench by the fireside, sweeping aside with his staff a stack of dusty parchments, some of which slid into the fire.

The Shaping reached after the calamity of parchments. Mauryl caught the reaching arm short of the fire. Parchment burned, with smoke and a stench and a scattering of pieces on an upward waft of wind, and the Shaping watched that rise of sparks, rapt in that brightness, but in no wise resisting or showing other, deeper thought.

Mauryl braced his staff between himself and an irregularity of the hearthstones, whisked off his own cloak and settled it about the boy, who at that instant had leaned forward on the bench, the firelight a-dance on his eyes, his hand . . .

"No!" Mauryl cried, and struck at his outreaching fingers. The youth looked at him in astonished hurt as the cloak slipped unnoticed to the floor.

A dread settled on Mauryl, then . . . in denial of which he set the cloak again about the youth's shoulders, tucked its folds into unresisting, uncooperative fingers. To his vexation, he had even to close the young man's hand to hold it.

"Boy." Mauryl sat down at arm's length from him on the bench and, seizing the folds of the cloak in either hand, compelled the youth to face about and look him full in the eyes. "Boy, do you understand me? Do you?"

The youth blinked. The dip of his head that followed might have been a nod of acceptance.

Or an avoidance – as the gaze skittered aside to the fire.

Mauryl put out a hand, turned the face toward him perforce. "Boy, do you recall, do you remember . . . anything?"

Another redirection, a blink, an eclipse of gray eyes, blank and bare as a misty morning. It might have been confirmation. It might equally well have been feckless bewilderment.

"A place?" Mauryl asked. "A name?"

"Light." The youth's voice began as a breath and grew stronger. "A voice."

"No more?"

The youth shook his head, eyes solemnly fixed on his the while. Mauryl's shoulders sagged. His very bones ached with loss.

The eyes still waited for him, still held not the slightest comprehension, and Mauryl drew a breath, thought of one thing to say, that was bitter, and changed it to another, that accepted all he had.

"Tristen. Tristen is your name, boy. That name I give you. That name I call you. To that name you must answer. By that name I compel you to answer. My name is Mauryl. By that name you will call me. And I do need you, I do most desperately need you – Tristen."

The gray eyes held . . . perhaps a spark of life, of further, dawning question. Mauryl let go the cloak, stared at the boy as the boy stared at him, open to the depths, utterly naked, with or without the cloak.

"Have you," Mauryl asked, "no thought of your own? Have you no question? Do you *feel*, Tristen? Do you feel at all? Do you want? Do you desire? Do you *think* of anything?"

8

For a moment the lips looked as if they might frame a thought. The brow acquired the least small frown, but nothing . . . nothing followed.

In the collapse of hope, Mauryl snatched his hand away, slid aside from the boy, fumbled after the staff that, rebel object, slid away from his hand away the wall.

Arm reached. Young fist closed on the ancient wood, flesh and bone certain as youth, quick as thought. Mauryl caught a breath, put out an insistent and demanding hand and clenched it on the staff, fearful of the omen.

He tugged gently, all the same, and the youth yielded the staff back to his grip, seeming as confused as before.

"You reflect," Mauryl said, holding his staff protected in his arms, regarding the Shaping with despair, "you only reflect, like still water. I was much too cautious. I restrained what I called, and it crippled you, poor boy. You've nothing, *nothing* of what I want."

There was no response at all but acute distress, mirrored maddeningly back at him. Mauryl turned his face from the sight, and for a moment there was silence in the hall.

A whisper of the cloak lining warned him, and the movement of a bare arm toward the fire . . . Tristen reached, and in a fit of anger Mauryl grasped the hand, hard.

"No. *No*, you witling! Do you at all understand pain? Fire burns. Water drowns. Wind chills you." He shoved the young man, he flung him from the bench, scattered embers as the boy fell, his hand against the fire-bricks.

The boy cried out, recoiled, made a crouched knot of pain, rocking like a child, while smoke went up about the cloak edge that lay smoldering within the fire.

"Fool!" Mauryl shouted in rage, and snatched the boy away from the leap of fire, stepped on the hem of his own robe and, betrayed in balance, clenched his arms about the youth to save himself as he fell to his knees.

Young arms clenched about his frail bones, young strength hugged tight, young body trembled as his trembled, in a stench of smoking cloth, a burning pain where a cinder

9

burned his shin. His own arms locked. He had no power to let go. The boy had no will to. That was the way they were, creator and creature, for the space of breath and breath and breath.

Maybe it was pain that brought water seeping from beneath his tight-shut lids. Maybe it was some motion of the heart so long ago lost he had forgotten what it was, after so long without a living, breathing presence but himself.

Maybe it was even remorse. That . . . was much longer lost.

Undo what I have done? Unmake this Shaping?

I might have strength enough. But it would finish me.

The boy grew quiet in his arms. The stray ember had branded his shin and quenched itself in singed cloth. The pain of the burning and the pain of everything lost became one thing, as if it had always been, as if there had been, in all his planning and preparation, no choice at all. It was foolish for an old man to sit on the floor in the ash and cinders, it was foolish for him to cling to a hope – most foolish of all, perhaps, for him to plan beyond so signal and absolute a failure.

With gnarled fingers, he lifted the boy's face. The tears had ceased, leaving reddened eyes, reddened nose. The face was no longer quite smooth. Something had been written there. The eyes were no longer blank. Awareness flickered, lively though pained, within that gray and open gaze.

There was before and after, now. There was then and now.

There was time to come. There was question and there was need, aching need, for some order in remembrance.

"I know," Mauryl said, "I know, a rude welcome – and you have everything to learn, everything to find." He lifted the boy's hand, passed his thumb over the reddened palm, working a small, soothing illusion. "The hurt is gone now, is it not?"

Tristen blinked. Tears spilled, mere aftermath. Tristen looked down, rubbing pale, smooth fingertips against each other.

"It will mend," Mauryl said, and felt with only mild foreboding – perhaps a fey, wicked magic lingered – a net settling over the net-caster as well. All his anger was pointless against the youth, all his long solitude was helpless against the spell of warm arms, the quickening . . . not of understanding, but of youthful expectations; the centering of them – on an old man long past answering his own. But he told the lie. He said in an unused, gruff voice, a second time, because the sound of it was strange to him, "It will mend, boy." He reached for his fallen staff, he struggled with it to bring his aching knees to bear, and stumbled his way to his feet.

Tristen also stood up – and let slide the singed cloak, as if such things in no wise mattered.

Mauryl smothered anger, caught the robe with his staff, patiently adjusted it again about the boy's bare shoulders. Tristen held it and moved away, his attention drawn by something else, the gods knew what – perhaps the clutter of vessels and hanging bunches of herbs in the room beyond.

"Stop!" Mauryl snapped, and Tristen halted and looked back, all unwitting.

Mauryl reached his side and with his staff tapped the single step to draw his attention downward, to the hazard he had never looked down to see.

"Tristen," he said, "now and forever remember: you are flesh as well as wishes, body as well as spirit, and whenever you let one fly without the other, then look to suffer for it. Do you understand me, Tristen?"

"Yes," Tristen said faintly. Tears welled up again, as if the rebuke and the burning were of equal pain.

"Tristen, thou –"

He discovered something long lost, long ago relinquished, and it swelled larger and larger in his heart until his heart seemed about to burst with pain. He tried to laugh, instead, who had neither wept nor laughed since . . . since some forgotten change, some gradual slipping away of the inclination. He made a sound, he hardly knew of what sort, knew not what to do next, and cleared his throat, instead – which left a silence, and the young man still staring at him. In the absence of all understanding, he put out a hand and wiped an unresisting face.

11

"An unwritten tablet, are you not? And a perilous, perilous one to write. But write I shall. And learn you will. Do you say so, Tristen?"

"Yes," the boy said, tears gone, or forgotten, cloud passed. There was tremulous expectation, as if learning should happen now, at once, in a breath.

And perhaps it should. Perhaps he dared not wait so long as a night.

"Come sit at the table," he said. "No, no, gods, thou silly, hold the cloak, mind your feet . . . " Calamity was a constant step away: unsteadiness threatened at every odd set of time-worn stones, so age must take the hand of youth, infirmity must guide strength that went wit-wandering in the search for a fallen cloak – and dropped the cloak again in utter startlement as a chair leg scraped across the stones.

Age found itself hungry, then, and warmed yesterday's supper in the pot. Shadows lurked and flickered about the edges of the room. The thunder of a passing rain wandered away above the roof. But such things the Shaping more easily ignored, perhaps as a natural part of the world.

Waiting, between his stirrings of the iron pot, he came back to the table, where the youth hung on every word he offered, eyes fixed with rapt attention on him when he spoke – though gods knew how many bits and pieces of that flotsam a foolish boy could store away, or how he understood them at all.

He poured ale, that being the best he had. The youth first tasted it with a grimace and a puzzlement. He served yesterday's beans – and the youth ate with a child's grasp of the spoon, then, with the bowl unfinished, upon one cup to drink, fell quite sound asleep, head propped against his hand.

Mauryl took the spoon away, took the bowl, moved the arm, left him sleeping with his forehead pillowed on his arm on the tabletop, wrapped in an ill-pinned cloak.

It was a minuscule beginning of wizardry. Mauryl stood, hugging his staff, asking himself in a small fluttering of despair what he had done and what he was to do to mend it.

Wrap a blanket about the boy, he supposed, condemned,

now, to simple, workaday practicalities. Ale had done its work. Magic had done what it could, and flesh and bone slumbered at peace, stirring forgotten sentiment in a wizard who had nothing to gain by it . . . nothing at all to gain, and all the world to lose.

CHAPTER 2

❧

Spatters of rain on the dust.

Trees whispering and nodding and giving up leaves, twigs sent flying. Smell of stone, smell of bruised leaves, smell of lightnings and rain-washed air.

Taste of water. Chill of wind. Flash of lightning that hurt the eyes. Boom of thunder that shook heart and bone.

It was like too much ale. Like too much to eat. Like too much heat and too much cold. Everything was patterns, shapes, sounds, light, dark, soft, sharp, rough, smooth, stone-cold, life-warm, and all too much to own and hold at once. Sometimes he could hardly move, the flood of the bright world was so much and so quick.

Tristen stood on the stone parapet, watched the lightning flashes fade the woods and sky and watched the trees below the wall bow their heads against the stone. Thunder rumbled. Rain swept in gray curtains against the tower, spattered the surface of the puddles and cascaded in streams off the slate of the many roofs. Tristen laughed and breathed the rain-drenched wind, raised hands and face to catch the pelting drops. They stung his palms and eyelids, so he dared not look at them. Rain coursed, cold and strange sensation, over his naked body, finding hollows and new courses, all to the shape of him.

It was delight. He looked at his bare feet, wiggled his toes in puddles that built in the low places of the stonework and made channels between the stones in the high places. Water made all the dusty gray stonework new and shiny. Rain made slanting veils across the straight fall off the eaves and played music beneath the thunder-rumble. Tristen spun on the slick stones and slipped, recovering himself against the low wall of the parapet and laughing in surprise as he saw, below him, where the gutters made a veritable flood, brown water, where the rain was gray. A green leaf was stuck to the gray stone. He wondered why it stayed there.

"*Tristen!*"

He straightened back from his headlong dangle, arm lingering to brace himself on the stone edge as he looked toward Mauryl's angry voice. He blinked water from his eyes, saw Mauryl's brown-robed figure. Mauryl's clothes were soaked through, Mauryl's gray hair and beard were streaming water, and Mauryl's eyes beneath his dripping brows were blue and pale and furious as Mauryl came to seize him by the arm.

He had clearly done something wrong. He tried to cipher what that wrong thing was as Mauryl took him from the wall. Mauryl was hurting his arm, and he resisted the pull, only enough to keep Mauryl's fingers from bruising.

"Come along," Mauryl said, and held the harder, so he thought saving his arm was wrong, too. He let Mauryl hurt him as he hurried him back along the parapet, Mauryl's black boots and his bare feet splashing through the puddles. Mauryl's robes dripped water. Mauryl's hair made curling ropes and water dripped off the ends. Mauryl's shoulders were thin and the cloth stuck to him and flapped about his legs and leather boots. The staff struck *crack, crack-crack* against the pavings, but Mauryl hardly limped, he was in such an angry hurry.

Mauryl took him to the rain-washed door, shoved up the outside latch with the knob of his staff, and drew him roughly inside into the little, stone-floored room. Light came only through the yellowed horn panes, storm-dimmed and strange, and the rain was far quieter here.

Mauryl let go his arm, then, still angry with him. "Where are your clothes?"

Was that the mistake? Tristen wondered, and said, "Downstairs. In my room."

"Downstairs. Downstairs! What good do they do you downstairs?"

He was completely bewildered. It seemed to him that Mauryl had said not to spoil them. Mauryl's were dripping wet. So were Mauryl's boots, and his were downstairs, dry. It had seemed very good sense to him, and still did, except Mauryl lifted his hand in anger and he flinched.

Mauryl reached for his shoulder, instead, and shook him, deciding, he hoped, not to hit him. Mauryl would indeed strike him, sometimes when Mauryl was angry, at other times Mauryl said he had to remember. It was hard to tell, sometimes, which was which, except Mauryl would seem satisfied after the latter and far angrier than he had started after the former, so he wished Mauryl had simply hit him and told him to remember.

Instead, Mauryl beckoned him to the wooden stairs, and led him down and down the rickety steps. The soaked hem of Mauryl's robe made a trail of rain drops on the wood, in the wan, sad light from the horn panes set along the way.

Clump, tap, clump, tap, clump-tap, downward and down. Tristen's bare feet made far less sound on the smooth, dusty boards. He supposed rain didn't spoil the clothes after all, and that he had guessed wrong. The water on the dust beneath his feet felt smooth and strange. He wasn't sorry to feel it. But he supposed he was wrong.

And confirming it, when Mauryl reached the walkway that led to his room, Mauryl banged his staff angrily on the floor. His robe shook off more drops and made a puddle on the boards.

"Go clothe yourself. Come down to the hall when you've done. I want to talk to you."

Tristen bowed his head and went to his own room, where he had left his clothes on his bed. The puddles he left on the board floor showed faintly in the light from the unshuttered horn panes. His hair streamed water down his back and down his shoulders and dripped in his eyes. He wiped it back and tried to squeeze the water out. It made dark tangles on his shoulders, and his clothes stuck to his body and resisted his pulling them on. So did the boots. His hair soaked the

16

shoulders of his shirt, and he combed the tangles out, to look as presentable as he could.

Maybe Mauryl would forget. Maybe Mauryl would forget he had asked him to come downstairs and tell him to go away. Sometimes Mauryl would, when he was lost in his books.

The thunder was still booming and talking above their heads, and the water was still running down the horn panes – the horn was yellowed and sometimes brown: it had curious circles and layers and fitted together with metal pieces. The horn colored the light it let in, and the shadow of raindrops crawled down its face, which he loved to see. A puddle had formed on the sill, where a joint in the horn let raindrops inside. Sometimes he made patterns with the water on the stone. Sometimes he let it stand until it spilled down off the sill and he waited and waited for the moment.

But he was cold now, and with his hair making his shoulders wet, he began to be cold all over. He took his cloak from the peg and slung it about his shoulders, hugged it about him as he went out into the wooden hall and clumped down the wooden steps, down and down to the study, making echoes that Mauryl couldn't help but notice. He was here. He was obeying, as Mauryl said.

Mauryl was standing by the fire. Mauryl had changed his clothes and wrapped himself in his cloak, too. Mauryl's hair had begun to dry, a silver net around his ears, not combed, and Mauryl had his arms folded, so he looked like a bird puffed up in its feathers, cold and cross.

"Sir," he said. Mauryl seemed not to notice him. He waited what seemed a long while for Mauryl to look at him, and wondered if Mauryl would after all forget he was angry. Or change his mind.

Then abruptly, fiercely, Mauryl turned his shoulder to the fire and looked him over, head to foot and back again, searching, perhaps, for another disappointment – disappointment was in the set of Mauryl's shoulders. Fault was in that stare. Tristen stood, hands clasped before him, downhearted, too, that he had so failed Mauryl's expectations.

Again.

His feet were numb with cold. He bent his toes in his boots, deciding he deserved to be cold, and maybe he could have fallen off the wall, but he did look where he was putting his feet, he truly did. Or he was quick enough to stop himself. He remembered slipping. He stood very respectfully in the archway, awaiting invitation to approach the fire, wondering if he should tell Mauryl how he'd saved himself.

He thought not, in Mauryl's current displeasure.

"I cannot begin," Mauryl said slowly, "cannot *begin* to foresee the things you invent to do. From waking to sleeping, from one moment to the next, boy, what will you do next?"

"I don't know, Mauryl. I haven't thought of that."

"Can you not think of consequences, Tristen?"

"I try," he said faintly. "I tried, master Mauryl, I did try to think."

"You great –" – fool, he thought Mauryl was about to say. But Mauryl shook his head, and hugged his arms about himself, cold, too, Tristen decided. Mauryl on his own, without the necessity of bringing him inside, didn't want to be cold, or dripping wet. So Mauryl hadn't noticed the wonder of the rain or seen the veils blow along the walls. Perhaps if he explained . . .

"The rain made curtains," he said. "The air smelled different. I went up to feel it."

"And the lightning could strike you Dead. *Dead,* do you hear?"

"Dead," he said. Sometimes Mauryl spoke Words he could hear and meanings came to him. This one did, with a shock of cold: Dead was a dark room with no candle, no floor, no wall, no ceiling. It drank his warmth, and wrapped him in, and took his breath. He couldn't get another. Then he found himself sitting on the floor across the room, and the fire crackling with more than usual sound in the hearth next to him. He saw the light on the stones and it proved he could see, it proved there was warmth.

He had blinked and he was here by the fireside, and

Mauryl was squatting in front of him, touching his face with a hand worn as smooth as the stones and the dusty boards, a hand as gentle as Mauryl's hand could be, sometimes, for reasons as strange as Mauryl's angers.

"Boy," Mauryl said, as if he were sleeping in his bed and Mauryl were telling him to wake up. "Tristen." Mauryl touched his cheek, traced the line of it, brushed his wet hair back behind his shoulder. The stone under him was warm from the fire. He didn't know why he was sitting there, but it seemed Mauryl had again said a Word, one of the soundless ones.

He had been standing in the rain, watching the lightnings flash. Mauryl had said lightning could strike him dead, but Mauryl had said a Word and sent him to that dark place. Then another Word had brought him back here to the fireside. Nothing so remote as lightning would have harmed him. It was Mauryl – only Mauryl he had to fear.

And to obey, *not* to make Mauryl angry again.

Thunder cracked, and he jumped, overwhelmed afterward with a shiver, hugging his knees against him until Mauryl pried one hand loose, clenched it in his, and wished him to stand up; but he was shivering too much of a sudden to straighten his legs. Thunder boomed out again above the towers and shocked the breath out of him, but Mauryl kept pulling at him until he found the strength at least to get his knee under him.

Then, clumsily, helping Mauryl, too, he could gain his feet and unwind himself out of the tangle of his cloak. But it was Mauryl who found him a place to go, taking him as far as the bench beside the fire and making him sit down, when he had no such wit left in him. Mauryl sat down by him and took his hand in his lap, clenched it tight, tight, while somewhere in the heights above them something suddenly banged.

He looked up, heart pounding in his chest.

"Only a shutter loose," Mauryl said, holding his hand. "Only the wind blowing it. Foolish boy, look at me." Mauryl caught his shoulders and, when a further crash distracted him, took his face between his hands, compelling his attention.

He shivered, teeth all but chattering, while the wind banged and hammered to get inside the towers, but Mauryl's eyes claimed his, Mauryl's whisper was more present than the thunder.

"Listen, boy. Listen to me. It's an empty wind. It's only rain. There are hazards in the storm, and you run such dreadful risks, boy, but not all in the storm. Be afraid of the dark. When the sky shadows, always be under stone, and always have the shutters closed, and the doors well shut. Have I not said this before?"

His teeth did chatter. "I took off my clothes," he said, deciding perhaps he had done that matter right. "I'm sorry yours got wet. I'm sorry you had to come into the rain."

He wasn't right. He hadn't understood. Mauryl's look said so.

"You were *Naked*," Mauryl said, and that Word came to him, and he felt Mauryl's keen disappointment in his mistakes.

The wind hammered and banged at the tower. The whole world was angry and dark, and confounded by him, who blundered clumsily from mistake to foolishness and back again to everything that made Mauryl angry with him. He wished again that Mauryl would hit him and be done. He didn't want more such Words, just the quick sting of Mauryl's hand, after which Mauryl would say he was sorry and talk to him in his softer voice again. Mauryl's blows were like the tingle in his skin when Mauryl made the tea taste sweet and he was holding the cup. Mauryl's blows stung, and tingled, and afterward, brought him that quiet certainty Mauryl could give him, of all things made right with the world.

But now Mauryl would not let him look away. Mauryl frightened him and made him look him straight in the eyes a long, long time.

"You know Words," Mauryl said, then. He didn't want Mauryl to know that. He was afraid of the Words. They came out of nowhere, and struck him in the heart, and made it hard to get his breath. He didn't know the Words Mauryl had.

Mauryl took them out of somewhere and said them and they were real, some making things sweet, some taking away pain.

Some struck him with understanding, and fear, or shame.

"Tristen. You know that you were naked."

"Yes, master Mauryl." He knew now he was wrong to be naked out of doors. He didn't know why. It was wrong to ruin his clothes. But he shouldn't have been outside without them. Mauryl had worn his. He thought he understood the bits and pieces of Mauryl's anger. It was, after all, about ruined clothes. He had been mistaken.

"You know there was danger."

"Yes, sir."

"Did you know you were in danger?"

"No, master Mauryl. And I'm sorry you got wet."

Mauryl shook at him. So it still wasn't the right answer.

"Boy. *Tristen.* Forget the cursed clothes. It's not the point. Fecklessness is the point. Putting yourself in danger is the point, boy. You're safe in here, inside. Whenever you're outside, you're not completely safe. Be careful. Watch your feet. Watch your head, don't forget what I've told you, and don't forget to think. Gods, every move, every breath, every foolish butterfly on the wind does not deserve your rapt attention!"

He remembered the butterfly. It was how he'd skinned his elbow on the stairs outside. He remembered everything, even the sting, and the tingle of Mauryl's fingers on his skin, and the way the sun lay on the stones when they were dry.

"Boy." Mauryl's fingers popped against his cheek, lightly, startling him into seeing Mauryl again. Mauryl's eyes were black-centered. Mauryl's face was grim and bitterly unhappy. "I won't be here forever, boy. You can't look to me for all the answers, or to tell you what to do."

"Why?" That was very unsettling to hear. It frightened him. "Where will you be?"

"I won't be *here*, boy. And you had better know what to do."

"I don't know what to do!" He was trying to be straight-forward with Mauryl, as Mauryl demanded. But he was beginning to be scared, now. "How long will you be gone, sir? Where will you go?" He did not conceive a place outside this place. He couldn't think of one.

"Things *end,* boy. People go away."

"No." He caught at Mauryl's hands. "Don't go away, Mauryl." He had never thought before that there was anywhere to go, or any other place to look down from, at the woods, or up from, at the sun and the clouds. But there must, then, be other places. "I'll go, too."

"Not by my choice," Mauryl said. "Not now. And if you're good, if you think hard, if you study – maybe I won't have to go at all. I could be wrong. I might stay after all. If you're very, very good. If you study."

"I will study." He snatched at Mauryl's hands. "I will. I'll try not to make mistakes."

"Do you know, boy, that your mistakes could open the keep to the Shadows, that you could leave a door unlatched, that you could be outside enjoying the breeze and the rain, and do something so utterly foolish by your inattention to the hour, that they could get *you* while you're outside, – and then what could I do, can you say? I had to come out in the rain just now to get you, foolish lad, and what if it were something worse than rain, what if it only *looked* good and *felt* good to touch, and what if it only felt good for the moment, boy, eh? What if it opened the doors and opened the windows and left you nowhere to run, then what would you do? Can you answer me that?"

"I don't know, Mauryl!"

Mauryl freed his own hands and captured his instead. "Well, you'd do well to figure it out before you do something so foolish, wouldn't you, boy?"

"I want to! I want to, Mauryl!"

"Wanting to won't be enough. Trying won't be enough. After it's got you is far too late. *Before* is the only time you own, lad, the only *before* you can trust is *now,* and you don't even know how long before is, do you, foolish boy?"

"No." He thought that Mauryl was telling him his answer,

22

maybe the very means to assure that he would never go away, but he could by no desperate reach of his wits comprehend what Mauryl was saying. "I don't know, Mauryl. I want to know, but I'm a fool. I don't understand anything!"

Mauryl bumped his chin with his finger, and made him look up.

"Then until you do understand, pay very close attention to doors and windows. Don't do stupid things on the parapets. Don't risk your safety. Don't go out in storms, don't let the sun sneak behind the walls when you're not paying attention."

"I won't, Mauryl!"

"Go practice your letters while the storm lasts. Read and write. These are useful things." Mauryl stood up and rummaged among parchments on the table, sending several off onto the dusty floor, along with a tin plate and a dirty spoon. Tristen dived down and rescued them, and put them up on the table again, but three and four more hit the floor immediately after, and Mauryl caught his sleeve, compelling his attention to a small codex Mauryl had pulled from among the parchments. Mauryl pressed it into his hands and folded his fingers over the aged leather.

"Here is the answer, boy. Here is your answer to all your questions. Here is the way. Learn it. Study it. Become wise."

Tristen opened the book to its center. Its pages were thick with copywork, a bold and heavy hand that was not at all like the writing on the parchments Mauryl trampled underfoot, not written in the delicate, rapid letters Mauryl used.

Someone else copied this, Tristen thought, and although that 'someone else' was not the thunderstroke of a Word, it was a thought he had never framed in his mind, a thought that there could be someone else, or anyone else, now, or ever.

But there had been. There were, in the same way there were, Mauryl hinted, other places. There must be other some-ones.

There must be, in those other places, as naturally as there must be a sun over those places and a wind to rattle their shutters, someone like Mauryl and someone like himself.

There was more than one dove, was there not, that lived in the loft?

There was more than one mouse in the lower hall. There were at least six, that Mauryl called sneaking little thieves, and yet put out bits of bread for them, because Mauryl said they were old, too, and moving more slowly now than they had.

So things had greater numbers than one, and mice grew old, and doves flew out over the woods Mauryl said to fear – and yet came back safe to their roosts in the loft, which had no shutters to bolt. There were many, many of them.

And someone other than Mauryl had written the copywork in this book, using straight, black letters that crossed the page in rigid dark masses, when Mauryl's flowed like the tracks of mice across the dust.

"Boy!"

He had walked straight ahead, thinking of the precious book in his hand, not the stairs before him. He had forgotten, first of lessons, the single step down. He caught himself, at Mauryl's voice, and made the little step safely, feeling shame burn in his face as he looked back.

Mauryl shook his head, out of patience with a fool.

So, shamefaced, he took his little book down to the table where the wall sconces were. He took the waxed straw from the holder and carried fire from the watch-candle, which was his task to renew every night and every morning, and lit the three candles.

Candles don't come like dewdrops, Mauryl had said, when once he left the drafty kitchen door open and the watch-candle had burned out. Mauryl had been out of sorts and had him light his straw instead off the embers in the hearth, which ate up half the straw at once, Mauryl grumbling all the while about fools leaving doors unlatched, and saying candles were hard come by, and they should be burning knots of straw by winter if his husbandry was so profligate.

Winter was a Word, howling white and bitter cold. Straw was a little one, yellow and dusty and hot. Dewdrops he knew from spiderwebs on the shutters, and the old keep had many spiders.

But where did candles come from, that they were at once so scarce, and yet vanished every handful of days for new ones to fill their holders?

They were like the little book, written in another hand, evidence of something outside, and of things more than one. Once he began chasing that thought, it seemed clear to him that candles came from somewhere.

And where then did their clothes come from, when Mauryl said, Mauryl had said it just this morning, that it was one thing to conjure something to do what it would do anyway, and one thing to make things seem better than they were, and quite another, Mauryl had said disgustedly, to conjure a new shirt, which had to come of a good many herb bundles, and which he'd torn on a splinter in the loft.

Mauryl had taught him how to patch it, and made him do it many times until he made it right.

Mauryl gave him such an important thing as this book, on which Mauryl said everything rested, and he thought only about shirts and candles, his thoughts skittering about as they always did, chasing down so many, many steps and stairs of his imaginings, into all the rooms that were there, that only had other doors behind the ones he knew. He tried not to go wit-wandering. He tried not to think of questions.

He sat down at the study table, in the old chair that was most comfortable, except for Mauryl's. He opened the book and smoothed flat the stiff pages. His own copywork, scattered all around him, was wearing the parchments down by layers in attempts at such orderly rows as this: he copied Mauryl's mouse-track writing and his fingers found ways to ink not only the parchment but himself, the quills, and other parchments. His quills threw ink into small spots he never suspected existed until he put his hand on them. He could write *Tristen* and keep it straight. But line after line, this marched straight and true, in masterful strokes of writing so heavy and dark it drew the eye straight to it and did not let it go.

This was wonderful in itself. Writing held Words, and one never knew when one might encounter such a powerful thing: writing like this was to fear, and hold carefully, and puzzle over, because some shapes were like Mauryl's writing and many had tails and straight, strong lines where Mauryl's had twists; and more had shapes he could not quite tell apart, or where one letter stopped and another began.

Certainly it was not Mauryl's writing.

Someone else's. Someone – of strong and straight strokes, lacking those whips and tails he'd thought were part of the letters, which he'd copied in his shaky attempts that turned the quill in wrong directions and spattered ink, or left a bead of ink that took sometimes a day to dry.

Another wizard? he asked himself. Mauryl said he was a wizard, and he, Tristen, was a boy, and that being a wizard, Mauryl knew what a boy needed to know.

Had he never heard what Mauryl had said? Not, The wizard; but, A wizard. Of course there was more than one of everything. Mauryl had always implied so. Mauryl had never told him there was only one.

Mauryl had said there were dangers and they came from outside. As the shadows did. And there was more than one of them. There were many more things in the world than one of each.

Mauryl spoke of this book as if it were a Word, filled with more and greater meanings than other books. This book was, Mauryl said, the source of what he needed. The Book itself might come from elsewhere and tell him what those other things were. Mauryl had said he need not go away if he could find the answers in this Book.

But try as he would to hook the letters together into words, puzzling out the strange ones, and trying them as this letter and that – he found not one word in it he could read.

The pigeons held the floor of the loft, and the doves held the highest rafters, up by the roof, in nooks the pigeons couldn't fit, living on different levels of the loft and filling it with their soft voices. The loft was a wonderful, dusty place. Shingles covered part of it. Slates covered one wing. Thatch covered some of the holes, but the birds that stole the blackberries stole the straw for nests, which they tucked into inaccessible nooks along the other rafters, and squabbled and flapped their wings along the dusty boards when they both wanted the same place.

All the birds of whatever sort had learned that he brought crumbs. So had a furtive few mice, which dared the owl – oh, the owl! – that held sway in the west end of the loft. But an inside wall divided the two, and the owl, which ruled the sunset side alone and grumpy, seemed not to hunt among the mice and the pigeons on this side, although, Mauryl said, owls ate mice.

That seemed cruel.

But the owl would take nothing that he brought and was a sullen and retiring bird, solitary on his side. He wanted not, evidently, to be disturbed, and glared with angry yellow eyes at a boy's offerings, and let them lie. Mauryl said he slept by day and hunted by night, and he was probably angry, Tristen thought, at being waked.

The owl flew out among the shadows at night and came back safely to sleep in the loft. But that not one bird and not one mouse crossed into Owl's side, and that all the boards were bare of nests or straw, might tell a boy finally that Owl wanted no company.

It might tell a boy that Owl was, if not content, not a bird like the other birds, but rather a mover among the Shadows, and possibly a bird other birds feared. Perhaps, Tristen thought, Owl was *their* Shadow, and the reason they flew home at twilight to stay until the sunrise. Perhaps there was a Shadow that hunted wizards, and one that hunted boys, and one that wanted mice and birds, and he'd stumbled on its daytime sleeping place – he supposed that, like Owl, Shadows had to have them. But if Owl was one of the dreadful things, he thought he should be glad Owl only flared his wings and glared at him.

Perhaps up in the rafters were other Shadows asleep, and if he waked *them,* they'd pounce on him. But there were rules for Shadows, as he could guess, that by day they had to sleep, and if one forbore to rouse them, then they forbore to wake.

So he went no more to Owl's side. He told Mauryl that he thought the Shadows might sleep in the loft: Mauryl said the Shadows slept in all sorts of places, but certainly he should be out of the loft well before the sun set, and he should be careful up there, Mauryl said, because the boards were rotten with age, and he might fall straight through and break his neck.

Mauryl was always thinking of disasters. That was what wizards did, Tristen thought, and boys had to learn to read, so he took his Book there and sat in the sunlight.

The mice grew tame, and the birds (besides Owl) liked the bread he offered, and fluttered and fought for it quite rudely (at least the sparrows), while the pigeons (better-mannered, Mauryl would say) puffed their chests and ducked and dodged about. The sparrows were full of tricks. But the pigeons' gray chests shone with green rainbows in the sun, and they learned to come close to him, and sit on his legs in the warm sunlight, and take bread from his fingers. The doves tried the same, but were far more timid, and the sparrows hung back and squabbled, thieves, Mauryl called them. Silly birds.

But the pigeons grew rather too bold in a very few days, and would land on his head, or fight over room on his shoulders, and he discovered there were disadvantages to birds. Mauryl said then that they were taking advantage of him, which was what creatures did if one gave and asked nothing – like some boys, Mauryl said. So perhaps he could learn to be thoughtful and to think ahead, which birds didn't do, which was why they had birds' wits, and not the wisdom of wicked Owl.

Be stern with them, Mauryl advised him. Bid them mind their manners.

So he became like Mauryl with them, well, most times. He shrugged them off his shoulders; he swept them off his knees. He tolerated one or two polite and careful ones and, he discovered, once the bread ran out, most were far less interested in his company. So he grew wiser about birds.

He said to Mauryl that the mice were more polite. But Mauryl said the mice were only smaller, and afraid of him because he might step on them by accident. Mauryl said that if they had the chance they might be rude, too, which was the difference between mice and boys; boys could learn to be polite because they should be polite, but mice were polite only because they were scared, and might be dangerous if they were as big as boys, being inherently thieves.

That saying made him unhappy. He lay on his stomach on the floor and tried to coax the mice out to him, but they were afraid of him and came only so far as they ever had. So he thought that Mauryl was right and that they expected harm of him, when he had never done any. He wondered why that was, and thought that Mauryl might be right about their character.

He read his Book in the intervals of these matters, or at least he studied it. He grew angry sometimes that he could understand nothing of it. Sometimes he found little words that he thought he knew. Sometimes he made notes to himself in the dust with his fingers.

And the silly pigeons came and walked on them, so they never lasted long.

Pigeons had no respect for writing, nor for boys. They feared him not even when he swept them off. They thought of him, he began to think, not as a boy, but like the other pigeons, flapping their wings to secure a place. And his wing-flapping, like theirs, did nothing but overbalance a pigeon. It never drove one away for good, not so long as there was the chance of more bread crumbs.

– Mauryl, the Wind breathed.

Mauryl stopped, seized up his staff and sprang up from the table in his tower room, parchments and codices tumbling in all directions.

Laughter came from the empty air, more clearly than its wont.

– You are weaker tonight, said the Wind. *Mauryl, let me in.*

He banged his staff on the wooden floor, tapped the gold-shod heel of it against the sealed shutters. The seal remained firm.

– Mauryl, the Wind said again. *Mauryl Gestaurien. I saw him today. I did.*

He scorned to answer. To answer at all opened barriers. He leaned on his staff, eyes shut, remaking his inner defenses, while the sweat beaded cold on his forehead.

– Once it was no trouble at all for you to keep me out. It must have been the Shaping that weakened you, Gestaurien. Do you think? – And was he worth the cost?

– You cannot read him, Mauryl thought, not meaning that to be his answer, but the Wind heard, all the same. He clenched the next thought tightly in his defenses, wove it firmly and strongly inside, armored as his own memory. The sense of presence faded for a moment.

– Come, let me in. The voice came from another direction, rich and soft and chilling. *You are failing, Gestaurien. Harder and harder now for you to shut me out. – And what is he to do for you, this flesh-clothed Shaping of yours?*

Dangerous to answer. Think nothing, do nothing.

– Ah, Gestaurien, Kingsbane, – What do you call him?

Tristen, he thought, and wished in vain not to have made that slip.

Laughter circled the tower room, rattling one shutter after another. *Tristen, Tristen, Tristen. Is he a peril to me, Gestaurien? This puling innocent? I think not.*

– Begone, wretch!

Shutters rattled, one after another. The wind chuckled, howled, roared, and stirred the shadows in the corners.

– Ah, secrets. The Wind sniggered, a mild rattling at a window latch. *Perhaps the great, the awesome secret is that you failed. So great a magic. So ambitious. And all so useless.*

– Begone, I say!

The shadows flowed back. The wind fell suddenly. The shutters were quiet. It had ventured too arrogantly, too soon.

Mauryl sank into his chair, bowed his head against trembling hands.

And then upon a dreadful thought –

– leapt to his feet, seized his staff in one hand, the candlestick in the other, tottering with the weakness in his knees. With his staff he ventured onto the creaking balconies, by flickering, precarious light that left the depths all dark.

He took the stairs much too fast for a lame old man and came down, aching and short of breath, feeling about him constantly with his magic, as far as the next balcony, and to Tristen's sealed door. He opened it and leaned against the door frame, breathless.

The boy was safely asleep, his breathing gentle and undisturbed. He could have heard nothing. The shutters of this room had never rattled, never attracted the wind.

With a shaking hand he set the candle down on the small table, next to the watch-candle, a candle pungent, like the one he carried from above, with rowan and rue, rosemary and golden-seal.

He tipped the cup on Tristen's bedside and found it empty, delayed to draw the coverlet over Tristen's bare arm.

Tristen stirred, a mere breath. The boyish face was always cold and severe in sleep, so stern, for such young features. But –

There was the shadow of beard on the smooth skin. When, he wondered, had that begun – in only so little time? Just tonight?

The magic was still Summoning, still working in him. Still – Summoning, that was the unexpected thing.

Mauryl dipped into the boy's dreams, precautionary on this night of strange intrusions. He found them nothing more violent than the memory of rain, circles in puddles, scudding clouds above the trees.

He took his candle again, softly closed the door as he left, renewed the seal with a Word.

The wind sighed about the towers, but it seemed a natural wind, now, and he climbed the creaking stairs back to his tower study, while the candlelight and candle smoke chased the shadows into momentary retreat, beneath and below and around and around the wooden stairs and balconies of the keep.

CHAPTER 3

~

Once a thought began it might go anywhere and every-where. Tristen despaired of better mastery of himself. His thoughts were not like Mauryl's thoughts, all orderly, hewing to one purpose. His leapt, jumped, flitted, wandered about so many idle matters, like the pigeons above hunting for dropped crumbs, pecking here, pecking there, in complete disorder. He found complete distraction in a candle flame or a butterfly, or, just after he skinned his elbow, the thought that elbows were very inconvenient to look at, and that there were parts of him he couldn't see, like his face, which was a curious way to arrange things.

It happened on that pesky step, and a fall right onto the stones of the lower floor with, fortunately, nothing in his hands. He gathered himself up, sitting on the stones, trying to look at his elbow, and finding red on his fingers. It hurt a great deal. He got up and went to Mauryl, fearing some permanent damage, but, no, Mauryl said, it was only a little Wound, and Mauryl told him to watch where he put his feet, and worked that tingling cure and put a salve on it. Wound was a Word, a scary one, that occupied his thoughts with dreadful images of red and ruin, and made him sick at his stomach, and made him remember how his elbow hurt.

But – he learned, too, that the skittering of one's thoughts could be a useful thing, to take one's mind off trouble – he still couldn't see his elbow.

So he went back to Mauryl, who was in the yard cutting herbs, and asked him if he could see *his* elbow.

"Not likely," Mauryl said. "Nor wished to, lately."

He began to walk away, rubbing his chin. Then he thought how, lately, he'd felt his chin grown rough, and it itched, and he couldn't see that, either.

33

"Mauryl, can you see your face?"

"No more than my elbow," Mauryl said curtly. The air smelled strongly of bruised herbs. "Stupid question, of course not."

He went away, noticing, not for the first time, but for the first time that he had ever wondered about it, all the stone faces set in the walls: some large, some small, grimacing visages that had sometimes frightened him on uneasy nights, when Mauryl was angry for some reason and when he sought his room alone; or when the wind was up and creaking in the roofs and the loft, and he was alone, lighting the sconces on the landings. The faces seemed to change with the candlelight when he walked past them, but Mauryl had said they were only stone, and harmless to him.

Some of them had pointed teeth and pointed ears. He had felt his teeth with his tongue and his ears with his fingers, so he was certain enough boys looked nothing like the images of that sort. Some of the stone faces had beards, and looked like Mauryl. Some were smooth-faced. Some looked more afraid than angry. Mauryl's face went through such changes of expression, and such changes portended important things to him – but the changing statues, Mauryl assured him, portended nothing.

He had been aware, too, in this growing curiosity about faces, that his hair was dark, where Mauryl's was silver, that Mauryl had a long beard and his face was, until lately, smoother than the statue's stone; that Mauryl's hands were wrinkled and his were not – his hands looked more like the stone hands that in places reached from the wall, not the clawed ones, but the hands with fingers. He was aware, now that he thought about it, that his face must be changing in some way, and different than Mauryl's in more than the beard.

He was thinking about such things when, the next day, he leaned over the rain barrel out by the scullery and saw just a shadow of a boy, hardly more than a shadow, but not, surely, a wicked and dangerous Shadow, as Owl was to the birds.

34

The shadow was his, true, but he could see in it no reason for his face to be rough or whether it was a good face or a frightening face. He thought that the sun was wrong, and his hair was shading the water, so he moved, and held his hair back at the nape of his neck – but it hardly helped. It was a dark barrel and the sun did little to light it.

But it did seem, looking critically, that his nose was straighter, and his skin was smoother, and his brows were thinner than Mauryl's. It was like and not like the stone faces. He made faces at the water-shadow. The shadow changed a little, where light reached past his shoulder.

The kitchen door opened. Mauryl looked out. He looked up.

"What are you doing?" Mauryl asked.

"Looking at my face," he said, which sounded strange. "Looking at the shadow of my face," he said, instead.

"Clever lad." But Mauryl's voice was not pleased. "Do you see all this wood?"

He looked in the direction Mauryl looked, at the large jumbled pile of timbers that had always stood by the door.

"Being such a clever lad," Mauryl said, "do you see this axe?"

The axe stood by the door inside. Mauryl came out with it in his hand. He thought Mauryl would cut wood, as Mauryl did now and again. Mauryl had always said the axe was too dangerous. Mauryl found it hard to work without his staff, but he would lean on it and pull out the smallest pieces and chop them into kindling.

So he stood and watched as Mauryl set one small piece of wood over the bigger one he used for a supporting piece and set to work, leaning on his staff with one hand, chopping with the other.

"You see," Mauryl said, "first to this side and then to that side." Chips flew. He liked to watch. The wood that came out of the gray beams was lighter, and the newest chips were always bright among those that littered the area around about. Mauryl made faces when he worked. The small piece became two pieces. "Do you see?"

"Yes, master Mauryl."

"You try a bigger one, if you're such a strong young man, with so much time to spare."

He took a fair-sized one. He set it where Mauryl said; he took the axe in his hand. Mauryl showed him how to hold it in both hands, where to set his feet, and showed him how to be careful where the axe swung. His heart was beating faster with the mere notion that Mauryl trusted him with Mauryl's own work. The axe handle he held was smooth and warm from Mauryl's hands. When he lifted it and when he swung very slowly at Mauryl's order, he felt the weight of it as something trying to weigh down on him.

"Very good," Mauryl said. "Now, always minding where you put your feet and mind the path of the axe, swing it faster this time and aim true. Never chase the wood. If the wood moves, stop and put it back. Never, ever chase it with the axe. That way you keep your feet out of the way of the blade. It will take your foot otherwise. Do you hear me, Tristen?"

"Yes, sir," he said, certain that was good advice. Mauryl stepped back and let him try in earnest.

It was far, far easier with the axe moving freely. He struck two strokes, to this side and to that side, and then Mauryl nodded, so he kept swinging, one pair of strokes after another, until the axe seemed to fly like a bird and he tugged it back, faster and better aimed with every stroke.

Mauryl watched him cut his piece through. Then Mauryl nodded approval and said, "Stack it against the wall. And fill the kitchen pan with water when you come inside. And wash before you come in."

Mauryl went inside again, and he pulled the rest of the beam along the supporting piece and set to work, making the whole courtyard ring to the strokes, because he liked to hear them. The feeling of the axe swinging had become almost like a Word, strength running through him with his breaths and with the strokes. The chips flew wide and stuck to his clothing. He chose bigger pieces, which were no trouble at all for him to lift, and none for him to chop, having two sound feet,

36

both hands to use, and the knowledge in his heart that he was going to please Mauryl by doing far more than Mauryl expected, far faster than Mauryl imagined.

He chopped only thick pieces, after that. He grew completely out of breath. The sweat ran down his face and sides, but he sat and let the breeze cool him, then attacked the pile again, until it made a taller stack than he had imagined he could make.

By then, though, it was toward time to be making supper. He washed the dust and the sweat off him; he washed his shirt, too, hung it out to dry, and flung the wash water away from the kitchen door as Mauryl had told him he should.

Then he filled the kitchen pan, and he ran upstairs to get his other shirt in time to run down again and help Mauryl stir up their supper.

It was the first time he had ever, ever, ever done so many things right in succession. Mauryl came out into the courtyard while the cakes were baking in the oven Mauryl's small kindling had fed, and truly seemed pleased with his huge stack of very thick wood. Mauryl had him carry a stack of both big and little pieces inside before supper, and after supper he took the dishes and washed them, and came back to sit at the fire and read until Mauryl sent him up to bed.

He was happy when he went to bed, happy because Mauryl was happy with him – he thought that as Mauryl gave him his bedtime cup and sat by him on the edge of his bed, saying how – but he was very sleepy – he was becoming strong, and clever, and he had to study hard to be not just clever, but wise.

"Yes, sir," he said.

"Do you practice every day with the Book?"

"Yes, sir," he said, feeling his wits gone to wool. "I read every word I can."

Mauryl smoothed his hair. Mauryl's hand was smooth and cooler than his forehead.

"Good lad," Mauryl said.

It was the most perfect day he remembered, despite the storm that threatened them, late, with lightning and thunder.

But Mauryl seemed sad as he lingered, sitting there, and that sadness was the only trouble in the world.

Then Mauryl said, "If only you could read more, lad, if only you could do more than read words."

He didn't know what more Mauryl wanted him to do than he had done. He felt suddenly desperate, but Mauryl rose from the edge of the bed as sleep was coming down on him thick and soft and dark, and Mauryl shut the door.

He heard the wind rattling at the shutters. He heard Mauryl's steps creak and tap up the stairs.

Trying wasn't enough, he thought as sleep came tumbling over him. Nothing but doing more than he was asked could ever satisfy Mauryl at all.

It had been a fierce storm, he knew that by the puddle under the kitchen door in the morning.

And when, after breakfast and morning chores, he went up to the loft with his Book and a napkin of crumbs – he opened the door and saw shafts of sunlight where no sunlight had been before. It was bright and beautiful. Pigeons and doves and sparrows were flying in and out of the openings.

But he saw the sodden straw and knew the storm had blown rain through the sheltered places. The little birds were all fledged and flying, but it had been a hard night for the nests.

And, worse, a glance toward the other wall showed a board down between the pigeon loft and Owl's domain.

That would not do, Mauryl would say. That would simply not do. He feared what might already have happened, and if it had not happened yet, because of the storm raging, it would happen tonight.

He could come and go safely with Owl. The board was not on this side of the dividing wall, it had fallen on the other, so he tucked his Book into his shirt for safekeeping, unlatched the door and came through into the huge barren loft that was Owl's alone.

There was a hole in the roof, a rib of the roof was down, and slates lay broken on the loft floor. Owl's den had become drafty and lighter, which he thought would not at all please Owl.

Owl sat puffed and sullen on his perch.

He picked up the fallen board. The pegs were still in their holes, and a little effort put it where it belonged and set the pegs back in their sockets, though not so far as they should sink. He took up a roof slate and pounded with it, and finally pounded the pegs with his fist on a piece of the slate, after it had broken, and the board settled where it had been.

Owl had ruffled up at the clatter and the thumping. Owl refused to look at him, perhaps because he had liked the hole into the pigeon loft.

But there was nothing to do for the hole in the roof, which Tristen found far beyond his skill. He went and looked out, and found the hole a new window, on a side of the keep he had never seen, a view of forest that went on and on, and, as he stepped closer, a view of a parapet of the keep he had never seen.

He wondered how one reached it.

He stepped up on the fallen beam, worked higher, with his arm on the roof slates, and from that vantage, with his head and shoulders out the hole in the roof, he saw a gate in the wall that ringed the keep, looking down on it from above. He saw a dark band of water lapping at the very walls of the fortress and, spanning that, a series of arches. From those arches outward into the woods that lined the far shore, he saw an aged stonework which vanished in among the trees.

He was astonished and troubled. He could imagine the course of the stonework thereafter. He saw a trace of a line among the treetops, where trees preserved just a little more space than elsewhere through the forest.

A Bridge and a Road, he thought, in the breathless way of Words arriving out of nowhere. A Road suggested going out, and then –

Then it came to him that if Mauryl went away then the Road was the way Mauryl would go, through the gate and over that dark water and through the woods.

He felt the Book weighing against him as he climbed down, reminder of a task on which Mauryl had hung so very, very much, and in which he had so far failed. But the Road was out there waiting to call Mauryl away and the Book could prevent Mauryl going, so he held it secret that he had seen the Road, as he feared that he had, by accident, seen something Mauryl had never told him, and which, perhaps, Mauryl would tell him only if he could not solve the matter Mauryl set him to do.

It was not in his power to patch the hole the wind had made. He put up a few boards, but for the most part the holes were out of reach. He had at least, for the pigeons, patched the one that would have let their Shadow in, and the pigeons and the doves as well as Owl would have to bear with the rain when it came.

He said nothing of the hole in the roof when he came down from the loft. He thought Mauryl might be angry that he had seen the Road, and it would make Mauryl talk of going away again: that was what he feared. He studied very hard. He thought that he read Mauryl's name in the Book, and came and asked him if that was so.

Mauryl said he would not be surprised. And that was all. So when he had studied the codex so long his eyes swam, he read the easy writings that Mauryl had made, and he copied them.

Some things, however, came much easier than others.

"Sometimes," Tristen said, one evening, brushing the soft-stiff feather of the quill between his lips, while his elbows kept his much-scraped study parchment flat on the table, "sometimes I know how to do things you never taught me. How is that, Mauryl?"

Mauryl looked up from his own work, at least to the lifting of a shaggy brow, the pause of the quill tip above the inkpot.

The pen dipped, then, wrote a word or two. "What things?" Mauryl asked him.

"How to write letters. How to read."

"I suppose some things come and some things don't."

"Come where, Mauryl?"

"Into your head, where else? The moon? The postern tower?"

"But other things, too, Mauryl. I don't know that I know Words. I see something or I touch something, and I know what it is or what to do with it. And sometimes it happens with things I see every day, over and over, only suddenly I know the Word, or I know how words fit together that I never understood before, or I know there's more to a thing. And some of them scare me."

"What scares you?"

"I don't know. Only I'm not certain I have all the parts. I try to read the Book, Mauryl, and the letters are there, but the words . . . I don't know any of the words."

"Magic is like that. Maybe there's a glamor on the Book. Maybe there's one over your eyes. Such things happen."

"What's magic?"

"It's what wizards do."

"Do you sometimes know Words that way, by touching them?"

"I'm very old. I find very little I don't know, now."

"Will I be old?"

"Perhaps." Mauryl dipped the pen again. "If you're good. If you study."

"Will I be old like you?"

"Plague on your questions."

"Will I be old, Mauryl?"

"I'm a wizard," Mauryl snapped, "not a fortune-teller."

"What's a –"

"Plague, I say!" Mauryl frowned and jerked another parchment over the first, discarded that one and lifted the corner to look at the one below, and the one below that. He pulled out one from the depths of the pile.

"Mauryl, I don't ever want you to go away."

"I gave you the Book. What does the Book say?"

He was ashamed. And had nothing to say.

"The answer is there, boy."

"I can't read the words!"

"So you have a lot to do, don't you? I'd get busy."

Tristen rested his chin against his arm, rubbed it, because it itched, and it felt strange under his fingers.

"Mauryl, can you read the Book?"

"You have no patience for your studies today, is that it? You worry at this, you worry at that – how am I to finish this?"

"Are you copying?"

"Ciphering. Gods, go outside, you've made me blot the answer. Enjoy the air. Give me peace. But mind –" Mauryl added sharply as he sprang up and his chair scraped the stone. He stayed quite still. "Mind you stay to the north walk, and when the shadows fall all the way across the courtyard –"

"I come inside. I always do. – Mauryl. – Why the north walk? Why never the south?"

"Because I say so." Mauryl waved a dismissive hand. "Go, go, and leave an old man to his figures."

"What figures? What do you –"

"Go, gods have mercy, take yourself and your questions to the pigeons. They have better answers."

"The pigeons?"

"Ask them, I say. They're patient. I'm not, young gadfly. Buzz elsewhere."

Another wave of the fingers. Tristen knew he would gain nothing more, then, and started away.

But he remembered his copywork and put it safely on the shelf, far from Mauryl's flood of parchments, which drowned the table in cipherings, with the orrery weighting the middle-most pile.

He hastened up the stairs, then, rubbing at the ink stains on his fingers, searching for wet spots that might find their way to his clothing or, unnoticed, to his chin, which still itched. He supposed he could ask Mauryl to make it stop, but Mauryl was busy, and besides, Mauryl's work felt stranger than the itch, which went away of its own accord when he was busy.

– *Mauryl,* said the Wind, *and rattled at the tower shutters, rattle, bang, and thump-thump-thump.*

Mauryl hardly glanced at the sealed shutters this time. It had been a shorter respite than he expected, and a far more surly Wind. There was no laughter about it now at all.

– *Gestaurien, let me in. Let me in now. We can reason about this foolishness of yours.*

It was worried, then. Mauryl drank it in and, still sitting, reached for his staff, where it leaned against the wall.

– *You know you can ruin yourself. This is entirely uncalled-for, entirely unnecessary.*

It tried another window. But that was simply habit, Mauryl thought, and thought nothing else, resisted nothing, like grass in a gale.

– *He's asleep,* the Wind murmured through the crack in the shutter nearest. *I passed up and down his window. Do you truly think there's any hope for you in this young fool? He knows nothing. I've drunk from his dreams, I have, Mauryl. You wish me to believe him formidable? I think not. I do think not. Not deep, not deep waters at all, this boy. He's all so innocent.*

– *Sweet innocence,* Mauryl said. *But out of your reach. Long out of your reach, poor dead shadow. Poor shattered soul.*

– *You've given me a weapon, you know. That's all he is. A* shutter went bump-bump, *and Mauryl looked up sharply, feeling the ward loosen, seeing the latch jump. If you had had the stomach to join me, Gestaurien, we might have raised the Sihhë kings to power they never dreamed of. The new lords would never have risen, and you and I would not be haggling over this rotting fortress.*

43

*It was more self-possessed than before, more reasoning.
That was not good.*

— Mauryl Gestaurien? Are you worried?

*— No. Simply not hurried. Patience I have in abundance. I
shan't enumerate your failings, or tell you what they are. Let
them be mysteries to you, like the counsel that I gave.*

*— Your mystery went walking on the wall. I saw him
there. Such a little push it would take, if I wanted to.*

*— If you had a body, isn't that the pity, Hasufin? You'd do
this, you'd do that. You're a breath of air, a meandering
malaise, a flatulence. Go bother some priest.*

— What was his name, *Gestaurien?*

*The spell-flinging startled him and disturbed his heart, but
he turned it with a thump of his staff, rose and thumped the
staff against the shutter.* Go away, thou breath of wind. Go,
go, even the pigeons are weary of you.

*Softly the wind blew now, prowling, trying this and that
window, for a long time.*

Far longer than on any night previous.

*And the stars . . . the stars were moving toward ominous
congruency.*

CHAPTER 4

~

After a dry spell, the rain built in the north and rolled up in a great, towering fortress of cloud, flickering in its belly with lightnings. Tristen saw it from the wall, and knew immediately that it was a dark and dangerous kind of storm, no sun-and-puddles shower.

He said as much to Mauryl, who said, gruffly, So stay indoors, – and went back to his scribing and ciphering. Mauryl had been scraping parchments all morning in preparation for whatever was so urgent, and had just scraped part of one he wanted by accident. Mauryl was not in his best humor on that account, and Tristen walked softly about his chores in the hall.

By evening the storm was crashing and thumping its way across the forest. Tristen made their supper as Mauryl had taught him, managed not to burn the barley cakes, and set a platter of them and a cup of ale at Mauryl's elbow in hopes of pleasing Mauryl; but Mauryl only muttered at him and waved his fingers, which meant go away, he was busy.

So Tristen had a supper of barley cakes and honey by himself, beside the fire, and since Mauryl evidenced no attention to him whatever, he left the pots for morning, when the rain barrel would certainly be full.

He decided nothing would happen in the evening. Then, Mauryl being so occupied he never had touched his supper, he took a candle, went up the stairs, lighting the night candles at each landing, so if Mauryl did come upstairs to his chamber, weary as he was apt to be, he should not have to deal with a dark stairway: that was Tristen's thought, and probably Mauryl would complain about the early extravagance of candles, but Mauryl would complain more if he failed to light them.

And he was bound for bed early, which gave him no chance at all of doing something to annoy Mauryl, when Mauryl was in such a mood.

So he opened the door to his room, lit the watch-candle on his bedside, sat down on the edge of the bed and tugged off his boots and his shirt, disposing the latter on the pegs behind the door and laying the Book which he carried on the table beside his bed.

The double candlelight leapt and jumped with the draft from under the door; Mauryl had said that was why the fire moved. It gave him two overlapped shadows and made them waver about the stonework. The floor creaked – it always did that when the wind blew strongly from the north. He had observed that mystery – Mauryl had called him quite clever – on his own.

And while he was undressing, he heard the rain begin to spatter the horn window, as the thunder came rumbling.

He stepped out of his breeches, and was turning down the covers when a great crack of thunder sent him diving into the safety of his bed and drawing up the covers about his ears, in the protection of the cool sheets. A second clap of thunder sounded right over his room as he shivered, letting his body make a comfortable warm spot.

The candles both still burned, the watch-candle and the one that sat always at his bedside. Beside them sat the cup that he was to drink – Mauryl made it for him every evening. But when he had blown out the candle he had brought, and by the light of the fat, dim watch-candle reached out an arm and picked up the cup to drink it – he found it empty.

Well, so, Mauryl had been preoccupied. Mauryl was very busy and bothered whenever he was at his ciphering, which involved lines and circles and a great many numbers that made no sense at all to his eyes. He wondered if he should take the cup down to Mauryl and ask him how to make it himself, since there had never been a night he had not had it, but he supposed that one night would not make all that great a difference. It was a comfortable thing, and Mauryl said he was supposed to drink it all, every night, but he was supposed to have breakfast every day, too, and there had certainly been mornings when Mauryl had quite forgotten, before he had learned to make it for himself.

So he gave a sigh and decided it was like the breakfasts, and that if Mauryl did chance to remember it, and if it were important enough, Mauryl would wake him and have him drink it. He lay back, abandoned and forgotten, and listened to the beating of the rain against the horn window.

But just then he saw lightnings making patterns in the rough horn panes, droplets crawling and racing across the fractured yellow surface, and he realized that the shutters that had turned up shut and latched every evening in his room – as the cup had always been waiting – were not shut. He had not seen it: the light from the candles had blinded him to anything so far as the end of his bed. The lightnings showed it plainly now that he was down only to the watch-candle.

And he knew that he ought to get up in the chill air and fold the shutters across the window and latch them tight, but the thunder frightened him, and the rain did, and the unguarded window did. He was safe in bed. He had always thought that if he stayed abed the thunder could not reach him and the Shadows had to stay away . . . but he knew better now: he was certain he should get up and shutter that window, and do it now . . .

If his eyelids were not suddenly so heavy and his breaths so deep and easy, the mattress gone soft, soft, soft as the water splashed off the window, which was a snug window, and latched, he knew that. He never unlatched it. Water ran down the gutters and down and down to . . .

To the cistern, he thought, then, and dreamed of the buckets he had to draw, and how the cistern smelled cool and damp when he took off the wooden lid . . . how it was dark and secret and he liked casting the bucket down, not knowing how deep the cistern really was, because the rope for the bucket was not nearly long enough to touch the bottom. He let it drop down and down, with a splash . . .

The rain barrel was for the kitchen. The rain barrel was for washing. The cistern, deep and dark, was a place of shadows . . .

. . . shadows that moved and flowed up like water overflowing, running along the stones the way water ran, flowing up the step and seeping, with the puddle, under the kitchen door.

He waked, in total dark, heart thumping in his chest.

The second candle had gone out.

It might have been the sudden plunge into darkness that had wakened him. He thought so. He heard no change in the rush of rain. The wind skirled about the perilous window; the lightning through the horn cast strange shapes, accompanied by thunder.

Something groaned, as if the timbers of the keep were shifting.

Wind sounds. Night sounds. The fortress was full of creaks and groans and scurryings that seemed loudest at night.

That was because the fortress was old; Mauryl had said so when he had come to Mauryl afraid. Old, well-settled timbers creaked with the changes in weather, and the mice came and went as they pleased in the walls. Owl flew out on better nights.

But he tried not to think of Owl, or Owl's fierce eyes glaring at him.

Again came that deep wooden groaning, which made him think the wind must be blowing from some direction it never had before. He lay shivering beneath his covers, warm enough, wondering why he was afraid, wishing that he dared jump out of bed very quickly and fling the shutter closed, but he imagined something at the window at just that moment, and himself standing too close . . .

He could run out onto the balcony and go looking for Mauryl, but he saw no light under his door, beside his bed. Light always showed far across the floor if the wall sconce on the balcony outside was still lit. It was dark outside his room, and he had no idea whether Mauryl was upstairs abed or down at the table.

The very walls groaned, and the groaning became a bellow that shocked the air.

"*Mauryl!*" he cried, and flung the covers off and bolted for the door, naked as he was, with that bellowing going up and down the hollow core of the keep. He flung the door open onto dark.

No light shone up from the great hall below: the heart of the keep was dark all the way to the depths and the nook of Mauryl's study, where lights burned latest. The candles were all out, even the watch-candles at the turnings of the stairs, and that bellowing echoed up from the depths and down from the rafters. He felt his way in panic along the wooden balcony, his hands following the cold stone of the wall, and he reached the turn where three faces were set together. He felt their open mouths and their pointed stone teeth, and groped out into utter blackness for the railing that should come before the steps.

His foot found the edge of the steps instead: he seized the railing for balance. The stairs went both up above and down to the depths from there, and he trusted nothing below. The safe place had to be Mauryl's room – if it was dark below, then Mauryl could not be there. Mauryl had gone to bed upstairs. Mauryl would tell him it was nothing, just a sound. Mauryl would call him foolish boy and calm his heart and tell him that nothing could get inside.

He ran stumbling up the steps, felt his way around and around the railing with the whole keep echoing and bellowing about him as if every mouth in every face in the walls had found a tongue at once.

His head topped the steps and he could see, by the light under Mauryl's door, the floor of the balcony above his. He climbed the last steps, he ran to that door, seized the handle and pulled – but it was barred from inside, and the bellowing hurt his ears, drowned his heart, smothered his breath.

"Mauryl!" he cried, and beat on Mauryl's door with his clenched fist. The dark was all around him, and he felt the balcony creak and shake as if something else were walking on it, something shut out, too, in the dark outside Mauryl's room. That thing was coming toward him.

"Mauryl!"

Something banged, inside, something shattered, steps crossed the floor in haste and the bolt crashed back. The door swung abruptly inward, then, and Mauryl stood, a shadow against the bright golden light that shone through the wild silver of his hair, the cloth of his robe.

The place was all parchments and vessels, charts and bottles on the unmade bed, the smell of ale and old linen and sulfur so thick it took the breath. The groaning was around them, deep and terrible, and Mauryl waved his arm in a fit of rage, shouted a Word –

The sudden silence was stifling, leaving his pulse hammering in his ears – his heart pounding. "You *fool!*" Mauryl shouted at him, and in utter fright he tried to leave, but Mauryl snatched at his arm and wanted him inside, where he was afraid to go.

Then somehow between the two of them the night table went bump and scrape and toppled over as Mauryl's hand left his arm, as pottery crashed, as parchments slid heavily out the door.

"Come back here!" Mauryl raged after him.

He fled in terror for the stairs, stumbled against the upward steps before he knew where he was, landed on his hands and knees on the steps and heard the furious taps of Mauryl's staff as Mauryl hastened down the balcony after him.

"Fool!" Mauryl shouted, and he clambered up the steps half on hands and knees before he even thought that it was the way to the loft.

"Tristen!" he heard Mauryl shout. He gained his feet and ran up and up the turns of the stairs, up the last rickety steps to the last precarious balcony and the highest secrecies of the fortress, dark steps that were always dark – except the light under the door.

It was lightning-lit, now; but the loft was his refuge, his place, full of creatures he knew. He fled to the door and burst into the wide space. Lightning lit his way, gray flashes through the broken planks and missing slates and shingles. Wind howled and wailed through the gaps, rain blew into his face from the missing boards, and rain fell down his neck as he felt his way among the rafters. All around him was the flutter of disturbed pigeons and doves.

The door he had left open blew shut with a bang, making him jump. But he reached the nook he most used, soaked and exposed as it was, and he dared catch his breath there, thinking Mauryl would never, ever chase him this far. His flight would not please Mauryl at all. But in a while Mauryl would be less angry.

So he sat in the dark at the angle of the roof, with his heart thumping and his side hurting. The birds could fly away from danger. If they stayed and settled, surely it was safe. The loft was a safe place, there was nothing to fear . . . and they were settling again. Lightning showed him rafters and huddled, feathery lumps, the blink of an astonished pigeon eye and the gray sheen of wings.

Thunder bumped, more distantly than a moment ago. The stifling feeling, like the sound, now was gone. His heart began to settle. His breathing, so harsh he could hardly hear the rain, quieted so that he was aware of the patter of rain on the slates just above his head, then the drip of a leak into straw, and the quiet rustling of wings, the pigeons jostling each other for dry perches.

A door shut, downstairs, echoing.

Then the stairs creaked, not the dreadful groaning and bellowing of before, but a sound almost as dreadful: the noise of Mauryl walking, the measured tap of Mauryl's staff coming closer, *step-tap, step-tap, step-tap.*

Dim light showed in the seam above the door: Mauryl carrying a candle, Tristen thought on a shaky breath, as he listened to that tapping and the creaking of the steps. The door opened, admitting a glare of light, and the wind fluttered the candle in Mauryl's hand, sending a fearsomely large shadow up among the rafters above his head.

Tristen clenched his arms about himself and wedged himself tightly into the corner, seeing that shadow, seeing that light. Mauryl was in the loft, now. His shadow filled the rafters and the pigeons made a second flutter of shadowy wings, a second disarrangement, a sudden, mass consideration of flight.

But he – had no way out.

"Tristen."

Mauryl's voice was still angry, and Tristen held his breath. Thunder complained faint and far. Slowly Mauryl's self appeared out of the play of shadows among the rafters, the candle he carried making his face strange and hostile, his shadow looming up among the rafters, disturbing the pigeons and setting them to darting frantically among the beams. The commotion of shadows tangled overhead and made something dreadful.

"Tristen, come out of there. I know you're there. I see you."

He wanted to answer. He wanted the breath and the wit to explain he hadn't meant to be a fool, but the stifling closeness was back: he had as well have no arms or legs – he was all one thing, and that thing was fear.

"Tristen?"

"I –" He found one breath, only one. "I – heard –"

"Never – *never* run from me. Never, do you understand? No matter what you heard. No matter what you fear. Never, ever run into the dark." Mauryl came closer, looming over him with a blaze of light, an anger that held him powerless. "Come. Get up. Get up, now. Back to your bed."

Bed was at least a warmer, safer place than sitting wedged into a nook Mauryl had very clearly found, and if sending him to bed was all Mauryl meant to do, then he had rather be there, right now, and not here. He made a tentative move to get up.

Mauryl set his staff near to let him lean on it, too – he was too heavy for Mauryl to lift. He rose to his feet while Mauryl scowled at him; and he obeyed when, his face all candle-glow and frightening shadows, Mauryl sent him toward the stairs and followed after. His knees were shaking under him, so that he relied first on the wall and then on the rail to steady him as he went down the steps.

The measured tap of Mauryl's staff and Mauryl's boots followed him down the creaking steps. As Mauryl overtook him, the light made their shadows a single hulking shape on the stone and the boards, and flung it wide onto the rafters of the inner hall, across the great gulf of the interior, a constant rippling and shifting of them among the timbers that supported all the keep. The faces, the hundreds of faces in the stone walls, above and below, seemed struck with terror as the light traveled over their gaping mouths and staring eyes – and then, the light passing to the other side, some seemed to shut those eyes, or grimace in anger.

"Go on," Mauryl said grimly when they reached the balcony of Mauryl's room, and Tristen took the next stairs. Beyond the outward rail, Mauryl's light drowned in the dark and failed, and Tristen kept descending as Mauryl's *step-tap, step-tap,* pursued him down and around and onto his own balcony.

It pursued him likewise toward his own open and abandoned door, as the light in Mauryl's hand chased the dark ahead of him, and in sudden dread of the dark in his own room, he let Mauryl's light overtake him.

"The candle blew out," he said.

"To bed," Mauryl said with the same unforgiving grimness, and Tristen got in under the cold bedclothes, shivering, glad when Mauryl, leaning his staff against the door, used his candle to light the remaining candle at his bedside, the watch-candle having burned down to a guttered stub.

"I didn't mean to make you angry," Tristen said. "I heard the noise. I'm sorry."

Mauryl picked up the cup from beside the candle and wiped the inside with his finger, frowning, not seeming so angry, now. Tristen waited, wondering if Mauryl would go away, or scold him, or what. The bedclothes were cold against his skin. He hoped for a more kindly judgment, at least a fairer one, by the look on Mauryl's face.

53

"My fault," Mauryl said. "My fault, not yours." Mauryl tugged the quilts up over his bare shoulder. So, Tristen thought, Mauryl had forgiven him for whatever he had done by leaving his room. He wished he understood. Words that came to him with such strange clarity – but the danger tonight, and why Mauryl was angry – it seemed never the important things that came easily and quickly, only the trivial ones.

Then Mauryl sat down on the side of his bed, leaned a hand on the quilts the other side of his knee, the way Mauryl had sometimes talked to him at bedtime, a recollection of comfortable times, of his first days with Mauryl. "You put us both in danger," Mauryl said, and patted his knee so that the sting of the words was diminished. "It was foolish of you to run. You startled me. Next time . . . next time, stay where you are. I know the dangers. I've set defenses around us. You attracted attention, most surely, dangerous attention – as dangerous as opening a door."

"Can't it get in the holes?" he asked. "The pigeons do."

"It's not a pigeon. It can't, no. It has to be a door or a window."

"Why?"

Mauryl shrugged. The candlelight seemed friendlier now. It glowed on Mauryl's silver hair and gave a warmer flush to his skin. "It must. There's a magic to doors and windows. When the foundations of a place are laid down, they become a Line on the earth. And doors and windows are appointed for comings and goings, but no place else. Masons know such things. So do Spirits."

They were Words, tasting, the one, of stone and secrets, but the other –

He gave a shiver, knowing then, that it was a spirit they feared. Other Words poured in – Dead, and Ghost, and Haunt.

He thought, Mauryl fears this spirit. That's why we latch the doors and windows. It wants in.

"Why?" he asked. "Why does it want to come in?"

"To do us harm."

"Why?"

"It's a wicked thing. A cruel thing. One day it will have you to fear, boy, but for now it fears me. Go to sleep. Go to sleep now. There will be no more noises."

"What were they? Was it the Shadows?"

"Nothing to concern you. Nothing you need know. Go to sleep, I say. I'll leave the candle." Mauryl stood up, reached toward his face and brushed his eyelids shut with his fingertips. "Sleep."

He couldn't open them. They were too heavy. He heard Mauryl leave, heard the door shut and heard the tap of Mauryl's staff against the door.

After that was the drip of the rain off the eaves, the soft groanings of the timbers of the keep as Mauryl climbed the stairs and walked the floor above.

It was back, and stronger.

Much stronger, Mauryl thought to himself, feeling chill in the moist air of the night.

There was no immediate touch. He waited, still weak from the latest encounter. Anger welled up in him. But he gave it no foothold. Anger, too, became a weakness.

– Your Shaping is helpless, the Wind whispered, nudging the shutter.

– Of course he is, Mauryl said to the Wind. Are you ever wrong?

– Wasted, Gestaurien, all your years were wasted. This Shaping is not enough. You work and you work; you mend your poor failed mannequin, but to what advantage? Where is your vaunted magic, now? All spent. All squandered. What a threat you pose me!

– Come ahead, then. Do your fingers still sting? – But there are no fingers, are there? No fingers, no heart, . . . no manhood. Mere food for carnal worms, a repast for maggots. A beetle has his home in your skull. He has your eyes for windows . . . A fat, well-fed beetle, a fine, upstanding fellow. I like him much better.

– The end of your strength, Gestaurien. Words, words, words, all vacuous breath. Shall I be wounded? Shall I flee in terror? I think not. – I see a loose latch. I do . . .

Bang! *went the shutter, and kept rattling.*

– Tristen, is it? Tristen. A boy. And careless, in the way of boys. He might forget a latch, the way you forgot his cup – and the shutter – tonight. Was that accident? Do you suppose it was accident?

The air seemed close, full of menace. The shutter rattled perilously. Mauryl rose up, seized his staff, and it stopped.

Thump, *went the next shutter, making his heart jump.*

– Worried? asked the Wind.

– Come ahead, I say. Why don't you? How many years did it take you to recover the last time you misjudged me? Twenty? More than twenty? Intrude into my keep again. Come, try again, thou nest for worms. You might be lucky. Or not.

It made no reply. It rolled in on itself with none of its accustomed mockery. It nursed secrets, tonight. It restrained something it by no means wanted to say.

Mauryl bowed his head against his staff and put forth all his guard, wary of a sudden reversal. But nothing came. He reached not a breath, not a whisper of presence.

He sent his thoughts further still, around the rock of the fortress, and through its cracks and crevices.

But no further than that. He found limits to his will that had never been there, perhaps the limits of his own defenses – or perhaps not his construction at all, but a prisoning so subtly constructed he had had no suspicion of it until now.

Sweat stood on his brow with the effort to catch the wind in his nets. But there was, no matter how fine he made them, not a breath within his reach.

He might believe, then, that the prison was illusory, that, as in the long, long past, he still found no limit but himself. But he feared not. He feared, that was the difficulty. Fear slipped so easily toward doubt – and doubt to the suspicion that his old enemy had no wish for encounter, not on his terms.

He would not be so fortunate, this time, in choosing the moment.

He had known as much, in his heart of hearts. His old student knew it, and sought as yet no direct contest.

CHAPTER 5

He could see Mauryl in the silver reflection, standing behind his shoulder. Mauryl waited, expecting him to cut himself, Tristen was well certain – *believing* he would cut himself. Mauryl had warned him the blade was sharp and showed him how to hold it.

He might grow a beard, Mauryl said, except Mauryl said that beards were for priests and wizards, that he was neither, and that, besides, it would not suit him. So Mauryl had given him the very sharp blade, a whetstone and, the wonder of the occasion, a polished silver Mirror.

Of course, he thought. Of course, and knew that men could, after all, see their own faces. Mauryl had said magic was what wizards did, and the mirror was clearly a magical thing. Tristen made small grimaces at himself, sampled his expressions to see if they were what he thought, and most of all noticed his imperfections: for one, that his mouth sulked if he frowned, and for another that his eyes had no clear color – unlike Mauryl's, which were murky blue.

But the beard Mauryl had set him to remove was only a few patchy spots, and a shadow of a mustache – that was the itching, and he agreed with Mauryl about having it off, seeing it looked in no wise like Mauryl's, no more than his dark, unruly mop of hair looked like Mauryl's silver mane.

There were virtues to his face, all the same, he thought, in such silver-glazed essence as the mirror showed him. It was a regular face, and he could make it pleasant. His skin was smooth where Mauryl's was not. His mouth – the mustaches shaded Mauryl's – seemed more full, his nose was indeed straight where Mauryl's bent, his brows were dark as his hair, with which he was well acquainted, since it swung this side and that when he worked, and fell in his eyes when he read.

There were certainly worse faces among the images in the walls. Far worse. He supposed he should be glad. He supposed it was a good face.

He guided a last flick of the bronze knife.

"Mauryl, it stings." There was a dark spot. He wiped it with his fingers and found blood.

"Now does it?"

He rubbed his chin a second time, feeling not the sting of the knife but the tingle of Mauryl's cures.

"No," he said, and washed his fingers and the knife in the pan, and looked again. His face seemed too . . . unexpressive. His hair was always in his way: Mauryl's behaved; but if he had as much beard as Mauryl, with such dark hair, he would be all shadows.

And Mauryl was shining silver.

He was vaguely disappointed, not knowing why he should care . . . but he had made up a face for himself out of the shadow in the water barrel, and he found his real one both more vivid and less like Mauryl's.

Maybe he should cut the hair, too, at least the part that fell in his eyes. But he doubted where, or with what effect.

"A clean face," Mauryl said. And as he offered the knife back, with the whetstone: "A proper face. – No, keep them. I have no need. And you will have, hereafter."

Mauryl had stopped talking lately about going away. But since the day Mauryl had threatened that, and given him the Book, every time he heard a hint of change, every time Mauryl talked about not needing this and not caring about that, no matter how small or foolish a matter, he felt a coldness settle on his heart.

He tried. He did try to read the writing Mauryl had said was his answer and their mutual deliverance from danger. But he made no gains. He had no swift answers, the way Mauryl's writing came to him. It had been days and days with no understanding at all, beyond what few words he thought he read, and he began to doubt those.

Most of all, Mauryl seemed weary with no reason, simply

weary and wearier as the days slipped by. Mauryl's eyes showed it most, and often Mauryl turned away from an encounter as if he carried some besetting thought with him. There was no spirit, no liveliness. Mauryl seemed to lose his thoughts, and to wander away from him in indirection.

"I have no need," Mauryl said, as if he had forgotten whether he had said that.

"Mauryl," he said, stopping him in his course to the study table, "Mauryl, what have I done? Have I done something wrong?"

Mauryl regarded him for a moment as if he had thoughts far elsewhere, saying nothing. Then he seemed to reach some resolution, frowned, and said, "No, lad. No fault of yours."

"Then what fault, master Mauryl?"

"A question," Mauryl said. "A deep question. – Someday, perhaps sooner than I would wish, Tristen lad, you must make choices for yourself. You must go where you see to go. Do you hear? You should go where you see to go."

It was by no means the answer he had looked for, none of this 'sooner than I would wish,' and 'go where you see to go.' It was not the way Mauryl had promised him.

"You said if I should read the Book, master Mauryl, you said you would stay."

"Have you read the Book?" A sharp, fierce look of Mauryl's eyes transfixed him. "Have you?"

"No," he had to say. "I know the letters. I see the shapes. But they don't go together, master Mauryl."

"Then it's very doubtful you can prevent my going, isn't it?"

"What am I supposed to do, master Mauryl? Tell me what I need to find. Tell me what I need to learn!"

"Something will occur to you. You'll know."

"Mauryl, please!"

"Over some things in our lives we have no governance, Tristen lad. Magic works by a certain luck and sometimes it fails by lack of that luck. What we individually deserve isn't as much as what we collectively merit. That's a profound secret, which few understand. Most people believe they live alone. That's very wrong."

"I don't understand. I don't understand, Mauryl. What people? Where are they?"

"They exist. Oh, there's a wide world out there, Tristen. There's a before and a now and a yet to come. All this matters. But in order to know how it matters, one has to know – one has to know more than I can teach you. Tristen lad, you have to find for yourself."

"Where? Where shall I look? If I found it, would you not go away?"

"Oh, I doubt that, Tristen lad." Mauryl seemed disheartened and made less and less sense to him. "I should never have feared your Summoning. It was my failing, when I Shaped you. Doubt, I swear to you, is a fool's best ally, and a wise man's worst. The work of decades, and I flinched. But mending, such as I might, I have done. – And if I go away, doubt not at all: take the Road that offers itself."

"But it goes south," he said. "You said never go on the south side."

"How do you know that it goes south?"

"Does it not?" It was the only Road he knew, a Word and a guilty secret that had troubled him ever since he had stepped up where he knew in his heart of hearts he was not supposed to venture. It was a Word that from that very moment had smelled of dust and danger and sadness. It was the way he thought Mauryl might go, if Mauryl made good his threat to leave.

Now he saw he had betrayed himself. He had thought because Mauryl had said what he had said that Mauryl might, after all, have meant him to discover it – but clearly not so, by Mauryl's quick and thunderous frown.

"And where, young sir, have you known about this Road?"

"From the loft," he said, shamefacedly. "– But I didn't go on the parapet. I looked through the hole the storm made."

"And said nothing of it to me?"

"I – saw it only once, Mauryl. I never looked again."

Mauryl still frowned, but not so angrily. "And what else have you seen from this vantage?"

"Water. Woods. – Stones."

"Ruins. Ruins of long ago. What more?"

"Mountains." That Word tumbled onto his heart, when he remembered the horizon above the forest.

"Hills. The *foothills* of Ilenéluin, which stretch far up to the Shadow Hills in the north. There are far greater mountains in the world. – What more have you found, in this escapade?"

"The sky. The clouds. Only that."

For a moment Mauryl stood with his arms folded, still seeming angry. "Names are power over a thing, for a wizard or for a man. This fortress has a name: Ynefel. The forest is Marna. A river lies between the walls of Ynefel and Marna Wood and it winds beyond Marna Wood again: Lenúalim is the river. These are their names. Do you take all of that, Tristen?"

They were not names. They were each of them Words – Words that came to him with dark, and cold, and terror; with trees and branches and depth and cold. They were Words that carried the world wider than he could see, and full of threats he did not guess, and animals and birds and creatures far more terrible than Owl.

Ilenéluin: stone and storm and ice.

Lenúalim: secrets and division, and dreadful dark.

Ynefel: –

He wanted not to know. He saw the stones around him, that was all, a place of rickety stairs and balconies spiraling up a stone-walled height, stone faces staring at them, stone hands reaching and never escaping the walls.

"Some things happen against our wishes," Mauryl said, "and some things we desired come in ways we would gladly refuse." Mauryl laid his hand on his shoulder. Mauryl wanted his strict attention, and that frightened him more than all things else. "Tristen, there will come a day. Soon. You have all I could give you, all I could mend afterward. Beware of trust, boy, but most of all beware of doubt. Both are deadly to us."

It was a stifling fear Mauryl laid on him. "I try to understand what you tell me, Mauryl. I do try."

"Go to your studies. Go find your Book. It's upstairs, is it not?"

"Yes. But –" He became convinced of secrets, of some deception Mauryl played at his expense. He knew his questions wearied Mauryl and his mistakes vexed Mauryl, and his slowness was Mauryl's despair. "Can you not help me a little, Mauryl, only a little? Show me just a word or two. Other things come to me without my even trying. This – that I most want to learn – I make no sense of it. It will not come."

"It will. In its own time, it will. Magic is like that." Mauryl's fingers squeezed his arm. "Be clever. Be no fool, boy. Tristen. Go."

He was disheartened at that. He took his gifts from Mauryl, the little mirror, the razor and the stone to sharpen it, he bowed politely, and went toward the stairs.

A sound rattled off the walls – a strangely muffled thunder that made him glance away to the study wall. Thunder, he thought. Rain would make the loft untenable. He would have to come downstairs to study, then, and perhaps, after all, Mauryl would take pity and give him at least a hint.

He laid his hand on the banister. And it was not thunder that made the banister tremble. He looked up in alarm as that rumbling came again.

"Go," Mauryl said.

"There's a sound, Mauryl. What is it?"

"Go upstairs."

"But –" He had almost protested it came from upstairs. But it came then from all about, and it rattled and thundered like nothing he had ever heard. Mauryl left him and stood staring toward the farther hall – it seemed to be coming from there, at the moment. It shook at the doors they never opened, never unbarred. It hammered. The thunder echoed through the stones.

"Mauryl!"

"Upstairs!" Mauryl slammed a heavy codex shut, and dust

flew out in a cloud. "These are no threat to me. A petty nuisance. A triviality. – Get upstairs, I say!"

The hammering had become a steady, regular thumping. The huge book had overset the inkpot as Mauryl shut it, and a trail of ink ran over the table, snaked among the parchments, and dripped on the floor as Tristen wavered between saving the parchments and obeying Mauryl – but then Mauryl shouted at him a Word without a sound to his ears, and a stifling fear came over him, a fear that left him no thought but to do what Mauryl had told him, while the hammering and banging racketed through the lower hall and shook the walls and the wooden steps.

He ran up the stairs faster than he had ever climbed. He reached his own balcony and ran for his own room – flung open the door and shut it again, trembling as he leaned against it, thinking then, by Mauryl's mastery of things, to have safety. But the hammering downstairs seemed to shake the wooden floor under his feet. The room felt dank and precarious – it smothered, it held him prisoner.

No safety, no hiding place, something said to him, and he felt a sense of peril so imminent he felt he had to have the door open again or suffocate. Mauryl had said no. Mauryl had said be *here*, but the thundering in the stone walls seemed to come from right below his window. He saw a crack run up the wall. To his horror he saw it advance rapidly along the mason-work and right up to the wooden frame of the horn-paned window itself – then around the latched side of the frame. The latch parted, the gap grown too wide, and white daylight came through.

He hardly knew what he was thinking, then, in that stifling terror, except of the Book, Mauryl's Book, that Mauryl had said was what he had to know, and he had to have – he snatched it from the table and thrust it into his shirt and grasped the door latch.

But after that nothing could stay the panic. He fled the room, sped down the balcony as the wooden supports quaked to the hammering at the doors – up, Mauryl had said, go upstairs, and his room was not safe. He ran the stairs that spiraled up and up past Mauryl's balcony, as the whole structure of the balconies creaked and groaned – he raced up into the high, mad reach of braces and timbers, and the narrow, low-ceilinged stairs that led into the shadow of the loft.

He could scarcely get his breath. He went to the boarded division of the loft, seeking a place sheltered from the holes and gaps in the shingles, a hidden place, a stable place. He clambered out under the eaves, guarding his head from the rafters, an arm braced against the dust-silked wood. Cobwebs, the work of determined spiders, tangled across his face and hair; he brushed them away, while all about him the fortress resounded to the hammering and the air tingled and rumbled.

Came a moaning, then, as if the entire fortress were in pain – and a rising babble, like rain dancing into the cistern, he thought, and crept further into his nook, tucked up with his arms about him. He shivered, as pigeons fluttered in alarm and more and more of them took wing out the gaps in the boards of the loft.

The babbling swelled, sounding now like voices, as if – as if, he thought, trying to reason in himself what it was – the whole fortress were full of people, all trying to be heard. The hammering had stopped, and began again, a sharp sound, now, ringing off the walls – the sound of an axe, he thought, and at first was bewildered, then knew, like a Word, that it was the doors that sound threatened.

Then – then the howling began, the same horrid sound that had frightened him from his bed – and if it was from inside, Mauryl must have called it, he said to himself. He felt it drawing at him. He felt Mauryl's presence tingling in the air around him. Wind swept in and scoured the straw from the floor; wind ripped holes in the shingles that patched the slates; wind sent a blast of straw out of the nests in the peak of the roof. He ducked and covered his eyes, and finally – finally in desperation locked his arms over his head and squeezed his eyes shut against the gale.

The howling hurt his ears, dust choked him – there were voices upon voices, rumbling, deep ones, and shrill and piercing: the stone faces everywhere about the keep, open-mouthed, might have come alive – stones might scream like that. He might have. He shook. He clenched his arms and legs up close, as the howling and the shrieking and the rumbling quivered through the boards.

The birds must have fled. They had wings. He had none. He could only stop his ears with his hands and endure it as long as he could.

Then the light he could perceive began to fade. He squinted through the wind, fearing if the sun was going it might never come back. A gust in that moment ripped planks loose from the facing, planks that fell and let in the howling of a stronger wind.

He recoiled and caught hold of a rafter, blinded by the flying straw and grit and dust. He felt the Book slip from his shirt, reached for it, saw, with tears running on his face, its pages whipped open by the wind. A crack opened in the floor, the dusty planks separating as the stones had parted in his room, and the gap spread beside the Book as the pages flipped wildly toward the opening. The Book began to go over –

He let go the beam to seize it, bending pages haphazardly with his fingers. He held it against him as the very timbers of the loft creaked and moaned in the blasts.

"Mauryl!" he cried, having reached the end of his courage. "Mauryl! Help me!"

But no answer came.

There was no more strength. Mice perished, poor surrogate victims, sorry vengeance for Galasien. Birds flew in the high reaches of the tower and battered themselves against the stone, falling senseless and dying to the floor far below . . . .

The wind roared, and Mauryl shuddered at the chaos that poured through the rents in the walls.

– Gods, he murmured, gods, thou fool, Hasufin.

– *The gods are gone*, the Wind said. *The first to flee us were all such gods as favored us, did you mark that, Gestaurien? But I may Summon thee back to my service. What do you think of that?*

– *Ludicrous*, Mauryl said, and slipped, perilously so, toward the horror always thick about the fortress. The imprisoned spirits wailed, mindless in their despair, wailed and raveled in the winds, powerless now.

– *So where is your Shaping, old Master?* asked the Wind. *Where is your defender, this champion of your poor crumbling hall? Cowering amongst the pigeons? Hiding from me?*

– *I thought you knew. Ask wiser questions. I wait to be astonished.*

– *Mock what you like. Banish me this time, old fool. Tell me this time who's the greater.*

– *Time*, Mauryl said, and drew a breath laden with dust. He cracked his staff against the stones, once, twice, three times, and the towers quaked, sifting down dust. *Time is ripped loose, fool, it is undone: we exist, thou and I, only for what will be; we dream, you and I, we dream, but no hand have we on the world. All is done, Hasufin, all for us is past, and failed, our candle is out, and worms are the issue of our long contention. Have done, thou arrant, prating fool, and let it rest here.*

The wind breathed in sudden hush between the gusts, sported about the courtyard, whirled among dead leaves that . . . for a moment . . . showed a dust-formed cloak and cowl.

– *Destroy the Shaping*, the man of dust said. *Do that, my old mentor, and, aye, we might together sleep the sleep. Will that content thee? Come, take my hand, let us kiss like brothers. Destroy him. And we shall sleep in peace.*

– *Whoreson liar. Worms, I say, worms for your bed, Hasufin, thou braggart, thou frail, mistaken fool. I weary of the war.*

– *Lies for lies, thou lord of delusion.*

The dust whipped away, stung the face, blinded the eyes. Mauryl flung it back, and Hasufin struck in kind.

The stones, the former inhabitants of Galasien, screamed with all their voices.

Chaos closed around. The thunder of the staff kept rolling, echoing, cracking stone.

Then came silence. Long silence.

CHAPTER 6

~

Tristen's ears still rang. His flesh still was chilled by the
wind. But the Shadow had gone, and broken straw prickled against his face and through his shirt and his breeches –
prickled until he was, first, aware of lying on the dusty
boards, and second, aware that one knee had gone through a
second gap in the boards, and third, aware that he still held
the Book safe beneath his body.

Holes were everywhere about the roof, letting in large,
dusty shafts of sunlight. Pigeons murmured, a handful going
about their ordinary business on the rafters and on the central
beam which upheld the roof. A quiet breeze stirred through
the loft.

The trouble was past, Tristen thought, and dragged himself
from his precarious position, gathered his knees under him
and sat up, holding the Book against him – Mauryl would be
pleased that he had saved it. Mauryl would have sent the
wind away. Mauryl would have held everything safe downstairs . . .

But Mauryl would be in no good mood.

He decided he should present himself very quietly downstairs, and straighten up the parchments and blot up the ink
before Mauryl saw it and lost his temper. He had had thunders
and screams and ragings enough: he wanted to please Mauryl,
and he most of all wanted calm and peace and Mauryl's good
humor.

He gathered himself up and crossed the creaking boards,
causing a quiet, anxious stir among the pigeons. He dusted
himself as he went, raked random straws from his hair, wanting to have no fault Mauryl could possibly find. But when
he went out and down the narrow stairs, and down again to
the balcony, the light was shining into the hall from holes in the

roof of the keep itself, which it had never done, and the balcony he walked had settled to a precarious, twisted tilt among the rafters.

"Mauryl?" he called out, wanting rescue.

But there was not a sound.

"Mauryl? I'm upstairs. Can you hear me?"

Rain would get in, at the next storm, and fall where it never had, on the parchments and the books in Mauryl's study. They had to do something about that, surely – some-one must climb up on the roof.

The balcony settled under him, a jolt, and a groan, sending his heart into his throat. He darted for the stairs, hearing little creaks and groans the while, which wakened other groans and creaks in the rafters.

He went down and down, as quickly as he could. The railing of the stairs shook under his hand, and the creaking boards on Mauryl's balcony roused a fearsome shriek of settling timbers; the triple stone faces at the turning of his balcony seemed changed, frozen in some new horror – or maybe it was the shadows from the myriad shafts of dusty sunlight that never before had breached the lower hall.

From overhead came another fearful thump and groaning. A roof slate fell past him and smashed on the stones below.

Tristen caught a breath and ran the steps, trailing his free hand down the banisters, clutching the Book in the other. He reached the study, where a chaotic flood of parchments from off the shelves lay crushed under fragments of slate.

Slates had fallen on the table and smashed the overset ink-pot. He bent and gathered up an armful of parchments, laid them on the table, then sought more, arranging them in stacks, making them, stiff and of varying sizes as they were, as even-edged as he could.

There was a fearsome jolt. An unused balcony came loose, one of the rickety ones on the far side, where they never walked – it groaned, and distorted itself, and fell in great ruin, taking down other timbers, jolting the masonry and raising a cloud of dust.

70

"Mauryl?" he called out into the aftermath of that crash. "Mauryl?" Mauryl should know; Mauryl would not abide it; Mauryl should prevent the timbers falling.

But light fell on him from his right since that crash, and turning his head, he saw a seam of sunlight, saw doors open, or half-open, near him, down the short alcove mostly cluttered with Mauryl's parchments.

He had never seen those doors ajar – had asked Mauryl once did those doors go anywhere, and Mauryl had said, Doors mostly do.

Anywhere in the world, Mauryl had said, is where doors go.

Another slate crashed on the stones, and another. He ducked under the kitchenward arch for safety as a third and a fourth fell.

Mauryl had never opened that south door, nor let him lift the bar. He had never guessed that sunlight was at the other side.

But the door was thrown from its metal hinges, and the bar was thrown down, one end against the stones, with the sun flooding through the crack – the sun, the enemy of the Shadows.

It seemed safer than where he was. He ventured a dash across the slate-littered floor to the arch of the alcove and, finding the gap almost wide enough to let him out, pushed and scraped his way through.

He stood on low steps in a place he had never seen – a stone courtyard within high walls, and a white stone path which led off at an angle through weeds and vacancy, as far as the gate that – he knew all too well – was the start of the Road that led through the encircling woods, the Road that Mauryl had said he must find and follow.

He had thought Mauryl would go before him. He had hoped Mauryl meant him to follow him when he went away.

And perhaps Mauryl had indeed gone, and expected him to have the wits to know that.

"Mauryl?" he called out to the emptiness around him.

Sometimes Mauryl did amazing things, things he never expected, and perhaps, even in this circumstance, Mauryl could speak to him out of the sun or the stones, or give him a stronger hint what he should do next.

Mauryl? – Mauryl? – Mauryl? was all the echoes gave him, his own question back again, the way the walls echoed with the axe.

He could not bear to call aloud again. The courtyard sounded too frighteningly empty.

But the Road was more frightening to him still, and unknown, and he did not want to leave by mistake, too soon: he was prone to mistakes, and it was far too great a matter to risk any misunderstanding at all.

So he sat down on that step in front of the door; he pressed his Book close against him, and told himself that Mauryl was surely still somewhere about, and that it was not time yet for him to go. He should only wait, and be certain.

Mauryl was not, at least, inside; the sun was high, and he was, he said to himself, far safer out here than inside where the roof slates were crashing down, and where the balconies were creaking and falling.

Mauryl could make the balconies stay still if Mauryl were not busy. Mauryl said that making things do what they did naturally was easy, and surely it was natural that things be the way they had always been.

Pigeons came down and walked about on their own errands, expecting grain, perhaps, but he dared not go in again under the chance of falling slates and cross the study to get it for them, not until the slates stopped coming down, or until Mauryl turned up to make everything right again – which he wished most of all.

"Please," he said faintly. "Mauryl? Mauryl, please hear me?"

It was the same as in his room, when the fear came. And no, Mauryl did not always arrive at the moment one would wish. Mauryl did not have every answer; Mauryl had tasks to do that a boy could not understand, and Mauryl's silence could well mean that Mauryl was busy. There had been a danger, but Mauryl had overcome it, and Mauryl would pay attention to him as soon as Mauryl found the time. He should wait patiently and not take hasty action, that was what Mauryl would advise him.

So he sat on the low steps, and he sat, and he sat, until the sun was behind the far tower and the shadow of that tower touched the courtyard.

While he sat, he tried earnestly, fervently, to read his Book, telling himself that now, perhaps, once the moment called for it, Words might come to him and show him everything Mauryl had wanted of him in his command to read this Book, things which would prevent Mauryl going on the Road, and which would prevent his having to go, as well.

But hours passed in his efforts, and in his fear. The shadow of the walls joined the shadow of the tower and grew long across the courtyard stones.

At last the shadow touched the walls, complete across the courtyard, and he knew that on any ordinary day he should be inside and off the parapets and out of the courtyard by now. He was thinking that when the wind suddenly picked up, skirled up the dead leaves from a corner of the wall, and those leaves rose higher and higher, dancing down the paving stones toward the tower.

And back again. That was odd for a wind to do. It was a chill wind as it touched him. The pigeons, while he read, had deserted the courtyard stones, seeking their towers for the night. The shadows, while he read, had come into nooks where no shadows had been at noon. The faces in the stone walls seemed more ambiguous, more ghostly and more dubious than they appeared by day.

Be certain, Mauryl had always said, that the shutters and the doors are bolted every night.

Be afraid of the dark. When the sky shadows, be under stone and have the shutters closed and the doors well shut. Have I not said this before?

He shivered, with the Book folded in his hands, his hands

between his knees as the wind danced back again. He looked up at the color stealing across the sky. The faces set in the walls changed their expressions with the passage of shadow. Now they seemed to look down in horror.

He looked up at the walls above his head – and saw Mauryl's face above him, stone like the others, wide-mouthed and angry.

He stumbled off the middle step, fell on the bottom one and picked himself up, staring at the face in horrid surmise – backed farther and farther across the courtyard stones, with Mauryl's face among the stone faces he had seen in the walls from the beginning of his existence here, wide-mouthed and wide-eyed as if Mauryl could at any moment scream in anger or in terror, either one.

"Mauryl?" he said faintly, and somewhere within the hall timbers fell with a horrific crash and splintering. Another balcony, he thought. "Mauryl?" he cried aloud, daring not admit he still could not read the Book. There must be an exception. There must be a way out. "Mauryl, what shall I do, Mauryl? Please tell me what to do!"

He heard slates fall inside, a lighter, sharper-edged ruin.

A cold skirl of wind went past him.

An immense mass of something crashed inside and knocked the door shut, as if someone had slammed it in his face. He stared in shock, terrified.

He had no recollection, then, of turning away, except he was walking toward the gate. Reaching it, he tried not the heavy bar but the lesser one, which closed a gate within the gate; that was enough to let him out. He shut it once he was through, and asked himself foolishly how he should bar it, and then – against what should he bar it? and protecting what? Mauryl had set great importance on locking and latching doors, but it was far beyond his ability to seal this one against harm. He turned and faced the bridge and the river, and the forest beyond it, already shadowing toward dark – and could only set out walking on the Road. Go where you see to go, Mauryl had said. Take the Road that offers itself.

And he did, over the rotten boards and stonework of the Bridge that spanned the river Lenúalim.

The water was dark beneath the gaps over which he walked, clinging fearfully to the stones along the edge of the high-arched bridge. The river looked murky green in the deep shadow and made patterns on its surface, swirls and ripples which on another day might tempt him to linger and wonder; but haste and dread overwhelmed all curiosity in him – haste – clinging to an ancient, crumbling stone railing, and with old mortar sifting from under his feet. If he should fall, he said to himself, he would slip beneath that surface, where it must be as cold and as dark as the rain barrel or the cistern, and where all that Mauryl had done with him and all that Mauryl had told him would come to nothing: he could not be so foolish.

A moaning sounded behind him, as if the gate had opened. He cast a look over his shoulder and saw it still shut. It might be the wind keening through some board up in the towers – if there were a wind, which there was not. He looked about again just as a stone left the railing ahead of him and dropped from the Road, for no cause that he could tell. It splashed into the water, making a plume, and it was gone, as he himself might be, without a trace, should the road give way.

He hurried feverishly, then, holding to the stones, and heard another fall of stones behind him: one, two, three splashes. He dared not waste a moment to look. It was the solid ground ahead that beckoned him, a shadowed shore where the Road went over safe earth, under deep-rooted trees, and his feet were very glad to feel that solidity under them as he left the bridge behind.

The moaning came to the trees then, making them toss their heads and whisper around him in a rush of sound he had never heard the forest make even in storm. Chill came with that wind, as leaves and fine grit went flying around him, stinging his eyes. The wind shouted around him, until twigs and then small branches flew like leaves. The whole forest seemed to shiver, and then –

Then it grew very quiet, no leaf stirring – a dank and breathless air as frightening in its lifelessness as all the previous fury of the wind. He hesitated to move at all, and when he hesitated, it seemed more difficult than before simply to move, or breathe, as if some soundless Word bade him stand still, and wait, and wait.

But, heart in his throat, he obeyed Mauryl. It seemed more important than ever to honor Mauryl's instruction, in the failing of all substantial refuges he knew. Dark was gathering in this dank hush, a convocation of Shadows that as yet had done him no harm, but he had no defense against them here, no stone to shelter him, no Mauryl to send them away, no light against the coming dark.

– *Tristen,* the Shadows mocked him, calling his name in tones that Mauryl might use. But Mauryl had never trusted them and he refused. He walked not because he knew where he was going but because that was what Mauryl had said to do. No harm had yet come to him doing what Mauryl said.

A shape glided after him, dark and silent. He felt it pass near. But when he looked straight at it, he saw nothing.

Shadows were like that, treacherous and evasive of the eye. But there was no Mauryl tonight to set a seal on his sleep, and no door, and no bed, no supper, no cup, and no means of having one – forever, so far as he knew.

The Road appeared and disappeared by turns in the dark. It seemed to meander aimlessly, but, Tristen thought, he had nowhere to go, except as his Road led him; it seemed to have no reason for itself, but then, he had none, so that seemed apt. If he had the wish of his heart all through the weary night it would be only to go back to Mauryl, and to have his room and his supper and to do forever what Mauryl told him – but it was not his wishes things obeyed, it was Mauryl's; and without Mauryl, he had to take what came to him and do as wisely as he could.

If, he thought, if he could have read the Book Mauryl had

given him, he might have prevented the ruin that had taken Mauryl from him. But he had not been able. Mauryl had known his inability. He was certain now that Mauryl had always known that he would fail in that most important task, and he was certain that that had always been Mauryl's unhappiness with him – for Mauryl had been unhappy. He had sensed, quite strongly at times, Mauryl's unhappiness and dissatisfaction in his mistakes, and, latest of all, Mauryl's despair and Mauryl's acceptance of his shortcomings. He should have been more able, he should have been quicker to understand, he should have understood Mauryl's lessons and done better. But he had not been good enough.

Follow the Road, Mauryl had said.

But Mauryl had also warned him to be under stone when the sun set, and as this one set and the world went gray, he saw no stone to be under. Mauryl had said avoid the Shadows, but he walked through constant shadow, and darker shadow – limped, finally, in a darkness deeper than any the fortress had held except in its blackest depths.

He was bruised through his thin shoes. His right ankle ached, and he had not remembered exactly where that pain had started, until he recalled his flight off the steps, and his fall off the edge of the step. Body as well as spirit, Mauryl had warned him, and the very hour that Mauryl had left him on his own in the keep, he had forgotten the first lesson he had ever learned, and fallen and done himself harm, exactly as Mauryl had warned him not to do.

He walked and walked, unhappy with himself, following the ancient stonework until the trees grew so close he could no longer find the next white stone to guide him.

So he had made another mistake. He had lost the Road. He was afraid, standing alone in the dark and trying to know what to do in this place where the path ran out. But it seemed to him that, if there were no white stones, still a long track stretched ahead clear of trees, and that seemed indisputably the right direction to go.

And, true enough, when he had gone quite far on that

treeless track he saw something in the starlight that he deluded himself was another of the white stones.

His heart rose. He went toward it as proof that he had solved the dilemma.

But it was only a broken tree, white inside, jagged ends of wood showing pale in the night.

Then he was truly frightened, and when he looked about him he saw nothing even to tell him which way he had come. He might have made, he thought, the worst mistake of all the mistakes he had ever made and lost the Road once for all, Mauryl's last, Mauryl's most final instruction – beyond which he had no idea in the world what to do.

At that moment a shadow brushed his cheek, substantial enough to scare him. It settled on a branch of that dead tree, hunched up its shoulders and waited.

"Owl?" Tristen said. "Owl, is it you?"

Owl, a sullen bird, only spread his wings and ruffled his feathers with a sound very loud in the hush of the woods.

"Do you know the way?" Tristen asked him, but Owl did nothing.

"Have you come on the same Road?" Tristen asked then, since they came from the same place perhaps at the same moment, and Mauryl had set great importance on his being here. "Did Mauryl tell you to come?"

Owl gave no sign of understanding.

He had never trusted Owl. He had never been certain but what the smallest birds disappeared down Owl's gullet, and he was all but certain about the mice.

But he felt gladder than he had ever thought he should be of Owl's presence, simply because Owl was a living creature as well as a Shadow, and because Owl was a force whose behavior he knew – and because he was despondent and lost.

"Do you know where the Road is?" he asked Owl.

Owl spread his wide blunt wings and, Shadow that he was, flew through the darkness to another tree and perched there. Waiting, Tristen thought, and he followed Owl in desperate hope that Owl knew where he was going. Owl flew on again, which he also followed. A third time Owl took wing, and by now he had no hope else but Owl, because he had no notion as he looked back where he had come from, or where his last memory of the Road might lie.

Owl kept flying in short hops from tree to tree, never leaving his sight – and by now he feared that he might have done something Mauryl would never have approved, and trusted a bird that Mauryl had never told him was acceptable to trust. One of the pigeons he might have relied upon, never questioning its character or its intentions; but Owl was the chanciest of creatures he knew, and he knew no reason Owl should go to such great difficulty to guide him to the Road. Certainly he would have helped Owl. That was a point: creatures should help one another, and perhaps Owl was constrained once there was such calamity.

He had never apprehended Owl to have great patience with him. He knew no reason Owl should not lead him far astray and then fly away from him. But Mauryl was often peevish himself, and yet Mauryl had never failed him or done him harm.

So he kept tracking Owl's flights through the woods, fending branches aside, scratching himself and snagging his clothing on thorns and twigs all the while. His ankle hurt. His hands hurt. Owl traveled farther at each flight now, and sometimes left his sight. He struggled to keep up and called out, "Owl! Wait! I'm not so fast as you!" but Owl only took that for encouragement to make his next flight through a low spot filled with water and to lure him up a muddy bank.

He was altogether out of breath now. "Owl, wait," he called out. "Please wait!"

Owl flitted on.

He tried to run, and caught his foot on a stone in the tangle of brush and fell to his knees, bruising them and his hands and sticking his left palm with thorns.

But the stone on which he had fallen was pale, a tilted, half-buried paving of the Road, and he sat there catching his breath, seeing other stones before him.

"Who?" he heard a strange voice calling. "To-who?" He had never heard Owl's voice, but something said to him that that was indeed Owl speaking his question into the night.

And it struck him that it was like Mauryl's questions, and that he had no answer, since the world was far wider and the Road was far longer than he had ever imagined.

"Come back," he said to Owl, rising to his feet. He tried to follow Owl further, but Owl left the pale trace that was the Road, and he gave up the chase, out of breath and sweating in the clammy night air.

But he could have no complaint of Owl. He kept walking, comforted that he was not alone in the woods, and hearing from time to time Owl's lonely question.

In the black, branch-woven sameness of the woods, the Road seemed finally to acquire a faint glow in the night, a glow against which Tristen could see the detail of branches in contrast. And slowly thereafter the whole world of black branches and pale stone Road widened around him until, looking up, he could tell the shadow of the trees from the gray sky. It was the dawn creeping through, not with a bright breaking of the sun, but a stealthy, furtive dawn that took a long, long time to insinuate itself into the black and gray of the woods. He might not have made any progress at all. Nothing looked different from where he had lost the light.

He had walked the night through without resting, and he supposed that since he had somehow reached the dawn unharmed he had done something difficult that Mauryl would approve, but he felt no comfort in his situation. He was very thirsty, there was no breakfast, he was bruised from his falls, and he missed Mauryl's advice and asked himself whether Mauryl had ever given any hint, any remote hint if, after Mauryl had gone away, he might ever find him again – because without Mauryl, he had no idea what to do next, or what he should be thinking of doing.

Use your wits, Mauryl was wont to say, but one had to

know on what question to use one's wits in the first place – like wondering how long his ankle and his knees would hurt when there was no Mauryl to make the pain stop, and wondering how long and how far the Road went, and wondering where Owl was and why Owl had followed him, out of all the birds he liked far better.

His thinking had become merely a spate of like questions with nothing to suggest the answers, and long as he walked, the sights around him never changed, one tree being very much like another to his opinion.

Sitting down, which he did when his legs were utterly exhausted, offered him only time to think up more questions, so he proceeded slowly and steadily, in pain that was more persistent than acute, pain that might, for what he knew, go on forever, as the Road might – in his worst imaginings.

But after a measureless time he found a little trickle of water running down from rocks beneath the roots of trees, at the side of the Road, a trickle that ran away and lost itself beneath a layer of leaves, but where it emerged from the rocks it was bright and clear.

And the mere fact it existed made this a Place, not just a part of the endless Road. It was not more trees and more Road; it existed as a difference in his condition, it offered relief from thirst, and he bent down by it and drank – then washed his face and his hands to the elbows and then his head and hair in the good, clear water, not caring that it chilled him through. He scrubbed and scrubbed until he began to shiver in the light breeze that blew, because Mauryl had taught him to love being clean.

He knew a Place along the Road, then, that offered him water, if he began to be desperate – clean water, as pure as that from the cistern at Ynefel, and it occurred to him that he could stay by it and not be thirsty today; at the very least, he could sit for a while and rest. He could let his head down against the mossy stones. He could shut his eyes a moment in the sunlight, knowing he could drink again any time he wished.

He found a dark gray nothing behind his eyelids. It shadowed with wings like the wings of his birds, quiet, dizzy movements, like their gliding in the sky, and he rode that for a precious few moments, content to be rocked in it, absorbed in it.

"Owl?" he asked then of that vision, remembering that Owl had followed him; and he saw the loft again, but they were only silly pigeons that came and went, and their voices lulled him deeper into sleep.

How strange, he thought, to dream of falling asleep. That was twice asleep. And very, very deep this sleep within a sleep seemed to be, layer upon layer of it folding him over like thick quilts on a chill night.

He looked for Mauryl in the grayness of the loft, then. He looked for Mauryl, but he saw only birds walking to and fro. He saw only dust on the boards, and there was a gap in the boards of the dividing wall that the storm had made, toward which he knew he ought not to look. He did not know why he ought not now, when he had ventured to explore the other side of that gap back at Ynefel. But it seemed to him that the gap in that barrier was a source of dreadful harm.

He hid in the loft, instead, and something came searching for him, something he could not put a shape to, or understand. He thought it was a Shadow. He tucked himself deep within the nook he had found between the rafters and hoped for it to go away.

It brushed by him. It came back again. It seemed he was not in the loft at all, but lying on moss-covered stone, among the leaves, and for some reason a deep leaf-shadow was on him, protecting him from the presence that paced along the Road. Looking for him, it was, he thought. He did not know what else it might be looking for.

The Book burned the skin of his waist where he had tucked it, as that presence paused beside his broad daylight hiding-place. It was not at all the loft now that sheltered him, and it was not the birds coming to and fro that made that strange sound, it was a patter of rain drops falling on the forest's discarded leaves.

And in the awareness of that sound the presence he had felt so strongly had ceased to be there.

Something loomed above him instead, spreading wings between him and the sky. It was Owl, out by daylight, perched on a leafless branch and peering fiercely off into the distances up the Road as Owl would do – Owl suspected things, and he seemed to suspect this one intensely.

"What do you see, Owl?" he asked, awake, as he thought, with his heart beating harder than a dream warranted. "What was it?"

But Owl flew off down the Road with a sudden snap of his wings and gave him not a second glance.

He was still afraid, then – of what, he had no idea, but the Place no longer seemed safe. Neither did the Road behind him, now that Owl had fled it in such haste. But he gathered himself up immediately and set out walking, following Owl.

The notion of danger behind him in the endless woods – and the notion of Ynefel also lying behind him and at the heart of the woods – was a new thought to him: the Road had at least one end, and he had come *from* there. The water was a Place. So he began to form in his mind then the notion that the Road might equally well go to Places, as doors did, and that *to* must be at least as important as *from*.

Then he thought that tomorrow or this evening must at least be at least as substantial as yesterday – and that *tomorrow* and toward a yet-to-find Place was where Mauryl had wanted him to go. Owl had gone, showing him the way in great urgency.

So there was somewhere to be, and somewhere to have been, and somewhere yet urgently to go, which Mauryl had assigned him. And his slowness had made him almost fall into the Shadow. It was another mistake to have delayed at all to rest – a mistake to have been wandering as much as walking, not knowing he had a place to be, not, he had to admit to himself, really wanting to follow Mauryl's instruction, not wanting to be anywhere but Ynefel, because he had conceived of nowhere else despite the Names that Mauryl had told him. Of course there were other Places. Mauryl had tried to tell him, but like rain off the shingles, it had slid right off his mind, as everyday sights did, until the Word was ready to come. Or – and this one had done that – a Word would come partway, and he would go on attaching more and more pieces of it all day or for days after, until a new and startling idea came to him with all its various pieces attached.

Now he feared that other Place he was going as possibly one that would take him in and close off to him forever the Place that he had been. He refused to imagine a world in which Mauryl was gone for good. It terrified him, such a Place, which could exist, now that he began to think about such things as tomorrow, and tomorrow after that.

Owl's precipitate flight frightened him. It drove him to desperate haste, far beyond his ordinary strength.

And when the dark came down again in his walking on the Road he was afraid to sit down and sleep, hungry and thirsty and miserable as he was, because the shadows were abroad. He kept walking until he was staggering with exhaustion and light-headed with hunger.

"Owl?" he begged of the formless dark. "Owl, can you hear me?"

It was the hour for Owl to be abroad. But perhaps Owl was busy. Or ignoring him, as obstinately as Mauryl would, when he interrupted Mauryl at his ciphering, and if he persisted, then Mauryl's next answer – and, he suspected, Owl's – would not be polite at all.

But he wished, oh, he wished Owl would come back. There were clearly sides to the Road which went on unguessably far, forest into which Owl could go, but he dared not venture. The air as he walked grew cold and the woods grew frightening. There were stirrings and movements in the brush where by day he had heard nothing. The place felt bad, the way the stairs and balconies of the keep, safe and familiar by day, had felt dangerous when the Shadows were free to move about.

No Owl, no Mauryl, no shelter and no door to lock. There was no safety for him tonight, and nowhere to stop. He sat down only when morning came sneaking into the woods, and he sat and hugged his knees up to his chest for warmth, his head both light and aching. He had no idea where he was, except beside the Road. He had no idea yet where he was going, or how far he had already come. The world remained measureless to him on all sides now.

And when he waked he was so light-headed and so miserable he tried eating a leaf from the bushes that sheltered him, but its taste was bitter and foul and made his mouth burn. He wished he had the water he had found yesterday, but there was no food there, he knew that for very certain. So he ate no more leaves, and after a long time of walking his mouth quit burning.

Then his stomach seemed to give up the idea of food at all. He was not quite hungry. He told himself he could keep going – he had gone farther than he had ever thought he could, he was stronger than he had ever thought he was, and miserable as he was, nothing had laid hands on him, nothing had stopped him, nothing had daunted him from Mauryl's instructions.

"Who?" came from overhead. Owl was back. Owl flew off from him with no time for questions.

Owl intended, perhaps, encouragement, since of Words there were, Owl was not profligate, and Owl asked his question without an answer.

Who? indeed. "Tristen! Tristen is my name, Owl! Do you hear me?"

"Who?" came from the distance now, beckoning him, a known voice, if not a friendly voice.

"Owl, did you eat the mice?"

"Who?" came again.

Owl denied everything, and flew away from him, too distant now for argument. Tristen saw him, a feathered lump, far, far through the branches.

But Owl guided him. Owl seemed to hold some secret, and constantly flitted out of his reach – but Mauryl had done that, too, making him learn for himself: he knew Mauryl's tricks.

He called out: "Are you Mauryl's, Owl? Did he send you?"

"To-who?" said Owl, and flew away out of sight.

But the mere sound of voices, Owl's and his own, had livened the leaden air, an irreverent fracture of the silence, and once the deathly silence was broken, from seeing for days now only the gray and the black of dead limbs, he began to see shafts of sunlight, green moss growing, and green leaves lit by the passage of sunbeams.

Perhaps the sunbeams had always been there, working their small transformations, but Marna, when it had first come to him as a Word, had seemed a name for darkness and loss; his eyes until this moment might have been seeing only the dark. But now that he looked without expecting gloominess, Marna showed itself in a new and livelier way — a tricky and a changeable place, as it seemed.

But then, Ynefel itself ran rife with terror and darkness, so long as the Shadows ruled it – and, again, Ynefel shone warm with firelight and smelled of good food, and Mauryl sat safe by the fireside, reading. Were not both . . . equally . . . Ynefel, to his mind? And were not both . . . equally and separately . . . true?

So perhaps Marna Wood could be fair and safe at one time and have another aspect altogether when the Shadows were abroad.

And if he could think – as he had – one way and then the other about its nature, and if the forest could put on an aspect according to his expectations, then it seemed to him much wiser to think well instead of ill of the place, and to expect sunlight here to shine brightly as the sunlight came to the loft at home, to fall as brightly here as it fell on the pages of his Book when he read his lessons among the pigeons.

And perhaps other things came from expecting the best of them as hard as he could.

So immediately he drew his Book out of his shirt, stopped in the full middle of a sunbeam, and opened it and looked at the writing, hoping that if one thing had changed, if he fully,

86

truly, with all his heart expected to read the Book, then the Words might come to him – just a few Words, perhaps, so he turned from page to page.

But the letters remained only shapes, and even the ones he had thought he understood now looked different and indecipherable to his eye. His expectation, he thought, must not be great enough, or sure enough, in the way that Mauryl expected bruises not to hurt, or Shadows not to harm them. He clearly had not Mauryl's power – but then –

But, was the inescapable conclusion, then Mauryl had never expected him to read the Book – or had not expected it enough. That was a very troubling point. Mauryl could expect his hand to stop hurting, and it would. Mauryl could expect that the rain would come, and it would. Mauryl could expect the Shadows to leave his room alone, and Mauryl could bar the door against them, and bang his staff on the stones and bid them keep their distance; the Shadows would obey Mauryl, if not him.

Yet Mauryl had doubted that he would read the Book?

Mauryl had doubted him and doubted his ability, but all else, including very difficult things for him to do, Mauryl had seemed so certain of. He no longer knew what Mauryl had thought of him, or what Mauryl had expected.

So he tucked his Book away fearfully and kept walking; and when the sun was at its highest overhead, he sat down on a fallen log in a patch of sunlight, took out his Book and tried again to read, tried, mindful of Mauryl's doubt, tried until his eyes ached and until his own doubt and his despair began to gray the woods around him.

But then the sun, which had faded around him, shone brightly and clearly in a new place farther down the Road.

So it seemed to him that the sun might be saying, as Owl had said, Follow the Road, and he rose up, tucked away his Book, and walked further, relying on the sun, relying on Owl, and hoping very much for an end of this place.

*   *   *

Came another nightfall, and the sky turned mostly gray again and the woods went back to their darkness. Tristen was growing more than tired, he was growing weak and dizzy and wandering in his steps.

He had begun, however faintly, to promise himself that at the end of the Road might lie a place like Ynefel, a place with walls of strong stone, and, he imagined, there might be a fireplace, and there might be a warm small room where he could sleep safe at night – that was what he hoped for, perhaps because he could imagine nothing else outside of this woods, and he wanted the woods to end.

Perhaps, in this place he imagined, there would be someone like Mauryl, since there surely would be someone to keep things in order. There would be someone like Mauryl, who would be kind to him and teach him the things he needed to know.

"Why did you go?" he asked that grayness inside him, speaking aloud and hoping faintly that Mauryl might be simply waiting for a question.

"What am I to do, Mauryl? Where are you sending me?"

But nothing answered him, not even the wind.

"Owl?" he asked at last, since Owl at least had been visible. It occurred to him that he had not seen Owl in a very long time, and he would at least like Owl's company, however surly Owl could be.

But Owl might be sleeping still, despite the dark that had fallen. Owl also failed to arrive.

So he followed his faintly visible path of fitted stones, which disappeared under forest earth, which reappeared under a black carpet of rotten leaves, which found ways along hillsides and threatened to disappear under earth and leaves altogether and forever. He was afraid. He kept imagining that Place like Ynefel. He kept thinking . . . of that fireside and a snug room where the candles never went out.

The Road lost itself altogether in nightbound undergrowth, where trees had grown and dislodged the stones.

"To-who?" a voice inquired above him.

"There you are," Tristen exclaimed.

"Who?" said Owl, and flew up the hill.

He followed, trying to run as Owl sped ahead, but he had not the strength to keep his feet. He slipped at the very top, among the trees, and tumbled downhill to the Road again, right down to the leaf-covered stones.

"To-who?" said Owl.

He brushed leaf mold from his fall-stung hands and his aching knees. He was cold, and sat there shaking from weakness.

"Are you different than the other Shadows?" he asked Owl. "Are you Mauryl's? – Or are you something else?"

"To-who?" quoth Owl. And leapt out into the dark.

"Wait for me!" Now he was angry as well as afraid. He scrambled to his knees and to his feet, and followed as he could.

But always Owl moved on. He had caught a stitch in his side, but he followed, sometimes losing Owl, sometimes hearing his mocking question far in the distance.

His foot turned in a hole in the stones, and he landed on his hand and an elbow, quite painfully. He could not catch breath enough to stand for two or three painful tries, and then succeeded in setting his knee under him, and rose and walked very much more slowly.

"Who?" Owl called in the distance. The fall had driven the anger out of him and left him only the struggle to keep walking. But he could do no more than he was doing. He hurt more than he had ever hurt in Ynefel, but that seemed the way of this dreary woods: pain, and exhaustion. He walked on until he had hardly the strength to set one foot in front of another.

But as he reached that point of exhaustion, and thought of sitting down and waiting for the dawn to come, whatever the hazards and in spite of Mauryl's warnings, he rounded the shoulder of a hill and heard Owl calling. And in scanning the dark for Owl, he saw a triple-spanned stonework with an arch at either end.

It looked to be a Bridge like that at Ynefel. His spirits were too low by now for extravagant hope, but it was a faint hope, all the same, that he had come to some Place in the dark. A lightless, cheerless Place it might be, but it was surely stone, and the arched structure offered shelter of a kind Mauryl had told him made the dark safe.

So he walked, wavering and shaking as he was, as far as let his eyes tell him the arch let through not into a building but into utter dark – and reaching the second arch, and seeing planks between, he could see that the dark to the other side of the rail was no longer the woods but the glistening darkness of water.

A Bridge for certain, he thought. An arch and a Bridge had begun his journey; and now, with a lifting of his heart, he remembered Mauryl saying that Lenúalim was at the start of his journey and that Lenúalim should meet him on the far side of Marna Wood. *Amefel* was beyond, and Amefel was a Word of green, and safety.

He pressed forward to reach that span, and when he stood on it, beneath the arch, he saw faint starlight shining on the water beyond the stone rail, and saw to his astonishment a living creature leap and fall with a pale splash in the darkness.

"Who?" said Owl, somewhere above him.

This bridge was not so ruined as the one at Ynefel. The second arch, looking stronger than the first, stood above the edge of the shore where the reflective surface of the water gave way to the utter dark of forest on the far side. He stood beneath the first arch with his knees shaking, and with all that water near at hand – and was acutely thirsty. He could see the stars – truly see the stars for the first time in his life, for there were neither clouds nor treetops between him and the sky. He saw the Moon riding among them – a knife-sharp sliver. He had seen it only by day, in its changes. Its glory at night was unexpected and wonderful, a light that watched over him.

He did not leave the Road to go down beside the river. He sat down where he stood, his legs folding under him. He leaned against the stone. He knew it was not wise to leave the

Road where he was, even to venture down to the river he could see. In the limited way the starlight showed it to him, it looked broad, and uncertain at the edges. Fool, Mauryl would say to him, if he fell in, after all this, and had not the strength to get out again.

Owl came and perched on the stone rail of the bridge. Owl came and went from there, and once brought back something which he swallowed with some effort. Tristen had no idea what it was nor wanted to know. Owl was a fierce creature, but Owl was all he had, so he tried not to think ill of him.

CHAPTER 7

❧

The water was brownish green and fast-running beneath him, as Tristen crossed the Bridge in the earliest glimmer of dawn, not trusting the middle of the boards – the loft had taught him that wisdom. Stone felt far safer, and he kept to the rim with the railing to hold to, where the planks lay on the stonework.

Owl had left him at some time last night and he had no guide in this crossing. But no stones fell. That heartened him. And oh, the other side of the river beckoned him, greener than Marna and lit in dawn sun. He was shaky with hunger, but he wanted to run, to rush whole-heartedly toward that green, bright place. Instead, he proceeded as carefully as he was certain Mauryl would advise him, all the way to the endmost span.

But only the width of the arch from a sunnier, younger forest, he asked himself, looking back, what if there were no way back, or what if he were, after leaving the bridge, at the end of all Mauryl's instructions?

He went. He saw no choice. The Road led him onto solid ground and up to a forest that smelled of life. The wan sunlight itself seemed greened by the leaves through which it came. The Road vanished momentarily beneath a thick blanket of gold-colored leaves, but beckoned reassuringly further on.

Marna Wood had indeed stopped with the bridge, every sense told him so as he walked onto that solid ground, and smelled a fresher, warmer wind. He heard a bird singing to the rising sun, and another Word flickered into memory, Wagtail, although it flitted just far enough he could not see it.

And desperately thirsty as he had been since last night, his first venture in this new feeling of safety was down to the water, among green reeds, where, having reached that edge, he stood and looked back a second time at the far side of the river.

Marna stood as gray and as black as it had felt when he had traveled it last night.

Then he saw a lump in a tree branch on that other side, down where the woods met the water.

"Owl!" he called, loudly, so Owl could hear across the river. He waved his arm. "Owl? Do you hear me? I'm here!"

There was no answer, and he was disturbed at the thought of leaving Owl. He hoped Owl knew he had crossed the bridge. He hoped Owl could find him tonight where he was going, wherever the Road would lead him.

He sank down then on the water's edge to drink, dry-shod on a spot of grass between two clumps of water-weed. In the shallows he saw brown and yellow stones. And before he could drink, a living creature swam up and looked at him from under the water surface.

Fish, the Word came to him. *That* had been the leaper in the river last night. It was brown and speckled and he sat very still as he would with the mice, until with a flip of a tail it sped away across the stones, free and very much in its own element.

One ate fish. That came to him, too, and he was repelled by the thought. He had no wish to be like Owl, who gulped down his neighbors.

The river as he drank made one sound, a hoarse voice of strength. The trees sighed with another. But those were not the only sounds. The air hummed with bees and a thicket by him twittered quite happily. He washed his head and hands and looked up to find the source of the commotion.

Birds had gathered about a bush, just up the bank, birds scolding and chasing one another, as he thought at first – but he saw when he came closer that berries were thick on the bush, and ripe berries had fallen on the ground, where birds lay, too, hale and well, but quite silly and flopping about, or sitting with feathers puffed, like pigeons on a chill morning.

The birds, though unacquainted with him, did not all flee him, being much too eager for the berries, and those birds lying and sitting about the bush scarcely evaded his feet, so he was careful where he trod. He took a handful of berries for himself – they were sweet, overripe, and stained his fingers, and he ate a double handful of them before the birds that had fled ventured back to take the ones he dropped.

He was sorry to take their breakfast. He sat on the bank and shared with them, tossing berries out where they dared snatch them. Some squabbled and fought over the ones he threw, while others, full-fed, scarcely reached after the ones he set in front of them. One let him pick it up, and he smoothed its feathers and set it on a branch, but it swung upside down, hung from one foot, and fell into his hands again. So he set it on the ground. It was quite puffed and quite silly, and very full, seeming completely healthy, except the sleepiness. He left some berries on the bush for the birds, and walked with something in his belly for the first time in days, feeling quite giddy, but very much better, thanks to the water he had drunk and the berries he had eaten.

He could have made cakes, he thought, if he had had flour and oil and fire. Cakes with berries. He had made them for Mauryl very often.

And the instant he thought of flour and oil and fire he thought of Mill, and Fields, and when he thought of Fields, then he thought of Men and Houses, Oxen, and Fences, recognitions that tumbled in on him disorderly as the squabbling birds, one thought chasing the other, one seizing a perch and fleeing or falling off in its turn, so chaotic that he struggled not to wonder about anything, and tried not to think beyond the necessity to place his feet one in front of the other and to keep moving, light-headed as he was.

But this morning, on this Road, the thoughts refused to stop coming. The whole woods chattered and rang with birdsong. It was full of Words for him, and Words brought thinking that conjured more Words. His wits wandered, his feet strayed. He turned an ankle painfully in a hidden hole in the pavings, which did nothing to stop the dizzying spate of Words – trees, mosses, leaves, stones, sky, directions, the names of birds and the track of a Badger – all these things crowded into his head until it ached, and he might have wandered in complete confusion if not for the stone Road that came and went beneath the leaves.

Long and long before the supply of Words seemed exhausted – before each had confounded the last – he knew Oak from Ash, knew Acorn and leaf and every sound that came and went. The knowing poured in on him more abundant than the recognition – but he could not, it seemed, exhaust the forest's store of Words.

In weariness of knowing things, in a muddle of sights and sounds, he sat down to rest and slept without intending to, until he blinked at a sky that had dimmed toward dark.

He had come through so much that was difficult and let his eyes close when the going became safer. Now he set out on another night of walking – he dared not sleep when the Shadows came, and he followed the Road as he had before.

Meanwhile the jumble of Words, though less than the rush by day, wanted to come back again, clamoring within that grayness in his mind, where Mauryl was, or might be. He knew Moon and Stars, and now he learned Marten and Fox.

But he tried to still the tumult and to hear only Mauryl, if Mauryl should send a Word to him out of that grayness.

He tried to hear Owl, who had not appeared all day long, but the creature that was singing now was, the song said to him, Frog, saying that it might soon rain.

He was thinking that when a wayward breeze brought the scent of smoke wafting down the Road – smoke, and the smell of something that might possibly be supper: he was not quite convinced that it was, but it smelled so like supper cooking that the hunger the berries had wakened in the morning became more and more urgent as he walked.

Fire was warmth and light, and fire also meant Men, his awareness informed him. Whatever seemed to be cooking – or burning, he thought from moment to moment – it *might* be good to eat. It smelled like that, although it certainly seemed overdone.

But he was still fearful, and not knowing how to call out to men who might themselves be afraid of Shadows in this woods, he decided it would be safer to go up soft-footed, as Mauryl's tempers had taught him, and to know them first, whether they were in a good mood or otherwise, or whether it was in fact supper they were about, and not just wood or rubbish afire.

He left the Road, and followed that smell of smoke up the wind as quietly and stealthily as he could over the dry leaves. He spied firelight shining through the brush and branches, and treading now with greatest caution, he slipped up to spy on the place.

They were indeed men. They had a small fire going in a spot cleared of leaves. They were not old like Mauryl. They were not young like himself. They went clothed in brown cloth and leather, clothes rougher than his own white shirt and breeches. They had beards, dark and full; they were cooking something on a stick above the fire, he had no notion what, but it struck the edges of a Word, and at once dismayed him and advised him that eating living things . . . was permissible. It was something men did by their nature – that *he* should perhaps do, if they offered him a share of their supper.

"Sirs," he said, stepping into the light, and instantly all four men were on their feet. Metal flashed – they had knives, and drew them and threatened him with them, with anger and fear on their faces.

"Sirs," he said, quietly, "please, sirs, I'm very hungry. May I have supper?"

"He ain't no woodsman," one said, and with a squint across the fire: "Who are you?"

"Tristen, sir."

"Sir," another said, and elbowed the first man in the ribs. "Sir, ye are."

"Where from?" the first asked. "Lanfarnesse?"

He pointed in the direction from which the Road came. "From the keep, sir. Mauryl's fortress. Ynefel."

One changed knife-hands to make a sign over his heart, hasty and afraid. The others looked afraid, too, and backed away, all to the other side of their fire.

"Please," Tristen said, fearing this meant no. "I need something to eat."

"His speech," the third man said, "ain't Elwynim, nor Lanfarnesse, nor any countryman's, that's certain. O gods, I liked it little enough bein' here. Lanfarnesse rangers be hanged, we shouldn't ever have come here, I said so, I said it, they's naught good in this forest, I told ye it hove on to Marna Wood."

The Names echoed through his bones, Words, confusing him, opening lands and fields and hills and Words Mauryl had said.

"You!" the first man said. "Whatever ye be, ye take yourself out away from here! We hain't no dealin's wi' you nor your cursed master. Get away wi' ye, ye damned haunt!"

"Please, sirs! If you could only spare a little –"

One threw something at him – it struck him and fell at his feet, a round, light something that he realized was a chunk of bread.

"Away, then!" the man cried. "Ye got what ye wanted, now take yerself away from us! Go back where ye belong!"

He picked up the bread, wary of more things thrown. "Thank you," he said faintly, and bowed. Mauryl would call it rude, not to give them thank you.

"Ye give us no filthy thanks," they said. "Ye got what ye asked. Now begone, away! Leave us be, ye cursed thing, in the name of the good gods and the righteous!"

"I mean no harm," he protested. But one bent and picked up a stick of wood and threatened to throw it, too.

"Get on wi' ye!"

The wood flew. He left the firelight. Something crashed after him through the brush and hit him in the back, painfully.

He began to run, fearing they were chasing him, fended

branches with his elbow, the bread in the other hand, as branches tore his hair and his face, snagged and broke against his shirt and trousers. He dodged through the trees upslope and down again the way he had come, and finding the Road, he set out running and running on the uneven stones until he caught a stitch in his side and his knees were shaking under him.

At least, he thought, looking back, the men had not chased him. He walked a while, with his knees still shaky and weak. A spot on his back hurt where they had hit him – the stick of wood, he decided, and was glad it had not been one of their knives. His mouth was dry, and now that he had bread to eat, between the dryness of his mouth and the lump of distress in his throat, he could scarcely swallow. Still, he was hungry enough that he tore off tiny morsels and forced them down, still walking, only desiring to be far away from the men and their anger as soon as possible.

They had had no cause to throw things at him.

They had had no cause to be afraid of him – unless they took him for a Shadow. He thought they should have been able to see he was not.

They called him Names, like Cursed, and Haunt, and spoke of Hanging, all of which made terrible pictures in his thoughts. They were angry with him for no reason at all, but he supposed that they were afraid, and perhaps having had no experience of Shadows, took him for something as dire and harmful as the worst ones, the noisy, hammering kind.

They might, truly, have thrown the knives. The stick had stung, but the knife might have –

Killed him, he thought, with a bite of bread in his mouth. Dead. Death.

Like the ragged black thing they were burning over the fire, Killed.

That was both Meat, and Dead.

Then he could scarcely swallow the bread at all. He forced down a few more bites and tucked it in his shirt along with his Book, and walked a long, long way before he felt like tearing off more bits of the gritty stuff and eating them to make the pain in his stomach stop.

He reached a point after which he no longer feared the men following. He kept walking, all the same, because he was certain those men were not what Mauryl had sent him to find, and because, all the same, they had waked important Words in him – Lanfarnesse, and Rangers, and Elwynim, that echoed and kept echoing and would not let him sit down and rest. They feared Shadows, which told him the Shadows did come into this place, and therefore he still had them to fear.

He heard frogs still predicting rain. He listened for Owl's return, and he had a great deal to tell Owl, who, however sullen, was far friendlier to him than men had shown themselves, and whose presence he felt as a bond to Ynefel itself.

If those had not been polite or proper men, there must be better ones. Words had shown him Houses, and he had not found that sort of men that lived in Houses, not yet, and certainly not at that fireside. Words had shown him Fields, and this thicket was certainly not that place.

Most of all – the thought of Fields had shown him great Walls, and a keep very like Ynefel.

That was what he looked to find. That was what he suddenly believed he was searching for.

He walked until he could scarcely keep his feet under him, rested and walked on. He smelled nothing more of men and heard nothing more of Owl, but he was looking to find Men of gentler kind, and most of all a Place and a Tower like Ynefel.

With a room and a soft clean bed, and a supper, and most of all a wizard who would know what to do next.

CHAPTER 8

❧

Morning came as the frogs predicted, with a sprinkling of rain through the leaves, a gray dim dawn, at first, with a slight rumbling of thunder. He ate most of the bread, fearing it might be ruined if the skies opened and poured as they had a habit of doing at Ynefel.

But before he was quite through, the sun was breaking through the clouds and shining through the leaves, dappling the gray stone of the roadway in patterns of light and shadow. Rain dripped at every breath of wind.

The birds sang, his clothing dried on his body and his hair began to blow lightly in the wind as he plucked the leaves and twigs from it.

And before he quite realized what he was seeing, with the cresting of another hill the trees grew thinner, gave way to brush, and then – a vision fraught with Words – to broad Meadows, where the Road ran, mostly overgrown with grass. The sky was dotted with gray-bottomed clouds that occasionally obscured the sun and sent patterns of shadow wandering the smooth hillsides.

He had never seen a meadow. He only knew the Word. Everything he saw was marvelous and new. He walked the Road, picking his way along the grass-chinked stones, listening to new birds, Lark and Linnet, marking their flight across an open sky.

Then, as his Road crossed between two hills, he saw a different land spread before him – a patchwork like the quilt on his own bed, in green and brown. Fields, he thought, and knew he had come indeed to something different, and a Place where Men lived.

He walked down to that land until it became browns and greens around him. His Road in places became a muddy track lined with fences some stones of which were white, like the Road – so the men had stolen them to make their own stoneworks, and he hoped they had not removed all the Road ahead.

Men were working in the fields. They stopped, mopped their brows and stared at him from a distance, but they came no closer.

In time he came to a Village that lay some distance from the Road. But his Road did not lead him toward it, so he decided that this was not the Place he was looking for. The houses were squat, and the color of their stonework matched the thatch of their roofs. He saw people very distantly, and a track did lead that way, but he had come to grief once from leaving the Road, so he did not let curiosity or hunger lead him aside.

He walked until dusk, and found green Apples on a tree and had two, leaving the Road just to cross a fence. He supposed that no one would mind. He slept by the roadside, under the shelter of that rough stone wall, as much shelter of stone as he had yet found on the Road, and in the morning had another apple, and one to take with him. They made his stomach hurt, but it was a different kind of hurt than having nothing at all to eat, and they eased his thirst.

He found berry bushes, and had a handful of berries. He found a brook, and drank.

He passed other villages, which never sat near the Road, as the fences never blocked it. He met a man on the Road, once, the only man he had seen on the Road at all. "Good day," he said, and that man dropped his load of sticks and climbed over the rubble wall and ran away rather than pass him, so he thought that he had been in his proper Place, but the man had not been in his, and the man had run for fear of consequences. He was sorry. He would have liked to ask questions. But at least the man had flung nothing at him, nor brandished a knife, and he walked as quickly as he could to be away from the village toward which the man had run.

But no one chased him and no one else appeared on the Road.

He passed another night beneath a berry hedge, and smelled woodfires on the wind, until the stars were turned in their courses. Remembering the man running and now smelling bread baking made him feel lonely and hungry, and reminded him that a few apples and a handful or two of berries was a very small sort of supper. The bread he had had from the men by the fire now seemed a very fine thing despite the grit, but it was long gone, and he hoped for more apples or more berries.

He walked in the morning, hungry and finding nothing at all to eat. His clothes, he had noticed, hung loosely on him, and despite his washing, showed increasing mud stains. He shaved every day. He had the razor and the little mirror, and when he found water to drink, as he did find frequently now, daily he would shave and wash and make himself presentable as Mauryl had taught him. But his face was going more hollow about the cheeks and more shadowed about the eyes, and he knew he looked more desperate and more untidy than he had begun.

On the third day since the Bridge, he came to a high place from which he saw the fields divided up in a great circle about a hill and a sprawl of walls and higher walls.

Fortress, he thought, and in his experience of strangers by now, he stood in some dread and doubt what he ought to do next.

But his Road, now a straggle of white stones, went inexorably toward it and, that being what Mauryl had said, as the Road was going, he gathered his courage and kept walking.

The narrow grass-grown track among the fields gave way to a broader path by afternoon, as he came down into the valley: a rough, earthen, common road, it became, running across others, between stone fences. On either hand were fields of sorts he had seen before: he knew Barley and Oats, which one could eat raw, though not pleasantly; he knew Orchards and Apples. He saw Sheep wandering white on the hillsides. He saw the walls in the distance ahead of him, wider and greater than he had imagined, vanishing behind low hills and rising again as he walked.

He saw other men in the fields, and he was anxious when he had to pass them working near the Road. But they were an occurrence more and more common, as if here the Road was permitted to them, or as if they had no fear of strangers.

In time he met a man who slogged along the road under a load of baskets slung on a stick. The man was coming toward him, and for very little persuasion he would have fled the meeting himself, over the fences and across the fields; but as the man came slowly, head bowed, he thought how the Road was his Place, and Mauryl had said go on it. So come what might, he kept walking and waiting for the approaching man to do or say something.

The man, white-bearded as Mauryl, just trudged past, with a glance or two toward him that said the man at least wondered at him, or suspected bad behavior in him, but over all the man with the baskets seemed no threat to him and did nothing.

Further along, he saw a man working and digging in the ditch beside the Road. That man stopped his work and looked at him in some evident surprise, as if he had expected him to do something remarkable.

He made a little bow, as Mauryl had told him was polite, and the man held his Hat in his hand and gazed curiously at him as he passed.

Nearer the walls, much nearer, he saw a double gate in the wall and slowly, the most dazzling, the strangest Word he had yet seen before him, he thought of Town, and then of People and Streets, of Walls and Defense, and gates and bars such as Ynefel had had. He saw a cart come out of those gates, a cart pulled by an Ox and accompanied by two men. It was piled high with straw and great clay jars. Its wheels wobbled and groaned with a squeal of wood on wood as, inevitably, they met and passed. He stepped off the track to give them room, anxious, because one man had a stick which he had no hesitation to use on the ox, for no fault that Tristen could see. He did not like that man and gave that man a straight, steady stare, wary and ready to move away if that man should strike at him.

But that man shied away from him instead, and the men went their way away from the town, as he went his, for his Road took him toward the gates – gates which still stood open, it seemed, to anyone who cared to come in or out, though Ynefel's doors and windows had been locked and barred for fear of Shadows.

Here there must not be such a danger, he said to himself; and though men seemed to look askance at him, no one harmed him or threatened him, perhaps being better-behaved men, of a sort Mauryl would approve. He walked, fearful but unchallenged, up to the stone gateway beneath the arch.

But there he saw that men with Spears – a dreadful Word – sat there talking with each other. Guards, he thought: Soldiers. Weapons and Armor, defenses and locks and protections. He was afraid of the guards, though they paid him no attention at all, seeming too busy in their conversation.

And he was not exactly deceiving them when he saw no reason to put himself in the notice of men busy at other matters, especially while he was obeying Mauryl's instruction. There being a cart with tall stacks of baskets stopped at the side of the gate, it was not exactly dishonest of him to duck behind it and walk past into the town without bothering anyone.

And there – were Streets, exactly as he anticipated them, but, oh, so different. He was confused for a moment, seeing no order in his choices, and settled on walking straight ahead, since it was the direction he had been going. Men stared at him, some very few, but most jostled him in their own urgent haste to be somewhere. He stared after one and the other, wondering whether he should be going there, too – but he saw nothing to attract him. Walking uphill, he entered on a place with narrowing daylight, where buildings increasingly overhung, where men spread out racks and jars on the side of the street and made those trying to pass dodge around the obstacles they posed.

Then his street opened out into a small level courtyard, in which he saw a Well, and men – no, Women – gathered there with buckets and jars.

Of course, women, and Children – *Children* . . . racing about the well, chasing and being chased.

His pulse became leaden, with a sense of profound wrongness into which he had no wish at all to question further. But wonder he must – as children dashed across his path, cutting him off a moment from his intended course. Two began to skip along beside him, singing some song of Words he failed entirely to understand, except the children in particular seemed to see an oddness in him which their elders ignored or failed to notice, and they sang about his oddness.

He dared not speak to them. They were creatures dangerous to him. He knew it as he knew that water would drown him and height would break him. He was glad when they gave up their game and dropped out of sight behind him, and gladder still when they gave up following. He walked as his street led him after that, with Names and Words ringing in his head: Wagon, Market, Carter, Blacksmith, Forge, Pieman, Pork and Chandler, Tinker, Aleman, Weaver and Warp and Weft – Youth and Age; Blindness; and Beggar and Ragman. Madness tumbled all about him, a confusion of images, of expectations. He had not realized at a distance how complex a Place a town was, how many dwellings it held, all narrowly separated by Streets and Alleys, none of which might ever see full sunlight, so closely they crowded together – and it was now late in the day, with shadows falling all across the streets and creeping up eastern walls, advising him day was ending. He should find a Place soon, but the town went on unfolding to him like a vast cloth spreading out with images and Words all about – Carpenter and Stonemason, Cobbler and Tailor, Fruitseller and Clerk and –

"Thief!" someone yelled, and Tristen jumped back as a Boy, shoving at him, darted past his elbow with a man in pursuit.

"Thief!" others shouted, and gave chase down a winding lane.

He stood and stared. Thief, it certainly was. Thief. And Stealing. Theft. And Larceny. Like the mice. Like the birds at Ynefel, stealing blackberries. He picked up a dropped chain of Sausages, and an angry woman snatched it back.

But it was far more serious here. They Hanged thieves . . .

Even a Boy, a Child . . . so small, and so mysterious . . .

The woman stalked back to a Butcher's stall, where dead things hung, strange to see, and frightening. Men walked around him as he stared. A man with a cart maneuvered on the cobbles, to have room to pass by him, the man saying not a word, but he realized he had made himself an obstacle, and he began to walk, wiping greasy hands on each other, that being all he had, since Mauryl had said, and most emphatically, never on his shirt.

He was shaky on his feet, after all the uphill walking, and he had found nothing to eat today. He had been hungry so often and so long it had become a condition, not a complaint. But hunger became acute as he smelled bread baking, and saw the basket of bread a woman carried, and saw where others were obtaining it. He saw it as a supper ready to be had – but as he walked closer and watched the exchange of Coin for bread, he realized that he had no Coin to give, and no prospect of having one. The Beggar down the street looked for Coins. He held out his hand as the beggar did, but no one seemed willing to give them to him for the asking. They shied away and looked afraid, and that warned him of harm to come, so he was quick to leave that place, and to dodge away through the narrow lanes.

It was now well toward that hour the Shadows came, and, supperless and desperate, he saw stone abundant, stone of the streets, stone of the gates, stone of the inmost walls of the Place, stone up and up about the great pale stone keep which dominated everything – all of which advised him that here Mauryl's warning about being indoors might hold true; but he saw nowhere yet to shelter him, no more than he had found anyone responsible to give him supper.

His path had wound steadily uphill, into narrow places where buildings on either side of the streets projected closer and closer in their second stories, plaster and beams above the stone, until they overhung most of the space between – giving Shadows ample refuge at this hour, the more so at the narrowest points of the side streets which extended on either hand. Some lanes were so dark they daunted him. The pavings underfoot were muddy and dirty, as Mauryl would never have permitted, the mortar-courses in many places running with water. He saw a man heave a bucketful out the door of a building – carelessly: children passing by skipped not quite out of the way, and shook their fists at the man, yelling wicked Words in high, thin voices.

The man slammed the door in their faces. The children threw stones at the door. It was not a happy sight.

At least no one threw stones or dishwater at him. A few women standing in their doorways looked at him mistrustfully, and one or two doors shut abruptly – but it was getting dangerously late, and doubtless they were anxious to be away inside, safe from the Shadows.

The Town was not at all like Ynefel. There were so many people, and it was not so clean as he had imagined. Not so noble as he had imagined. Not so helpful as he had hoped. His stomach ached with hunger, and he was afraid of the coming dark. He thought of going up to a door of anyone, man or woman or even child, who looked kinder than the rest, and asking if he could have supper and stay the night – but he feared their anger, too.

Now the sun was gone even from the highest walls, long past that time that Mauryl had always said he should lock the doors and come inside. Prudent men and women were doing exactly that quite rapidly now, and it all said to him that he should find his own shelter for the night, and quickly. Whatever Mauryl feared had not touched him in the woods, so either he had been fortunate, or perhaps Mauryl still somehow looked over him, since Mauryl had had power over the Shadows.

But perhaps, equally to be believed, keeps and towns were the unique abode of Shadows. He saw a great many lurking in the narrow streets and in the rare spaces between houses, and he feared he had never been in such danger in the woods as he was now.

He kept walking, that being all he knew to do while he formed some plan for the night. He became aware, then, of a sound following him.

He looked back in apprehension – looked down into the small, dirty face of a child, a boy with ragged sleeves and breeches out at the knees, who had been copying his steps through the twilight. The boy tucked hands behind him and grinned up at him.

He was hopeful then, but not too hopeful, and ventured a smile in turn. The boy stood fast, rocking on his bare feet.

"Where ye from?" the child asked.

"From the Road." He had learned to be cautious with Names, ever since the men at the fire, and the first man he had met on the Road.

And sure enough the boy's eyes widened in alarm. "Gods bless, Yer Lordship, – ye are a gennelman, are ye not?"

"Tristen," Tristen said, fearing the boy would run and accounting that he heard Words of respect, but equally of fear from the boy. He reached out, but dared not touch him or hold him. "My name is Tristen. Is there a place safe to spend the night? Might I stay in your room, boy?"

The boy looked surprised, and began to rock again, hands behind him, then gave an uneasy laugh. "My *room*, Yer Lordship? I hain't got a *room*, but I knows them as has."

"A place to sleep, something to eat. Please. I'm very tired. And hungry."

"Oh? So why don't ye go uphill? Up there's for lords like you. Hain't ye spoke to them at the Zeide?"

The Zeide. He looked up at the walls. But Zeide was wrong. It was only half a Word. *Kath*seide. The Kathseide was the fortress of the Amefin – and it echoed with other Words: Eswyllan and Sadyurnan . . . Hênasámrith . . .

"I could take ye there, Yer Lordship," the boy said.

"Thank you," he said fervently. "Thank you, boy."

He was profoundly relieved, having met practical-minded rescue at the very last before the dark. The boy, for his part, wasted no time, but bobbed a sort of bow, turned on one bare foot, and swung along extravagantly in front of him – it was more alley than street where the boy led him, darker and fouler yet than the gate-road he had generally been following. Every shutter and almost every door here was shut. But the boy swaggered his way ahead with a bold, a confident step, as a vast, somber sound boomed out, brazen and measured and frightening.

"What is that?" Tristen asked, recalling the hammering and wailing of the Shadows in the keep, and looked up at the strip of fading daylight above them. The sound seemed, like the groanings in the keep, to come from the very walls.

"Naught but the Zeide Bell, Yer Lordship," the boy said, in a tone that said of course it was that, and he was a silly fool to wonder at it. "The Zeide bell tells folk the lower gates is shut."

"But not the Zeide gates?" he said, concerned for their safety, and distracted by the thought of Bell, Alarm, and warning. "Are they shut, now, too? Are we too late?"

"Nay, nay, Yer Lordship, she don't never shut most times. Ye follow, – ye follow me, Yer Lordship, is all."

He caught perhaps half of that, except that the boy would guide him, and no, there was no danger. He followed, re-assured and relieved when the alley let out on a broader, cleaner street, upward bound. The boy strode along, and he walked briskly beside him, with hope, now, that things might turn out as Mauryl had wished. There would be some wise man, there would be someone Mauryl knew, there would be stout doors and clean sheets and supper and a bath.

Oh, very much a bath. He could never lie on clean sheets as dirty as he was. There might be hot bread and butter and ale and turnips; but he would be, oh, so content with a piece of bread and a bit of cheese, and he would invite the boy in, who badly needed a bath and clean clothes, too. Surely the wise master to whom they were going could find something for the boy, a good dinner, a room to sleep in, and the boy could show him all manner of things and talk to him when the master was busy, as wizards often were.

He saw a high stone wall before them, and indeed a gate that swallowed up the street. That – a shiver of recognition came over his skin – that was the Kathseide, he thought when he looked through the gates and saw the keep inside. The fortress on its hill. The Place like Ynefel.

There was nothing crumbling or ramshackle about these stones. There might be grime in the streets outside its wall. There might be washwater thrown carelessly in the town streets, but not here. The buildings below on the hill might be shuttered in fear of the coming night, but the Kathseide's windows showed bright with colors, a beautiful notion. He thought how it would have brightened the old gables and the shuttered windows of Ynefel had even his humble horn window stood unshuttered to the night.

He saw before him what Ynefel might have been.

Except for the people. And women and children.

Except for the smoothness of the walls, which showed no faces, none. It was pristine. Beautiful.

His knees ached as they climbed the last steep stretch of cobbles, this road being steeper than Ynefel's, as the walls were taller than Ynefel's. Within the open gateway he saw stones pale gold and clean, unweathered, a cobbled courtyard, beyond a thick archway, and inner buildings, pale stone glowing in the twilight.

He was looking at that instead of watching around him, when dark movement came from the side and, out of nowhere, metal-clad men suddenly confronted him.

"I brung 'im," the boy said. "I brung 'im, master Aman."

He was frozen with fear, facing such grim expressions, like Mauryl's expression when he had done something wrong. The boy was looking quite proud of himself and seeming to expect something of the men, who were holding weapons and waiting, he supposed, for him to account for himself.

"My name is Tristen, sir. Are you the master here?"

One of the men grinned at him, not in a friendly way. The other:

"The master, he wants?" that one asked, leaning on what spoke other Words: Pike, War, and Killing. "Which master in particular, Sir Strangeness?"

"I suppose . . . the master of all this Place."

They laughed. But the men seemed to be perplexed by him. The one leaning on the pike straightened his back and looked at him down a nose guarded by a metal piece, eyes shadowed from the deepening twilight by a metal-and-leather Helm. The third, helmless, had never smiled, not from the beginning.

"Come along," that one said, and motioned with his pike for him to enter the arch of the gates.

"The boy," he said, remembering his manners, "the boy would like supper, if you please, and a place to sleep."

"Oh, would he, now?"

"He has," he said, finding himself wrong, and chased by one of Mauryl's kind of debates, "he has nowhere to sleep. And he wants supper, I'm sure, sir."

"He wants supper." The man thought that strange, and dug in his purse and flipped a coin to the boy, who caught it, quite remarkably. "Off wi' ye. And no Gossip, or I'll cut off your Weasel ears."

Weasel was four-footed and brown.

And there was, clearly, another way one found coins. The guards had coins to give. For himself, he saw no such chances, but he was prepared to go where they asked and wait until the men could make up their minds what to do about him.

"Come along," said the one the boy called master, and another shoved him, not at all kindly or needfully, in the shoulder. He thought how pigeons fluttered and bumped one another. If this man was indeed master here he seemed a rough and rude sort. But he remembered how the men at the fire had behaved, and how they had grown quite unfriendly once they became afraid of him, and the weapons these men had were far more threatening than knives.

So he thought he should do what they asked and not give them any cause to be afraid; and then, he thought, he might find out whether this man was the master of the Kathseide, or whether he was only master of these men. Perhaps there was someone else, after all, who might ask him inside and talk to him much more reasonably than men outside, and perhaps even be expecting his arrival.

He walked through the gateway, believing they would go through into the courtyard and straightway to the inner halls of the keep, but he was no more than under the gateway arch when the one man dropped the staff of his pike in front of his face and made him stop – a roughness which he was not at all expecting, and which might be misbehavior on their part.

But he was not certain. He might have been in the wrong. He let the other man take him by the arm and direct him toward a doorway at the side in the arch, which his fellow opened, showing him a room bright with candlelight, a plain room with a table and chairs, and another man sitting – curious sight – with his feet on the table. Dared one do such a thing?

Not, he suspected, at Mauryl's table.

"We've an odd 'un," the helmless man said. "Wants to see the master of the Zeide, he says."

"Does he?" The man at the table wrinkled his nose. "And on what business, I'd like to know. – Is this our report from about town?"

"Seems t' be our wanderin' stranger."

"Has either of ye seen 'im before?"

"Never seen 'im," one said, and the other shook his head. "Truth t' tell, 't was Paisi picked 'im up, led 'im up to us wi' no trouble to speak of."

"Paisi did. Led 'im up, ye say?"

"I was surprised meself. I figured the little Rat could find what smelt odd, so I sent him out. But I never figured he'd bring it himself. Clever little Rat, he is. An' this 'un –" The man sat half on the table. "Him talking like a Lord," the man said. "Airs and manners and all. He wasn't at all meetin' wi' anybody of account in town. Talked to some on the streets, as of no account at all, wandered here, wandered there, ain't no sense to it, by me, what he was doin' or askin'."

"A lord, is he?" The man slowly took his feet off the table – Mauryl would have been appalled, Tristen decided uneasily. He was surrounded by behavior and manners he began to be certain that Mauryl would not at all approve, manners which far more reminded him of the men in the woods. And from one master, now there seemed two, and they wondered whether he was a Lord, which held its own bewilderments.

But, then, they had brought him in under stone, where he was safer. They might have shoved him about quite rudely, but they had not harmed him.

"And what," the man in the chair wanted to know, "what would be your name?"

"Tristen, sir, thank you. And I came to find the master of the Kathseide."

The man frowned, the grim man looked puzzled, and the one sneezed or laughed, he was not certain which.

"Is he the Mooncalf all along? Or only now?"

"A mooncalf in lord's cloth, to us at least. All up and down the town, nothing of trouble nor of stealin' that we've heard yet, and the boy had no trouble to win his copper. But he come strolling up from the low town, bright as brass, and he had to be through the gates sometime today, though Ness an' Selmwy don't report seein' 'im."

"So how long *have* ye been lurkin' about the streets, rascal?"

"Not lurking, sir," Tristen replied, he thought respectfully, but the man at his back fetched him a shove between the shoulders. "Walking."

"How long have ye been in the town?" the foremost man asked, and he was glad to understand it was a simple question, and anxious to lay everything in their laps.

"I came in from the Road, sir. I walked through the gates down below, and the boy led me up to this gate to see the master of this Place before the dark came."

"Did you, now?" the man said, leaning back again, and one of the other two shut the door, a soft, ominous thump, after which he heard the drop of a heavy bar.

"Paisi certainly done better 'n Ness an' his fool cousin," the grim man said.

"And how, pray," asked the man in charge, "did you pass through the gate, sir mooncalf?"

"I walked through, sir." He remembered ducking behind the cart. He knew he was in the wrong.

"Is that so?" The man brought the chair legs down with a thump and waved a hand at the two who had brought him in. "Is he armed? Did you make certain?"

One man took him by the arm and held him still while the other ran hands over him and searched his belt and the tops of his boots. That began to frighten him, the more when the man, searching the front of his shirt, discovered the Book and the mirror and razor.

"Now what's this?"

"Mine, sir." He saw the man open the Book and anxiously watched him leaf through the pages, turn it upside down and shake it. "Please be careful."

"Careful, eh?" The man laid the Book on the table, showing it, open, to the man in the chair. "It don't look proper to me."

"Foreign writin'."

"It's mine, sir. Please." He reached to have the Book back, and the man behind him seized his arm and twisted it back, hard.

It hurt, and it scared him. He turned to be free of the pain. The man shoved him into the wall, hurting his other shoulder, and he tried then to make them stop and to have his Book back.

But they began to strike him and to kick him, and they tried to hold him. He had never dealt with men like this, and he had no notion what to do but run: he swept himself a clear space, swept up his Book and fled for the door, trying to throw the bar up.

A heavy weight hit him across the neck and shoulders and smashed his forehead into the door. He came about with a sweep of his arm to make the man stop, but in the same instant arms wrapped around his knees, hands seized his belt, and the weight of two men dragged him down to the floor. A third landed on his side and, setting an arm across his throat, choked him, while the other struck him across the head.

The dark went across his sight. He fought to breathe and to escape, he had no idea where or to what, or even how. But blows across his shoulders and across his head kept on, making the dark across his eyes flash red.

One man ripped the Book from his hand. The other kept sitting on his legs, not hitting him, and the third man had given up hitting him, and rummaged all over him, continuing his search. He was too stunned and too breathless to protest. He was willing to lie still in the dark and catch his breath if they would only cease the blows.

The dark, meanwhile, began to be dim light – and his head hurt, the more so when the man above his head seized him by the hair and hauled him not to his feet nor quite as far as his knees.

"Can ye make aught of it?" asked the man holding him, and the man in charge, turning the Book this way and that:

"I'm no Scribe. Nor's he, by the look of 'im. A thief, I'd say."

Thief. Stealing. Theft. Crime. Gallows. Hanging.

Dreadful images. Terrifying images, from his position, in pain and unbalanced – the man had a knee in his back, and his eyes were watering with the pull on his hair.

"Well?" the man asked him, shaking him. "Where did ye come by it, thief?"

"The Book is mine," Tristen said. "I am no thief, sir."

"It ain't like honest writing to me," the grim man said.

And the other, holding it out in front of his eyes: "What's it say? Eh?"

"I can't read it."

"Ye can't read it, eh? So you *are* a thief. A brigand. A

robber. Who did you kill to get them fine clothes, eh?"

From Stealing to Killing. He shook his head. "No, sir, I killed no one."

"Another lurking after the Marhanen," one said to his fellows.

"He might be," the third man said. "He might, that, but do they send a fool?"

"I am no thief," Tristen said. The very word was strange to his mouth. He fought to get a foot and a knee beneath him, and the man let him, but no more. "It is my Book, sirs. Please let me up."

"And what would you do wi' a book, hey, if you can't read it?"

"A novice priest, by 'is talk, I'd say," said the man at his head. "Stole a book an' run, by me. Killt somebody for the clothes."

"No, sirs," Tristen said desperately. "It belongs to me. I'm not to lose it."

"Not to lose it," the man in charge said. "And who said?"

"My master, sir."

"Ah. Now His Lordship has finally owned a master. And who would that be?"

"My master said –" He knew dangerous questions by some experience now; and not to name Names carelessly. "My master said – I should follow the Road."

"And who said this?"

"My master, sir." He truly did not want to answer that question. He feared that they had their minds made up that he was in the wrong, and the men in the woods had liked least of all where he had come from. He was light-headed from hunger and from exhaustion, and he began to fear they would hit him again. "Please give me the Book, sir."

"He's mad," the man on his feet said.

"And never will answer the question. – Who is this master, man? Answer, or I'll become angry with you."

He feared to answer. He feared not to. He had no knowledge how to lie.

"Mauryl," he said, and by the look on the man's face once he said that Name, he feared it would have been far better for him to have kept still, no matter what they did.

CHAPTER 9

~

The assizes were done, the evening headache, promoted by a boundary dispute and a squabbling lot of voices, had given way to a pleasant warmth of wine, and a wind from the west stirred the air from the open window-panels above a candlelit tumble in the silken sheets. Orien and Tarien were a red-haired bedful, a welcome diversion on this night when Cefwyn felt the need to forget the day's necessities. Together the twins had the wit of half the council combined, a more astute judgment, a keener humor; and their perfumed oil, Orien's hands and Tarien's lips were a potent, delirious persuasion to think of nothing else at all and hold himself as long as he could manage –

Which he could do, thinking of the water rights of Assurnbrook and two border lords at each other's throats. He could distract himself quite effectively for perhaps a breath or two, asking himself whether bribery, diversion, or main force was the appropriate answer to fools – a mandated marriage, perhaps: Esrydd's light-of-wit son, the thane of Assurn-Hawasyr, and Durell's plump wayward daughter, both with ambitions, both lascivious, both –

Was it through the female line the lands of Payny could descend? The earl's daughter by a second wife . . . that could pose a problem.

The intricacies of Amefin titles were another source of headache, the thane of this and the earl of that, and the province of Amefel as a whole ruled over by the Aswydds, ducal in the Guelen court at Guelemara in Guelessar, and styling themselves aethelings, though discreetly, in their own provincial and very luxurious court . . .

"Gods," he moaned, the vixen proving she had teeth. The other threatened Tarien with the pillow, and he took the game for what it was, rolled Tarien under and suffered a buffeting of feathers and a flank attack, Orien complaining she was slighted. Or was it, after all, Tarien?

He let himself be wrestled onto his back, and a furious battle ensued between the twins, in which he was the disputed territory, and in which he had an enchanting view of both well-bred ladies, before they smothered him in unison, and not with pillows.

He was taking random choice, then, perilous decision, when came one thump at the inner door, and a second.

And a third. Which roused his temper, which defeated other processes in midcourse, and left him utterly confused between the twins, who wanted him to continue, and his door, at which some fool continued a hammering assault.

"Gods damn you!" he cried, flat on the battlefield, over-whelmed and unhorsed. "Gods damn your knocking and battering, what do you want that's worth your neck?"

"M'lord," came from the other side of the doors. "Forgive me . . . "

"Not damned likely!"

" . . . but there's a stranger in hall. Master Emuin said you should hear this."

"Master Emuin has no natural impulses," he muttered, and drew a pillow over his face, momentary refuge. "Master Emuin has no –"

Thump. "My lord?"

He groaned and tossed the pillow aside. Orien – or was it Tarien? – kissed him on the mouth and clung to his arm. Her twin tossed a wealth of red-gold hair over a sullen shoulder and gathered the wine-stained sheet about her, rising.

He rolled to the doorward end of the bed, sighed as his feet found the fleece rug, searched blindly down the bed for remnants of his clothing.

"My lord?"

"Idrys," he said to the batterer, "– Idrys, damn you, go down, tell them I'm aware, awake, bothered, duly alarmed, and duty-bound, I shall be there in a gods-cursed moment – I can dress myself, I learned at my lady mother's knee, curse you all —"

Orien cried out as he snatched her by the wrist, squealed as he fell atop her and recovered his moment, at least enough to serve.

After which . . . after which: "I'm duty-bound," he said. "Tomorrow night."

"Perhaps," said Orien – he believed it was Orien. Lord Heryn's sisters did as they pleased, and she would please herself again, or Tarien would, or both together. They played pranks on their lovers, which were more numerous than Heryn Aswydd accounted of . . . but not many more, one could guess. Their lord brother, His Grace the Duke of Amefel, aetheling of the Amefin, was much about the court himself, in and out of this bed and that, trading gossip in every profitable ear.

One talked no affairs of state with the twins, who never asked gifts – least of all from him, whose acceptance they courted, oh, so gladly, since Luriel's abrupt departure from the court . . . but wager that *this* untimely knocking would clatter straight to Heryn's ear for whatever value it had.

Emuin, about at this hour. A stranger, with some matter of import, enough to bring the old man from his bed.

Idrys, moved to rattle his doors to have him to some meeting.

Business with a stranger smelled of assassins, aimed at him or aimed at someone who wished to point a finger. Conspiracy was constant in this gods-cursed and often rebel district, and it could well wait until morning – late morning. Or three mornings hence for what he cared tonight. The headache was recurring.

He pulled on his hose, struggled, servantless, with the boots, and found the shirt . . . not overly rumpled. The doublet – no. He damned such formalities. He wore the shirt-tail out, splashed cold rose-scented water into his face, groped after the towel and blotted his beard and eyebrows dry – a cursory brushing of his hair, then, an apology to a braiding on his way out of the bedroom and to the door – the hell with it, he decided, and left the bedroom for the foyer doors.

A clash of arms resounded as, passing through the foyer, he left his apartment, four guards relieved at least of their night-time boredom and mandated to endless discretion. The senior two went with him without asking. The junior and less privileged pair, with a second noisy salute, settled back to night-watch over his rooms as he went toward the east stairs.

The twins would dress and find their way out, and his guards would ignore their departure as they ignored their presence.

Such tedious games they played, when it involved dynasty, and heir-getting, Amefin ladies, and the Marhanen prince's bed.

Avoiding gossip. Avoiding . . . public acknowledgment of a known situation.

Down the hall he went with his guard about him, boots resounding on marble, and down the broad white stairs, on which the Guelen staff, instigated by his majordomo, made profligate expenditure of candles (your father the King, they began, when he protested the cost).

His father the King, in the capital at Guelemara, a province away, in the heart of the realm of Ylesuin, had an extravagant fear of the dark. And of assassins.

Entirely justified, as it happened, by Grandfather's example. Hence the guards. But it had not been for want of candles that Grandfather had died.

Clatter and rattle down the steps behind him: his bodyguard, ready to defend the Prince of Ylesuin from axe-wielding priests and jealous lovers.

Himself, he dreaded only the dank, after-midnight chill of the marble halls, undiminished by the candles. He walked, followed by clatter and clank, toward the open doors, the gathering of guards, the fuss and bother of wakened staff in the lower halls. A page overtook him, clearly wakened from sleep, having brought his cloak, which in summer and after the heat of his exertions he could well have done without, but the cloak was there, the air was always cooler in the audience hall than elsewhere, and he slung it on, freed his hair from it, encountered Emuin just inside the doors, along with a clot of night-staff and guards.

"This had better be worth it," he muttered to Emuin, whose habit, in former years common cloth and perpetually inkstained, now was the immaculate gray of the Teranthine order – although within the court he wielded secular power his monastic and meditative order abhorred.

"I assure Your Highness . . . " Emuin began, but he brushed past, sleepy, by now, and not in any good humor.

"My lord Prince –"

His captain of the guard, Idrys, slipped up to him like a pike to a passing morsel, a black pike, wily, and veteran of hooks. Cefwyn waved a hand, a limp, circular signal that said to Idrys what he had just said to Emuin, in less polite terms, and stalked up the dais steps to the gilt, antique and unwarrantably uncomfortable throne, on which he disposed himself in no formality. He hooked a knee over the arm, heaved a sigh, and blinked, bleary-eyed, at the scatter of political expediencies that cluttered this midnight audience. He could list agencies that might be behind this undoubted ploy to obtain the unaware, uninformed state in which he found himself. Certain courtiers would have the stomach to play these games, such courtiers as aimed for his ear, his table, his bed, such noble families of the Guelenfolk from the capital as constantly plied their politics in this chamber; such of the Amefin locals as lurked in the aisles on feast days to catch his attention, hand him a petition – offer him an assignation with their sisters.

Little difference, one from the next, except he mortally loathed the ones that arrived after midnight, determined to have his ear privily and at unusual length regarding some piece of skullduggery gone awry before the other side of the business, no more nor less at fault, could counter it with appearances and protestations of their own.

Emuin. With Idrys. One did hope for consideration from one's intimates, at least. And was disappointed.

One did expect, being roused at this ungodly hour by those same intimates, at least something of spectacle, an Elwynim assassin, a clutch of lordly conspirators . . . a ravished and indignant lady of high degree.

And what was there? A dark-haired and dirty fellow in the ruins of good clothing restrained by two of the Guelen guard, a desperate case, to be sure, but hardly worth two armored men.

Tall for any Elwynim. Lanfarnesseman, perhaps; many were tall and slender, although most were as fair as the Guelenfolk and very few Lanfarnessemen went beardless. The prisoner stared consistently at his feet and one could not be otherwise certain of the features, but the bare, well-muscled forearms and the slender hands, alike the face, said young; and youthfulness said maybe fool enough – counting nine skulls of would-be assassins bleached and raven-picked on the Zeide's south gate, in his year-long tenure here – to carry some personal pique against him, for hire or for, gods save them, the ancestral Amefin grudge.

He truly hoped not to have that old business begin again.

"So what have we?" he asked, swinging his foot in deliberate contempt of amateur intrigues. "A stolen mule? A pig-napper? And two of you to restrain him? Good gods."

"Highness," Idrys said. "This were best heard in private."

"Well, well, my bed chamber was private, at least, the while. Morning would not do for this? Nothing would serve but I come down myself, over cold floors and colder –"

"Highness," Emuin chided him, his tutorial voice.

Cefwyn waved his hand. "Have your play, then. Proceed." The hall was emptying of servants and of the curious, a last few lingering near the door; but scribes, the borderland of needful elements of the court, and occasionally discreet, stayed. "Out," he ordered the lingerers. "No record of this. Back to your beds. Shut the doors."

The doors shut. He swung his foot, and frowned at the

prisoner, who still studied the marble steps in front of him. "So what have we?" he addressed said prisoner, but it was unproductive of answers.

Idrys came to him and offered him a small book, a codex, leather-bound, old, the worse for wear. He flipped the pages open at random, saw a blockish, antique hand, a forgotten – perhaps wizardly – language.

His heart skipped a beat – a little skip, true, and he would not betray the fact, nor mend his posture, no, not for this, which he began to suspect as some priestly game with him. He did *not* think it was Emuin's doing. It had the smell of a priestly matter, illicit and heretical practice, meaning the Bryalt faith, dominant in this province, could again be afoul of the orthodox Quinaltines, who had probably come a long and dusty ride from the capital to urge some obscure point of theology and rant to the Prince about cults and conspiracies on the borders.

But that it came through Emuin set it above the inconsequential and the purely theological.

He shut the book, left it idly in his lap, and cast a narrow look at his old tutor. "Well, old master. I take it the pig-thief came bearing this. And of course I must be roused out most urgently."

"He claims it as *his,* Highness."

Not likely his, Cefwyn thought, the youth being a youth, and lacking in every sense the plausibility of the occasional graybeard who gulled the villagers and roused – if merely for a season – Amefin expectations and Amefin disaffections from the Crown.

He considered Aman and Nedras, the gate-guards who were the anomaly in this gathering of court and guards – not the restrainers of the culprit, but those whose part in this doubtless intrigue-ridden malfeasance he had yet to hear. They were the ones who had brought with them, as he supposed, this head-hanging, straw-bedecked youth, the unwilling center of all this commotion. He would have thought, absent the gate-guards in the affair, that the Quinalt and the Teranthines were at odds over some point of abstract logic – but, gods, he had thought better of Emuin than to wake *him* for some priestly rivalry; and the matter did look to be some arrival at the Zeide gate.

"Man," he said, curiosity aroused, "pig-thief. Look up. Look up here. Whose book is this?"

The prisoner had been considerably knocked about. He seemed to need the guards' holding him on his feet, and needed a shake from Aman to have his attention.

That brought his head up, jolted him to alertness . . . and for a moment in Cefwyn's awareness there was nothing – nothing – but that pale gaze.

Fear, Cefwyn thought, heart racing in his breast, his sense derived of judicial experience reasserting reason. It was fear he saw in most faces that came before him under such compulsion; far rarer, however, was the courage to look him in the eyes; and, he was ready to swear, although he had never met it in this court . . .

He saw innocence. Absolute, stark, terrifying innocence.

He had moved without thinking – had dropped his knee off the arm without knowing it; had held his next breath and feared the whole assembly in the hall had seen, did see. He was not accustomed to be so moved by anyone, and he was vexed with himself. He felt no threat in the stare, only an uncanny, helpless attraction toward this creature, an attraction all but physical, unprecedented, and intimate, so acute that he felt exposed in that motion of his heart. He had never been so set aback in his life; and he was afraid, as this creature seemed afraid, this . . . youth, this . . . man, this . . .

He had no way to name what he felt or what he saw; he had no reckoning even how much time had passed in the creature's looking up, and shaking back his loose and tangled hair, and meeting him stare for stare.

But he knew that the men who held him were no restraint at all, if this bedraggled, fragile, glorious creature should decide to contest them.

Did no one but him see it? Did not Emuin, who was

reputed wise in such matters, know that this threatening youth was not in any sense held by the guards? They had beaten him. There was straw in his dark hair and dirt on his clothes. If his guards had no terror of him, they were fools.

But maybe they had after all felt afraid – had they not, clearly, exhausted their chain of command?

And had those superior to them not called others, until the affair of the prisoner racketed to Emuin?

And had not Emuin insisted, through Idrys, that His Highness needed to be dragged from bed urgently to intervene in the matter? This was *not* an ordinary case. In any sense.

"Come. Come here." Cefwyn beckoned the young man closer, and the two guards brought him to the lowermost step. The young man gazed at him again, that intimate and terrifying stare – as if the young man – which he could not possibly do – knew secrets that would damn his soul. The impression was so strong that almost he would have disposed the guards from the hall for fear of the youth speaking too much, or bringing some business worth lives – and he did not even know he owned such dreadful secrets. He found no reason for such a fear; and the youth, besides, seemed weak and uncertain on his feet, apt at moments even to fall to the marble floor without the guards' steadying hold.

A moment while his thoughts raced, that silence continued in the room, until one could all but hear the snap of candle flames, until the melting of wax – like the melting of flesh just now in chambers above – made the air cloying sweet. It was Orien's perfume. It clung to him. His thoughts scurried like mice, this way and that, desperate, looking for an approach to the problem – and found it under his fingertips.

"Is this your book?" Cefwyn asked, lifting it from his lap.

"Yes, sir."

"And are you indeed a thief?"

"No, sir. I am not."

"Where were you and what were you doing, to be arrested by my guards?"

"I was at the gate. I asked to see the master."

The Guelen guards were unhappy with that. They shook him and cuffed him, saying, "Mind your manners, man. Say, 'yes, Your Highness' and 'no, Your Highness', and 'Your Highness, if you please'."

Cefwyn winced, almost protested – but Aman, of the guard, added: "'E's a wee bit daft, Your Highness. We had a notion he might be some Elwynim wi' that writing, if ye know, Your Highness, him and his clothes and his speech and all, and his being a stranger."

"Who brought him in?" Cefwyn asked, and had a confused and apologetic muttering from an officer of the gate-guards, and an avowal from Idrys himself, to which he waved a negligent hand: he knew the chain of command, and by now so did the young man – too well, he was sure.

"And you think him Elwynim? Walking in by daylight, in those clothes?"

"Your Highness, he flew right by the town guards, like their eyes was blinded, Your Highness, and them good men. He said he had old Mauryl for his master. He says he come down the road out of Marna, right from the cursed tower."

His heart skipped a beat, but it was only confirmation. He knew now that there was omen and worse in the young man. He had seen it in the book. He had been certain of it with never a breath of a name. And to judge by Emuin's urging to come intervene in this matter – Emuin also had opinions, and fears to disturb his sleep, he could rely on that, too.

"From the old keep," Cefwyn said, with the gooseflesh prickling on his arms, and a sense of peril and moment now to every move he made – not acute, not inescapable, but there. The young man was looking at him, and he avoided those eyes with a glance at his captain of the guard. "And them knocking the man about. Hardly prudent. One might make him angry."

"This is not a jesting matter, my lord Prince."

And Emuin, unbidden: "Ask him his business, my lord Prince. He asked for you."

That was not news he wished to hear. He rested his chin on his hand, assumed a stony indifference and slid a glance at the youth, trying – trying to see flaws and faults in that countenance, in that overwhelming force of the youth's expectations.

That was what it was: expectation. Unmitigated. Unquestioning.

Faith. Appalling, utter faith, directed at *him,* in the gods' mercy, who was not accustomed to such impositions.

"So. And what is your name, young stranger in my lands? And what are you to rouse me out of my well-earned bed at this midnight hour?"

"My name is Tristen, sir."

"No other name?"

"None that I know, sir."

"And do you live most times at Ynefel, or do you travel about the land, rattling gates and conversing with honest guards?"

Incomprehension grew, and fear became foremost in the youth's eyes. "I did live there, sir. But the wind came, and the roof slates fell, and Mauryl –" The youth's voice faded altogether, not into tears, although the young man was distraught – simply into bewildered silence.

"So how *does* Mauryl fare?" Cefwyn asked him.

"I fear – he is not well."

"And the roof slates fell," Cefwyn echoed him.

"Yes, sir. They did. Not all. But –"

"Because of the wind, they fell."

"Yes, sir."

"And what brought you here to my hall?"

"I wish a place to sleep, sir. And supper."

There was anxious laughter among the guards. But the young man seemed quite, quite fragile. Childish of manner, now, and altogether overwhelmed.

Cefwyn did not laugh. "Supper," he said. "Did you walk all that way for supper?"

"And a place to stay, sir."

"Bringing one of Mauryl's books."

"I didn't steal the book. Mauryl gave it to me. He said I should read it."

"Did he?" He could not find in the young man's face the innocence he had seen before. He might have deceived himself. It might be an Amefin-sent deception, challenging his dignity and his authority. So he challenged it in turn. "How many days did you walk from Mauryl's tower?"

"Four. Five. Perhaps five."

"Walking? One takes it for twice that many days. At least."

"Days and nights, sir."

"Days *and* nights."

"I feared to sleep, sir."

"One does doubt this," Idrys said coldly, and a spell seemed broken – or provoked. Cefwyn felt uneasiness at what he heard, but although it seemed to him that, if his maps were true, the youth's account was far short of the truth – still, the youth's remembrance might be in question. He felt more uneasiness at the habit Idrys had of provoking a situation. He saw it building.

"He does seem unlikely simple, Your Highness," the chief of the gate-guard said, "from time to time. An' then again, he don't."

"Well-acted, though," Idrys said. "Quite well-acted, boy."

"The book," Emuin said, "the book."

"Oh, the book." Idrys waved his hand. "I'll have you two its like by morning. Amefin maunderings. Lyrdish poetry. Gods know. Save it for the library. Some musty priest will make sense of it."

"I think not."

"Monastic pantry records," Idrys said under his breath. "Household accounts."

"A plague on you."

"Enough," Cefwyn said, watching the youth instead, whose glances traveled from one disputant to the other.

A Road there was indeed in Marna Wood, and legend held that no matter where one found that Road, it went to Ynefel, and not easily away again.

And by his speech, by his manner, by that unreadable book in his possession –

Had Mauryl had a servant? Cefwyn asked himself.

Or, gods save them, an apprentice?

– Or – worse still, a successor?

Not even the Amefin locals, with the old Sihhë blood still, however thin, in their veins, would readily venture that Road, that forest, far less go asking admittance at Ynefel's ancient gate. If an apprentice, surely no ordinary lad had come asking for the honor. But reputedly the old wizard had stirred forth, from time to time, though not to court, and reputedly the old wizard still dealt with those willing to risk the river – if indeed it was, as some credulous maintained, the same Mauryl who had dealt with his grandfather, still dealing in Sihhë gold and wizardly simples, and having Olmern lads bringing baskets of flour and oil and such like goods as far up that river as they dared go.

And never would Olmernmen cheat the old man, or short a measure. In truth – so his spies' reports had it, they made the measures as much as possible, and tucked gifts in as well.

So the Olmernmen, particularly those of the village of Capayneth, still honored the Nineteen, the wizards' gods, as did the rural folk of Amefel, – while the local Quinalt priests, for a share of the gold, looked the other way. As a deity, Mauryl had been demonstrably efficacious for centuries – at least, skeptics said, the many who had had the name of Mauryl and occupied the tower since the legendary rise of the Sihhë kings. More, on the medicines and spells the old man sold, Capayneth's sheep bore twins, Capayneth's women never miscarried, Capayneth's crops somehow never quite headed-out and dried before hail that flattened other fields, and Capayneth's folk lived long and healthy lives. So they said.

And mutter as the Quinalt would, it could not prevent the veneration that outlasted the Sihhë themselves.

Mauryl fallen? The sun had as well come up in the west. Comets should fill the heavens.

The youth's acute attention had flagged now. The youth's head had drooped under his study as if bearing himself on his feet was all that he could do. If this lad was local deity, heir to immortal Mauryl, he bore the wrong name and showed himself a mortal and weary godling, smudged with mud and traces of blood, wilting before his eyes. The spark that had leapt out of the youth for that moment seemed utterly irrecoverable now, the force all fled, – for which the Prince of Ylesuin could be grateful. Here was only a tired young man with an unkept look and a convincing innocence at least of pig-theft, wife-beating, and petty banditry.

"Tristen."

"Sir?" The head came up, the eyes met his, and that moment was indeed almost back, that intense, that unbearable innocence – so appalling and so unprecedented that a man was drawn to keep looking, wishing to be sure, from heartbeat to heartbeat, that it was truly there or had ever been there.

But he could not find it again, not with the same force. Perhaps the young man did have secrets. Perhaps the young man had discovered them in himself, and was not quite so innocent.

Or perhaps he had found that his hosts were not what he had hoped.

"Aman."

"Your Highness?"

"This young man is not to be harmed in any way. Do you understand?"

"Yes, Your Highness." There was true commitment in that answer. Aman knew when the Prince of Ylesuin was completely serious, and when default would entrain sure consequences.

"Idrys. The west wing, the blue room."

"My lord Prince, –"

"Idrys. The west wing. The blue room."

"Yes, my lord Prince."

"Tristen."

"My lord?"

A change. An awakening to proprieties. A wit wakening – or a pretense abandoned. It could betoken lies. Or utter ignorance. Cefwyn did not so much as blink. "Tristen, these several honest men will take you to a room, and servants there will provide you whatever you reasonably need. Your requests *will* be moderate, I trust . . ."

"Supper?"

"Assuredly." One did not interrupt the Prince of Ylesuin when he was speaking. There were breaths bated. Not his. He became imperturbable. And equally plain-spoken. "I also suggest hot water." The young man looked to have been accustomed to cleanliness – and if he had himself walked five days and five nights through the woods, as the youth had claimed to have done, a bath would have ranked foremost among his requests.

"I would be very grateful, my lord."

Ah. Politeness. Courtly politeness. And a moment, all unanticipated, to set the hook.

"These things," Cefwyn said, "if you will answer a question."

"Sir?" Back to the first mistakes of protocol, in such an audience. And in an eyeblink, the young man's self-possession began to fray about the edges. In vain, perhaps, the guards' knocking-about: threats of harm had not shaken the youth's composure or come near the truth. But now, in the diminishing of threats, the offering of comfort – then the abrupt withholding of it – the young man's voice trembled.

Not a chance tactic. Nor kind. No more kind than a prince could afford to seem, in getting at the facts of a case.

"A simple question, Tristen. An easy question."

"Yes, sir?"

"Who sent you?"

"Mauryl, sir."

"Is that the truth I am to believe?"

A hesitation. A careful, apparently earnest, rethinking. "No, sir."

"What is true, then?"

"Mauryl said to follow the Road."

"And?"

"Nothing more, sir. Only to follow the Road. I thought –"

"Go on, Tristen with no name. You thought –"

"Thought, since the Road came here, through the gate, that this must be the place he meant me to be."

Mauryl's student. Possibly. The young man could dice his reasons quite, quite finely, point by point, and say what he chose to say. A common villager did not do that. It came of courtly records. Priestly teaching.

And a prince could parse reasons down the list – I, thou, he, whence, why, and to what end – quite, quite well on his own.

"And for what purpose, Tristen of no name, did Mauryl Gestaurien send you – ah! – *bid* you to take to the Road?"

"He never told me that."

"Did he say – go left or go right?"

"No, sir. It only – seemed – as the gate showed me."

"And Mauryl is not well, at the moment."

"No, sir."

"In what way is he not well?"

"He –" Clearly they had reached an abrupt precipice of reason. Or a brutal wall of understanding. "I – saw his face above the door. In the wall, my lord. Like – like the other faces."

From an improper 'sir' to a presumptuous 'my lord.' And on such a chilling declaration. There was consternation at various points about the hall. He hoped there was none from him – he tried at least to maintain calm. The matter of the faces was well-rumored, the work of the last Galasieni – or the succession of Mauryls all hight Gestaurien: accounts varied, none of which he had taken as truth, and he would not be daunted, not by the claim, not by the innocence in the voice.

"Like the other faces. Most remarkable. Or not, in that venue. Do casual strangers inhabit the walls? Or only outworn wizards?"

"I – have no idea, sir."

"Are you a wizard yourself?"

"No, sir."

"What are you, then? Beggar, servant, – priest of unwholesome gods?"

"No, sir." The gray gaze was frightened, now, as if this Tristen were well aware of mockery and yet had no means to discern wherein he was mocked.

"Come," Cefwyn said, "even the score, sir wayfarer. Ask a question of me."

"Are you the master of this place?"

"Yes," he said, as plainly as the youth asked, and ignoring the ducking of heads and hiding of expressions all about the hall, stood fast in this assault of the wizardous and incredible. "I am. Cefwyn. Prince of Ylesuin, for that matter, but, yes, master of this hall, this town, this province. – And if I give you welcome, you are indeed welcome, Tristen late from Ynefel. – Mauryl indisposed. Immured. This is astounding, even momentous news. Is there perchance more you should tell me?"

"I fear," the youth said faintly, "I fear that Mauryl is lost. I think he would come back if he could. But he's in the wall."

"What of the rest of Mauryl's books?" Emuin asked. Like a pebble in a still pond, that deftly-dropped wizardly concupiscence. Emuin was likewise refusing to be daunted. And the young man's eyes were at once wary and alarmed.

"I suppose inside, sir. Everything was falling. I sat on the step outside. I feared to go back inside. When it grew dark – I went to the Road."

"I wager you did wisely," Cefwyn said, keeping his voice quite sincere. "Mauryl was our neighbor for many years, vastly preceding my tenure here. Or my father's or my grandfather's, for that matter. He kept his own borders and stayed out of mine. One can hardly ask for more in a neighbor of long standing. – Idrys, perhaps instead of the blue room, which is doubtless musty – is the gray hall in good order for a guest?"

134

He himself doubted that was the case, but it signaled to Idrys the quality of hospitality he meant. "Cedrig's chamber," Idrys suggested, "is far airier, Highness."

Meaning to Idrys' knowledge it was clean, unoccupied, – and might have advantages as far as the guard being able to keep a close eye on things, being upstairs and at the end of a cul de sac hallway. That would far better satisfy Idrys' concerns – which were certainly not to ignore.

"See to it," Cefwyn said lightly and, keenly aware Emuin wished the young man disposed otherwise, and that Emuin wished his own hands on the book, held out the book to their guest. The guards – simple men but no dullards – let him go then, and the young man set an intemperate foot on the second and the third step. Cefwyn held the offered book so he must ascend to claim it, not leaning forward to give it. It was a trap, and even as the youth laid hand to the book, Cefwyn did not let the book go, wishing the young man face to face and in privy conference with him.

"Did Gestaurien teach you his arts?" he asked in a low voice, not for other ears. He looked at close range at the prisoner, at the reality of grimed skin and tangled hair and those eyes that had no barriers in them. "The truth, Tristen from Ynefel, as you wish my hospitality. Are you a wizard?"

"No, sir."

"And what is in this book?"

"He said I should read it. I make some sense of the letters, but I don't know the words. – Can *you* read it, sir?"

Trapper became trapped – in an earnestness, an expectation he had never met in anyone.

"A few words." He by no means could do even that. "Surely Emuin knows more. – Perhaps he would teach you – if you asked."

"I hope so, sir."

"What did Emuin say to you regarding it?"

"He said I shouldn't answer the guards' questions any longer. He said I should come with him, and he would see you took care of me."

"*Did* he?" He cast a look toward Emuin, standing, hands folded in his sleeves and looking like the fabled cat in the creamery. "And why would I take care of you?"

"I suppose because you're master here, sir."

"If he said so, why, of course it must bind me, must it not, master Emuin? – Believe him, young traveler. Like Idrys, there, do you see? Idrys is a very grim fellow – a very dangerous fellow. But if he likes you well, and if I say so, nothing will ever come close to you in this hall that would harm you, do you follow me?"

Tristen looked briefly askance at Idrys, and seemed not in the least reassured. "Yes, sir."

"I promise you." He let go the book into Tristen's keeping, locked his hands across his lap. "Idrys, take our guest upstairs. – Aman, thank you, and thank your captain for the astuteness at last to call Emuin. Good night, gods attend, back to your posts, all. – And, Emuin, . . ."

Emuin was, ghostlike, halfway past the door he had not ordered opened. Emuin stopped still, and ebbed silently back into the audience chamber while Idrys took their guest and the guards away out the selfsame door and out of his immediate concern.

"I take it," Cefwyn said as the door was shutting again, leaving himself and Emuin alone, "you do read somewhat of the book in question."

"I say we should go riding tomorrow."

Not to discuss within walls, Emuin meant.

"Not a word tonight, old master?"

"Not on this."

"A caution?"

Emuin walked from the door to the dais and stopped, arms folded. "In specific? You are in danger."

"From *him*?" He sprawled backward, legs apart, the calculated image of his student, sullen self. "Master Emuin, surely you jest."

"I swore, no more students. I'll not have you acting the part. Gods, you affront me!"

"I affront you, good sir. *Whence* this midnight call, with no counsel, and now my decisions affront you? Now we have dire secrets? I am not fond of being led." He thumped one booted ankle onto the other. "I am not fond of being hastened into conclusions, nor of having advice presented me on the trembling, *crumbling* verge of decision, nor of being a pawn of others' ambitions, which –" An uplifted finger, forestalling objection. "– of course the Teranthine Brotherhood does not possibly have, nor you within the brotherhood, nor Idrys toward me, nor, gods know, the captain of the night-guard, whatsoever, toward anyone. So I confess myself entirely nonplussed, master Emuin. *Why* the book, why the secrecy, why this midnight alarum out of the hearing of my more slugabed courtiers?"

"Ah, is that why you were so prodigal of your hospitality? To confound me? – I had rather thought it a glamor on the young man."

It stung, that Emuin had seen that moment for what it was.

It warned him that others might have seen him bemazed.

And it made him ask himself what he had felt – still felt, when he thought about it: an affinity of the soul for an utter stranger, a young man linked, moreover, to a wizard of dubious repute and legendary antiquity. For a moment in that audience he had felt as though some misstep might take their visitor away from him, and felt as though, if he should by that chance let him go, forever after he would know he had lost the one friend his fate meant him to have.

Which was foolishness. Men were, among the chattels of which the Prince of Ylesuin had usage, the most fickle and the most replaceable. Let Emuin fall utterly from favor, as sometimes, hourly, seemed imminent, and two-score applicants would rise out of the hedges by sundown seeking Emuin's office and bearing their prince's humors far more philosophically.

So he told himself – hourly. But Emuin knew him, Emuin had no fear of him, and that, while a sin in a councillor (Emuin had been that in the court at Guelemara), was a virtue

137

in his privy counselor and a necessity in a tutor – which Emuin still was, when m'lord Prince needed a severe lesson read.

His fortunes *bound* to some wizard-foundling-apprentice with feckless trust writ all over his features?

"I've no *need* of him," he protested to Emuin.

"Said I *ever* you had need of him?"

"I have *need* of advice, master grayfrock, from your ascetic and lofty height, doubtless superior to fornicating mortals. What *is* this creature, why at *my* doorstep, why in the middle of *my* night, why bearing grammaries of unreadable ill, and why in the name of the unnameable in *my* tenure in Amefel? He could have gone to the Elwynim. He could well have gone to the Elwynim. He may *be* Elwynim, for what we know – and needs must come to my gates begging supper? Damn the luck, sir tutor, if luck has anything to do with it!"

"There is no violence in him," Emuin said. "Peace, Cefwyn. I do not yet know the cipher he is, but it would be well to treat him gently. I do much doubt he is the witless creature your men believe. *Ynefel*, he cried out, and *Mauryl*. And your guard in an access of wit roused their captain, who, after a candle's time lodging this boy in the prison's stench and squalor, became uneasy, roused the magistrate of the hour, and so quite rapidly they came to the staff, and to Idrys, who broke my sleep, and I, after much shorter interrogation, yours. But in all this time, save a disagreement with the gate-guards, no defense did he use, neither by hand nor by word."

"What is he?"

"My suspicion?"

"I will take your chanciest and rarest guess at this point."

"Mauryl's Shaping."

Shaping was a word that belonged to dark ruins and forests . . . not arriving in a man's own downstairs hall, not standing at his feet, looking at him eye to eye.

But it did accord, he thought with a shiver, with a face without the lines that twenty-odd years of living should have set into muscle and mouth. It could become anything – as it had varied quickly between apprehensive, or bewildered – but nothing stayed there. *That* was the innocence that attracted him.

And chilled his blood now.

"A revenant."

"So the accounts say: the dead *are* the source of souls."

He rested his chin against his hand, feeling an unstoppable roused-from-bed chill, a quivering of his skin, as if – he knew not what he felt. It was not a terrible face. It was not a cruel face. It had been – childlike, that was his lasting impression.

"Are such things evil, master grayrobe?"

"Not in themselves."

"Why?" His arm came down hard on the arm of the throne. He was disturbed, not alone for the realm, and for the guest under his roof; he was – personally disturbed that the visitor had that much moved him.

More than moved him. He would not sleep tonight. He knew he would not sleep easy for days after meeting that intimate stare – and hearing what Emuin claimed.

"Why?" Emuin echoed his question. "Why would Mauryl call such a thing? Or why would it come here?"

"Why both? Why either? Why to Mauryl Gestaurien and his mouse-ridden hall? What did the old man want, living there as he did, when the Elwynim would have received him? What does this thing want here? And why did you let me give it hospitality?"

"I gave you my guess, lord Prince. Not my certainty."

"A plague on your guesses, Emuin! This is, or this is not – a man. Is it a man – or not?"

"And I say that if I knew all about that matter that Mauryl Gestaurien might know, I should be a very dangerous man myself. I merely caution. I by no means know."

"And counseled me take him in, allow him that cursed book, set him upstairs from my own apartments –"

"At least," said Emuin, "if he takes wing and flies about the halls you should have earliest warning."

There was no abating it. There was no more Emuin knew for certain, or, at least, no more that Emuin was willing to say. It was time for sober, direct questions.

"What do you advise?" he asked Emuin. "All recriminations aside, what do you advise me do, since you were so forward to bring him to me?"

"Keep him here; treat him as gently born, but keep silence about him. There are things he does not need to know. There are those who do not need to know about him. Inform His Majesty of particulars if you must, but none other. None other. And put strict limit to what order Idrys gives. Idrys does not approve this guest."

"And do what with him, pray, in the event he does begin to fly?"

Emuin looked up from under white brows in that sidelong way that cautioned, reminding an old student that the old man was no fool. "Mauryl served Ylesuin for his own reasons. And yet did he ever serve Ylesuin at all? Or why did he turn so absolutely against the Sihhë? Mauryl is the question here, still."

Mauryl the recluse, the incorruptible; Mauryl the murderer of his own kin; Mauryl the peacekeeper on the marches of the West. Accounts varied. Nothing in Mauryl had ever been predictable.

Neither was his death, at the last, predictable, nor, one could well surmise, was Mauryl's last gift at all predictable – if it was indeed his last and not a wellspring of further gifts of dubious benefit.

Cefwyn let his breath hiss between his teeth. "And back to my question: if he begins to fly, or to walk through walls, what in bloody and longstanding reason shall we do with him?"

Emuin bowed his head, ironic homage. "You are the ruler of this province now, young Cefwyn. You say all yeas and nays. I am here merely to assist."

"In this I purpose, I swear, to take your advice, Emuin. What does this Shaping want here?"

"I am certain I have no idea." Emuin brushed invisible dust off his gray robes and off his hands. "Time I should attend my devotions, my lord Prince. I grow too old for such nocturnal excitements."

"Emuin!"

Emuin stopped at the bottom of the steps, looked back in the attitude of a father annoyed by a favored son. "Yes, my lord Prince?"

"You brought him here. I want a plain answer. What manner of thing is such a Shaping, what is he likely to do, and what are we to do with him?"

"Ah, no, no, no," Emuin said softly. "I by no means brought him. Dismiss that notion from your calculations, my Prince. He brought himself. He has no idea what he is; nor have I; and we are safest if we do well with him."

"Is he personally dangerous?"

"You know as much as I, my young lord." Emuin turned his back a second time, which no sober man in the town of Henas'amef would have dared, and ambled away, dismissing his prince as the pupil he had once been. "I am for prayers and bed. Patience will unravel this; force has had its chance. And yes, he is perhaps very dangerous, as Mauryl was very dangerous. Win his love, Cefwyn. That is, in binding dangerous things, always wisest."

"Emuin."

The door closed. Cefwyn swore, stamped down the steps and stalked out the echoing door through the confusion of abandoned men-at-arms, who gave way in prudent haste before his anger.

He was well up the stairs to his west wing apartment before he realized that, in the disarray of the men-at-arms' general instructions and posting, the guards below had not followed, Idrys was on the uppermost floor with the prisoner, and he himself was unguarded. No prince of Ylesuin walked alone or slept without steel at his threshold.

"Kerdin," he hailed the captain below. "Attend me. Now."

And as the man scrambled to gather up a force of guard

and overtake him, he turned and stamped his way up to his floor, his hall, his rooms, where, with a clatter and martial thump, an abundance of guards changed outside his foyer. He stormed through the two sets of foyer doors, seeking the doors of his bedchamber, where a rumpled bed and a lingering musk recalled the twins.

He slammed the last doors, seeking unachievable privacy. The musk smelled as fetid as the prison-stench. He took off his cloak and his boots, stripped the bed, flung sheets this way and that in a fit of incoherent temper, and cast himself down on the bare mattress on his back, still fully clothed.

The candle was all but spent. It flared brightly for a time, then dimmed in fitful spits and spurts. Cefwyn lay with his hands locked behind his head and his eyes fixed on the painted ceiling, his heart still beating for combat, not sleep.

He could not rest with the like of that creature on the floor above him.

Wizardry. Summonings. Shapings. Unreadable grammaries. Every village had its sorcerous pretender here in Amefel, who by sham and sleight of hand and an occasional – perhaps even credible – cattle-curse or -healing, maintained an Amefin tradition of pot-wizards and generally harmless simples-sellers to which the established Bryalt faith turned a blind eye. Poisonings by such practitioners were generally accidental, the occasional curse or healing was inevitably undocumented, the tin and silver amulets were far too numerously displayed in windows and scratched on sheep-bells to credit for great threat to public decency or the common weal.

But greater magics, Old Kingdom wizardry – the Marhanen had rid the land of that and slammed the lid on that box of terrors once and finally, in the fall of the Sihhë, in the fall of Althalen.

That his own house, the Marhanens, had used Mauryl's help once to gain the throne – well, that debt of his family lay far in the past, two long generations before his own, as happened, and in the living memory, so far as he knew, only of Mauryl Gestaurien, Emuin, and the Duke of Lanfarnesse, who was stretching the point; besides, in the countryside, a handful of gaffers grown fewer and more incredible as the years rolled by. Wizard . . . well, yes, Emuin himself could be accounted as such, and of the Old Magic; but Emuin had renounced wizardry and taken the gray robe of holy orders.

And as for Mauryl Gestaurien, arguably the greatest wizard alive, Mauryl had retired from the world to raise cabbages or, gods save them, wayward ghosts, once the old Sihhë hold at Althalen stood in ruins. Ynefel had been for hundreds of years the haunt of owls and mice, nothing more, its dreadful walls a subject of rumor and legend along the border. Mauryl had never come to Amefel's court, nor the King's court in Guelemara, not even to renew his oath to the Marhanen Kings; and one had hardly, except for the Olmern rivermen, spared a thought for the old man's doings.

Yet, more worrisome than the amulets and the sheep-bells, the countryfolk of Amefel burned straw men at harvest, reminder of other, bloodier customs; and despite the ban on wizardry in Marhanen lands, the Sihhë star still appeared in fresh paint on rocks out in the Amefin countryside.

And the old silver and copper coinage that bore that mark turned up worn as amulets about Amefin necks despite the threat of the Marhanen King's law and the ban of Quinalt priests. Such charms the countryfolk sold in open market even here in Henas'amef, as well as other, more dreadful charms, claimed to be bones of the offered dead.

There might well be, in the remote and folded hills of Amefel, a few places remaining where the Nineteen were worshiped openly: a Guelen patrol not a moon ago had found in the ancient shrine at An's-ford a saucer of something noxious, red, and only slightly dried. Horses and stout ropes had sufficed to pull the old stones apart and scatter them, which would, one hoped, discourage a continued observance at that site, but it had, a reminder how things always stood in Amefel, needed Guelen guardsmen to perform the dismantlement. The Amefin, even those who served to guard the gates at Henas'amef, had refused to aid in it.

Cefwyn tossed on his bed, cursed the whole benighted province, and wished the visitation instead on Efanor his brother, who sat comfortably in the far more entertaining court in Llymaryn (father's dearly beloved son, Cefwyn thought bitterly) and who needed not endure this provincial exile, this plagued, wizardous frontier with assassins lurking in the streets and poison likely in the wine.

Wine offered by smiling lords and ladies of the Amefin court at Henas'amef, of course, who sat across the table from him on state occasions and heartily wished it might be softer-handed Efanor, just Efanor, *faraway* Efanor, who would inherit the Marhanen throne.

Or wishing they might sup instead with the hostile land of Elwynor across the river, which once, along with Amefel *and* much of the rest of Ylesuin, had been under Sihhë rule. Nine bleached skulls adorning the Zeide's South Gate (which had gained from them a grim new name) and twelve of his own Guelen guardsmen dead preventing them: that was the Elwynim contribution to his peace of mind.

Mauryl Gestaurien had occupied the land between the new and the old and occupied a loyalty between the new and the old – servant, some said, to the first Sihhë lord who had overthrown Galasien; uneasy and absent servant to the Marhanen, who had overthrown the last Sihhë king.

And Mauryl dead – one could only believe, from the young man's account – dead. At least immured.

What could kill such a man, in such a dire and unnatural way?

If one believed the youth, who seemed as sincere about his account as he knew how to be, the report that wizardry had overwhelmed Mauryl Gestaurien was more than ominous, and suggestive that the old business at Althalen was perhaps still simmering, and that wizardry which few living men had seen was not simply tales of peasant folk and riddling tutors. Emuin himself, one supposed, as young as a student of Mauryl could possibly be, had seen Althalen fall, and Mauryl had been even then no young man, if he were only the last of his line, and not far, far older, as the peasants claimed – as Emuin hinted sometimes to believe. Mauryl had not been Sihhë himself, but a native of lost Galasien, last of its fabled builders – so rumor said.

Rumor said Mauryl had served the Sihhë from the witchlord Barrakkêth to their fall in the death of Elfwyn – deserting them for crimes only wizards understood.

Wizards like Emuin, who would not speak of it, and who, legend now held, had entered holy orders soon after the dreadful night.

Which was not true. Even he could give the lie to that: Emuin had been quietly active in his art *and* at court in Guelessar for ten years of his own young life, and had taken to the gray habit and religious retreat only lately . . . but so readily the Amefin took rumor and legend-making to their hearts that the years between events, most of which had transpired in the very midst of Amefel, mattered nothing to the bards: it fit their expectations, that was all that mattered. If the truth did not fit, why, – cast it out.

As gods knew they would take this truth with no small stir.

Mauryl dead. And this, this vacant-eyed youth come in his place . . . one could hear the rumors starting. One could hear the gate-guards gossip to their Amefin cohorts, and the lower town guards to the baker and the butcher, and them to the miller and the pigherds, and from there, gods knew, over the fields to the villages, to the hills, to the Elwynim across the river and the Olmern who supplied the old tower with flour, and back again. By the time it had made three trips, Mauryl would have perished in fire and sorceries. Mauryl would have cast himself in stone. Mauryl would have set a curse on the precinct of the tower to entrap any fool who ventured there, Mauryl would have raised cohorts of the dead –

Mauryl would have sent this young man –

For what? For what purpose, in the gods' good name, did Mauryl send this innocent-seeming creature, and to him? To *him*, when all Mauryl's legendary interventions had been to the ruin of kings Mauryl served?

The candle began to drown and sputter in its own wax, the ceiling to dim at the corners. Cefwyn rolled aside and rescued the flame, tipped the wax out, let the candle flare and the wax puddle and dry on the marble tabletop. He did not trust his reason in the dark, and sleep, as he had foreknown, was entirely eluding him.

In the small, secret shrine contained within the Bryaltine fane, Emuin sat on a low bench, hands locked upon each other, and the sweat stood on his face.

His thoughts strayed persistently from the meditations he attempted and other thoughts crept in like hunting wolves, in a darkness that pressed upon the light of the candles. It was a nook of solid stone, all about it thick stone containing other nooks dedicated to other gods, a place permeated with diverse beliefs. It was isolate, it was silent, it was surrounded by other prayers that should have made him immune to fear or to sorcerous intrusion. He clenched his hands and muttered the ancient ritual aloud, trying to prevent the wit-wandering that was suddenly so dangerous, so permissive of fatal indiscretion.

Mauryl, Mauryl, Mauryl, his thoughts ran, with more grief than he had ever remotely thought he would feel for the old reprobate; and for a moment despite the candles blazing at arm's length on the altar in front of his face the darkness in the shrine felt almost complete. Such was the distress in his soul.

I am the last of us, he thought, trying to foresee the personal, moral import of Mauryl's passing; and in doing that, met another realization, inevitably that other name: Hasufin.

The sweat broke and trickled down his temples, and his hand moved to the Teranthine sigil at his breast, silver that – whether chill, whether hot – seemed to burn his hands. He opened his eyes on the candles he had lit and set in a pattern about this private shrine, a pattern itself of obscure significance even in Amefel, whose ancestral roots went deep. There were thirty-eight candles that burned hot and bright, that drowned in light the memory of murder, that drowned in their heavy scent of incensed wax the remembered stink of blood.

But the years ran like water. They trickled through the fingers when a young man shut his fist, and then he was old, and men were knocking at his door at night and showing him a young man whose mere existence told him the extreme, the consummate skill which Mauryl had reached – a knowledge which no wizard before him had attained, not counting Hasufin's abomination at Althalen. Mauryl had done this – created this – Summoned this.

Without telling him what he planned. Without asking help.

But did Mauryl Gestaurien ever ask help of him?

Only once.

Damn him! Emuin thought, and caught a breath and smothered his anger in prudent, clammy-handed terror. Even yet, he felt fear of the old man's cruel rages. Fear of the old man's skill. Fear of the old man's deep and mazelike secrecies about his past, his present, his ambitions.

Fear . . . counting the state of young Tristen's wits, or lack of them. Fear of his innocence, his unwise trust. Fear that Mauryl might have fallen short of his ultimate, perhaps killing effort, to Shape this creature, then, and last and cruelly cynical act, passed the flawed gift to him.

Damn him twice.

Mauryl gone from the world. It was thoroughly incredible to him.

It must be done, Mauryl had whispered that night, three generations ago, as men reckoned years. Destroy his body. Trap him where he wanders. Leave him stranded forever. It's our only chance against him.

Gods, how had he listened to Mauryl? How had he broken through the spells that ringed that chamber and that sleeping child, and carrying silvered steel, which should have blasted the hand that wielded it?

I will hold him a time elsewhere, Mauryl had said. Only be swift, – and do not flinch. He is not the child he seems. He is not a child, mark me. Not for nine hundred years. Hasufin is the spirit's name. The child died – fourteen years ago. At its birth.

The body had had so much blood, so much blood. He had never imagined that blood would strike the walls, his robe, his face – he had never imagined the feeling of it drying on his skin when for the entire night of fire and murder he was waiting for Mauryl to rescue him from the collapsing wards, an entire night not knowing whether that eldritch soul was indeed banished or loosed within the chamber with him.

Go, get you away, Mauryl had said to him, after. Man of doubts, get you away from this business. Doubt elsewhere. Doubt for those with too much confidence. You will never want for usefulness.

That spirit had, Mauryl swore, gone back to a very ancient grave, dispelled, dispersed – discomfited, but not, it had become very clear, destroyed. Mauryl had taken the tower of lost souls and Sihhë magics, had held the line for decades against that baneful, outraged soul.

It had seemed it would hold forever. That no more would ever be required – of him, at least. Mauryl had not entrusted the dreadful tower to him, nor offered to. Mauryl had not called him to further study. After his obedience, after his survival where all others perished, Mauryl had harshly dismissed him, bidden him live his life in modest quiet afterward and to barrier his soul by whatever means he could.

I shall not call you, Mauryl had said. An end of us. I take no more students. An end of folly, for this generation.

For *this* generation. For *this* generation and two more. He had held the truth from two Marhanen kings – and taught their heir . . . at once more and less than he wished.

Emuin thrust himself to his feet, limping in the aches and stiffness of old age he had, for a dozen heartbeats and in the grip of potent memory, forgotten. He wiped a gnarled hand across his lips, cast his thoughts this way and that from the path his devotions and his conscience directed as his personal salvation.

148

I cannot manage this, he thought, refusing this new thing as he had tried to refuse new things the night Althalen fell. Mauryl had chided him for his trepidations. Called him coward. And relied on him because Mauryl had no one else fool enough – wizard enough – to attempt that warded chamber while Mauryl fought by less physical means.

And now that Mauryl had attempted this Shaping without advising him and without seeking help from him – now that Mauryl was dead and his work came down to a feckless, hapless youth, at risk and unguarded, – *now* did Mauryl have the audacity to send the unformed and vulnerable issue of his folly to *him* to guard?

Where was Emuin the coward in *that* reckoning? Where was the contemptuous advice to defend his own soul and renounce wizardry in favor of pious self-defense?

Save himself for this moment? Was that Mauryl's reasoning? Unnoticed, out of the fray, moldering his youth and his time away in self-limiting meditations, preventing himself from what, unchecked, he might have been, losing the years he *might* have added to his life – all the while waiting for Mauryl's hour of decision?

And Mauryl never telling him?

He felt for the door and leaned there in the fresher air, slowly taking his breath. There was a pain in his chest that came with passions and exertions. It came more frequently in this last year.

Mortality, he thought. He might well have lived a century longer, might even have reached Mauryl's fabled years, had he not renounced his arts in favor of – what? A fabled but insubstantial immortality – a priest's immortality – which priests could not in concrete terms describe, could not produce, could not remotely prove? His outrage for the waste of his life frightened him. His doubt made mockery of all his deliberate, studied years of abnegation. His doubt raised up anger, and impulse to action, and separated him from all the choices he had ever made.

Still turning away? he could hear Mauryl ask him. Still running, boy?

Still the hand on the latch, boy, and will not open the door?

But all wizardry since that night had held peril for him such as he could not bear. He did not wish to contemplate it, knowing he had bathed himself in blood, betrayed a trust, crossed thresholds each one of which could lead him to darker and angrier magic than he wanted to contemplate – to sorcery and damnation indeed.

His weakness was his own strength. His weakness was his own knowledge. It was fear of both which had led him to the Teranthines – seeking tamer certainties.

And he had found believers who linked their hopes to milder things. Oh, indeed, believers. Unquestioning believers who thought they questioned everything, unhearing believers who heard nothing that in the least degree questioned the tenets of their sacred quest toward a salvation they predetermined to exist. What denied that, – why, shut it out. What threatened that, never was; what threatened that, never had existed. What threatened their confidence had no validity at all for the true and determined believers.

And came this, – Mauryl's *evidence* of an access to souls departed, a power the Teranthines denied existed?

Came this, – calling up the nightmare that was Althalen, the ruin of the last of the Old that had flickered on this side of Lenúalim, and the death of the one wizardling among Mauryl's students who might have been the greatest of them . . . who might, if he had lived, if one could believe the promises that still came whispering in one's dreams, have restored lost Galasien and undone the spells of the Sihhë?

Hasufin would have become, so far as the Teranthines remotely imagined such power, a god.

But for doubt, they – who, through Hasufin, might have inherited the Old Magic – had murdered Mauryl's old student and stranded him in a second death: at least that was the belief Mauryl had urged upon them. A second death – because Hasufin was not the fair, soft-spoken child he seemed to be, a mere fourteen years in the world, and was by no means the Sihhë king's young brother. They had died, all the wizards at Althalen, all but himself and Mauryl, in that desperate assault on Hasufin's wizardry, while the Marhanens ran through the halls with fire and sword. The wizards had all perished, except himself, except Mauryl, who had parted from him thereafter and called him coward.

Him – coward. He still trembled with the indignity of it.

Ask – what this Shaping was. Ask about its innocence, this wayfarer with Mauryl's stamp and Mauryl's seal all over him – in a book on which he felt Mauryl's touch.

He felt a clammy chill despite the heat of the candles. He turned from the door and fought down the smothering panic that urged him to flee all involvement, panic that urged him to seek retreat at the shrine at Anwyfar among the pious, the modest Teranthines, and to take refuge in the semblance, at least, of godly and human prayers.

Why? the essential question pressed upon him. Because Mauryl knew he was dying?

Because somehow, by some means, what they had trapped and banished had found a Place to enter again that they who bound him had not thought of?

Temptation offered itself: there were ways to find those answers. He could even yet set himself mind-journeying; that art did not leave a wizard, once practiced. It seemed reasonable, even sanely necessary, to look however briefly at Ynefel, where none of Cefwyn's patrols dared go, to confirm or deny human agency in this . . . apparent wakening of an old, old threat.

It was appallingly easy to make that slight departure, that drifting apart from here . . . they had gone far beyond illusioning, the brotherhood at old Althalen. He had not been the least of Mauryl's students, only – for a time, only for a time, evidently, after that dread and bloody night – the last.

Out and out he went faring, through gray-white space.

And drew back again, shivering, an impression of blinding light yet lingering in his mind, a glimpse of something too well remembered – too tempting – that final reach for power, first, to govern those who had no power, and then to contend with each other for more power, the greater against the lesser, for the ambition of gods . . .

He carried the Teranthine circle to his lips, clasped it in his two hands, warming it with his breath, attempting again the peace of meditation. His mind was too powerful for easy diversion into ritual inanity, endless repetition of prayers. That was the reason he had sought the once-obscure Teranthines – not a confidence in their pantheon, which was in major points of belief the same as the Quinalt's – but rather interest in the intricate, interwoven and demanding patterns of their approach to meditation, which sought, in their most convolute supplications, all gods, lest any be neglected.

For one who did not, in any case, believe in the new gods the Guelenfolk had brought to the land, it had been very attractive. For one who did not wholly desert the gods of his youth and his art – it had given comfort and stability in a world he perceived as entirely conditional.

Now, considering what he knew and what he feared of Mauryl's workings, he found his meditations at once terrifying – and liberating, to wizardly powers the Teranthines did not remotely guess.

He had continually, in his devotions, approached the Old, the Nineteen, seeking answers to questions which would have horrified even the all-forgiving Teranthines: it was in consideration of their sensibilities that he had never explained to them that the Sihhë icon for which he had asked – and bought – their secret indulgence, for its presence in a Bryaltine shrine . . . was not mere honor to an ideal. That this particular form of the Sihhë star was older than the Sihhë, who had needed no gods – he had not mentioned that. He never murmured Old names aloud in his devotions. He applied himself to intricate and many-sided rituals the origin of which the eastern-born Teranthines, jackdaws of all religion, had themselves appropriated from the western-bred Amefin. Sometimes he provided them innovations of meditative practice that were not innovation at all, with methodology and exercises of focus that, from his writings, slipped into orthodox Teranthine practice across all Ylesuin. The Bryaltines were exclusively Amefin, heretic to the Quinalt eye, and practiced dangerous meditations and collected gods like talismans because they feared to lose anything. The Teranthines, meditative and truly less interested in proselytizing, gave him respectability in the royal court and a comfortable life: they had the Marhanens' patronage, and they let an intelligent man think. He had respect within the Brotherhood: the Teranthine ritual constantly evolved and grew, now with scattered pieces of Galasite belief set into it – his own.

He should, he thought, feel profoundly guilty for those inclusions, for the Teranthines were innocents born of the new age and he was not; but he had until now found his appropriations from the Galasite practices small matters, nostalgic for him, and unlikely to do the Order harm or bring it into conflict with the Quinalt – he was very circumspect, and argued with a jurist's knowledge of the Quinaltine belief. And indeed, he had cherished his small deviations as the last connection of the world with the Old, to bequeath something of their practice to safeguard the new, a silent and precaution-ary gift, like this shrine, that his donative had established in the face of changes and persecutions. The candles here never ceased, through all the years, day or night, in his absence. It kept the light of wizardry burning – literally – in this ancient land: it strengthened by its little degree the wards and barriers wizardry had never abandoned, not through all the Sihhë reign, not through the Marhanen ascendancy: and the age of those reigns together was, almost precisely, a thousand years.

His gnarled hands clenched. So easy it was, if he willed, to fall into the old thoughts, the way of wizardly power so easy to a man once practiced. Hasufin had been very old, very evil, Mauryl's student once in Galasien, who had aimed at power nine centuries ago and come back from the grave to have it: it was still necessary to believe what Mauryl had told them, and not that they, in the circle of Mauryl's disciples, might conceiv-ably have destroyed a wizard who could have restored the art to its former, enlightened glory – and given all the world to them.

Refraining from power is, he thought, gazing at the eight-pointed star shining on the altar shelf, the sole virtue I have achieved in all these years. Mauryl would not have lied to us. I *believe* that. But . . .

Doubting is my sole defense, the only effective barrier against the unequivocal dark. I am all grays.

And the safest, wisest thing to do now is to go into retreat at Anwyfar and to have nothing to do, for good or for ill, with this thing of Mauryl's.

I shall die soon, – soon, at least, as men reckon years. I have seen to my own soul. I need not risk it in Mauryl's service. I need not fling myself into Mauryl's designs, against Mauryl's enemy, ancient – unknowable to my age.

How dare he? How *dare* he do this to me?

Then he thought of his own students, of Cefwyn and others that were young, without understanding of the deeds he had done, without defense against the enemy Mauryl had himself fostered, and against whom once before Mauryl had enlisted his unthanked help; and in that thought he clenched his hands and wept for sheer pent-up rage.

The servant passed from sconce to sconce, touching a waxed straw to a new set of candles, others, half-consumed and long-unused when they had arrived at the room, having been taken from their sockets and replaced.

Which Tristen thought profligate, and entirely unneeded.

There was a large table at one side of this room, nearest the fire, which he thought was a table for food and for study. Beyond a slight sort of archway was the bed, where, if he were at home, he would have gone and simply flung himself down with or without the sheets, daring even Mauryl's displeasure.

But he feared now even to move without the leave of Idrys, who waited, armed and grimly patient, in a hard chair near the door.

It seemed forever that the servants had worked – the room

would have done very well for him, dusty as it was. Ynefel had been dusty. He would not have cared for dust on the tables or even on the bedclothes, as he would not have cared that the candles were old and half-burned. There was dark behind the unshuttered windows, long since, and the knowledge that a bed awaited him – with servants arranging new sheets, new comforters – made him nod toward sleep even sitting and trying to be on his best manners.

They had laid a small fire in the hearth, they said, to burn freshening evergreen and to take the mustiness away. If there had been any, it must have long since done that. They fussed over candles that were perfectly good. Before that, they had kept him waiting in the hall an unendurable time, arranging this and that, bringing in stacks of linen. Now he sat by the fireside warming the shivers and the aches of travel from his bones and growing sleepier and sleepier as they found still more things to dust and polish.

But, oh, at last, at last, now, the servants looked to be finishing their business and looked to be leaving. With eyes that burned with exhaustion and a hope that like the rest of him trembled with repeated demands, he watched them all gather by the door as if they were about to leave.

He hoped that Idrys would go, too, but he did not.

And servants left, but at the same time more servants came in bearing a huge brass tub, which – an interminable wait – they set in a corner behind a screen, and filled, with successive pails of steaming water. Then they told him they would help him with his bath.

"I can bathe, sirs," he said to them. He would bear with anything they wished, only to get to bed, but he had had enough of strangers laying hands on him, and he was bruised and sore.

"Do as they ask," Idrys said darkly, Idrys seeming weary himself and out of patience. So he did as they wished, stripped off his filthy clothing and settled into the bath – wonderfully warm water which smelled strongly of pleasant herbs. He bent and ducked even his head. Offered pungent soap, he washed his hair and scrubbed the lines of dirt from his hands and everywhere above and below the water.

Idrys came and stood over the tub, hands on hips. "Wash well. There are doubtless vermin."

"Yes, sir," Tristen said, taking it, on reflection, for some sort of a peacemaking, and a very reasonable request from Idrys. He scrubbed until his skin turned red, the cloudy water turned brown, and he felt himself at last entirely clean and acceptable.

Idrys walked away, apparently satisfied – while Tristen almost lacked the strength afterward to rise from the tub. But with two servants' unanticipated help he managed it, and wrapped gratefully in the sheet they offered, shaking from head to foot in the cold air, but, oh, so much relieved.

He sat where they wished then, and they toweled his hair, during which he nearly slipped from the bench asleep.

"Here," said Idrys, pushing at him to make him lift his head, as the door opened and yet more servants came in, and one pattered closer. He saw food offered him, he put out a hand and took a wedge of cheese as from the other side a second servant offered him a cup both pungent and sweet. It seemed when he tasted it much finer than the ale Mauryl had given him sparingly. He drank, and ate a mouthful of the cheese, and tears began to flow down his face, reasonless and vain. He wiped at them with the back of the hand that held the cheese, gulped the wine down, because he was thirsty.

Then his fingers went numb, so that he could hardly hold the cup from falling.

Idrys caught it before it hit the floor, the servants caught him before he did – but he was still aware as they carried him to a soft, silky and very cold bed.

Then he slept, truly slept, for the first time since his own bed in Ynefel.

CHAPTER 10

~

Idrys occupied the chair opposite him when he waked – Idrys sat with arms folded about his ribs, head bowed. But not asleep. Tristen caught a sharp glance from that black shape near the light of the diamond-glass window and recalled uneasily both how he had come to this bed, and why this man sat watch over him.

Idrys did not move. Even with no cause but his waking, Idrys' lean, black-mustached countenance held no expression toward him but disapproval, a coldness that seemed to him far greater and far more fearsome than that of the gate-guards or the Guelen soldiers, who had toward the last of his ordeal sometimes laughed, or touched his shoulder kindly, or offered him a cup of water. He imagined that he smelled food. But mostly he smelled burnt evergreen. He supposed that, over all, this room was far finer than the guards' quarters, and that the things over which Idrys presided were far more extravagant than the soldiers had offered – but he had, he thought, far rather the Guelen soldiers, if he could only have the bath and the bed, too.

He pretended to sleep a while longer, in the vain hope that Idrys would lose patience and leave, or call someone else to watch him sleep. Idrys had to be bored. He hoped to outlast him.

"There is food and clothing," Idrys said finally, undeceived, "whenever you feel so inclined."

"Yes, sir." Thus discovered, Tristen dutifully sat up, aching and sore, and followed with his eyes Idrys' consequent nod toward the table in the other room, where a breakfast was laid – he saw from where he sat – on large silver platters.

He was chagrined to have slept through so much coming and going.

And he supposed if they gave him breakfast they were going to take care of him and that if they took care of him he must have duties of some kind that he was neglecting lying abed.

So he rolled stiffly out onto his feet and wrapped his tangled sheet about him as he cast about looking for his clothes.

"Have your breakfast first," Idrys said, so without demur he went and looked over a far too abundant table of cheeses and fruit and cold bread, while Idrys, never rising from his chair, watched him with that same dark, half-lidded stare.

He gestured at the table. "Do you not want some too, sir?"

"I do not eat with His Highness' guests."

That seemed as much conversation as Idrys was willing to grant to him, and Idrys seemed impatient that he had even asked. In embarrassment and confusion, he sat down, gathered up a bit of bread, buttered it, and ate it with diminished appetite, for he had little stomach left after days of hunger, and he felt Idrys' eyes on him all the time he was eating. He drank a little, and had a piece of fruit, and had had enough.

"I am done, sir." He was appalled at the waste of such delicate food. "I could hardly eat so much. Will you eat, now?"

"Dress," said Idrys, and pointed to a corner where a stack of, as he supposed, towels rested on a table.

He found it clean linens and clothing – not his own dirty and torn clothes, but wonderful, soft new clothing of purest white and soft brown – along with a basin and ewer, a wonderful mirror that showed his image in glass, and all such other things as he could imagine need of. But most pleasant surprise, he found his own silver mirror and razor and whetstone, which he thought the gate-guards had taken for themselves; he was very glad to have the little kit back, since Mauryl had given it to him.

And all the while there was Idrys at his back, arms folded, watching his every move. He tried to ignore the presence as he reached for the razor and tried to ignore the stare on his back as he began, however inexpertly, to clean his face of the morning stubble. Idrys remained unmoved, a wavery image in the silver mirror he chose to use.

He combed his hair and dressed in the clothing that lay ready for him – which fit very close and had many complications and required servants to help him. It was not as comfortable as his ordinary clothing.

What they had provided him was like the fine clothing that Idrys wore, like that Cefwyn had worn: gray hose, a shirt of white cloth, boots of soft brown leather, a doublet of brown velvet, – far, far finer and more delicate cloth than that Mauryl had given him, and his fingers were entranced by the feeling of the clothing. But he would have rather the things he knew, and the clothing Mauryl had given him, and Mauryl with him to tell him not to spoil his shirt. It was a thought that brought a lump to his throat.

"Your own had to be burned," Idrys told him when he asked diffidently where his own things were. And he wished they had not had to burn what Mauryl had given him, and thought them very wasteful of good food and clothes, and candles, which Mauryl had said were not easily come by. But he dared not argue with the people who fed him and sheltered him. He supposed there were new rules for this Place, in which such things counted less.

Idrys regarded him with the same coldness when he had finished and when he stood shaved, combed, and dressed. He found no clue to tell him whether it was fault Idrys found or whether it was impatience with his awkwardness, or merely – it was possible – boredom.

"What shall I do now, sir?" Tristen asked. He hoped for answers to his questions, for a settling of his place and duties in this keep – perhaps to speak at length with master Emuin, who reminded him most of Mauryl.

"Rest," Idrys said. "Do as you wish to do. Pay my presence no heed. I shall stay at least until His Highness calls me. He will probably sleep late."

"Did you sleep, master Idrys?"

"I do not sleep on duty," Idrys said, arms folded.

Tristen wandered back to the table and found the little food he had taken, and perhaps Idrys' at least moderate and reasonable answer to him, had further stirred his appetite. He sat down and buttered another bit of bread and cut a very thin bit of cheese. Idrys had settled in a chair nearby, still watching him the way Owl might watch a mouse.

"Master Idrys," he found courage to say. "If you please, – what is the name of this place?"

"The town? Henas'amef. The castle is the Zeide."

"Kathseide."

"So men used to call it. Did Mauryl tell you that?"

"No, sir. Master Idrys." Tristen swallowed a suddenly dry bit of bread, still terrified of this grim man, and was very glad that Idrys' mood had passed from annoyance to this sullen, idle companionship.

"Why have you come?" Idrys asked him, then, as swift as Owl's strike.

"For help, master Idrys."

Idrys only stared at him. There seemed one reasonable thing to say to Idrys, and to all the people whose sleep he had disturbed.

"Or if you will only let me go," Tristen said in a small, respectful voice, "I will go away. If I knew where to go. – Am I in the wrong place? Do you know, master Idrys?"

Idrys' face remained unchanged, and in that silence Tristen's heart beat painfully. Idrys finally said, "Ifs count nothing." But Tristen did not take it for his answer, only a sign that Idrys had heard his offer and, pointedly perhaps, ignored his real question regarding his permanent disposition.

But in that moment came a rap at the door, and Idrys rose and went to see to it. There was some ado there: servants, Tristen thought, were waiting outside, or perhaps guards; but the fuss came inside with an opening of the inner doors, and it was Emuin.

He rose from the table, glad to see the old man, who had listened to him patiently last night, who had been kind and pleasant to him and kept his promises to bring him to the master of the keep. Emuin smiled at him gently now and dismissed Idrys to wait outside – as behind Emuin came Cefwyn himself, whom he was not quite so glad to see, and who looked reluctant and unhappy to enter. Cefwyn clapped Idrys on the shoulder in passing and spoke some quiet word to him, after which Idrys nodded and left.

The door closed. Tristen stood still, looking for some cue what to do, what to say, what to expect of them both or what they expected of him.

"Much the better," Cefwyn murmured then, looking him up and down. "Did you rest well?"

"Yes, master Cefwyn."

Cefwyn looked askance at that greeting; Tristen at once knew he had spoken amiss and amended it with, "My lord Cefwyn," as Cefwyn sat down in the same chair Idrys had lately held. Emuin settled on a chair near the table, and Tristen turned the chair he had been using and sat down quietly and respectfully.

"You may sit," Cefwyn said dryly, in that very tone Mauryl would use when he had done something premature and foolish.

"Yes, sir." So he had been mistaken to sit. But now Cefwyn said he should. He had no idea what to do with his hands. He tucked them under his arms to keep them out of trouble and sat waiting for someone to tell him what he was to do here.

"We come to unpleasant questions this morning," said Emuin gently. "But they must be asked. Tristen, lad, is there nothing more you can tell me of Mauryl's instruction to you?"

"No, sir, nothing that I know, beyond to read the Book and follow the Road where it would lead me."

"But you cannot read the Book."

"No, sir. I can't."

"And what was Mauryl's work? What was the nature of it? Did he say?"

"He never told me, sir."

"How can he not have known?" Cefwyn snapped, but Emuin shook his head.

"He is very young. Far younger than you think. Not all seemings are true. Listen to him. – Tell me, Tristen, lad, do you remember Snow?"

Snow was a word White and Cold and Wet, lying on the ground, clinging to the trees, falling like rain from the skies.

"I know what it is, sir. It comes to me."

"But you have not seen it."

"No, sir."

"Ever?"

"Not that I remember. Perhaps the shutters weren't open."

"This is an unnatural business," Cefwyn said, locking his arms across his chest. "I tell you I have no liking for it. Emuin, can you judge what he says?"

He feared Cefwyn, whose eyes were sometimes cold as Idrys' eyes, whose voice very often had an edge to it, and whose speech had many, many turns he failed to follow.

But Emuin's voice was gentle and forgiving. "He was Mauryl's, my lord Prince, and Mauryl was not wont to lie, whatever his faults."

"He never stuck at worse acts."

"Peace," Emuin said sharply, and turned on Tristen a gentler look. "Lad, I've told you that I knew your master. That he was my teacher, too. He would not have you lie to me."

"No, sir," Tristen answered. "I wouldn't think so."

"You have no idea why he died."

"I don't know that he is dead, sir."

"What do you think befell him? Why do you think he might be alive?"

"I don't know, sir. I know –" It was difficult to speak of his reasons and his guesses. He had never said them aloud. He had persuaded himself not to speak them aloud, not so long as the guards questioned him. But Emuin said he was Mauryl's student, too, so surely he should tell Emuin the truth.

"I know that Mauryl believed he would go away somewhere. I thought he meant the Road. He gave me the Book and said he might not have to go if I could read it. But I failed." It was a difficult failure to admit. He was deeply ashamed and troubled with a thought that had worried at him ever since he had come to the guards' hands. "Perhaps I was mistaken to go out the gate. Perhaps I was mistaken about when he wanted me to go. I would have asked him, if he were there, sir. I wish I might have asked him."

"I do not think you were mistaken," Emuin said, which he was glad to hear. "You did exactly as Mauryl would have had you do, and very wisely, too."

"I hope so, sir."

"I am very sure."

Tears welled up in his eyes and a knot came into his throat. He looked down, because Mauryl had said men did not show their tears, and Mauryl had said he was becoming grown. But the tears escaped him and ran down his face, so he wiped at them surreptitiously, as quickly as he could, and tried to pretend they had never happened.

"You see," Emuin said to Cefwyn. "He is still a child in many respects. Mauryl did not gain everything he wanted in his working."

He had no idea what Emuin meant. He looked to see whether Emuin frowned or not, and in that moment Cefwyn leaned back and folded his arms, regarding him coldly. "You will stay here," Cefwyn said sternly, and then cast a glance at Emuin. "– How much, then, can he comprehend?"

Heat mounted to Tristen's face. "Sir, I do understand you."

"Do you?" Cefwyn seemed always on his guard, as Idrys seemed to be. Perhaps Cefwyn was angry about his mistakes in manners. He knew he had made them, even in recent moments.

"Lad?" Emuin said. "What do you understand?"

"I understand most things, sir, but there are some Words that come slowly, so I lose the sense of them. But," he added quickly, lest Emuin think he was more trouble than he possibly wished to undertake, even on Mauryl's wishes, "I am not slow to learn, sir. Mauryl told me otherwise."

"Cry you mercy," Cefwyn said in a breath. "So you do answer for yourself, sir."

"Yes, sir. – Yes, m'lord."

"Apprentice to Mauryl?"

Apprentice. It came muddling up out of somewhere. "I think after a kind, m'lord, but – Mauryl called me a student."

"Did he?"

"Yes, sir."

"If I give you liberty of the keep, of all this vast building, will you agree to stay within its walls?"

He suddenly realized Cefwyn was asking him to stay. And Emuin had just said that he had done what Mauryl wished. He began to hope for a turn for the better – that after all he had not failed Mauryl's order. "Yes, sir," he said, with all attention, all willingness to obey.

"You will undertake not to speak to others than myself and Emuin, in any regard."

"I will not speak to others, no, sir."

"Lad," Emuin interposed, "Prince Cefwyn means that restriction for your protection. There are some few people about who are not to be trusted, who would use you very deceitfully, and some would do you harm. You must trust the two of us, and only us."

"Not Idrys, sir?"

"Idrys serves Prince Cefwyn. You may speak to Idrys. He is Lord Commander of the Prince's Guard. And you may always tell the servants what you want and what you do not. His Highness means simply that you should not converse with chance strangers you meet in the halls."

"Yes, sir. I understand." In Ynefel – in all the world before – there had been only Mauryl. He had never had to understand there were safe people and dangerous people, but on his way to this new place he had learned that abundantly, and he was glad to know there was a rule he should follow. It would be ever so much easier to please these men and avoid trouble if he had a rule.

"Good." Emuin rose and, as Emuin had done before, patted his shoulder in leaving. Cefwyn got up to go, Tristen rose, and Cefwyn delayed to look back, frowning as he studied Tristen from head to foot.

Then Cefwyn shook his head and left, as if he still disappointed Cefwyn's expectations.

He stood staring at the door after it shut, hands clenched on the back of the chair. He should not, he told himself very firmly, be angry or upset with Cefwyn, who had given him everything he presently had; who had, in fact, given him everything pleasant and good.

Everything . . . but welcome.

Their leaving was the first time he had been altogether alone since he had come here last night, the first time he had stood in the middle of a room which – he supposed – was to be his. It was a far, far different and grander room than any Ynefel had had to offer, as large by itself as the downstairs hall at Ynefel. The whole keep had no wooden balconies, but stone floors throughout, which stayed up by some magic, he imagined, and did not tumble down of their own tremendous weight.

But the moment he wondered about it with a clear head, he thought of Arches, and Barrel Vaults, and Coigns and all such Words as masonry and mason-work, and the scaffolds he had seen in the town below, all, all those many Words and memories of the town and Ynefel pouring in on him. Like pigeons fighting over bread, his thoughts were, as he remembered the space outside the walls, and he put his hands to his head and turned all about – finding no more Words, at least, everything safe and known, bed and table and chair and Curtain, indeed, there was a Curtain, of which Ynefel had had none such embellishments.

There was Leading, and Gilding and when, on a quieter breath, he dared look out the window, one knee upon the bench there, he saw, distorted through rippled glass, slate roofs, and chimneys, and, oh, indeed, there were pigeons walking on the ledges.

He went at once to the table and the remnant of his huge breakfast and took bread, and carefully unlatched the little section of the diamond windows that had a separate frame and latch. The pigeons flew away in alarm when it opened, but he put the bread there on the ledge below the glass and trusted they would find it soon.

He was very glad to find them. He wondered were any of them his pigeons, that might also have escaped from Ynefel.

He wondered whether Owl would come, and what place there might be in this place that would be possible for Owl to sleep by day, as Owl preferred to do. Perhaps there was a loft somewhere in the buildings nearby. Perhaps there was a loft even in the Kathseide itself. He stood and watched, and, certain enough, the pigeons gained courage to come close, and then advanced to the roof slates below the window, and landed on the sill beyond the diamond-glass panes. He was very still, as he had learned to be in the loft at home, and watched them make short work of the bread.

He brought them more, and frightened them again, but they would come back: pigeons could be quite brave, he knew, where bread appeared.

After that, he explored every detail and secret of the room and (none too early) the practical necessities in an unlikely cabinet with a most ingeniously made swinging shelf, a shelf which could, he found on his hands and knees, be reached from the outside hall. But that door could be latched from inside by a very strong latch.

And bothering that small door must have alerted men outside, guards in brown leather and red cloaks, who came in immediately through the foyer and the inner doors to ask if he wanted anything.

"No, sirs," he said, embarrassed. And then asked if he might go outside a while.

"His Highness give permission, m'lord, excepting to talk, that ain't permitted, even to us, begging your pardon, m'lord. And us is to be wi' ye wherever, to keep ye out of difficulties."

M'lord, they called him, and respected *him*. That was a different thought, and relieved him of fear somewhat.

He decided to take it for granted, then, that he was set free as Cefwyn had said, and he did venture into the hall. Idrys was not there, to his relief, and he walked down the hall with two guards remaining behind at the room and two guards trailing him, guards who declared they were not to talk to him and who seemed also forbidden to walk beside him. He wished that they could do both. There were questions he would have liked to ask them. But there was, his consolation, a great deal to see in all this great place.

He explored the polished upstairs hall, where echoes rang with every step. None of the servants returned his attempts to smile, but shied from him as the townsfolk had, and he supposed that they had had their orders, the same as the guards had, not to speak with him.

He went cautiously downstairs, and met the stares of finely dressed men and women who stood in groups, stared with cold eyes and spoke words guarded behind hands and turned shoulders. They seemed to measure him up and down and did not want him among them, that was clear. He had as fine clothing as they, but no gold, no embroideries – he supposed that as they saw things what Cefwyn had given him was very plain. And perhaps they knew that he was from Ynefel, which no men but Emuin seemed to trust. The men when he did walk past them gave him only cold faces. But the women, some of them, looked over their shoulders at him, and one, with remarkable red hair, did smile.

He stared longer than he should have, perhaps, drawn by that one pleasantness and wishing to speak to her. But he remembered Cefwyn's instruction, and the woman walked away with a swaying of remarkable bright skirts. Men that witnessed the exchange gave him very cold, very angry stares and made him certain that he should not have smiled back at her. There seemed to be a rule against looking at him. Perhaps Cefwyn had made it.

"Was I wrong, sirs?" he asked his guards. And they looked confused, and one said,

"Certainly not by us, m'lord." At which the others laughed, but not in an unpleasant way. So he felt he had not done wrong, at least not so the guards could tell where the fault was, and he continued right in their eyes.

But he had, the moment he thought of it, broken Cefwyn's commandment to him, just by speaking to them. And he heard Mauryl chiding him, saying, Can you not *remember*, boy?

He seemed to have learned very little, over so much time. Mauryl would still despair of him. Mauryl would still shake his head and say he was a fool, chasing after butterflies again, and forgetting to mind the many, many things he was supposed to remember.

But he did not retreat to his room. There were things still to see and things still to know. There could be no learning if he did not try new things, and there could be no safety, he thought, if Cefwyn did not will him to be safe: Cefwyn was clearly lord of all these people as Emuin was master, and if either of them said that he was free to walk where he would, then he went where he would, trying to ignore the angry looks that came his way.

He walked further, to a place in the downstairs hall where the marble pavings changed to worn flagstones. That dividing line in the plan of the building struck him like a Word: it felt that strange, that important to him. He stopped still, and looked about him across that Division at walls less ornate than the walls elsewhere. He expected doors where there were no doors, he expected a hall – and found one, but hung with Banners out of place there, and the stones were plastered over and painted. It was not right. The doorway was not Right.

There's a magic to doors and windows, Mauryl had told him. Masons know such things. So do spirits.

"M'lord?" he heard his guards say, faint and far to his ears. He heard the clank of armed men walking. He saw Shadows there, and turned a frightened look to the men with him.

The hall changed. It was only the hall again.

"Are ye well, m'lord? Will ye walk back again? There's no outlet by this way."

There was not. Not now. The Place he knew had had a further door. But the door let them only into what seemed a blind end, bannered and hung with weapons of every sort. He knew another Name, but clearly it was not the right Name, as Kathseide was not right, and men knew what he said, but named it differently, so they thought him a fool, too, and simple. That was what they called a man who lost himself in hallways and stumbled over sills that to his reckoning did not belong there.

He feared that flagstoned hall. He was glad to leave it. It felt wrong, in that doorway. It was fraught with the chance of Words, and he had had enough of Words for a few days: he truly hoped to settle the ones he had, and perhaps to find Owl, if Owl could find his window.

He did not know why the place down there had made him think of Owl. And then he knew: it had been like the loft. There had been a high, peaked end, and exposed rafters. Sunlight had streamed in where now there was stone. Birds had gone in and out that opening that did not exist, Hawks had lived there, and fed on pigeons and on mice, being birds fierce as Owl.

Those were the shadows he saw, the bating of wings, not the still, straight display of dusty banners. Owl might have come there. But Owl could not find an entry, no more than he had found a way to summon Owl.

He thought the more time passed, the stranger and wilder Owl might grow, until Owl quite forgot him.

He wished he could ask his guards if they had seen a large lump anywhere about the eaves, a very unhappy lump, Owl would be.

But, no talking to them, Cefwyn had said. He had learned something. The place where Owl might have been at home in the Kathseide was shut to him, with the coldness with which shoulders turned to Owl's master.

Again . . . no welcome. No hint of welcome, not for him, nor for Owl. They would become lost from one another. The windows were too tight, except for here, and here it seemed things should be wood and very little stone, there should be an airy passage, and it should smell of straw. It frightened him. Words and Names had never betrayed him before. It made him doubt other things he thought were sure.

But there was, absent Emuin, no one he thought might advise him what he saw.

And Emuin did not come that day or the next, nor the next.

The size of the building was deceptive. It sprawled its wings and corridors in unexpected directions, and made courts and narrow shafts and mazes of halls in which it was easy, except for the presence of his guards, to become lost.

But six days was sufficient to wander every permitted hallway of it. There was a tiny cramped library filled with parchments and codices, occupied by two old men who had no love for each other. There was, on a seventh day, when his guards became involved in a dice game in the hall below, a great room of sunny windows where brightly dressed ladies sewed and infants played, but he was not welcome there, and he distressed his guards, two of whom he did not see the next day; he counted it his fault and sent in writing to beg Cefwyn's pardon, but Cefwyn sent back to him, also by written message, saying they were men, not children, and they knew their duty.

He took that for severest rebuke, and a sign that he was not himself a man, in Cefwyn's opinion.

He had found the kitchen, a ready source of food at any hour, Cefwyn's orders refusing him no luxury.

There were Barracks which he avoided, where the guards exchanged long and easy conversation with their fellows, but he could not speak, and he found it tedious and uncomfortable, and full of harsh and disquieting Words.

There was the Armory, which smelled and echoed of Weapons, and his guards said that was no place for him. But there was the Forge not so far from it, where the master Smith and his helpers worked metal glowing bright and almost transparent, making it grow and change, and where sparks flew like stars.

There were Stables, which excited his interest the moment he saw them, but soldiers barred him and his guards from that yard, saying they had had orders. So there were exceptions to Cefwyn's grant of freedom, and one involved Weapons, which did not appeal, and the other involved Horses, which were a Word of Freedom itself, a Word of Hay, and Leather, and soft noses. They were a cascade of Words – Heavy Horse, and Light; Mare and Foal; Hoof and Hock and Pastern, and he could have stayed and watched for a long time and drunk in those Words, but the guards had their orders, and he had no more than a glimpse of creatures that set his heart to racing and his hands itching to touch and know.

There was a long wing of Warehouses dusty with grain, a place of pleasant smells and an occasional furtive rat; he liked to be there, and he had discovered it on the third day, but the records keepers of that place seemed likewise anxious to have him gone, and the guards were bored, so after the fifth day he came no more to the granaries.

In all his explorations, he found no loft, only upper floors, and they said there was nothing higher, no place better than his own windows from which he could see the other roofs and a narrow space of courtyard. His windows could not be opened, except the small square that could let a breeze in; he supposed that was for safety.

He did not like it that the windows had no inside shutters to latch, and reading by candlelight or lying abed in the dark, he cast looks askance at that glistening dark glass on nights when the wind blew and sighed about the eaves, but evidently the Zeide had less fear of Shadows, and no one but he seemed worried about the matter. He even opened the window one night and left a bit of sausage out on the ledge, closing the little window quickly. He hoped Owl would find it and he would know by its being gone in the morning that Owl had been there – but it was still there when the sun rose, and by the next afternoon it was gone, after the servants had been there tidying up, so he thought that they and nothing baneful had found it.

One sanctuary he discovered where he could walk and sit at will: the west garden – which he came upon quite by accident, and which he most loved of all the places he could go. It was like a small, safe woods grown within walls, the trees carefully trimmed, even the pond neatly bordered. Birds from beyond the walls came and perched in the trees and hedges as he could not imagine they would do in the cobbled streets of the town down the hill. His pigeons came down, too, five at least that he recognized from his ledge on the other side of the building, and with the freedom of the garden and no opening pane to scare them, they began to take bread quite fearlessly from his hand.

But others disapproved the pigeon-feeding, and showed it by their looks. The lords and ladies of the Court resorted to the garden in the shady hours, jeweled and beautiful to see, at distance, in clothing with gilt threads that flashed and sparked in small patches of sun; but their stares at him were disdainful when he sat on the ground feeding the birds, which, when he thought about it, they, in their fine clothes, could never do.

The pigeons came to him now when he simply sat on the bench by the pond – there was a pair of titmice that grew more and more clever, and he fed them and fed the fish that lived there, while the lords and ladies (for those were the titles one did call them) along with earls and ealdormen and such, simply ignored his presence, and he theirs. He read his Book in the bright sunlight – or dutifully tried to read it – and on further days tempted the birds with grain that he asked the servants to bring him.

They were, he said to himself, mostly town birds, never so trusting as the birds of Ynefel, and would not bear a sudden movement, except the tits and the pigeons, who became entirely sure of him and very daring.

No one in all these days had broken Cefwyn's rule and spoken to him. He watched the lords and ladies in the assurance of safety here and studied their manners and their better graces such as he could puzzle them out, thinking that if he were more like them, he would become more acceptable in this place. Since in all these days, neither Cefwyn nor Emuin had troubled to call him, and the servants, the cooks, the archivists, and the granary keepers all dealt with him as quickly as possible and in silence, it did seem to him that it might please Cefwyn if he were more mannerly, and more like the people who lived here.

But he would not abandon the birds, who chattered to him, and buffeted his ears with their wings.

Came a day he sat, as often he would, by the pond, once he had exhausted the birds' appetites; and he had two books to read – one being Mauryl's, of course, which he would try every day until his eyes grew tired. But the other was a book he could truly read, and which spoke about Truth, and Happiness, and he daily lost himself in that, once the birds were well fed and the fish in the pond were sated. Each afternoon, now that his guards had found occupation to themselves in the old stone arch, a comfortable place where they sat and tossed knives idly at the dirt and talked freely to each other, he read, laboring over the Words that concerned the manners of men and of Philosophy and right and wrong, tangled reasonings, not all of which made sense to him. Words came but slowly out of that maze. But they seemed to be very important Words, and he chased them where he could.

He was thinking of Justice when a shadow across the page startled him, and made him look up in alarm.

He had not been listening for any approach. He looked around at brocade skirts and dainty slippers and up into a fair lady's face that smiled on him, red lips and dark eyes, and masses of auburn hair. It was the lady who had smiled at him before.

"Good day," she said.

He laid his book aside and quickly gathered himself up, having now to look down at her, for she was not so tall as he. She was beautiful, bright and dainty, with a light in her eyes that seemed mirth just about to break forth. He was entranced, delighted – and dismayed, because he very well remembered the condition of his freedom, and spread his hands in apology.

"I cannot," he said.

"Cannot what, sir?"

"Talk with you. Cefwyn forbade it."

"Did he, indeed?"

"Forgive me. Please go. My guards will be unhappy."

Auburn lashes swept over dark eyes and lifted again, restoring an intimate moment. She smiled at him, such a smile as held friendship and mockery at once. "Your guards will be unhappy. – I am Orien Aswydd. And who are you, sir, that Prince Cefwyn keeps so isolate in *my* house?"

"Your house?" It upset all the order he had made of things; and his question immediately brought a frown from her.

"My house, indeed, sir, and what is your name?"

"Tristen," he murmured, and m'lady was what he thought one called a lady, be she a thane's lady or an earl's, but he feared offending her, having made one mistake already.

"Tristen of Ynefel? Do I hear true? Mauryl's – what? Apprentice?"

"Student, m'lady. I was his student."

"And Prince Cefwyn keeps you prisoner here. Why?"

"I don't know."

"What, don't know?" She laughed and lost the laughter in gazing past him, where someone had walked close.

His guards had moved, and one put an arm between, wishing him to turn away. He bowed slightly before doing so. He knew that he had lingered longer than he should.

"Lady Orien!"

Emuin. Tristen looked, dismayed as the old man came strolling down the path.

"Your Grace," Emuin said, also with a nod, "good day to

you." And after a silence, and sternly, "Good *day,* Lady Orien."

Orien stared at Emuin with what seemed intense dislike, whisked her beautiful skirts aside and walked away with small precise steps down the gravel path. The sun on her auburn hair shone like a haze of fire.

Tristen stared after her, and Emuin set a heavy hand on his shoulder, demanding his full and sober attention. "What was said?" Emuin asked.

"I told her my name, sir. She asked why I was a prisoner. She said this is her house. I thought it was Prince Cefwyn's."

Emuin seemed slightly out of breath. Emuin drew him to a bench and sat down, drawing him to sit beside him. "Do you feel yourself a prisoner?"

"I promised Prince Cefwyn I would not leave, and I –"

"Do you wish to leave?"

"I know nowhere else, sir. But if I am not welcome here, I know how to go back to the Road – if you give me leave."

Emuin studied the gravel at their feet. "Do not," he said at last, "trust that lady. She is one of the chiefest Prince Cefwyn meant when he warned you not to speak to strangers."

"Yes, sir," he said. He must say. Emuin commanded Orien, and Cefwyn perhaps commanded Emuin; he had tried in all he heard to make sense of it. Emuin was still out of breath, and he suspected that his guards, less attentive to their talk than he had thought, might have called Emuin, or Emuin might have seen what was going on from the windows above. He had never seen master Emuin in the garden before.

"As for going back to the Road," Emuin said, "believe me that you are ill-prepared to wander it, young sir. There are very many dangerous people to account of."

"Like Lady Orien?" He truly wanted an answer to his question. But surely Emuin remembered what he had asked, and chose not to answer.

"Lady Orien," Emuin said, "and her sister, are Amefin, and this is, in good truth, their brother's house. Heryn Aswydd is Duke of Amefel, and lords of Amefel did formerly style themselves kings – petty ones, but kings. Now they style themselves aethelings, which is the same thing – but they do so quietly. Prince Cefwyn is Lord Heryn's guest, by the will of the King in Guelemara, who is *not* a petty king: Ináreddrin is King of Ylesuin, which is eighteen provinces, most of them far greater than rustic Amefel, which he also rules, above any duke. Prince Cefwyn is King Ináreddrin's heir, and he does the King's will here in Amefel as the King's viceroy, which means the Duke of Amefel is obliged, being a loyal subject, to quarter the prince *and* his court, *and* his Guelen guard, both the Prince's Guard, and the regulars. It also means the west wing of the Zeide is Prince Cefwyn's so long as Prince Cefwyn pleases to remain in Amefel, which he will please to do so long as the King wills it. So you are the prince's guest and ward, by right of Mauryl's title in Ynefel, which His Highness chooses to honor at least by courtesy. So you are not answerable to Lady Orien except through him."

There were a confusing number of Words in what master Emuin said. But it meant Prince Cefwyn had taken care and charge of him. That was comforting to know. And he supposed that if he had to choose who was telling him things most true, it would most likely be master Emuin.

"I am glad to know that, sir," he said.

"What are you reading? Is that Mauryl's Book?"

"Yes, sir. But I still make no sense of it. The other the archivist lent me."

Emuin picked the other book up from beside him and looked at it. "Philosophy. Hardly a novice's book. And you read this one, do you, with no difficulty with the words?"

"It seems a great deal of argument."

"Argument, indeed." Emuin seemed both thoughtful and amused. "Do you like the scholar's argument?"

"It seems to me, sir, the book is about Words, and I learn them."

"And how else do you fill your hours?"

"I feed the birds. I walk."

"You must be lonely."

"I wish Mauryl were here. Or I were with Mauryl."

176

"You Miss him."

His throat went tight. "That is the Word, yes, master Emuin." It was difficult to speak more than that. He looked away, wishing to speak, now that he had someone, if only for a moment, to speak to. But the words stuck fast. He thought Emuin would leave him in disinterest.

But Emuin set his hand on his shoulder, and left it there while he struggled to clear the lump in his throat, a strangely difficult matter now that there was someone beside him to notice.

"This morning," Tristen began, as calmly as he could, "this morning I was thinking that, in Ynefel, I knew very little. I thought things changed a great deal. But now that I've been Outside, things inside the Zeide seem to change very little."

"Very perceptive." Emuin lowered his hand. "Things do change. But mostly common and noble folk alike live their lives inside safe walls, and never seek to go outside or travel as you've traveled ever in their lives."

"Are most folk happy, sir? I see them laugh. But I can't tell."

"Nor can I," Emuin said somberly. "Nor can I, Tristen."

"Emuin, I've seen children."

"Yes?"

"A man should have been a child. Ought he not? – And I never was."

Emuin did not move, but stared at him with that troubled look any appearance of which he had learned to dread in people: it presaged fear. But as if to deny it, Emuin smiled warmly and patted his knee. "If there is fault, be it that old reprobate Mauryl's, never yours. Your consent was neither asked nor given. You exist. What you do now is in your power. What Mauryl did regarding you – was not at all in your power."

"Was I a child, Emuin? I don't remember. Mauryl called me boy. But I think I never was."

"Think of now, young sir. Now is yours. The future is yours."

"But I was not a child, master Emuin. – What *am* I?" He began to shiver and Emuin's hands seized hard on his arms.

He wanted the old man to draw him into his arms as Mauryl had, to shelter him as Mauryl had, but there was, he believed now, no such shelter left in the world. Held at arm's length, he saw mirrored in Emuin's eyes his own terror; he felt the grip that held his arms for comfort push him back more than draw him in – impossible either to escape or approach this man. Cefwyn had claimed him. Emuin had not.

"Ask no questions now," Emuin said.

"You know, master Emuin. You could answer me. Could you not? All these people know. And they fear me."

"Therein –" Emuin let go his arms and tapped him ungently on the chest. "There. Therein lies what you are, Tristen. Therein lies cause for them to fear you, or to adore you, or to trust your judgment as true – which is not the same thing, Tristen. And, believe me, you have more of choice in those matters than seems likely to you now."

Tristen blinked; the pain in his chest unknotted at the old man's rough touch and for a moment he breathed more easily. It was very much the sort of thing Mauryl would have said, and perhaps, though it lacked the tingle Mauryl's cures had always set into him, there was a bit of healing about it.

"Important now that you stay here," Emuin said, "mind what you're told and stay safe while you learn."

"You knew Mauryl. Did he speak to you about me? Did he warn you I was coming?"

"I last saw him years ago."

"But you said that he taught you."

"When I was as young as you seem now, he was my teacher. That was a long time ago."

"And not after?"

"I couldn't stay with him." Emuin shook his head, and fingered that silver circle that he wore. "We differed. I walked the same sort of Road that you walked, my boy, the Road back into the world. Don't be frightened here; this is a far less dangerous place than Ynefel."

"I was never in danger there."

"Truth, lad, you were in most dreadful danger. As was

Mauryl. As events proved, I fear. Mauryl protected you. Mauryl saw to your escape. Mauryl could do no more for you, and less for himself."

Memory of that place was all he owned and Emuin's words threatened to change it. "I was happy there. I want to be back there, master Emuin."

"He was a demanding master, and he could be a terrible man. And well you should love him, if only that you never saw that other side of him. Patience never came easy for him."

"He was good to me."

"Tristen, you will hear hard things of him; they are many of them true. He was feared; he was hated; and most of the ill that men say of him is true. But so, I very much believe, are all the things you remember. I tell you this because you will surely hear the ill that men do speak of him, and I would not have you confused by it. Hold to the truth you know of him; it is as true as any other truth, as whole as any truth men know, and I am vastly encouraged that you reflect a far gentler man than the master I knew."

It was the same as when he had touched the hearthstones. The hand that had met the fire was never the same as it had gone in, having knowledge but never again the same joy of the light. That hand had been burned. The pain had entered his mind. And a little smooth scar remained of that moment, despite Mauryl's comfort. In the same way he heard the truth about Mauryl, that Mauryl had existed before him, and outside him, and had had other students, who liked Mauryl less. He had no reason to think Emuin lied in his harsh judgment of Mauryl, who was his arbiter of all past right and wrong – as Emuin was his present master.

"Tristen," Emuin said, "you say that you sat outside on the step the day Mauryl left you."

"Yes, sir." The sunlight turned colder. "I did."

"What did you see there? What did you hear? What did you feel?"

"Dust. Wind. The wind took shape. It broke and became

leaves. And the wind blew through the keep, and stones began to fall."

"The wind took shape. What manner of shape?"

"It was a man."

Emuin said nothing, then. Emuin's face seemed more lined with age, more somber, more pale than he had been. He knew Emuin had not liked to hear what he had said. But it was the truth.

"It is too much to ask," Emuin said, "that Mauryl in any sense prevailed; but he sheltered you, and I trust guided you to reach this shelter. Do not think of going from this place. Whatever happens, do not you imagine going from here. I believe everything you say is the truth. I do not see falsehoods in you. Will you do as I say? Will you take my judgments in Mauryl's place?"

"Yes, sir." Tristen gazed at him, waiting for explanation, or instruction, and hardly felt the old man's grip. The bearded face so like Mauryl's swam in his eyes and confounded all memory. "Will you teach me as Mauryl did?"

Emuin held his arms and drew him to his feet. "You and I should not stand in the same room. Not now." With reluctance, the old man embraced him, then embraced him tightly. Tristen held to his frail body, not knowing why Emuin said what he said, but knowing Emuin's embrace was unwilling until the very last, and knowing now that desertion was imminent.

Emuin set him back again, and for a moment there seemed both sternness and anger in Emuin's eyes. "Cefwyn will care for you."

"Yes, sir," he said. He could think of nothing worse than being abandoned to Cefwyn's keeping, not even wandering in the woods. He looked down and Emuin shook at him gently, as Mauryl would.

"There is a good heart in Cefwyn, Tristen. He was my student, and I know his heart – which is a fair one, and a guarded one. Many people try to gain his favor, not always for good or wise intentions, so he makes the way to his favor full of twists and turns, but there is, once you have overcome all barriers, a good heart in him. He is also a prince of Ylesuin and his father's right hand in this region, and you must respect him as a lord and prince, but mind, mind, too, – now that I think on it, – never take all that Cefwyn says for divine truth, either. He will be honest, as it seems to him at the moment, but his mind may change with better thought. Like you, he is young. Like you, he makes mistakes. And like you, he is in danger. Learn caution from him. Don't learn his bad habits, mind! – but expect him to be fair. Even generous. As I cannot be to you. As I dare not be."

"Yes, sir."

The place they stood grew brighter and brighter, until it was all white and gray, like pearl; and the light came out of Emuin, or was all through Emuin, and through him.

– You are indeed, Emuin said, seeming, *finally well-pleased in him. You are indeed his work, young Tristen. Hold my hand. Keep holding it. Keep on.*

He could scarcely get a breath, then, and was standing on the pondside beside the bench. But Emuin was far away from him, halfway to the door; and with his back to him, walking away down the flagstone path.

– There is no leaving, young sir. You cannot find Mauryl again. But you can find me, at your need. Do not come here oftener than you must. I strictly forbid it. So can your Enemy reach this place. Do not bring him here. And do not linger in the light. At your urgent need only, Tristen. To do otherwise will put us both in danger.

It was like a brush of Emuin's hand across his face. Like a kindly touch, as Mauryl had touched him. And a warning of an Enemy that frightened him with scarcely more than that fleeting Word. He knew that Emuin was going away, but not as Mauryl had gone – there was a Place that Emuin would go to, and it was measured across the land and down the Road, and was not here – but it was not death.

He knew that something had happened to Mauryl, and that there was a danger, and that it dwelled in the light as well as

181

in Ynefel, rendering that gray space dangerous for him to linger in.

Emuin vanished within a distant doorway, rimmed with vines, a green arch above the path.

And a gust of wind skirled along the gravel, kicking up dust. There was a fluttering sound, as the wind went ruffling callously through the pages of his abandoned books.

He had been careless. He did not like such breezes. He went and gathered up Mauryl's Book and the Philosophy both from the bench, closed and pressed the precious pages together, under the watch of his patient guards.

But he had nowhere he had to go, nothing now that he was bound to do but what Emuin had bidden him do. He sat on the stone bench and thought about that, watching the fish come and go under the reflections on the surface until the shadow from the wall made the water clear, and he knew his guards, who had no interest of their own in books or birds or fish, were restless, if only to walk somewhere else for the hour.

CHAPTER 11

〜

He heard a clatter in the yard in the morning, and a great deal of it. It brought him from his bed and sent him to the door to ask the guards, who, in their way, knew most things that went on.

"We ain't to talk," the one named Syllan chided him, "m'lord."

"Master Emuin," said Aren, the one who would talk, sometimes, in single words and with his head ducked. "Leaving."

"Leaving," Tristen echoed, distraught, and flew inside to dress without the servants, without his breakfast, without attention to his person. He was in his clothes and out the door, as quickly as ever he had dressed in his life, in Ynefel or in Henas'amef. "I wish to go downstairs, sirs."

"Young m'lord," Aren said. "Ye know ye ain't permitted down there wi' the horses –"

But he was already on his way, and his guards followed. "Only from the steps," he said, walking backward for a breath, then hurried down the hall and ran down the stairs, his guard overtaking him on the way.

The lower floor was echoing with activity, the doors at the middle of the hall were wide open, and when he went out to the great south steps, which he had never attempted to visit before, the courtyard was echoing and a-clatter with horses. He heard shouts and curses, not the angry sort, but the sort of curses men made when there was haste and good humor about a task. He went halfway down the broad steps before one of his guards interposed his arm and stopped him.

"Just a little further," he asked of them; but they drew him over to the side, out of the jostling current of people coming up and down on business; and held him there – until straightway they fell into conversation with some of the soldiers waiting for a captain who had not shown up.

He watched the gathering of horses, and the men climbing into saddles, sorting out weapons and banners; it was bright and it was noisy, a show he would have been curious and delighted to see if he were not so achingly unhappy with the reason of it.

Emuin had shown him a way that he might find him even in a commotion like this if he really, truly wished –

No, he said to himself, that was not so. Emuin had said that it was dangerous to do and to do it only if he really, truly *needed* to reach him.

So he stood, doing as people had told him – until – just at the very bottom of the steps he saw Emuin walking past, and he moved two steps down before he even thought that he was testing the limits of his guards' patience.

But Emuin had looked up and beckoned to him, so on that permission he ran down as far as the bottom of the steps.

"Remember what I told you," Emuin said, taking him by the arms.

"Yes, sir," he said. He looked Emuin in the face and saw neither disapproval nor anger, but anxiousness; and he wanted never to be the cause of Emuin's concern. "Mauryl taught me about dangers, and to shutter the windows."

"The Zeide has no shutters," Emuin said. "But be careful of dark places, young lord."

"I shall," he said earnestly. "Please, please be careful, master Emuin."

"I shall, that," Emuin said, embraced him again, this time with a fervor Emuin had denied him yesterday, and walked on toward the tall, spotted horse they were holding ready for him.

Emuin climbed up, then, with a groom's help. The mounted soldiers closed about, the Zeide gates opened, and the column filed out with a brisk clatter of horses' hooves.

In the same moment Tristen found his guards near him again, ready to reclaim him, and he climbed calmly halfway up the steps with them, then stopped to look back at the last of the column.

The iron gates clanged shut. His guards began to talk again to the soldiers standing there. All real reason for him to be in the yard was done, and most people were going up the steps and inside or off through the courtyard toward the stables, but he had nowhere urgent to go.

A darkness touched the corner of his eye. He looked up and saw Idrys frowning down at him from the landing.

So did his guards see, and looked chagrined, caught in serious fault, Tristen feared. He went up the steps in company with them, as Idrys' cold eyes stayed fixed on him the while.

"It was my fault, sir."

"Do you take the prince's order lightly? A matter to ignore at will?"

"No, sir," he said. He feared that Idrys would do something to restrict the freedom he did have. Or that Idrys would unfairly blame his guards. But Idrys went inside the doors ahead of them, and did not look back.

"That were good of you, m'lord," Syllan muttered, and Aren said, "Aye. It were, that, m'lord."

"It was my fault," he maintained, because it was, although he was also glad to have seen Emuin at least once more, and glad to have had that embrace of Emuin, which made him feel that Emuin did care for him and would, truly, be there at his need.

But he said no more of it, since the guards were supposed to say nothing at all and were breaking another order.

He went to the garden then, and found it as trafficked as usual. People laughed and talked, where there was often quiet for thinking. It seemed as if everyone who had taken leave of ordinary business to see Emuin leave now congregated to gossip about Emuin and his reasons, and they stood about in clusters, chattering together in voices they wanted not to carry.

But the garden, usually his refuge, reminded him only that Emuin would not chance here again, in this place which had, to him, seemed overwhelmed by Emuin's presence and now was dimmed and made small by his absence.

He would not abandon the birds, who looked for him. But he went away after he had fed them, and took to his room.

He read, sitting on the bench in the light of the diamond-paned window, with the latched section, not even large enough to put his head out, open beside him. He had lured the pigeons almost as far as the inside sill, but the boldest was still too wary. He had a secret cache of bread crumbs, which he set out on that windowsill now and again. That was his day's entertainment.

He thought, too, that Idrys must have spoken sternly to his guards, because they were very quiet and had kept their eyes downcast when he walked back with them from the garden.

The next and the next days were as lonely, and as silent. He truly *needed* speak to no one. The servants brought him food, in which he had no choice, nor knew how to ask – it was delicate fare, on which he was certain the kitchen had spent much effort, but he picked over the plates with diminishing appetite, and on the third evening after Emuin's departure he rejected his supper entirely save for a bit of bread, which seemed enough.

Servants cared for his clothing. Servants renewed the candles. When, in his desperate loneliness, he ventured to bid a servant good day, that man flinched and bowed and turned away; knowing he had caused his guards a reprimand, he feared to speak to the guards more than to say where he would go, and they kept very silent now, even among themselves.

Owl had never come. That was better for the pigeons, but he was sad to lose Owl. He reckoned Owl probably hung about where he had seen Owl last, at the edge of Marna, where the bridge was. There were birds and small creatures on the shore, on which Owl could make his suppers, and Owl had likely become a terror about the bridge, Shadow that he was. He hoped that Owl was well.

Came a fourth morning, when he went down the stairs to begin his day of wandering about, in the escort of his guards, and he stopped and lingered at the foot of the stairs, lost and wholly out of heart this morning for the ordinary course of his walks, finding nowhere to go, nowhere at all he cared to go, nothing that he cared any longer to do, or see, or ask of anyone.

He walked down the hall, watching the patterns in the marble at his feet, finding shapes in them, knowing his guards trailed him as always, protected him as always, deterred conversation as always.

"Sir Tristen," a soft, light voice hailed him – a forbidden voice, ahead of him in the hall.

He had no choice but look up – his heart having skipped a beat and reprised with dread of Idrys' displeasure. It was, as he feared, Lady Orien; but now he saw two Oriens, the very same, hair quite as red, both alike in green velvet corded with gold, and both smiling at him.

"I mustn't speak with you," he said, and started to go down the hall away from them, but with a rustle of her skirts, Orien – or was it truly Orien? – closed the gap between them and hung on his shoulder, smiling at him.

"Tristen," she said. "Where, in such a hurry? Musty books?"

"Mauryl bade me –"

"Oh, Mauryl," the lady said. "Pish."

And the other, exactly like Orien: "So sad of countenance, Sir Tristen."

"M'ladies," he said, trying to brush first the one and now the other lady from his arms, "I have explained. Please: I am not permitted to speak to anyone."

"Such cruel hospitality. How have you offended the prince?"

"Please," Tristen said, and broke from them and walked quickly through his disturbed guards, back the way he had come. He had offended Orien Aswydd, he thought, yet Emuin had said she was to be avoided. And magic had made two of her. He did not look back. He hurried to climb the stairs.

Face to face with a pair of the gate-guards.

One he knew, a face out of his bad dreams; he met the

man's eyes without willing it, and turned and fled down the steps, taking the side hallway toward the garden.

No one but his own guard followed. On the bench near the pond he sat down and clenched his hands behind his bowed head until he could draw a calm breath.

The gate-guards, he told himself, would not come for him. They had not seen his misbehavior. They had not reported him. His own guards would not. They stood silent, as they must, now, but they were his own, such as he had, and they would have rescued him from the encounter if they had had time, he told himself so, as they had intervened before to save him from untoward encounters, and he hoped that they themselves would meet no reprimand.

He stayed by the pond all the day, save once going to the kitchen to ask a bit of bread, of which he fed half to the birds and the fish, who never knew his foolishness or his failures or his indiscretions.

And in the afternoon he tucked up his knees and rested his head on his arms, risking a little sleep finally in the sun's warmth, for he had ceased to sleep well of nights. Breezes blew through his dreams. Wings fluttered in panic, and beams and timbers creaked. Stones fell from arches. Shadows crept among the trees, soundless and menacing, and the wind roared through the treetops, rattling dry twigs and leafy boughs alike, making them speak in voices.

Here – the wind was pent in garden walls, the trees were trimmed by gardeners, the voices were all of passers-by who cared nothing for him.

But someone walked near on the gravel poolside.

And stopped.

He looked up into Idrys' grim face and started to his feet. He stood with heart pounding, for never had Idrys approved anything he did.

"Prince Cefwyn has sent for you," Idrys said, then, the shape of his worst fears.

* * *

Guards stood at the door of Cefwyn's apartments, downstairs from his room, grim red-cloaked men with gold and red coats and a gold dragon for their insignia: the Guelen guard, they were, which attended the prince. Idrys went through their midst without a glance, and Tristen followed him through the doors they guarded, through an anteroom and into a place of luxury such as, even imagining the ornament of his room done thrice over, he had never imagined existed.

Patterned carpets, gilt embellishments across a ceiling that was itself adorned with countless pictures, furnishings carved over in curling leaves, a fireplace faced in gold and dark green tiles and burnished brass. Idrys took up his station by that fire, arms folded, waiting, and Tristen stood still, not daring stare, only darting his eyes about while pretending to look down.

There were windows, tall glass windows such as he had seen in the solar downstairs, clear in the centermost panes and amber and green in the diamonded margins – amber and green that recalled, most inappropriately for his conscience, the ladies' gowns. The windows looked down, he saw, upon the roofs of the town below the wall, varishadowed angles of black slates and chimneys from which individual plumes arose to mass into a haze of smoke smudging the evening sky.

A door opened to the left, next that alcove in which the windows were. Cefwyn came into the room, stopped, looked at him –

Tristen bowed, as he knew men should with Cefwyn.

"Good day," Cefwyn bade him, walking to the table.

"Good day, lord Prince."

"Emuin asked me to see to you."

It was not, then, the discovery of his wrongdoing that he had feared.

But now, after Emuin's departure, now the prince unwillingly took direct governance of him? He supposed that was the way things had to be.

He had far, far rather Emuin.

"Do you want for anything?" Cefwyn asked.

"No, sir."

"Anything?" Cefwyn repeated, although clearly Cefwyn was not pleased to be concerned about him, and clearly he might best please Cefwyn by making himself very little trouble. He knew such moods. Cefwyn threatened him. He had lost Emuin. He was content himself if Cefwyn forgot him for days and days.

"No, sir," he said dutifully.

"If there is ever anything you need, you will tell me."

"Yes, m'lord Prince." He thought perhaps that that last was his dismissal, and he should go, but Cefwyn was staring at him in such a way as said there might be something more.

"You have remembered your condition," Cefwyn said, "to speak to no one in the halls."

"Yes, sir." It was not quite a lie. He trod closer to the truth. "Sometimes people speak to me, but I don't seek them out."

"What do you do with your days, sir student?"

He shrugged, feeling a lump of anger in his throat, and kept his eyes fixed past Cefwyn's shoulder, beyond the windows, on the roofs and the smoke haze. "I feed the birds."

"Feed the birds?" Clearly Cefwyn thought it was a joke.

"They are grateful, m'lord, as birds know how to be. And polite as birds know how to be."

"Is this insolence?"

"No, my lord Prince. I do not intend to be insolent."

"Do you want for anything at all?"

"No, my lord Prince."

Cefwyn frowned and jammed his hands into his belt. "Idrys."

"My lord."

"Have Annas bring wine. – Sit down," he bade Tristen, suddenly indicating the group of chairs in the corner of the large room.

Tristen unwillingly chose that nearest him and sat down. Cefwyn sat down facing him, crossed his booted ankles and leaned back, hands folded on his stomach.

"You have no diversions," Cefwyn observed then. "You

cease to eat; I have had report. You pace the halls or sit in the garden doing nothing."

"I feed the birds, sir."

"You've not tried to leave," said Cefwyn.

"No, sir, never."

"Emuin claimed that there was no malice in you. He left you in my keeping. What am I to do with you?"

Cefwyn wanted to have an answer that would let him dismiss the matter. That was all.

"I need nothing."

"What would you wish me to do?" Cefwyn asked. "Damn what you *need*, man. I have power. What would you have me do?"

"Have others speak to me."

"You are gentler company than most. I cannot set you out among these Amefin lords. They would rend you like wolves."

"I would not speak to the lords, sir. Only to my guards. If you would, sir."

The door opened; the aged servant brought the wine and poured two cups, offered to Cefwyn and then to him. Cefwyn lifted his cup and drank, deeply and full; but Tristen only sipped at his, for he had eaten but little in two days, and it came very strongly to his stomach.

"Idrys," Cefwyn said suddenly.

"Your Highness?"

"Be at ease. I judge no harm in him."

Idrys unfolded his arms and sank down on a bench by the fire, tucked up one knee and rested his arm against it. His dark eyes did not cease to watch and his frown never left him.

"There are no civilized diversions in Henas'amef," Cefwyn said. "Only the hunt. No hunting about Ynefel, I'll wager."

Tristen shook his head. Hunting was a Word of blood and death. It shivered down his spine.

"Gods, what *did* you do there? – Grammaries? Wizardry? Unholy sorceries?"

"I read, sir."

"Would you ride, Tristen?"

Horses, and open land. Moving air. Sunlight. "Yes," he said at once.

"My lord Prince," Idrys said, sitting upright.

"With full escort," Cefwyn said.

"The area is not secure, m'lord. Even so."

Cefwyn frowned, folded his arms tightly across his chest, and scowled, rocking his chair back. "Doubtless. So we ride with the guard."

"M'lord," Idrys protested.

"No, no, and no." Cefwyn was angry now, and looked not at Idrys, only at the table, his face mad-eyed like Owl's sulk. "Damn it, I am strangling in this Amefin hospitality. *With* the guard, with a troop of heavy horse and the Dragon Guard to boot, if you like, but I shall ride, Idrys. Tomorrow. Gods." He slammed the chair legs down and turned his face toward Tristen with a frown and an exasperation that Tristen did not take for anger directed at him. "Tomorrow," Cefwyn said. "Tomorrow morning, at first light, we will ride out to the west, have a glorious day in good weather and come back to a good supper, does that suit you?"

"Yes, m'lord Prince."

"Idrys is careful with my life. It's his business to suspect everything. — Idrys, is Annas waiting dinner, or has he deserted to the Elwynim? What is keeping him?"

"Is my lord done with business?"

"Yes. Finished, writ, waxed, sealed, and quit of. Not another lord with complaints, not another tax roll. I refuse. I deny them. I consign them to very hell. — No, damn it, *you* will stay, Tristen. You'll have your supper here. Will you?"

"Yes, sir," he said, bewildered. He had started to rise, thinking himself surely dismissed with this flood of complaint and exasperation, but with Cefwyn's offer of supper, and perhaps someone to talk to, he suddenly found that he had appetite, even with his trepidations. He sank back down; he drank the wine: his mouth was dry. Idrys had gone to call Annas in, and in the attendant commotion of trays, bowls, plates, and pages, a page hurried to fill Cefwyn's cup and his, without his asking.

"So what have you done with your time here – besides the birds?"

"I read, sir," Tristen said.

"Do you gamble? Play the lute? Do you do anything but read and feed the pigeons?"

"I – don't think I have, sir."

"The court is abuzz with you. The men are jealous. The women are smitten. I receive inquiries."

"Of what, sir?"

Cefwyn looked at him as if he had said something remarkable or perhaps foolish. He sat still, and Cefwyn ran out of questions.

But the old servant Annas and the pages had laid a glittering table in the next room in a magically short time, and Annas announced their supper ready.

So following Cefwyn's lead Tristen went and took his place at the end of the table. Cefwyn took the other, while the man Annas walked between, serving them a delicate white soup that smelled of mushrooms. It was very good. It was, he thought, the best thing he had tasted in days.

Meanwhile Idrys stood guard, as if his legs never tired and his back could not bend. Tristen turned from time to time to see him, wondering at the man, disturbed to have his eyes constantly on his back.

"He will take his supper after," Cefwyn said to his concern. "You don't understand the manners here."

"No, sir."

"That is a virtue."

"Yes, m'lord."

"Is that all your speech?" Cefwyn asked. "Forever and ever, – sir and m'lord without end?"

"I – *can* converse, m'lord Prince."

Cefwyn shook his head. "Idrys' silence is comfortable since I know its content; and yours is, if silence pleases you. – Idrys."

"My lord?"

"No ceremony. You make our guest uncomfortable. Sit at table. This is no Amefin. For that reason alone I trust him."

Idrys walked over to the sideboard and with a clatter disburdened himself of his sword. He sat down at the side of the long table and Annas set a place before him. He loosed several of the buckles of his black armor and held up his cup as a page poured him wine.

"Idrys is a man you should trust, Tristen," Cefwyn said. "You should understand him. He is another fixed star in the firmament. And there are very few. He and Emuin, and Mauryl, each after his own fashion. – I think we shall ride out to Emwy, tomorrow, Idrys. That village has made complaint of sheep losses. I think we would do well to look into it."

"Too near the river," Idrys said. "Too far. It would require a night."

"Near the river. Near the hills. Near the woods. There is nowhere on the gods' good earth someplace is not *near*, Idrys." Cefwyn took a calmer breath. "It would be politic in the countryside, would it not, for me to show a certain – personal – concern in local affairs? I refuse to be seen cowering from the attempts against my life. Or relying on Heryn's assurances – or Heryn's maps."

"Not overnight. Not this place. Not with an untried horseman."

"Emwy."

"My lord Prince, –"

"Emwy, Idrys. Or Malitarin. Now *there's* a village loyal to the Marhanen. And only four hours' ride, do I recall?"

"Emwy overnight," Idrys said stiffly, "might be better."

"A peaceful village. Missing sheep, for the good gods' sake. In the Arys district. I've been looking for excuse to see the hills there, from safe remove, I assure you. I want very much to know how that land lies – how wide that precious forest is, apart from Heryn's maps. And I had as lief know what the local grievances are, beyond the missing sheep. How they think the border stands recently."

"A double Patrol would be at minimum wise, my lord

Prince. – And lodge *in* Emwy, not on the road. Walls and an armed presence in the village."

"I grant you. But no advance warning. No word to anyone where we ride. And polite and moderate in our lodging. I'd have this village stay loyal."

"May I point out your guest has only light clothing?"

"See to that." Cefwyn's quick eyes darted back. "You've never ridden?"

"No, sir. M'lord. Mauryl had –"

"No skill with horses. Have never handled weapons."

"No, lord Prince."

"Idrys chides me that there is at least a possibility of Elwynim on our side of the river. Not in force. But best we do have some caution."

"The Elwynim are not safe, m'lord?"

He amused Cefwyn, who tried not to laugh, and struggled with it, and finally rested his forehead on his hand, shaking his head.

"There is hazard," Idrys said, completely sober.

"Indeed," Cefwyn said, and soberly: "Ynefel once prevented that sort of thing. But my captains believe now there will be a set of trials of that Border – which is still far from Emwy, and I doubt there is anything to be feared there at the moment."

"Your enemies pray for such decisions," Idrys said. "And I remind you our young guest is not – without any impugning of his good will – entirely discreet."

"And I," said Cefwyn, "doubt anything at all in Emwy's strayed livestock but a straggle of hungry Outlaws, pushed out of the woods, if anything, by our real difficulty over on the riverside."

"Outlaws," Tristen said, lost in the notion of Mauryl and Elwynim, sheep and Borders. "Men in the woods."

"Men in the woods?"

"I did see some. They were cooking something over the fire. But I know it wasn't a sheep. It was much smaller. They gave me bread."

"Near Mauryl's crossing?" Idrys asked, so sharply attentive it startled him.

"I suppose, sir, near the bridge, but not – I was walking so far –"

Pages had whisked away the soup bowls and served them instantly with a savory stew and good bread. The smell was wonderful, and he had a mouthful of bread and sauce. His stomach felt better and better.

"Most probably," Cefwyn said, "there is the cause of Emwy's strayed sheep. Bandits. Outlaws."

"The gate-guards thought I was one," Tristen said.

"Well you might have been," Idrys said, "but for that book. How *fares* that wondrous book, Lord Tristen? Still reading it?"

No question from Idrys ever sounded friendly. No question from Idrys *was* friendly.

"Do you read it?" Cefwyn asked. "Emuin said you made no sense of it."

"I do try, sir," Tristen said faintly, and swallowed a mouthful of bread, which he had made too large. A page had refilled his wine cup and he reached for it and washed the bite down. "But nothing comes to me."

"Nothing comes to you," Cefwyn echoed him.

"Not even the letters," Tristen confessed, and saw Idrys look at him askance.

"Emuin said nothing?" Cefwyn asked. "Nor helped you with it."

"No, sir, but I still try."

"Sorcerous goings-on," Idrys muttered. "Ask a priest, I say. The Bryalt might read it."

"Damned certain best not ask the Quinalt," Cefwyn said. "Eat. Plague on the book. It's doubtless some wizardly cure for pox."

"Mauryl said it was important, sir."

"So is the pox."

"If I learn anything of it –"

He saw by Cefwyn's expression he had been foolish.

Cefwyn had stopped eating, crooked finger planted across his lips, stopping laughter.

Tristen stopped eating, too. Cefwyn composed himself, but did not seem to be angry.

"Sometimes," Tristen said, "I don't know when people mean what they say."

"Oh, you've come to a bad place for that," Idrys said.

Cefwyn was still amused and tried not to show it. "Tristen. I care little for pox, except as I could apply it to Lord Heryn. – Which," Cefwyn added, before Tristen found a need to say anything, "is a very boring matter and a very boring man. – Eat."

"Yes, sir." He felt foolish. But Cefwyn said nothing more about it, and the stew went away very quickly as Idrys and Cefwyn discussed the number of men they should have along on their proposed excursion.

But the Name of Elwynim nagged at him. So did the accusations the gate-guards had flung at him. So did his recollection of the men in the woods. He reached for wine. He recalled the guards that had thrust that Name at him amid blows. It was a Name that would not, as commoner things did, find the surface and explain itself. He pulled at it, as something deeply mired.

"Are not –" he ventured to ask finally. "Are not Elwynim and Amefin both under Heryn Aswydd?"

"Mauryl's maps are vastly out of date," Cefwyn said.

Idrys said, "Or perhaps the old man never quite accepted the outcome of matters."

Cefwyn frowned. "Enough, sir."

"They are no longer under one lord," Idrys said. "The Aswyddim are no longer kings. The capital has moved. Did Mauryl never say so, master wizardling?"

"You see why he does not sit at table," Cefwyn said, leaning back with the wine cup in his hand as pages began to remove the dishes. "He provokes all my guests."

"Only to the truth, my lord Prince."

"But –" Tristen said, confused and not wishing to provoke

a quarrel. "Why should the Elwynim be crossing the river to steal sheep from Heryn Aswydd?"

"Easiest to show," Cefwyn said, and thrust himself to his feet. Idrys pushed back his chair to rise, and Tristen did, in confusion, thinking they were leaving the table, and looked for a cue where to go next; but Cefwyn immediately found what he wanted among the parchments stacked on a sideboard and brought a large one back to the table, carelessly pushing dishes aside to give it room as pages frantically rescued the last plates. The salt-cellar became a corner weight. A wine pitcher did, moisture threatening the inks. There was an up and a down to the words, and Tristen diffidently moved closer as Cefwyn beckoned him to see.

In fair, faded colors and age-brown lines, it was a map; and Cefwyn's finger and Cefwyn's explanation to him pointed out a design that was subscribed Henas'amef; and a pattern that was the Forest of Amefel, and then, differently made, and darker – Marna, and the Lenúalim which wound through it.

"Here sits Ynefel and the river. There is the old Arys bridge. Our realm of Ylesuin ends here –" Cefwyn's finger traveled up where the Lenúalim bent through forest, and Marna Wood stopped. In that large open land were divisions of land, drawings representing fortresses, and the whole was marked Elwynor. He saw one fortress, Ilefínian, that touched recognitions in him. Ashiym was the seat of a lord, a place with seven towers, but they had only drawn six . . .

Names: Names, and names.

"This is Elwynor. Did Mauryl show you nothing of maps?"

Cefwyn's voice came at a distance. He tried to pay attention, but the map poured Names in on him. "A few. I know he had them. He never showed me. But I know what they are, sir. They –"

A haze seemed to close about his vision.

"Tristen?" he heard.

"Elwynor was much larger once," he said, because it

198

seemed so to him, but that was not what he was seeing. His heart pounded. He felt the silence around him.

"Yes," Cefwyn said, in that awkwardness.

He could easily find Emwy. It was where it seemed to him it should be. He ventured to touch that Name, which he had not known, though Cefwyn and Idrys had spoken it, until he saw it written on the map – Words could be elusive like that: there, but not there, until of a sudden they unfolded with frightening suddenness and he saw them – he saw all of Amefel, and the air seemed close, and warm, and frightening.

"Emwy, indeed," Cefwyn said. "That's where the sheep go wandering."

"More than near the river," Idrys muttered. "The *stones* of that place are uneasy. I still would speak with you privately, m'lord, on this matter."

"Pish. Sihhë kings. Before my grandfather. – Did Mauryl teach you the history of Althalen?"

"No, m'lord, nothing." Tristen felt faint, overwhelmed with Places, and distances.

"Probably as well. It – are you well, Tristen?"

"Yes, sir." The haze lifted as if a cold, clear wind had blown onto his face, and now the solidity of the table was under his hands. He caught a breath and set his wine cup farther away from him. "Mauryl said I should be careful of wine. I feel it a little warm, sir."

"Gods, and us straitly charged not to corrupt you. – Annas, open the window. The fresh air will help him."

"No," Tristen said quickly. "No, I am well, m'lord Prince, but I have drunk altogether enough." He made himself stand straight, though the dizziness still nagged him, a distance from all the world. "I've not eaten today. Not – eaten well – for several days."

"So I had it reported. Cook is a spy, you know."

"I had not known, sir." He found Cefwyn's humor barbed, sometimes real, sometimes not. He feared he was being foolish; but he truly had no strength and no steadiness left.

"A dangerous young man," said Idrys. "My lord Prince,

for his sake as well as yours, do not bring him into your society. His harmlessness is an access others can use. And will, to his harm and yours."

Trust this man, Cefwyn had said. Yet Idrys called him dangerous, and spoke of harm, when he had only looked for a little freedom. Idrys might be right, by what Cefwyn said. It might well be that Idrys was right.

"I shall go to my room, sir, if you please, I want to lie down. Please, sir."

"He has not drunk all that much," saïd Idrys.

"Much for him, perhaps. Perhaps you should see him to bed."

"Aye, my lord."

Tristen turned, then, to go to the door, and had to lean on the table, bumping the salt-cellar. "Sometimes," he tried to explain to them, "sometimes – too many Words, too many things at once –"

"Too much of Amefin wine," Cefwyn said with a shake of his head. "Debauchery over maps. That you'll sleep sound tonight I don't doubt. Idrys, find some reliable Guelen man that can stand watch on him personally, someone he *can* confide in, and mind that the man is both kind and discreet. He's utterly undone. Have care of him."

"Sir," Tristen murmured, yielded to Idrys' firm grip and made the effort at least to walk, foolish as he had already made himself. He wondered if Cefwyn would after all take Idrys' advice and send him back to solitude.

But Idrys' advice he already knew, and asked him no questions.

Idrys escorted the wobbling youth to the care of the assigned guards – one could take that for granted, as Idrys knew his duties.

And for no particular – and more than one – reason, Cefwyn wandered to the clothes press in his bedroom, and to a chest that, with a turn of the key set in its lock, yielded up a small oval plaque set in gold, with a chain woven through with pearls.

Ivory, on which an Elwynim artist had rendered black hair, green gown, a face –

A face lovely enough to make a man believe the artist was bewitched himself. A face fair enough to make a man believe in Elwynim offers of peace and alliance, while Elwynim bones bleached above the gate for trying to cut short his tenure in Henas'amef.

A face of which one could believe gentleness and intelligence, wit and resolve alike. Could such clear eyes countenance assassins? Could such beauty threaten?

There might for all the prince knew be a bewitchment, not on the artist, but on the piece itself, which warmed to his hand. He should have sent the piece back with the last dagger-wielding fool, or flung it in the river, but he had not. He had not been fool enough to reply to it, save by the means of word passed to suspected spies that he wished to hear more – how should a man or a prince wish not to hear more of such a face, even from his mortal enemies? – but no answer had come, either floating the river, flying pigeon-fashion, or trudging down Amefin roads.

And, failing such elaboration – he should have tossed the miniature out the window, lost it, forgotten it at least, and kept the chest, which was finely done, of carved wood and brass.

But at certain moments he still resorted to it, asking himself – what in fact was this offer of the Regent in Ilefínian, what was the scheme that had the sonless Regent offering his only daughter to prevent a war his lords and advisors seemed bent on provoking, a war the Elwynim march lords invited in daggers, in poison, in cattle-theft? Count the ways: Elwynim found occasions to make his tenure difficult, and he counted this proposal among the tactics, a way to ruin his father's digestion did he even mention it in court in Guelemara.

Perhaps, on the other hand, Elwynor thought to create a better chance for its assassins, and that was why the chest had come to him secretly, by an Amefin carter, who said a man had given him the box and said the prince in Henas'amef would pay more than Heryn Aswydd to have the piece.

That was the truth. One wondered what other rules of commerce the Amefin commons had understood.

The door opened and shut. Idrys walked back in.

"Ah," Idrys said, having caught him temporizing again with the border.

"Ah, yourself," Cefwyn said. "I take oath that he knows nothing of Elwynor."

"Oh, that one? Sir mooncalf? I take oath he knows nothing Mauryl did not tell him."

He had, in fact, rewarded the messenger handsomely for this ivory miniature, carried to him from the border by an Amefin peasant. And he doubted not at all that Heryn Aswydd wished to have intercepted that box.

But no paintings in ivory comprised Heryn's offer of alliance. Heryn's offer came straight to his bed. Often. And twice over.

Cefwyn tossed the miniature back into the chest and closed the lid and locked it, insofar as the lock could serve to protect it from general knowledge.

"Is there a reason," Idrys asked, "my lord contemplates such Elwynim gifts, on the eve of a ride so near the border?"

"I might, of course, wed Orien instead. Or Tarien. It would secure the province."

"My lord jests, of course."

"Heryn counts it no jest. Nor does Orien. As my Lord Commander knows." Cefwyn walked to the window, where the sun went down into sullen dark. The window showed the far horizon and a seam of red light.

One could not see Ynefel from here. One could not know for certain, except as one believed Tristen's tale, that the fortress had fallen. And one did, in such unsettled times, want to know what the situation was, bordering Marna, and what the locals saw and surmised about changes in their sheep-meadows.

Though in the wizardly fashion in which Emuin knew things, Emuin had confirmed it was so, that Ynefel and its master had indeed fallen – and a prince could become so utterly dependent on such attesters as Emuin, and Heryn, and even Idrys, with all his attachments and private reasons.

By far less arcane means a prince knew that the twins had their own designs, independent of Heryn, and knew that their brother Heryn, who could not keep his tax accounts in one book, had his private reasons, and his none-so-private ambitions. And all the cursed pack of them, Elwynim, Amefin Aswyddim, and the Elwynim barons, had a notion how to secure in bed and by other connivance what they could not win of Ináreddrin's heir in war – unless Ináreddrin's heir grew careless about personally verifying the reports others gave him.

One wondered what effect Mauryl's fall had had on the border – or if they were remotely aware of it.

Or what the inhabitants of such villages as Emwy thought their taxes were, that Heryn collected for the Crown.

And how far the Crown Prince of the kingdom of Ylesuin should ignore the situation.

It was given as truth among every borderer that Ylesuin would eventually have to marry and mistress some sort of agreement to settle the ancient question of the border heritance. That such an agreement was imminent and due in this generation was an article of faith among borderers; that the Prince of Ylesuin had no more choice in the matter than Lord Amefel's sisters had was an article of faith on his father's part – but the heir of Ylesuin did *not* accept that role yet: the heir of all Ylesuin had other ideas, which involved bedding the Aswydd twins, enjoying the labor, and affording the Aswyddim the confidence that their habitually rebel province had secured useful influence.

And if the heir of Ylesuin was bedding the Aswydd twins, the heir of Ylesuin thus became too valuable to offend or assassinate, at least for the Aswydd partisans in Amefel, if not the other Amefin nobles who hated Heryn and his taxes.

It was thus far a comfortable and tacit bargain, one he was certain the Aswyddim had no wish to see the Elwynim outbid with a marriageable daughter. Heryn Aswydd had lately betrayed two Elwynim assassins who thought they could rely on Aswydd aid; and thus far (at least until, at his pleasure, the matter of Aswydd taxes racketed to Guelemara and the King's exchequer) Heryn's sisters, particularly Orien, the eldest, were a pleasant dalliance, so long as Aswydd excesses and Aswydd ambition stayed in bounds. It was all Amefin sheep Heryn Aswydd sheared, and thus far none of them had complained to the Crown.

But now Mauryl entered the game, with this wizardling – for that was a very good guess what the youth was – casting his own sort of feckless spell over sane men's credence and doubts, and saying, all unexpected, Believe in *me*, lord Prince. Cast aside your other plans, lord Prince. Mind your *former* allies, Marhanen Prince, in Ynefel.

"He might be Sihhë," Idrys said, out of long silence, and sent a chill down the princely spine.

"He might well," Cefwyn said, looking still into the gathering dark, at the last red seam left of the sky, far, far toward Ynefel. "But Mauryl did serve us."

"Mauryl Kingmaker. Mauryl the sorcerer."

"Wizard."

"The Quinalt will have apoplexies."

"Priests seem to recover quite handily."

"Three bids, Cefwyn prince. Do you realize? The Elwynim, the Aswyddim, – now Mauryl. How many directions can you face at once?"

He made no answer for a moment. The light was going. To see the horizon became, through the distortion of the crown glass, a test of vision.

He said, then, "Only guard my back, master crow. I'll care for the rest."

CHAPTER 12

❧

Words trembled in air, writings black and red, Names, that were Ashiym, Anas Mallorn, Ragisar, Malitarin . . . villages, that were Emwy and Asmaddion, and sheep were there, but Anas Mallorn ruled the riverside –

Owl flew above a parchment and faded land. Owl's wings were barred and blunt and shadowed villages at a time. Owl, Tristen called to him, standing at some vantage he could not at the time understand. But Owl was on a mission, or hunting mice, and would not heed him.

Owl eluded him and kept flying, opening up more and more of the land to him, Names that writhed in red ink and fortresses in black. Streams snaked under Owl's broad wings to join the Lenúalim, and all, all went under him.

"M'lord," someone called to him. But he was losing Owl.

Owl, come back! he called, for it seemed to him that Owl would leave the edge and enter the dark. But the map kept widening, Words and Names and lands like Guelessar and Imor . . . Marisal and Lanfarnesse . . .

"M'lord." Someone touched him, and he blinked, realizing it a gruff voice and perhaps one of the gate-guards, standing over him by dim candlelight.

It still might be, as he opened his eyes wide and gazed on a scarred and broad-nosed face, fair-haired, but gray and bald on the crown. He feared the man at first glance.

But it did not seem an unfriendly face.

"Uwen Lewen's-son, m'lord. The captain sent me. He said I should wake ye. Sorry. But it are toward dawn. And ye'll be ridin' wi' His Highness, so best ye be up and breakfasted."

"Yes, sir."

"M'lord, I ain't sir yet, no wise. Uwen's all. Servants is waiting wi' a small breakfast, and I'll fit ye for the ride, if ye please."

"Thank you," he said, if Uwen would not be called sir. Still – he was going out riding, Cefwyn had kept his promise, and for the first time in days he was glad to get up. He rolled out of bed and went immediately to wash and dress, while the servants were bringing breakfast in and lighting more candles in the early-morning darkness.

"Here's a robe, m'lord," Uwen said, flinging a robe about his shirted shoulders. "Ye have a bite, now. Ye'll be regretting it halfway through the day, else ye do."

He thought it sensible advice, and he sat down to a breakfast of hot bread and butter and honey, while Uwen was working with something of padded cloth and oil and metal, taking up laces, as it seemed.

He finished his breakfast more quickly than usual. He stood up, and Uwen gave him a padded undergarment, such as he had seen the soldiers wear about the barracks, such as, he thought, Uwen also wore under his mail and leather.

He was disturbed and fascinated at once, exchanging his robe for the soldier's padding. Uwen snugged the laces tight around him, saying, "Well, ye're slighter 'n ye seem, m'lord. Breakfast an' all. Does that seem fitted, here, m'lord?"

"Yes," he said, and Uwen took up a mail shirt.

"Watch your hair, m'lord," Uwen said, twisted his loose hair into a rope and helped him on with the shirt. The shining metal settled on and shaped itself about him like water, like –

His fingers traveled over the links, smooth going one way, rough-edged going the other, and as he breathed, he found the weight – like a Word, like a Name, settling about his shoulders and about his ribs and becoming part of his own substance – but he was *not* this Thing. He was not this Weight. He was Mauryl's, not a soldier . . . he was not this thing that enveloped him in steel.

"Ye'll get used to it," Uwen said. "Here's rough land, m'lord. We got bandits, we got Elwynim, we got Amefin who could mistake ye for a target, silly lads. Here."

Uwen had a coat in his hands, and Tristen put his arms in

like a shirt. Uwen buckled it on, then looped a belt around his waist and snugged it tight.

"His Highness has got you a nice, quiet horse. She don't do no nonsense. Ye ready, m'lord? Ye set fair?"

"I think I am." The coat was red, like Cefwyn's guard, and like what Uwen wore. He looked like another soldier, except the brown hose and brown boots where the soldiers wore black.

"Them are house boots," Uwen said, following his downward glance. "But the captain didn't warn me 'a that. They'll have to do, begging your pardon, m'lord, just stay t' horseback and mind ye got light feet."

"I will," he said. Uwen certainly must have leave to speak to him. Uwen chattered in a friendly way, in a manner of speech he found like singing to his ears, and when he went out, Uwen spoke in the same way to his guards, knowing them all, it seemed, laughing, clapping the one named Lusin on the shoulder as they left.

They walked down the shadowed hall to the stairs. The sun was just coming up. Servants were removing last night's candles, hurrying about on early-morning errands, some bearing linens, some coming from the kitchens. Guards were changing watch downstairs, and a few early-morning clerks were on their way to archive.

Uwen led him down the outside steps, past guards who also knew Uwen, as it seemed, and down and around to the stable-court in the first light of dawn, where a troop of soldiers and another of stableboys were saddling horses, and pages were standing with banners and bringing other gear.

Uwen picked up weapons by the side of the stableyard, weapons which had a worn, well-used look; and Uwen buckled on a sword and a dagger as Tristen watched, queasy at his stomach and hoping no one expected him to go likewise armed.

The mail surrounded his breathing, reminding him constantly that there was danger as well as freedom in the outside. In Uwen's close company he walked among the red-cloaked guard . . . saw Cefwyn, who looked little different than his soldiers, with brown leather and a gold dragon, like that his guards wore, on his red coat. All, armor and arms alike, that distinguished him from the soldiers at all was the silver band on the plain steel helm.

"Tristen," Cefwyn hailed him, and strode through the others to meet him.

Idrys walked like a dark shadow at Cefwyn's back, hand on hilt, where that hand always, even indoors, seemed most comfortable.

And at Cefwyn's orders a man brought up a horse, red from crown to feet, with a clipped mane and a look of stolid patience. "She will bear you gently," Cefwyn said. "Her name is Gery and the stablemaster swears she's easy-gaited."

Tristen took the reins in his own hand, rubbed the red, warm shoulder and threw the reins over, set foot in the stirrup and swung up as he had seen, dizzy for a moment at the mare's shifting of weight – a haze of sensations, of smells, of sounds. He looked down at Cefwyn's anxious face, at Idrys' frowning one.

"Well enough," Cefwyn said then, patting him on the boot, and patting Gery. Cefwyn turned away and a groom brought Cefwyn's horse and held it as he swung up. It was dark – Bay – the Word came to him; it had black stockings and a black mane as bays did. Idrys mounted a big black; and Uwen another bay – it was a color common in the guard's horses.

Idrys gave the order, the Zeide's iron gates swung open, and horses grouped together, stringing out as they passed the narrow gate.

"Ride to the fore," Idrys ordered, passing by him, and Tristen set himself as near Cefwyn as he could, almost at the head of the column, save that Idrys and a handful of the guard rode before him; but suddenly a number of men thundered past on either side and increased that number in front. Shod hooves echoed down the cobbles of the hill, disturbing the streets, where townsfolk early from their beds scurried from their path. Shutters came open. It was strange to see the town from the height of a horse's back, and to ride swiftly

208

down the very street over which he had walked, sore-footed and hungry.

A child ran from their path and a woman cried out. Tristen took Gery aside with his knee and turned in the saddle to look back, frightened by that cry of alarm, but the child had made the curb safely. And in that glance back –

He saw Bones. Skulls – above the gate. The bones of men.

He all but dropped the reins, and caught his breath as Cefwyn said sharply, "Tristen!" and Gery bumped Cefwyn's horse – his fault, he knew. His knee in Gery's ribs had caused Gery to drift; the uneven hand, the uneven seat – he suddenly knew with exquisite precision where his hands were and where his knees were, and how Gery had understood every move, every shift of weight he made. He straightened around, found his balance, found the right stress on the reins that made Gery know where to be and Gery at once struck a different, confident stride.

Gery looked to him, he thought, as he looked to his teachers; Gery, like him, wanted to do right, and wanted to understand, and he was talking to her with his knees and the reins alike as they went clattering at a fair speed through the streets, past all the buildings, all the scaffoldings and the shuttered windows and the fine buildings and the less fine, all the way down to the level courtyard by the main town gate, which he had once passed behind an idle cart, slipping past the guards.

But the gates stood wide for them and the guards there stood to attention as they went out with a rush onto the open and dusty road, out through the fields, toward his Road –

But not onto it. They went along the wall, and they went past the town, toward the horizon of rolling fields.

Then Idrys and the men in front slacked their pace, and Cefwyn did, and all the column behind.

Men outside the walls were already at work, already walking the roads, carrying hoes or mattocks or other such. The countryside was awake far and wide as the light came stealing over the fields.

"You ride well," Cefwyn said, "Tristen."

"Sir?" He shook off the haze that had come on him, blinked and brought the morning into clarity again, the fields, the creak of leather and the ring of harness – the give and substance of mail that surrounded him.

"You ride well. In the streets, you rode well. And you say you have never sat a horse."

"Some things come to me." He patted Gery's neck, overwhelmed with the feel of her, with the smells and the sounds around him. He was trembling. He wished to make little of it, but Cefwyn cast him such a look that he knew he had not succeeded in indifference; and he feared that calculation in Cefwyn's eyes.

"Mauryl's doing," Cefwyn said. "Is it?"

"I know things. I read and write. I – ride." Gery's warmth comforted him. He kept his hand on her. He felt her strength and good will under him. "I didn't know I knew, m'lord Prince."

Cefwyn frowned. The horses kept their steady pace and if Idrys or Uwen heard what passed between them, they gave no sign of it.

"You know it very damned *well*," Cefwyn said. "For down a hill and out a gate."

"It's like Words. I know them, sir. I know things."

"Am I to believe you?" Cefwyn said at last.

"Yes, sir," he said faintly, fearing to look at Cefwyn. Good things seemed always balanced on edge, always ready to leave. He did look, finally, as they rode, and Cefwyn stared at him in a way different from other people, even Mauryl, even Emuin – afraid of him; but not angry with him, he thought, nor willing to abandon him.

He knew not what to do or say. He looked away, embarrassed, not knowing whether he should have perceived this fact of Cefwyn. They rode in silence a time, well past the walls, now, and out along a narrow track where men rode two by two as the road went around the west side of the town and toward the rolling fields and pastures. The Dragon banners fluttered and snapped ahead of them, carried by young men. The morning sun glanced silver off a small brook in the valley. Hills rose on the eastern horizon, just past their shoulders, and beyond them – perhaps the Shadow Hills, perhaps even the mountains Mauryl had named to him, Ilenéluin, drifted in morning haze.

In the west were lower hills. The forest was that way. Marna Wood lay that way, and south. He knew. He gazed in that direction, remembering that dark path, remembering the wind in the leaves.

"A long walk." Cefwyn's voice startled him.

"Yes, m'lord."

"A fearsome walk."

"It was, m'lord."

"Would it fright you now?"

"Yes, m'lord." He did not think they would ride that way. He hoped they had no such plans. "The horses could not cross the bridge." That thought came to him.

"Bridges can be mended."

"The stones are old."

"Wizardry raised them. Wizardry could mend them, could it not?"

"I don't know, sir. Mauryl would have known. Emuin might know. We never saw any men, ever."

"Elwynim press at us. The skulls above the gate? Those are Elwynim."

"Did those men steal sheep from Emwy?"

"They came to kill me."

He found it shocking. "I don't know about that, sir."

"Don't you?"

"No, sir. M'lord Prince. I don't at all."

"Mauryl knew. Mauryl assuredly knew."

"He didn't tell me, sir. He didn't tell me everything." He became afraid, here, riding alone with Cefwyn, with no advice from anyone, and with the talk drifting to killing and stealing. "What should I know?"

"Uleman."

"Is that a name, sir?"

"One might say," Cefwyn said, seeming in ill humor. Then Cefwyn said:

"The Regent of Elwynor. That must mean something to you."

Names, again. Words. Tristen shut his eyes a moment, and there was nothing in his thoughts, only confusion, Words that would not, this morning, take shape. "I don't know. I don't know, sir."

"I thought you just – knew things."

"Reading. Writing. Riding. Words. Names. But I don't know anyone in Elwynor, sir. Nothing comes to me."

He was afraid to have failed the test. For a time Cefwyn looked at him in that hard and puzzled way, but, unable to answer, he found interest in Gery's mane. It was coarser than a man's hair. It was clipped short, and stood up straight. He liked to touch it. It was something to do.

"Tristen," Cefwyn said sharply.

"Sir." His heart jumped. He looked to find what his fault was. Perhaps even his respectful silence. Cefwyn kept staring at him as they rode side by side. He was afraid of Cefwyn when Cefwyn looked like that.

"Ninévrisë. Does that name come to you? Does Ilefínian, perchance?"

"Ilefínian is the fortress of the Elwynim."

"And Ninévrisë? What does that name conjure?"

He shook his head. "I have no idea, m'lord. Nothing."

"Such names don't come to you."

"No, m'lord."

"Do you take me for a fool?"

"No, sir. I don't think you are at all."

"And where do you find your truths? Do they come to you –" Cefwyn waved his hand. "– out of the air? The pigeons tell you, perhaps."

"My teachers do."

"Your teacher is *dead*, man. Emuin is gone. He fled to holy sanctuary. Who teaches you now?"

"You, m'lord."

"I? I am many things – but no teacher, I assure you. And damned certainly no moral guide."

"But I have to believe you, my lord. I have no other means to know." He was afraid, and shaken by Cefwyn's rough insistence on what he knew must be the truth. "The philosophy I read makes no sense of Names. Rarely of Words."

"Gods witness," Cefwyn said after a moment, "gods witness I am a man, not a cursed priest. Choose some other. At large and random you could fare better."

"Emuin said to listen to you."

"Then damn Emuin! I am not your guide, man. Moral or otherwise. – Would you believe anything I told you?"

"I believe everything you've told me, m'lord Prince." The prospect of doubt in things he had taken for true was sufficient to send sweat coursing over his skin. "I must believe you, sir. I have no other judgment, except to judge the people that tell me."

"Gods." Cefwyn slumped in his saddle, then suddenly took up the reins. "Follow me!" he said, and spurred around Idrys and past the vanguard.

Tristen followed; Idrys and Uwen would have, but Cefwyn turned and shouted, ordering their separate guards back. Their lead widened until they two rode alone with the escort far too distant to hear.

"Do not," Cefwyn said, "*ever* confess to any man what you have just told me."

"Yes, sir."

They rode in silence a time. "I have never lied to you," Cefwyn said at last, and quietly. "At least that I can recall. – Do you know who I am, Tristen? Do you really understand?"

"You are the King's son," Tristen said, looking at him, "of Ylesuin."

"Of Ináreddrin, King of Ylesuin, son, yes, his heir; and of Amefel, by His Majesty's grace, his viceroy in Henas'amef and over Amefel and its uneasy borders." Cefwyn looked down his nose at him, a narrow stare. "Most men – and women, oh, especially the women – have ambitions to share that grace. I have a vast multitude of devoted followers, and from none but a handful of my guard would I take untasted wine. What say you, Tristen?"

"Of untasted wine?"

"Poison. *Poison*, man. Poison in the cup, a knife in the dark. I defend this cursed tedious border against old resentments, and the Amefin, in particular those Amefin who are opposed to the Aswyddim on account of their burdensome taxes, would prefer another heir, since me they cannot manage, and they have discovered that. Now with nine heads on Henas'amef's gates, the Elwynim sue for peace and the Regent offers me his daughter. And the Amefin like that well, save Heryn Aswydd and his lovely and well-traveled sisters, who like that least of all." He lifted his hand to the east, where Henas'amef itself showed small and remote, now, falling behind them. "And should you lack for suspect affections or affiliations, or even bedmates, why, my dear sir, consider Guelemara. The capital. My father, my kith and kin, another pack of wolves, but with far better and courtly graces. The capital is vastly more civilized than here. They poison only fine vintages. You've been treated far more shabbily, having experienced Henas'amef's rough hospitality."

"I find it kind," Tristen said, "mostly."

"You are quite mad, you know."

"Most have been kind to me."

"Mad, I say."

"I think I am not, sir, please you."

Cefwyn's hand moved to a medallion he had at his throat, like Emuin's. "Do you not suffer midnight impulses to revenge? Do you not resent what certain folk did to you? Do you not think remotely of serving them in kind?"

"Who, sir?"

"A man has a right –" Cefwyn's words tumbled one over the other in a passion and fell to a halt.

"Sir?"

"Don't look at me like that! I am *not* Emuin. Don't look to me for answers, damn you, don't you dare look to me for answers! I'm no arbiter of virtue! You'll not trap me in that!"

"Emuin said you were a good man. But he said not to copy what you did."

Cefwyn's mouth opened. And shut. Cefwyn stared at him.

"I ought not to have said that," Tristen said. "Ought I?"

"Gods. You will terrify the court."

He was terrified, too. And lost. Cefwyn used words very cleverly, very quickly turning them from the course Tristen thought they would take.

"Or is such your humor?" Cefwyn asked.

"What, sir?"

"Cry you mercy, Tristen. I have never met an honest man."

"You confuse me," Tristen said. He felt cold, despite the sun. "I don't understand, sir, I fear I don't."

"I don't ask that you understand," Cefwyn said, "only so you don't ask too much of me. Emuin did tell you the truth."

The sun climbed the sky, and far past the view of the town, even beyond the reach of the fields, they took a westward road that ran up among low hills. The guard had long since swept them up again within their ranks and Idrys rode with a small number out to the fore, sometimes entirely out of sight as the road bent back and forth.

But it seemed the land declined, then, and in very little time the hills gave way to meadow, where a breeze that had made the day a little chill grew warmer and stronger, and lifted the banners and pennons.

They kept a moderate pace over an hour or so, between pausing to rest the horses. One such rest, as the sun passed its zenith had bees buzzing about a stand of white and pink flowers, and the horses cropping grass and the blooms of meadow thistles. Their company disposed themselves on a grassy slope and shared out a portion of the food they had brought.

It was wonderful, in Tristen's mind: he sat on the grass next

to Cefwyn and Idrys and Uwen, and felt a pleasant cama-
raderie with these rough soldiers – a joking exchange which
Cefwyn and all the rest seemed to find easy, and in which the
respect men had to pay Cefwyn seemed quickly to fall by the
wayside. There was laughter, there was nudging of elbows at
what might be cruel remarks, but the object of them rolled
right off a stone, feigning mortal injury, and got up again
laughing. Tristen was entranced, thinking through the way
these men joked with one another, laughter a little cruel, but
not wicked: he understood enough of their game to see where
it was going, involving a flask that emptied before its owner
regained it; there was mock battle, the man laughed, and
Tristen thought that if he were so approached, he could laugh,
too. It was good not to be on the outside watching from a
distance, and Cefwyn laughed – even Idrys looked amused.

It was good not to be protected into safe silence. He wished
the men would play jokes on him. He had not understood
jokes before, not this sort. Mauryl had had little laughter in
him.

But he saw Cefwyn easier, saw Uwen grinning from ear to
ear – even Idrys flashed half a grin. He hadn't known the man
had another expression; and he doubted it after he had seen it
– but it made him know other things about the man.

Afterward, though, when they were mounting up again,
Cefwyn said they should go warily, and Uwen said he should
stay close, that thereafter they were crossing through more
chancy territory. There was a woods ahead, which the King's
men had wanted to cut down, but Heryn Lord Aswydd, as
Tristen gathered Uwen meant by naming the Duke of Amefel,
had lodged strong protest, because of the hunting and
because of the woodcutters of Emwy village and others, and
had undertaken to keep the law there himself.

"So," Tristen said, "can the Duke of Amefel not find the
sheep?"

And Idrys said, "Well asked."

Cefwyn, however, looked not at all happy with the question, so he guessed he had wandered into a matter of

contention between them, and he was well aware that Idrys had begged Cefwyn to choose some other direction.

But Cefwyn, unlike boys growing up with wizards, was a prince and did what he pleased, when he pleased, and what he pleased was to ride in this direction. So Tristen thought, and began to worry —

Still the soldiers seemed to take the news of their direction as a matter of course, and Idrys had almost laughed at noon. It seemed, at least, the men felt confident of accomplishing what Cefwyn wished at Emwy village, whether that was finding lost sheep, or Elwynim, or outlaws.

He thought about it as they rode, and patted Gery's neck and wondered if the horses thought at all about danger: it seemed to him, one of those things he knew along with riding, that he might rely on Gery's sense of things, and on all the horses to be on the watch for danger of a sort horses understood.

In late afternoon they had woods in sight on their left hand, and the land grew rougher, less of meadows and more of stony heights, on which forest grew.

They traveled until forest stretched across their path. The woods was not Marna, Tristen judged: it was green. But it was very likely part of that forest that lay on Amefel's side of the Lenúalim, a thick and deep-looking forest all the same, reminding him of hunger and long walking.

The men talked about the river lying close.

"Is it the Lenúalim?" he asked Uwen.

"Aye," Uwen said. "And Emwys-brook. And Lewen-brook's not far. Not a good place we've brushed by, the last hour and more, m'lord."

"Because of the woods? Or because of the Elwynim?"

Uwen did not answer him at once. "Ghosts," Uwen said finally, which was a Word of death and grief and anger. It disturbed him. He looked at the trees on either hand as they rode into that green shade, and so did the men, who said very little, and seemed anxious.

But he looked to the green branches, even hoping to see a

feathery brown lump somewhere perched on a limb. Since their excursion planned to stay a night near this wooded place, he even hoped for Owl to find him – if Owl would haunt any place outside Marna, such a place as this seemed exactly what Owl would favor. The whispering leaves sounded of home to him. It made him think of standing on the parapet at Ynefel and listening to the trees in the wind. And he thought it would be a very good thing if he could find Owl and bring him back to Henas'amef. But the men around him looked not to be comforted at all by what they saw or heard.

"It's not so dark as Marna," he said, to make Uwen feel safer.

"Few places would be," Uwen said, and made a sign folk made when they grew frightened. So he did not think he dared say more than that.

But in a little more riding, the track they followed, leaf-strewn and hardly more substantial than the Road he had followed through Marna, brought them through a thinning screen of trees and brush, into yet another broad valley, with fair grasslands and fields and hills open to the afternoon sun.

"This is Arys-Emwy," Uwen said. "They're mostly shepherd-folk."

So they were still in Amefel, Tristen decided. He remembered the pale lines on the map. He saw the Name in his memory. Sheep had left their tracks about the meadow and on the road, although they saw none grazing.

They came on stone-fenced fields beyond the next hill, and crops growing, and further on they could see the thatched roofs of a village – Emwy village, Uwen said, which seemed a pleasant place. It had no outer walls, just a collection of low stone fences. The buildings were gray stone, two with slate roofs and a number with thatch. Shutters were open in most of the houses, and many of the doors likewise were open. Men and women were working in the fields closest to the village, and thin white smoke was going up from a few of the chimneys.

Folk stopped work as they saw what was riding down their road, folk came in from the fields, and dogs ran and barked alongside the horses, as slowly the people gathered.

"Hold," Cefwyn said, and the column halted; he gave some order to Idrys about searching the houses, and Idrys and the men around him, with none of the banner-carriers, went riding off quickly into the single street of the village.

"Where are the young men?" Cefwyn asked of the silent villagers, who leaned on hoes and gathered behind their stone fences.

And they were all old, or young women or children.

"Answer the Prince!" a man of the guard said, and lowered his spear toward the people.

"Off wi' they sheep," an old man said. "Off seekin' after they sheep, m'lord."

"Who is the head man, here?"

"Auld Syes. *She* is, m'lords." The man nodded toward the village, and all the people pointed the same way.

Cefwyn drew his horse about and bade them ride on toward the village itself, where Idrys and his men going in advance of them had turned out a number of villagers from their houses, a number of children, Tristen saw. Dogs were barking.

"This ain't good," Uwen said. "If village lads is off searching for any sheep, they should have the dogs along. They're lyin', m'lord."

What Uwen said to him echoed in Tristen's head as they rode up on the village and into its street. There were two girls – a number of children, many very young. There were old folk. Cefwyn's men, those afoot, who had been searching, and others sitting on their horses, were looking this way and that, hands on weapons. Idrys came riding slowly closer to them.

"Not a one of the youths on the rolls," Idrys said, out of some far distance. "So much for Heryn's law-keeping."

Tristen drew a sharp, keen breath, feeling a shiver in the air. Dust moved aloud the street as a stray gust of wind blew toward them. The gust gathered bits of straw, whipped a frame of dyed yarn standing by a doorway, and one woman, one old woman was in that doorway.

"Are you Auld Syes?" the sergeant asked.

"I am," the old woman said, and lifted a bony arm, pointing straight at Cefwyn. "Marhanen! Bloody Marhanen! I see blood on the earth! Blood to cleanse the land!" The wind danced around her rough-spun skirts, it skirled through the tassels of her gray shawl and the knots of her grayer hair. She wore necklaces not of jewels but of plain brown stones and knots of straw. She wore bracelets of knotted leather. Tristen looked at this woman, and the woman looked at him. She feared him. He knew that look. She stretched out her arm at *him* and pointed a finger, and cried a Word without a sound; and now in dreadful slowness Cefwyn's men were making a hedge of their weapons.

The wind wrapped around and around the old woman, winding her skirts and shawl about her until she was a brown and gray bundle in the midst of the dust.

The Word was still there. He couldn't hear it. People were screaming and running and Gery was plunging and snorting under him, crazed, as the wind whipped away from them, taking straw and dust with it, still blowing in and out among the houses, still whipping at the skeins of yarn. The frame fell over on the woman, covering her in hanks of yarn. Dogs were growling and barking, but some had run away. A handful of old men and women and a boy with one foot all stood where they had, and Cefwyn was shouting at the riders – "Up the lane! Catch one!"

– *Mauryl's damnable tinkering, the Wind was saying, with a hundred voices. Mauryl's meddling with the elements. Unwise. He would never take advice.*

– *Who are you? Tristen asked it, and thought of Emuin – it was like that gray place. But Gery was with him, Gery refused to go further, shied back and turned –*

"Tristen!" Cefwyn was shouting at him, and the wind whipped about, blinded him with bits of straw that flew and stung. Gery jolted so strongly forward he hit the cantle, and he fought to hold her as old women hauled the sputtering woman out from under the hanks of yarn and young women bolted down the lane between the houses and fled.

"She –" Tristen began, but had no words to say what the wind had said to him – it was all fading in his mind the way dreams faded, except it had spoken of Mauryl, and home.

"M'lord Prince," Idrys said, sword in hand, "this is no longer a ride for pleasure. Take an escort. Ride out. Now!"

Cefwyn was incensed. "Damn it! I'll not be chased by a pot-wizard and a gust of wind!" Cefwyn's horse was fighting the rein and he brought the animal full about in the midst of them. "She's a foolish old woman!"

"Lost sheep be damned," Idrys shouted at him. "It was a lure, m'lord Prince! They wished nothing but to draw you here. Your life is in danger. No one dragged their sons across the river. They've gone, they've taken to your enemies. – No, Your Highness!" Cefwyn had gone aside from the road, and Idrys went so far as to ride in front of his horse. "Go up in those hills and you'll be feathered like a goose. That's their purpose. That's what they want!"

"Do not you dispute my decisions, sir! The women know where to go!"

"Straight to their brothers and husbands!" Idrys said. "Give over, m'lord Prince. This profits no one but your enemies! If there's aught to learn, the patrol I've sent will find it!"

The wind came near them. The air seemed to buzz and hum like insects on a lazy day. Uwen caught Gery's rein, and Cefwyn was still disputing Idrys, but Idrys seemed then to prevail.

Two riders who had left them were still chasing across the fields, jumping fences, but the banner-bearers and the rest of the troop gathered around Cefwyn.

They were alone in the village, then, with the old villagers and the lame boy and the dazed old woman staring at them.

"Where are your men?" Cefwyn asked again, and had a

confused babble of pointing, and swearing, oh, indeed they were up with the sheep.

"The lost sheep?" Cefwyn shouted at them. "The sheep that strayed, that you complained of? Or was I ever to see that message? Was it to Heryn Aswydd you sent? And what was it to say to him? Treason? Do we speak of Elwynim, and not of sheep at all?"

The villagers were afraid. Tristen was afraid. The air still seemed to him to be alive with threat. The elderly villagers kept protesting their innocence. But the air tingled. The light was strange.

"Uwen Lewen's-son," Cefwyn said then, "take your charge and ride as fast as the horses can bear. Tell them at Henas'amef we've stayed in this village asking questions, and we'll hold these people under guard until the patrol comes back with you. – Take Tristen with you!"

"Aye, Your Highness." Uwen turned his horse, reached out, leaning for Gery's rein, and drew Gery about with him perforce.

"No!" Tristen said, fighting him for the rein.

"M'lord," Uwen said, and would not give the rein up as Gery jerked and shook her head, hurt, Tristen saw, and abandoned his attempt to hold her back. "We're ridin' for help for the prince, m'lord! His Highness don't need no argument. Come on!"

Gery went, fighting a step more, and then Uwen let go the rein and expected him to follow. He knew that Uwen had no time to spare for his fear. He steered Gery with his knee as Gery joined Uwen's horse in a brisk gait, back along the road.

"Prince Cefwyn will manage," Uwen said. "Unarmed and unschooled ye ain't much help, m'lord. We're bound to do what we're told, ride to the other side of that damned woods, and fast back as we can."

"What are they looking for?"

"Just you leave the village to His Highness!" Uwen said to him. "An' stay wi' me, m'lord. We got to get us past them trees. If we start summat from cover up there in the rocks, that woods is all one woods, clear to the other end of

Lanfarnesse, and full of trails. – Can ye stay a fast ride?"

"Yes," Tristen answered. His breath was coming hard. Idrys had spoken of enemies, and that word he did know – Mauryl had had enemies. The Shadows were enemies, and the forest seemed the most apt place for them to hide. He rode with Uwen, and glanced back as two more of the guard came riding breakneck down the road and their own horses picked up pace to match.

"Hawith, Jeony," Uwen said, waving his arm toward the road and the woods ahead. "Get yerself out to the fore of us, we got a m'lord to get through here." He took off his helm as they jounced knee to knee and offered it to Tristen across the gap. "Put that on, m'lord. No disputing me on this."

Tristen settled Uwen's helm, warm and damp with Uwen's sweat, on his head, and made Uwen no more trouble. They were coming to the woods, with the danger of some sort to pass, he understood well enough, trouble which might try to stop them. He understood the concern to know where the village men were, if they were supposed to be in the fields, but some of Cefwyn's men had gone up in the hillside meadows chasing those who had run – and what they thought those fugitive women had done or might do, he did not understand. Their own course seemed the most dangerous, a road winding past gray rocky knolls and through thick forest shadow, and as they approached the forest, with the horses already tiring, Uwen reined back, jogging a little distance, letting the horses take their breath.

"We'll ride hard through," Uwen said. "Fast as we can. Ain't no deceiving anybody. If they come on us, if happen I don't come through, ye ride straight on for town, hear me? Woods or fields, overland, wherever ye can find a way, ye get to the Zeide gate and tell the Lord Captain of the Watch – his name is Kerdin, he's always on duty at night, and he'll get us help. Mind the village is Emwy, and ye don't talk to no Amefin officers, ye hear me, young m'lord?"

"Yes, sir," he said. They were passing into the green shade, and Uwen took a faster pace. The men, Hawith and Jeony, had vanished ahead of them through intermittent shafts of light that hazed the way ahead.

Their own horses' hoofbeats sounded lonely on the earth. Sounds began to come strangely, and the sunlight seemed brighter, the edges of things unnaturally sharp and clear. Gery caught-step under him and threw her head, and that sharp-edged clarity was all around them, making things dangerous.

"Uwen!" he said, caught in strangling fear.

He reined back in fright, heard a hiss – before or after his hand had moved. Something hit his side in a whistling flight of missiles and Gery jolted forward, crashed through brush and under a branch.

He spun over the cantle sideways and crashed down into brush on his back as he held tight to Gery's reins. Men were shouting, rushing downhill, motley clothed and motley armed. Stones whisked through the leaves, cracked against trees. Arrows hissed and one thumped and sang near him.

He got up again – found the stirrup and hauled himself, winded as he was, to Gery's back. He reached the road, ducked low and hung on as Gery ran.

He heard nothing of the hoofbeats. He was in that bright light, that grayness, he and Gery both, though brush stung his face and raked over his shoulders. He had lost Uwen. He had lost the other men. Gery broke out of the woods and he saw not the road home, but the village where Cefwyn and the others were.

He had gone the wrong way. But there was no choice, now. He rode up at all Gery's speed, and Idrys' men swept him up with them, in what he only then realized was safety.

"They Shot the men." He could scarcely speak. He was trembling. So was Gery. But no one had followed him. There were no arrows here. "Uwen might have gotten away," he said, teeth chattering as with chill. "I don't know, sirs. I'm sorry."

"Damn them," Cefwyn said.

"Overland," Idrys said. "We go overland. I *know* the map, m'lord. We can make it through. Damn the village and their witch! They'll wait for night."

Cefwyn was not pleased. Cefwyn was taut-lipped and furious.

"Call the searchers back!" he said, and a man lifted a horn to his lips and sounded a quick series of notes that echoed off the hills.

He hoped Uwen was alive. He had heard the sound of arrows: he would never forget it in all his life. He shivered still, held Gery as quiet as she would stand and felt her shiver, too. Breezes brushed against his face, and he felt it chill, but that was only fear, not – not the stifling foreboding he had felt in the woods.

The men Idrys had sent out came back over the hills, down the lane beside the orchard, six men filling out their number again, on tired horses.

"Overland," Cefwyn said. "As best we can. Idrys! Take the lead."

It had not been the outcome Cefwyn had wished. They had not gained anything. The old woman, tottering on her feet, still disheveled, came out from among the others and down the street, calling out,

"The King, he come again, he come again, Marhanen lord, ye mark me well! *The King, he come again*!"

"One should silence that crone," Idrys said. Tristen caught his breath up to plead otherwise, that the woman was old and she was afraid and she sent only a little presence into the air.

But Cefwyn said, "Let be," and that stopped it. Idrys took the lead in leaving the road, back down the lane that led downhill past the village and toward a meadow pasturage.

The banner-bearers followed. Cefwyn led the rest of them, down this lane that sheep recently had used.

He thought he should have tried to help Uwen, but he had thought he was doing what Uwen said.

He had made a mistake, a foolish, foolish mistake, when, after getting back in Gery's saddle, he had turned back instead toward Cefwyn, blinded by fear, mistaking his direction. Fool, Mauryl would say.

Deservedly.

225

CHAPTER 13

∽

One of the men said he knew the way, and that he had ridden patrol here, so, he said, he could lead them around the woods and they would come to the road again before it entered the trees.

"We'll have our reinforcements," Cefwyn said to Idrys, "by morning. No use our riding south to the road and back again. We'll have these horses staggering under us, riding there. Make camp!"

"We are not armored against arrows or shepherd Slings, m'lord Prince. I want you safe away. We'll fire the haystacks. *That* will keep these people busy: *you* ride out of here, m'lord Prince! If Lewen's-son fell, we've no one in Henas'amef to ask our whereabouts until tomorrow late. We do not know their numbers – but I can busy them and ride clear."

"Then we both can!"

"No, my lord Prince! Do not be risking the King's heir after some ragtag troop of women in a sheep pasture! There are battles worth a prince and there are those not, and this is *not*, m'lord. I pray you use the sense your uncle had not, and live long enough to reign!"

There was silence for a time. Uwen might have made it through, Tristen thought. There might be help coming. But it would still be late. And Idrys and the prince stared at each other, glowering.

Finally Cefwyn said, "I'll not draw off men you may need. We'll go by the eastern valley. I can find that in the dark. You overtake us on the road. That is an order, sir. No lingering. I need you. I'll take Tristen, and two men beside."

"The wizardling is not a *man*, not in wit, not in experience – he's a risk, m'lord. A maid ten years old would do more than fly back down the road for rescue! A blushing maid might have stayed with her escort!"

"Sir, –" Tristen said, stung.

"Tristen," Cefwyn said. "Nydas. Lefhwyn. That is my word, Idrys."

"And Brogi," Idrys said. "At least *three* men, m'lord Prince. And six more, for safety."

Tristen bit his lip, unable to protest. Cefwyn said, shortly, "Later, master crow," and put his horse to a quicker pace as Idrys and others dropped back to ride back to the village.

But six more than two men followed them; Tristen followed, not wanting to leave Idrys' assessment of him unchallenged, but not having any argument against it, either. He had not done well, losing his way in the woods. He had fallen into that gray place, and he had thought he was facing the right direction, and he had ridden out in the wrong one. He did not know now whether he had turned face about in that Place, or had simply lost his sense of which side of the road Gery had gone to, and gotten turned wrong in the terror of the moment. He felt the fool – as Idrys had clearly said he was. But he had resources he had not used. He might call to Emuin, if things were going wrong.

But Emuin was very far away, and could send them no soldiers, nor any other help that he knew. Emuin had said the gray place was a dangerous place to linger. He wondered if Cefwyn knew of it, or if Cefwyn could go there, or if any of the other men could; he wondered whether he should tell Cefwyn that possibility or whether Cefwyn was privy to Emuin's doings with him, or should be.

Meanwhile their case was not desperate: ground flew under them, green grass and gray stone and black earth, over meadowland interspersed with rocky knolls perhaps too small to have names. The map still echoed Words to him, Words running in red and black and brown, with fine lines that blurred and ran and tried to find accordance with the land.

Wrong, something said to him. Wrong, wrong, this map; but he had been wrong once about directions: Idrys had said he was a fool and a difficulty to whatever party included him. And he had no way to say Idrys was wrong.

The horses could not long sustain the hard pace Cefwyn had set riding clear of the village and its stone pens. It was across the fields and pastures they went, away from the rocky hills to the north, and Cefwyn set a slower pace, still in no good humor, speaking to the men Idrys had sent only to indicate direction and prospects of reaching the point they sought, using a certain hill as a landmark. The man who claimed to know this land maintained that the road by which they had come lay due south of that mark.

That was wrong: it was south after some long distance east, Tristen thought: but he found it prudent still to hold his peace. Cefwyn was not in a pleasant mood, and south would do for a while, at least to get them *toward* the road.

They rode for a long while, until they had come where they thought they should find the hill, and failed to see it; and the man was begging Cefwyn's pardon just as they actually came in sight of it, and became sure where they were.

I know, Tristen thought. Owl's flight over the map in his dream had shown him all this place. It had shown him where hills should be, and the brooks that emptied into each other until they met on Lewen plain, somewhere the other side of the village, if they were going as far as the river.

Which they were not. They were still going directly south, which would lead them into rough land, Tristen thought. It would not be quicker. But no one asked his opinion, and Cefwyn was still short-tempered. He thought Cefwyn had a very good reason to be, counting the men lost and his argument with Idrys.

He was thinking about that, and they were passing quite close to the hill in question, a hill remarkable for a treeless top capped with stone – a bald hill, the men called it, and had a name for it: Raven's Knob – when they rode across a dark trail in the grass, left to right across their path. He saw it, wondered about it, as the only feature of disturbance in grasstops otherwise as smooth as velvet, a track such as their own horses made. Someone, Tristen thought, had made a recent passage through the meadow and away from the track they took. The trail they had left went up around the shoulder of Raven's Knob.

Cefwyn saw it too, and while they proceeded, one of the lead men rode out for some distance off their course and looked closely at that trail before he rode back again and rejoined them on their way.

"One rider," the man – Brogi – said. "Maybe two, Your Highness. Light horse, gone over the Knob and down the other side, by what I mark. I'd not be disturbin' things further without your order, Your Highness. That's a lookout over all the valley, that place is."

It was not good news, a fool could gather that much, too. Cefwyn frowned more darkly than he had, since, surely, Tristen thought, men on horses no matter what their business ought properly to be on the roads and not following sheep-paths across the land, unless they were trying to avoid something, as they were.

There had been no horsemen in the village. But he could not say whether there had been in the woods.

"It were made a few hour back," Brogi said, further. "I'd take oath on that, Your Highness."

"Perhaps it was Uwen," Tristen ventured in a quiet voice. "He said leave the road if need be."

"I judge it earlier than that, Highness," Brogi said. "The sergeant's apter to have gone off south before now. If it's his, he's lost. Maybe Lord Heryn's folk, but I wouldn't take anything anywise on trust, Highness, not wi' what we've seen."

"If Heryn's men," Cefwyn said, "still, I don't trust them."

"Highness," said another, older man, "our horses are tired. There'll be no running far or fast. If we can avoid stirring this nest, far better we could do that, and get on to the road."

"One or two horses, you swear."

"That left tracks back there, aye, Your Highness. Not more
'n three, but that isn't saying where they come from or how
many might be in camp further on."

The men were all saying be careful. The soldiers could by
no means argue directly with Cefwyn, but they spoke their
minds as much as they dared. "M'lord Prince," Tristen said
quietly, very faintly and respectfully bidding for Cefwyn's
attention. "Master Idrys doesn't know this is happening. Is
there any way to tell him?"

"Master Idrys is gods know where at the moment,"
Cefwyn said shortly. "Run hither, run yon across the meadows, and we may gather ourselves gods know what for
notice. Idrys may still be engaged at the village, he may have
gone south to the road, or he may even have hared off on his
own devices for very good reasons, damn his sullen, secretive
ways. We go as we are; we stay to the sheep-paths, and bear
as we can toward the road where we *hope* master Idrys will
meet us. Gods know what's encamped hereabouts, or
whether they've spied us out from the height."

"Margreis," Tristen said. That Name came to him, a
village he remembered from the map. "Isn't it near Emwy?"

"Ruins," Cefwyn said shortly. "And how do *you* know?"

"From the map, sir."

"Margreis is a haunt of outlaws from time to time. And it
is near the Knob. No, best we ride slowly, put no demands on
the horses until we reach the road. We risk no breakneck
speed on a cursed sheep-path."

That was the order Cefwyn gave, then. It still seemed to
Tristen it was far wiser to turn back to the village, where
there were walls and doors to lock against men or Shadows.
It seemed to him that being out in the land when dark came,
as coming it rapidly was, might not by Mauryl's instruction
be the best choice. It seemed to him by what he did remember
of the map that they would not find the road before dark even
at better speed than they were making, and the notion of

them wandering these sheep-paths in the dark looking for hills the man recognized did not seem in any way the wisest thing to do.

But making camp and lingering seemed the worst of all choices – sitting where their enemies could come up on them in the dark. He was glad at least Cefwyn was of a mind to go somewhere, if he would not go back to walls and doors they could lock.

Besides, he did not know that he was right; his notions were often right – but Names and impressions were coming to him now from moment to moment: bits and fragments of the map, details of land and cover shaping themselves from what he saw as if of a sudden the land around them had become that map of Cefwyn's, and he could see beyond the hills, guessing which way villages lay, and where the river was.

Cefwyn's men were still not exactly right about the direction, but the way they were going seemed the shortest they could manage without going through the low hills to the west, closer to the deadly woods: Cefwyn kept them proceeding as quickly as the horses could carry them, over ground stonier and less easy as the shadows lengthened.

And at deep dusk, the sheep-track on which the man had guided them played out at a brook with a high rocky shelf on the other side, so they had to ride along the lower bank and then cross and climb steeply up a sheep-path among the trees.

But that brought them up where there was rapidly no through track at all, only a tumbled lot of stone that nature had not made, with a scattering of trees. It was not the woods they had met before, only a copse of willows that gave way to stone and brush.

An old wall showed through the brush. Paving stones were all along the ground, like the Road, but pale gold. Some stones along the base of the wall were carved with leaves, and some with birds and some with circles. Some had faces, one with pointed teeth peering out from the leaves as if it lurked there in ambush.

The air tingled. That gray place of Emuin's was so easy from here; it rippled along just under the air, and it frightened him. The soldiers made signs against harm and Cefwyn wore a hard and unhappy face. The way became overgrown, steep and stony, and they had to find their own way through a tangle of half-buried stone in the gathering night.

But it was more directly toward the road they were going now. Tristen was certain of it. "I think this is right," he said. "The road is straight on from here."

"Damn the luck," Cefwyn said, refusing to be reassured. "This is not at all where I'd intended to go. We should bear more easterly and get out of this warren."

Immediately after, they found the walls of a building, which had not at all a good feeling. Soot stained the vacant windows and doors, as if the place had burned.

"Althalen," he heard one of the men say. "This is Althalen, gods save us."

It was a Name. Not a troubling one. But it seemed so to everyone else.

"They're stones," Cefwyn said sharply. "Dead stones. They harm no one. Look sharp for ambush. That's the danger here."

The light had all but gone. Shadows established their hold on the ruins and crept out of holes where they lurked by bright day. I dislike this, Tristen thought, and would have said so, if he had thought anyone would listen, or if it would have done anyone any good, but it was like the time before: all along, they were doing the best they knew to do, going generally south before they could turn east, and they were far enough along their track now that there seemed no choice, or only worse choices left.

Idrys might miss them on the road, Tristen thought. He hoped that Idrys might come after them. The ruins were all around them, and more and taller ruins lay stark on a hill above. The place felt worse and worse. The sky was the color of dirty water. The air turned dank and chill as light left the land.

And throughout, Shadows ran along between the stones, leaving their lairs in the deep vacancies of broken masonry.

Lines upon the earth, Mauryl had said. Secrets known to masons and stoneworkers. But what restrained a Shadow once the building was overthrown and once horses and men rode where doors and windows had not been? Surely such a calamity weakened their magic.

Wind blasted up, out of nothing. The horses whinnied and fought the bits, wanting to run.

Something was following them. He felt it. The horses felt it. He cast a look back, feeling terror gathering thick about the stones, a sense of presence the like of which he had felt once before in the forest, that time that something had passed him on the Road in Marna. But no more than then did he see anything substantial. Gery's skin twitched against his knee as Cefwyn led the way down an eroded slope. They passed into a dark, tree-arched gap between the lines of overthrown masonry and fire-stained ruin.

Wind blasted suddenly at their faces, skirling through the trees, sighing with a voice of leaves. A horse whinnied from far away. Tristen smelled smoke and heard voices raised in alarm, faint and far, but many, many of them. He thought of what Idrys said about burning the haystacks.

"Something is burning," he said.

"Nothing's there," Cefwyn said, sharply. "Stay with me."

A well-worn path went along the foundations of another set of walls. The smell of burning was overwhelming. It clung to them as they went, the horses all panting with the pace Cefwyn set, white froth flying from the bits in the gathering dark.

"I surely wisht I had me a bow," said one of the soldiers.

"Keep ahorse," breathed another. "Ain't no arrows to touch the cursed dead."

"Quiet," Cefwyn hissed.

"Fire," Tristen insisted.

The air seemed gray, then, and he knew he had slipped again into that dangerous place. Worse, it had become full of Shadows.

He saw fire spreading through the shadow-woods, pale and

dimmed, sickly orange in a white and gray landscape of shadows, and he could no longer find Cefwyn nor the men with him as he rode.

– *Stay, a voice said to him. Stay, fledgling. Feel your feathers singed, do you? The fire will not touch you. I would not let it touch you. Believe me. Trust me. Follow me. I'll lead you safely home.*

– *Emuin? he called out. Emuin, are you there?*

"Stop him!" voices cried.

Hands reached, Shadows rippled and rushed through the gray and the smoke and the pale, pale glow of fire against the pearl-colored sky.

He saw a gulf of darkness ahead of him and sent Gery flying across it, riding for the only gap in the fire he saw.

He struck a level plane where Gery fairly flew, away from the fire, away from the flames, away from the voices and the Shadows that reached for him.

But Gery and he went soaring through empty air, and a way loomed in front of him through breaking branches, a way of escape with fire on either hand, a path that went on and on, into the pearl-gray air.

Darkness loomed up; the bodies of horses checked Gery's forward rush. *Catch the reins!* he heard one shout, and hands dragged at Gery, hands dragged at him, too, until Gery stumbled and slogged to a stop.

The gray was no longer clear but charged with man-shaped shadows, full of harsh voices and reaching hands . . .

"Stay," Idrys advised in a voice hardly recognizable for its rawness. "Stay, damn you! Enough! M'lord Prince!"

Other shadows came up behind him. He was still on Gery's back. The whole sky spun and wove with lesser Shadows, the sort that men made: pale gray, not the deadly black of the true ones. The air echoed with voices reporting riders in the hills.

"Cursed ground," someone said, and: "They're Sihhë dead," which was a Name potent with their fear. "What's it to *him*?" another asked. And another: "He's right with 'em all. He'd have led us to very hell!"

"He led us to the road," a louder voice said. "Shut your damned mouths."

And amid all those voices he heard Cefwyn ask, "How did you chance here?" and heard Idrys answer: "The woods and damned good fortune. There was manure that no sheep nor goat made, m'lord Prince, horse manure spread about Emwy's orchard, bold as you please. I fired the hay, sent ten men after you overland and took the short way after – four good Guelen men, m'lord Prince, four good men lost on this cursed venture not counting Lewen's-son!"

He was no longer holding Gery's reins. Gery moved, and he swayed and Gery moved out from under him as someone called out warning, but he found nothing at all to hold – he was drifting in that gray place, and a hand pushed him until he was straight in the saddle and Gery moved back under him.

More men came riding up, enemies, some thought, but they were not. He knew them, not their names, but he felt their presence and knew them for Cefwyn's men. They were men Idrys had sent to track them through the countryside, and they complained of ghosts, and haunts, and swore they had smelled smoke, too, that it clung to their clothes. That they had heard voices and children screaming.

The night came clear about him, then: a place, a road, open to a sky beginning to show stars. They were on the road, and Idrys spoke of ambush. "We should be on our way, m'lord Prince," Idrys said. "There's nothing to gain, few as we are. We've tripped something before they'd like – so let us have the advantage of it, not throw lives away in chasing ghosts. It's phantoms you're seeing."

"A plague on Heryn's lost sheep," Cefwyn said, and, "We'll have questions for Emwy district. If they won't respect my banner, they'll pray for me back again. *And* they'll answer my questions."

They rode away from the place. Things came clearer as they went, the dark of ordinary night succeeding gray in his vision. But they were going, they said, back to the town, back to safety, where they might send men to find out the truth of business about Emwy district.

"Althalen," he heard Idrys mutter. "A fit place to murder the Marhanen heir."

A Name, a Name that rose up and coiled along the road, a Name that cast the night into confusion and distrust.

A Name that wrote itself on aged parchment, and shadowed with Owl's broad wings.

The gray was more, then, and the light in that place breathed with voices all striving to tell him something, but so many spoke at once he could not hear a single word.

He was sitting on a rock, and horses were nearby. He swayed as he sat, and a hand touched him – he reached to feel it, seeking something solid in the reeling, giddy light.

A blow stung his cheek. A second.

"Cold as the dead," Cefwyn breathed. "Tristen."

"M'lord," he said. The world was clear, if only the small dark space of it where Cefwyn was kneeling on one knee – that was not right. Cefwyn should not do that; but all else was gray, and cold, and went and came by turns as Cefwyn fumbled at his own collar and drew out a circlet of metal on a chain.

"Here." Cefwyn drew the chain off and pressed the object into his hand perforce. He felt the shape. He felt it as something alive and potent. Numbly he clenched it tight, pressed it to his heart and breathed, seeing the world dark and overwhelmed with Shadows and starlight.

"I was lost," he murmured, trying to make them understand. "Cefwyn, –"

– The Marhanen. We are betrayed once and twice, creature of Mauryl Gestaurien. You are deceived if you trust in these. Mauryl cannot have intended this, of all things else he would have done. You are in the wrong place. Leave them. Come away.

"Unnatural," a soldier muttered. "They's ghosts about. They's no good for a Marhanen nor a Guelen man on this road."

"Get him up. Set him ahorse," someone said, and Tristen tried to see, but the Shadow was around him. He knew he stood. He knew Cefwyn took the object and the chain from his hand and put it over his head, and about his neck, insisting that he wear it. It chilled him through the mail. "I am afraid," he said. "Cefwyn, I don't know the way from here. I can't find the road home."

"Hush," Cefwyn said, or Mauryl said. He was not certain. Rough hands pulled him, guided him, lifted him up and across a saddle which he struggled at the last to reach, knowing it was his way to home and safety.

A long time later he heard the sound of horses. He said as much, but no one would listen. Later, after another rest, and after they were on their way again – it might have been hours – they heard them, too, and he heard men curse and some invoke the gods. He heard metal hiss and knew the sound for the drawing of swords.

He felt at his side, but he had no sword. As in the loft when Mauryl died, when others took measures against the danger, he waited, not understanding, searching through the grayness to know whether the riders that came toward them were friend or foe.

Someone hailed them in the distance. "M'lord Prince?" that voice said, then closer. And eventually another called, rough and grown familiar since a morning that now seemed a world past, a voice that had called him out of a safety amid the bedcovers, out the dark of his room yesterday morning.

"M'lord Prince? Lord Commander? Is that you?"

He trembled, recognizing Uwen's voice. He saw Uwen with a bandage about his head, ahorse and leading other horsemen toward them out of a faint coloring of dawn above the hills.

Among the riders was His Grace Lord Heryn in velvet hall-clothing. Heryn made haste to get down and kneel on the roadside and to offer Cefwyn his respects and his concern.

"Well you came," Cefwyn muttered. "And with the Guelen guard. How kind of you to bring my soldiers. Or was it my soldiers who brought you?"

"I heard the news," Heryn said. "Your Highness, I had no inkling, none, of any disaffection in the area. My men have come and gone there with no hint of their doings. I swear to you I'll find out the truth. I'll get to the heart of this. I'll find the ones responsible *and* their kin. Damn them all!"

It was not the last word that Heryn said. Cefwyn also gave some answer to him. But the sound of voices grew dim. Uwen had ridden close, and asked if he was well.

"I think," he began to say, but did not finish.

*– Tristen, the Wind breathed. **Tristen, Tristen.***

He felt the chill, and struggled against the touch.

*– No, said the Wind, and there was fear in it. **Tristen is not your name.***

"Uwen, –" he found wit to say. He stood on the ground. He had gotten down from Gery at the rest they took; but he stood foolishly with Gery's reins in hand, and could not manage them, he was shaking so. "Uwen. Help."

"Aye, m'lord. Here's a stirrup clear. I got ye." A hand reached down to him, took Gery's reins, and lingered to take his hand. "Put your foot in 't, m'lord, I'll pull."

He set his foot in Uwen's stirrup. Uwen pulled on his hand as he tried to rise, pulled until he could catch a grip on Uwen's coat, and then on Uwen's arm, as he came astride the horse. He settled, taking a grip on the saddle, not knowing what else to do with his hands, but Uwen bade him to put his arms around him – "The horse can carry us both a ways," Uwen said. "Ye ain't got but a mail coat, nor me much more, m'lord. Rest forward against my back, there's a lad."

He let his head sink again, trusting Uwen, trying with all his will not to fall into that grayness again. It had become a deadly place. He knew this as he recognized Words when they came to him. The gray space, which Emuin had warned him was not their own, was not a refuge here, this close to haunted things. He had not reached Emuin. He could not

238

attract Emuin, only that hostile Voice that called and urged at him, and of all things else, he dared not listen to it.

But it was safety he had found at Uwen's back, at long last, after long running. Uwen offered him protection, a trusted, a kindly presence, strong enough to chase the shadows for him.

He slept, utterly, deeply slept, then, his head bowed against Uwen's shoulder.

CHAPTER 14

∼

"I done what I knew," Uwen said. The veteran's voice shook. And Uwen Lewen's-son, Cefwyn thought, was not a man who feared that much of god or devil – or the lord court physician. "I talked to 'im all th' way home, Your Highness," Uwen said, "I told 'im, don't you fear, I told him, Don't ye go down, lad, and he clung on. He hears what ye say. – He ain't deaf, sir." The latter to the physician, who tucked his hands in his black sleeves and scowled.

Cefwyn scowled at Uwen and at the physician alike, as the learned fool shook his graying head and withdrew from Tristen's bedside.

"In sleep, despite the protestations of unlearned men, there is no awareness," the physician said. "It is perhaps a salutary sleep, Highness. There is no hurt on him that mortal eye can see, naught but scratches and bruises, doubtless from the falls –"

"A fool can see that! Why does he sleep?"

"Nothing natural can cause so profound a sleep. I would say, ensorcelment. If he would bear the inquiry –" The physician moistened thin, disapproving lips. "I should say this far more aptly is a priest's business. Or – failing that – the burning of blessed candles. The Teranthine medal – is that his choice?"

"I gave it to him," Cefwyn said sharply, and whatever sectarian debate the physician was about to raise died unsaid. "Holy candles, is it?"

"He needs a priest."

"He needs a physician!" Cefwyn snapped. "I engaged you from the capital because I was assured of your skill. Was I misinformed, sir?"

"Your Highness, there are –" A clearing of the throat. "– rumors of his unwholesome provenance. – And if it is true that he came from Ynefel, I understand why you have engaged no priest. Yet I have risked the inquiry, Your Highness, and made the recommendation. Perhaps a lay member –"

"A plague on your candles. What in the gods' name ails him?"

"Not a bodily ill."

"A priest, you say."

"I would not for my own soul stay an hour in Althalen; the feverous humors of that place, particularly at evening –"

"Out on you! You've never come near Althalen!"

"Nor ever hope to, Your Highness." Secure in his physician's robes, his officerships in the guild, and in his doddering age, the man gathered up his medications, restored each vial, each mirror, each arcane instrument to its place, while the patient slept unimproved and an unlettered soldier did the only things that seemed effective, kneeling by the bedside and talking, simply talking.

Baggage packed, the dotard pattered to the door and opened it.

Guards closed it after him. They were Guelen men, of the Prince's Guard, men he trusted – as he would have thought he could have trusted the Guelen physician not to be affrighted by the unorthodox goings-on of a largely heretic province.

But Uwen stayed, on his knees, arms on the bedside, pouring into the sleeper's ear how red Gery was to be let out to pasture tomorrow with his own horse for a well-earned rest, how she'd taken no great harm of the run Tristen had put her to, and how he was very sorry to have left Tristen in the woods, but he'd had the prince's orders to ride to town and he had done that.

Uwen had indeed done that. With two of Uwen's comrades dead and Uwen himself struck on the head with a sling-stone that might have cracked a less stubborn skull, Uwen Lewen's-son had ridden his own horse to the limit and roused Lord Captain Kerdin and a squad of the regular Guard in an amazingly short time. Then, instead of pleading off as he well might have done with his injury, Uwen had changed horses and ridden with the rescue, joined of course by His Grace Heryn Aswydd's oh-so-earnest self.

Uwen Lewen's-son had stayed with his charge all day and night after, besides his breakneck ride and a lump on his skull the size of an egg. Uwen had bathed the man, warmed the man from the chill that possessed him, and talked to an apparently unhearing ear until he was hoarse. Uwen had hovered and worried without the least regard to his captain's casually permissive order to retire, and not expected a prince's reward for his staying on duty, either.

"You've done him more good all along than that learned fool's advice," Cefwyn said. "But there's no change. I'll have reliable men watch him. Do go to bed, man."

"By your leave," Uwen said in his thread of a voice. "By your leave, Your Highness, I had to leave him in the woods. I'd not leave him to no priest who won't stir for thunder. I'd rather stay."

So Uwen Lewen's-son had looked Mauryl's work in the eyes, too, poor ensorcelled fool. Idrys had called Uwen a longtime veteran of the borders, a man of the villages, not of the Guelen court, but long enough about the borders to know wizard tricks and sleight-of-hand; and to know now – a shiver went through his stomach – what the hedge-wizards only counterfeited to do.

He recalled the gust of wind that had skirled around the old woman in Emwy. That was either a timely piece of luck, or it was something entirely different. Tristen had been involved. Therefore Mauryl had. Kerdin, in a moment out of Heryn's hearing, had wanted to send a force of Guelen men to occupy Emwy and poke and pry into local secrets; Idrys, having seen the area himself, had wagered privately that such a force would find bridges as well as witches, and advised them, in colder counsel and with his prince safe in retreat, that they ought well to consider how much they wished to discover, and when.

Heryn, during that ride home, had said the horsemen whose sign they had seen near Raven's Knob might have been nothing more sinister than his own rangers, going about their ordinary business and keeping out of sight.

Then where are Emwy's young men? he had asked Heryn plainly, himself, and Heryn, always ready with an answer, had said they were in fact hunting outlaws, that Emwy district had indeed lost numerous sheep, and that the prince was entirely mistaken and misled if he thought there was possibly aught amiss in Emwy.

That meant that the prince, the Lord Commander, *and* his company had foolishly panicked at the sign of friendly Amefin rangers, that they had fled those friendly forces in confusion, and outlaws – outlaws, where supposedly Heryn's rangers were thick! – had shot and slung from ambush, killing the prince's men, for which they would pay – so Heryn Aswydd swore.

The bedside candle, aromatic with herbs, not holy oil, broke a waxen dam at its crest and sent a puddle down the candlestick and down again to the catch-pan beneath it. The puddle glowed like the sleeper's skin, pale, damp, flawless.

Heryn had implied, by what he had said, that the prince and the Lord Commander of the Prince's Guard, who, himself, had led His Majesty's forces in border skirmishes before this, were fools, starting at shadows.

Or Heryn thought to this very moment that the prince and his Lord Commander were fools to be *tricked* by shadows.

Shadows of which Amefel had many, many, in its secret nooks and clandestine observances – and in its ancient alliance with the Silver Tower. Mauryl's tower, as men had called it since the Sihhë kings died.

Heryn thought the prince did not delve into such secrets. Heryn thought the Marhanen prince, out of Guelen territory, sanctified by the Quinalt, had no conduit to such strange wells as Heryn Aswydd drank from in his countryish meanderings. But the prince had had Emuin for a tutor, the prince had learned enough to safeguard himself from pretenders to Emuin's craft – and the prince, more lettered in many respects than Heryn Aswydd, he would wager, was not complacent or blind.

The prince wondered, for instance, considering the luxury

hereabouts which did not find its way to royal coffers, where Heryn had found the means. The polished stone – oh, well, there were quarries. The carvings, to be sure – the artisans of Amefel were skilled, if heretic, and the patterns traditional to the region were . . . ornate, and devoid of symbols nowadays that might offend the Quinalt, whose local patriarch had such carvings in his own residence, set in gold and pearls, of course. One wondered with what hire Heryn bought them, or where the gold flowed before and after.

The Sihhë kings had hoards unfound – they said. The Sihhë kings had had means to call it out of the sea – or less savory places.

The Sihhë kings had had such wealth as Heryn used – Heryn, who might, like the Elwynim, have a little of that ancient, chancy blood in his veins, as he had such ancient, chancy connections to various villages of Emwy's sort, hung about with curious charms and observing strange festivals regarding straw men and old stones.

Heryn appeared to tax the villages white – and a Marhanen prince was not certain, with all the work of his accountants, whether that appearance was as simple as even the second set of accounts showed, or whether there was a reason villagers were to this day more ready to cut the throat of the hated Marhanen than they were to overthrow Aswydd taxes. Treasure trove was due the Crown – but one could prove nothing in the damned books. Heryn appeared to pay his taxes. Amefel appeared to be richer than its fields.

"M'lord," Uwen was saying, patting the sleeper's cheek. "M'lord, d' ye hear?" At the bedside, Uwen took the sleeper's hand, which the physician's ministrations had left prey to cold air, and, tucking it across Tristen's chest, drew the blankets up to his chin.

Like chiseled stone the face was, too perfect – and seemed older sleeping than awake, curious perception of Mauryl's creature. It was a grimmer, more hollow-cheeked visage than when the curious, gray eyes were open, entrapping, ensor-celling the unwary eye to look into them, not at the features, not at the stature, which was tall, nor at the shoulders, which were broad – nor at the hands, fine-boned and strong and sure on red Gery's reins.

Mauryl's piece of work had fallen ill in the Sihhë ruin, complaining of smoke which only some of them had smelled before or after that warning, but which he could now imagine clinging even in this room.

Mauryl's piece of work had ridden a good mare a course that should have broken her legs and his neck, through sapling woods and over ruined walls, along starless trails, over thorn hedges and dead-on to the road they were looking for – staying just out of their reach and with uncanny accu-racy arriving to meet Idrys, who was desperately looking for them.

Thereafter – an increasing swoon, moment to moment waking to be with them, then gone again, like a candle gutter-ing out, wit and resource all spent. Uwen had had hard shift only to keep his charge ahorse; and it had taken two men to carry him, yestereve, to this room.

Tristen had not waked since that last time on the road, still far from Henas'amef; had not waked though taken through the clattering town streets and through the gates; had not waked though borne by the guard upstairs and undressed and settled here; had not waked through the ministrations of three separate physicians, the last of which had been the prince's own resort.

Cefwyn looked at Uwen and let go a breath, giving a shake of his head.

"A priest would call this a dangerous place to be. Are you a pious man, Lewen's-son?"

"Not so's I'd leave him, Your Highness. I seen wickedness. I seen it where I had no doubt. This 'un don't 'fright me."

"They say he's a haunt, you know that."

"Who says, Your Highness?"

"Oh, the wise, that might know. Gossips in the hall.

"Servants in the scullery. Men in the guardroom. — Priests at their prayers. Some might say your soul was in danger. Some might say he'd bewitch you. Or that he already had."

"Some might say they're full of wind. — Wi' all respect, Your Highness." Uwen ducked his head and his ears were red. "I misspoke."

"Idrys called you honest. I respect that."

"I don't know that, Your Highness, but if the Lord Commander says."

"Servants will attend tonight. Tell them if you have need of anything for yourself or for him. Anything. Do not be modest in your requests. His belongings are under guard in his own room, upstairs. My guard, across the hall, will rouse me if he wakes — or worsens."

"Your Highness." Uwen gathered himself up to his feet. "Thank you, Your Highness."

"Bed down by him, on the mattress. You've need of your own rest, man. He'll not mind."

"Aye, Your Highness. — I —"

"Yes?"

"The physician didn't hint at any cause, Your Highness? I seen men hit on the head, m'lord, or knocked in the gut, and I seen 'em sleep like this." Uwen's scarred chin wobbled. "I didn't think he'd fallen, Your Highness, and I couldn't feel aught amiss, but maybe he sort of cracked his head, or one of them slingers —"

"He had a good soldier's helm till he lost it, Lewen's-son. Where was yours?"

"I guess I give it him, Your Highness."

"So your own head is the chancy one, isn't it? No, Lewen's-son. This is Mauryl's working, and by Mauryl's working he lives or not."

"They say Mauryl's dead, Your Highness."

"That they do. And perhaps the old man's work is unraveling. Or maybe it isn't. If we knew, then we'd *be* wizards and our own souls would be in danger, so I'd not ask, man. I'd just keep the fool covered and pour a little brandy wine down him if he wakes. You could bake bread in this room, gods, and it won't warm him."

"I been thinkin' of warming stones. Summer 'n all, Your Highness, if we could once get 'im warm . . . "

"It could do no worse. Tell the servants." He gave a shake of his head and walked out, through the anteroom where Lewen's-son had a bed he refused to use, and across the hall where Guelenmen stood guard over his own quarters. It was a larger room he'd allotted Tristen. It was a finer room, but that was beside the point for a man who might not wake. It was – the holy gods knew, a twinge of conscience, that he'd so failed Emuin's simple behest to take care of their visitor.

He'd sent to Emuin, last night, post-haste, a royal courier, one of twelve such silver tags which the King in his expectations of calamity had allotted his son and heir. They allowed a courier anything he needed anywhere along his route, under extreme penalty for refusal of his demands. He'd not used a one, before last night.

He'd not needed one before last night. Or had, counting what had been quietly going amiss over in Emwy district, and he had failed to see it growing.

Outlaws. Using shepherd weapons. And, if one believed Heryn Aswydd, rangers on horses, unusual enough in a woodland district. Rangers who didn't show themselves even to the prince's banners plainly and unequivocally displayed?

Not proper behavior, as he added the tally.

He crossed through the anteroom of his chambers and inside, where the servants were disposing bath and bed, and where Idrys was poring over maps on the sideboard.

"No change in him," Cefwyn said.

Idrys said nothing. Cefwyn unlaced cuffs, collar, side laces, and hauled off shirt and doublet together, before the staff could receive all the pieces thereof.

"The men I wanted?" Cefwyn said to Idrys. "I'll see them between bath and bed."

Idrys frowned. They had had their argument already: it

was bootless to dispute it in front of servants. Idrys said, "Yes, my lord Prince," and turned and went.

Four messengers.

To four lords of the south besides the Duke of Henas'amef, proud Heryn Aswydd. There was a lesson to be taught, and it began now, before the sun had risen on this silken-smiling Amefin lord, who asked with such false concern after his safety, who rode in hall clothes out to the windy road to ask after a Marhanen's welfare.

Cefwyn shed the rest of his clothing, stepped into the bath and ducked down under the tepid surface long enough to scrub the sickroom heat from his skin and hair, long enough to count to twenty, and to want air; and to find the bath too warm for pleasure after the stifling warmth across the hall. Gods alone knew how Lewen's-son stood it.

"Your Highness," Annas said, alarmed as he broke surface again – expecting a near drowning, perhaps; but Cefwyn found the draft from the open window vents more pleasant than the heat of the water. He clambered up to his feet, reached for the linen which a servant, taken aback, was slow to give him, and snatched it around himself, splashing the marble floor and the plastered walls as he stepped out. Servants mopped to save the woven mats and other servants scrambled to offer his dressing robe and more dry linens. The bath smelled of roses and hot oils. It cloyed. The water heated the air around him. He shrugged the dressing robe about him and mopped his own hair with the linen towel, ignoring the servants' ministrations as, in his wake, Annas ordered the just-poured bath removed, the bath mopped – the linens taken away.

"Leave it," he said, and tossed the towel at the boy nearest him. "It can cool." It took six servants half an hour to empty the cursed tub. "Do it in the morning, Annas, please you, I prefer quiet."

Annas understood. The three pages seniormost in his service understood. The latest come, he doubted. But he sat down in front of a window vent in his double-layered robes, and endured, still damp, the noxious airs of the night breathing from the open windowpane, despite his physicians' earnest disputations and predictions of the upsetting of his humors – his humor was vastly upset already, and if anything, the damp wind cleared his wits and made him less inclined to order summary execution for the servant who escaped Annas with an offer to light the, he was assured, already-laid fire.

"Out!" he shouted, he thought temperately, and moving to his desk, taking up pen and uncapping the inkwell, he wrote four brief notes to four provincial lords, affixed the seal of his personal ring, which precluded tampering with the ribbon he wrapped about each. Then he waited.

The chest was in front of him. The Elwynim chest. The bride offer.

And perhaps it was imprudent and tempting his own immoderate anger to lift the lid and to take out the ivory miniature, and to test his mood against that wide-eyed expression, the full lips, the midnight cloud of curls and swell of bosom daringly portrayed to entice a man, an offer of luxurious peace – to snare the heir of Ylesuin.

And ask – *ask* whether there were old bridgeheads being refurbished across the Lenúalim. Ask what this offer meant against the arrant folly of Heryn Aswydd who, if he were wise, might know his two sisters, fields for every plow, were temptation to lesser lords, but *not* to the heir of Ylesuin, *not* to promote His Grace Heryn Aswydd of rebel, perpetually heretic Amefel up to high estate in the court at Guelemara.

All that Heryn expected, in return for no more than a tumble in the bedclothes, for the latest gossip, for a whisper of Heryn's ambitions, for a night few whores could match for invention or few councillors for wit: oh, well indeed the twins (who came in a set, he had always believed, principally because neither trusted the other) were full of plans. By what he had heard, Tarien never, *never* forgave her sister her minute precedence into the world and would knife her in an instant if she thought Orien might gain anything above her.

Mothers thereby of a royal heir? No. That was for ladies richer, less versatile, more religious, less profligately trafficked, and certainly of larger, more influential and orthodox provinces. He could name an even dozen candidates of higher degree; ladies virginal, well-brothered and -fathered and -uncled –

Close-kneed, religious, limp and meek.

But – this – Elwynim. This – ivory bewitchment at which he stared, at odd moments, imagining that face alive with hints of both virginity and hoyden mischief – a crown of pearls and maiden violets, mirth dancing in the eyes, lurking about the edges of the mouth ...

The Regent's maiden daughter and only offspring, a bid for peace, an end of the old rivalry.

Meanwhile the vicinity of Emwy seethed with so-called outlaws, that near the ruins of Althalen, that near the Lenúalim's dividing shores, open defiance aiming at seeing the Prince of Ylesuin come to the same end the Sihhë had met – while the Aswydds simply pursued kin-ties, bed-sharings and bastard offspring (who might be worth lands and money in the coffers of the Aswydds, if nothing else) and endlessly embellished this great gilt palace which, the prince would greatly suspect, came not only of hidden Sihhë gold, but of other sources.

Foolish offer, this ivory Elwynim loveliness. A message had come with it that Elwynor did not propose to yield up its sovereignty, but that the Regent's line, having come down to a daughter with no other royal prospect, considered a matrimonial alliance and separate title for the heirs.

Audacious. Damned audacious of a man waiting all his sonless years for the Sihhë to rise from their smoky pyre, or for Mauryl Gestaurien to mend his treason and send them a King.

The more to worry – considering the feckless young man across the hall, who'd shown a seat any rider could envy and a skill at riding he claimed not to have.

Damn Emuin. *Damn* Emuin for kiting off to prayers and

piety and leaving him a young man so full of mysteries. Every possibility and every fear he owned was potentially contained in the young man lying cold as a corpse in that bed – who might be fading, for what he knew, with Mauryl's power leaving the world, who might be ensorcelled by gods knew what, who might be afflicted by some malady that – naturally? – gods! came on the raised dead.

The source of souls, Emuin had said.

And fallen into languor at Althalen, the very place where the last Sihhë king perished?

He heard the sound of men entering the antechamber and knew by the plain fact there had not been a rush to arms among his guards outside that it was Annas or Idrys, and by the scuff and clump of soldierly feet that Idrys had come back with the men he had asked Idrys to find.

He disposed the miniature to the chest; he closed the lid; he looked up as Idrys shepherded his choices to his desk. Idrys took a stance with arms folded, his eyes disapproving; and Cefwyn ignored the pose as he had ignored Idrys' objections to his decisions.

Four men, plainly armored and armed, Guelen men. So was the patrol that was going out in pursuit of the bandit remnant that had official blame for the attack on the Marhanen prince. They were Guelen men, too, that patrol, with orders to believe nothing too fantastical of bandit origins, and to look closely at kinships with Emwy and with Henas'amef did they take any bandits – did they take any, which a gold sovereign would wager they did not.

But these four men would not ride all the way with the patrol.

Nor would the four parchments bearing the Marhanen Dragon and Gillyflower personal seal of Cefwyn Marhanen, the King's viceroy – who did have specific authority to do what he proposed, but who . . . *with* the King's grant of a viceroy's power in Amefel . . . held the royal command over this whole uneasy border, with authority the southern barons would ignore at their peril.

"A patrol will go out under sergeant Kerdin Ansurin," Cefwyn said. "And once out of view of the town, you four will go your ways, avoiding all eyes; that is important. You, sir: this to Pelumer in Lanfarnesse; you, to Sovrag in Olmernhome; you, to Cevulirn at Toj Embrel, in his summer residence; you, fourth, to Umanon in Imor Lenúalim. Say nothing of this to anyone, not to man, nor woman, nor lover, light-of-love, nor your own barracks-mates. Walk from this room to your horses and join the band at the gates. A good opinion and reward if you discharge your missions faithfully and discreetly. The patrol you will leave is seeking the bodies of your comrades up in Emwy district. Believe there is danger. Believe there are those seeking Guelen lives. Be prudent, be quick, seek water only at brooks and springs, and lodge nowhere but under the sky."

Heads nodded. Grim looks confirmed their purpose. Young, these men, but Idrys had chosen them, and he knew Idrys' standards.

"Further," he said, "say no word of departure to any but your officer on the road, and if the lords to whom I send should ask you further of my business or the reason of the message, say that you understand that the summons is general; no more than that. You know no more than that. All else is surmise which cannot be profitable. – Have you any question? Ask now."

There were shakes of heads, and "No, Your Highness," faintly from two.

"Go, then." Cefwyn leaned back in his chair the while the men filed out.

And waited, foot on the rung of the table, one ankle on the other.

Idrys came back and lingered, arms folded, a shadow in the doorway.

"You've given me your opinion," Cefwyn said.

"Surely now you will need a fifth messenger."

"How and where?"

"To your father the King, to explain what you've done."

"Blast your impudence! You do surpass expectation."

Idrys remained unmoved. "He will surely send to you then, my lord Prince."

The bare foot slipped off the rung. He drew a deep breath and tucked his feet under him, canting his head at Idrys. "Tell me truth, master crow. Are you my man or his?"

"Yours, my lord. Of course I am."

"Then grant I have some wit. Grant I do what I must."

"Perhaps so, my lord Prince; but you know that it will not at all please His Majesty. You did well to send for Emuin."

"Because he will *listen* to Emuin?"

"Because the situation on this border is increasingly unsettled. And it would be wise."

"I am summoning the lords to consult."

"You are raising an army to intimidate the Amefin, and there is no one who will fail to understand that. Best it were a Guelen army, not provincial, raised of their neighbors and quartered about this town."

"Yield this inquiry back to my father? Come crawling to his knee and say I could not manage it?"

"You would win far more by filial humility than by what you propose, my lord Prince. An appeal for more troops would not be accounted an admission of fault or failure."

"Are you my man, Idrys?"

"I have given you my oath, my lord Prince."

"Then act like it."

Idrys inclined his head slowly, with just irony enough to sting.

"My lord, a second time: wait for Emuin."

"Because I will not take your orders, Idrys?"

"Because you are in danger here and I am not given resources enough to protect you from it. When danger comes into these chambers, I am one man, my lord Prince, with no more resource. The Guelen forces have lost man after man: niggling losses, but good men. You've just sent patrols out into the countryside. The remaining men will be on longer shifts, under the constant knowledge that they are few among these Amefin. The kingdom could lose its invested heir here, my lord; and that would not well please His Majesty, either. I do not know how I should explain it to him. Forgive me, sire, but I seem to have lost your son? I think *not*, Cefwyn prince."

"I hope to save you the necessity. Bear no reports to my father. Give me time to summon the march lords in. Once done is done, once I have the necessary troops to impose peace – my father *and* my brother will accept the settled state they see here."

"That is not the way I know my lord King."

"He loves me well," Cefwyn said with a twist of his mouth, "only so I make no errors. My brother, now, – Efanor . . . is the one who will fret himself hollow at my maintaining an army here."

"One cannot possibly see the cause."

"I am the heir. Am I not? And shall I not, in I hope not imminent prospect, command the armies of eighteen provinces, including the ones I've summoned tonight? And why should my brother be anxious about four, now, as if I had cause to fling over my duties here and leap upon his privileges? Should I care, in his place, if he raised armies? But I do think he will care, Idrys; he was all out of countenance that I had had *you* to my household when Father posted me to this province. As if my brother should need a general in Llymaryn. And good gods! we have sworn *oaths* of our brotherhood. I do find it curious what men surmise one will do that they would do, Idrys. Do you ever ponder such curiosities? It seems to forecast *their* inclinations more than mine."

"Your brother has unhappy precedent. Your uncle's death –"

"Was chance."

"His advisers believe not."

"And Father loves Efanor. Let us say the truth. Father loves him and would not mourn overmuch if some Elwynim put a dagger in my back."

"Fathers often dote on the lastborn. So I'm told. This does not make him first."

"So my father set me this duty to teach me responsibility. So he said."

"I heard."

"Well, then, duty leads me to this measure, and my royal father knows he need have no fear of my diverting that army off the Elwynim border and against him or Efanor. Whatever he thinks of me, he does at least believe me sane, and my brother can learn so."

"Your father is old, and it does not well agree with his years or your brother's anxious fears, my lord Prince, to have one son amassing troops in the countryside while the other son is living quietly in Llymaryn. Whatever your father knows or believes of your intentions, there will be concern about this among the northern barons. That is the plain truth."

"I am the invested heir; if trouble comes of what I do, then let Father look to the ambitions of the barons whose advice he's leaned upon too much, – including Heryn Aswydd, chief among them, Heryn Aswydd. I don't know whether Father has me watching Heryn or Heryn watching me, and, damn it! I have nothing to gain that is not already mine."

"It would still be more politic, my lord Prince, to use only Guelen troops."

"And what will that say? Dear father, send me your armies? I promise not to bring them home?"

"I shall sharpen my sword." Idrys made a second ironical bow. "You will have Heryn and his men buzzing about your ears when word of this flies free. You raise the wind, my lord Prince. And there may follow rain. Perhaps a frost."

"Given this present situation, Idrys, – how would you secure the Zeide from disturbance, without reinforcements?"

"Disarm the Amefin – now, before they can hear what you have done. Put the Guelen on guard at all posts, and bar the Amefin guard from duty and from the armories."

"Do it. Tonight."

Idrys' brows lifted. "That is extreme, my lord Prince."

"You claim to be my man. You give me advice. Then you

have my authority for whatever needs be done to make it clear to all Ylesuin where this mustering of forces is aimed – at Amefin treachery, not my brother's feverous fancies of an enmity I do not bear him. The one is a family matter. The other – is an order to me to hold a province with two hundred thirty men. Folly, Lord Commander, and letting Amefin fill out the posts after the business at Emwy – I think not. They cherish no thoughts of our good will, only hopes of our timidity. Hence my summons to the southern provinces, which my father may count his elder son's folly, or his elder son's premature ambition, but not if I turn up sufficient stones quickly enough. Lest you marvel, I do not believe Heryn – not his rescue, not his protestations."

"Is this recent disbelief or longstanding?"

"Oh, growing apace. Nor patient of further incidents. I take to heart all your warnings about the Amefin. Say to all who ask that the armory is locked to prevent thefts. We have had recent thefts, have we not?"

"If you say so, m'lord."

"Say, too, that we suspect an Elwynim spy among the guard. I should hate to offend the honest among them. Just let the next shift – be Guelen. Will that not make a quiet and quick transition? They won't know the replacement is general until they go back to their barracks. Review all rosters for patrols or issue of equipment. Better we have short patrols for a few days than lose our knowledge of what tidings have flowed to what place in Amefel. – And set up the sergeants *with* the scribes to take down a list of our loyal Amefin guard, man by man, accounting their villages, their residences, their relatives, persons who may vouch for their provenance and behavior, and question the men they name to vouch for them, and check back again. We are foreigners here. How else can we tell loyal men from trespassers? – Appoint Mesinis to the task."

"Mesinis? Mesinis, do I hear correctly?"

"This should take sufficient time for a muster of foot out of Far Sassury, if we needed send so far."

"My lord," Idrys said, "Mesinis it is."

"Wake me," he said, "promptly – if it goes amiss."

"My lord Prince, I am well certain, if our guard-change goes amiss, you will hear the alarms in the night."

"But alarm among the Amefin will give my brother far sounder sleep. Will it not? And Heryn certainly less?"

"*If* success tonight goes to our side, m'lord, and not to Heryn's. The man might take action, my lord Prince."

"See it does go to our side. – *And*, and, Idrys, . . . have master Tamurin take yet one more look at Heryn's tax accounts, past years as well as this. Have master Tamurin go directly into archive without warning, and appoint him pages to carry all relevant books to his premises, no matter the protests of those dotards Heryn appointed. Including the books of the town accountants, this time. *That* will divert m'lord Heryn from his petty grievances over Emwy and his guard appointments, and set the rumors flying among his earls and his thanes and his what-nots, some of whom may come to us in their distress."

Idrys actually lifted a brow, looking pleased and amused. "As you will, m'lord Prince."

"Good night, Lord Commander."

Idrys went without further objection. Cheerfully. That was rare.

Afterward Cefwyn lay in the broad bed, threw a coverlet over himself against the breeze from the window, and stared at an unrevealing mural on the ceiling, a trooping of fairy and a breaking-forth of blossoms, wherein smaller fay lurked under leaves and made love in the branches. A star was in the painted sky. A gray tower – or was it silver? – was on the hill. A star and a tower were the arms of the Sihhë, alike the arms of Mauryl, the Warden of Ynefel, were they not banned throughout Ylesuin. But surely Heryn would not lodge his prince in this chamber, under that painting, if they were more than chance elements of the piece. Perhaps the prince was suspicious and uncharitable even to suspect Amefin humor in the arrangement – as he was suspicious and uncharitable to suspect Amefin humor in Heryn's riding, oh, in hall velvet, and lightly cloaked, with the guard, risking danger –

– only in his tardiness to make his claim of innocence. Heryn had faced no danger of alleged outlaw weapons, the real nature of which he would wager his royal stipend Heryn knew.

He had laid out his riding clothes, his sword and his leather coat on the bench nearest the bed, without advising Annas or asking the servants' or the pages' help. He wanted no rumors running the halls until a bolt was on the armory door.

He did not take for granted at all that he could, without a blow struck and with but a handful of loyal guard, collar Heryn Aswydd – who was no novice in deceit and who had far cannier and hereunto unknown advisors. Even relying on Idrys' skills to avoid surprise, he knew Idrys' failings in diplomacy toward recalcitrant outsiders, and knew he risked stirring resentment where none had existed – at least where none existed to any extent that would prompt Amefin to assail the prince of a realm that had been, if not loved, at least peacefully and reasonably obeyed.

It seemed to him urgent, however, to act. His household officers generally had thought it best to tiptoe about the secrets of Amefin disaffection and map all the edges of it before making any move, all for fear of starting something far larger than Heryn from cover – meaning Amefin collusion with their ancient allies the Elwynim – and stirring themselves up a far wider conflict than a bandit or two in Emwy's bushes.

Disarm the Amefin by night, simply by moving them off watch as they turned in their weapons at the armory. That in itself would provoke outcry and dismay by morning, but it would frighten the Amefin, who had seen Marhanen vengeance in prior generations. And to confound their wildest terrors, the scribe he had assigned to the questioning and registry was far from vengeful – a kindly and grandfatherly old fellow, fine for small details. Mesinis was the absolute soul of patience, . . . and incapable, one suspected, of taking accurate notes long before he became slightly deaf. Moreover, Mesinis did *not* deal well with Amefin names or the Amefin brogue.

He liked that stroke; he truly did. If one was bound to create consternation among one's enemies, it seemed, after outright terror was established, best to aim that consternation at small, maddening obstacles like Mesinis, which obscured the more outrageous acts – small, maddening obstacles in which the prince could graciously create exemption and ease the way, making Amefin *grateful* for Marhanen intervention on their behalf.

Hourly he expected some alarm from the halls, some wild threat from Heryn and his minions, or worse, some rising in the town at large that would invade the halls and tear them all limb from limb.

They were not thoughts on which a man could sleep. But when the hour for the guard change passed without alarm, that matter at least seemed settled. The one patrol was out by now, riding by night, and his messengers would leave that column and spread out to the barons of the adjoining provinces, who in their lordship of their provinces did not directly owe him fealty.

But if His Grace of Amefel were allied with some Elwynim lord slipping *his* Regent's leash (as well Amefel *had* once been, with Elwynor, ruled from Althalen), and general war broke out, then be certain that His Royal Highness Cefwyn Marhanen would bear the lifelong reputation for losing a province, and be certain that his royal father would regain it, to his father's credit but to his own lifelong disgrace – and lasting trouble in his own reign. His father had set him here to prove himself or fail, with hopes, at least on the part of certain barons in Guelessar, Llymaryn, and elsewhere in the realm, that the elder prince of Ylesuin, known for debauch, might most spectacularly fail in the temptations of Heryn's court – or die and never sit the Dragon throne.

But those were northern lords who opposed him, while the barons of the more religiously diverse south readily distrusted that coalition of established and orthodox Quinalt interests that had moved into the court at Guelemara during his father's reign. Even in heretic Amefel, he suspected, many hoped for Good King Log to establish his rule in Ináreddrin's quieter younger son Efanor.

While if there was any personal advantage he himself had in undertaking this oversight of Amefel, it was the expectation of the southern barons that the Crown Prince, having ruled in the south, supported by the south, might reward the south and send such influences packing. Efanor never saw it. Efanor had lately become piously Quinalt. Efanor, turning to the gods, had no real heart for conspiracy. It was why the northern barons so loved him.

It was the reason *he* was so desperate as to send those messages.

And twice in the night he roused poor Annas to go inform himself how Tristen fared. Each time the answer was the same: He has not wakened, my lord Prince; and, reliably, His man is with him.

Mauryl's gift. *That* cuckoo in the Amefin nest was yet to fledge – and a frightened small portion of his heart wished the wizard-gift might come to nothing, while the greater, the nobler part of him feared losing that gift, whatever it might mean, whatever uncertainties it brought him.

Came a noise somewhere that caught him with his eyes shut and his thoughts drifting. He was not certain he had not dreamed it. The fire in the hearth had burned down; he roused himself to tend it, not troubling Annas, and looked and found gray daylight in the windows.

The noise repeated itself. *Thump.* The guard was admitting someone to his chambers, and he cast a thought toward his sword. He rubbed his eyes and his face and reassured himself with the remembrance that the guard had changed at least once in the night, and nothing had raised alarms or rung the muster bell.

The inner door opened, that from the foyer; and it was Idrys, shadow-eyed and unshaven, but fully armored and bearing his sword.

Idrys bowed with his usual grace. "My lord Prince. Amefel applies to see you. He frets in his disfavor."

"And my orders?"

"Executed. While the Zeide slept, at the watch change, as you ordered, the Guelen forces took the Zeide gates, the armory, the stables, the storerooms and the kitchens, and stand guard outside Heryn's and the twins' rooms. The Amefin guard is disturbed, needless to report, but awaits its orders from Heryn, and Heryn . . . is awaiting your pleasure, my lord."

Idrys had rarely looked so pleased with a situation.

"Well done," Cefwyn said.

"My lord."

"I think," Cefwyn began, and nudged the brass kettle and last night's tea water over last night's coals to heat. He tossed on a few sticks of wood from the heap beside the hearth, while Idrys took up watch over him, arms folded. "I think that Heryn may seethe in his own juices a time. How long, do you think, is prudent?"

"Enough time to see Your Highness breakfasted and well sated with tea."

"Perhaps I shall invite him to breakfast."

"Shall I relay that invitation, Your Highness?"

"Carry it yourself. He fears you."

"Most gladly, my lord Prince."

Idrys departed, and Cefwyn thoughtfully investigated the kettle of water, hesitating still, in the weariness of a long night, to call in the clatter and conversation of servants and pages.

But he rang the bell, and when Annas turned up from his bed nearby: "Breakfast," he ordered, "for myself and Heryn Aswydd. A guard will escort you, the cook, the pages, with every pot and every cup and source. There is dissent and division afoot."

"I shall take good care," the old man murmured, "my lord Prince."

Cefwyn went back to the wardrobe to revise his selection of clothing while Annas arranged an early cup of tea. Pages arrived, seeking use, and by their grace he bathed, merely an affair of a hot towel: the bath which he had left unused and cold still stood. Over his linen went bezainted leather, nothing approaching the two stones' weight of the shirt he had worn on the ride to Emwy. It was for lighter weapons, the kind that came from close at hand, and it glittered with suitably decorative but martial effect.

It did sit well, at least, between the Amefin and a Marhanen heart.

The breakfast arrived in the hands of Annas, two senior guards and two pages; the maps were discreetly rolled – except the one for Emwy district, which he deliberately left in plainest view – and he had had the pages move the dining board into the sunlit alcove beneath the windows.

Annas provided them a simple meal and a hot one, easy to eat a quick sufficiency and end the meeting early; or, if he pleased, to linger over the breads and jams. Cefwyn settled into place at the table and waited, sipping at a cup of tea.

Shortly Idrys arrived with Heryn in tow, a sullen and scowling Heryn, who stopped and bowed at formal distance from the table while Idrys continued to the warm window-side, where he took up his station, arms folded, waiting.

Cefwyn rose, bowed, and gestured to the seat at the far end of the table. "Welcome, Your Grace."

Heryn came to the offered seat, stood with his hands clenched on the back of the chair.

"Your Highness, –"

"Sit, sit down, Amefel. No doubt you have questions."

"With armed guards –"

"You could not protect me, Your Grace. That Amefin patrols were in the area of Emwy I do take your word for, but I do think they would have regarded our displayed standards and my banner. I fear you have been misinformed on the nature of the attack at Emwy, which casts into doubt not you, of course, but certain assumptions. Therefore I've moved to secure the premises until we learn whether there has been compromise of your informers. Surely your own life is not secure. Trust my guards. They are honest men."

The color had utterly fled Heryn's handsome face.

Cefwyn smiled, lips only, sure that Heryn took his double meaning. "Sit, sit down. I assure you that this apartment is at least as secure as your own."

Heryn sank into the chair, picked up the cup and carried it almost to his lips as Annas began to serve the breakfast. Heryn stopped in mid-sip with a look at him, guarded, terrified.

"Your health," Cefwyn said, still smiling, lifted his cup and drank.

The sweat stood visible on Heryn's face. And Cefwyn half-turned, looking at Idrys.

"Idrys."

"Your Highness."

"Any sign of the horses out of Emwy?"

"Aye, my lord, a few. The dun and three bays made their way back last night. Peasants brought them for reward, knowing the King's mark."

"You rewarded them."

"Amply, my lord."

"Excellent." He looked at Heryn and divided up a sausage. "It's clear that the general countryside still has reverence for the Crown."

"I would assure Your Highness so," Heryn said.

"Our patrols will be searching the country round about very thoroughly. We wish to find that bandit group and question them."

"I would have thought all your men were on duty here," Heryn said bitterly, while the sausage went down quite well. "So many in the halls."

"I assure you, it's to your own advantage that the Crown should take direct responsibility for my welfare. The cost to the town for losing the Marhanen heir would be bloody and extreme, and – regrettable as it might be, and no matter your efforts – there would be that certain cost to pay. His Majesty and I have quarreled, but the depth of our quarrel is vastly exaggerated. Vastly. Marhanens may quarrel with each other. Attack us – and he *is* head of our house."

"I assure Your Highness –"

"Oh, we do believe your efforts might well succeed. But I refuse to put that manner of responsibility on this province and on you, Amefel. The Guelen are seasoned men. They know the extent of their duty, and they'll stand their posts indefinitely, until we are sure the persons responsible have been hunted out and hanged. – Sausage, Your Grace?"

Annas made a trip to Heryn's end of the table, but Heryn took only bread.

"Your Highness," Heryn said, "surely your personal guard will be under hardship. I assure you my own men are sufficient for myself. You might at least relieve the ones at my door –"

"I will not hear of it. The welfare of this province is my special concern. My guards stay." He filled his mouth with bread and honey and ate, enjoying the breakfast. "Amefin honey. I shall send some to my father with personal recommendation."

"Thank you, my lord," Heryn murmured, although he seemed to have difficulty breathing, let alone eating.

"You must not take the issue so to heart. You have done your best to guard me. Now I shall do mine. – Do you not care for the bread, Lord Heryn?"

Heryn gathered up the knife and his knuckles were white on the handle as he dipped into the butter.

"I have," Idrys said, "set Anwyll to watching Tarien and Sergeant Gedd to Orien's door."

Cefwyn smiled grimly. Anwyll was immovable, and Gedd was by his preference immune to Orien and all her servants.

"I've made certain promises of liberal reward among the ranks, m'lord Prince," Idrys added, "once this period of double watch is safely carried. The men are in excellent spirits on that account."

"Promise it on my authority." Cefwyn gathered up his sword and buckled it on. "I will see that reward paid."

"Where are you going, m'lord Prince?"

"To see to our guest."

Idrys' frown was instant. Cefwyn started to the doors, and Idrys shadowed him past the guards and into the hall.

"Be rid of this ill-omened guest," Idrys said. "Send him to Emuin's retreat. Send him to the Quinalt in Guelessar, if you ask my advice in this matter, m'lord."

"Not in this."

"I wish you would wait for Emuin's arrival."

"You have mentioned that." He had glanced at Idrys as he walked out the door of his apartments. He looked back, and stopped in what he purposed to say next. There was but one pair of guards at Tristen's door. "What's going on here?" he demanded of those men. "Where are the other two?"

"Gone wi' him, Your Highness," said one man. "Wi' Uwen."

"He waked."

"Natural as morning, Your Highness, and ate breakfast and left."

"I left word to wake me!"

"You had a guest, Your Highness. We was told not to interrupt."

"Damn." He was aware of Idrys watching and forbore to scatter blame for what were doubtless contradictory instructions. "Where did he go?"

"To the stables, Your Highness. Something about his horse."

Cefwyn swore. "Stand your post," he ordered, and strode off for the stairway, with Idrys and an anxious pair of the Guelen guard close at his back.

CHAPTER 15

❧

Guards snapped to attention at the doors, and another pair at the stableyard gate: evidence of Idrys' efficient arrangements. And at that clash of weapons, old Haman came out in a scatter of stableboys – the man was at his post, to Cefwyn's mild surprise – but Haman had no frown nor seemed other than cheerful.

"Your Highness." Haman bowed. Amefin, Haman was a man of the land, not the Amefin court. His politics was the care of his animals and he cared for absolutely nothing else. A Prince could restrain his temper in respect to such a man. And in the replacement of Amefin guards from their posts, both Cook and stablemaster were left unquestioned.

"Haman. My guest, the young man. Where is he at the moment?"

"Come to see to his horse, Your Highness. And gone back inside again."

Cefwyn bit his lip, refused to turn immediately and acknowledge Idrys' self-sure stare, which he was certain awaited him. He drew a slow breath and looked instead toward the stable, where his own Danvy was putting out his head. He walked to that stall door, lingered to give his favorite a pat and an apple from the barrel.

"He's fit enough, Your Highness," Haman said. "Throwed a shoe in that affair, no more. Smith's already seen to him. I'm for putting him out to the far pens for a sennight, by 'r leave, Your Highness."

"Give him good care, master Haman. I've no questions. Pasture it is. And best you give both my horses good exercise. Work the fat off Kanwy. – Did my guest say nothing of his further business this morning?"

"No, Your Highness. Concerned for the horse, he was.

266

Wanted to see her before we sent her down to pasture. He walked to the paddocks back there, he brought her some grain with his own hands and he spoke wi' her a while, and then he and his man, they went back inside again. – He were fearful pale, Your Highness. I thought then of sending word. But his man and your guard was with him all the while, and I thought he was there on proper business."

"I'm certain he was. Thank you, master Haman." He turned to go, met Idrys' eyes by complete accident, and scowled. He brushed past Idrys, stalked across the yard and heard him and the guard following as he mounted the steps again into the lower hall.

"My lord Prince," Idrys said as they came into the corridor above, "leave it in my hands. I'll find him."

"*We* will find him." He cast Idrys a look over his shoulder and found precisely the expression he had thought to find.

"Warm this egg in your bosom, my lord Prince, and you may find it hatches something other than a sparrow. We've done quite well with the lord of the Amefin. I advise you confine this fledgling of Mauryl's. Confine him in whatever comfort you deem suitable, but confine him closely, at least until Emuin is at hand to deal with him. This man will surprise you with some action you will most assuredly regret."

He glanced away and strode ahead, seeking the windows that had best view of the garden, ignoring Idrys and his advice.

Tristen was not in the garden, either.

In the end he was compelled to stand and wait, chafing while Idrys consulted with a chance-met group of Amefin servants in the hall, who pointed down the hall toward the archive and bowed in frightened confusion, uncertain in what affairs they were involved on this chancy day, with Guelen guards posted everywhere and rumors by now running the halls.

"The library," Idrys reported, "m'lord Prince. The horse . . . and the archive."

Cefwyn exhaled shortly, relieved, as they walked toward the east wing, to think that it was nothing more sinister than books that drew Tristen . . . until he began to wonder with what insistence Tristen must have prevailed upon his guards and Uwen, and why, rising from a profound sleep, so unnatural a sleep, he had insisted after fatuous poesies, philosophies . . .

Books, in these particular hands, were not harmless . . . which was exactly what Idrys was thinking, he knew it. He could hear it hanging in the air in Idrys' very tones.

He could see, with the same clarity, Tristen's unlined and sleeping face yestereve – which Idrys had seen; and he could see that wild-eyed visage at Althalen, that same face with horror all the way to the depths of those uncommon eyes when he overtook him on the road. Idrys had also seen it.

He did not forget it, nor ever would. And now, lo, the unnatural sleep, leading straightway to, the guards had said, a natural waking and the visit to the paddock, which was perfectly of a piece with the gentle moonstruck youth he'd taken under Emuin's less than explicit instructions and led out into conspiracy and eldritch ruin.

Now books. Archives? Gods *knew* what the Amefin archive might hold in its dusty stacks and pigeonholes.

He quickened his step, came through the door into the musty precincts of the archive, where books and chaotic piles of civil records shared a room that had not, by reports, known order in ages, a room where tax records had been most effectively misplaced, and where, pursuant to last night's orders, his own accountant still commanded a battalion of pages rummaging the west wall of the archive.

"Your Highness," Tamurin said, mistaking his mission and the object of his inquiry. "I am immediately requesting the records necessary – immediately, m'lord Prince."

"And in good haste, master Tamurin. I approve all you need do."

Master Tamurin passed from his acute attention. In the dim light that came through a cloudy window some distance down the east wall, at a reading table almost overwhelmed with stacks of parchments and codices and towers of decaying paper ... there, run to earth, sat Tristen, with a massive codex open on the overloaded table, with Uwen and the two guards leaning against chairs on either side of him, peering at the work as if they could possibly read much more than their pay vouchers, and waiting as if at any moment Tristen might pronounce some extraordinary wisdom.

"Out," Cefwyn bade them, and included Uwen with that princely sweep of his arm.

Tristen lifted his head, his face lost in shadow, his hair a darkness in the dusty sunlight. It was – a chill touched Cefwyn's skin – a stranger's face, with the light touching only the planes and not the hollows: it was a man's face, a forbidding face.

The guards, conspirators in Tristen's wanderings, perhaps at last recalling that they were to have reported a change in Tristen's condition, eased past, trying to slip unobtrusively out of the way. The guards he had brought with him held their position, but somewhat to the rear. Only Idrys pressed close enough to involve himself in the situation, and Cefwyn considered banishing him as well. But on principle and to have another opinion of the encounter, he decided otherwise.

"Lord Prince." Tristen rose and started to close the massive codex. Cefwyn took two steps forward and thrust his hand into the descending leaves as Tristen stood stock still. Cefwyn dragged the book across the table, reopened the heavy pages and turned the book on the table, dislodging clutter, to look on the crabbed Amefin script, the crude illuminations, the miniature map of the Ylesuin that had once been, when it had been a mere tributary to the wizard-ruled west, the wide realm of the Sihhë kings.

He half-closed the book, then opened to the first page and the title: *The Annals of the Reign of Selwyn Marhanen.*

"Ah. Grandfather," Cefwyn murmured wryly with a look at Tristen's shadowed face. Still standing, he turned back to the pages that Tristen had been reading and angled the page to the light of the dust-clouded windows. "*Althalen,*" he read aloud, and Tristen's face had a strange, now fearful expression, still shaped in shadows.

Cefwyn set his foot in the seat of the chair, dragged the great codex up on his knee and inclined the whole face of the page to the light of the same dusty window. *"The account of the taking of Althalen by the Marhanens."*

He looked up to see Tristen, whether that face was contrite, puzzled, angry, or any other readable expression. Window light made it still a white, forbidding mask. He took a loose parchment from the table and laid it on that open page for a marker, closed the codex and gave the massive volume into Idrys' keeping, dust and all.

He looked at Tristen to see what Tristen thought of that – which seemed no more than Tristen thought of his intervention here at all. The frightened Amefin chief archivist stood in the shadow of the stacks by the other archway.

"How did he find this book?" Cefwyn asked, fixing that man with his stare. "Did he ask? Did you suggest it him?"

"He – asked for a history of Althalen, Your Highness."

Cefwyn cast a look about the other volumes stacked high on the tables all around him: census files, tax records, deeds of sale, meager books of poetics, science, and philosophy. And history. Oh, indeed, Amefel had history.

He looked toward Idrys' black shape and frowning countenance. "There are witnesses," Idrys cautioned him, meaning that his questions were already too full of particulars and betrayed too much.

"Tristen," Cefwyn said mildly, "walk with me."

"Yes, m'lord," Tristen said meekly. He looked into light as he bowed and the gray eyes seemed as naked as ever they had been. Fear was there. Cefwyn thought so, at least. Bewilderment. All the things that might placate an angry prince.

Tristen turned, started to pass Idrys on his way to the door, but Idrys, unbidden, set down the book, laid a hand on Tristen's arm, and roughly searched him for weapons. Tristen endured it, stone-still, in midstep.

It was carrying matters too far, unordered: a protest leapt

to Cefwyn's lips, in Tristen's defense, this time; but on a morning like this, in a hostile hall, a prince was a fool who blunted his guards' attention to his protection. When it was done, Tristen continued down the aisle of the library, seeming only mildly disturbed by an indignity that would have racketed to the King's ear had Idrys inflicted it on Heryn or Heryn's familiars. He walked behind with Idrys while Tristen walked ahead in a downcast privacy and careless dignity that, had Idrys stripped him naked, he did not think Idrys could have breached. It was no astonished, defenseless youth such as Emuin had brought him that night in the lesser hall. This morning the jaw was set. The broad shoulders, in velvet and silk, declared a restraint of self, emanating not from fear but from fearlessness, and he did not think Idrys failed to be aware of whether a man feared or disregarded an outrageous interference in his affairs.

Tristen walked down the aisle of cluttered tables, past the business of account-gathering and agitated archivists, and the guards joined them at the door, escorting them down the corridor and up the stairs.

Anger blinded him, Cefwyn saw that in himself now, anger he had not let break. Anger had gathered in his chest and dammed up his reason; and now came a strange sense of grief, of betrayal, if he could lay a word on it: loss – of some rare and precious treasure that he had briefly seen, desperately longed for in this man.

Mauryl's gift, he reminded himself, in a morning fraught with dealings with traitors, in a morning after breakfast with Heryn Aswydd. It was Mauryl's Shaping of present flesh and something other; and, given he had adequate wit to rule a province, he should have seen hazard in Tristen's fecklessness toward all and sundry threats; he should have seen it did not come of helplessness, but of Mauryl's work. He should have armored himself and steeled his heart.

And had not, had not. Had not.

* * *

Upstairs, safe behind the doors of his apartment, he looked again into that too-clear gaze and met the absolute challenge to trust that Tristen posed.

"Out," he said to the guards, but Idrys did not budge. "Out, Idrys."

"In this alone I am your father's man, my lord Prince. I *will* stay."

Tristen stood alone by the table. The book lay beside him. Cefwyn sat down by it, laid his arm on the leather, fingered the edges of it.

"Why," he asked, looking up at Tristen, "*why* did Mauryl send you to me?"

"He did not send me to you, sir, not in anything he told me."

"One forgets. The road brought you."

"The road did, yes, m'lord."

"Did you sleep well last night?"

"I slept, yes, m'lord."

"Rather long, as happened."

"Uwen says I did, sir." There was the least edge of distress, now. "I had no knowledge of it."

"What happened in Althalen? What did you see? Ghosts?"

"No, m'lord." Wariness crept in. "Nothing happened."

"You rode with the devil on your heels. You rode such a course as I've scarcely seen and none including myself could overtake. And you never having ridden. How did you manage?"

"I don't know, sir."

"Wizardry?"

"No, sir." The voice was faint. Respectful. Convincing, if less in the province were amiss. "I was afraid."

Tristen had a faculty for adding the unexpected, the ridiculous, that tempted a man even in the heat of temper to burst out in laughter.

"Afraid."

"There was something very bad there, m'lord Prince."

"Something bad," he echoed. A child's word. A child's look in eyes gray as a boundless sea. He refused to be turned from anger this time. "So you broke from the company, you risked lives, you deserted me, you deserted the men guarding you, and rushed onto the road into the hands of you knew not whom, because something bad frightened you."

"Yes, sir."

"'*Yes*, sir.' Say something more than 'yes, sir,' 'yes, m'lord,' 'beg your grace, m'lord Prince.' These are serious matters, Tristen, and I refuse to be set aside with 'yes, m'lord.' If I ask you, I want a full and considered answer in this matter. What frightened you? Something bad? Good living *gods*, man, credit me for good will, and tell me what you saw."

A breath. A settling. "I don't know, sir. I don't remember all that I saw or all that I did, or where I was. I thought I was doing what I ought. But I thought you and the soldiers were behind me. I thought you were there."

"Damn you! you knew. You knew where we were!"

"No, sir. I did not."

"Men *die* for such mistakes, Tristen."

"Yes, sir," the answer came faintly.

"You damned near killed your horse, damned near killed *me*, and half the men with us. If it wasn't wizardry that carried you safe over those jumps, I should assess that mare's foals for wings. – And, damn you, don't look at me like a simpleton! You say you're not simple. You claim Mauryl for your teacher. You say there's nothing unnatural about your riding, your appearance, or your coming here. You say there was nothing unnatural in your sleep nor in your waking. What do you think me? A fool?"

"No, sir."

Fainter still. More contrite. Cefwyn averted his eyes from that look that compelled belief. He opened the huge book and turned to the place the loose parchment marked.

"What did you seek in this book?" he asked Tristen without looking up. "What do you seek in the one Mauryl gave you? – Who *were* you before Mauryl set hand to you?"

There was no answer. He looked up and saw Tristen's face had turned quite, quite pale.

"I don't know, sir."

"What did he send you to do?"

"I don't know, sir."

"I want more answer than that. I want your honest, considerate opinion."

"I know, sir. But I don't – I don't understand – what I was to do. I don't even understand – what I am. I think – I think –"

Finish it, Cefwyn thought, his own heart beating in terror, because Tristen had gone beyond what he asked, went beyond, in his wondering, what he would ever want to know of wizard-work – because there *were* answers, and there was, he suddenly realized it in the context of Tristen's vacillations between feckless acceptance and that severe, terrible self-confrontation, – there was somewhere a truth. He was Emuin's student as Tristen was Mauryl's. He had learned no wizardry but he had learned its peculiar logic. There was a reason Tristen had not read Mauryl's strange book. There was a reason Tristen had gotten onto the red mare uncertain of the reins and hours later terrified him in a hellbent rush he could not match with a better horse.

"I think," Tristen said in a thin, small voice. "I think other men are different than I am."

It was another of Tristen's turn-about conclusions, the sort that could tempt a man to laughter. But this one stuck in a prince's throat. This one echoed off walls of his own circumscribed world, and he thought to himself, too, – he, the Prince of Ylesuin – Other men are different than I am; while the look in Tristen's eyes mirrored his own inward fear. That, he saw facing him and, much, much worse, the look of a man who could say that honestly, the look of a man who had gone to that archive and asked for that book.

Alone. Mortally alone. He understood such fear. He had to fear Tristen's declaration for what it was, but he respected above all else the courage it took to face that surmise and seek an answer, with all it might mean.

"Tristen, certain folk say it was bandits who attacked against my banner. Certain folk say it was otherwise, a mistake, only

274

the movement of Amefin patrols and lost shepherds. What do you think?"

"There *was* harm meant."

"I agree. I've set guards to protect certain people, and you will aid me best, understand, if you do not go wandering about the halls against the advice of your guards."

"Yes, sir. I'm sorry."

"Are you *well*, Tristen?"

"Yes, sir."

"You said you could not recognize a lie. Now I ask you to discover the truth, truth, as you would speak to Mauryl. Say it to me or never again ask me to trust you. What did you see that frightened you?"

"Smoke. Fear. Fire. I wanted us to come *through,* sir. I wanted *you* to come through, and I thought you were behind me, I did truly think so." There was a moment's silence. "I believe I thought so."

"You thought you were leading me to safety. – Or, if you were only running, Tristen, I forgive it. Only say so."

"No, sir. I thought that I was going toward safety – I believed that you were behind me, and that if I turned back . . . if I turned back . . . I don't know, sir. That's all I remember."

"Conveniently so," Idrys said, forgotten in his habitual stillness. Cefwyn flinched, the spell broken.

"But you did follow me, sir," Tristen said.

"And you fell straightway into a sleep no man could break," Idrys said coldly. "Is this wizardry? Or what is it?"

"I –" Tristen shook his head, and there was – there was – Cefwyn would swear he detected guilt, or subterfuge in that look; and if this was guilt, the other things were either lies or hedgings of the truth.

"Did you dream?" he asked, and Tristen looked at him like a trapped deer.

"No, sir."

"What did you do? The *truth,* Tristen. As you told me before. Trust me now or never trust me. You have no choice."

275

"There were names. There were too many names. I grew tired. I slept. I sleep when there are too many names."

"Names of what?"

"Althalen. Emwy. Other names. I might know them if you said them, m'lord. I can think. I can try to think of them."

"Did this dusty book tell you anything?"

"Not yet, sir."

"You didn't read it."

"I hadn't time, sir."

Cefwyn leaned back and bit his lip, flicked a glance to Idrys.

"Be rid of him," Idrys said. "At least confine him until Emuin returns. Neither you nor I can deal with something Mauryl Gestaurien had his hand in. This Shaping is no hedge-magician's amusement. Be rid of it."

"Damn you, Idrys!" He saw Tristen's face gone ashen. "Tristen."

"Sir?"

"Would you do me harm?"

"No, sir, in no way would I."

"Go back to your rooms across the hall. Do not leave them on any account. I'll have your belongings delivered to you."

"Yes, m'lord Prince."

"This evening . . . " Cefwyn said, impelled to soften his order, which was arrest and confinement. And he had not intended to agree with Idrys' cursed advice, nor at all to appear to – but it seemed the only safety for Tristen and for the Crown and the peace. "This evening I shall expect you at dinner, if you will accord me the pleasure."

"Sir." Tristen rose from his chair, seeming reassured. Idrys saw him to the door with complete if cold courtesy.

Then Idrys came back to stand in front of the table, arms folded, impossible to ignore.

"Do not give him that book, m'lord Prince. Don't send it to him."

"You are a useful man to me, Idrys, but do nothing to harm him. *Nothing.* – And *whose* man are you?"

"Where it regards your safety, . . . yours, of course. – What says that book, my lord Prince?"

"Blast you, – must *none* come near me but you?"

There was a moment's silence. Idrys drew a long and quiet breath while Cefwyn tried to catch his.

"You suffer strange attractions, my lord Prince, mindfully stubborn attractions toward those things which are most likely to harm you."

"You suspect everything and everyone that comes close to me! You and Emuin –"

"Orien and Tarien, my lord?"

"Damn you!" He looked aside, feeling a burning in his eyes he cared not to show to Idrys.

"My lord Prince," Idrys said, coming to lean too familiarly against his chair back, "the last of the Sihhë kings died at Althalen at the hand of your grandfather. That is what he will read in that book."

Cefwyn swept the parchment aside from the place it marked, and smoothed the heavy page. The letters swam before his eyes, a script that cast back to the Galasite foundations of *all* writings, a history once safely remote from his present-day concerns.

"The Marhanen," said Idrys, "were not kings then; they were trusted chamberlains to the long line of Sihhë halflings in Althalen. As your grandfather was to Elfwyn. Perhaps our innocent lad would like you to resume that post to him."

"Push me no further, Idrys. I warn you."

"I warn *you*, m'lord Prince. Not so long ago, not so long ago that cursed place sank in ashes: men are still living who remember. Emuin for one. *He* was at Althalen. Ask him. *Mauryl* was certainly there to open the gates to your grandfather and make him King; and for that pretty treachery, your grandfather appointed Mauryl only the ruins of Ynefel and banned his arms from civilized precincts. A fine jest, was it not? And for all these years the woods have grown over Althalen and cloaked all the bloody Marhanen sins."

Cefwyn looked up sharply. "Speak so freely to my father, Idrys."

"Murder has been done for far lesser things than thrones. Most dangerous when the possessors of thrones forget how they came by them. Your father, like your grandfather, decreed death for bearing the Sihhë arms or practicing the old arts."

"Yet employed Emuin!"

"What says the book, my lord Prince?"

"Blast your impudence!"

"It serves you. *What says the book, my lord?*"

Cefwyn covered the page with his outspread palm, stayed a moment until the swimming letters became clear again and his breathing steadied.

"I have need of Emuin."

"Now, *now,* you are sensible, my lord Prince."

He whirled on Idrys, making the chair turn. "But likewise you shall wait for his advice, hear me, Idrys. You will lay no hand on Tristen!"

"My lord Prince." Idrys stood back, implacable. "For your own safety –"

"For *yours,* do not exceed my orders."

"Do you know, my lord, *why* Emuin made such haste to escape Henas'amef? Do you know *why* he retreated out of Amefel before this Shaping of Mauryl's asked him too close questions?"

"You make far too sinister a design. He has gone to retreat to consider."

"To consider what, my prince? Your messages?"

"He will come back, damn you, when he has thought this matter through . . . "

"My lord, *I* have thought on this. I have thought long and hard on this: if Mauryl could summon something out of the last hour of Althalen, think you that of the two thousand men who died there, it would have been some humble spitboy out of the kitchens? This Shaping is deadly. Mauryl was no true friend to the Marhanens, nor to the Elwynim, either. He served the Sihhë until he turned on them, out of some quarrel with his fellow wizards. He killed his own king. He locked himself ever after in Ynefel, brooding on gods only know what resentments or what purposes; and dying, sends you *this,* this Shaping with lordly graces? Ask his *name,* m'lord. I urge you ask his name."

"He does not know his name."

"One can guess."

Cefwyn pressed his lips together, the sweat started on his brow. He wiped at it. "You suppose. You suppose, Idrys."

"A Sihhë, my lord. What worse could he send you?"

He had no answer for that.

"No stableboy," Idrys said. "No scullion."

"Then why for a halfling king? Why not the first five Sihhë lords – those of full blood?"

"Why not, indeed, my lord Prince? A good question."

Cefwyn left the chair in temper and went to look out the window at something less troubling. At pigeons walking on the sill.

"They still burn straw men in this district," Idrys said. "You see the old symbols on boundary stones, to the priests' abhorrence."

"I have seen them. I have had your reports, master crow. I do listen."

"Read the chronicle, m'lord Prince. The Sihhë were gentle lords. Some of the latest, at least. Barrakkêth's blood ran thin at the last. They ate no children. They went to straw men and not captives for their observances . . ."

"They never ate children. That's a Quinalt story."

"But were they always straw men, at festival?"

"None of us know. Histories may lie. My grandfather was not immune to the malady, you know."

"Elfwyn, was, they say, a very gentle sort. Dead at Althalen – as were they all. Last Sihhë king. – Last of the witch-lords."

"Then no hazard to us. A gentle man. You say so."

"One doubts he even blamed Mauryl for his death. And perhaps he was the only one of that line Mauryl would regret."

"If he were Elfwyn, if he *were* Elfwyn –"

"It was Elfwyn's younger brother Mauryl wanted dead. So did Emuin, and all that circle. So I'm told. They insisted the youngest Sihhë prince was a black wizard, whatever that means, if not a sorcerer. And of course Mauryl and his circle had no wizardly ambitions, themselves, whatever makes wizards ambitious. But the child prince died in the fall of Althalen, and so did Elfwyn and all the Sihhë who could claim the name, since the wizards could come by Marhanen help *and* arms no less bloodily. Marhanen ambition was satisfied with the crown. The Elwynim councillors drew off to shape a Regency until the Sihhë should rise from their smoky grave, I suppose, and sit on the throne of Elwynor. I wonder what satisfied Mauryl. A tower in the woods?"

"Who knows what Mauryl wished or wanted?" Cefwyn retorted. "One supposes he got it, since he left us in peace."

"But, if one believes the Elwynim, –"

"One has no reason to believe the Elwynim."

"Even for bride-offers?"

"Have I accepted it?"

"Yet the Elwynim claim the Sihhë kings *will* return. Who do you suppose promised them that?"

"The Elwynim chose to believe it. It gave legitimacy to the lord of Ilefínian, who otherwise had no royal blood, no more than any other Elwynim lord. The lord of Ilefínian chose to call himself Regent because there was nothing else he could call himself – certainly not king – not even aetheling."

"As of course the Marhanen were royal to the bone."

"Treason, master crow."

"Treason for the commons. Loyalty – in an adviser to the Crown. Look at the *reasons,* m'lord Prince. Mauryl raised up this Shaping. Perhaps the old man was atoning for his crime, bringing *back* the King he helped to murder – an excess of your grandfather's zealotry, or his ambition. Perhaps Mauryl *did* promise the lord of Ilefínian a King to Come."

"You must have spent hours on this. You've kept yourself awake with these fancies, master crow. I suggest a roll in the sheets. 'T will help you sleep."

"A prince with two thoughts to his own safety in this rebel province would help me sleep, m'lord. A toadstool tea for this Summoning you take to your bosom would help me rest at night, but you will not take that advice."

"Have you read this book?"

"I know the history of all claimants and lineages alive, m'lord Prince, who might come into serious question. Now I see I must study the dead ones."

"And if Mauryl *has* raised Elfwyn of the Sihhë? What can you say of him, beyond a short reign distinguished only by his calamity?"

"A weak king, who wasted his treasury on shrines and supported scholars and priests of any persuasion at all. He lost three towns to the Chomaggari in his first year of reign and still kept his scholars fat and his army nigh barefoot. If it were not for Mauryl Gestaurien he would have fallen sooner. But then, if it were not for Mauryl Gestaurien, he might not have fallen at all, and the Marhanen would still *be* lords chamberlain to the Sihhë. Rebellion wanted an able general. Which your grandfather was. Unfortunately for the Sihhë king – your grandfather was *his* general."

"As you hope to become mine?" Cefwyn asked, and had the satisfaction of seeing Idrys blink. "On the tide of a war on this border?"

Idrys' chin lifted. "I trust I serve a wiser lord. The latter-day Sihhë put all their trust in Mauryl, and thereby, my trusting prince, the gates flew open to the Sihhë successors and the Sihhë died a terrible death along with their king, next Althalen's burning walls. – You invite – whom? – to your table, my lord Prince?"

"A well-spoken and civil young man, whose converse is pleasant, whose company I find far less self-serving than, for instance, Heryn's, whose presence you have generally approved."

"Your grandfather tossed Sihhë babes into the flames," Idrys said, "hanged the women and impaled the men above the age of twelve in a great ring about Althalen's walls. And

281

even from the grave, would the Sihhë bear you love, Cefwyn Marhanen? He does not remember these things. He could not remember these things with that clear, innocent look he bears you. Think of *this* when you trust too much. That account is, I will wager you, in that book, m'lord Prince. That is the chronicle your guest has been reading, and I will wager you he *is* Sihhë, with *all* it means."

"Then what do we do? What do we do, hang his head at the gate? I am not my grandfather! I do not murder children! I have no wish to murder children! Elfwyn in life was a gentle man. He haunted my grandfather to his dying day. My grandfather on his deathbed swore he heard the children crying. I do not want a death like that. I do not want dreams such as he had or a conscience such as he had. He never slept without holy candles burning in his room."

"He had a peaceful reign. His enemies feared him. Consequently his taxes were lighter than Elfwyn's or your father's. Ylesuin remembers his reign as golden years."

"Golden on Sihhë gold – consequently his taxes were lighter."

"And his enemies were all dead or in terror of him."

"I will not be such a King."

"M'lord Prince, – what became of the ivory miniature?"

Another of Idrys' flank attacks. Thwarted on one front, Idrys opened another. And the devil where he was going with it.

"A lovely thing," Idrys said. "Is it in the chest yonder? Do you still keep it? Or have you sent it to your father for his word on this – Elwynim bride-offer?"

"My father, as you well know, would fling it in the midden."

"Ah. And therefore you keep it? You temporize with this offer?"

"I do not see what this has to do with my grandfather *or* my guest."

"A marriageable daughter, a sonless Elwynim king – ah – regent. Uleman of the Elwynim sees the ravens gathering – knows he cannot command his own lords, who are more apt to war with each other over fair Ninévrisë's hand – so, oh, aye, offer you the daughter, offer the bloody Marhanen the last Sihhë realm with no more than a wedding and an heir-getting. Whatever has prevented you from leaping to that offer, m'lord Prince?"

"Nine skulls on my gate is not enough?"

"And, of course, you are the heir of Ylesuin. And wish no witchly get out of a marriage bed."

"It did somewhat cross my mind."

"And would cross your father's. And your brother Efanor's. No witchly offspring to sit the Dragon throne. Yet you still keep the ivory."

"A lovely piece of work. A pretty face. Why not?"

"Still temporizing with the matter. Asking yourself how more cheaply to gain a claim to Elwynor."

"I do not!"

"You doubt that Uleman countenanced the assassins. You said so yourself. Internal dissent. Angry lords, jealous fellow suitors for the lady's hand . . . "

"I am no suitor, for her least of all! And what has this to do with Tristen, pray, master crow? What edifice of fantasies are we now building? Or have you quite forgot the track?"

"'Tristen,' is he now, and not 'Mauryl's gift'?"

"Insolent crow. Crow flitting about the limits of my tolerance. What has this business of assassins and Elwynim to do with him?"

"Ah. Mauryl's motives. That's our worry."

"What? A stray piece of work from Mauryl's tower? Mauryl's dying maunderings? – Mauryl's rescue of a Sihhë soul from wherever Sihhë go when they die? Emuin said treat him gently. I take that for the best advice, and until you have more substantial complaint –"

"Mauryl's motives. And Uleman King –"

"Not King. As you well know. Find your point."

"Oh, you have taken it, m'lord Prince. Elwynor has no kings. Only Regents, a Regent in waiting for a King, like his father before him, and his grandfather. Waiting for what? A

283

King your grandfather murdered. I ask what dealings Uleman had with Mauryl before Mauryl died, or what the promise was that's kept Elwynor under a Regent for all these years. Not so foolish and stubborn as we thought, if they were waiting for something Mauryl promised them – and now has delivered."

"Then why send a Sihhë revenant to *me*, crow? Your logic escapes me."

"Mistakes are possible. Mauryl dead – perhaps the Shaping went down the wrong road. Or perhaps he did not. Who knows but Mauryl? And perhaps Uleman."

"Then Uleman's logic escapes me. Why this proposal to *me*?"

"Why, because Mauryl had not yet fulfilled his promise. Or if he had, Uleman had no idea of it. He sees his kingdom foundering for want of an heir – and, my lord Prince, if he had such, he needs no marriage with his longstanding enemy. I'm certain he desires no Marhanen in his daughter's bed. But Uleman is an honest and doting man, as I hear, fond of his wife, fond of his daughter, with his lords chafing at the bit, wanting more than a Regency for some King to Come. Each of his earls seeing, as mortality comes on the third and sonless Regent, that marriage with this – we dare not call her princess, only the Regent's daughter – would legitimize any of them as an Elwynim King. *This* is what they see. And – if one believes in wizardly foresight – dare we believe that the third generation is the charm, that old Mauryl laid a sonlessness on the Elwynim Regent so that it *would* come down to this, just at the time Mauryl should produce a claimant and fulfill his magical promise."

"Gods, I should have you my *architect*, not the Lord Commander of my guard. Such a structure of conjecture and hypothesis! Shall we put towers on 't?"

"And shall we not think that this Shaping of Mauryl's *is* a rival for your father's power? That *he* is the bridegroom for this bride? That Uleman will know this, the moment he knows this Shaping exists? Send now to Uleman accepting his

284

offer and see whether he sends the bride. I think he would see her wed a dead Sihhë king rather than a live Marhanen."

Cefwyn drew deliberately slow breaths and leaned his chin on his hand, elbow on the arm of the chair, listening, simply listening, and thinking that, whatever else, Mauryl's childlike Shaping had least of all the knowledge what to do with a bride, Elwynim or otherwise.

But – but – Tristen had had no knowledge of horses, either, until he climbed into red Gery's saddle. Tristen rode – a prince could be magnanimous toward such skill – far better than he did, on far less horse. That stung, more, actually, than any prospective rivalry for the Elwynim Regent's daughter, who was, as an ivory portrait, a matter of mere theoretical and aesthetic interest –

But interest enough to risk a taint of Sihhë blood in the Marhanen line – no. The Quinalt would not accept it. The Quinalt would rise up against the Crown.

"It may be true," Idrys said, "that Mauryl robbed this Shaping of his wits. But Mauryl gave him a book which I concede may *not* be Mauryl's household accounts. This Shaping is, however you reckon his worth, not the feckless boy that came here."

"Oh, come, would you set Tristen to guard the larder from the kitchen boys? Far less set him to govern a kingdom! And now you fear wizardly curses and prophecies? You were never so credulous as that before."

"My lord Prince," Idrys said broadly, "I did not believe in such things. I did not believe that the Mauryl Gestaurien who betrayed Elfwyn was that Mauryl who betrayed Galasien after very similar fashion. Now I do take it so."

"On what evidence?"

"Good gods, m'lord, we talk and sit at table with a Shaping, in broad daylight and by dark. What is more probable? That Mauryl is the same Mauryl – or that you have invited a dead man to your table tonight?"

"It is a question," he conceded.

"And if Mauryl has robbed him of his wits, still this

Tristen is not the young man that came here. That compliant boy is gone, my lord Prince. Look at him carefully tonight. You were far safer dining with Heryn at Heryn's table. At least you never believed Heryn to the exclusion of your own advisers. If I were a credulous man – and I am fast becoming a believer in more than ever I did – I would say you were bewitched."

"I *and* the Elwynim Regent. – So what profits us to wriggle? We are foredoomed, we cannot stray from our wizard-set actions. I do not believe that, Idrys! And I have seen a portrait of Elfwyn, likewise in ivory – my father had it from Grandfather and keeps it in a chest with other curiosities of Althalen's unspendable treasures. I see nothing *like* our guest in that face, as I recall it. So what *is* a Shaping? If the Summoned soul's the same, then why not the flesh that clothes it?"

"Because the flesh is gone to *worms,* my lord, and whether a Shaping need resemble the dead it clothes I leave to wizards. But should the soul not have something to do with Shaping the flesh about it, all the same? I should much doubt he was a Sihhë *princess.* A king, well he could be. The King the Elwynim believe will come again. Go, go, accept the Elwynim marriage. I'll warrant no bride comes across the river."

"Then why should Mauryl not send him to the Elwynim? And how could a wizard who could raise the sleeping dead so broadly miss his target?"

"Perhaps he didn't miss."

"How not?"

"To wreak most havoc, my lord Prince. I'll warrant worse than happened at Emwy comes by spring, and I'll warrant bridges are building at least by spring thaw, if not by now, else I would have counseled you more emphatically than I do not to call the border lords in. Let your father the King take this move of yours for foresight – and so it is. But foresight against only one of your enemies, m'lord Prince. The worst one of all you lodge next your own bedchamber. The King who should come again, my lord. Well that you've called Emuin."

"Emuin was Mauryl's student." He wished not to listen to Idrys' fancies. But once the thoughts were sailing through his mind, they spread more canvas. "And dare I trust Emuin, if this was all along the design? Whom shall I trust, master crow? You, the arbiter of all my affections?"

"Few," Idrys said. "Trust *few,* m'lord Prince. And only such as you can watch. You say very true: Emuin *was* Mauryl's student."

"Leave me. I've thoughts to think without your voice in my ear."

Idrys rose, bowed, walked toward the door. Anger was in Cefwyn's mind. Petty revenge sprang to his lips . . . harsh belittlement of Idrys' fears. But Idrys had never deserved it.

He let Idrys go in silence to the anteroom that was his home, his narrow space between the doors. Sword by his side, Idrys slept, every night ready to defend his own life and the heir's should the outside guards fail or fall in their duty. Little wonder Idrys' every thought was deception and doubt.

He had sent for Emuin and had now to wait, first for the message to reach his old tutor, and then for Emuin to gather his aged bones onto a horse and ride back. He was not certain now whether he wholly welcomed Emuin's intrusion into the matter. He needed time for all that Idrys had told him to sink into bone and nerve. He needed time to know in his own heart what he had taken under his roof, or what manner of situation he had made for himself.

Win his love, Emuin had said. Win his love.

Gods, how much had Emuin known, or guessed, or foreseen about Mauryl's work? He had questions to ask. He had very many of them.

And it was still, all things considered, a good thing to have sent to Emuin. But more than trusting Emuin to solve matters – he had to solve them in some way that preserved the peace on the border, if in fact Mauryl had aimed at overthrowing the present order.

Wizards and spells. Like Uwen, he had been disposed to believe the accounts of magic as exaggerated, the wizard arts as no more than he was already accustomed to see in Emuin's warnings and in the likes of the woman at Emwy – a great deal of show, taking advantage of a fortuitous gust, claiming credit for natural events and natural misfortunes.

But if one did take Tristen for exactly what Emuin claimed him to be – and certainly Tristen's continually changing skill argued for something unnatural, as Tristen's manner argued for his personal honesty – then all disbelief was foolish, and a prudent prince should take careful consideration, Idrys was very right, even of folk tales and superstitions which might forewarn him what else Mauryl might have done, and *how* Mauryl might do it: whether spells worked at long or short range, and whether they could grow in strength even after the wizard was dead. He knew the wizard of Ynefel could do far more than cure cattle or luck-bless a pregnant sow. The village of Capayneth had certainly enjoyed far more than luck in Mauryl's favor.

One dared only so far ignore the possibilities of what Mauryl might have done less beneficently. One dared only so far treat a wizard-gift as what it seemed, and all Mauryl's purposes as friendly and generous.

Win his love, indeed, win his love. What Emuin had said was not the pious Teranthine sentiment it had sounded. It was a wizard's direct advice.

CHAPTER 16

❧

Fawn-colored velvet stitched with silver thread, blue hose, a silver chain and a pair of soft brown boots: for tonight, the servants had said, when they laid out the clothing. Tristen was amazed.

Cefwyn had sent it, and the servants, with other clothes and other gifts, including finer clothing for Uwen, all for the expected dinner summons.

"Surely fine feathers for the like of me," Uwen said with a shake of his head. Uwen had shaved, and a servant had trimmed his silver hair. "Such as," Uwen said, rubbing the bald spot, "such as there is, m'lord." Uwen's hair shone pale and silver with the preparations the servants had brought, and they smelled, both, of perfumed oils and bathwater.

It pleased him that Uwen was pleased. He loved the touch and feel of the fine cloth and the softness of the new boots, and he was only a little anxious as they crossed the hall, assured by the servants that it was the proper hour for supper with the Prince, and that the table was waiting for them.

The guards let them in without delay, and they walked into a room fragrant with delicious smells, scented candles, the table set with candlelit gold – a Harper sat in the corner, and began a quiet Music. The Words came to Tristen with the first sounds – and the sounds transfixed him, went through his ears, through his heart, through his bones, so that he stopped still, and stared, and did not move until Idrys came beside him and brushed his arm, directing him to the table.

It was so beautiful. It was so unexpected a thing.

He bowed to Cefwyn before his wits thought to do it – he recovered himself, saw that Cefwyn's habitual russet velvet had given way to red with gold embroidering. Even Idrys' sober black now was velvet picked out with silver. The music washed at his senses, the smells, the glitter of light on gold and beautiful colored glass – hearing, smelling, seeing, remembering to be polite – all flooded in on him.

"Sit," Cefwyn bade him, taking a chair at one end, while the harper kept playing softly, sound that ran like water, caressed like the harper's fingers on the strings.

He sat. Cefwyn bade Uwen and Idrys to table. Annas was there, and servants young and old, who poured them wine and served them food in little dishes made of silver and gold.

Between such servings the harper sang for them, sang in Words, a Song of a shepherd with his sheep, a Song of dawn and evening, a Song of traveling on the river, and of a man far from his home. He was entranced. And after that, Cefwyn talked of horses and how Gery fared, and how he had two horses, Danvy and Kanwy, and how he had Kanwy's brother Dys up at another pasture, and they should ride up there someday and see.

It was so much coming at one time, so much to listen to, so much to imagine that he found it hard to eat – taste was another flood into his senses, sweet and bitter, hot and cold: there were so, so many things to listen to and to look at, from the glass on the table to the several colors of the wine, and the sound of the harp, and a rapid conversation in which he only knew how to say, Yes, m'lord Prince; or, No, m'lord Prince – foolish, helpless answers to what he was sure were Cefwyn's efforts to draw more conversation than that from him.

But even Idrys was soft-spoken, even Idrys smiled and laughed and, uneasy as Uwen had looked at the outset, Uwen became willing to laugh, even to speak from time to time. The harper played more songs, these without words, cheerful and bright, and Cefwyn told Annas take the dishes, and bade Idrys and Uwen sit still at table – "Stay," Cefwyn said. "Tristen and I have matters to discuss. Annas, whatever they might wish. Two soldiers can pass time over a wine pitcher. – Tristen, come over here and share a cup with me."

"Yes, sir," he said, and, following Cefwyn to a group of chairs remote from the table, sat where Cefwyn bade him sit.

Annas came and offered him a cup of wine, different than that he had left at table – but he only sipped it, and poised it in both hands so more wine could not come into it without his noticing: he had learned to be wary of Cefwyn's generosity.

"So," Cefwyn said, crossing one ankle over another, in possession of his own cup, which he held in similar fashion, "how *does* Gery fare?"

"She cut her leg," Tristen said. "Master Haman says it's slight. But I shouldn't have ridden her so hard. I'm very sorry, sir. I'm sorry she was hurt."

"I'm glad you didn't break your neck."

"Yes, sir." It sounded like one of Mauryl's sort of utterances, with rebuke directly to follow.

"Do you remember Uwen taking you to his saddle?"

"Not clearly, m'lord Prince."

"You seem to have cast your spell over Uwen. The man and your staff had strictest orders to report to me if you waked, and, lo! they go following you about, here and there, upstairs and down, with never a thought of my orders in their heads. Did you bid them do that?"

"I beg you don't blame him. It was my fault. He asked me to wait. I disobeyed him. He was trying to catch me. And I knew better, sir. I did know better. Not about your order. But I knew I made him chase me, because I wanted to go outside. I know it was wrong."

Cefwyn's brow lifted. A long moment Cefwyn simply stared at him. "You know that Uwen is at your orders as well as mine."

"I know, sir."

"But you obey him, do you?"

"He's my guard, is he not, sir?"

"He is your man." Cefwyn waved his hand, dismissing the question. "He chose this morning to take his allegiance with you. Therefore I release him to give oath to you, and, for good or for ill, *you* provide for him. – Racing about just ahead of us, out to the yard and back again to the archive and searching up a book – hardly the place I'd seek a young man in a soldier's company."

This was not, then, a casual questioning. He wished himself back in his own room, his old room, not this huge place opposite Cefwyn's apartment. He perceived he had brought Uwen into difficulty.

"Do I distress you?" Cefwyn asked. "Why did you go to the archive, out of all places you could go? What sent you there, instead of – say – the garden, or anywhere else of your habit?"

"I wished –" He found himself on ground more and more frightening. "I wished to know more about Althalen."

"Why?"

It was hard to speak. He had not been able to explain to Uwen. He tried, at least to explain it to Cefwyn. "It's a Name, sir. I know it. I asked the archivist was there anything to tell me about Althalen. And he gave me that book. – Was it wrong?"

"Not wrong. Perhaps it's not what you wish to find. It's my grandfather's history. Did you know that?"

"No, m'lord Prince."

"My name is Cefwyn Marhanen. Does that mean anything to you?"

"No, sir." It did not. "Not except that you have two names."

"Elfwyn. Do you know that name?"

"I don't know that name either, sir."

"Sihhë."

"People say that I am Sihhë."

"Are you?"

"I've read –" He sensed in all these questions that this was purposeful and far more important than Cefwyn's simple curiosity, and he suspected now that all this evening had been leading to this strange chain of Words and Names. "I read in the book that the Sihhë were cruel wizards. And it's a Name, sir, but I don't understand it – not – that it makes sense to me. Mauryl was a wizard, but he was never cruel. He said I should be polite, and I should think about others' wishes and not touch what doesn't belong to me. I don't think that leads to being cruel, sir. So it isn't Mauryl, either."

"No. It doesn't seem so." Cefwyn gazed at him and sipped

292

his wine, and went on looking at him, seeming strangely troubled. "Mauryl brought the Sihhë kings to power. Have you heard that? Do you think that is true?"

"I – don't know, sir."

"But it doesn't trouble you."

"I don't see how it should, sir."

"Do you not *remember* things? Isn't that what you told me – that you hear names and you know them?"

"That's true. But some Words – time after time they mean nothing to me, and then, on a certain day, in a certain way, they – unfold."

"Unfold."

"Yes, sir."

"And has the word Sihhë unfolded at all to you?"

"It –" It did trouble him. That Word lay out of reach. He knew it was there, that Name, and that he had part of it, but not all. "I think that I might be Sihhë. People in the garden mostly said so."

"And therefore you believe it?"

"No, m'lord. I don't know what it means. – Can books be wrong?"

"Egregiously wrong. And mislead men – egregiously."

"Like lying."

"Or making mistakes."

"I make mistakes. I make far too many, – Mauryl said. And I still do. Don't be angry at Uwen."

"You say you're not a wizard."

"No, sir. I'm not."

"Then what *would* you be? If you could choose – what would you be? A prince? A king?"

"On the whole, sir, – I think I had rather be Haman."

Cefwyn's chin rested on his hand as he listened. A crook of Cefwyn's finger came up over his lips, repressing what might be a smile. Almost.

"You are remarkable," Cefwyn said. "Rather be a stable-master."

"I've said something foolish."

"And honest. – Can you yet read that book of yours? The one Mauryl gave you?"

"No, m'lord Prince. I can't. I tried, this afternoon. But I can't."

"Are you my Friend, Tristen?"

It was a Word, a warm and good one. "Yes, m'lord Prince, if you like."

"Had you a name once, besides the one Mauryl gave you?"

"None that I know, sir." He could hear his heart beating. Suddenly he was tired, very tired, and wanted to sleep, although sleep had been the farthest thing from his mind a short breath before.

"Tristen, tell me, why did you come to Henas'amef rather than, say, to Emwy?"

"It seemed the right way."

"Does it still seem so?"

"I think so, sir."

"You might have lived at Althalen before Mauryl called you forth. I should tell you – you most likely did. Hundreds of the Sihhë died at Althalen. Elfwyn died there. Mauryl and Emuin were there, and they helped my grandfather, Selwyn Marhanen, become King of Ylesuin. They killed Elfwyn and his queen and all the Sihhë they could find for three years after. Does this surprise you?"

He was afraid. He wanted Cefwyn to talk about something else. "I'd not heard that, sir, no."

"There was fire. The hold of Althalen burned. And you smelled the smoke when we rode there. You remembered how to ride. You were most certainly a horseman, and a fine one. You're clearly a scholar, versed in letters and philosophy. You have graces that mark you as well-born. Your speech is liker Amefin than not, but then, you learned it of Mauryl, didn't you?"

"Yes, sir," Tristen said. Surmises flooded at him, too many to think of and still follow Cefwyn's skipping from point to point.

"My father is King," Cefwyn said. "I shall be. I by no

means know what Mauryl intended in sending you here. Many in this province of Amefel would be pleased to see me dead. Would that please you? More to the point, – would it have pleased Mauryl?"

"No, sir." He found it hard to breathe. "It would not. I don't think so."

"The medallion I gave you. Do you still wear it?"

"Yes, sir." Tristen felt it against his skin. "Do you wish it back, m'lord Prince? I didn't know –"

"No, no, wear it. Wear it every day. Let me show you another." There was a small table beside Cefwyn's chair, and Cefwyn took from it a white medallion on a gold chain woven with pearls. Cefwyn leaned forward to show it to him. "This is Ninévrisë. Did Mauryl ever mention that name?"

"No, sir. Not at all." He steadied the medallion slightly with his fingertips. It was a beautiful face. It was no one he knew. But he liked to look at it. "She has a kind face."

Cefwyn leaned back again, put the medallion again on the table. "Her father is regent of Elwynor. He offers her to me in Marriage."

Marry. Marriage. Husband. Wife. Bed.

Children.

"Will you Marry her?" he asked.

"I did consider it. That we were attacked at Emwy, that things have gone amiss in that area – might be because certain Elwynim are opposed to it. Or it might be because certain Amefin are opposed to it."

"Do you *wish* to marry her?"

Cefwyn's brows lifted, if only mildly, and he took a sip of wine. "It would certainly set certain teeth on edge. You understand – lords marry not for love but to get heirs. And an heir of both Elwynor and Ylesuin – would be very powerful."

It was a nest of Words. Of ideas. He listened.

"Equally," Cefwyn said, "a prince to rule well and long needs a loyal group of lords on whom he can rely. You said, did you not, Tristen, that you would be my friend? You would Defend me from my enemies?"

"Yes, sir."

"Would you Swear that in the sight of strangers?"

Swearing was a word about gods, and it fluttered about Truth and Lies and making strong promises. It was wider than that, much wider, and the threads kept running off into the dark, so he knew it was a large idea; but it felt entirely reasonable: of course he should defend Cefwyn, if someone tried to harm him.

"Yes," he said. And that pleased Cefwyn greatly. Cefwyn looked to have set aside the worry he had had in asking him.

"Do you hear?" Cefwyn asked in a loud voice of Idrys, who had been talking with Uwen over at the table. "Do you hear, Idrys? He will swear to defend Ylesuin's heir."

Idrys left the table. So did Uwen. Tristen stood up, then, as Cefwyn did. He had thought the declaration of no great moment, but Cefwyn thought so, and Idrys frowned and looked not quite so pleased with the matter.

"And keep his oath?" Idrys said. "Can you keep an oath, sir wizard?"

"I am no wizard," Tristen said. "And, yes, sir, I know what it means."

Cefwyn went to the table, where he dipped pen in ink and wrote something rapidly on parchment. Tristen stood up and walked over to watch as Cefwyn heated sealing-wax over a candle and dripped it onto the parchment. He impressed his seal on it. "Call Margolis," he said. "She can keep a matter to herself. And we have not that much time. Tristen has agreed to swear me his allegiance, and *you* – " he said, looking at Tristen. "You will have a name, hereafter, sir, subject to my father's confirmation – which I do not think he will withhold. By my grant the lordship of Ynefel and of Althalen is filled. Tristen, Mauryl's sole and undisputed heir, inherits. Both holdings are within my jurisdiction. The grant is, subject to the King's will, lawful."

"And will the Quinalt stand to bless this?" Idrys asked. "Or had you rather the witch of Emwy?"

"Their little storm will pass, master crow, as all storms do.

296

And these Amefin rebels will have a new bone to gnaw; so will the Elwynim. Damn me, but they will!"

"My lord," Tristen protested, bewildered in this debate of his fortunes and the approval of people he by no means knew; but Cefwyn's hand closed on his shoulder and Cefwyn hugged him close in a way Mauryl might have done, which quite shocked him, and touched his heart and chased thought from his head.

"You will stand by me," Cefwyn said. "This is my *friend*, master crow. Treat him well, Emuin said, and do I not? Lord Warden of Ynefel, Lord High Marshal of Althalen, *Tristen* aetheling, entitled to the honors and arms and devices thereof."

"Oh, the Aswydds will be *delighted*," Idrys said.

"Be *still*, crow. Margolis will see to all the details. She'll work the night through." A second time Cefwyn pressed his shoulder. "Tristen, I'll send such servants as a lord might need. And, Uwen, –"

"M'lord."

"Have extreme care that they are *Guelen* servants. None of the Amefin, by any mischance. And no word of what we've agreed. Not to them. Not where you could be overheard by anyone. – And no wandering about without sufficient guard. Certain people will not be pleased by this. – Go, good night, good rest. – Uwen, I release you from your personal oath to me; you'll stay in my guard; I set you over *his* household, gods witness he will need you – give your oath to him and gods keep you. – Tristen, keep that medal I gave you about your neck day and night."

"Yes, m'lord Prince." Tristen made a bow, on his best manners. "Thank you." He went with Uwen, who lingered for a bow of his own, and so to the doors, which Uwen opened, and let them out to the foyer.

The inner doors closed behind Tristen and his man.

The outer doors closed, after that, assuring privacy within the apartment.

Alone with Idrys, Cefwyn looked in his direction, finding exactly the expression he expected to find – which was no expression at all.

"Well?" Cefwyn asked.

"I do not dispute my lord's decision," Idrys said softly. "Only his wisdom."

"Not even that, my lord Prince. I find it a clever move. Even a ruthless move. You astonish me. The Aswyddim and the Elwynim set down at one stroke. – Do you give him the bride-offer portrait, too?"

"You heard him. He knows the meaning of a promise. And you saw that he bears me no ill will."

"I doubt that he knows what an oath is," Idrys said.

"And is more bound by what he promises than Heryn Aswydd sitting on a heap of holy relics."

"Oh, indeed, my prince, I'd believe his lightest word above Heryn's solemn oath, if ever one word he says he has the knowing governance of. Perhaps he *will* serve you wholly. But he is defenseless now, my lord Prince. Wear him for armor and something will, through him, find your heart. He is still Mauryl's. I still advise, wait for Emuin, and do *not* release Uwen Lewen's-son. He likes Mauryl's piece of work too well. This blade will turn in your hand."

"If Emuin will bestir himself and make haste I shall consult Emuin. But the lords of the south will ask about Tristen's standing in my company, and soon, – and I have to tell them something."

"And will you raise his standard? The arms you've granted him cannot be displayed, m'lord Prince, by the King's law, they cannot be raised – here in Amefel, most particularly."

"And are, throughout the province."

"On farmhouses! Not under this roof! Not in the prince's grant of honors!"

"He *is* the promised king. He *is* the King the Elwynim look for, by your own reckoning."

"He is Sihhë. And mild and good as Elfwyn may have been, not all their line was so civilized: good gods, m'lord Prince, of the five true Sihhë kings of legend, Harosyn flung his father on his mother's pyre, Sarynan hunted his two brothers like deer through his woods. Barrakkêth immured his enemies alive in Ynefel's walls, and his son Ashyel added to the collection with half a score of his less pleasing lords, among them an ancestor of the Marhanen line, for no fault but riding before him at the hunt. So they say. I've not seen the faces, but Olmern folk swear they exist, and move, at times, and in recent days I hold fewer doubts than ever I brought to this benighted province. I would most gladly see you home to Guelemara, my lord Prince, without an Elwynim bride, without a wizard tutor, most of all without a friend with a claim on the Sihhë throne."

"Emuin said, Win his love."

"Master Emuin is not here to advise. Master Emuin is not here to see the imminent result of his advice. Love has not prevented Sihhë excesses."

"Black silk for Dame Margolis. Black silk and white. Silver thread. I trust there will be such in the Zeide's ample warehouses."

"My lord, I agreed to this wild plan. But the arms you grant him cannot be displayed, not without royal dispensation."

"I give it. I am my father's voice in this province, if some do forget it."

"Send to your father before you raise the Sihhë standard at Henas'amef. Even if it were the best of plans, you are not King. Perhaps he will approve your plan. But you will do far more wisely not to take this on your own advisement. Even with the royal command you hold, you dare not repeal your grandfather's order."

"I cannot lose a province, either. Ask which my lord father would countenance."

"We are not to that, m'lord Prince. We are far from that and have much more resource."

"Then I will send tonight advising him. I shall say that I have all confidence of his approval – it will secure this border. It will *do* what my royal father set me here to do, and I know that the Quinalt will buzz about him like an overset hive, and

299

I *know* that they will be at my father's ears before my lord father can think through this matter. He gave me to rule this province and to hold it against all threat. I take it that includes levying troops to defend it."

"I am not so certain it extends to nullifying a royal decree."

"He will bear the arms of Ynefel."

"Better you should style him with the phoenix. Do we add the crown?"

"Your wit lacks, sir."

"It has a point. I still say – do not surprise your father in this matter."

"Apply to Margolis. Say I have need of this most urgently. Say if she or her maids betray me I'll marry them to Haman's louts. See to it."

"The message," Idrys said, "to His Majesty the King, my lord Prince."

"Master crow, you do try my patience."

"By your father's order, m'lord Prince. The letter."

He went to the table. He wrote, *Most Gracious Majesty and dearest father, I have won on Emuin's advice the allegiance and oath of fealty of the King for whom the Elwynim have waited, and have granted him rights and lands and the raising of his own standard. I pray you trust me whatever you may have reported to you that I bear you filial affection and all loyalty.*

That too he sealed with wax and stamped with his signet.

"For what good you can wring of it. He may not like my success. But there you are, master crow. I may yet disappoint him sorely, and win over my enemies instead of dying here."

"He is not your enemy, m'lord Prince. He is no fool, to set aside his heir."

"So you dare say. But I am not his favorite son." He cast himself into the chair at the table and extended the scrolled message. "By the time this reaches him – I will be right, or most fatally wrong."

* * *

There was a to-do among the servants and the guards that Uwen was dealing with, and by the darkened window, which showed a very little gray slate beyond the rippled panes of the bedchamber, Tristen stood finding new textures in the glass, new shapes of candle-shadow about the walls.

Servants. Silk and velvet. He thought of the pigeons which, haunting the window on the floor above, on the other side of the building, must have missed the bits of bread days ago. He was sorry for that. He missed them. He hoped they would be clever enough to find this window. He always seemed to be moving on, always seemed to be finding a new bed, a new window, a new arrangement for his life, which unfolded with a swiftness that foiled his ability to plan for anything, do anything, hope for anything.

But Cefwyn had called him his friend tonight. Cefwyn had hugged him, not tentatively like Emuin, but as warmly as Mauryl once had, and he had been afraid no one would ever do that again.

Cefwyn had filled his head with Words and Names and told him what he had to do, as Mauryl had. Cefwyn had placed demands of obedience on him as Mauryl had. In one hour the world seemed to have reeled back to an older, more comfortable night, when the walls were not bright white, casting back the candlelight, when the air had been dank and dusty and Mauryl's pen scratched away at the parchments, louder than the crackle of the fire in the hearth, Mauryl telling him Words until the air hummed with them.

But then, then, Go to bed, lad, Mauryl would tell him; and he would take the candle. Mauryl would send him aloft to light all the candles on the balconies, at which time the faces would seem to move, or to change.

Swear, Cefwyn had said, and named Names that meant nothing to him as yet, but they might, in the way of things that came closer and closer and then unfolded themselves wide around him.

Cefwyn had named Names and said Words until the unshuttered dark of his new room seethed with them.

A door opened, perhaps the servants going out: the candle wavered, and Shadows crept along the joints of the black-paned window and into the joints of the masonry. He knew no magics such as Mauryl had had to keep them at bay. He was defenseless against them, except for the candles and the window latch.

He had always thought the candles Mauryl had had him light had been his defense. But it had been Mauryl. He knew now that, threaded through every stone of Ynefel, it had been Mauryl's power keeping him safe and keeping the Shadows out. And there was none such here. And things were changing so fast.

– *Emuin*, he said, reaching for that gray place. *Emuin. I need you.*

He could see before him a pale spot in the gray, and he tried to go toward it. A weight sat on his shoulders, cold and crushing, and he knew there was something behind him. He knew that Shadows raced along the corners of the room, and sniggered at his mistakes.

– *Emuin, Cefwyn calls me his friend. He says I should defend him. And I would gladly do that. But it always seems that people have to defend me. I should know how to do the right things I know to do, master Emuin. And I don't know how to make this room safe.*

He hoped for an answer. None came. He tried again.

– *I answer Cefwyn's questions with foolish answers, master Emuin. And I still can't read the Book. I still don't know what Mauryl would have me do. I had Owl for a guide and I lost him. I do wish you would tell me how to be wiser.*

– *Could you not, sir, answer me – just once?*

There was attention. He felt it, then. Emuin was far distant and busy at books – an absolute tower of books. Like Mauryl. Like Mauryl, Emuin was searching for something that he had forgotten. And Emuin had become aware of him.

– **Go back, boy!** Emuin's voice said, and something less friendly came faintly through the gray. **This is not a safe** *place now. Stay out of dark places. Go no more to the old palace. His remains are there. And he sees you. He sees you, boy. Get away!*

He fled, as Emuin had said. Shadows poured after him, almost caught him, and a voice not Emuin's and not Mauryl's said gently, – There you are. Changed rooms, have you?

He fled the gray place, went careening back to the room and the window.

Something made the latch tremble. It rattled, if ever so slightly.

It stopped, as if his eyes had tricked him.

His heart hammered against his ribs. His face and his arms were clammy with sweat. He heard quiet in the next room, where Uwen had been talking to the newly arrived servants, beyond the open bedroom doors. He started to walk to the other room. But, feeling dizzy, he sank down into the nearest chair and rested his head in his hands, struggling with that gray light that kept trying to establish itself in his mind.

He heard Uwen's step. "M'lord," Uwen said, kneeling by him. "Are ye ill?"

"I am cold, Uwen."

"Silk shirts is damnable cold in a draft, m'lord. I think I like linen best. Here, lad." Uwen rose, and with a gust of cool air, a coverlet from the bed, he supposed, came whisking through the air and landed about his shoulders. Uwen snugged it up close about his chin and set his hand to hold it. "You have this about ye, m'lord. I'll make down the bed. It don't take no servants for that."

"Uwen, – light more candles. I don't want it dark."

"Aye, m'lord." Uwen pulled down the covers on the huge bed, another waft of cool air, made it smooth, then took the sole burning taper from the table and walked about the room, lighting all the candles, making the Shadows retreat.

Then he came back and went down on one knee. "There ye be. – Ye feel any better, m'lord?"

"Cefwyn has given me Ynefel," Tristen said. "He calls me his friend. Did you hear?"

Uwen's scarred face was frowning. "I suppose His Highness has it to dispose, m'lord."

"Uwen, tell me. Is it Ynefel men fear so? Or is it Mauryl? – Or is it me?"

"I don't know, m'lord," Uwen said. "Ynefel hain't a good reputation. But hereabouts is a superstitious lot."

"Go," he said finally. "Uwen, if you fear me, go."

Uwen looked up, in fear of him, he was sure of it, and with something else, too, that had once touched Mauryl's face. Uwen scowled then, spoiling it. "Ain't never backed off from no man. And not a good lad like you, m'lord."

"You don't have to run, Uwen. You can just stand outside with the other guard, no more, no less than they."

"Ain't leaving ye. And enough of foolishness, m'lord. Ye'd best get ye to bed."

"No." He clenched his hands before his mouth, remembered the little scar and rubbed at it with his thumb, staring into the candlelight. A face like his own came to him, dim and mirror-like, as if it were reflected in bronze. He shut his eyes the tighter, and opened them, and it left him.

"Uwen, Cefwyn believes I'm Sihhë."

"So folk say ye might be."

"What does that *mean*, Uwen?"

"Old, m'lord. And wizards."

"I'm not. I wish I could do what Mauryl could. But Mauryl's lost, Emuin's left me and *he's* afraid. Uwen, I have no way to ask anyone else. What is Althalen and what does Cefwyn think I am? Why does Idrys think I lie? Why does Cefwyn ask me Names over and over again? Why does he talk about killing and burning? Why does he want me to swear to be his friend and defend him if he thinks I'm something he won't like, Uwen?"

Uwen's face was pale. He drew from his shirt an amulet and carried the thing to his lips. "My lord, I fear some mean no good to ye. I don't say as the prince means ye ill, but others – others ye should watch right carefully."

"Do you feel so? But I will swear to be his friend. I have to do it. Cefwyn is m'lord Prince, and I must do what he wishes, is that not so?"

"Aye, m'lord," Uwen whispered. "That it is. But ye don't understand what they intends, and I'm sure I don't. I don't think m'lord Prince has authority of his father the King to do a thing like he's done. The King will hear, sure enough, and then gods help us."

"So what should I do, Uwen?"

"Ye do what Prince Cefwyn bids ye. Ye swear and ye become Cefwyn's man, and 't is all ye can do. He's a good lord. Ain't none better. But ye don't cross 'im. Marhanen blood is fierce, m'lord. And there ain't no living Sihhë. The Marhanen damned the name, and damned the arms that he give you. For that reason, His Majesty ain't apt to be pleased in what His Highness has done."

He listened. His heart hurt. "Then I shall send you away. You were brave to stay with me, tonight, in Cefwyn's apartment. But I don't want you to come to harm, Uwen. I never want you to come to harm."

"He won't harm me, m'lord. For his honor, he won't be laying hands on me. I was his before he give me to you. I'm still in the guard, and he ain't one to dispose his men to trouble. But that ain't reckoning His Majesty the King. I've no wish to be watching them set your head at Skull Gate. I don't want to see Prince Cefwyn's there either, after the King learns what's astir here." He touched lips to the fist that held the medal. "Don't repeat none of this. Maybe ye hain't no sense of it, m'lord, but growing up in Ynefel surely taught ye some sort of caution. Don't ye cross Cefwyn. Don't think of crossing him."

"I can't, I shan't, Uwen."

Uwen's hand pressed his. "Lad . . . m'lord, . . . I give ye my oath t' be your man, right and true, by the good gods, by their grace. That's my word on 't. But ye be careful. Ye keep the prince and the Lord Commander happy wi' ye. For your own sake."

"I shall. As best I can, I shall, Uwen."

"Let me get them boots off. Ye'd do better abed."

Tristen thrust out his foot and braced himself for Uwen's pull on one and the other. He shed his clothing and let Uwen put him to bed. He shivered between the cold sheets.

"Shall I blow out the lights, m'lord?"

"No. Uwen, please. Let them burn. Let them burn until morning."

"Aye, m'lord. If 't please ye, I'll send for more candles. We'll light 'er like a festival, only so's ye sleep."

CHAPTER 17

~

The bell at the lower town gates tolled arrivals. Cefwyn continued to sift through the revenue reports, ignoring the bell until one of the guards outside opened the door and crossed the foyer to report that Lord Heryn Aswydd was demanding admittance.

Idrys was otherwise assigned. Cefwyn considered, finally rose and gave instructions to grant the demand, with appropriate precautions.

The lord of the Amefin had brought his twin sisters. Heryn bowed, Orien and Tarien curtsied, and Cefwyn folded his arms and leaned against the dead fireplace, secure if nothing else in the guards who had trailed this trio into the room.

"What is this at our gates?" Heryn asked.

"I do hardly know, Your Grace, being here, and not there, and not prophetic, but I will assume they are several of the neighbors."

"Send these men of yours away."

"Patience." Cefwyn returned to the table and perched on the corner, amid the tax records. "Though I have limited patience myself. Your tax accounts are exceedingly nuisanceful, Lord Amefel. My master of accounts daily assails me with new complexities of records-keeping. – Do believe that my humor today is not the best."

Heryn's face was all formality. "I shall have my seneschal make account to me where this fault may lie. But do rest assured, my lord Prince, that the Crown has always received its due."

"You've furnished this hall in grand style, Amefel. I would rather iron and horses than gilt and velvets, with matters as they stand on the far borders. – Or perhaps you don't count the Elwynim a serious danger to your interests."

"I have constantly maintained the requisite levies." Heryn drew a quick breath and made a wide gesture. "This is not the issue, Your Highness. There are strangers at my gate, that you may call neighbors, but I do not. I protest this treatment of me and my house. I protest the dismissal of my personal guards. I am treated like a lawbreaker. I cannot but believe that Your Highness has lent his ear to malicious influences."

"Idrys, mean you? Pray don't attack him. I fear he's not here to defend himself. He's pursuing business you set him."

"M'lord prince?"

"A messenger you managed to dispatch." Cefwyn raised his voice and the twins backed away. "Where is your man Thewydd?"

Heryn went white, and for a time no one moved, neither he nor his mirrorlike sisters nor the equally mirrorlike guards who escorted them.

"Dispatched to your father," Heryn answered after a moment, "that His Majesty the King may know my situation, my duress, and my complaint."

Cefwyn let go a long breath, angry, and hoping that a message to Guelemara was the only truth. "You have the right to appeal any grievance to the King. You hardly need subterfuge to effect that, no midnight departures or disguises."

"I have the right to walk my own hall unimpeded, but your treatment of that right makes me doubt the others."

"You may say so, Amefel. You may complain to my lord father. I'll seal and stamp the message myself if you like. But you will give account to me *and* to my father the King when the accounting comes."

"I am prepared to do so, Your Highness, in clear conscience."

"You have hazarded your man's life," Cefwyn said. "If taken, he will pay for your lack of trust in me, since Idrys, as you well know, is not a patient man."

"My lord Prince." Heryn spread wide his hands in an attitude of entreaty. "I protest this arrest. I have done nothing –"

308

Cefwyn gestured toward the records. "Nothing improper? You've bled this province *white*, sir. You've made the Crown look rapacious and you've appropriated to yourself taxes you declared to the province to be due to the Crown. Is that of advantage to us in our defense of a dangerous border? Does that win the loyalty of the peasants? Have I even cavalry to show for it? No. Gold dinnerplates." He stalked as far as the windows, lest his anger choke him, turned and paced back, and Heryn stood with Orien and Tarien on either hand, a whey-faced lot and suddenly loathsome to him. "You may regret having appealed to His Majesty, Heryn Aswydd, since, having invoked the King's law, you will now be unable to stop it. And I, my finely-dressed lord, and ladies, have begun a long list of questions in which my father the King will interest himself when he summons you to Guelemara. We speak of *treason*, sir, as well as theft."

"My lord," Orien began, and winced as her brother gripped her arm and pulled her back.

"Do not involve yourself," Cefwyn advised her. He turned his shoulder to them. The bells rang down at the outer gate, distant and clear on the air, but there was another bell pealing out now, that of Skull Gate, and a clatter of hooves echoed off the inner walls.

"What have you done?" Heryn asked him.

Cefwyn looked out the window, ignoring Heryn and all he represented.

The doors opened. One of the Guelen pages entered, out of breath. Sasian, his name was, an earnest lad. Cefwyn signed to him. "Your Highness," the lad breathed. "It's Ivanor's banner, and Imor's."

Cefwyn's lips made a taut smile. Cevulirn and Umanon together, neighbors and allies, the horsemen of the southern plains and their city-dwelling allies from across the Lenúalim.

Here. Safe. Answering immediately to his summons. Breath left him in a long sigh, and he cast a look askance at Heryn's pallid face.

"We have *guests*, Amefel."

"To be entertained at my expense?" Heryn cried. "You are quartering Ivanim in my town?"

"Expense, expense, matters with you do seem to have a single song, Lord Heryn. We are conferring on matters of import to all the region; the others will doubtless be arriving before twilight."

Heryn opened his mouth and shut it quickly.

"No," Cefwyn agreed, "I would not object in your place, Amefel." He made a chivalric gesture toward Orien: pale, russet-haired, *ambitious* Orien. "You will have the opportunity to play hostess to all the region; an opportunity to use all that grand gold dinnerware, all this surplus of servants and display. You should be delighted, dear, vain . . . lady."

Color rose to Orien's face. Tarien turned white.

"Out!" Cefwyn said to her and her sister, and she whirled and fled, remembered to curtsy, and fled again. After an opening and closing of her mouth Tarien left in her wake, and two guards went with them.

"My lord Prince," Heryn said, choked with rage. "Your treatment of my sisters does you no honor."

"Your sisters are charming whores, and do you cry honor, who made them serve where you could not?"

Heryn swore. The guards moved with a clash of metal and Heryn's hand stayed from the dirk he wore. For a moment Heryn seemed on the verge of that fatal madness, then wisely mastered his impulses in favor of more diplomatic assault. Cefwyn regarded him with disappointment.

"You are dismissed, Your Grace."

"I am not your servant, to be dismissed so rudely. Or do you fancy yourself already King?"

"Surely *you* fancy I shall *not* be."

For a moment Heryn's face was void of expression, and a chill came on Cefwyn's skin. A mistake, to have baited the man. He had misjudged the threat. Coxcomb, liar, usurer and outright tax-thief that he was, Heryn Aswydd was in fact dangerous.

Nine assassins, and the last a troop of them, in lands Heryn patrolled.

Of course the man would not be provoked to draw – and the man knew the prince trod on fragile ground, raising armies.

Heryn did *not* know other things shaping quietly in the handiwork of women. He trusted that Heryn did not know. But in those books of account there were debts at outrageous interest that other lords and even tradesmen owed that *kept* the nobility of Amefel swilling at Aswydd's trough.

Cefwyn turned to the page, who stood the while frozen in horror. "Go back, lad; see the lords at the gate offered all courtesies and welcome. Have the master-at-arms run up the flags of all our guests beside mine and Amefel's, as they arrive. Go. Haste."

The boy sketched a hasty bow and fled. Cefwyn returned to his table, sat down, and found his place in the records. "Perhaps," he said to Heryn, "you would care instead to assist me in my reckonings of the proper tax. Doubtless you can explain these accounts and the source and disposition of these revenues."

There was absolute silence. No one moved, neither Heryn nor the guards. Heryn leaned insolently against the table by the door, red-bearded, elegant Heryn, who had succeeded after all in surprising him with an audacity and mental quickness greater than he would have believed in the man.

Cefwyn, seething with anger, turned a massive page, the numbers on which swam in front of him.

Tax the people at more than the Crown rate, then lend them money back to pay the tax – collecting interest through the town's moneylenders who let the income out again through *their* fingers. Those books also his men were searching for, this time in town. Well it was to have probed the man to the quick, he decided. Almost he had regretted pressing him thus far, but now at least he knew the temper of the man, underestimated as it had been.

"We shall go down," he said, "and meet Amefel's other guests. It should be time. Will you join me, Your Grace?"

"Of course, Your Highness," Heryn said.

He closed the book, and swept up with his own guard the Guelen guardsmen with Heryn, men whose eyes were shadowed with a service in which they alternated sleep and duty. The duty would be lessened with the arrival at that gate, with troops other than Guelen and Amefin available to dispose about the Zeide.

They went out and down the hall at a brisk pace, down the steps, and got no further than the turn toward the doors before, shadows against the light, a troop of men came in.

Cevulirn and Umanon together, travel-stained, dusted from the road, and weary from a day's ride. "Pages!" Cefwyn called out. "The lords' baggage to their quarters. Rouse out Lord Kerdin and see to their men!" He met the lords with a handclasp and a clap on the arm that raised dust, the consequence of a large troop in a dry spell on the roads. "Welcome, welcome, both. A long day, a long ride. You are the earliest. I trust my men have been down by the gate to provide your captains what they need."

"Prompt and well-prepared, Your Highness. Your Grace." The latter Cevulirn addressed to Heryn, who met them as if he had remained undisputed lord in Henas'amef.

"Your Highness, Your Grace." Umanon was a smallish, stout man with drooping mustaches and the figure of a wheel blazoned in white on his green surcoat: lord of Imor Lenúalim, and a master of rich farmlands and the great high road. Cevulirn stood at his shoulder, a thin, tall man whose colorless hair and mustache and gray surcoat made him curiously obscure to the eye; his device was a white horse that betokened the wide plains of Ivanor, the good grasslands and sleek horses that were the wealth of the unfenced south.

"We've arranged water and wood for your encampments," Cefwyn said. "We trust you'll leave your captains in charge and enjoy the hospitality of the hall. We expect more of your brother lords to arrive, and this evening we'll make formal reception in the grand hall, granted the rain stays at bay and our other guests arrive in timely fashion. At worst, good food and good company for those of us who do meet."

"At your pleasure, my lord Prince," said Umanon; and in his dark eyes, as in Cevulirn's gray stare, was keen curiosity; but they were too prudent to ask questions where answers had not been advanced in the letters or put foremost in the meeting.

"It is not war," Heryn said, "nor is anyone taken ill. I am as puzzled as yourselves at this gathering. But welcome, my lords, welcome, all the same."

Cefwyn smiled tautly at Heryn's conscious malice and brazen effrontery, and saw dismay leap into the lords' eyes, a second glance at him, – and caution.

"His Grace Lord Heryn is not in favor, today, as you see. He even sends to His Majesty in protest of my orders. But I am jealous of my life, my lords, as I assure you is my royal father, and Heryn has lately been most careless in that regard. You surely noticed the ornaments of our south gate. I urge you take precautions for yourselves: assassins of some stamp or other have been a damned pest in Amefel this summer. Heryn does of course swear they're Elwynim. But overtaxed farmers can grow desperate, and even blame their prince for their plight."

There was a lifting of heads, scant glances toward Heryn: there was no great bond among the southern lords, and with that handful of blunt words he marked Heryn as plague-touched. Heryn's poisonous tongue merited him a visit to the cellars, but to have the man delivered to prison in his own hall, particularly under witness of the neighbors, was extreme. Heryn's boldness so far had saved him from his own prison, and his answer had, as happened, neatly warned the visiting lords, always jealous of their privileges, that they well might be cautious: that the Marhanen prince might be exceeding the authority the King had lent him.

But now Heryn bowed, all humble, and was oh, so far from the drawing of a weapon that alone would give the prince clear cause to remove a baron of Ylesuin to his own well-stocked cellars. Clever man, he thought, and far braver than he had reckoned him.

"This evening, my lords," Cefwyn murmured, and they

bowed in courtesy, prepared to go off with an assortment of pages and attendants.

Heryn, too, took his chance to leave under that general dismissal, bowing and sweeping up the Guelen guards assigned to him, so that his treatment in his own hall would be clear to his unasked guests. The man had a gift and an instinct for epic.

Heryn was Amefin, he was noble, accepted by the Amefin lords as well as by the peasants he abused, at least as one of their own.

There had not been another choice but the Aswydds and their ilk to rule the province. There might be, now. Annas had been instructing Tristen in protocols, in manners, in courtly matters, and Annas reported him a quick and gracious hearer. "A pleasure, m'lord," was Annas' assessment of him.

He climbed the stairs, went back to his apartment and to, as he planned, the cursed books, wherein his accountant had placed small papers and notes explaining the artistry with which the Aswyddim had entered here and entered there their meandering sums.

He left his guard at the doors, went through with the sergeant of the detail to open the door for him, and went inside.

A movement, dark and unexpected, by the window, caught his eye.

Idrys.

Cefwyn dropped his hand from his dagger and the beating of his heart began again.

"My lord," said Idrys. "We could not overtake the messenger. A horse was hidden for him at the Averyne crossing."

"He is to my father," Cefwyn said, on his second whole breath. "So swears Heryn."

"That was his direction, my lord." Pale dust overlay Idrys' black armor and etched lines into his face, making his eyes starker and more cruel than their wont. "I returned when I saw that there was no likelihood of my both overtaking him and reaching the town again by dark; I dispatched men in pursuit, but if he rides to the limit, on that horse, he may escape them. That he is bound for your father may be the truth; but that is not the assumption the guard will make if he lags within arrow-flight of them. Unfortunate man."

Cefwyn frowned and folded his arms. "We have come to a point of final reckoning with Heryn. He trusts he knows my limits. He is about to learn he does not. I am glad you did return."

"You have reckoned the consequences, my lord, both personal and general, of a breach with the Aswyddim?"

"I have reckoned them. This Heryn Aswydd is a soft-surfaced man, but there is steel beneath the velvet, Idrys. We were well rid of him as Duke of Amefel. He trusts I dare not do it. And he thinks he knows my resources. He's probed for Tristen's provenance as other than Ynefel, he seems to hold suspicions that I've contrived accusations against him merely as a threat, nothing of substance I dare actually carry through. And in that matter he is very ill informed."

CHAPTER 18

The sun was far declined and red when the remaining lords arrived. Black-bearded Sovrag of Olmern and his rivermen hit the town out of the northwest, having navigated the Lenúalim through Marna, and having caused the gate wardens of the lower town great consternation when he insisted to bring a large clutch of his own guards about him into the town, the men of the Black Wolf banner, rougher and less mannered than their lord.

So Cefwyn heard on a message run up from lower town. He sent down to the Zeide gate to let the man and his escort in, and met him in the lower hall, himself, to his guards' dismay.

"Ha, Marhanen-lord," Sovrag called out – he towered over most men, this black wolf of Olmern, who had taken his lordship rather than inherited it. He was nearly as wide as two men: no common horse could carry him, and he most-times went by boat, where boats could carry him. His voice was fit to rattle the glass of Heryn's fine windows.

But Idrys, turning up at Cefwyn's shoulder, murmured, "That escort of his is show for Cevulirn and Umanon," for there was bad blood there, and no secret of it – and the camp he had designated for the Olmernmen was to the town's north, on the river approach, well away from Umanon.

Cefwyn walked forward and gave his hand to the lord of Olmern – "Well," he said, "well, my lord of Olmern, welcome to the hall. I doubt you'll need quite so many men – but I would most gladly borrow them for posting; my own guard is stretched thin, and I trust your folk had sleep on the river, true?"

He had last met Sovrag on the occasion of his investiture as heir. Sovrag had seemed truly giant then, less so now, grace of a span or two he had grown.

Likewise he knew that Sovrag in days past had raided on the river as much as he now traded on it. And trade with Elwynor he might, too, but never quite hide the fact: he was an unsubtle man.

A greeting hand-to-hand was surely not the welcome Sovrag usually met, and certainly not the one he knew he was due for his armed incursion. It was a test, Cefwyn reckoned; a test of his welcome and possibly a test of the Aswydds, with whom relations were not cordial. But his bearded face split in a grin. "Your Highness," Sovrag said, and clapped him on the arm fit to leave marks. "If you've use for these scoundrels of mine, be sure they'll follow orders. Gods, ye've grown to a proper man, Marhanen-lord."

"You'll find water and wood at the north gate, space for you and your bodyguard in the southwest tower – ample space there. The Ivanim and the Imorim are lodged easterly, and *I* am lodged between."

Sovrag burst into laughter. "Aye, m'lord Prince!" he said.

"I'll send you there, then. Boy! Show m'lord to the southwest tower, and put him in the hands of the staff."

And, dismissed to the guidance of an apprehensive Guelen page, Sovrag went his way with his escort shambling about him, loaded with rivermen's canvas bags, and armed with the dirks and hooks their trade made more useful than swords.

Within the hour a fight erupted between an Ivanim and a riverman of Olmern in the stableyard, and Pelumer's folk of Lanfarnesse had ridden into the midst of it.

"Can they stand?" Cefwyn asked of Idrys.

"The Ivanim and the Olmernman? Scarcely but they will live, m'lord Prince, except your justice. Guelenfolk separated them. Amefin were laying bets."

"Bring the two. I will see Pelumer here, too."

Idrys went. Cefwyn shook his head and called Annas for wine, and when it had come, drank it slowly to settle his stomach.

He feared now for what he had done, having the actuality of the lords of the region within the Zeide, a troublesome mix of highborn men within, and old feuds seething among their men camped without the town.

There were, added to the mix, the inns, the wineshops, the Amefin women, peasant cottages, and the Olmernmen in force inside the walls, who were never more than river pirates save by the grace of the King's grant of a township to the man Sovrag had knifed in a dice game.

The prince, meantime, feared Heryn's subtlety, if he invited him to the formalities tonight: Behold me, how I am wronged. He feared as well the subtlety of Heryn's staff, if he excluded the lord of the Amefin from festivities in his own hall.

Orien and Tarien would ply their talents to the same end. Cevulirn was too cold for them, and Pelumer too wise, but Sovrag and Umanon, each with a different sort of vanity, both were vulnerable.

Men approached the door. He took a chair at the table, in front of the account books, still with the wine in hand, and with a sidelong glance surveyed the bloody pair that the Guelen guard brought him, men chained together.

And ignored them a time, in favor of the accounts – while their wounds doubtless ached and they had time to realize together that they had broken the peace of the house with their brawling, under the hospitality of the Crown.

There was hanging for that offense.

"My lord," said another page, "Pelumer Duke of Lanfarnesse."

And that was superfluous, for there immediately, past the overwhelmed page, was Pelumer at the door, and Cefwyn left his chair and his wine with a quick smile and a welcome. Pelumer was the oldest of Ylesuin's barons, white-haired and bearded – with his Heron banner, a frequent winter visitor at the court in Guelemara. His sun-seamed face was a sight, as it were, from home, though Pelumer's land of Lanfarnesse was southernmost of all of the southern lords.

It was more than a handclasp: he embraced the aging lord

with the same warmth he had felt when he had been a boy and Pelumer's hair had been darker. Pelumer had given him his first lesson at archery. Now he felt the warmth of a friend of the Marhanens, and of safe company.

"Ah, Pelumer, how good to see you!"

"Gods bless," said Pelumer, his frown-lines cracking into a broad smile. "And how weary you look."

"You are the shield at my back, Pelumer. The only man in the realm who has, I can say before them all, no feud with any other. And I need your rangers out along the border; I need their furtive watch over the river and the woods."

"I've had reports, m'lord Prince. Some of which you should be made aware of. And my rangers are already out."

"I will hear. I will most gladly hear them. – My page will guide you to quarters for yourself and whatever guard you feel sufficient – many of them, if you please. Guard yourself as you see fit. Warn your men as I know you do. And we meet tonight in hall. In an hour. Time for you and yours to settle, but only that."

"No word of the cause?"

"Not yet."

"Your Highness," Pelumer said, and bowed, and withdrew.

In all of this the malefactors remained. And counting that the prince had yet to dress for hall, and that he had need to make some disposition of the case before him to make a hard point with dissent among the common men:

"Olmernman, your name."

"Denyn, m'lor'."

"Yours, Ivanim?"

"Erion Netha, my lord Prince, of Tas Arin. – But, I assure Your Highness, I was not the one who –"

"Be still!" he snapped, and the men stayed motionless as fawns in a thicket.

"Who draws in despite of the Crown or the Crown's officer, dies. That is the law, for lord and man. Erion and Denyn, you have disrespected my hospitality. I claim your persons from your lords for my justice. That is the King's law."

They were pale, those two, but no word came from them. They were alike in stature, but the Ivanim Erion was a slim, hard-eyed man in his prime, and the stocky Olmernman Denyn was a youth whose beard had hardly started.

"A hanging offense, no honorable death there, none that your kindred could cherish for their comfort. Is it, sirs?"

The boy's lips trembled, but the boy set his jaw. From the Ivanim there was a tightening of the jaw but no more protest, no bravado either.

And the waste of such men – one young enough to be on his first muster, and perhaps too young to restrain his temper or his foolishness, and one old enough to know better than the fight he'd gotten into – filled his mouth with distaste.

"You are mine," he said, "and for your mockery of my law you will learn to serve it, both of you. You will stand guard at my door."

"My lord," the guard sergeant protested.

"Dead, they avail nothing. You will stand that duty, sirs, until Idrys sees fit to relieve you. You will eat with that Guelen unit and bed with them together, chained as you are. No one will remove that chain for any cause, and should one of you die for any cause but in my service, I will flay the survivor alive and burn his father's house. Do you hear me, Erion and Denyn?"

Tears brimmed in the boy's eyes, and the Ivanim's bloodless face looked numb as he nodded.

"Then take up your post," Cefwyn said, and they bowed and went, limping and bloody and unwashed as they were, and still chained together.

He passed them that evening as they stood among the Guelen who would watch the room and not attend him to hall. Blood had dried on their wounds and their faces were ashen with pain and fatigue. He lingered and looked on them, and they gazed on him with apprehension.

"The Guelen do not love their company," Idrys said as they walked together.

"Does any province of this realm love another?" Cefwyn asked. "This is the third generation since the Sihhë kings. Look you back at them. Is this not a perfect type of my father's kingdom?"

"Will you mend it by being murdered by them?"

"You will not move me, Idrys."

"By your own will, you risk your life."

"Go. You know what I will have you to do."

"My lord." Idrys stopped at the stairs. Cefwyn did not look back. The guards that stayed with him were sufficient, and failing those, there was still the bezainted leather and the dagger and sword at his belt.

CHAPTER 19

～

There was formal display in the grand hall, which was Heryn's, like all else; and Cefwyn had not used it since his formal reception by the Aswydds last fall: Heryn's gold and lavish ornamentations were most evident here, the wealth of the province on bold display. So was Heryn himself, with his Guelen-imposed guard, and with Orien and Tarien, joined by a thin surly scattering of Amefin earls and thanes of Heryn's retinue among the crowd of visitors and ealdormen of the town itself . . . the Amefin now being outnumbered by the guests and their attendant bodyguards who crowded the guest quarters and who would soon crowd the hall for the banquet to follow. The tables for that affair were not yet brought in. It was all a standing crowd.

Cefwyn drew a deep breath and walked that center carpet, not looking to the sides, and wondering the while about the safety of his back, on which he felt Heryn's stare, not unaccompanied by the stare of outraged Amefin nobles.

He reached the middle level of the dais and turned, seated himself in the right-hand seat of the throne set there. Then, stiff with hatred, Heryn advanced as far as the third step from the top, bowed to him, and took that place which the Duke of the Amefin had to accept with the prince-viceroy occupying the throne above him.

"My lords," Cefwyn hailed them, and the Amefin chamberlain rapped the floor with his staff until silence reigned.

One by one the lords were proclaimed, in order of honors and precedence – himself, Heryn, Pelumer, Cevulirn, Umanon, and Sovrag, with trumpet flourishes and unfurling of banners from their standards, pronouncements of lengthy titles and proclamations of ancestral rights, an ordinarily tedious business, one through which the Crown Prince, and likely the lord being named, might watch the candles, or add chains of figures, or parse antique verbs, or do any number of things to maintain himself awake.

But tonight was an uncommonly late assembly, beneath huge chain-anchored circles of oil-filled lamps, which lent their own odd pungency to the war of perfumes and the aroma of foods waiting in the east hall. Tonight there was a perilous rivalry of voices, of display, of elaboration and martial character, each trying to outdo the other. Cefwyn sat still and watchful throughout, acknowledging compliments and appeals to his personal attention as required, his eyes straying often about the vast ornate hall – easy to become distracted in the forest of serpentine columns and the flash of banners of lords and minor lords. The crowd of Amefin and outsiders alike shifted at each new name, anxiously to estimate each other, to see who was named and who was not, and with what honors. His eyes were not for that detail so much as for the strategic location of his guardsmen, the steel glint of businesslike weapons, the movement of Amefin servants and messengers about the room on, one assumed, needful errands.

As prince, he had to face this assemblage. As prince, he had to hope that no one trod on disputed titles or territory that might bring the knives out. – Sovrag was the one to watch for outright provocation, Umanon for a test of the prince's authority to summon them – but grant Umanon would be here among the first if he thought that business might be discussed that could work against him. Wild bulls, his father was wont to call the lords of Imor; and having them in yoke meant contentions his father was accustomed to handle. Watch them, he thought: the barons would try him, they damned well would try him.

"My lords," he said at last, when all ceremony was done, "we bid you welcome in the hall."

"My lord Prince." That was Sovrag's booming voice, coming from the left-hand assembly, and he looked toward the man, whose blue breeks, gilt-edged green cloak, and dark red doublet made him seem more appropriate to brigandage than to the lordship of a province.

And he foreknew exactly what the matter was that Sovrag would bring; he could, with a little deftness, shift it aside. But Sovrag was unsubtle and in his way easier to manage than, say, Cevulirn, on whom one could get no hold at all. So he nodded assent, beckoned, and the big riverlord came forward and set hands on hips in the center of the hall, upheaving all business, all ceremony, on a point of personal interest.

"My lord Prince, in all respect, welcome we may be, but there's a man of mine in question. I'd know about that matter before we set hand to matters of the court. He's a boy, no more'n that, and some Ivanim's got his nose in the air because my boy walked in front of his damn horse."

"A hanging offense, my lord of Olmern, that's the issue. Not the damn horse. Nothing else but the drawing of weapons under the King's peace. Yours is not the only lordship involved."

Cevulirn stepped forward, as colorless in gray and white as Sovrag was garish. His pale regard was chill and angry. "Since the matter is now public," said the Ivanim lord in a voice for which others made silence, soft and piercing as a slight. "You have shamed a man of honor and of long and personal service to me, Your Highness. You would have received my protest privily this evening, and it is doubtless awaiting your attention through appropriate process, but since the lord of Olmern brings the matter in public, and since it seems Your Highness' pleasure is to hear it, I will say that I have had a report of the incident. The law decrees hanging. It does not decree the shameful state which you have accorded him."

"What, shame to be taken to my service? I think not."

"He was the innocent party, my lord Prince."

"I judge both guilty. And I give you clear notice now, my lords, in all love and confidence in your good will, if there is further fighting in this town or in this hall, I shall see the surviving participants personally, and deal with them by the King's justice. These two, Olmernman and Ivanim, I make an example of my mercy. If they serve me well, they will find me a generous lord; if they do not, I have already made judgment of the survivor, and it is severe indeed, Your Grace, be it your man, be it Olmern's. I am completely impartial as to which. I will not have weapons drawn or blood shed in this hall or anywhere within this gathering of forces."

There was silence in the hall.

"Do you challenge my claim on their persons?"

Cevulirn made a bow. "No, Your Highness."

"Olmern?"

"Aye," said Sovrag. "You may have the lad, m'lord Prince, and welcome to him. He's a good boy." Sovrag frowned at Cevulirn. "But if there be any provocation of my men – from His Grace, there –"

"I am determined," Cefwyn said, raising his voice, "that there be peace in this hall. I trust you hear me. Shall I have it proclaimed by the herald, whose voice is louder?"

"Beware, lest we all have Guelen guards," Heryn said.

"Dear Lord Heryn," said Cefwyn, leaning back on his throne and giving Heryn a sidelong glance. "I rely on the honor of our guests, who are all honorable and proven honorable in good service to the Crown; but such is the love I bear you, Heryn Aswydd, that I shall continue to lend you Guelen guards. Indeed – such is the prevalence of assassins in your domain," he added, looking around at the others, "that I advise you all to sleep with guarded doors. Mauryl Gestaurien is dead. Doubtless that sad rumor had reached you. There have been now ten attempts on my life, of which the south gate is witness, save the last, where we lost good men in my stead, and yet Lord Heryn swears the district under his control – ah, what else of gossip have I forgot? Armed bandits in the countryside, of which there now are fewer. Perhaps you have had such difficulties, my lords. If so I earnestly pray you advise me."

"We passed a village at the border south," said Pelumer, "Trys Ceyl was the name of it – Trys Ceyl and Trys Drun – and the folk in that area begged us stay, grace of a good neighbor, so of that grace and my knowledge ye'd approve, m'lord Prince, a handful of my men did stay there. We've had our troubles the last two years on the forest marches: brigandage, livestock stolen, skulkers about the haystacks. Our rangers report no substance we can pursue on any large scale. Movements in the woods, shepherds startled, lost goats. But two of the village folk at Trys Ceyl seem to have disappeared without trace, they say there, man and son, and I thought it worth leaving five men to see."

"Well done, and I hope they find nothing so grave as we did by Emwy. Aught else observed by any of you?"

"Naught but quiet on Lenúalim's south," said Sovrag. "Upriver . . . I wouldn't say. It's eerie and quiet at Ynefel and all through that wood, and we sailed past it by broad day and set no foot on that shore. Ynefel's always chancy, and things come unhinged lately. A lot odd's come to us by rumor."

"Odd things among the Elwynim?"

"I heard, leastwise third-hand, aye, m'lord Prince, troubles and outlawry pourin' out of the fringes of Marna. Which of course we don't directly see, lord Prince, respecting as we do Mauryl's dividing of the river. Except you call us north, of course."

He chose not to challenge that. Or to say what his spies knew of Sovrag's occasional goings and comings. "And by bridges to the south?"

"Bridges, aye, well – I don't know. We sailed that stretch out of Marna at night, but I'd swear there wasn't decks on 'em. Looked open to the sky, to me, and showin' stars through, lord Prince."

He looked at the frowning lord beside and behind Sovrag, whose lands were also on the river and bordering both Amefel and Olmern to the south. "Imor?"

"In the south," said Umanon with a sour glance at Sovrag, "our only troubles are local, and, unlike some, we never fare north. We have had misgivings of Olmern's adventures, however limited, and I do not hesitate to say so."

"Much of our trouble, too, is local," said Heryn unasked. "Good my lords, look to your own rights and do as pleases you, but, as for me, I do nothing until the King responds to my inquiries. You should know this assemblage is without the King's knowledge or sanction."

"But lawful." Cefwyn held up a finger.

"But lawful," Heryn admitted. "As in the matter of the Ivanim and the Olmernman, what my lord Prince wills becomes lawful."

There was deathly silence in the hall. Heryn awaited some reaction to his brazen defiance. The barons and the Amefin lords alike waited to see what would result. Cefwyn let the silence go on. And on.

And suddenly in the outer hall was the tread of guards. Cefwyn leaned back then, a smile on his face, for the timing, thanks to Heryn, was far better than his precise order could have arranged. Heads began to turn.

It was Idrys, and Uwen, and following them, startlingly pale-skinned in black doublet and short black cloak, Tristen, escorted by the red-cloaked Guelen guard.

And the arms that Tristen wore on his shoulder for this oath-giving were arms unseen in the court of Ylesuin for more than two generations, the silver Tower of Ynefel in chief, above the eight-pointed Sihhë Star.

A page carried in and unfurled a banner, black and argent, bearing the same. A murmur of consternation erupted as Amefin townfolk and lords of Ylesuin together realized what banner they were seeing. The chamberlain pounded for order. Heryn had moved a step down from his entitled stance on the dais, and more slowly Cefwyn arose, walked down to the last step and held out his hand for Tristen.

Look neither left nor right, he had personally warned Tristen, and Tristen's pale eyes were locked now on his as a drowning man's on a sole promise of safety.

Their hands met, and Tristen, as he had been told, went to one knee on the step and pressed Cefwyn's hand to his lips.

"What manner of sham is this?" Heryn cried aloud. "This man is a wandering idiot, a halfwit known to everyone in Henas'amef!"

Cefwyn closed his hand on Tristen's and drew him to his feet, prepared to turn and deal with Heryn, but to his astonishment Tristen himself turned, fixed Heryn with a cold and clear-eyed stare, and swept it then on all the other lords.

A silence fell strangely in the hall, so that suddenly the chamberlain's staff rang loud in the silence.

"Tristen Lord Warden of Ynefel and Lord High Marshal of Althalen," Cefwyn said into the silence. "Confirmed in those honors by me, to the lordships thereof and to all rights and inheritances in those lands to which he is as Mauryl Gestaurien's heir entitled."

"No!" Heryn shouted above the instant tumult. "My lords, this wretch came to the gates babbling Mauryl's name, and upon that sole evidence this whole invention is made! He is no son or heir of Mauryl Gestaurien! And he is no kindred of Elfwyn Sihhë, only some peasant halfwit who may or may not have been Mauryl's servant – hence his gentleman's speech! We all know that Mauryl had neither wife nor heir, legitimate or otherwise, unnatural that he was, – if in fact the old hermit at Ynefel *was* Mauryl Gestaurien. If, if, if, and upon those *ifs* this *perhaps*-servant of the man who was *perhaps* Gestaurien who was *perhaps* of Ynefel and *perhaps* the same Mauryl who was the ally of the Amefin is confirmed to equality with us, whose service to the Marhanen house is long and honorable. I protest it bitterly, my lord Prince! I do more than vehemently protest – I refuse to recognize this travesty on the honorable dead of this province, until I see more proof!"

The resultant murmur of voices quickly died in the crash of the chamberlain's staff. Cefwyn lifted a hand, unhurried, unmoved, satisfied in the attention.

"He was Mauryl's, but no servant," Cefwyn said. "And indeed the old man was Mauryl Gestaurien and indeed he had neither wife nor *natural* heir."

There was silence, profound silence attendant on that announcement, and about the room no few of the hearers made pious signs that rapidly became a contagion. The patriarch of the local Quinalt made the same signs, and stared round-eyed and set-lipped at the proceeding. The rival and obscure Bryaltine abbot, close to the earth of Amefel, stood his ground among his supporters, a knot of three black robes in the shadows. The Quinalt patriarch looked to be gathering himself to speak.

"Please you, my lords," Cefwyn said before that could happen. Least of all did he want the priests to fling pronouncements into the charged and anxious air. He caught the eye of the patriarch and glared a warning. The old man, who was, only yestereve, the recipient of a truly munificent Crown donative, closed his mouth and continued to glare. "My lords, Heryn has said there is no sufficient cause to have summoned you; in some quarters of Heryn's domain, my motives are suspect, it seems – and surely he but reports the sentiment of his lords; but consider how you will fare, my lords, if bridges are being built in secret, and if the Elwynim do plan incursion – as certain ones would urge on me is the case. Mauryl has fallen, our borders to the west are undefended; and now assassins work to remove me from command and lately to defy Mauryl's will and succession. Lord Tristen himself could tell you what he has seen. Question him if you will."

Utter silence; Heryn first, Cefwyn thought, he will attack.

"How came Mauryl dead?" Sovrag leapt in first, daring where even Heryn had caution, and Tristen turned in that direction.

"The wind came," Tristen said, "and the balconies fell. It was wicked, that wind, sir. – And Mauryl said I should follow the road. That was what I did. The road brought me here, and I came to Prince Cefwyn. And to master Emuin."

There was silence still. Cefwyn realized his hand was clenched painfully. He relaxed it. The spell of Tristen's voice had fallen over the hall. He knew then that he had not misjudged Tristen, that Tristen's very artlessness had power; that there was ensorcellment in his look and in his voice that had stopped far less gentle men in their tracks; and most of all that Tristen would, if asked, tell exactly what he believed to be the truth, come hell, come brimstone, wizardry, or the Quinalt's blanched faces.

"Do you intend to send him to Ynefel, my lord Prince?" asked Pelumer suddenly. "Is he to take Mauryl's place?"

"No," said Tristen. That was all, in a silence made for a much longer remark.

Sovrag cleared his throat. "There's been no immediate trouble, I can say. Aye, we trade with Mauryl, aye, there being no King's law against it, I'll own to it, a boat to the landing by Ynefel's bridge, and by morning the goods are gone and there'll be a batch of simples and weight of gold in the boat, our own man never knowing how . . . ."

There was a murmur, Umanon with his guard, but it died.

"And by morning, I say, the goods'd be gone, but now – now, I suppose, there's an end of that trade."

"Not Sihhë gold, of course," Cefwyn said softly, the Crown claiming all such hoards, where found.

"No Sihhë gold, m'lord Prince, no Star on 't. But fair weight of gold she were. And we give tax on it, as m'lord Prince can know by the accounts, same as any trade: we writ 'er down wi' the King's man. But I say this: there were peace with Mauryl and peace with the border yonder, only so's we stayed out of Marna Wood except as we was supplying him. I know men of Elwynor to try to come south and never come through. Not a year gone, some of mine got greedy and came off the boat and tried the old man's gate, but no one that went in came out – and I got the word of the man that stayed wi' the boat that there was shrieking and screaming aplenty in the keep, fit to chill his blood. But no harm come to him, and he fell into a sleep as always and waked wi' the goods gone, and the gold and the simples as always in the boat with him. The men that left that boat never come back. I can swear to ye, and so would that man swear, that that were Mauryl indeed, that old man in Ynefel. And I say, too, Mauryl's demand of flour and oil and all did double this spring, to the wonder of us all."

A murmur went through the hall, at that. Cefwyn paid sharp attention, thinking to himself that here was a source very few consulted – a source on that river that saw more than he admitted to seeing, because he was most often breaking the King's law and hedging on breaking Mauryl's partition of the river into two parts eighty years ago – north for Elwynor's commerce, and south for Ylesuin's, to the profit of Olmern and Imor.

"Thank you, m'lord of Olmern," Cefwyn said. "And, Tristen?"

"My lord?"

"Will you offer peace to all the lords assembled, for Ynefel and Althalen?"

"Most gladly, sir."

"And be a loyal subject of the Marhanen Crown?"

"Yes, m'lord Prince. Most gladly."

"And a pious subject of His Majesty?"

"Most gladly, m'lord Prince."

It was very quiet, for a questioning of rite and ritual. It was more quiet than attended a royal heir's investiture, he could attest to that; more quiet, more sobriety, and more careful attention to implications of words the lords all, at one time or another, memorized and mouthed, believing in the oath, it might be, but never understanding as applicable to themselves the prohibition against sorcery.

A second kneeling, a second impression of Tristen's lips against his hand and placing of hands within hands: he raised Tristen up, set a brotherly kiss on his cheek, and the whole hall breathed with one breath.

There was a move at his left then, and he glanced aside in alarm, recoiled a step sideways as Heryn cast himself to his knees at his feet – his first thought was for the hands, a weapon, but the hands were empty, and there were Guelen all about as alarmed as he, whose hands *were* on weapons. Pikes had half-lowered.

"My lord Prince," Heryn said in the dying murmur of alarm. "I beg forgiveness of you and of him. I thought – I most earnestly thought this was a sham meant against this

331

hall. Gods witness I was wrong. I am a loyal man to the King, and to his sons. Gracious Highness, forgive my suspicion."

"It is late for that."

"I withdraw my protests, and will swear so."

"I do not withdraw my Guelen, and will swear so."

"I must bear that, then," Heryn said, and when sarcasm might have prevailed, there was no apparent edge to his voice, only anguish.

Something must be done with him; the whole hall waited, anxious, skeptical of Heryn alike, perhaps embarrassed in Heryn's fall from dignity, perhaps thinking of their own weapons: Cefwyn knew the volatility of the region all too well; but he considered rejecting Heryn and his offer, and his tax records, a moment or two longer than he might ordinarily contemplate a move to fracture the peace.

But after such a delay, enough to make Heryn's face go to pallor, he beckoned the man to rise, and, still frowning, gave him the formal embrace courtesy and custom demanded after such an accepted capitulation.

Still there was a cold feeling next his heart while Heryn touched him. He was very glad of the leather armor he wore, and he said to himself angrily that he had indeed been in bed with but two of the Aswydd whores, and them less shameless.

He set Heryn back coldly and turned his shoulder to him as other lords and their adherents came to the steps, quick to protest their support in more dignified terms than Heryn's example. Even dour Cevulirn came and offered more than ritual support against, Cevulirn said, the rumors of bridge-building.

Came, too, one town official of Henas'amef, creaking with age, who seized Tristen's hand, to Tristen's clear astonishment, and knelt and kissed it, tears running down his face.

"M'lord Sihhë," the man hailed him. "We believe in ye."

Mark that for remembrance, Cefwyn thought angrily, wondering at the man's brazen act; and then saw Tristen's look, which was touched by the gesture and was completely bewildered as the old man's tears wet his hand.

Shame reproved him then, as he saw that there was no

politicking at all in the old man's tears and trembling. It was
no treason, only an old man who had waited a long time to
see what he was willing to agree the old man had indeed seen
– and a better age for the folk of Amefel and Elwynor if it
were true and accepted by the Marhanen: *that* was what he
had held out to the population of Amefel. He saw it clearly
now. The frail old official knelt and kissed his hand, too, and
he helped the man up, and, more, embraced him. He was
frightened – disturbed to the heart – by his own jealous
impulses.

He knew his grandfather's mind, the quick suspicion, the
angers, the jealousy with which the old man had brought up
his two sons – the same jealousy that worked within him and
within all the Marhanens. It was their curse. It was their
besetting fault. He kissed the old man on the cheek, in a cold-
hearted demonstration of Marhanen recognition of the native
Amefin.

He was Marhanen. He couldn't help the politicking. It,
along with temper, ran in the blood.

All about him after that was tumult. A press of Amefin
bodies unnerved his guards. He, with Tristen, received the
respects of Amefin who never before this would have dared
approach the Prince of Ylesuin.

The hour was his. He had made peace in his district. A Sihhë
banner was on display in a hall where it had once hung as
sovereign, now grouped with the banners of Ylesuin. A Sihhë,
aetheling in the minds of the people, had sworn fealty and allegiance to the Marhanen prince and been recognized and legit-
imized – a prince himself: that went with it. The prophecy on
which Elwynor should reunite with Amefel – was fulfilled, but
not as the Regents of Elwynor would have it.

Servants were carrying in the tables, meanwhile. Annas
was in charge. Annas could read the subtleties of a situation
the way master Tamurin could read accounts, and knew when
to make distraction, and when to make it loud and urgent.

*   *   *

333

There was venison, there was pork, there was rabbit and there were partridge pies, a specialty of the region. There were pitchers of wine, wheels of white and yellow cheese, white bread and black. Plates whisked off and onto tables with the precision of weapons-drill, and there was an endless succession of courses, a loaf of eggs-in-sausage, a course of roast veal and another of fish, delivered not alone to the huge hall, but to the adjacent Zeide weapons-court, where the gentry of Henas'amef, in all their finery, had had the prince's invitation to the tables set up since evening.

There were Guelen guards at every entry, and weapons not in urgent display, but the guards were sober, watchful, and well convinced every potential assassin or hirer of assassins among the Amefin was likely a guest tonight in hall or out in the common court. But festivities and food abounded in the courtyards as well as in the hall, not to mention the kettles of stew set up in the lower town court, offering supper to any bringer of a bowl and supper and a trencher of bread to those who had none, on the prince's largesse.

Pay due courtesy to the guards, weary and sleepless as they had already been: Idrys had admonished them, to a man, on the prince's orders, that there were to be no complaints of pushing, no press with pikes or weapons, no hesitation if needed, but no temptation of Amefin tempers. And cheer spread throughout the Zeide's courts, audible through the windows above the tumult inside: there were cheers raised, there were toasts, there was moderate tipsiness, but only once so far was there a breach of the peace, and that over a young damsel of the town and a trio of suitors. There might have been a resort to the King's law. There might have been arrests.

But, informed of the cause, Cefwyn chose not to notice it, nor to have the guards acknowledge seeing it. He had Heryn on one side and Umanon on the other, with Sovrag and Pelumer within easy distance, Cevulirn and Tristen out of easy speaking range at the high table.

He also had Idrys at his back, constantly, as Uwen held anxious watch at Tristen's, and other lords' men hovered in similar fashion. If there was to be amanita in the sauce or a knife drawn at table, there was at least sufficient force to be sure of revenge. But Heryn had no Amefin, but a Guelen man to watch his back, and it might be well, Cefwyn thought, that Heryn had that for his own protection. Before he had even come down to hall to hear Heryn's protestations of undying affection, he had set the Guelen servants free to gossip to their Amefin counterparts of Heryn's account books, a dispensation of gossip loosed with the same mindful intent with which he would have signed a death warrant.

And if there was tonight any anxiousness in Henas'amef, particularly in that courtyard, besides the raising of a Sihhë standard contrary to the King's law, it surely revolved around those books. Two messages thus far had come to him from the Zeide doors, stating that the sender had information on usury, if the prince would send messengers to this appointment and that on the morrow.

The prince tucked the small missives in his shirt and measured his wine consumption, while Heryn drank far too much and Umanon far too little to be pleasant.

Sovrag leaned up the table, jeopardizing a goblet. "M'lord Prince! D' the Elwynim know about this Sihhë lad?"

"I wager they will," he called back.

"Ye wisht 'em t' know, m'lord? We can 'complish that by mornin', an ye will."

"I think we can wait, m'lord Sovrag, on the ordinary flow of gossip. On the other hand –" A thought came to him, not a new thought, but new to the moment.

"Eh?" A page was serving sweetmeats. Sovrag's fist seized a full share and two, and Sovrag never moved from staring at him. "Eh, m'lord?"

"Bridges! I'd know for certain about those bridges!"

"Along the Elwynim reach, me lord?"

"Oh, aye, on the Elwynim reach. No, I was asking for the Arachim's bridges! I'd know if there's preparation for decking – such as could be brought up quickly, laid on or taken off."

Sovrag grinned. "Well, I passed right under Emwy's, and

335

saw nothing – but, then I wasn't looking for decking stowed out of sight. I could have a boat have a look there and on upstream, m'lord Prince, if you was to promise 'em lads a sovereign."

"You have it," he said, to the scandal of lord Umanon, past whom the unlordly barter flowed. "Two sovereigns if they don't tell the Elwynim!"

Sovrag pounded the table and laughed aloud. "Ye got 'er, m'lord, ye got 'er! Brigoth!" He summoned his man close, seized him by the front of his doublet to bring him closer, and shouted into his ear something about a boat and launching by moonset.

"Idrys," Cefwyn said, and Idrys leaned into range. "Two sovereigns."

"Yes, Your Highness." The stress on his title said what Umanon's silent outrage said, that the Prince of Ylesuin had no need to haggle with a subject lord, or to pay him for his services. But the two sovereigns would find their way to Sovrag's purse, he was well certain, and he by the gods liked a lord who for once put a simple price on his work.

"He seems a pleasant enough witchling!" Sovrag said next. "He don't look more 'n a lad."

"He's honest," Cefwyn said back, knowing the voices were carrying. "And fair-minded."

"Mauryl always dealt fair," Sovrag said. "If he come by Mauryl's will, and if the gold from that trade be done, then what he says is so, the old man's gone. So say I. And him sworn t' you, me lord, and to the King?"

"By his oath, sir, yes."

"'At's a neat trick," Sovrag said, at which there were several shocked faces. And then seized a page. "Pour for the Sihhë lord," Sovrag said. "A health for His Lordship of the Sihhë!"

The page ran to do as he was bidden, by a man of Sovrag's size. Lie down with hounds, Cefwyn said to himself, sorry now he'd set the man in motion, but, refusing to be set aback by the riverlord's raucous good will, he rose himself and proposed the health, of the King first, of the company second, of the Sihhë lord third.

Annas himself poured Sovrag's cup full, one of the big ones, at each toast, and at each health, after his prince's own lengthy praise of the King, of the company, and of Mauryl's unexpected heir, Sovrag drained his cup to the dregs.

Cefwyn proposed the health of their Amefin hosts, at last, not mentioning Heryn, who doubtless smoldered in indignation.

Which saved him the decision, finally, whether to toast Heryn last, for Sovrag collapsed off the bench, and he had drunk every toast, himself.

But started with fewer. Which, he heard remarked as the banquet dwindled down to the determined drinkers, might well become legend, how Prince Cefwyn, standing, had drunk Sovrag of the Olmernmen under the table.

It was not at all the report he wished his royal father to receive.

But the evening, he judged, when he declared the lords all duly welcomed, was otherwise a success.

Still, afterward, walking up the stairs to his apartment with Tristen at his side and Idrys and Uwen Lewen's-son at his back, he could not shake the conviction that the evening had not gone quite as well as he would have wished, and that the lords liked each other no better than they had in the beginning.

Heryn was the poison, he said to himself. Heryn had no reason to be pleased with the evening, far less reason to be pleased with Tristen's appearance under forbidden arms and, what had surely galled Heryn, Tristen's health being drunk quite willingly by the other lords.

And least of all could Heryn be happy in the slights heaped on him by the prince under his roof and in the failure of the southern lords, especially the lesser lords of Amefel, traditionally fractious against the Marhanen, to rise in support of his challenge. That such a man as Heryn had accepted the

337

humiliation of apology was not incredible after the rest of Heryn's performance; the sincerity of it, however, was far from credible, and he felt uneasy even with the guards around. He asked himself how he had fallen into the trap of accepting Heryn's public contrition, or how he had gone from being certain he wished to be rid of Heryn to envisioning ways to keep Heryn, momentarily forgetting his sins of taxation, in favor of the functions Heryn and his predecessors had very aptly performed for the Marhanen, namely keeping a key and very troublesome province quiet. Heryn knew the Amefin rebels well enough to prevent any untimely rising. In point of fact, Heryn might have no interest whatever in rebellion against the whole Marhanen line. It was most particularly Cefwyn Marhanen that Heryn wished dead: Cefwyn who was onto his tricks, Cefwyn who had probed into his books, Cefwyn who would be far too active and aggressive a Marhanen king. If Efanor became King, Efanor, who hated the borderlands, would never visit here, and *that* would suit Heryn Aswydd well. As their royal father had suited the Aswydds – until he produced an heir perhaps too forward in his opinions and too public in his excesses, an heir whose edges King Ináreddrin wished to blunt against provincial obduracy and the facts of rule in an unwilling and witch-haunted border district.

But Heryn was (postponing the decision on Heryn's fate, at least) safely under guard. His sisters, ordinarily the bright moths to lordly flame, had flittered away to guarded quarters and lordly virtue was safe under this roof tonight, at least from the Aswyddim.

They reached the crest of the stairs, the safe territory, the vast torchlit hall stretching away into intermittent darkness. They walked together in separate silences until the guard which escorted Tristen necessarily parted company from that which stayed about him, going to the opposite side of the hall.

Then he realized how very absorbed in his own thoughts he had been, and looked up to bid Tristen good night, to – as he realized he should – tell him his hours of study with Annas had done well for him.

But he had waited an instant too long. Tristen had his back to him now, and walked on with Uwen and his escort, head bowed, a tall, formidable shape, did one not know how gentle-spirited – black sparked with silver, under the dim light of the wall-sconces, which seemed far too grim a color for their childlike guest.

So somber Tristen seemed, so strangely sad and defenseless in that company of soldiers, though he towered over the most of them.

Elfwyn, the thought came unbidden, and a chill came over him. Feckless, murdered Sihhë king.

Elfwyn would not even fight for his own life, at the last. He would not leave his hall or his studies until the Marhanen soldiers came for him, to bring him out to die. Elfwyn had cared only for his books, and they had burned those with Althalen.

So, so much knowledge and lore of the Sihhë had been lost there.

He had launched war – or peace – this night. He had raised the standard his grandfather and his father alike had banned for fear of Elwynim pretenders.

But he had granted what he had granted to Tristen even to the good of the Elwynim. In Tristen, in this sonless dwindling of the Regents' line in Elwynor, he had a chance for peace and resolution of the old dispute, and Mauryl had sent it to him, perhaps a test of Ylesuin's willingness for peace – and a test of his kingship, what he would be, what he might be, if he could settle that old dispute and make a lasting peace with the realm of Elwynor – itself containing six provinces – that had once, with Ylesuin, Amefel, Marna, and lands west and south, constituted the Sihhë domains.

The chained men at his door jarred his muddled thoughts: the Olmern lad and the Ivanim were still on watch. He saw the boy's eyes glassy in the glare of candles.

He stopped.

"Is this man ill?"

The Ivanim lordling maintained grim silence. The boy said, "No, Your Highness."

He looked to the Guelen sergeant. "Change guard, sergeant. Idrys has, I presume, given you my conditions to them?"

"Yes, my lord Prince."

"They're to receive the same standard fare and the same watches as your own. Do gently to them if they are gentle men with each other. If one kills the other, report it to me. They know the consequence."

"Highness."

Cefwyn went into his apartment, seeking the warmth of his own fire. He wrapped his arms close about his sides and stood with head bowed, suddenly feeling the weight of the metal-studded leather. His joints ached.

"M'lord."

Idrys startled him. He had not known Idrys had come in yet.

"Guards are to remain as set, m'lord Prince?"

"Gods, yes, they remain."

"Yes, my lord Prince."

Idrys left him, seeming satisfied. Cefwyn walked into the other room, his bedchamber, his eyes automatically searching the shadows for ambush. It was lifelong habit. He expected to die by assassination – someday. It was the common fate in his house. He did not fear the shadows – as his grandfather had and his father did. He needed no candles. He had no faith in the Quinalt or in candles blessed by priests. It was his inherited nature, perhaps, to grow gloomy and fatalistic.

But he had perhaps solved Mauryl's riddle, this Shaping the wizard had cast on the Marhanen doorstep. He was the third generation after Althalen, the generation in which all curses and chances, by all the accounts, ultimately came home. He was the King-to-be of Ylesuin. And Tristen – Tristen could become the surety the Marhanen King had on this border, perhaps a provincial lord, even a tributary king, himself, over a diminished realm, in which men of the east would not be subordinate to Sihhë lords or Sihhë kings. It was peace he had begun to build, it was a settlement of ancient disputes. It was the dream of a kingdom without the need to keep half its peasants constantly under arms, or with weapons within reach; a kingdom without the need to dread their own western provinces as a breeding-place of assassins. He had seen enough of assassins, attended enough executions, seen enough funerals.

And if his father the King had meant a year here to blunt his heir's untried edges, then his father equally well might know that granting him an independent command might not bring the two of them into congruency of thought. He grew less, rather than more, like his father. He tinkered with mercy. He temporized with witches. He – gods, only to think of it now as done – had raised the forbidden standard in the sight of the Quinalt and the southern lords.

He could hear his brother say, Father, he's lost his wits. He's bewitched.

But he could by no means hear his brother say, Father, send me to set things right. Efanor had no liking for Amefel or long discomfort.

Efanor, younger brother, was sitting well-appointed to Llymaryn, a province where no hint of rebellion stirred the leaves of summer, where vineyards thrived, where pious Quinalt orthodoxy ruled the land and no one had contrary or troubling thoughts. Conscience sat easy on Llymaryn, in the holy heart of a people of entirely Guelen descent, a land without foreign borders to ward, a district where the lords vied with each other only in complimenting the King's younger son, in telling him he was right, and good, and just, and that divine justice approved him.

Efanor spent his year of administrative trial in paradise, praised and pampered – and probably still virgin: the Quinalt ruled Llymaryn, and lately it seemed to rule Efanor's every thought.

He stripped off the red doublet and dropped it – not on the floor: he had more regard of the pages who likewise suffered this crucible of his heirship, lads who grew wary, and thin about the cheeks, and learned to go in pairs. "Boy!" he shouted, and a page, sleeping on the bench, leapt up and rushed to catch the garment. And his shirt, after.

Idrys came in. He heard the outer door shut and heard Idrys stirring about in the other room – heard Idrys talking to one of the pages, probably filling his head with instructions to watch the prince's guest.

Idrys did not approve what he had done. But Idrys was not his father's man. He began to believe that. Idrys had gone very far with him tonight, across a boundary of decision that, now, either admitted them to negotiation with the Elwynim, or committed them if not to war, at least to a period of very unsettled peace. He had the forces now to make the point. He had demonstrated he could summon them. He had demonstrated his willingness to do new things.

He would be interested to see what Sovrag's lads turned up, whether there were, as he feared, bridges built or reinforced, ready to receive decking which could be brought up very quickly, and whether the Elwynim were in fact preparing for war, behind the cover of this bride-offering.

He would, he resolved, see whether the bride was still waiting, or what Elwynor's Regent would do, once he knew the Sihhë King-to-Be was in Marhanen hands.

CHAPTER 20

The sun flooded through the panes of a room grown familiar over days of confinement. The pigeons were far less frequent on this straighter side of the building, where ledges and slants were less convenient and fewer. Tristen lay a time abed and stared at the daylight through the glass, seeing no reason this morning that he should rise from bed, no particular reason that he should do anything. He had performed last night as Annas wished. He supposed that he had pleased Cefwyn. He supposed he had pleased the lords Annas had named to him, and perhaps even the lord regarding whom Annas had warned him.

But that was done. He had no permission to do anything. There had not, at least, been such permission yesterday; he expected none today.

Hearing the servants stir about, and hearing Uwen's voice, he knew that Uwen would be walking in, attempting to be cheerful, asking him – as he had asked him in days past – what he would do today, and making idle talk to fill the time.

He was grateful for Uwen. And he would send Uwen down to the library to bring him another book of philosophy or poetry, since Cefwyn denied him books of other sort. He would attempt to read Mauryl's own Book, of which he had less and less hope.

He told himself, or had told himself once, that if he could read it, all conditions would change, and he would become wise, and make no more mistakes, so that Cefwyn would approve him, and he would become, as Cefwyn had said he would be, his friend.

But since he had agreed to be Cefwyn's friend, he had heard a great deal of how he should bear himself and what he should answer, and how not to make mistakes – and he had seen very much of Annas, who was kindly, and patient – but very little of Cefwyn.

A prince was busy a great deal of the time, so Uwen said.

A prince had a great many people wanting his time and his attention. Mauryl had been busy with his calculations – and he had learned to be content just that Mauryl was there. He should be content that Cefwyn was there, that was all.

And that was too anxious a thought to stay in bed with. He gathered himself out of the sheets, crossed the cool floor barefoot to the fireplace and poked up the small fire, a pile of ash and ember dwarfed by the size of the hearth, that let them brew tea and warm water, – all of which servants would gladly bring from downstairs. But then it was cool by the time it reached him; and sometimes it came so late he had forgotten any want for it. He much preferred to do that duty for himself, and liked the fireside; he had seen that Cefwyn maintained a small kettle, too, in his very fine apartment, with all the servants at his beck and call, so he decided no one minded.

Uwen came in before the servants, and wished him good morning. Waiting for the water to warm, he shaved himself with mostly cold water, a task he would not allow to the servants, while Uwen chose his clothing for him and servants stood by to offer it. He washed. He saw his reflection not in the large glass mirror the room afforded, but the little silver one Mauryl had given him, which he had kept through all the changes of accommodations. And it showed him a soberer, a more thoughtful face than it had first reflected on the day that Mauryl had given it to him. It was his mirror of truth. Small as it was, it showed him only his face, not the fine clothing, not the change of room. It showed him the changes in himself, not in what men gave him, or lent him, or the manners others showed to him.

He wondered if Mauryl would approve of what it showed.

He longed to take his books to the garden. They allowed him no such excursions nowadays. They allowed, *they* allowed, and did not allow, he insisted to think, but he knew in truth that it was not *they,* it was Cefwyn who did and did not allow. The *they* who disallowed his wishes and pent him in this room had assumed a faceless impersonality in which he cloaked all Cefwyn's less kind acts. Cefwyn had been kind to him. Cefwyn had hugged him about the shoulders. Cefwyn had treated him as he treated important men. *They* forbade him to go to the garden.

They could without much stretch of imagination at all include Idrys, whose resentment and distrust of him he knew.

They could well embrace the stranger-lords, who breathed war and violence and, last night, had compelled Cefwyn to be like them. He was not certain he liked them.

They could encompass the servants and the guards, who wished him kept out of sight, out of mischief, out of the way of doing foolish things. Mistakes when he was with Mauryl had threatened his safety and Mauryl's, so Mauryl had warned him; now he perceived that his mistakes might have caused the deaths of the men up by Emwy village – he was not certain, but something had caused such things to happen, and mischief was (at least it had been so in Ynefel) his fault, of his inexperience.

So he knew that he might have been at fault, and that his continued confinement might well be justified, or even precautionary, because he was foolish, even though for the brief while on the ride to Emwy, and even afterward, he had had the conviction he knew what to do. That absolute conviction had often led him straight to a fall.

So he persuaded himself that Cefwyn did not will him to be miserable. Cefwyn had no wish at all but to give him fine clothes and to see him take his place among skilled and competent men.

And he thought he had done, last night, everything they wanted of him.

Except – he had not at all liked the undertones of anger; or Heryn's cold defiance of Cefwyn. He had been set aback by Sovrag's roughness, and by Cevulirn's coldness. He was not accustomed to meet such contrary behavior. He saw no one to call them to task – except Cefwyn. Or perhaps the King, whom he had never met.

He did not think Cefwyn had been entirely happy when he left the hall. He did not think the evening had been successful in all regards. He knew that Cefwyn did not like Heryn, and he wondered why Cefwyn had asked him there, or why Heryn had been so provocative of Cefwyn's anger. There were a good many things about the gathering he did not understand, and he hoped that he had, at least for his own part, done what Cefwyn wished.

Defend Cefwyn. Perhaps he should have spoken when Heryn had objected as he had. He thought that he might have been remiss in that. But he had not been certain at the first that Heryn was doing anything amiss. He was always slow to understand such things.

He stood still gazing off into the distance while Uwen was offering him his shirt, and he realized it and pulled it on.

"I don't like the black," he said, regarding what Uwen laid out for him on the bed.

Uwen shrugged helplessly. Uwen had a black surcoat that bore the Sihhë arms minuscule in silver. Gray mail was under it, and the old, worn dagger was at Uwen's belt. Uwen's person was, if not as immaculate as last night, passably so this morning; his scarred face was close-shaven, his gray hair was clipped and combed.

That transformation he had not expected to last, and he knew Uwen was not comfortable or happy in the new finery. So he accepted the offered clothing – he was ordered to wear his mail shirt constantly, another misery that seemed excessive, particularly since he had no permission to leave his apartment. He sat down to pull on his boots, stopped with one on, and stared into the distance, thinking on Ynefel and his own room, and wondering what had become of the pigeons, and where Owl hunted now, and whether, if he went to that river shore, and the bridge, he could find Owl.

The other boot. Uwen stood waiting. He smelled food. It

came unwelcome, arriving with an opening and closing of doors and a clatter of servants in the anteroom.

He thought despondently of sending a direct appeal to Cefwyn, asking to be allowed at least to walk about and see these newcomer lords.

Perhaps they did interesting and lively things.

Perhaps there was someone of the many people who had come in with them who would talk to him.

But he supposed that was exactly what Cefwyn wished him not to do.

Olmern, that name was new to him. But Toj Embrel, Imor, they were Names fraught with curious import in his mind. He recalled the face of the lord of Toj Embrel, the Duke of Ivanor, and wondered if he liked the Duke of Imor – he suspected not, but he had no grounds for that opinion, except Umanon's generally frowning countenance and disdainful expression.

And the men that Cefwyn had chained outside his door: that also had come with these strangers, this unaccustomed touch of cruelty in Cefwyn, an image which frightened him, and had haunted him to bed last night. He wondered if the men were still standing their post in the hall.

"M'lord, are ye well?"

He looked up at Uwen's anxious face. "Well enough." He rose and let Uwen help him on with the coat, the one from last night, with the Tower and the Star on it. Uwen said they would take off the sleeve and the velvet pauldron with the arms, but they had no plain sleeve ready yet.

He cared nothing for whether or not his sleeve had the Sihhë arms. It mattered nothing to him what it did and did not bear. He belted it; he slipped into this belt the silver-hilted dagger that had arrived with the clothing. He stood a moment looking toward the window, until he realized Uwen was still waiting, and that Uwen wanted his own breakfast.

"Have them serve," he said, weighted with mail, smothered in velvet. He wanted most to go outside and into cool air – perhaps down to archive. They might permit that.

"Yes, m'lord," Uwen said solemnly. And winked. "And if ye eat your breakfast proper, His Highness said ye could fly free of tutors and tailors the while. That the garden was safe, and they've led Gery up from the pasture. Thought ye might wish to ride down to the east stables, outside the walls. *If* ye eat your breakfast, m'lord."

"Do they promise?" he said. He had gotten used to *they*. His heart had leapt up, all the same.

"Sure as a holy oath," Uwen said. "You come sit down to breakfast and drink your tea, m'lord. None of this eating standing up like a horse."

The gate bells pealed out. It was far from noon. Such off-hours ringing had previously marked strangers' arrivals.

"I thought all the lords were here," he said.

"I thought they was," Uwen said. "But you have your breakfast. No runnin' off. I have my orders."

He dutifully sat down and let the servants serve him. "Sit down," he wished Uwen, too, and Uwen did, gingerly, and not truly comfortable with the notion.

He had morning tea, he had eggs and fresh rolls and honey. He did not, as Annas had taught him to be careful, spill a drop. But his thoughts were on the bell, as well as the stables, and seeing if he could find the pigeons later today. He slipped a roll into a napkin, and thought to go down to the garden after he came in from his ride.

But then came the Zeide bell itself, that announced arrivals at the fortress gates. "I've finished," he announced, and went to the window to watch that little space that he could see of the aisle toward the stables, just between the west tower and the stable wall.

He heard the clatter of horses on the cobbles, excited, reckoning when they should pass, that he not blink and miss the foremost. Grooms were running, flinging open the gate. There were well-dressed men, too, from the hall.

"Ain't no patrol, m'lord," Uwen murmured. "They don't make no commotion for that. More visitors is coming."

He waited, and just when he thought they would, there

was a flash of riders passing the gap, red banners flying.

"Guelen," Uwen exclaimed. "Good me gods, they be Guelen riders coming in, and under the Dragon. 'At's the King's men."

"From Guelemara?" Tristen asked.

"Aye," Uwen said. "Have to be, someone of the King's own household at the least."

"Emuin."

"It might well be."

Tristen turned in haste from the window, and hurried for the door.

"Lad!" Uwen called after him.

But he was past the servants taking away the breakfast dishes, past the startled door guards with such speed that the two who were duty-bound to follow him were hardly quicker than Uwen to overtake him. He raced down the marble stairs as nimbly as he had run the wooden steps of Ynefel, startling every sentry along the lower hall, but only those at the outer steps moved to bar his way.

"Let me through!" he said, and Uwen and his own guards overtook him just then.

"Let be," Uwen said to the guards, who gave way in confusion, and while Uwen was negotiating himself and the two house guards past the door guards in different colors, Tristen was down the steps.

It was an astonishing commotion in the yard, the red banners, the fine horses, and the finely dressed men – he had not had leave to be down in the yard when the other lords were arriving. He was overwhelmed with the color and the movement, and looked for familiar faces, for soldiers he might recognize, most of all for Emuin.

– *Emuin,* he thought, *reaching for him in that gray space.*

– *Boy?* he heard. *Boy? Where are you?*

But it was instantly clear to him that he was mistaken – Emuin was not near. Emuin was somewhere – by a brook. Under a gray and shadowy willow. Emuin was sitting down and washing his face in water he could not see.

349

– Emuin, I thought it was you. I'm sorry.

– Boy, what's happening? Emuin was at once concerned. Emuin was getting to his feet, batting at insubstantial willow-fronds – his boot was in one hand, his book falling from his lap. Tristen! Who's there? Be careful, I say!

One man in the courtyard sat a white horse and was clad all in red and gold – that man leapt off his mount right at the steps, startling him, drawing his attention back to the courtyard.

But before the lord had gone a step, the white horse reared up, and the man turned about and seized both reins and stableboy, separating one from the other and swearing with such invention as even the soldiers failed to match.

It was amazing confusion; Tristen stood staring as Uwen and his other two guards reached him. Master Haman came from the stableyard to reason with the angry lord in red. Haman took personal charge of the beautiful horse, and the lord, graceless and angry, turned and stamped back to the steps, his fair face scowling.

Tristen backed a step and meant to give the man ample room – but the lord stopped on the steps and looked up directly at him with such surprise and anger that Tristen froze where he stood.

"What in hell are you?" the lord asked him. "What manner of sorry joke is this?"

He lost his tongue, facing such rage as had just stormed through the stableyard and frightened even master Haman.

"M'lord," Uwen prompted him in a low voice and from behind, "this is His Highness Prince Efanor, Prince Cefwyn's younger brother."

"My lord Prince," Tristen began: if this was Cefwyn's brother, he was willing to like this man well for Cefwyn's sake.

But Efanor backed up and set a hand on his sword. "Who are you, I say?"

"Tristen, sir. I assure you –"

"Your Highness," Uwen began, edging past on the steps, offering an empty and an open hand. "If it please Your Highness, –"

"Emuin's foundling." Efanor had eased his posture, but the hand stayed on the hilt and the haughty look and the frown remained. "I would have thought you somewhat younger, by the reports that reached us. Ynefel's cursed badge I do not find amusing, sir. Whose idea? Whose permission?"

Tristen stood completely confused.

"Your Highness," Uwen said. "Your Highness, your pardon, he don't readily understand."

"But I do understand," Tristen said, out of fear for Uwen's safety. "Nothing at all is Uwen's fault. Cefwyn gave me permission for whatever I do, sir."

"Do not," a voice rang out from overhead, higher up the steps. "Do not vent your spleen on him, brother. I am here. Welcome to you." Cefwyn came down beside him. "Tristen, go inside."

"Stay," said Efanor, a brittle and biting voice, like and unlike Cefwyn's, as they two were like and unlike in other particulars. "The man – if it is at all a man – intrigues me. So do these warlike preparations. On whom are we marching? And when? Am I asked to join? Or is this solely a local matter?"

"Ynefel having fallen," Cefwyn said, "the stability of the province is threatened. These are simply precautions."

"Precautions," Efanor said, sweeping a hand at the crowded stables. "No proper room for my horse. Camps about the town, threatening productive orchards and good pastures. You have no patent to raise armies, brother. And this –" He swept the hand toward Tristen. "Amid your army-making, this peculiar precaution. – Is the Sihhë star your new banner – or are you still using the old one?"

"Oh, come, shall we discuss policy in the stableyard? Discourse with the stableboys below? I should have reckoned you would be instant on the road once Heryn's rumors found you. You must not have paused day or night. And how fares our royal father?"

"As quickly. Ahead of me, in fact, with Guelen forces in his command, good brother. Which may or may not please you to hear."

"What, Father's coming *here?*"

"Does it give you pause?"

"In unsettled conditions, it does, yes, brother. Whence this peculiar notion? Where inspired? Surely not Emuin's advice."

"A message of your Amefin host – that said the King might well inquire of the situation on the Lenúalim. That there was serious incursion which you were not able or disposed to contain, at Emwy."

"At Emwy." Cefwyn was puzzled; and Tristen also thought that that was not the truth. "At *Emwy.*"

"Is this not the truth?"

"Where *is* he?"

"I would gather, farther down the road than I, since he purposed to ride straight through. And, laggard I, I determined to take my leisure and find out the situation here. I had thought you on the border like a good commander."

"He will come here first."

"No, I think he purposed to go right on to Emwy itself, and see for himself how things stand."

"Damn his suspicious nature! He must not go there! Efanor, on my oath, I cannot guarantee my own safety there, let alone his."

"And should he lodge here? Rebellion in Amefel, Mauryl dead, villages plundered, general lack of order, imminent dissolution of –"

"Heryn? *Heryn* sent this word? And he believed Heryn Aswydd and not *me?*"

"Aye, Heryn Aswydd. The lawful Duke of Amefel. Say Heryn had complaint of you, and Father would see, before coming here. You know our father. – And I, good brother that I am, I thought at least to shake clerkly matters into order here, and cover at least your minor sins, such as I found . . . "

But Cefwyn was looking elsewhere, as if he heard not a word. "Oh, gods," Cefwyn breathed. "O blessed gods. The old road. To Emwy. Man. *Man!*" he shouted, seizing on the sergeant of the guard who had followed him. "Arrest Heryn Aswydd, his cousins, and his sisters. See to it! Now!"

"Whence comes this?" Efanor demanded. "Blessed *gods*, Cefwyn –"

Cefwyn started down the steps, caught Efanor's arm, brushing past Tristen. "How far ahead of you? How *far*, Efanor?"

"I've no notion I should tell you. I expected *you* to be out on the border. I don't know what I see here!"

"I *live* on the border, brother! This *is* the border! There are no safe places here! What do you think I do here? Heryn Aswydd has asked Father to come to find me at Emwy, on the old road to the border, do you comprehend me in the least, brother? *Yes*, there's trouble there. Sheep-stealing and stone-throwing, most recently. But maybe the building of bridges . . . *my* reports are yet to come in. *How far ahead, damn you?*"

"I lingered in An's-ford. I have no idea. – Cefwyn, in the name of the gods, what's toward? Why should I trust you?"

"Then stay here!" Cefwyn snapped, and cast about desperately. "Guardsman, find Idrys. He's off about the lower hall somewhere. If you can't find him, – send an officer! – Master Haman! Saddle light horses, the fastest, for myself and twenty of my personal guard. Now!"

"Fresh horses!" Efanor shouted suddenly at his men and the stableyard. "We're for the road again!" He overtook Cefwyn and the two of them went side by side down the steps as Tristen stood aside in confusion. "I'll trust you, Cefwyn! But if you lead me out there and make me look the fool in front of Father –"

"Nine heads over the south gate witness what's happening in this province. Heryn lied, lied to cast suspicion on me and draw Father out to the border. Damn the man, I'll explain on the road, brother. There's no time. None! – Tristen, –"

"I'll go with you," Tristen began.

"No!" Cefwyn said angrily. "Uwen, take him out of here and keep him *close*, damn you!"

"Stay," said Efanor. "No, you'll *not* keep your sins at home! I'd have Father see this guest that bides at the heart of this mystery. Let our father judge what you've raised here

353

before he rides into your keeping. Heryn's arrest I abide until I see the truth. But Mauryl's witchling goes with us, brother, or I swear to you I'll advise Father to avoid your hospitality until he has the truth from you – as he is already disposed to demand."

"Brother, I've no time for this!"

"I warn you, this man goes with us or my men arrest him where we stand and take him all the same! It's King's law he's broken, with or without your complicity!"

Cefwyn glared, distraught, then turned to shout orders at others of the guards that stood at the gates.

"Bring him!" Cefwyn shouted over his shoulder, which Tristen thought meant himself.

"My lord, m'lord," Uwen muttered, staying him with a hand. "Beg off from this. I'll go with 'em and speak to questions. There's great danger, d' ye not see? You should go back. Cefwyn could keep you back if you plead ill. He'll not let 'em arrest ye. Ye've every reason to be ill, m'lord, and Efanor hain't th' viceroy here."

"I wish to go," Tristen said, and went down into the yard as he was. "I want Gery, Uwen. Is she able to go?"

"Aye, m'lord. I think so. I'll tell 'em." Uwen sounded not in the least pleased, and that was painful – but so was it painful to stay pent up: he understood arrest, and had had his fill of it at the Zeide gate, his first night. He heard Uwen shouting orders to the stableboys, amid all the other clatter and shouting about the horses being taken into stable, horses being brought out, forty-four in all, horse gear being called for – it was a flood of motion and color, with the kitchen staff and the house guard and finally the Amefin noblefolk and even a straggle of boys from the town, who should not have gotten past the open fortress gates, coming to see what was the clamor.

But after they had gotten the horses from the stable saddled, and just as Uwen and no few others were coming back from the armory, all but running and still buckling buckles and tightening laces, the grooms led red Gery in from the pens and flung her saddle-pad on. Gery stood flicking her ears and staring about at the noise and clatter. Tristen soothed Gery with his hands and let the grooms saddle her. Meanwhile they had found the banner-bearers and Cefwyn's own pages had come running down with Cefwyn's riding cloak and his gloves, while Cefwyn had come back from the armory with a shield, a helmet, and a pair of light-armored leather breeches like the gear Efanor and his men wore. The Guelen guard were fitting out in like gear, men continuing to fit straps, settle gear on horses, while grooms sweated and tightened girths.

In all it was very little time until the escort formed up. A page brought Cefwyn a packet of some kind, a sword and his gauntlets. Uwen had put on his plain leather and metal, with the Marhanen Dragon still blazoned on leather at his shoulder. Uwen had a sword. Tristen had none. But now the troop was mounting up, the banners were up, the standard-bearers were moving to the fore, where he understood he should be. Tristen climbed up on Gery's back as all around him men were mounting up.

"Idrys," Cefwyn said. "Where is Idrys?"

"They have not found him," someone said.

"Damn. – Boy!" Cefwyn shouted at a page. "Boy, you stay – inform Idrys when you find him. Have him tell Cevulirn, and bring a hundred light horse up to Emwy crossing. Inform the rest of the lords, in whatever order you find them. Bid them stay alert, and be careful – this is important, boy! – be careful of men riding without a banner! There may be Elwynim across the river, but they may equally well be King's men, spying."

Cefwyn pulled his horse about and rode for the gates to lead as much of the Guelen guard as there were at his command, the twenty or so men he had ordered. Six men of Cevulirn's White Horse blazon fell in with them, and Efanor came with his two squads all on remounts and borrowed horses, twenty or more. By now the head of the column was beginning to go out of the gate, sorting itself into order, for there was no room in the courtyard for a file of half a hundred men to spread out. There was no passing room at the gate, either, but Tristen rode after Cefwyn as closely as he could, and Uwen tagged him close behind.

Cefwyn was afraid. And on Efanor's word Cefwyn rode for Emwy, where they all knew there was danger, and in a great hurry, with very few of the men who had gathered here. Worse, by Tristen's estimation, Cefwyn rode with Efanor's men.

Men lied. He had seen that in his brief life. Lie was a Word, as Treason was a Word, involving lies told to kings.

And someone had surely lied. Heryn Aswydd, beyond a doubt. But – by all he knew – Brother and Father should mean Love, but Cefwyn had not spoken at all well of his relatives, and it seemed to be the truth: he did not see love or trust in great evidence between Cefwyn and his kin.

CHAPTER 21

❧

Curse his father's damnable suspicion, Cefwyn thought: and jerked back Danvy's reins as Efanor's borrowed mount shied into him in the streets of Henas'amef, missing a potter's shelves and a startled dog. Efanor was in no good humor, the high-spirited black Efanor had picked out of the remounts was sideways as much forward, and Efanor, the great horseman Efanor, picked this creature on show, not on common sense, all because Efanor had to cut a princely figure on a cross-country run – damn him, he was going to fight the beast all the way.

Stubborn pride. Stubborn temper. Play every piece against the other. It ran in the family. His father came out here without telling Efanor why, with no trust in planning with any adviser. Haste in execution, with no one, not even his allies advised: Ináreddrin had a reputation for finding information his enemies thought he could never find; and for moving swiftly, for moving ruthlessly, and for striking before a traitor or an enemy looked to see him –

It was legend and it had succeeded as a tactic, in a long life fraught with petty rebellions and uneasy borders on every hand. But to have Efanor aware of their father's suspicion, and not the son accused; to have their father move so strongly on an Amefin lord's word – and against *him,* after he had sat a year on this cursed, hostile, witch-ridden frontier of the realm, dealing with Heryn Aswydd's tax records, and have their father believe Heryn Aswydd instead of him?

That stung. That fairly stung, and he knew not whether it was filial duty, personal alarm or heartfelt outrage that sent him out in his father's own kind of unheralded haste, the other lords unconsulted and unadvised, save Cevulirn, who had the light horse that might avail something quickly enough.

But what did he say to the others? Pardon, my lords, but my father calls me to task for summoning you to do my father's business?

Pardon, my lords, but my father the King believes a man whose father before him cheated his own people?

Pardon, my lords, my father believes all men cheat, and if they cheat in ways he knows about he trusts them more?

Is all this because I have called Heryn's account due, which my father has tolerated for years?

Gods, was *that* my mistake, Father? Have I stumbled on something you allowed, all to keep the Amefin cowed under a thief and his usurers?

The horses hit a traveling stride as they made the road outside and went along the walls past Cevulirn's camp, sending up a cloud of dust in this dry spell that gritted in the teeth even of the foremost. Men of the White Horse, encamped near the gate, turned out to stare.

"Tell the captains," Cefwyn bade the Ivanim with them, calling them forward, "tell them all you know, bid them saddle a hundred horses against your lord's arrival, and follow as you can. This may be a chase for no reason, but it may not."

"Aye, m'lord Prince," the sergeant said, who rode briefly alongside him, and dropped away again, to bear messages where they needed to go.

Peasants working in the fields stopped and stared as they passed. Along the wall-road, the camp of Lanfarnesse turned out men to shout questions at them, asking what proceeded in such haste.

Granted Heryn fell quickly under arrest, they had left Pelumer as senior of lords in the Zeide: Pelumer, then Umanon and, third, gods help them, Sovrag. Pelumer's chiefest and most immediate duty would be to keep Umanon and Sovrag from each other's throats; and gods knew where Idrys was, but he would gladly dispose Idrys to duty between Umanon and Sovrag, if Idrys could not rapidly overtake them. The Guard Captain, Kerdin Qwyll's-son, had the command second to himself now, a man no stranger to Amefin roads: Guelen patrols had been sent full-circuit of Amefel and its neighboring districts, keeping watch on the King's subjects – and learning the lay of the land.

Ambush? He looked on his brother, on that damned fancy-footed horse, that had already worked up a lather getting down from the town. Efanor would be heir if something befell him, and, for all the boyhood loyalty they had sworn and all the love they'd vowed to hold to – he had to ask himself what would be the case if it were not Elwynim that Heryn had supported, all along, but another, more agreeable prince? A prince who could appreciate Heryn's gold dinner-plates and his high-blooded horses, a prince who had never slept in mud, never faced a bandit ambush, never discommoded himself from what his religion told him was right.

At least Efanor's love of their father, he did not doubt – love and the lively suspicion of conspiracy that ran in Marhanen blood. He saw Efanor cast a glance at Tristen, who came up on his other side, and saw Efanor frown – clearly trying to hold brother-love and Sihhë in the same mouthful.

"Emuin counseled us to do him no harm, brother," Cefwyn said. "Emuin said deal fairly with him."

"Emuin's advice has not always been godly advice," Efanor said. "He *was* the old wizard's disciple. What *else* should he say?"

That, from the prince the Quinalt loved much better than it loved Ináreddrin's elder son.

"Emuin should say what benefits the Crown," Cefwyn shot back as they rode side by side, "not what serves others' revenues and their power. Beware those godly sorts, younger brother. The Quinalt line their nests no less than the rest of their ilk and they've far more nests to line."

"What do they *teach* in this province?" Efanor asked him in dismay.

"Clear-sightedness," he retorted, but the brother who'd once traded him barb for barb looked offended and self-righteous.

This is Efanor's one chance, he said to himself. Should I fall from grace, and Heryn's charges prove true, then he and his men fly nobly to Father's side, and I am put to disgrace and worse. The Quinalt would declare festival on that day.

The *priests* have stirred him up, the cursed *priests* have shaken Efanor from his meditations and been at Father's ear, too, once Heryn's protestations gave them the chance.

Hence Efanor arrives – to do what? rescue me from imprudent book-keeping? What has Heryn said to them?

Good gods grant we be in time. This is Heryn's most desperate move: attack the King, blame the heir. Gods witness I never thought the man had it in him.

Only Heryn never believed his own arrest was possible. Heryn never believed that I would move. Take that for a lesson for all years to come.

He hoped to the gods, too, that Idrys had found Heryn, and that he had not fled to shelter somewhere troublesome – like Elwynor. Please the good gods he could reason with his father, and not run head-on into that Marhanen tendency to trust blackguards before another Marhanen. Heryn had questions aplenty to answer, questions that he remotely feared might involve Efanor, once he began to talk, even if they were lies; and there might also be talk that his father the King would wish to silence, Cefwyn said that to himself, too, – if his suspicions were true just how the Aswyddim had evaded detection in their fraud for two, perhaps three generations.

He did not want to think that Ináreddrin would sacrifice his own heir to keep Heryn from saying what that arrangement was: he did not want to think his father knew the extent and evil of Aswydd's pilferage, the way he still, on the strength of a childhood only intermittently rivalrous, did not want to think that Efanor himself was secretly in Heryn Aswydd's friendship.

But he dared not confront anyone around him with such possibilities – except Idrys, damn him, who might have agreed with him, but who was not here for reasons he *hoped* were duty elsewhere. He was worried for Idrys' safety. He knew that Idrys might be the first to suffer in a plot to bring him down. He could not discuss matters with his brother. He did not want the Guelen guard and Ivanim alike to witness the Marhanen at each other's throats.

The hills enfolded them softly on all sides, the same craggy tree-crowned hills that they had passed on a much more leisurely ride to Emwy, and again at the end of a nightmarish ride by night. When they crossed the old Althalen road (though no one spoke the name) where it joined the road to Emwy district, they began to ride over the recent tracks of a fair number of riders – their father had a hundred twenty men with him, Efanor said, and that was where, if their father had wished to pass by Henas'amef unnoticed and unreported, he would have picked up the Emwy road.

By then they had passed beyond cultivated fields and into pasturages, and into the pastures of remote and smaller villages. They aimed the horses for a brief pause for breath and a limited watering at a stream that crossed the road, and came in on ground trampled by horses and now occupied by sheep. The shepherd was waving his staff and calling his dogs to gather the flock back again. The sheep bleated in panic and scattered from their horses down the narrow banks of the streamside.

"Have you seen riders today?" Cefwyn called out over the racket, as he got down from the saddle.

"Aye, m'lord," the shepherd said, with his dogs yapping and his sheep in a panicked knot, climbing over one another at the high bank, "yea, m'lord, I seen a great lord wi' red banners, a great lord, like he was a king . . ."

"That he is," Cefwyn said shortly. "How long ago, man?" and the man glanced at the sun and swung his stick at a growling dog.

"Oh, not so long. I was up to there on the height, m'lord, an' I was bringing the sheep down – but 'is silly ewe had got herself down a bank, an' I come down and around the long way, m'lord . . ."

The tracks of horses, filled with water where the sheep had not trampled, told their own story. "Not that long," Cefwyn called out, having walked a little distance up the stream and had a close look. He kept Danvy moving, not letting him fill up on water. But Efanor had not gotten down, and had let his horse stand, instead arguing with the reins – which itself annoyed him. Blessed chance his lordly brother Efanor would ever ask an Amefin shepherd the evidence of his eyes, or understand the man's brogue if he did. The brother who had adventured in the sheep-meadow with him had gone; the younger prince of Ylesuin had rather argue with his horse than soil his boots, or deign to company with him and read the clues with him. He did not understand, or want to understand, Efanor's state of mind at the moment. "We can overtake them before Emwy," he said, rising into the saddle. "The horses have rested all we can afford."

But banners at a distance was not the only thing the shepherd had seen today; he was looking straight at the emblem Tristen wore, and, on the sudden resolution of their remounting, tried to approach him. But Uwen prudently turned Tristen toward the horses and set himself with his back to the man, affecting not to see his approach.

Then Tristen looked back, on his own, staring at the shepherd, who, thus confronted, reached for amulets of gods knew what sort at his neck – until Uwen maneuvered the red mare between, put the reins in Tristen's slack hand and gruffly bade him mount at once as Tristen went on staring.

Not one of his fits, Cefwyn prayed, not a lapse in front of Efanor, and not a shepherd going on his knees to an outlawed symbol. They were near Althalen, and cursed ground, and he damned the whole miscarried day, as he rode Danvy between, to head off unwanted peasant adorations.

"Uwen," he said, leaning from the saddle to catch Uwen's attention, "well done. Keep him from all mischief, either speaking or doing. Hear me. Althalen is very near this road.

Do not, do *not* let him ride apart from us, and do not indulge his fits or his fancies if you must take the reins from him by force."

It was all he could afford to say, for immediately there was Efanor riding close as the column formed. He said, "Good you should mention it," to Uwen, and put Danvy across the stream, as the standards, his and Efanor's, grouped to move to the front.

"What was that?" Efanor asked, overtaking him. "What do you fear? Heryn? Or some other?"

"At Emwy," he said, "men of ours died for reasons I suspect were Heryn's malfeasance if not his maleficence. We have men in the region now trying to find answers. Our father may well fall in with them – or fall afoul of them, gods know. But by what this shepherd says we have every hope of over-taking him before he can ride into Emwy. His start is longer but our horses are fresher."

"What happened there?" Efanor said. "What happened at Emwy? A plague on your evasions!"

"Treason," he said. "Bluntly, treason, brother. Heryn is dealing with the Elwynim. No evasions. And high time you should ask. Heryn's a thief and the son of a thief. He's either conniving with certain of the Elwynim to kill me, or conniv-ing simply to keep profitable hostilities going. If I knew which, I'd have beheaded him before this."

"On what proof?" Efanor asked. "On what damned *proof*, brother mine?"

"The books. His books. I'd written to Father. If anyone read my reports. Or if my men, gods help them, ever got through to him."

"And the reports of Elwynim marriage offers?"

"Is *that* what brought this on?"

"That? *That*, do you say, as if it's nothing?"

"It's nothing until I answer the offer, one way or the other, and I've not answered it, nor would have answered it without Father's advisement. But that was *not* my report. Who said so? Heryn?"

"I heard it in Father's camp. Last night." Efanor lifted a gloved hand. "I know nothing. No one takes *me* in confidence."

He bit his tongue. He did not say what he thought, which was bleak and accusatory: At least you knew Father was coming. At least you heard, brother, at least he aimed no inquiry at you, after setting you to investigate your host.

Or was Heryn to spy on *me?*

"Was it not," he said instead, as they rode knee to knee, "the way Grandfather dealt with *his* sons? And did we not swear together Father should never do the same to us?"

"Yet here we are," Efanor said. "And you suspect *me,* and never a reason for it. I swear to you, I did come to warn you, as well as to secure the books, brother."

"There was no warning of this whim of our lord father's?"

"None. "

"I believe your word, brother. Forgive my doubting nature."

Forgive that the desire of their father's heart was for Efanor to succeed him as King of Ylesuin, and forgive that no few of the northern and eastern lords their father played off one against the other likewise wanted Efanor to succeed to the Dragon throne, for much the same reasons as Lord Heryn would doubtless prefer Efanor.

How could he say to Efanor, They do not love you. They believe you a fool. Wake up from your pious dream. You have duties besides your own salvation. The kingdom needs a prince with his wits about him.

And yet that blunt challenge of Efanor's just now had rewakened hope in him. The younger brother he had known in childhood had played their grandfather's game right well, by seeming not to have an opinion. Facing every direction was surely Efanor's chief attraction to certain lords, as his piety attracted priests. But he had known his brother's real nature, before manhood added reticences and other considerations, and – dare he remotely hope? – possibly even the veneer of his piety. If *that* were in any degree a pretense,

Efanor might be many things, but not, toward the ambitions of the northern barons, at least, a fool.

Desperate as they were to overtake, they could not push the horses to the limit and have anything left for fight or pursuit: already the column was threatening to string apart, the slower horses and the heavier riders making the difference. They held to their sensible pace, slacked back a little at intervals, then picked up the pace and kept moving, steadily, riding with all the skill they had. The sun declined another hour at such a rate, and it was a question in Cefwyn's mind whether they dared assume their father had gone to Emwy, and whether they might save more time going overland and through the haunted precinct; or whether the easier going of the road would make up for the distance. He gambled on the road as the better choice, and they went another hour on.

Then as they came atop the rise, with the turn toward Emwy a ridge away from them, there appeared a haze of dust above the hills. Cefwyn saw it at the same moment Efanor and several of the other men called out. There were riders ahead. They could believe it was the King's party. But they still dared not ask the horses for more than they were giving.

They kept moving, and the interval lessened. They were on the rise of the hill between them and the other force, the horses hard-breathing on the climb when, under the noise of their own horses, they heard the hammering of arms that was like no other sound on the gods' earth.

"Ambush," Cefwyn exclaimed, and bitter fear was in his mouth, for here in one place were both Princes of Ylesuin, and the King was under attack. "Efanor, take ten of your guard and ride clear!"

No, Efanor began to say. But:

"Brother," he said sharply, "ride back to Cevulirn on the road, and take Tristen and his man with you. Too many of the Marhanen are at risk here. Come for us with that force. You can trust Cevulirn."

Efanor dropped back then, and Cefwyn turned his head and shouted at Uwen to take Tristen and ride with him. He saw them fall behind, and turned his attention forward, for they were coming over the hill, with the woods and the road and the embattled forces perhaps two, three hundred in number, before them.

He rode hard then, hard as he dared to have his guard around him as he came down toward the fray. He saw light horsemen, well-armed, with no colors evident, attacking the bright scarlet of the Dragon banner. He set his shield on his arm, he drew his sword, and rode into the oncoming horsemen, Kerdin and other men with him.

The meeting was a blur of motion, of bone-jarring impact to wrist and elbow as his sword struck, a flash of bodies in the press, racket of arms and the squall of angry horses on every hand as they plunged into the motley-armed lines.

Like quicksilver, the bannerless attackers melted aside from their charge and let them see the center, where red and motley engaged in a crush that threatened to overwhelm with numbers the knot of men and red banners. There was the King his father. There was the danger.

Cefwyn hauled on the reins to turn Danvy to that quarter and plied the spurs, wishing to the gods at this moment for Kanwy and not Danvy under him. The light horses were faster in pursuit, and they would not have been here in time – but they could not deliver the shock of heavy horse in driving straight for that embattled center, where the King's banner was, and where the enemy would resist – while the hostile outriders skewed aside from them and let them through. He knew he was riding into a trap and a trick older than the Amefin hills, to fold in on them when they reached that center, but for his father's life, he had no choice.

"Sound our presence!" he bade Kerdin. "Loud as you can!" He hoped to gain his father's attention and have his father try to fall back toward him, but he dared not stop his own charge for fear of losing momentum and bogging down in a separate envelopment.

Danvy stumbled and regained his feet on the rutted road-side as Cefwyn pushed him for more speed, and more attackers, nightmare sight, came down from their right flank, down off a hillside.

Then he had view of a red horse, black rider, sweeping along the side of that hill toward those threatening riders – it was Tristen, with Uwen close behind: perhaps Efanor as well, was his instant, frightened thought. He damned them for fools if they had not retreated.

But he could not help them – he had to reach the King's force, a disarrayed mass, banners askew in the midst of a furious assault of light-armed riders, and to that sole objective he put the spurs to Danvy, swearing. He had no time to attend Tristen's folly: he was about to lose a friend, and maybe the other heir of Ylesuin – but his father's lines had been folded in, packing men in on each other so that lances and well nigh swords and shields were useless at the center, around the King. He wrung the last from Danvy to come in hard with what men could stay with him, to batter his way toward the center of that closing entrapment, to open it up and give the King's men a chance to use their weapons on the envelopment he knew was now coming around both their forces, separately and fatally if he could not break that knot around his father.

Danvy hit shoulder to shoulder with another horse. Cefwyn took a hit on the shield and shoved and swung blindly, felt the sword bite as Danvy staggered, recovered, and stumbled his way over yielding bodies. After that, he hacked and shoved whatever was in his path until it became a solid press of horseflesh and bodies and he could go no further.

He was in danger of being cut off, now, from his own companions. Danvy went almost to his knees on a body, recovered his footing, and a blow came down on the shield, an axe stuck fast in the gap. He struck back at what target he could see past the encumbrance, wrestling with the axe-wielder for possession of the shield until the man's sheer strength dragged him into clear sight of the man and half out of Danvy's saddle.

One of his men hacked at his attacker, who left the axe and reeled aside. Danvy struggled for footing and Cefwyn tried to clear his shield, laying about him half blind and encumbered, until it was red badges all about him, red banners, and he knew the King's men as well as his own guard were bringing their forces to bear.

Danvy jolted hard then as a horseman careened into him, and Danvy stumbled and went down. Cefwyn sprawled, rolled from the path of oncoming hooves and staggered up, still owning his sword by its wrist thong, still with the remnant of his shield on his arm. He had wet haze in his eyes, blurring the riders coming down on him.

I die here, he thought with strange amazement, and, clearing the drip of blood from his eyes with a shake of his head and a pass of his sleeve, realized he had lost his helm and the half-shield was the defense he had – his own lines had been driven back and it was only the enemy in his view. He braced his feet among the dead, facing that gray and brown wall of horsemen coming at him, every detail astonishingly clear, as if the last moments of living must be stretched thin till they broke, till a prince had a chance to know he had led his kingdom's forces to disaster.

A red horse plunged between. Tristen's black form cut across his view, Uwen close on his heels . . . Tristen swung the red mare about; and Uwen was trying to reach him as Tristen rode Gery head-on into the oncoming riders.

A blade swung. Unengaged, Cefwyn watched helplessly as Tristen ducked under and kept riding, the edge passing over his body by the narrowest of margins – he was going deep in among the enemy; and Uwen accounted for the man who had missed him.

"M'lord!" a voice cried near at hand; a second horseman rode across in front of him and slid to a stop. The guardsman leapt off, and Cefwyn swung up to the offered saddle, took a new grip on his sword and braced himself for the onslaught about to come down on both of them.

But it had fallen back. Among those motley horsemen,

from the dead or the living, Tristen had found a blade and wielded it, shieldless, turning the red mare with his knees this way and that, the blade swinging dark and deadly in the light, as enemies went down. Tristen kept pressing, a dark and terrible force cutting into the enemy's ranks, methodically taking man after man, forcing the red mare further. There began to be space about him – a rider in black velvet, and with a single man beside him and no shield at all.

"Sihhë! Sihhë!" the shout was ringing out from the enemy ranks now. They had seen, Cefwyn guessed, the emblem he bore. But Tristen gave no mercy to the rout that began around him. The red mare did not cease to weave and seek openings in the retreat and the sword did not cease to take lives. The arm was unerring, hewing down men, no move wasted. The clash of blades that did oppose him became a distant music, and the turning movements assumed a strange beauty, like a dance, the movement of a natural force of destruction that swept the enemy back and back.

The scene hazed, with a sting of salt in his eyes. Cefwyn struggled for breath, left with no enemies, no battle for him to face. He sat the saddle, arms limp, battered beyond the strength to lift sword or shield, and he realized a remote sting and swelling in his leg as his strength ebbed. He tasted copper, realized that he had been hit, and that the pain had yet to reach him – but the leg obeyed him when he signaled the horse with his heel, and turned, looking for the King.

More riders thundered up. He looked about in horror, lifted an arm that weighed double, and saw then the White Horse of Cevulirn sweeping onto the otherwise silent field.

A horseman came up beside him. A hand seized him, stayed him in the saddle, and he could not see the man until he blinked his vision clear.

"Idrys." He recognized his black-armored would-be rescuer, who, late to the field of combat, held him ahorse until others could dismount and come about him. "No," he protested, not willing to be lifted down. He refused their ministrations and, laying his sword across the saddlebow because he had no strength or steadiness to sheath it, he rode with Idrys for escort this way and that among the corpses and the knots of men still ahorse.

He saw the Dragon banner, then, and put the horse to as much speed as it could make over the trampled, littered ground, realizing that men around that banner were standing silent and with heads bowed. He saw Efanor among the men kneeling there – Efanor would have come in with Cevulirn's men – and by Efanor's grief-stricken demeanor he foreknew the worst.

He dismounted – Idrys was instantly at his elbow to take his arm, to help him limp forward to where his father lay. The Dragon Guard had fallen thick about their King. He walked over bodies of men whose names he might know well if he looked. But his father's white hair was the only thing truly clear to his eyes – their father was only exhausted, he said to himself: their father was hurt, not dead; their father was a force of nature, a fact of their lives – he could not die.

Men gave back from him as he arrived, and he saw what he did not want to see, dark blood welling from the gut, a wound beyond any physician's skill. Efanor was white-faced, tears making trails beside his mouth. Cefwyn fell to his knees with a gasp of pain, leaned on Efanor's shoulder, and for a moment their father looked on both his sons kneeling over him.

The King's feeble hand reached out and closed on Efanor's.

"My son," Ináreddrin said.

No look, no single glance to spare for him. Cefwyn bided silent as in that instant the light faded from Ináreddrin's eyes and the strength from his hand. The watching circle of men waited.

A moment more. A last breath. Quiet, and that sudden relaxation no sleep could counterfeit.

"Help me up," Cefwyn muttered angrily. He had lost his sword – dropped it, forgotten it, he cared not except he had nothing to lean on to get up, and was trapped, kneeling in the dirt. He reached out his hand for Idrys and Idrys raised him up by a heavy effort as the pain of grief in his heart and the numbness in his leg together all but overwhelmed him. He had a desire to lay about him, striking anyone, everyone remotely witness to his father's spite, to his father's lying there in the shameful dirt, among the mortal dead.

But there was no enemy. There was no argument. He was the object of attention now. Guelen guard and Ivanim together, Cevulirn, among the others, all looked to him to know what he thought, what he was, what he would be and do next.

Then Cevulirn bowed the knee, and went down, stiffly. Others knelt. Someone – he was not certain who – took the battle-crown from his father's blood-stained head and offered it to him in a grimed fist.

Cefwyn took it in one hand. It was a gold band. He could bend it if he chose. He could cast it in the mud and grind it under his foot and bid them *have* Efanor. But he took it in both hands, solemnly set it on his brow – it rested on the cut, and hurt, but he was all but numb to it. There were no cheers.

Efanor had risen, and stood by, doing nothing, only look- ing down at their father, tears running on his face. The King's guard and his own awaited some first move, some gesture of omen, some order to bring the world into sense again. He reached, cold-bloodedly conscious of his choice, and took his brother's hands, which he woodenly held as Efanor knelt, as Efanor dutifully, going through the play, kissed his hand, as Efanor rose and looked him in the face. He made his eyes distant and void of anger as he kissed Efanor's bloody cheek in turn and let go his hands, which were cold as ice. Their father's dying slight seethed in him with bitter, burning jeal- ousy, and armored Efanor with self-righteousness and sacri- fice before these men, in whose witness – damn them all – he would shed no tears.

But why feel the sting? he thought then. In death, no differ- ent truth than in life. Father loved him, never me.

Father practiced Grandfather's tactics down to his dying breath, and gave Efanor his one victory, his sole recompense to be by one year not the heir.

But no man on the field chose to regard that last gesture as negating the sworn succession. Cevulirn, the Duke of the Ivanim, was a southern man, and his own. And Efanor had knelt, and kissed his hand, and owned to the legal truth – righteous priestling that he was; though he had been nowhere – *nowhere* when their father was fighting for his life, not priestly Efanor.

But that was manifestly unfair. He had sent Efanor for Cevulirn. Efanor had followed his orders. He had brought Cevulirn – too damned late. Efanor had come to the field with Cevulirn's men, on a horse he'd just worn down with a ride back to reach the Duke of the Ivanim and then, anxious for appearances, would not, he would personally swear to it, have sensibly bidden Cevulirn leave him ignobly on the road and make all haste to their father's rescue without him.

Which was also unfair to suppose. He was looking for someone to blame.

Idrys steadied him. Someone had found a linen pad to tuck into the gash on his leg, and a bandage to wrap about his leg, over the reinforced leather. The pain as the man jerked a knot taut hazed his vision, then lessened, over all, as the wound found firm support.

"Get me to a horse, Idrys," he said, and with a sweeping glance about him at the Ivanim, and to Cevulirn, he said, "Well that you heard my message and followed. I thank you."

"My lord King," said Cevulirn, and sent a chill through his blood.

"I heard late," Idrys said on his other side. "Your message did reach me." Idrys' hands were gentle as he helped him.

"Is Danvy gone? Did he go down?" He heard himself sounding like a small boy asking after a favorite pet, knowing as a man knew, that miracles did not happen on a field of battle.

And he remembered then, upon that thought of miracles – or of damning wizardry: "Gods, Tristen. *Where's Tristen?*"

"He's well, Your Majesty," Idrys said calmly, coldly. "I'll have men look for Danvy."

"Stay," Cefwyn said thinly, and caught a breath, insisting

372

to stop at an ankle-high hummock on which he could stand and where Cevulirn and his father's officers could both see him and hear his orders. "Take up the King. Make a litter. We'll carry him –" He lost his breath and his clarity of thought both at once and stood shaking like a leaf.

"To the capital, Your Majesty?"

The notion dazed him, as for the first time he considered that he had personal and royal obligations suddenly far wider than Amefel. The capital: Guelemara. Halls safe from Elwynim assassins.

And, at least for a while, safe from a rebellion in Amefel. Or from any incursion across its borders.

But this was a murder from which a King who meant to reign long – could not retreat.

Delegate their father's funeral, in the capital – to Efanor, with the Quinalt orthodoxy free to stage everything to their satisfaction, and say what they liked?

Let Efanor go home to the capital? Let him stand alone with the Quinalt to bless the proceedings and the northern lords to stand with him, bees around Efanor's sweet-smelling, pious influence, with their lips to his ear?

"No," he said. He would not give up his brother. He would fight for Efanor, if nothing else. "To Henas'amef," he said, and saw looks exchanged, subtle consternation among his father's guard.

And no one moved.

They question me, he thought in anger. And then in utter, wild overthrow of his reason: They came here on Heryn's accusations of me. And my father is dead. They think I – *I* – am at fault for this.

"Surely," said the Commander of the Dragon Guard – Gwywyn was his name – "Surely we should send word to the capital, Your Majesty."

His heart was beating fit to burst. He was angry. He was shaken to his soul, and in pain. But he stilled the shout and the anger he wanted to let loose. His hands were still shaking and he tucked them in his belt to hide the tremor.

"Lord Commander, surely we shall do that, but we shall send to Guelemara from Henas'amef, where this attack was ordered. I will have answers as to Heryn Aswydd's involvement. He is the source of the message my brother advises me brought you here. Credit my brother for my presence on the field." He gave Efanor his due. Entirely. And aimed a stroke straight to the heart of Heryn's false report of him. "I rode here from Henas'amef, as hard as I could. I would to the gods you'd sought me there, Lord Commander, not here."

"I would to the gods, too, Your Majesty." The Lord Commander seemed both overcome by the loss and relieved in his mind by that small though significant piece of information, and went on his knees and swore him fealty and kissed his hand as he should have done earlier; but this was an honest man, Cefwyn said to himself. He had not known Gwywyn well, but this courageously late acceptance told him this was a man well worth winning to his side. He lifted the man to his feet, confirmed him as continuing among his high officers, and Gwywyn gave orders to his father's men.

To *his* men, he thought in anguish.

There was more to do, quickly, much more, – but first the necessity to move them clear of further attack. "Cevulirn!" he said. "Men of yours to ride ahead on the road, men to lag back, by your grace, Ivanor! We've yet to know whether this is all they have in reserve in this cursed place. Either they swam these horses across, or we've a bridge decked and in use – and we're not in strength to find it out now."

"Leave it to me, Your Majesty," Cevulirn said, and gave orders more rapidly and more astutely than he had managed. He had babbled. He had given not commands, but reasons. It was not a way to order soldiers, or lords who might be tempted to give back contrary reasons and not actions. It was not his father's way. It was not a king's voice he had, or a king's confidence-inspiring certainty on the field.

But the things he ordered were being done. He tried to

think what he might have omitted to do. The crown worked at the wound on his head when he clenched his jaw or when he frowned, and was its own bloody misery.

"Efanor," he said, and his brother came to him. Red-eyed, Efanor was, pale of face, still leaking tears, like the little boy who'd suffered tragedies enormous at the time – the little brother who'd been his constant ally in the house. On an impulse he embraced his brother, as he had rarely done since they'd become men. "Efanor, with all my heart – I would we had all come even moments sooner." He said it consciously and publicly to remove any sting Efanor might have felt in his late arrival, and to remove any doubt Efanor had had of his acceptance. But Efanor was stiff in his embrace.

"My lord King," Efanor said through the tears. The face had hardened in that instant of that embrace. The voice had gone cold. It was clearly not a time to press Efanor on anything, least of all with an appeal to familial loyalties which Efanor had ample familial reason to doubt. He had loosened his hold on his heart once: he could not risk it twice, or he might break down in the witness of these men, and perhaps Efanor felt the same. He made himself numb, incapable of further grief or astonishment, in favor of calculation that told him that trouble for Ylesuin was far wider than the loss on this field. He felt sweat on his face, that began to dry and stiffen on his cheeks, and he did not let expression fight against it.

"I will grieve for this tomorrow," he said then. "Forgive me, Efanor."

"You have no tears."

"I shall have. Let be."

"Where is your Sihhë wizard, Cefwyn king?"

He was still dazed, conscious of Efanor's attack on his associations, and of the bitter nature of that attack – and at the same time keenly reminded of the question of Tristen's whereabouts. Looking about, he saw no sign of him.

"My lord King," said Idrys, "we can make a litter for you, too, if you need. You need not ride."

"No," he said. "Where has Tristen gone? Where is he?"

"Majesty," Idrys said, "we're searching for him. No one's seen him since the fighting."

"The man saved my life, damn it – saved the lot of us! I want him found!"

The buzz of flies hung in the air. Men coughed, or cursed or grunted in pain, bandaging their hurts. Men and horses wandered at apparent random through trampled, bloodied grass, seeking order and direction. One such whisper through the grass and accompanying jingle of bits brought him Danvy. A man had found him, Danvy showing a cut on his shoulder but nothing that would not heal, nothing that even precluded him being ridden home, and he wanted not to part from Danvy again: he patted Danvy's neck and gathered up the reins, guilty in recovering a creature so loved, so dear to him, amid other, more grievous losses to the realm.

A man helped him into the saddle. Other men were mounting up. Their dead were too many to take with them, the danger in the area too great to detach more than a squad of Cevulirn's cavalry from their main body to stand watch over them against village looters. He had heard Idrys give necessary orders for the removal of weapons from the dead, so as not to meet them coming back in hostile hands – and to search for clues of allegiance among the fallen enemy.

But that was Idrys' concern and Idrys was giving all the orders for those that stayed: Cevulirn and Efanor were ahorse. Still he saw no sign of Tristen, and could not ask again, petulantly, like a child: Idrys was doing all he could to be sure of the area, and who was in it, and if Tristen and Uwen were among the fallen or the wounded, the men staying behind would advise him and do more than he could do.

The Crown meanwhile had other obligations too urgent, among them to secure his own safety, and Efanor's, as the only two Marhanen, and them without issue. "Shall we move?" Efanor asked him, prompting him to issue orders which no one but he could give, and numbly he said, "Let's be on our way."

So the King's litter began to move. The elements of Cevulirn's men and the Guelen guard sorted themselves into order, the King's Dragon Guard with their tattered red standards, the men of the Prince's Guard, who now – he realized with faint shock – must attach to Efanor as heir to the throne (but not Idrys, he swore to himself: Efanor should never inherit Idrys). The two red-coated Guard units came first, with the gray and white contingents of Toj Embrel and Ivanor at large riding under their own banners and under their own lord.

At some length Idrys overtook him, and rode beside him, apart from Efanor, who rode with Gwywyn.

"You are not fit to ride," Idrys grumbled. Idrys' face, whitened by the road dust, was a mask. "You should have taken the litter. The bleeding is worse."

"Where were you?" Cefwyn snapped. His leg hurt him, now, swelling against the bandage, muscles stretched by sitting the saddle.

"Heryn almost eluded us. He led me a chase. We did overtake him. And he dispatched another messenger. Heryn's man babbled treason – and will say more."

It was news that flooded strength into him. Vindication. Proof, for his father's men. For all the realm besides. He drew a deep breath. The hooves scuffed deadly slow in what had become a warm day, belying the clouds in the west. The flies pursued them. The band about his head seemed a malicious and burning fire.

"He will believe me," he said, thinking of Efanor. "My brother will believe me now."

"My lord?" Idrys asked.

But he chose not to answer. He had said too much, in that, even to Idrys.

They came up behind a pair of horsemen on the road, riding ahead of them so slowly that even at their pace they were gradually overtaking them. Cefwyn watched them from his vantage at the head of the column, and knew who they were, long before the interval closed enough for anyone to see the red color of the mare, and the black of her rider, and the stocky figure of the man on the bay.

"Your Majesty." It was Gwywyn. "Shall we ride forward and find them out?"

"No," he said, "I know who they are. Let be." So the Lord Commander fell silent riding on one side of him with Efanor, and Cevulirn arrived beside Idrys on the other, to hear the same. They drew steadily nearer.

"Majesty," his father's Lord Commander whispered, justifiably apprehensive, for there was indeed an eeriness about the pair, who had never looked to know what rode behind, as if a king's funeral cortège and the procession of his successor were nothing remotely of interest to them.

The stocky man looked back finally. The other did not, but rode slumped in the saddle, dark head bowed.

He is hurt, Cefwyn thought in anguish, and yet – and yet – in the trick of the setting sun and the dust the two horses raised in the trampled roadway, it was as if two ghosts rode before them, beings not of this time or place, nor accessible to them.

Not Elfwyn, he thought. Whatever soul Mauryl had called – it was surely not Elfwyn's unwarlike soul that had ridden to save their company. It was not the last Sihhë king whose hand and arm and body had found such warlike skills as drove armored enemies in panicked retreat.

Sihhë! their attackers had cried, falling back in consternation. He would never forget that moment, that the enemy about to pour over him had given way for fear of two men, one of them having ridden out unarmed but for a dagger.

Tristen rode loosely now, as if sorely hurt, as if he expected no help, Cefwyn thought, and would rebuff what aid might be offered him. But gingerly he moved his horse forward, while the main column kept the pace it could best maintain.

He rode alongside, met Uwen's anguished face . . . saw Tristen's profile in a curtain of dark hair. Tristen's head was bowed against his breast, as if only instinct kept him in the

378

saddle. His face was spattered with blood like his hands, and the black velvet was gashed, showing bright mail underneath. Blood had dried on the velvet, and on the mane and neck and feet of the red mare. Tristen's hands did not hold the reins. They clenched a naked sword, on which sunset glinted faint fire, and blood sealed his hands to it, hilt and blade across the saddlebow.

"Tristen," Cefwyn said. "Tristen."

The dark head lifted. The pale eyes behind that blood-spattered mask were unbarriered and innocent as ever as they turned to him.

Cefwyn shuddered. He had expected some dread change, and there was none.

"This, too, I know," Tristen said distantly, and raised the bloody sword by the hilt in one hand. He let it down, then. And without any expression on his face, without any contraction or passion in the features, tears welled up and spilled down his face.

"You saved my life, Tristen."

Tristen nodded, still without expression, still with that terrible clarity in the eyes, fine hands both clenched upon the sword.

"My father is dead," Cefwyn said, and meant to say in consequence of that – that he was King. But suddenly the dam that had been holding his own tears burst when he said it, as if with his saying the words, it all became real. He wiped at his face, and the tears dried in the dusty wind, as he became aware of the witnesses closing up around him.

"Are you hurt?" Cefwyn asked.

"No," the answer came, faint and detached. Tristen's eyes closed as if in pain, and remained so for several moments.

"Uwen, care for him."

"Your Highness," the soldier whispered, and fear was in his eyes as he corrected himself. "M'lord King."

Riders had còme up behind him. Only the leaders had overtaken him: the column was falling behind them. The pace they had taken was a hardship on the wounded.

379

"My lord," said Idrys' cold voice as he reined back with Efanor and Cevulirn. "The Sihhë should not precede you, not in this column, not into the town. It will not be understood. You have fostered this thing. Now it grows. Better it should vanish. Kings need no allies such as he is. Send him to some quiet retreat where he will be safe, and you will be."

"He was by me," Cefwyn replied bitterly. "He rode between me and the assassins. He almost saved my father. Where were you?"

"Serving Your Majesty, not well, perhaps. Better I had left Heryn to others. I deeply regret it. – But, all the same, he should not precede you. For all our sakes, my lord King."

It was truth. It was essential, even for Tristen's future safety. He surrendered, still angry at himself, at Idrys, at fate or the gods or his father for his dying act: he was not sure. "See to it."

Idrys rode forward. Cefwyn watched as Idrys spoke briefly to Uwen, and immediately after the pair went to the side of the road and let the column pass.

He could not see Uwen and Tristen, then. He must trust that they would come in safely, that Uwen's good sense would fend for them both, however far back they had been pushed by the succeeding ranks, and that Tristen would find his way home with the rest of them, when of all persons he most wanted to know was safe, it was Tristen. He was King. And he could not protect the things he most wanted safe.

A wind began to blow at their backs, a chill wind out of the north, kicking up dust in clouds, flattening the grass beside the road and making the broad Marhanen banners crack and buck at their standards, so that the standard-bearers fought to hold them.

Idrys dropped back into place. He said nothing. Efanor was on the other side.

They spoke no words. The journey now did not require them.

*   *   *

The sun was rising as they came into Henas'amef, with the gate bell tolling, and the Zeide bell picking up the note as they rode the cobbled streets.

A Marhanen king, Cefwyn thought, seeing the townsfolk gathered. A Marhanen king is visiting this town for the first time since the massacre of the Sihhë.

Now the Marhanens bleed.

He had sent Idrys ahead, to deliver word up to the Zeide. But, perhaps uninformed, the townsfolk had run out to gawk and cheer as the column came in with banners flying and numerous strangers to the town. The crowd was excited, then struck silent and sober at the sight of wounds; they muttered together at the King's banners; and as the cortège passed, somewhere a voice cried out, "The King is dead!" and the cry went through the town, with an undertone of fear – well it might be fear, if the province were held to blame.

And hard upon that, "Sihhë!" went rippling through all the rumors, beneath the tolling of the bells, until he knew that Tristen had likewise come within the gates – knew that it was more than Tristen's presence that stirred the people. A Marhanen King was dead and a living Sihhë had ridden in from battle. To them it might be omen, even verging on prophecy.

The Zeide gates up the hill gaped for them; the grim skulls looked down victorious from the south gate, and the Zeide's many roofs behind that arch were a mass of shadow against a pearl-colored sky. "I will show you justice here," Cefwyn said to Efanor as they came beneath the deathly gate. "I promise you an answer for the treachery responsible for this."

Efanor did not look at him, nor he at his brother. They preserved funereal decorum as the procession labored its way up and around the front of the Zeide, to the east façade and the holy and orthodox Quinalt shrine where – he had already given orders to Idrys – the body would lie in state within the Zeide's walls.

"Promise me another answer," Efanor said finally, when

they had come clear of bystanders, in the cobbled courtyard, "an answer for the questions that brought our father here."

Now, now the bitterness came out. And the suspicion.

"Was it not enough, what you saw, Efanor? They were lies that Heryn used to lay a trap for you – playing on our family's cursed suspicions. There was nothing true in anything Heryn reported. Our own distrust was his ally, Efanor. Do not go on distrusting me."

"I saw brigands without a crest. I do not know why our father is dead. But you need not work over-hard to please me, brother. I am obliged now to be pleased at whatever you do."

It was the bravest, most defiant speech he had ever heard from Efanor as a man. It gave him as thorough a respect for his younger brother's courage as he had for Lord Gwywyn's. And it grated on his raw sensibilities.

"Stay by me, Efanor. I beg you. I am asking you. Courage is well enough, but face our enemies with it. Not me. We swore not to be divided. We swore Father should never do it."

Silence.

"Efanor."

"I would not wish," Efanor said coldly, "ever to leave your side, brother. Never fear I shall."

Torches were lit in front of the Quinalt shrine. Fire whipped wildly in the dawn. The bier was loosed from the horses, a loose, soldierly thing of spears and belts and cloaks. Men took it up and bore it toward the doors. A priest confronted them, as ritual demanded he do. Wind whipped at his robes, rocking him in his hooded and faceless decorum.

"The King is dead," Cefwyn said, disturbing the thump and flutter of banners and fire. "He perished by assassins on the road to this town. Have it proclaimed. Make prayers for his soul."

His father's body entered first. The bearers laid it on the altar and disposed the banners on either hand, those of the

Dragon Guard, the Marhanen house, of Guelemara, Guelessar and Ylesuin.

He went inside to burn incense and make prayer, feeling the words for the first time in years. He kissed the worn silver letters set in the stone altar and rose, stopped dead as he saw a dark figure standing in the shrine door, with the flash of the silver Star and Tower on black velvet. A second figure joined it: Uwen.

"Lo, your ally," said Efanor, at his shoulder.

Tristen waited. Cefwyn limped a step toward the foreboding figure, conscious of Efanor's witness. The family curse, he thought, feeling trapped. Alive and with us.

"Cefwyn," Tristen said. The voice was faint and bewildered. He heard only terror, the childlike quality that was the gentle man he knew.

He embraced Tristen as he could not embrace his brother at the moment, he rested his aching head on Tristen's shoulder, looked up at him then and saw in Tristen's eyes all the compassion and tenderness he longed for in his own brother.

I have nothing but this, he thought. In all the world there is no gentleness toward me but this. Efanor will not reason with me.

"My friend," he said to Tristen. "You should not have come here. – Uwen, take him to his room. I have other business tonight."

Tristen lingered, but Uwen tugged on his arm and, like a tired child, Tristen yielded and went where he was bidden.

The priests' chanting echoed in the vaulted hall. Torches fluttered and scattered sparks of windblown fire about the bier, stinging where they chanced against living skin.

Cefwyn turned and met Idrys' grim stare.

There was duty. Idrys had something on his mind.

"The messenger," he remembered then. "Heryn."

"Both under arrest," Idrys said. "My lord, see to necessities and mourn later. The messenger could not have been going to the ambush on the road. It was too late for that. It was surely elsewhere he was sent."

Cefwyn delayed a moment, his eyes on the haze of wind-whipped torchlight and then on Efanor, standing among the silent Crown officers.

The great bell of the Quinalt shrine began to toll, solemn and terrible.

"Learn where," he said to Idrys.

CHAPTER 22

T here were dreams.
Tristen fled the clangor of metal and the sounds of men and horses, woke, and still heard the iron bells peal out their dreadful sound.

Dark had fallen while he slept. He pressed the heels of his hands against his eyes to drive away the images of the dreams, and at last dragged his aching limbs from the safe and comfortless sheets, shrugged on a robe and went to the hearthside. He stirred the embers and threw on another small piece of wood, for the light, not for the warmth.

The candles had burned down to one guttering stub. He sought others in the cupboards, barefoot on the chill floor. To his relief he found a few, and pulled out the spent candles and set the new ones in the sconces, lighting them, one to the next, so that they chased the Shadows into the corners and beneath the bed and as far as the shutterless window.

Uwen slept, he was certain, since Uwen had not stirred out with his fire-making or his search after candles. He would not disturb Uwen for any reason of his discomfort. Uwen had done too much, and was sore from bruises. So was he, from exertion, and from the unaccustomed riding. He had taken a few bruises: his arm was sore from the shock of encounters, several, as he thought, from wresting a sword from a man. But that was all. He had no wounds. He had gone to bed soon after reaching his rooms. He could not tell what hour it was.

The sound of riders echoed up off the cobblestones, briefly overwhelming the relentless tolling of the bells. The sound passed and dimmed; the Zeide, a maze of alleys and roofs and wings, echoed sounds in deceptive fashion, but it was a large number of riders going somewhere in the night, by the stable-court, he thought.

He had dimly heard armed men tramping about the halls earlier . . . coming and going from Cefwyn's apartments, he had judged. He had heard, half-waking, the bells ring out from the lower town as well as from the shrines and from the Zeide gate.

He would have stayed by Cefwyn, but Cefwyn had wanted to be alone, except for Annas and Idrys. Cefwyn had most emphatically told him to go to bed and rest.

And perhaps, Tristen thought, it was because he did not understand having or losing a father, or the questions that proper men had to discuss with each other at such times.

He knew at least what it was to lose and to be lost. He would comfort Cefwyn if he knew how – but he had not known how to comfort himself when he had lost Mauryl except by walking and walking until he had to sleep, and by days coming between himself and that time. He supposed that was not very great wisdom, and that he had, after all, nothing but the perpetual difficulty he posed to offer to anyone – which was no great gift to Cefwyn, when Cefwyn was suffering his own pain.

He shivered as he sank down on his knees by the hearth, seeking warmth. The flames had taken the wood and made a golden sheet before his face, bright, moving, distracting him from memory.

Almost.

He shut his eyes tightly against the remembrance of the noise, the dust, the faces. He buried his face in his hands and stayed so a moment, not breathing until the need for breath made his head spin and he dropped his hands and gasped like a man drowning – flesh as well as spirit, Mauryl had said.

A naked sword stood in the shadows beside the hearth, leaned point-down against the wall. Uwen had cleaned the blood from it.

It was the sword he had wrenched from a man who had attacked him. He had carried it away from the field, not of any real purpose at first, only that his hands held it, and eventually his thoughts lit on it, possessed it, and he had not, in the end, cast it away as useless to him: such a thing was not useless, in such events as moiled about him.

He had bathed, among first things when he had come home. Even so, and after all the scrubbing, the reek of blood lingered in his nostrils and he could not, no matter the perfumed oils the servants supplied him, feel clean. He looked at his hands in the firelight, at his arms that bore no wounds to betray the thing that had happened to him. He was dismayed at his own unscarred existence, and was most of all appalled that he bore no mark of it, while so many, many others had taken wounds that would mark them forever.

I do this well, he thought. I do this very well. And through his mind flitted the memory of Ynefel, his untutored hands struggling to write, and soon finding that they knew the art.

Mauryl had approved his work. Mauryl had said –

But Mauryl had no longer any clear face in this memory. The whole of Ynefel seemed strange to him and beyond recovery. He was cut off from its good memories. There was no way now back to those days, that innocence. He could not but ask questions, and questions, and questions of men less wise than Mauryl, and the questions led him, every one, farther and farther from home and safety.

Cefwyn said, Idrys said, men all said, and it was probably true, that he was Sihhë; that all the Sihhë had died terribly, and that Mauryl had called him out of death and given him a shape and substance; the servants said, and Cefwyn said, that he did not so much learn things, as remember them.

If I go on, he thought with a shiver, I may remember dying. I would not wish that.

The servants spoke when they thought he was not listening, and he knew that they greatly feared his nature, even if they regarded him kindly. He knew they thought him a wizard. They believed his name had been Elfwyn, and they said that he had died at Althalen.

And perhaps it was true – he thought that they had overheard it from those who knew – but the name of Elfwyn was not a Name to him, although he remembered clearly that

Cefwyn had said it to him, trying, he knew now, to discover whether he would remember it – and he had not. Althalen itself, though a Name, was a place he thought ought to prosper, not lie in overgrown ruin. His thoughts were cluttered with far worse places than that, Names he could not recover, and others – Galasien, Aryceillan, Arachis – Names he had never heard anyone use, hovered on the edge of his awareness, and came near him at sleepy moments, like birds that tried to light, but found no footing in recent memory.

The servants said perhaps he had had his last fit because he had come near a cursed site, and the ghosts that lingered there had made him ill, as ghosts were, he gathered, reputed to do, stealing life from the living. But it was not theft that had afflicted him there. It was no ghosts that had afflicted him at all, but a surfeit of Words, Words in horrid profusion, violent Words that had not confused him at all today, when he had seen Cefwyn in danger. Once he had seen the fighting in front of him, once he had seen the King's banners all grouped together and the troops helplessly drawn in on each other, with Cefwyn trying to breach that knot, he had known clearly what to do. He had known in the way he had known, once the pen was in his hand, how to write, and in the way he had known, once he had found a horse under him, how to ride. He had known in such clear order the things that had to be done to unfold that foredoomed battle-line and bring it to bear on the enemy again.

He had known not only the use of the sword, but the process and the direction of the battle. He had known where to go, and what had to be done to let that embattled knot break open – and he had seen without a doubt on that field the specific men he had to take down to confuse the attackers and drive them in retreat.

A sweat broke out on him that had nothing to do with the fire. The wind that had swept down on them on the road had been cold, and that wind still blew – he could hear it against the windows.

He had done what he knew to do. He had not read

Mauryl's Book, but he had found a skill in him for wreaking dreadful harm – he had found a capability latent in his hands, in this present sinew and bone that Mauryl had made. He knew that things were still unfolding to him, and that he might discover more things still. He was not the feckless boy who had fallen on Mauryl's wooden steps, and skinned knees on the stone floors of Ynefel. He was coming to what Mauryl had wished him to be, perhaps, but he was not yet aware of what that was. He did not think his present being was linked as tightly to his past as Cefwyn and the servants feared – he did not think it mattered that much who he had been, though it was a start to knowing who he was to be, and what he might expect himself to do.

That was the thing that set him shivering: not knowing what other abilities might unfold in him. He had discovered today that he was not a slight man. He was tall, and strong, and might seize a man and break his hold on a weapon; he was quick, and could strike faster than a man who came at him. He rode without needing to think – in motion, Gery was part of him, coming through for him by her bravery when other men's horses shied into trouble. She had gone over the dead, on uneven ground – he had not failed Gery and she had not failed him, and that was the terrible thing. While they did together what he knew to do, it had felt like flying, the sword had weighed nothing to him, and Gery had done what Uwen swore she was never trained to do, because he had the gift, as Uwen had said the Sihhë lords had had, to speak to horses and to enchant them.

He thought not. He thought it was only because he knew how to sit a saddle and because he had once, alive at some other time, ridden for many, many hours, and loved it best of anything he did. He didn't know how he could have risked Gery the way he had – he didn't know how he could *not* have risked her and himself and Uwen, to go to Cefwyn's defense, when Cefwyn was in deadly danger – so many, many things he did not know how to weigh one against the other. He could not weigh the value of taking the sword, and saving the men, and killing others, who were, at the end calling out, "Sihhë! Sihhë!" and refusing to fight him, so that his chief weapon then became the vacancy he could create with his mere presence, where he rode, where he made Uwen follow, where he forced a horse to go, who had become dear to him – as Uwen was, as Cefwyn was, as the peace was, that he had found in Cefwyn's presence.

He shut his eyes tight, feeling moisture squeeze between his lids. He wiped it with both his hands and pressed against his eyes so the red light that made would take away the sights from him. He inhaled the wood smoke, and it made him remember Althalen. He felt the stone of the fireplace against his back, and it was all that told him he was not drifting in the black and red, knowing the value of nothing, knowing not what to do, or how to weigh what he had done, or the lives, or the pain, or the fear. Words and abilities were breaking out in him so rapidly he could not master them – they were, the opposite, near to mastering him, sending him careening wildly through choices he could not reconcile, into events every turn of which violated Mauryl's precepts of right and wrong. He met necessities that caused him to do terrible things, even – even enjoying the feeling of Gery under him, or the loft the sword could attain, like a living thing, like that day in the courtyard, when he had learned to use the axe, and found it weighed nothing to his hands. He had thought it good. He had thought that day good, and never known where it might lead him.

Or was every choice like that, when one truly, truly ventured into the wide world beyond the woods? Was there no clean, clear line to tell him right from wrong? Was there no way to make right choices without scattering harm in his wake – without making even Uwen afraid of him?

He made himself clear rules to guide him in a world of confusion: I shall not harm Cefwyn, he thought. I shall not harm Uwen. It was a modest beginning, surely.

But harm meant such complex things, and extended in so many directions. Was harm thwarting Cefwyn's wishes, or doing what one thought best, even when Cefwyn objected? Was harm risking Uwen, saving Cefwyn?

He heard Idrys' voice, accusing him, and demanding he come in the gate last, because otherwise it would disrespect the King – but which King, had not been clear to him then or now.

"Sihhë!" the people in town had cried, out of joy to see him, the very people who had shunned him in their streets when he had been in such desperate need, alone, and hungry. "Lord Sihhë!" they shouted, like the men on the field, but the ones had rushed toward him and the others had fled. "Lord King!" they cried out, when the one King was dead, and the other King was Cefwyn, but he was not their king, nor wished to be, that least of all.

The wind rattled at the windowpanes. There seemed menace in the night, and the wind reminded him of the wind that had hovered around the towers of Ynefel. The wind blew now as it had blown there, in violent and angry gusts, and rattled the window latch.

– *Sihhë, it said. Open the window.*

– *No, he said, and wondered at its simplicity. He was far wiser than that.*

– *Sihhë lord, the Wind whispered to him; and then it whipped away with a sinuous force, leaving an impression of its terror behind it.*

But not, perhaps, fear of him. Something else came. He sprang to his feet, transfixed with the realization that the presence was not at the windows, it was with him in the room.

It found no barrier. It brushed past his attention, weak, gentle, and reasonable.

– *Tristen. Tristen, welcome me, quickly. I have not much strength.*

– *Emuin.*

– *The King* – the presence began to ask him, and grew thin, and almost left.

– *The King is dead, master Emuin. Cefwyn's father is dead. Now Cefwyn is King.* He stood in that place of blinding *light, where was neither life nor time. He looked about him slowly. There was a shadow in the light, a presence which had no shape, but essence which from moment to moment threatened to dissipate, and he thought that this was Emuin. Hold on, master Emuin. I need you. I very much need you tonight, sir. I've tried before.*

Emuin seemed to grow more substantial, then. And seemed dismayed at him. Oh, gods, Emuin murmured. Gods, lad. What have you done?

– I did everything I knew, sir. He held out his hands to draw Emuin closer, but the bloodstains showed dark on the light that was his skin, and he stopped reaching, appalled at what he saw. I fought, sir. I thought it was right. I knew how. And Cefwyn was in danger.

Emuin frightened him with his fear. He thought Emuin might flee him as the men had on the field.

But Emuin came closer then, and a touch brushed his stained fingers, and a silken touch folded fingers into his, and closed, almost substance. A touch brushed his face, and it seemed that Emuin's arms folded him close, as Mauryl would, as Cefwyn had – but never was the fear Emuin felt so evident as now.

– I don't know how to help you, Emuin said. You've gone far beyond what I understand, lad. I don't know what to do.

– Tell me what is right! he asked of Emuin, but Emuin said, That's the difficulty, isn't it? What's right? I don't know, young lord. I never knew, myself.

It was not the truth he wanted to hear of Emuin.

Then he felt something else creep near. It listened to their thoughts, a presence that lived in this white place and was a danger once they were in it.

– Go back! Emuin said, pushing him away. You must go back. Immediately. I'll be there as I can.

He saw something twisted and moving, nothing but shadow. He knew that it had been a man – or something like. That is Hasufin, he heard Emuin say, but far away. Be careful. Tristen. Be careful.

Emuin's voice faded. He saw Ynefel. The fortress seemed very near, visible through a shadow woods, a place by tricks of the eye new and substantial, then shimmering and fading into mist and deeper shadow. Something dreadful sat there now. He saw Mauryl's face in the stones of the wall, and all his certainties that this was where he wanted to be fell away from him. He wanted to escape. He felt Emuin behind him, in that strange sense of place and whereabouts. And he dared not leave Emuin undefended in his flight.

– Inborn in the Sihhë, a voice whispered, is the skill to touch other planes. The old blood runs true. Shaping that he is, he has substance here and there alike, does he not, Emuin?

– Nothing that should interest you, Emuin warned him. Young lord, believe nothing it offers you.

Tristen stopped in mid-impulse, drifting close to that familiar place, and Mauryl's features began to shade and warp until it was another and younger face that looked on him.

He was aware of all the land then, stretched out like the map on Cefwyn's table, and little tendrils of darkness ran out from Ynefel, curled here and there in the woods and lapped out into Elwynor – while another thread ran through Amefel to Henas'amef itself, growing larger by the instant.

He felt threat in that single black thread, as if it touched something familiar, something close to him. Or was himself. He was not, single chill thought, certain.

Other threads multiplied into Elwynor, a complicated weaving of which he could not see the end.

– Tristen! Emuin commanded him.

He had grown attracted to the voice. He tried now to retreat toward Emuin. He risked becoming as attenuated as the threads.

– Tristen! This is Mauryl's enemy – this is your enemy! Come back to me! Come back now!

A hand seized his hand. It pulled him through the air faster than he could get his balance, and he fell.

He struck the floor on his side. His limbs were sprawled on

393

cold stone, aching. He moved his hands, as amazed at the play of tendons under flesh as the first time he had seen it – and felt strong arms lift him up and strong arms encircle him, a shadow intervening between him and the fire.

"M'lord! – Guard! Damn, get help in here, man! He's had one of his fits!"

He heard Uwen's voice. Uwen's shadow enfolded him. He blinked at it dazedly and languidly. Other men crowded about him, lifting him from Uwen's arms, but not quite – all of them together bore him somewhere, which turned out to be back to bed, down in the cool, tangled covers, which they straightened, tugging them this way and that.

Most left, then, but Uwen remained. Uwen hovered over him, brushing the hair back from his face, kneeling at his bedside. Uwen's seamed face was haggard, pale, and frightened.

"I am safe," Tristen said. It took much effort to say. But he found the effort to say it made it so. He drew a freer breath.

"Ye're cold, m'lord." Uwen chafed his hand and arm violently, tucked the arm back beneath the cover and piled blankets on him until the weight made it hard to breathe. Uwen was satisfied, then, but lingered, kneeling by his bed, shivering in the chill of a night colder than Tristen remembered.

"Uwen, go to bed. Rest."

"No. Not whiles ye go falling on floors in fits."

Uwen saw through his pretenses, he was certain, although Uwen made light of it. It filled him with sudden foreboding for Uwen's life. "Uwen," he said, "my enemies are terrible."

Uwen did not move. The fear did not leave his look. But neither did he look overwhelmed by it. "Oh, I know your fits, m'lord. They don't frighten me. And who else knows ye the way I do? And where should I go, worrying about you, and no way to do anything, then? I ain't leaving for any asking, m'lord, so ye might as well forget about it. Not for your asking. Not even for the King's."

Uwen was too proud to run away. Tristen understood so.

He had no urge to run away himself when the danger came on him, because in the moments it came, he saw no choices. He understood this, too, and did not call it bravery, as it was in Uwen. That place of no choices was very close to him now. It still tried to open behind his eyes, and he shivered, not from fear, but because flesh did not well endure that place.

And bravely Uwen held to his hand until the tremors passed, head bowed, his arms rigid. Uwen would not let him go into that bright place again, and that, he thought, was very wise on Uwen's part, even if Uwen could see none of it, and could not reach after him. Uwen could hold his body, and make him aware of it, and keep him from slipping away.

"How near is it to morning?" Tristen asked, when the tremors had passed.

"I don't know, m'lord. D' ye want I should go ask?"

"There must be soldiers. I must have soldiers."

"M'lord?"

"There's an enemy at Ynefel. He mustn't stay there."

"Gods, no." Uwen hugged him tight. "Ye can't be goin' again' that place, m'lord. It ain't no natural enemy, whatever's there, and best ye leave it be."

"I am not natural," Tristen said. "Whatever you have heard of me, I think it must be true."

"That ye be Sihhë? I don't know about such things. Ye're my good young lad, m'lord, ye ain't nothing but good."

"Can I be?" He spread the fingers of his hand wide, held it before them, against the firelight. "*This* knows what I am. It fought for me. And I dreamed just now of Ynefel. I saw threads going out of it. My enemy lives there now and he wants this land. He reaches into all the regions around us. He reaches even into this room, Uwen. I felt it."

"Then tell m'lord Cefwyn. He's the King, now. He can call on the priests. Or master Emuin, what's more like. He could help."

"No. Cefwyn doesn't understand. I do. Leave me, Uwen. Go back to the guard where you were. Of all the soldiers I must take there – not you."

"The King won't have ye go wi' any soldiers," Uwen forecast with a slow shake of his head. "This is priest's business. Little as I like 'em, they got their uses, lad, and this has to be one."

"Priests." He recalled the priests he had seen – those he had met only today in the Quinalt shrine, where the King's body was, priests scattering before him, cringing, lest their robes touch him. "They fear *me*. How could they face my enemy?"

"Then I don't know, m'lord. King or no, His Majesty hain't got no soldiers willing to march that road."

He found nothing to say, then. He had no plan, else, if even Uwen said he was wrong.

"M'lord," Uwen said, "m'lord, – I'd go wi' ye. I'd go wi' ye t' very hell, but I wouldn't see ye go there. I'd put meself in your way right at these gates, wi' all respect t' your lordship, I won't see ye go there. No."

"Uwen, what if this enemy comes out from Ynefel? What if he comes across to Althalen?"

"I don't know nothing about that, m'lord. I don't know nothing about wizards, and I don't want to know. I'll guard your back from any enemy I can see wi' my two eyes and smite 'im wi' whate'er I find to hand, but, gods, I don't like this 'un. Send to Emuin, m'lord. He'd know what to do. He's a wise 'un. He ain't no real priest."

He shook his head. "Emuin doesn't know at all what to do with this. He's afraid."

"Ye don't know that, m'lord?"

"I spoke with him. I spoke with him just now, Uwen."

"M'lord, you was dreaming. That was all."

"I did speak to him." The ceiling seemed more solid now, a pattern of woodworking and lights. "I'm warm now. Go to bed, Uwen."

"I'm comfortable here, m'lord."

"I'm in no danger now. Go rest. Think about going back to the guard. The servants can manage for me." He reached for Uwen's scar-traced arm, pressed it, careful of new cuts, and a bruise that, the size of his fist, darkened the side of Uwen's forearm. "I want you to be safe, Uwen."

"I hain't got no family," Uwen said finally. "The guard's me mistress. But I couldn't leave ye for the barracks again, m'lord. Couldn't. Wouldn't be nothing then. I'm getting old. I feel the cold in winter, I think on my wife and my girls and my boy that the fever got, and there ain't no use for me beginning again. Damn, no, I couldn't leave ye, my lord."

And he tucked the blanket about him and got up and wandered away to his own small room between the doors.

Tristen watched him. He had never known about Uwen's wife or children. He had made Uwen remember them, and he saw that Uwen had attached to him a feeling that Uwen had nowhere to bestow; as he had had for Mauryl, and had nowhere now to bestow it – not on Emuin, who had not Mauryl's wisdom, and not Mauryl's strength: Emuin had fled him and refused to be known, or loved, or held to, and he respected that wish, even understood it as fear. Cefwyn asked him to be his friend, but Cefwyn had so many people he had to look out for and to take care of.

But Uwen had only him. Uwen by what he said had lost everyone else. Uwen was not so wise as Mauryl: he was as brave as anyone could ask, but somehow he had ceased to depend on Uwen for advice as much as Uwen had begun to take orders from him.

And when had that happened? When had he grown to be anyone's source of advice in the world, when he did not understand the world himself?

He lay still in his bed, and longed for daylight. Time – of which he had rarely been acutely conscious – again seemed to be slipping rapidly toward some event he could not predict or understand.

Far away he heard movements in the halls. From the yard came the occasional clatter of hooves, horsemen abroad in the dark, bound to or from the lower town or countryside or the camps – there was no cause to be dashing about on horses within the Zeide courts. Perhaps messengers, he said to himself, and tried to think what might be going on that had so much astir.

He had no inclination to sleep and confront another bad dream. Sweat prickled on him, the blankets weighed like iron. The beats of his heart measured interminable time, and he lay and stared at the lightless glitter of the windowpanes.

The darkness seemed a little less outside, a reddish murk, but not in the east, a glow that reflected on the higher roofs and walls – and from outside came a noise he could not at first recognize, then decided it was many voices shouting at something. Thunder rumbled. Rain spattered the glass, a few drops, and the air stayed chill – he could feel it with his fingers to the glass, and the fire seemed more than convenience tonight.

The glow outside was much too early, unless, he thought, in this wretched day the laws of nature were bent and that murkish light was an ill-placed dawn or an effect of storm he had never seen.

But whatever the cause of it there was less and less chance of sleeping or resting in such goings-on, with the accumulation of unanswered questions and unidentifiable sounds and light. He rose from bed, determined at last and least to know what was happening that kept other people awake, and searched out clean, warm clothes. He had half dressed before, probably because of his opening the clothes-press, which had a stubborn door, Uwen arrived from the other room, rubbing his eyes and limping.

"M'lord," Uwen murmured, "what's the matter?"

"I don't know," he said, and thought of going quickly, taking just the door guard, not wishing Uwen to have to dress and break his sleep, but then he remembered Cefwyn's order about wearing the mail, and it was too serious an order to dismiss lightly. He went to get it. "There's a great deal of going and coming. I'm going downstairs to see."

"I will, m'lord. Ye don't need to stir out."

"I want to see, Uwen. *I* want to know." It seemed to him his whole life until now had swung on his ignorance of the things around him – that too often he had taken others' seeing and others' doing, and not always had the result of that turned out for the good. He knew much too little, now, when Cefwyn was becoming King and Cefwyn's brother was entering the household. So much else was changing, not alone in Henas'amef, as he knew it to be, but in Elwynor and the whole of the lands he had ever heard about.

While he was putting on his boots Uwen had stumbled back to his own space, and came back fastening his breeches and carrying his boots and his coat – Uwen did not intend to let him go alone, that was clear, and of all orders he could give Uwen that he knew Uwen would obey, he had had clear warning that Uwen would disobey him wide and at large if he bade him stay.

There came an outcry from some distant place. They both looked toward the windows. "M'lord," Uwen said, "don't be going out. I don't know what's happening. I don't think it's nothing good. I swear to ye, I'll go down fast and see, and report to ye before ye could dress and be down."

"No," Tristen said, wound his hair out of the way as best he could and began to struggle with the mail shirt himself until Uwen came to help him.

The mail came down on his shoulders and shaped itself to his body, becoming no weight, a part of him. He picked up a coat that had turned up in the clothes-press, velvet and black like all else they gave him, the heaviest thing he had, against the chill in the night. He put it on over the mail, and Uwen, shaking his head, fastened it snugly down his chest, not pleased with his going, but helping him to be presentable, all the same.

The halls upstairs were deserted except for the guards appointed to the various doors. Noise of shouting drifted up from the lower floor, and they walked to the stairs, two of the guards from their own door walking behind them as the guards always did when he went outside.

Half of Cefwyn's door-guards were missing, too, meaning an empty apartment and the likelihood that Cefwyn had never yet come to bed – or that Cefwyn had had to leave it after that clattering of men up and down the hall.

Cefwyn's father lay dead. He thought that, however exhausted Cefwyn was, however strongly Cefwyn had rejected the offers of people who wanted to stay these lonely hours with him, it was unlikely that Cefwyn would have slept at all tonight.

But that Cefwyn would be up wandering the halls – he had not expected.

They descended the stairs into the main hall, where soldiers gathered and servants and lords and ladies stood in knots whispering together, weeping, some of them. He smelled smoke, and recalled Althalen, where Cefwyn swore no fire had come since the Sihhë had died there. But this did not seem ghostly smoke. It made the eyes sting.

The noise came from the halls beyond.

"No farther," Uwen counseled him. "My lord, stay and I'll see."

He knew by Uwen's warning that there was no pleasure to come to him by going any farther. But all safety tonight seemed illusory; and his danger was worse, he had already persuaded himself, in biding ignorant of what happened in the place in which he lived, whether Cefwyn acted or others did without Cefwyn's knowledge. Defend him, Cefwyn had bidden him swear: and how could he do that in utter ignorance?

Guards stood in the central hall. He went past them unchallenged, and Uwen stayed with him. So did his personal guards, into the main doors at the Zeide's heart, those that let out into the front court.

Those four doors lay wide open. Their access and the whole corridor was jammed with mingled soldiery and residents of the hall in brocades or velvets or priests' plain habits. Lamps lit the place, as they did in all places where the wind blew through, but the glow outside the doors was the red glare of a larger fire on vast billows of dark smoke, the stench of which reached far inside the hall.

Voices roared, outside, a wash of sound in which no words made sense.

It was impossible to keep together in the crowd. He plunged past a knot of lords out onto the landing and down the stairs, searching for a clear space to stand, at first, then found himself swept up in the rush, realizing that the crowd was carrying him toward the heart of the disturbance.

"M'lord," he heard Uwen call to him, one clear, thin voice in that din of voices, but he had found a clearer vantage at the side-facing steps and did not wish to yield it up.

Wind rushed at him in that exposure, cold, rainy wind warmed with smoke. Ash and sparks flew. He wondered if the far wing of the building itself was afire – but he saw as he came past the crowd on the steps that it was a large fire set at the side of the courtyard. Men came and went sparsely in proximity to its light, showing him how large that fire was, a pile of wood more than the height of a man; and the flames lit figures that hung on the curtain wall above it, men dangling from ropes, against the stones of the defenses of the Zeide. While he watched, one plummeted into the fire, in a plume of sparks.

Men. Men hanged by the neck from ropes. Men burning in the fire.

The crowd behind him shouted. Guards broke forth from the doors, jostling him. In that press, for one frightening moment, he saw a distorted face, a bloody wreckage of a man hastened along by armored Guelen guards. Red hair, the man had, and the ruin of fine clothing. For an instant the man had looked straight at him.

Heryn, he thought in horror.

Heryn Aswydd. Cefwyn had blamed him for the men who had attacked the King.

Soldiers keeping the crowd back pressed him against the wall, and he stayed there, his back against it, following with his eyes the progress of that company of soldiers and others across the yard. Raucous laughter shocked him. He came down the steps, seeking to go closer, in the smell of smoke-warmed wind. There came a rumble he realized belatedly was thunder. Droplets of rain began to fall – it will put out the fires, he thought. It will save Lord Heryn. It will clear the smoke. It will make things clean.

And then he knew that it could not, because it could never bring things back the way they had been, simple, and clear and becoming utterly safe at a word from the men who ruled his life. The fires were not going out for any rain, and the burned men would not come back to life.

"M'lord." Uwen reached him and caught his arm. "M'lord, best you go in."

"They mean to kill him," he said, unable to accept that Uwen was so calm, as that last group mounted the steps toward the fire, taking Heryn with them. His voice choked. He was trembling. "Orien? Tarien, too?"

"That's in King Cefwyn's hands, m'lord, come. Come wi' me. This ain't no place for you."

He could not let Uwen or anyone conceal any more truths from him. Uwen frightened him with his calm voice, his evident belief that such things as he saw now were ordinary and right. He broke away from Uwen and began to walk across the yard. Rain was falling, pelting him with large, cold drops, spotting the cobbles, making him blink as the wind carried rain into his face.

Uwen caught his arm, forcefully, this time. "King's justice, m'lord, ye can't help here!"

Justice? Was this the Word from the archive's Philosophy? Was this the Word that went with Happiness?

He feared the violence around him, he flinched at the loss of life – he feared the passage from life into death that he had already caused, and saw it happening again before his eyes, and he could not explain or understand it – but the knowledge that it did happen was inside him, a Word racing around a doorless dark and trying to come out. Men feared that passage as they feared nothing else – and he understood the dying on the field as much as he understood death at all. But in the Zeide, where he lived, Men had gathered to cheer as other men burned – and Uwen seemed to think it was nothing remarkable, but nothing he should look at.

Rain began to pelt down about him, but it had no effect on the fire – the blaze sent out waves of heat too great for any rain to stop.

Then lightning whitened the stone of the top of the fire-stained wall, thunder cracked right over the yard, and rain began to sweep down in fire-lit sheets. Drenched onlookers began to retreat, some running, to the doors. A man slipped and fell on the steps. It was confusion, and in all that crowd was no one he would wish to find, no one whose answers he would want to know. He began to move instead against the crowd, trying to reach that proximity of the fire where he knew he was forbidden, as he was forbidden all harsh things.

But Uwen caught him a third time, pleading with him, half-drowned by a peal of thunder, and in defeat he went with Uwen back to the steps, up under the shelter of the arch.

In the doorway a shadow accosted them with such absolute authority he stopped cold, standing partly in the rain.

It was Idrys.

"Your guards report more faithfully than your man does," Idrys said. "And what provokes this bloody curiosity, lord Tristen of the Sihhë?"

"Where is Cefwyn, sir? Where shall I find him?"

Idrys' eyes raked him over. "I shall take you there, my lord," Idrys said with no more than his usual coldness, and turned and led the way, not a far distance once they were inside. Guards with Idrys cleared their way through the gatherings of men and women who shivered and complained in the corridor.

They passed the intersection of hall and stairs and came to that chamber they called the Lesser Hall, where the guards had brought him to meet with Cefwyn the first night he came here.

"Wait outside," Idrys bade Uwen.

"Uwen, do so," Tristen said, because Idrys' tone had not been polite. Uwen was soaked; he was; he wanted to have answers from Cefwyn while Cefwyn was to be found; and as quickly as possible take himself and all his guards upstairs into dry clothing. He did not expect it would take long, or that Cefwyn could spare much time for him, but he was determined that Cefwyn should know what was done outside, if Cefwyn was in any wise ignorant. He did not wholly trust Idrys, regardless of Cefwyn's word. He saw reasons the lords around Cefwyn might wish not to inform Cefwyn of everything that happened, and he still found it hard to believe that Cefwyn knew of that horror outside.

He entered the hall behind Idrys, into a space which now held a large table. He brought smoke with him, the reek clinging to his clothes, but he could not be certain he was the sole source. The lords from the south and strangers who had come with Cefwyn's brother were gathered about the table, and their armed escorts stood about, crowding the walls, some of them rain-draggled, proving that they, too, had been outside.

So perhaps Cefwyn did know. But there was no dampness about Cefwyn. He saw Cefwyn and Efanor among those standing at the table, over a collection of maps, and before he could approach, Idrys arrived at Cefwyn's side and whispered something precautionary in Cefwyn's ear.

Cefwyn looked about at him in anger. "I told you stay to your room!"

He was shaken by the anger, dismayed, and he did not thank Idrys for whatever Idrys had said. He remembered that Idrys clearly knew what was going on in the courtyard. But he still held out hope Cefwyn did not. "They've hanged Lord Heryn," he said to Cefwyn. "And other men. I don't understand, m'lord."

Cefwyn seemed disturbed, and still angry. "They've *beheaded* Lord Heryn. Noble blood does have its privilege. But you've clearly passed the bounds of things you need to know, sir. – Idrys, why did you bring him here? Damn it, why isn't he in his room?"

"Your Majesty, Lord Tristen begged urgently to have personal audience with you. I thought it might be of more moment than it seems."

"No, sir," Tristen said, and evaded Idrys' reach to come to the table between Cefwyn and lord Pelumer. "No, sir. I need to speak with you."

"Not now, Tristen."

"Sir, – Emuin –" He had diminishing confidence he had any argument at all regarding Lord Heryn, but that was not the only cause he had of disturbance tonight, and it was not the only thing Cefwyn needed to know. But he recalled that Uwen doubted his hearing Emuin, and Cefwyn did not look patient of his stories or his questions at the moment. "Emuin warned me of a danger – and this –"

There was a murmur among the assembled lords.

"What danger?" Cefwyn asked. "When?"

"Tonight, sir, now."

"Is Emuin here?" Cefwyn asked. "Has he come?"

"M'lord King," Idrys said, "Emuin is not here." Idrys took Tristen's arm, and his fingers hurt. "Let me take you upstairs, young lord."

"No! M'lord, I saw it –" He resisted Idrys' attempt to draw him away, and it was clear on faces all about that no one of them believed him, or thought it likely he had spoken with Emuin at all. He kept the struggle between himself and Idrys a quiet one, and kept the pain Idrys caused entirely to himself. "I shall wait my turn, m'lord King, if you please. I think I might know something useful, but I don't wish to speak what I don't know." He thought of Uwen shivering in the hall. "Only let me dismiss Uwen and my guards upstairs. They're wet through."

"So are you."

"Yes, sir, but I want to stay."

"Dismiss your men," Cefwyn said. "Page. Get him a cloak."

"From his quarters, Your Majesty?" the page asked.

"Give him mine! Good gods!" Cefwyn was in pain, and

405

limped when he moved – Cefwyn ought to be in his bed, Tristen thought, but Cefwyn was trying to decide something with his maps that were strewn across the tabletop, and with these men, not all of whom were pleasant or agreeable. Tristen took his small permission to go to the door, and put his head out.

Uwen was there, shivering till his teeth rattled. So were the two night guards, in no better case.

"Cefwyn's guards will see me back," Tristen said quietly, for there was business and argument going on behind him, among the lords in the room. "Please go upstairs and go to bed, Uwen. Have the guards change clothes. I'll be safe."

"Ye're sopped, too, m'lord. Shall I bring a cloak down?"

"They have me one. I'll not be long. – Or if I am, please go on to bed. The guards here will see me upstairs. There's no need of you to stay."

"Aye, m'lord," Uwen said, not sorry to be sent for a change of clothes, he was certain. Uwen was shivering and miserable, and gave him no argument about it.

He shut the door to the hall and took the heavy cloak from the page who waited at his elbow. He wrapped the thick, lined velvet about him with relief and went back among the others in the room.

"What happened inside Amefel and on the border," Cefwyn was saying, "we must answer, early and strongly. Heryn claimed his frauds against the Crown frightened him to such a desperate treason. Heryn claimed that his only intention was to call the King here and to arrange an attack of a small Elwynim force – he swore that he meant to be there with his own forces, to come to my father's rescue. He had the effrontery to say –" Cefwyn drew an angry breath. "That had my father not moved early and had I not had him under arrest, the plan would have worked and my father would not have died."

There was a muttering among the lords. Tristen thought it a foolish plan on Heryn's part, a dangerous and desperate plan. He saw the motions of troops in his mind, he saw the lay of the land.

And he thought that there had been far more enemies than seemed likely for a false threat against Cefwyn's father.

"This was Heryn's claim," Cefwyn said, "and we could obtain no other word from him. From two prisoners, common men, we have a name, Lord Caswyddian of Lower Saissonnd. Style of shields and various leavings on the field do indicate the river provinces of Elwynor. The prisoners did not see him on the field, but avow a son of his led them in what was given to be a retaliation for the execution of five Saissondim under flag of truce – this never happened, but this was what they were told. Sovrag's men are not back with a report, but either by bridge or by barge, the Elwynim have at least light horse across the river in numbers. Which they may have withdrawn. Disregarding the question whether Heryn told the truth, whether this story of the prisoners reflects something Heryn did, which he denied, or whether the Elwynim betrayed Heryn and advantaged themselves of his folly to do far more than he wished – a possibility which I do not discount – I am not in either case convinced the Elwynim Regent was behind the attack. That – is behind my reasoning."

"M'lord," Efanor said, "this was not a rag-tag element. These were well armed. We have names."

"Of a lord and men bearing no device, no banner. This is not the Regent. It *is* a sign of the Regent's lords with the bit in their teeth. It is a sign which way the wind is blowing should the Regent die."

"Our father is dead!" Efanor said. "What matter *which* cursed Elwynim crossed the river? The Regent is ultimately responsible! You do not consider accepting any marriage offer from them! You would not *do* this!"

"Did I say so? Have I done so? I point out that we are not dealing with a well-organized enemy, brother, and that a message to the Elwynim Regent possibly – if it cannot produce us names – may still produce action, even strengthen the hand of the Regent against troublesome elements within his own realm and get us the justice we're due."

"These are murderers! These are godless, heretic murderers!"

"Who, if certain Elwynim lords have acted without their Regent or in spite of him, have committed treason against him, brother. Before I commit men to the field, I'd know against whom we are sending troops, and why, and whether there is another choice that will not plunge the realm into a war along half its borders – with gods know what allies, at a very unstable time in our affairs and theirs!"

"You are temporizing with murderers. You are expecting truth from a man who does not worship the gods!"

"One can hardly be both godless and a heretic, brother. And this is Amefel."

"You've been in this heretic land too long, brother."

"Efanor. Efanor. You're mortally weary. So am I. And heart-sore. I know that. Go upstairs."

"I'll not be dismissed!"

"I'll not be lessoned! For the love we bear each other, either offer counsel without reading me scriptures, Efanor, or offer me no counsel at all. If I want a priest I'll call for one!"

Efanor was pale. His hands shook. "This is not a joking matter, my lord brother."

"Trust I know it is not. Trust that I make my prayers as they're due, good brother, and trust that I know Amefel as having more worthy lords than the Aswyddim, the Elwynim as having many worse lords than the Regent, and that if we allow any fledgling in that nest to raise himself by the death of our father, we not only sully our father's memory, we promote his murderer to fortune and to power. If we attack and kill the Regent, we may well put our father's murderer in power, because we have at one stroke given whatever villain bears the guilt both a war and a kingship to fill."

"Or," said Umanon, "we throw the Elwynim into confusion, and we attack across the river."

"Look at the map, Your Grace. Having conquered all of Elwynor, shall we arm twelve-year-old maids and send them out to stand duty? Elwynor is a vast, vast land, as great as our own kingdom. We do not do well to pull the dragon's tail."

"Empty land. Pasturage. It is not that populous."

"But it is not now hostile and *we* are not in it. How far apart must our patrols ride through these pastures to prevent seditions? And if we found one nest of sedition, would they not move into the unpatrolled land? We cannot occupy Elwynor, sir. You dream."

Cefwyn was right, Tristen thought. But there was more. He burned to say so, but the argument was already bitter.

"Fear," said Umanon, "makes fewer patrols necessary."

"I cannot agree," Cefwyn said. "And I will not be disputed in this. To take Elwynor would be a disaster to us."

"Not if they fear us."

"Sirs." Tristen could bear it no longer. "Sirs, there's more than Elwynor. There's Ynefel."

"Who is this stranger," asked Umanon, "that we should trust him? He's Sihhë, you say, and does he not most properly stand with the Amefin – at best?"

"We trust him," Cefwyn said, "because he saved our life. Because he drove the attackers off the field and saved the lives of all of us near my lord father."

"He did that," a captain said.

"But," said a finely-dressed lord Tristen did not know, one who had come with Cefwyn's father, "does he stand as a member of this council, my lord King? He has no real holdings. Althalen and Ynefel are a domain of mice and owls."

"Lord of Murandys," Cefwyn said softly, leaning forward, "his titles are by my grant, and by inheritance – titles by *blood*, m'lord."

There was chill silence.

"Or something like unto it," Efanor muttered.

"Brother," Cefwyn said.

Efanor ducked his head and folded his arms, the image of Idrys.

"My lords," Cefwyn said, "I have not slept tonight, nor have you. I have sent messengers informing the northern lords of my father's death, and of my resolution to hold this town and settle matters on the borders before returning to the capital.

The press of events here affords me no respite for an official mourning nor for the receiving of their formal oaths, which I hope they will tender in intent, at least, by messenger. The danger to the realm is here, whether in Amefel, whether on the river. Our decision is made. My father –" Cefwyn's voice faltered. "My father will be interred here –"

"M'lord!" Efanor's head lifted.

"Here, I say, in a Quinalt shrine earliest of all Quinalt shrines in Amefel, a place of great import, great and historic sanctity, and presided over by the southern Patriarch, who will conduct the services as soon as we have built an appropriate vault, brother, in which our father may lie until I have dealt with his murderers! The King of Ylesuin will *not* be carried home, sirs, murdered, and with no penalty dealt his killers. The Kings of Ylesuin living *and* dead will not quit this province until they have justice, sirs, and on that I take holy oath! You will not dissuade me."

Heads bowed, even Efanor's, in the face of Cefwyn's anger. Tristen ducked his head, too, but he had caught Cefwyn's eye, and Cefwyn seemed not angry at him, nor as passionate as his voice had sounded. "The rest, the rest, sirs, I shall inform you after I've taken more sleep than I have yet. Good night to you. Gods give you peaceful rest."

The lords bowed, murmuring polite formalities. Tristen wondered if Cefwyn had changed his mind and wished him to leave, too, but when he had caught Cefwyn's eye, Cefwyn shook his head and caught his arm. Efanor also remained, exempt from the order, it seemed; and Idrys – constantly Idrys stayed at Cefwyn's shoulder.

The door shut. They were alone, save the Guelen guard.

"Efanor," Cefwyn appealed to his brother.

"Have we secrets to share at last?" Efanor asked. "Now am I in your counsel, brother? Am I at least privy to the secrets you bestow on the Sihhë?"

Cefwyn made a curt motion of his hand: the guard withdrew and closed the door.

Then Cefwyn leaned on the table, head bowed above the

map in an attitude of profound weariness. "Efanor, trust me. After the funeral, I shall send you to the capital, while I pursue matters here. Is that not trust? I shall give you highest honor. I forget our quarrels. Only do not *ever* oppose me in council on matters we two have already discussed, – and bear me some small patience now, as I bear it with you."

"What moves this sudden liberality?"

Cefwyn's face had been weary. Now it went hard and angry and he straightened his shoulders. "The gods' grace, Efanor! I cannot fight outside enemies and you at once. Grant me this. Our father's death will be repaid. I do not say it will be repaid tomorrow, but that it will be repaid – give me this much trust. Give me your affection, if you have it to give. But I shall take your duty, if you offer at least that."

Efanor's eyes wandered to Tristen and back again. "Whatever influences work here have mellowed you – or your experience in this land has vastly increased your subtlety."

"I am tired." Cefwyn eased a chair behind him, extended his wounded leg, and sat down, holding it. "Gods."

"Better you had followed your physicians' advice, Majesty," said Idrys. "The guards should bear you up to bed."

"No." Cefwyn reached to the crown about his brow, rubbed it, where it left a mark and bloodied a cut. He settled it on again. For a moment he rested his eyes against his hand, wiped at them, looked up again. "I have no subtlety left at all, Efanor. This province has undone it. I pray you be my loyal brother, nothing less."

"I am astonished," Efanor said dryly. "I am truly astonished. But bear you good faith, I shall, if you bear it to me. I had not expected your trust, Cefwyn."

"I need all such allies as I can trust. We are under attack. Mauryl – was a grievous loss. – Tristen."

"Sir."

"You were out there. Tonight."

"I saw, sir."

"It was justice," Cefwyn said.

"I believe you," Tristen said, knowing nothing else to say.

"You had news of Emuin. A messenger? To you and not to me? Or what?"

It was not Cefwyn and himself, it was not Cefwyn who could be his friend and bear with his imprecisions and his foolishness.

Nor was he the same as he had been, even days ago. He said, with cold at heart, "No, sir. Emuin does speak to me. He tries to help me. But he can't, always. I think that's why he went away."

"Wizardry," Efanor said.

"No, sir," Tristen said, "I don't think so. I don't feel so. Just – he hears me."

"How can you dispute such things?" Efanor demanded, not of him, but of Cefwyn. "How can you countenance such arguments – wizardry and not wizardry? Do natural men hear wizards?"

"We had no natural man at issue in Mauryl," Cefwyn said in a hard voice, "and damned well we should consult, brother, both Tristen and Emuin, where they have something of significance to say."

"Consult as you like, then. *I'll* none of it!"

"I'll warrant you'll hear nothing to imperil your delicate holiness. Stay. As a wizard, Tristen is gentler than Emuin is."

"I saw his gentility on the field."

"And he ours, and *yours* tonight, brother! Forbear. Father gave me a province next a wizard and Emuin for a counselor to help hold it. Now Mauryl's fallen, and left me Tristen for a ward – whom Emuin approved. Tristen swore to be my defender, and kept his oath like a good and godly man, or this realm would have no king, not you, nor me, nor Marhanen at all – and Heryn would lord it over a realm of his own tonight, snugged right close to Elwynor. Wherewith the Regent would go down, some pretender would rise up with the marriage-able daughter, and Heryn would become bulwark of an Elwynor no longer held at bay by a river that Mauryl, I have long suspected, defined as their border until his overdue but

unwelcome departure from these mortal bounds. *That* is my
fear – that whatever stricture the old man laid on the Elwynim
no longer holds. But it is not a fear I wish to rehearse before
the Amefin lords –"

"Whom I would not have admitted to counsel, let me tell
you."

"Brother, I know these men, that some are in dire fear of
being tied to Heryn's sins, and others hated Heryn bitterly for
reasons of their own and thought until today that he had had
unquestioned Marhanen support. As perhaps Father did find
him useful, Father not well knowing the inner workings of
Amefel – but, to be quite pragmatic about Heryn Aswydd, I
have been in this province long enough to have known too
much about his excesses in office and to have received at least
tentative approaches from the lords most desperate of those
excesses, so that *I* no longer needed him. Therefore his head
will adorn the gate."

"And in your manipulations you drew Father into this –"

"Do not you *dare* say that to me!" Cefwyn brought his
hand down on the maps, hard. "Father chose to believe
Heryn instead of me. Ask Father's councillors if they could
dissuade him, or whether they fed the fires. Ask them! I do
not ask where you stood."

Tristen clenched his hands together, wishing he knew what
to say to prevent a fight. But after a moment Cefwyn said,
more quietly,

"I do not ask, brother. I take your presence here as exactly
what you said, coming here to make things look better than
you feared they were. But I do not think you looked to find
me in Henas'amef."

"I did not," Efanor said, also quietly.

"To what an extent we have left our childish trust. We
swore, you and I – we swore not to let Grandfather divide us."

"I keep that oath," Efanor said. "I do not know if you do,
brother."

"I shall. Nor shall I believe the lies men tell. Heryn finally
realized that small change in his affairs, tonight. I fear that

413

Father did trust him. But I would not. – Tristen. Tristen, my friend. What do you need of me?"

He was confused in the flow of Words, Words that made great sense in the instant he heard them, and faded the next, but that advised him that far more had passed than he knew, and that nothing in these chambers was so clear or unequivocal as matters had seemed on the battlefield. How alike these two lords were, he thought, Efanor and Cefwyn, alike in features, alike in stature, in small turns of expression – but for Efanor's smooth chin and the crown on Cefwyn's brow.

"I came to say," he began, and his thoughts were still chasing the matter of Heryn and the fire, and the hanged men, and Heryn beheaded because he was noble. And the Marhanens. "I came to say, sir, I fear – fear –"

"Be at ease," Cefwyn said.

He could not but look at Efanor, who he knew disapproved him. At Idrys, who frowned. And, distractedly, last at Cefwyn.

"I saw Ynefel," he began. "I saw Mauryl's enemy reaching out of it."

"How do you know that?"

"I saw it, sir."

"You were nowhere near Ynefel. You dreamed, you mean."

"I dreamed awake, sir. And I think the harm never left Ynefel when Mauryl – died. Mauryl said I should go, I think, to keep me from it. It's not a good thing, to let his enemy stay there. His enemy is reaching out into Elwynor. Even here. My window rattled, more than once, and it did that in Ynefel. He did it."

"The man's mad," Efanor said in disgust.

"No, now," Cefwyn said. "Tristen. Go on. He, you say. This danger. What should we do about it?"

"You ought to have shutters, sir. Mauryl closed them every night."

"Shutters," Efanor said. "Of course. Shutters will save us. Good gods, brother!"

"Be still, Efanor. You are *no* help to his good sense. – Tristen. What about the windows? Are we speaking of magic, here? Is it something Mauryl did?"

Efanor made it hard to remember things in order. Idrys was staring at him, listening to everything he said and ready to find fault with what he could scarcely explain in words. He tried to gather his points in order. "Mauryl's enemy, m'lord King. He came to Ynefel, usually with storms. He rattled the shutters at night. Now the windows rattle here."

"Wind does that!" Efanor said, and Cefwyn: "Hush, brother."

"Mauryl said – Mauryl said that holes in the roof were no matter. That there are lines on the earth Men make when they build, and so long as you take care of them, the enemy can't get in. You ought to close all the doors when the Shadows go across the courtyard. You should have shutters, m'lord, and close them. Everyone in the town should. Doors and windows let a spirit in. It can't cross at other places."

"And it seeks to come indoors."

"I don't think it has, here. People are careless in town – but I don't think it's powerful here, yet. I think it could become powerful, if people started listening to it. I think Heryn was listening to it. I think that someone in Elwynor might be."

"Is this a god, this creature?" Idrys asked. "Or what?"

"It was a man. I think it's a ghost. A haunt. Emuin calls it Hasufin. But I'm not certain that's its name."

"Hasufin," Cefwyn said.

"Gods forfend," Efanor said, and he no longer sounded scornful. "I said there would no good come of this place. It's the whole cursed province. But past the holy shrines, no ill will come."

"It wants a Place, sir, that's what I know. But it's not just staying there. I'm afraid it's not. I don't know if it has help to go outside Ynefel, or even if it wants to. If you'd give me soldiers, sir, I'd go find out."

"No," Cefwyn said, "no such thing. I've sent for Emuin. I expect him soon. He'll deal with whatever it is."

415

"I don't think so. Emuin can't deal with it by himself. I think Mauryl did. But he was so old. He wasn't strong enough. I think —" He was trembling, and folded his hands under his arms to hide it. "I think that's what I was brought here to do. But I can't read the Book, and I don't know how."

"Gods bless," Efanor muttered.

"I would go," Tristen said. "I would go back to Ynefel. If you would give me soldiers. I would go there and find out what the trouble is."

"Well offered, Tristen, but what would they do?"

"I don't know, sir. But I would try to send it away."

"Try you would. But it's not a task for soldiers."

"A task for priests," Efanor said.

"No, sir," Tristen said. "Soldiers are more apt than priests. I do think they are."

"Against unholy magic?"

"Against whatever this is, sir."

"Tristen," Cefwyn said, "I fear no men would follow you. You ask far too much of them."

"Uwen said so. But I think – sometimes – I shouldn't have left there. I think – if I were what Mauryl wished me to be – I should have known what to do."

"Believe Uwen in this. Leave it to experienced men."

"To priests," Efanor said.

"I don't find any strength in them, sir. They seem more afraid than helpful. I've seen this thing. I saw it in the courtyard."

"Here?"

"No, sir, at Ynefel. It was a man made of dust. And it fell down into leaves."

There was long silence. "Sihhë," Efanor muttered finally. "And here we are, brother. The old ills, the magic, the wizardry, are all returned with him. What next?"

"Tristen," Cefwyn said, "you will not work against me. Whatever you do, you will not work against me or against the realm of Ylesuin."

"No, sir, I would not."

416

"You saw nothing of my father's death, by fact, hearing, rumor, or conjury before it happened. You would have told me if you had any warning at all."

"No, lord King. I never saw it. I would have told you."

"Nor have you plotted with Heryn."

"No, sir. I would not. I would have stopped him if I could."

Cefwyn had seemed to believe him all along. He thought that Cefwyn wanted him to say all these things for Efanor's sake.

"Heryn named two names," Cefwyn said. "Those when pressed may name others. In the meanwhile, – in the meanwhile – we can hope the Elwynim will not dare another move, since none has come by now. I say we go to bed, brother. And, Tristen, I say you leave matters to Emuin. He will come. And you can ask him what to do." Cefwyn stood, favoring his injured leg, and embraced him. "I never thanked you. I do that now, from the heart. Go back to your bed and have better dreams. We'll talk on this again when Emuin comes."

But, Tristen thought, but – Cefwyn had never yet understood him. Cefwyn had never understood there was imminent danger, and Efanor certainly had not. He looked to Idrys, who was holding the door, as first Cefwyn, then Efanor, left the room.

"Sir," he said to Idrys, "sir, please tell him –"

"M'lord King has his father lying dead," Idrys said coldly. "He has his pious brother to deal with, no easy matter. He has fractious lords chafing to establish their influence, and to add to his problems he has the Quinalt aghast over your influence as it is, m'lord of Ynefel. I suggest for the moment and in days following you keep very quiet and do not offer advice on priests again in Prince Efanor's hearing. This is a religious man, to whom priests mean much. I would not, *not*, sir, say again what you said to him about the ineffectuality of priests."

"But it is *true*, sir. If they could have kept *me* out of the shrine they would have, this morning. And they could not."

"M'lord of the Sihhë, if you persist, you may find what priests can do in this world. They can move princes to do the bloody things you saw in the courtyard, and they can move lords to speak and act against your King, to whom you swore fealty and obedience, sir. That you saved my lord on the field counts much with me and I honor that. But you will do as much harm to Cefwyn as you did good today if you turn the Quinalt priests against him with your talk, and well you might. I shall oppose you in that, I do warn you."

"But the danger, sir, –"

"Is in no wise as urgent as you have presented it. If you can prove otherwise, come to me with it and I shall batter His Majesty's doors down to gain you audience with him. Otherwise admit that while you may know Emuin's thoughts from afar you know nothing of Quinalt orthodoxy, on which rock you will founder if you persist in speaking such opinions, true or not. Good *night,* lord of Ynefel."

Cefwyn was going away with Efanor and with the guard, upstairs. Idrys left the door and followed, already well behind and hastening to overtake Cefwyn.

There were men of the Guelen guard still about the council door who might take him to his room, separately. And he sensed that Idrys had listened to him, but Idrys was telling him that truth or falsehood did not matter, and against all Mauryl's teachings – it did. There was no equivocating with thunderstorms and less with the Shadows.

And least of all, he feared, with what he saw in that gray realm which Cefwyn did not see, which no one but Emuin seemed to travel with him.

He did not know how to make Idrys understand, when he did not understand the threat himself. He did not know how to make Cefwyn believe what he himself could only half believe was so. He held Cefwyn's cloak about him, thinking of doing as Cefwyn expected him to do, and asking the guard to escort him back to a place where he could be guarded, and kept, and, he feared on his experience with Men, locked more securely away from seeing unpleasant truths.

418

That meant that he should know less of Cefwyn's affairs, not more, and he should have none of his questions answered, and none of his warnings heard: the more ignorant they kept him the less they would sensibly heed his warnings of what little he did see.

He moved away from the doors and left the guard, who had not questioned him and perhaps did not think of doing something without someone asking them to move, for someone who was not their assigned duty – he had learned of Uwen how the guards thought, and what they were told to do.

He walked to the massive central doors. The rain was still coming down, but the fire was not wholly drowned. It burned sullenly, and a handful of men, some well gone in wine or ale, stood in the shelter of the arches, watching the fires. There were guards, but they were watching the men, or talking with each other. And, he thought, he had Cefwyn's cloak about him, with the Marhanen Dragon blazoned on the leather edges.

So it was no difficulty to walk out onto the steps in the drizzle, and to walk down the steps in the shadow of the wall, and then to walk around the corner of the wall, and to walk on in that shadow, along the puddled base of the wall, to a dividing wall and a gate that always stood open by day.

It was open by night, too. He walked through, past the steps and the doors at the end of the wing, doors which were shut, their guards inside in the dry warm air, where sensible men had rather be.

The gate to the stable court was latched, but not locked: he supposed there were so many guards about and there was so little place to take a horse without leave that, absent the chance the horses would stray from there, no one cared. The stable door was shut, but that had no lock, only a latch. He went inside, and heard a stirring in the straw.

He thought at once of Shadows. Then he thought that the horses who lived here would not stand quietly if there was harm about; and it proved only a sleepy, half-scared stable-boy who called out asking who was there.

"Tristen," he said.

"Me lord?" The child came as far as the door and shoved it open to the drizzly night. "They don't 'low no lamps, m'lord, on account of fire. What would ye be wantin'?"

"I need a horse," he said.

"Aye, m'lord." The boy-shadow sounded doubtful, and scratched his ribs. Lightning lit the aisle, shone off the white-edged eye of a heavy-headed and dark horse that looked out of its stall, waked by the goings-on. "Ye want 'im f' far or fast, m'lord?"

"The best you have," he said. "A horse that didn't work today."

" 'At sure ain't many, m'lord. We brung Petelly here from pasture. He's a big fellow, fair fast. 'E don't mind th' weather, but 'e's a stubborn mouth, and 'e sure don't like the spurs, m'lord, 'e pitches like a fool."

"I wouldn't like them, either," Tristen said. The boy went to the horse who had put his head out; and who regarded him with a wary eye as the boy led him out in the flickers of the lightning. Petelly stood patiently while the boy searched up the tack, stood sleepily through the saddling and bridling – sniffed over Tristen's hands as Tristen took the reins and heaved a sigh as Tristen climbed up, moving into a sedate walk as Tristen rode out into the rain.

He tucked Cefwyn's cloak about him and over as much of Petelly's back and gear as he could make it cover. He rode Petelly quietly to the Zeide gate, and the guards, surprised in a dice game, let him through with only a question who he was and a look at him by lamp-light from their open gatehouse door.

"Tristen, sirs, from the Zeide."

"What business?" one asked.

"My own, sirs."

But one plucked at the other's arm and said, " 'At's a King's messenger, don't ye see?"

The second man held the shielded lamp close, and said. "Pardon, sir."

Perhaps it was the cloak. He did not think they knew him. They were not the guards who had been on duty the night he came, and it was at least the second, if not the third, watch of the night. But he did not quarrel with their notion he was a messenger – which was, he supposed, wrong, but, then, he was doing nothing he ought to be doing, and it was, he supposed, too, less wrong than running off with Petelly, which he knew was going to perturb master Haman, and probably get the poor stableboy in trouble.

But he could not do other than he did, and did not tell them the truth: they opened the gate for him, and he rode Petelly slowly down the slick cobbles of the town's main street to the town gate, and the gatehouse there.

"Who goes there?" the challenge came to him. The gate-house door opened, its lamps sending out a feeble light onto flooded cobbles, water pocked with rain, where the drainage was not good. One resolute man waded out into it, carrying a lantern and dutifully looking him over.

"Gods, didn't know ye in the dark, m'lord. Hain't you no escort?"

"None tonight," he said. He did not know the guard's name, but the guard seemed to know him. "Open the gate, sir."

The other came out, saw him and made a quick sign over his heart. "Gods bless, 'at's the Sihhë." The thunder was booming off the walls, and the lightning lit the faces, whiter than the lantern-light.

"The gate," Tristen said.

The guards' faces were fearful. They both made signs against harm, and hurried to lift the bar on the little gate, the Sally-port, the Word came to him. He rode through, and they began quickly to shut the gate after him. But he had thought of one trouble he had not accounted of when he had begun to evade the watch Cefwyn set over him.

"When my man comes here," he said, "as I'm sure he will, tell him I did not go to Ynefel."

"Where *is* ye goin', m'lord?" one asked, under the stamp and splash of Petelly's restless hooves.

421

"Searching," he said, which was at least a part of the truth. "Tell him I will be back."

He turned Petelly along the wall-road, and at his asking Petelly picked up his pace, laying back his ears at the thunder-strokes, but shaking his neck and wanting to run.

"Go," he said, and let Petelly have the rein he wanted. Petelly stretched out and ran, splashing through puddles and tearing along the road beside the Ivanim camp.

He had at no point of his evolving escape been sure he could escape and ride out past the guards, and past the camps – but no one now put his head out of a tent, no sentry prevented him in this downpour. He passed the Ivanim. He passed the camp of Lanfarnesse. The guards in town were not at fault, if no one had told them not to let him out. The sentries of the camps outermost, watching Cevulirn's horses, and those watching Pelumer's, had no reason to challenge him: he had come from the town, past other sentries.

And with the last tents and the last picket lines behind him – there was nothing but open road and the night ahead of him.

Now he had no one to account to and no one to harm but himself: his greatest fear had been Uwen's finding out, and rushing after him in a mistaken and utterly dangerous direction, because they had talked of Ynefel. He was sure that Uwen, hearing Cefwyn and others come in, as he must have done, would be wondering already why he had not come back. Uwen would have begun to worry; and probably already Uwen would have dressed and gone downstairs to look.

Then Uwen would ask close questions of the guards, who perhaps had not seen where he went. But once they began to search as far as the stable-court, which was a favorite haunt of his, and far more likely than the garden in the dark and the rain, then the boy would surely say at once that he had given him a horse.

But after that – after that, Uwen had to ask for a horse, too, and Uwen was not a lord: Uwen could not obtain a horse for the asking. Uwen would have to go to the commander of

the watch, who might have to wake someone of more authority, like Captain Kerdin.

Or Idrys. Idrys would be angry, and cast about very far and
very fast looking for him, bringing his cold wrath down on
those who should have asked more questions. He was sorry
for that, he was very sorry for it.

But there was no way at least Idrys could blame Uwen,
who had not been on duty. It was, if it was anyone's fault for
not watching him – Idrys' own fault, though he did not think
it would put Idrys in any better humor. Idrys would send
down to the town gates to ask where he had gone, and they
would surely say, He went west, and Idrys would know at
once, the same as Uwen would, where besides Ynefel he
might go.

Then Uwen would beg a horse and orders that would let
him and the guards ride out to catch him. He hoped that
Idrys did not ride out himself.

But the boy had said that they were bringing in horses from
the pastures, horses that were not the best; and if the boy had
given him one of the strongest and fastest horses they had, in
Petelly, that meant whoever of the guard chased him would
not have the best. And Uwen was not a foolish man. Uwen
would not rush ahead of other riders.

What he was doing was disobedient. Mauryl would say so.
Dangerous. Uwen would say so. But it was clever. He thought
so.

Not wicked. Or – not as men reckoned wickedness. He had
harmed no one, except, perhaps, the guards who had let him
do what they thought he had a right to do. He had disobeyed
Cefwyn's order to go back to Cevulirn's forces, and not to go
with him, and Cefwyn had thanked him for it, because he
should have done that. And if they would not listen to him in
their council, still, someone had to do something, because the
enemy was not waiting for a more convenient time – and
Cefwyn had acquired new advisors who urged Cefwyn to
listen to the priests, who knew least of all about Mauryl's
enemy.

And once Emuin arrived, Emuin also would forbid him to try, even enough to find out what that enemy was doing – he had begun to perceive the reasons of Emuin's retreat far from him, and it was because Emuin doubted he could do anything. Emuin was afraid of his enemy, and did not want to face him.

But if Emuin waited until the enemy did more than rattle the windows of the Zeide, then the threads he had seen going out of Ynefel would be very many, and very dark. And *that* was not good advice.

He had been at two places where he had felt the Shadows most powerfully. He had gone on Mauryl's Road as far as Henas'amef, but he thought now, tonight, that Henas'amef was not, after all, the end of his travels, only a resting-place, a place to learn. He could not rest too long, or remain too safe – Mauryl had not brought him into the world to be safe; he knew that now: Mauryl himself had not been safe. Mauryl had been fighting an enemy all unknown to him, an enemy that had finally overwhelmed him, and now, though he had never yet been able to read Mauryl's Book or understand Mauryl's reasons, he knew at least something of Mauryl's fight.

The rest of the answers were not, he assured himself, at Henas'amef. He had been closer to them at Emwy than he had been anywhere since he had left Marna, in that place where the Emwy road came closest to Ynefel.

CHAPTER 23

~

The rain was a misery, pouring off the tent, finding ways under the edge to soften the ground around the stakes. The holy brothers had already been out in the rain, struggling to reposition the stakes at the end of the tent, and a man who had not begun his life's work as a priest reflected that prayers and the brothers' inexpert efforts did less for tent-stakes than minor wizardry could. Sit in the shelter of this rock, good father, rest yourself, good father: leave the tent to us, good father, in the gods' good grace, father.

Emuin was more and more tempted to fix that corner stake himself, suspecting that the good brothers would not feel a twinge or a tingle in the air if he did.

But there were powers in the air tonight that might. He did not think that they had reached as far as Arreyburn, but he was not willing to wager on it.

"Rocks," he called out finally, impatient, and wishing he had closer attended the setting of the tent in the first place. He had trusted woodcraft in two seventh sons of some town mayor, gods save him, and let them position it when the gale came down on them and drenched them.

"Pardon, father?" one asked, rain-drenched gentility.

"Rocks. Good bloody *gods,* boy, you set the left-side stakes in a runnel down the damned hillside, what do you expect?" He brushed past the pair and slogged into the rain himself, gathered up three sizable wet rocks from the hill and jammed them, one after the other, tightly up against the three tent stakes and trod on each of them, hard.

After that he retreated, drenched, inside the tent, stripped off his sodden clothing, and seized up a relatively dry blanket to wrap in while he pulled off his boots.

He had a change of clothing in the baggage. The good

brothers among whom he had been in retreat had given him no hired guards, who might have known how to set a tent. The hired guards had been off seeing to the protection of ten brothers going to the blessing of the harvest in this end of season, and the assessment of land-rent for the abbey's tenants. Collecting the annual rent was a mission occasionally fraught with high passions, and occasionally beset by banditry, and the soldiers were reasonably called for. The abbot had not anticipated a message from His Highness or, now – if one believed Tristen, and he did – the King, bidding him come to a place and a danger he had tried very hard to avoid.

The brothers shivered in modest propriety in their wet robes, scorning the tyranny of the flesh. They lit the lamp after its overset in the collapse of the tent end: they were at least good for that. The oil had not caught fire, their tent had not burned down, and the brothers thanked the gods in their constant muttering of, "Thank you, sweet gods, thank you, dear gods," that could drive a man to desperation. The muttering, as of doves, increased in times of trouble. They blessed the lamp, they blessed the tent pole, they blessed the oil-sopped carpet that, with the mud, was going to have the lot of them looking like mendicant friars by morning.

"In the gods' good name, sit down and be warm, brothers. Don't press against the canvas. It makes leaks." Emuin tucked his own dry blanket around him, and wished the lamp oil had not had attar of roses added. It gave off a cloying perfume that had the closeness of the grave to a man who was holding the grave at bay with such difficulty tonight.

The pair settled. They heard the beating of the rain on the canvas. Thunder boomed, and the good brothers made prayers, quietly, at least.

But true gods, unlike spirits, did not permit themselves to be summoned, did not manifest at a wizard's whim – or a priest's – did not answer a mortal's demand; and did not know, perhaps, mortal needs, or mortal fears. Even the Nineteen, They of Galasien, the hidden gods, were wisps in the ether, a breath, an unanswering, unanswerable riddle.

426

And a wizard-turned-priest began to ask himself – then what earthly good were they? Were they more or less than Hasufin? Was *that* what wizards prayed to, and what the Elwynim held sacred? He no longer knew, and now doubted his years of prayers and all his attempt to save the old lore.

Ináreddrin dead, Cefwyn King – and Tristen set at liberty in the midst of it: none of the news that had flooded toward him by earthly messenger and unearthly summons could give a wizard-priest peaceful dreams. He felt the danger in the ether, where Tristen's every disturbance of that expanse of dream and substance gave advisement to the enemy which sat gathering forces at Ynefel. Every breath of wind through the insubstantial realm informed the power they least wished informed, and Tristen had no inkling what a powerful presence he was there. Tristen could not see himself – Tristen could not see the disturbance he made, could not, at least, understand that his manifestation was not ordinary, that it shouted to the heavens and drew attention. He was Sihhë. He was indubitably Sihhë, and that power was born in him – if he *had* been born. That power was in his bones, if he had had them shaped in anything but the womb of air and Mauryl's will.

If he had ever personally doubted since he laid eyes on Tristen, it was only regarding the order of presence he had to deal with – not its potency.

No, Tristen was not a wizard. He did not need to be. No, Tristen did not work magic. Tristen willed things, and the ether bent, bending the earthly realm with it – even when Tristen was unaware he was doing it.

Like a young man, Tristen had reached out to the only elder he saw; or he, like an old fool, had sensed the troubled ether and reached first. He could not now remember how it had been – but he had become ensnared, and then Cefwyn had, and after him, others, the ineffectual gods save them.

Now Tristen had begun searching the mortal earth for a force he could not master in the unearthly realm, searching – although he was certain Tristen did not know it in so many words, and likely did not think of it in anything like the way a wizard thought of it – for points of Presence in the earthly realm where the enemy was most vulnerable.

And where the enemy was consequently most powerful: unfortunately. One went with the other.

If Tristen would not be so rash as to dare assail Ynefel itself, still there were even in Amefel places almost as fraught with the enemy's presence. He could name one very dangerous site without an instant's hesitation.

The boy was on the road. He caught impressions now and again as an unskilled presence tried to keep from attracting notice and achieved – if not the opposite – at least a very qualified success.

The boy – the Shaping, the Sihhë-lord, the power that a dying and desperate master had released on an unsuspecting world, where men thought that priests could hold back the dark without being shadowed by it – was looking for answers in a physical realm that could only lead him to trouble. There were places of potency. But in very truth, there was no dark to hold back – at least – the dark that there was had no wellspring and no dividing line that this wizard had ever found. The dark that he knew was general. It was ubiquitous. It had its frontier in every soul that lived and had lived, and the good brothers yonder in their goodness were a pale, powerless nothing if he cared to look. They were all but invisible in the ether, as all but a few of the Teranthines were invisible.

Once he had thought it a refuge, once he had thought it holiness, and a sanctuary where a wizard once stained with his craft could find a lodging for his soul that the Shadows could not find or touch.

But now he began to suspect that the good brothers did not shadow the ether not because they were good, but because they had masked themselves *from* everything, had carefully erased their stray thoughts, had poured out their human longings, emptied themselves of desires and become so transparent an existence that they had not only ceased to be evil, they had ceased to be good. They had ceased to fight the battles of everyday life, and simply weighed nothing. Not a feather. Not a grain. They had given up everything, until they vanished from the scale of all that mattered, having given away themselves long before any power declared the contest.

There were those who did cast a shadow in the ether. There were those whose presence could become a Place, and whose Places, however many they created in their lives and the leaving of life, were links to the physical world. Advantageously situated, they could make a power both elusive and unpredictable – like Hasufin.

He could recall a young, smiling boy whose shadow had loomed among wizards at Althalen, a Shadow trading on its child's shape, and on human sympathy and human scruples, Mauryl had argued, when the most of them among Mauryl's students saw only the child, and argued that its natural, childish innocence might protect them long enough to let them, through moral teaching, change its character.

Then Mauryl had said a thing which echoed frequently through his nightmares nowadays, that innocence answered no questions, nor wished to, and that a very old soul counted on their reluctance to harm the housing it had chosen. No other disguise could have gotten it to that extent through their defenses.

Most of all he recalled how a child's body had lain still and helpless while the indwelling spirit ranged abroad in the halls of Althalen, killing men armed and unarmed, ordinary men and wizards, old and young, with no difference, up and down the halls, stifling their breath, stealing the force in them for the strength to break the bonds Mauryl had set on him.

That spirit is almost as old as I, Mauryl had warned the six of them that night. My student, yes, he was that, long ago, in Galasien. He was a terror to his enemies, but mostly, most of all, Mauryl had said to them on that dreadful night, Hasufin was a despiser of all restraint. As his teacher, I set him limits he immediately disdained. I set him work that was too tedious for his artistry. I set him exercises he overleaped as irrelevant and unengaging to his ability.

This spirit ruled in Galasien. Oh, he was noble-born. He

would be a king over Galasien. And as I raised up the Sihhë kings to bring him down, now I bring down the Sihhë because they temporized with him, and nothing less than their destruction tonight will prevent him.

Mauryl had fallen silent, then, and gazed into the fire – a younger Mauryl, he had been, with gray instead of silver about him; and much of gray Mauryl had always been, dealing in powers which he advised his students never to attempt to manage. *It will stain the heart,* Mauryl had said. *Of the soul I do not speak: the corruption of the living foredooms the dead. We are none of us safe.*

None of them, in that dreadful hour before the fall of Althalen, had dared breach Mauryl's inner thought, not knowing for certain, but sensing that Mauryl wandered just then free of the bounds of the room. And true enough, Mauryl had come back to them with a hard face and an iron purpose.

I shall tell you, for the youngest of you, Mauryl said, and laid out for them all an incredible tale, how, journeying to the north, he had brought back the five true Sihhë-lords; how in one night of terror he had brought down the Galasieni and raised up a more potent wizard than Hasufin himself; how Mauryl had, shivering in the heart of the citadel of Galasien, helped the bright towers fall and the people perish, locked within the very stones of Ynefel, Hasufin seeking lives upon lives to increase his magic against the Sihhë-lord who bent his will against him, and Mauryl sealing all the people in the stones of the remaining tower – the Sihhë fortress, after that night: Ynefel.

And long the Sihhë kings had ruled, unnaturally long, as men counted years. After them had come four halfling dynasties still able to keep their power intact, whether by innate Sihhë magic, or by conscious and learned wizardry – until (unnatural and, to a wizard mind, fraught with danger) a Sihhë queen gave birth to a babe that died, and was alive again – a miracle, oh, indeed. But in such unhingings of natural process more things might come unhinged, and all

Mauryl's skill could not pry the queen's mother-love (another force of fearsome potency) from a child which cast that terrible shadow in the gray. Talented, the queen maintained – and by the age of ten that child, uncatchable and clever, had murdered two of his elder brothers.

He was a spirit more precocious and more cruel thus far in his young years than, Mauryl swore, the last time this spirit had walked the earth. This spirit remembered its skill, and its former choices, and all . . . *all* . . . moral instruction was wasted on it.

Mauryl had opened the doors of the secret chambers, that heart of Althalen in which the Sihhë housed their greatest mystery, and let the Marhanen, lords of the East, loot and burn and kill without mercy those who escaped the wizardly struggle that resulted; Mauryl had simply cared little, one suspected, that the Marhanen seized the opportunity in the opening of those doors and the theft of *something* the present location of which one feared to surmise.

Mauryl had persuaded the lords of the Elwynim, who had Sihhë blood in their veins at least as much as the last dynasty, not to attack the Marhanen in the persecutions that followed. Mauryl swore to them that he had not utterly betrayed the Sihhë, that a King should come of Sihhë blood and inherent wizardry – a king to whom magic should be as ordinary as breathing, as it had been to the true Sihhë, who were not Men, as Men were nowadays. And that King-to-Come would save his own.

A Man such as he was learned wizardry as best he could. A Man and a young Man beginning in the craft simply did as elder wizards bade him and tried to guard his soul from the consequences.

Now there were no elder wizards – or, rather, and more troubling still, *he* was eldest. Mauryl was gone and Mauryl sent him – sent him Tristen.

I think, Cefwyn's last and pleading message to him had said, *that our guest is becoming what he will be, and he remains affectionate and well-disposed. He repays loyalty with loyalty, and is a moral creature. You bade me win his love, old master, and I greatly fear he has won mine in turn. Is this wise? You ignore my letters. I have the faith of the messenger that you do receive them. Why this silence? I need your presence. I need your counsel. Come to Henas'amef and help me advise this gift Mauryl gave us.*

So he came. He had been on his way when that one found him on the road. But it was too late, he began to fear. What Tristen did now, Tristen had chosen to do. He had evaded Tristen so long as he feared Mauryl's spell was still working in him – hoping for virtue. And now in one terrible day Tristen had learned killing and fled the prospect of meeting with him in the earthly world, where he might affect his heart, and where Men under Cefwyn's orders or his might lay physical restraint on him.

Tristen had run, whatever his reasons, toward Hasufin's domain, for that was the nature of Althalen, running as a deer would run when the dogs were baying at its heels.

No. Not a deer. Nothing at all so defenseless as that.

Tristen was doing what was in him to do, whether by Mauryl's Shaping or that he was moving now beyond Mauryl's intent and toward – toward something unpredictable. Sihhë were not natural Men. However they had arisen, out of Arachis as rumor among wizards had held, or from whatever source Mauryl had called them, they were not limited to wizardry and could act without learning. The egg, as Cefwyn put it, had indeed begun to hatch, and once that happened, a man such as himself, who had learned his wizardry as an art, not a birthright, could only keep himself as securely anchored to the world as possible.

CHAPTER 24

~

The leg ached, a constant pain that preyed on temper, with occasional sharp pain that brought a cessation of reason, whereby Annas and the pages walked softly about the place. There had been no sleep. None. After a late, last converse with Efanor, who had gone off to his third-floor rooms, Cefwyn had not so much as gotten out of his clothes in the hours before dawn, when Uwen Lewen's-son had come hailing his door-guard, reporting a horse gone from the stables and Tristen out the Zeide gate.

If any other man in the Zeide had slipped the gate on any ordinary night, Cefwyn would have concluded the man was off to some merchant's daughter. If any other lord had taken a horse from the stables he might have concluded that the man was some partisan of Heryn's, and that his gate guards and the camp sentries that let him pass were fools.

But the guards knew this man as his partisan, Sihhë that he was, and had never questioned, never *questioned* Tristen's right to take a horse from the stables or to ride out two guarded gates in succession, because Tristen wore the King's own cloak and was known throughout the town to have the King's friendship. If it had lacked any help in the calamity, Tristen had worn a new riding-coat which had the Tower and the Star on it, plain as plain for any gate-guard who failed to know the Sihhë and any Amefin who would for the blink of an eye think of arguing with him.

And because, he had to admit it, he had abandoned Tristen downstairs to the care of a rank of guard that had never received the cautions the guards in the royal residences had had regarding Tristen – with Uwen dismissed upstairs, and on a night of driving rain and turn-of-season cold that had persuaded sentries at two gates to keep their noses inside gate-houses and under canvas – no one had asked the right questions, no one had challenged him, and no one had advised Captain Kerdin, who alone might have raised an objection.

If there was wizardry in Tristen it must be the sort to rob sane, preoccupied men of their better sense, and to convince otherwise sensible and experienced gate-guards that here was the most innocent urgency they had ever met – on the King's business at that. If he had ordered Tristen's escape himself, he could not have found more plausible stories than the various guards had raised in their defense, and he could only hope that Marhanen cloak did not prove a source of danger in a countryside where armed soldiers on the King's business went in bands for safety. That was the kind of law Heryn Aswydd had kept in his province, and peace was fragile most of all with Heryn Aswydd's corpse and six others hanging at his own south gate and no lord at all in power over the Amefin.

Meanwhile Uwen Lewen's-son, on little sleep and in an agony of failed responsibility, had taken to the road on one of Cevulirn's better mounts with a captain and an élite fifty of Cevulirn's light cavalry in search of Tristen. And thank the gods, the lower town guards, damnably lax in other points, swore convincingly that Tristen had left specific word that Ynefel was not his destination.

So where *did* Tristen know to go in the world, if not to Ynefel? There was Emuin, for one, and in a contrary direction from all the others. The best information they had said that he had gone west, and that only left Althalen, Emwy, and Elwynor, a pretty choice of troubles.

Ask whether lying and evasion were, like swordsmanship and horsemanship, two more lordly arts Tristen had unfolded from his store of amazements. Not that it surmounted the shocking ills of treason and regicide and the consequences that Tristen had seen around him in the last two days, but it was disturbing, all the same, that Tristen had committed such acts so masterfully and so successfully.

And his own restless staring out the window this morning after such events, for a view of, above the wall and the surrounding roofs, gray-bottomed clouds which at least were showing blue sky between, did nothing to ease the ache in his leg or the impatience he felt. He wanted to reach Tristen himself, to have a word with him apart from the officers and the allies, to know what reasoning had prompted Tristen to have left – and to ask what Tristen believed he might do, given what little Tristen knew of the attack against him or the doings up by Althalen.

He paced, bereft of further information on which to decide anything. He leaned on a stick which he refused to use before outsiders, and it had already made his hand sore and did nothing to mend either the pain in his leg or his ill temper. Walking hurt; it was a different hurt from the throb of the limb while he sat, and that was the variance an ill-humored fate gave him on the first day of his reign over a divided realm, a dukeless province, and a pious brother he had as lief, if Efanor crossed him this morning, drown in the nearest deep well.

"Go back to bed," Idrys said first, when Idrys decided to report in, red-eyed and dusty.

He did not answer Idrys. He was not in a humor to be chided to bed and he was not in a humor to be told, as he could guess by Idrys' face, that there was no better news in the search after Tristen.

"I take it there is no news of him," Idrys said.

"I do not have to tell the Lord Commander. You know there isn't."

"Lewen's-son won't give up. I have every confidence."

"Would that I had."

"Would Your Majesty care for other news?"

"Is it better?"

"I have searched for this name Hasufin," said Idrys. "For some few hours. I have made brief inquiries of the annalists and the archivists, rousing them from their beds, and I and my most reliable clerks have run through, in short, the Zeide archives, the local Quinalt library . . . and the Guard records. *Then* with notes in hand, and with a fair familiarity with the *Red Chronicle* of Guelen record, I visited the Bryaltines, reckoning the Amefin's local breed of priests might recall items our godly and proper Guelenish Quinalt has forgotten. And, m'lord King, as you may see, I did my own searching." Idrys brushed at his doublet in distaste. "I am coated in age and cobwebs."

"And gained something? Damn it, get to the point."

"There are Hasufins woven through the warp and weft of the genealogies I plumbed – including, in the Bryalt *Book of Kings*, one Hasufin, called Heltain, a wizard, rumored as some sort of spiritual antecedent, or, indeed, namesake, of Aswyn, the fourteen-year-old brother of Elfwyn Sihhë of the Guelen *Red Chronicle*, which, let us recall, our guest had in his hands."

"And had no time to read. If you believe he made up this tale –"

"By no means. I merely point out he has an interest in the old accounts himself, and one wonders for what he was searching."

"To the point, crow!"

"I'm arriving just now. And I confess I was surprised to see Hasufin as a name of such surprising persistence in the Bryalt accounts – even back hundreds of years. As, let me say, I found several Mauryls of various repute before the records go back into the old Galasite tongue – for which, m'lord, you must obtain a priest. There are Bryaltine clerks who claim to read that language fluently, but without your orders I declined their assistance. It would have necessitated questions and names named which I did not judge you wished made a matter of gossip."

"The hell with the Bryaltines. *Tristen.* Is there anything naming him, while you were about it?"

Idrys heaved a sigh, then, leaned on the back of a chair and ducked his head a moment, evidently gathering patience to deal with an impatient and very short-tempered lord; and Cefwyn repented his curt tone. Idrys had been as sleepless as he.

"No, my lord King," Idrys said. "I found Triaults, Trisaullyns, Trismindens, and Trisinomes, all married into four Sihhë dynasties, but not a single Tristen under any spelling, in any age, in any chronicle, although I certainly do not claim to have made any exhaustive search in my few hours. I would say the old man plucked his Shaping's name from his own fancy – or out of Galasien's long history. Who can know? In any case, I no longer think Elfwyn is at issue. I fear Mauryl sent us a soul far less gentle."

"Yet this Hasufin supposedly at Ynefel is one certain name we do have in this business. You can remember accounts I can't. I wasn't *born* until Father and Grandfather were speaking to each other only through the Lord Chamberlain. If they weren't shouting. I had *nothing* of the gossip after the event. What *are* you looking for?"

"If," Idrys said, "if the Hasufin of our Sihhë's mysterious dream is indeed at Ynefel, those records we cannot possibly find without a perilous venture to Ynefel itself, where Lord Tristen swore – reliably, let us hope – he was not going. But the matter that set me so urgently searching last night – the name Hasufin has the ring of Amefel about it, and, it turns out, by the Bryalt record, it might even be a kinship name for one of the Sihhë of Althalen, though I am hard put to know how a dead prince signifies, or how he could overwhelm Mauryl. But – to confound matters further, the name turns out to be as prevalent as Mauryl's in the Bryaltine records – which I must say are anecdotal and fragmentary – but," Idrys said in some satisfaction, "many of that name are reputed to be wizards, all supposedly descended of a very early Hasufin Heltain who studied with someone, yes, my lord King, someone named Mauryl, reputedly in a district which the Bryaltine record called Meliseriedd – a name I've never heard attached to it, but I hazard a guess the district it describes is Elwynor. At least it lay to the north of the river. In delving into civil records the one wisdom I have learned is to join no names into one name until I see proof."

"But it is well possible that our Mauryl is all one Mauryl. So is it not possible that this Hasufin Heltain is one man?"

"A far leap, Your Majesty. I still refuse to make it, or to

attribute anything to a name I cannot otherwise put shape to. So to speak."

He ignored Idrys' wry humor. "Yet the name is in the Sihhë line. That proves some connection to my grandfather, to Mauryl, to Ynefel, and to Tristen."

"Suggests a connection, my lord King. Which might mislead us. All those things are possible. But none are proved."

"Still, –"

"Worth inquiry."

"Prince Aswyn called Hasufin in the Bryaltine book. *Was* there possibly also another still-living Hasufin when Althalen fell? A namesake uncle? A cousin of the same name? Or *was* this Aswyn?"

"I looked for all manner of references. One must know, m'lord King, the records, particularly the early ones, are all anecdotal, nothing of a chronicle in the way of the Guelen book, just the notation that a wizard named Mauryl did this or that, a wizard named Mauryl lifted a cattle-curse at Jorysal in a certain year. A wizard named Hasufin was supposedly associated with the Mauryl who may or may not be the same Mauryl as ours. The trouble is, there are Hasufins aplenty associated with the district for as far back as the records go. And Aswyns. Four at least. Elfwyn's youngest – not younger, but youngest – brother, the *Book of Kings* reports as still-born. And then the same book turns up an Aswyn as brother to Elfwyn with no mention of the stillbirth – typical of the records-keeping."

Cefwyn leaned heavily on his stick, sank into the nearest chair, and adjusted his leg before him, deciding that this would not be a simple report. "And the lad who died at fourteen?"

"According to the *Red Chronicle*, which we know, Mauryl's partisans killed the fourteen-year-old younger brother of Elfwyn king, during your grandfather's attack. According to the Bryaltine record, the *Amefin* record, mind you, yes, the one Prince Aswyn died at birth, and turns up in further records as living. Then in that record – the Bryalt one, mark you, m'lord, he has the surname or gift-name Aswyn

Hasufin. But no further mention for good and all does the record make of him between two and seven – if it *is* the same Aswyn and not a third. Two brothers of Elfwyn died by accidents. We do not have their names, though I remotely remember hearing in my youth of one called Hafwys or something of the like. Possibly Hasufin – who knows? I was not born either when Althalen went down."

"Fevers. Childhood mishaps. In a house reputed for wizardry – one would expect, would one not, fewer fevers and fewer fatal mishaps?"

"There was mention of vows made by the Sihhë king for the life of that infant, some sort of offense to the Galasite pantheon, some hint of an unholy bargain with the gods, the usual sort of thing – but this is a Bryalt record that talks about divine judgment." Idrys was not a superstitious man. It had the flavor of irony. "From the Bryalt – they might know. The Sihhë king was unlucky in the rest of his reign, at least, lost two sons and died, which brought Elfwyn to the throne within a span of – perhaps fourteen years. That much is not coincidence. And, it seems, even in a royal household, chroniclers grow careless and namesakes confound the record – I've searched archives before, on various accounts, and, understand, I find this confusion nothing unusual, Majesty. An entry goes in, no one records the death. A second child is born, they assign the same name, the chroniclers fail to rectify the account, and someone later attempts to mend matters, further confounding the confounded."

"Elfwyn's younger brother was always given, in every account I've heard from Emuin and my mother, as Aswyn, no mention of Hasufin."

"If we for a brief moment assume the *Red Chronicle* can be reconciled with the Bryalt account, and that this is Elfwyn's only surviving brother who appears as Aswyn, and that it is also Hasufin – though they give the age as nine, not twelve – at Elfwyn's coronation, and that it is not a cousin I found also named Aswyn – an Aswyn who *is* the right age does appear in further record, a prince among princes, and there were dozens honored with the title but remote in the succession. He was a student, as Elfwyn was, of Mauryl Gestaurien, as who in that court under the age of his majority was not a student of Mauryl? – But, but, lest I forget, my lord King, in this prolific confusion of Aswyns and Hasufins – another name of note: an Emuin, called Emuin Udaman in the chronicle, named as Mauryl's apprentice, aged thirty-four at that time, if the chronicler made no other mistakes. Is that not remarkable? If that were our Emuin, and not a cousin, that would make his age –"

"Over a hundred."

"One might certainly ask. And dark-haired still in *your* memory as well as mine. I debated mentioning that. And must."

He recalled Emuin of the immaculate Teranthine robes – but more the graying man in ink-stained roughspun, making a most unwizardly ascent of a willow in which his king's son's first hawk had entangled its jesses and tried to break its wings.

Emuin, skinny legs in evidence, retrieving the wayward bird, which bit his thumb and his ear bloody for the favor.

"You find conspiracy under every leaf, master crow. You cannot doubt Emuin. He'd laugh at you."

"A man whose ambitions and actions, like Mauryl's, may be older than the Marhanen reign? I find at least a question in the coincidence and a duty to report it."

"I find nothing at all sinister in it. He always claimed to have been Mauryl's student. Why should he not be in the account? And if we accept that Mauryl was as old as the Amefin believe – as by our experience, he might be – what's a mere hundred years? Why quibble, if we accept Mauryl saw centuries? If we accept that Tristen is – whatever he is – why, gods, indeed, why balk at anything? Our search through archive is for a dead man!"

"One observation more, my lord. I may yet astound you. Emuin, most certainly our Emuin, indisputably, paid a visit to the Bryaltines in this very town when he left Mauryl and came seeking service with your grandfather. But, what is not in the *Red Chronicle,* but in the Bryalt book, he recorded a curious wish among them: that for a sum of gold, provenance unknown, a sign be written on the wall in letters of curious shape, that the Sihhë star be set in silver there, and that candles in certain number be burned day and night."

"You jest."

"Certainly not the sort of shrine one could bribe the Quinaltines to establish. And not one even the Teranthines would countenance."

"Was it done?"

"Oh, it is there, m'lord. The size of a man's hand, that star, with odd symbols, in a remote corner of the crypt. To this hour the candles, thirty-eight is the specification, burn day and night – tended by someone in constant care. The sum of money must have been considerable. It does go back eighty years, during your grandfather's reign. Perhaps, too, the Bryaltines are very general in their worships; in the villages, I have observed, Bryaltine priests seem very little distinguish-able from hedge wizards. Most of all, this is Amefel, my lord, and never did I feel it so keenly as standing in that small shrine."

"Thirty-eight. Why thirty-eight?"

"Why, twice Nineteen, my lord King. A second Nineteen. A return of the old gods? Another ascendancy of wizardry over men?"

"Damn."

"Aye, m'lord."

"Emuin is *Teranthine*. A rational man, not a religious. I know him, my teacher, my –"

"The record is there to be read, my lord, in the shrine, if you will I bring it to you. – My lord, granted the Teranthines do shelter him and attest his piety. But they were an obscure sect before he came to them and brought them fame and fortune. As Emuin has grown in favor, in two, now three reigns, so they have prospered in donatives and courtly devotions of lords who would not omit a respectable order, especially now, one favored by the Marhanens. And so blessed, would the Teranthines denounce him willingly for his private devotions, to whatever powers? A minor peccadillo, one of those small

441

matters I doubt Emuin told your grandfather – or your father when your father made Emuin your tutor. I know him well. And I doubt Emuin has ever confessed fully his sins to me – or to the Teranthines, who doubtless do not wish to bear the burden thereof, even if they suspected it. I am tolerant, but not where it regards the overthrow of the realm or fealty to dead wizards."

"Gods," Cefwyn muttered, and touched his chest where once he had worn a silver circlet, a Teranthine amulet. But he had given the amulet to Tristen. It had been comfort to him as a child afraid of dark places and his grandfather's nightmares of burning children. It had become a luck-piece when he became a man, if only because Emuin had given it to him. He had seldom thought of the religiousness, only of the friend and counselor. Now he did think of it. Now, perhaps belatedly, he questioned to whom he had given something he treasured, his personal attachment to Emuin.

Emuin had been a father to him, more than his own had been; and to lose both his father and Emuin in a matter of days –

Now, he thought angrily, eyes stinging and hazed, – now you have me to yourself, do you not, master crow? My bird of ill omen. My jealous shadow. Now you have discredited even Emuin. And of course you speak against Tristen. Shall I trust only you, hereafter?

"Emuin is at Anwyfar," Idrys was saying. "I can send the message. I can summon him. If he is not already on his way, on the news of your father's –"

"Let Emuin be. Let be, Idrys! *Gods!* You have an excess of zeal for turning stones."

"My lord is too generous for his own safety's sake. Go back to the capital, where a King of Ylesuin belongs. Leave your brother this thankless frontier. Above all, I counsel you, do not let Efanor go to Guelemara without you. Far better he stay here in Amefel with you, if you will not go."

"If Efanor dies here, well-sped? Is that your meaning? Is that what you say?"

442

"I am my lord's man, none else."

"You do not trust Efanor as my representative? Even absent the chance for my father's funeral?"

"He is, straight from his devotions in godly Llymaryn, a naïve and believing man. To send him alone among the machinations of your father's courtiers *and* the western lords is not wise, my lord king. Hold him here in the place of danger and go yourself back to safety. Hard duty is the lot of superfluous princes, especially if they are contrary-minded. And if Lord Tristen of the Sihhë asks you lend him soldiers to lead, why, give him the Amefin and march them against Ynefel as he wishes. It would please the Amefin commons and most of the lords, who do not mourn Heryn Aswydd or his taxmen or his usurers, and give them common purpose against an enemy not yourself."

"And if Tristen should succeed, and *take* Ynefel from this purported enemy – this – Hasufin of various chronicles?"

"Why, good success. I should applaud it, since I cannot counsel you against this Sihhë gift. And if your Lord Warden of Ynefel should instead join with your more numerous enemies across the river – at least your enemies will all be facing you, not standing at your back."

He drew a deep breath. "And as we spin out this skein of distrust, what should we do with Emuin?"

"Oh, by all means, bring Emuin here. Your Sihhë lord might well need him *and* his shrine."

"Idrys, –"

"I am entirely serious, and I pray you take me so. Any other course may make your reign a short one."

"Already men of my father's court think I had a hand in my father's death."

"I have not heard that said today."

"Oh, but it was said often yesterday. It was the reason of Efanor's coming to Henas'amef, master of all suspicion! Maybe it was an empty court my brother hoped to find, where he could ensconce himself and his Quinalt advisers, while Father caught me consorting with Elwynim and Amefin sorcerers. Maybe he was honest in his hope to save me from sorcery and heresy. Killing Heryn did not prevent my enemies from shaping their own belief, nor will it in future. So shall I likewise murder my brother, my black and bloody counselor? A pious and believing man Efanor may be, but he is no innocent in intrigue. He and I survived my grandfather together, and my uncle is in his grave. Do not talk to me of courtiers besieging Efanor's sweet innocence! I will not have you of all people fall under his spell!"

"I am not unaware of his abilities, nor blind to his ambitions – nor to his Quinalt supporters. Do what you will. You are King. When you are an old king, none will dare remember it to you."

"*I* would remember. And they would write it, after I am dead."

"What care you then? Likely they will write it anyway."

"But I would know. I have to sleep of nights. *I love my brother, damn you!* Is that a fault in me?"

"My lord King, leave this place, leave Amefel and all its influences. There is too much of the Old Kingdom here. You belong eastward, in Guelemara. When you can breathe that air, you will forget all these morose thoughts – and this Sihhë revenant."

"Are you afraid, Idrys? Have I finally gone where you fear to follow? Have I possibly gotten ahead of you?"

"I am my lord's man."

"Your advice to me once had more than retreat in it."

"Shall I give you the advice I like best? Kill Efanor, kill the Sihhë, and be rid of Emuin all at one stroke. But you would never hear that. Kill Orien Aswydd and her sister. But you will not. Kill Heryn's four feckless cousins, who will lie down with conspirators and get up with ideas, but you will not."

"No," he conceded. "I *will* not."

Idrys frowned. "So. Who is to the fore now, m'lord King? I, or you?"

"There is yet," Cefwyn said, "no news from Sovrag?"

"No, my lord. Nothing."

"It is possible, you know, that even Tristen's fears are born of too much rich dessert and a disposition to dream of that place on uneasy nights. It may be nothing. He may come back on his own, confounding us all."

"You dismiss all my advice out of hand, then complain I am too timid. What shall I say else? Dream, my King, of a safe and pleasant province."

"I hear you, Idrys. I warn myself by everything you've said. And hear me, now: I would rather my brother in court with the northern barons about him than to see him command the southern barons in the field. These marchlanders, excluding Amefel, are the most formidable troops in the whole of Ylesuin, and Efanor is far more to Amefel's liking than I; I know it; Efanor is everywhere better loved than I –"

"How not? He has never had to use the hard edge of authority: he can be fair weather to every man. Prince Efanor simply listens and lets every man shape his own desires about him. A reigning king has no such luxury."

"So there is no remedy."

"No, no, no, m'lord King. Give Efanor *real* authority. Give it too much and too early. Let him fail – save his life. Then he will also appear in your debt."

"What, fail at the cost of my southern lords? Of this border? If he did try to general the south, provoked a war with the Elwynim, and decimated the best troops we have, – then where should we be, Idrys, thou and I? In the capital, – with battalions of courtiers?" The leg hurt at a sudden shift of weight; he winced and eased it, and shook his head. "I will not give him the south."

"Ah, but release the lords home. They'd not answer a second summons this season. It's coming up harvest-time, and winter. They will sit in their capitals. Meanwhile let him loose his Quinalt legalists on the Amefin, and he'll not be the beloved prince by spring. Not in Amefel."

"Let him loose the Quinalt on the Amefin and I won't able to hold Amefel."

"My lord, –"

"I have made up my mind, Idrys." He waved a hand at the table. "I have signed orders for levies on the villages and master Tamurin has made you lists, names and ages. I do not invoke them yet, understand. But they are there, against need, and can go out at any hour, as faithful a list as the Aswydds' taxmen own. – Ah! and speaking of Orien and Tarien –"

"Yes, m'lord King?"

"The ladies Aswydd are mortally penitent, have you heard? They apply to be freed of arrest."

"Surely Your Majesty jests."

"Oh, I am considering it. Better them than their rivals, whose account books we have *not* discovered. – And the mayor of the town wishes to see me. So do various of the Amefin thanes, earls, lords . . . whatever they style themselves and however they relate to the Aswydds, who've been in *every* bed in the province. Likewise the local patriarch of the Quinalt wishes audience – I can guess that matter. I shall make donations for services in the capital. And, no, I'll not send my father's body with Efanor when he goes – I stand by my word in council. No funeral until I bring our father home, no chance for Efanor to display his extravagant grief in public show, even unintended, to raise hopes of him and rumors about me, have no fear. – Gods! I find this gruesome."

"But wise, my lord. Not to remove your father from the province without justice done him – is a good and pious thought. I did applaud it."

"I have learned from you." He moved, and winced. "I do thank you, Idrys, for all your dusty labors. I am warned, regarding Emuin, and I shall not forget – but I look for him, I do look for him. I shall thank you, also, if you advise me at whatever hour he arrives."

"My lord King could thank me well by taking himself to bed before he lames himself."

"Take to your own for at least two hours. I need your clear wits, Idrys."

"Majesty." Idrys bowed, unsmiling, picked up the lists and the levy orders, and departed.

Cefwyn wrapped his arms about his ribs, cursed, and then in febrile restlessness, rose up and began to pace the room, cursing his sore hand at every other step with the stick, which took his mind from the ache in his leg and the greater ache in his sensibilities. He wrapped himself in righteousness and anger sufficient to deal with the Aswyddim and the Quinalt conjoined.

Then he went out into the anteroom and opened the door, little caring now for the pride that had kept him from using the stick in view of others. The pain was more. He gazed across the hall, where guards still stood at Tristen's door, awaiting what – gods alone knew, doing what, the gods alone cared. They were assigned: they were on duty. No matter that there was no one there to guard.

Soldiers, Tristen asked. *Soldiers*, for the gods' sake. In so short a time Tristen's concerns had changed so much.

He remembered the methodical rise and fall of a blade in Tristen's hands. A dark figure wreaking destruction without pity.

The bowed, sad figure that rode ahead of them homeward, on the tired red mare.

He leaned painfully on the stick and turned, furious with his own pain and faced with the innocent guards at his own door, two Guelen guards, still of the Prince's Guard, and, part of the lending of trusted men of other commands, two Lanfarnessemen, giving him Guelen of the Dragon Guard and the Prince's Guard to spare to other posts.

Then, on unremitting duty, there were the two in chains, lordly Erion and the river-brat Denyn, horseman and pirate, keeping at least the semblance of peace between themselves – and looking anxious under his close notice.

"How do you fare?" he asked them, fighting the pain, compelling himself to be patient and soft-spoken, when an outcry of rage was boiling behind his teeth.

"Well, Your Majesty," Erion murmured.

"The wounds are healing?"

"Yes, Your Majesty."

447

He looked at Denyn. "How do you deal with your companion?"

"Very well, Your Majesty."

Erion's right wrist and Denyn's left were wrapped with leather against the galling chain.

"Do they," Cefwyn asked the Guelen sergeant, "keep the peace?"

There was a little hesitation, a tense regard from the sergeant. "Aye, m'lord King." He did not entirely believe that report, and regarded the pair skeptically and at length, but it was unprecedented that a Guelen sergeant should lie for two miscreant foreigners. He had made matters clear to the fractious barons. What remained was cruel, and a difficult matter for his own guard, and it challenged his own pain. "Free them of the chain," he said, and walked away – insisting to himself that he was himself free, that he was *not* bound to Tristen; that he owed nothing to Tristen; that Tristen's apprehensions were of no substance and Tristen's appearance in his court in this most perilous time for Ylesuin was more related to an old man's natural demise than to any immutable destiny of the Marhanens – and that Tristen's fears were no more than innocence confronted with the very frightening sight of the King's justice.

Which . . . had not stayed Tristen's hand on the field at Emwy. He was, if one believed anything about Tristen, a conjured soul who had shown a frightening skill at arms, a conjured soul who was mostly surely *not* the feckless, bookish Elfwyn of the *Red Chronicle*. There had been defenders in that hour who had fought for Elfwyn – some of them his heirs; but Tristen had defended *him*. Tristen had saved him from certain death. Was *that* the action of an enemy? Was that a man he should doubt, no matter what Idrys found or did not find in archive?

Perhaps he should have listened to Tristen. But to send troops to combat Tristen's nightmares of Althalen would do no favor, not to the men nor probably to Tristen's reputation.

And if Tristen's fears owned more solid form, if such a

band met not with nightmares but with living enemies, come on reconstructed bridges across the Lenúalim, it would engage Ylesuin prematurely on a front he was not ready to open – which he did not wish to open at all if he could delay the matters he had with the Elwynim Regent into sensible negotiation. He was not, whatever his anger, whatever his passion said, about to lay waste the whole Lenúalim valley in retaliation. He had a kingdom of provinces in precarious balance, he had a southern frontier with the Chomaggari always looking for advantage. He could not, for a gesture, for vengeance, for any consideration, give way to temper and attack Elwynor, even when his own spies said Elwynor was in extreme unrest: he dared not lock both their kindred peoples in a struggle the coastal kingdoms would see as their opportunity to take lands long disputed on his own borders.

Meanwhile there was hope: the Regent was old. If the Sihhë prophecy were the substance behind this uneasiness and this resurgency in wizards, if the Elwynim knew the Sihhë standard was brought to light in Henas'amef, and that a Sihhë lord stood high in council, something might well begin to change on the Elwynim side of the river, and peace that had been impossible for two generations might be possible in the third.

Give me opportunity, he asked privately of the gods he privately doubted – because in two generations of Marhanen rule no King of Ylesuin had had sure command of the western marches.

In two generations of Marhanen rule no King of Ylesuin had had a hope of establishing lasting peace on any border.

And he could not allow Tristen to leave him – not in respect to his hopes of peace and a reign that would not be remembered for its disasters.

Nor for his own sake, he found; it was a large part of his anger and distress that, absent Tristen, he could see no one – no one he could look to for his own happiness. Emuin would ask him common sense. Idrys would lay out cruel choices and remorseless reason for taking them. Tristen asked him simple questions that made him look again at simple things he thought he knew.

He had no friend, none, in his entire life, that his father had not minutely examined and appointed to serve that function. He had no prospect or enterprise to draw him from day to day except the duty of a king. And of men who crowded close about an heir apparent, and those, far more numerous, who must settle their future hopes and daily needs upon a king, he had three he relied on: Annas for his comfort and his good sense; Idrys for his dark and practical advice, Emuin for the knotty questions of justice a king could face – but of all he knew, he had never found any man who reached the less definable needs of his heart, until, that was, Tristen asked him foolish questions and touched those things in him he had thought men gave up asking. Tristen had brought the wondering of boyhood back to him, and he found himself *thinking* about things and looking at them in odd ways, when for years he had simply defended his own thoughts, taken wild pleasures to give his detractors a less vital bone to gnaw, done his duty to the Crown and barred his soul against those with something to gain of him.

A king could live without a friend: gods knew his grandfather had, and his father, by what he knew. He might reign long, might become well respected, might die in a productive, peaceful, perhaps safer, old age, alone.

But his heart would have died long before that day.

CHAPTER 25

❧

Petelly had tired, long since – had run as far as he could and went at long, brisk walks along the Emwy road, among the wood-crowned hills. Petelly was not as fast as Gery, but he was strong. Perhaps Uwen could overtake him, Tristen thought. Uwen was good at things a soldier did. But for the while he was free, and he had no wish, at least for a day or two, to be near anyone who knew him, though dearly he loved the sound of Uwen's voice, and already missed him. He worried about him, as well, if Uwen followed him too closely or somehow failed to hear his message; but he counted on Uwen to be wise, and to read the trail he was leaving on the muddy road.

Such a din of things had begun bearing in on him, so many echoes and voices had begun clamoring for his attention and his understanding, that he longed for his space of silence before Uwen or someone of the Zeide did overtake him. He no longer made sense of any single voice. He felt drawn thin, overwhelmed with pieces and shattered bits of knowledge of Henas'amef and of things that meant nothing to him, that everyone believed should be vastly significant.

Now – now, deep in the hills, at last with only Words he knew about him, and no one speaking to him, he could draw a peaceful, considered breath.

He could not have borne, last night, some new constraint of Cefwyn's fears holding him locked in his rooms. He could not bear some new, more dreadful event tumbling in on him before he had understood the last.

Most of all, he could not bear Cefwyn making some new demand of his unquestioning belief – or Emuin arriving to take charge of him and severing him from Cefwyn – for Cefwyn might well yield him up to someone who could occupy him for a time; and then forget about him and his advice for days upon days. He did not fault that Cefwyn would abandon him: he knew that Cefwyn was busy. But he knew that his concerns were important. And it occurred to him that, absent, he would weigh far more heavily on Cefwyn's thoughts, and what he had said might weigh far more than it ordinarily did.

But if Cefwyn could lock him away and know where he was, Cefwyn would cease to think about what he had said. So, absent, he decided, he was far more present than if he were at Cefwyn's elbow.

Here he felt free, no longer hedged about with constraints, no longer so unremittingly battered by chance. He rode in both fear and anticipation of what lay ahead of him, at least to discover more truths of the world than he knew now, and, by that, to be less helpless than he was among men who knew who they were.

It was not without discomfort, this journey: he was still soaked through, although the sun warmed the cloak and Petelly's body warmed him. He had eaten very little on the road to Emwy, nothing on the way back, had missed his supper asleep yesterday evening, and his breakfast this morning, and after that his noon meal, so that by now he was a little light-headed, but he did not at all miss the clatter of his well-meaning and kindly servants. He had been hungry before, on the Road. He took it for no great hardship. He let Petelly graze a little for his midday meal as they went. Petelly had left a warm, dry stable and run both far and fast for his asking, and was surely as glad as he was to see the sky clearing and to feel a warm afternoon sun touch his back. Petelly had mouthfuls of thistle-bloom, one after another – he seemed to favor the purple, feathery sprays, and they grew profusely on the hillsides and along the road, silvery, jagged leaves, and tassel-like puffs rising above the gold and green of the grass and the thickets of broom.

He had wrung water out of Cefwyn's beautiful cloak, and knew he owed Cefwyn both its return and an apology for its condition. He had taken off his coat as he rode this morning and wrung it out, but wearing it, rumpled as it was, and wearing the cloak spread out on Petelly's rump was the only way he could find of drying them, save this early morning when he had let Petelly rest. Then he had spread the cloak out on stones under the sun, so it had become merely damp instead of sodden. His new coat with the silver stitching seemed ruined for good – it was soaked, the padding under the mail was soaked, – his boots had stayed somewhat dry during the ride, but walking in the wet grass this morning, leading Petelly, had soaked through their seams, and he did not want to get down and walk on the road, and gather mud that would end up on Petelly and his saddle-skirts.

Fool, Mauryl would say, fool, out in the rain again.

But Mauryl's rebuke carried no sting at all now. It had become a bittersweet memory of an old man who had been very patient with him, and with his own perpetual failure of Mauryl's desperate expectations.

He could hear Mauryl in the quiet of the countryside: at least the memories of Ynefel had begun to come clear to him in greater detail and with more color than in Henas'amef. He had had his head and his ears all stuffed with the presence of Henas'amef, the Words of Henas'amef, the Names of Henas'amef, some of which had touched him and taught him and made him wiser.

But now, in the hills, under the sky, he found himself thinking very clearly of Ynefel, and Mauryl, and the things of his earliest memories. The advice of Men had filled his ears with a clamorous assault in town. Here, he listened to the Lark and watched a Fox trot along the hill and thought – how Mauryl had said it was very easy to make things do what they wanted to do.

And if Men in Henas'amef called that wizardry, he never recalled Mauryl calling his work that, though Mauryl had called himself a wizard. Mauryl had simply expected a thing to be as it wanted to be. And it was. Mauryl never seemed to think it remarkable. He didn't think it remarkable, either.

So perhaps it had been easy to make himself be here – because this was what he wanted to do, and this was the direction he wanted to ride. Nothing had been able to stop him last night and nothing had prevented him this morning.

He recalled Mauryl saying he would know what to do when the time came for him to go. And he had indeed known. He had followed the Road and found Emuin. So what Mauryl had promised him had come true.

And now that he thought about it, it did seem that he might know when it was time for him to do other things, and to take other Roads, even to take up the one he had been on, which he had once thought led through the gate of Henas'amef.

But perhaps his Road had only turned there, and gone along beside the wall of the town. Perhaps that was why it now drew him out again, and perhaps the clamor and clatter of the town and the gathering of lords and their men had troubled him because they were all outside Mauryl's wishes.

That was one state of his thoughts. There were two. One state of his thoughts was calm and safe, and he knew he could rest as he rode, and do as he pleased, and arrive where he wished to arrive, and ask the questions he wished to ask. That was the freedom.

The other state of his thoughts was not calm. The other was full of jagged edges and Words half-unfolded and things that might and might not be, and all the ties he had made to people. That state of his thoughts was full of Cefwyn's expectations of him, and Emuin's, and Uwen's, all unfulfilled. He did not know where good or bad resided, whether with the things Mauryl had wished him to do, or with the things that bound him by friendship to Cefwyn. The thoughts did not at the moment seem compatible.

He knew that in the simplest thinking of all, he should have stayed for Emuin and accepted Emuin's advice, even if it was to stay in his room and keep silent.

But it seemed to him – leaping to that other way of thinking – that he had found his way past the gates without hindrance because that too was the way things wanted to be. If that indeed was wizardry, then Mauryl had done it or he had.

Lady Orien did not expect visitors this afternoon. That was evident. Maids snatched at sewing and scattered, white-faced, from the benches at the solar windows. Orien herself cast aside her laprobe and rose up in a scattering of colored threads.

Orien was not at her best. There was little color in her face, and her clothing was gray, looking old and outworn, a gown chosen for comfort, surely, not show. The red curls were drawn back severely and braided in a long braid. Small bruises marked her left cheek and her chin, marks the source of which Cefwyn did not know, but guessed as possibly one of his guards. She seemed entirely unnerved at his sudden intrusion. Her fine hands locked together as if to stop their movement. But she was never at a loss for argument.

"I should have thought you would pay me some courtesy of announcement, Your Majesty. But, then, you own the guards and doubtless you will make free of my door when you will."

It was by no means the contrition he had had reported to him. The soft, even voice had little quaver in it; the eyes, none.

I misjudged Heryn to my father's ruin, he thought. Have I likewise misjudged my act of mercy? It grows late to order other deaths; now it would have the taint of persecution.

"You are safe here," he said coldly. "Do not presume too much on my patience. You asked to be heard. I am here."

"I thought it was myself who would be summoned," she said, and brushed at her gray skirts. "This is all I can do for mourning." Now, now came the quavering voice. Worse, it did not have the sound of pretense. "Do I learn now what will be done with me and my sister?"

"What would you ask, Lady Orien?"

455

Her head came up; her chin lifted. "I would *ask*, my lord King, for Amefel."

Her audacity astounded him. He recalled with shame how she had flattered her way into his bed, while she plotted with her brother against his life and against his father's life. His gullibility appalled him.

"I am Aswydd," she said. "Like other Aswydds, I can divorce sentiment and policy. Give me Amefel for my holding. I shall mourn my brother and bow to circumstance. It will save Your Majesty division and confusion within the province at a time when Your Majesty has greatest need of unity. And it will prevent contention among other lords as to who may claim the spoils – with all the feuds and history entailed."

"I need no advice from you or your sister on policy."

"No, my lord King, since you well know these things to be true."

What she said made clear sense, but he did not stop hating the woman. "Have what you ask," he said then, and was gratified that it surprised her. The color quite fled her face and she looked as if she would gladly sit down; but she could not, in the King's presence, and he did not give her that leave. "Your cousins I shall banish, all, far eastward, stripped of all properties, which I give to you. That will doubtless give them great love for you, Orien Duchess of Amefel, and constant hope of your charity. But extend them none, on pain of death. Your sister Tarien will have no estate. It is yours, and you may not bestow it in your lifetime. You will remain under arrest, Your Grace of Amefel and Henas'amef, until it pleases me to release you. You will be in all particulars . . . sole holder of the title."

"So that there will be no lord to face you in council but myself, and no man to stand for me."

"Ah, but I shall stand for you. Is it not the ancient custom of Amefel that a man who deprives a lady of her male kin must see to her welfare? A Crown wardship for you, Your Grace. And Lady Tarien's wardship and that of your cousins to you. No one will harm you. But I would not have a dozen of my lords competing for your tarnished favors, or have you

456

or your sister politicking between the sheets. When you wed, Your Grace, if *ever* you know another man – and I shall take a dim view of impropriety – it will be with my approval; and the Aswydds' rule over Amefel *ends* with your name, by one means or another. Be assured, you are lord *and* lady in Amefel."

Orien's face had gone quite pale. She made a slow curtsy. "My lord King, –"

"I let you live. I let your sister live. If you were Heryn's brother, Your Grace, you would fare differently, I assure you. Cross me again and you'll find no further mercy. That I would execute a woman – never doubt. But your brother swore in dying that you no more than obeyed his orders as lord of Amefel; and therefore you and your sister and your cousins are alive."

"My lord," she breathed, and her face was rigid.

"Never grow arrogant, my lady. You will never have any champion for your opinions but myself, and I like them little. Your head is insecurely set and might make pair with your brother's on the south gate at any moment."

"I beg my lord King, his body for burial."

"That I do grant. Neither I nor the ravens have more use for it. But on condition the burial be private and seemly. Yourself, the priests, your sister, . . . my soldiers."

Orien swept another curtsy, slow and deep, showing her breast. He lingered, looking at her, wondering what had ever attracted him to this cold, scheming woman, or why he let her have her life now. The look she gave him was not Heryn's, but something more direct and more defiant.

"The bloody Marhanens," she said in a soft voice. "Always extravagant in revenge. I thank my lord King, that I have discovered a gentler nature to moderate your justice."

The fact of her sex was there again, and mitigated the epithet generally used and seldom dared to the Marhanens' face. Again a different Orien flashed into memory, pale skin and silks and tumbled hair. Her bruised face offended his sensibilities.

"We have beheaded women before, we Marhanens. Remember that. I shall never trust you. But neither will I persecute you, Lady Orien."

"My women and I," she said gravely, "will make prayers of gratitude for that."

He cast a sharp look at the servants in the shadows of the room – well-born, some might be, even bastard cousins. But two were peasant-looking, darker-haired, of Amefin blood and maybe older, wearing such talismans as Amefin women wore. He looked at Orien, lady of Amefel in more than in his grant, and feared their curses, and witchery.

"Pray rather that my good humor continues," he said. "Where is your sister?"

"At her own prayers, my lord King. For our brother's soul. We are a pious people."

"Horses may fly," he said, "but I am little interested in pious Aswydds."

He turned then, conscious of the limp that would not bear him from them with any authority. He made his departure all the same deliberate and casual, and lingered at the door for a backward look. None of them had moved. Most looked frightened, even Orien.

Petelly had had his fill of thistle-tops, at least for a while, and moved along with ears up as the forest shade drank up the road ahead. Tristen felt only a little shiver of apprehension, knowing that this was the place that had claimed lives of his companions, but as a woods it beckoned green and living, not like Marna, of which it might even be an outgrowth. He went cautiously on both accounts, and he had not gone far inside that shade before he saw, recent in the mud of last night's rain, the print of another horse.

He knew that Cefwyn would send men up here to bring back their dead. He knew that Heryn had claimed to have rangers in the district – as Cefwyn might have men here that he had not known about.

There were also the men who had killed Cefwyn's father. There were reasons aplenty to fear the shade ahead. He vividly recalled the arrows that had flown at him when he had ridden with Uwen, when men very near him had died; and he recalled that track of a horse that had appeared as a dark line in the grass near Raven's Knob that evening he and Cefwyn had fled from Emwy, a warning of someone besides themselves out and about the hills.

But Heryn must have sent a message to Cefwyn's father, to urge him to come to Emwy. It was even possible, he thought, that Cefwyn by going to Emwy had fallen into the trap prematurely: if Cefwyn had died there, the King would have come, all the same, to Emwy; and there – possibly – the King might have died all the same, and Efanor would have become King. That was the way he put Cefwyn's suspicions together, to explain the uneasiness he had heard between Cefwyn and his brother.

But ifs, Idrys had said to him, counted nothing. It had not happened the way Heryn wished. And Heryn would not plan anything else. Nor, he thought, had Efanor done anything to harm Cefwyn.

It did not mean, however, that the Elwynim Lord Heryn had dealt with were done with their actions.

He thought of that as he rode Petelly further and further into that green shade.

He thought of it with great urgency when, in the mud which the rain had made an unwritten sheet, he saw a man's footprint on the road, one place where someone had trod amiss, and slid on the mud, and then recovered himself and gone up onto the leaves. He looked up on the hillside where bracken hid further traces.

It might be someone from Emwy village. There were surely reasons for the villagers to be out and about the woods, pursuing their claims of lost sheep, and there were indeed signs of sheep about. But there had been a horse's track earlier, and he could not but worry about the safety of Uwen following him, along with whatever other men Uwen might have swept up. He was not concerned for himself. But Uwen would not turn back at a sign like this: Uwen would search the more desperately, and come into trouble.

He said to himself now that he should turn back, wait on the road for Uwen and see what Uwen thought, now that he had chosen the meeting, and now that there was something else at issue besides himself. He might persuade Uwen to wait, send someone back, supposing that Uwen came with soldiers, as Cefwyn's men seemed generally to travel about the land – and if Uwen did, then he might see whether, having gained, however indirectly, the soldiers he had asked Cefwyn to give him, he could stay on the fringe of Marna a time with wise and experienced men under his orders and discover the secrets the woods had. They were important secrets, he was certain, secrets that might tell him much more about himself, and about Mauryl's intentions; he could talk to Uwen, and Uwen would scratch his head and offer Uwen's kind of sensible opinions, which were different than Emuin's, but no less thoughtful.

That was the best thing to do, he thought, and he began to turn Petelly about on the road.

But that gray place flickered across his sight, an uncertain touch like the light through leaves, like a brush of spider-silk across the nape of his neck.

He turned Petelly full circle.

A gray, shaggy figure stood among the trees, in the green light, a figure in ragged skirts, wrapping her fringed shawl closely about her. It was the old woman of Emwy. Perhaps *she* was the reason he had had to persist on this road – as he might be the reason of the old woman's coming here, into this perilous woods.

She said nothing. She turned and walked uphill through the bracken.

He touched Petelly and rode him up the gentle slope. He did not trust himself safe from harm in doing so. Nor, he thought, did she trust there was no harm to fear from him, but surely she had some purpose in coming out into this green and gold and breathless forest.

She stopped. She waited by a spring that welled up out of

the hill, where someone had placed rocks in an arch. The Sihhë star was carved on the centermost, and one stone was a carved head, while others, separately, had acorns, and bits of vines, and one, a hand. The pieces did not belong together. But they made an adornment for the fountain. Someone had brought them there, perhaps from Althalen, he thought, where there were such things.

"Auld Syes," he said. He had not forgotten the name. "Why did you act as you did against us?"

The old woman hugged her shawl about her, bony hands clenched on the edges. Her hair was gray and trailed about her face, which was a map of years. Her mouth was clamped tight. Her eyes were as gray as his own.

"Sihhë lord," she said in a faint, harsh voice, "Sihhë lord, who sent ye?"

"Mauryl, lady."

She laughed, improbable as it was that such lips could ever laugh. She turned once full about, spread her arms, and her skirts and the fringes of her shawl flew like feathers in the green light. It might have made him laugh. But the feeling in the air was not laughter. It was ominous. The place tingled with it. She bent down and from among the rocks about the spring took a silver cup. She filled it, and drank, and offered the same cup up to him, on Petelly's high back.

"Drink, drink of Emwy waters, Sihhë lord. Bless the spring. Bless the woods."

He did not think the drinking mattered so much. He took it from her, and drank the cool water. He gave it back, and the old woman was pleased, grinning and hugging herself, and he felt that tingle in the air that Mauryl's healings had made. In that moment all the weariness of the road fell away, and Petelly, who had put down his head to drink, brought his head up with a jerk and a snort, the white of his eye showing as he looked askance at the old woman and backed away with more liveliness and willing spring in his step than he had had since last night.

He quieted Petelly with an unthought shift of his knees,

and found himself brushing at that gray space again, himself and Petelly both, where white light shone, and fingers of light flowed through the old woman's fringes.

Came a child through the light, then, skipping through the gray shadow of the woods, as if a mist had moved in: in the gray place, the child moved, and yet the trees were in that place as well.

— Seddiwy, lamb, the old woman said. Show the Sihhë lord the paths ye know. Ye know where the good man is, do ye not?

— Aye, the little girl said, aye, mama, I do. I can. I will. The lord ma' follow me.

The child skipped away through the shadow-trees, playing solitary games of the sort children played.

He was not aware of having turned downslope. But Petelly began to move. He saw nothing but a breeze going along the hillside, a light little breeze that only rustled the leaves of the trees.

Down across the road it went, disturbing the trees on the other side.

He did not trust children. But there seemed no harm in this one, who existed in that gray space which was no place for the innocent and the defenseless, but she had not stayed there long. She was a flutter of leaves and a skitter of pebbles on the lower slope, a little disturbance of the dust, that danced and skipped and danced.

She was a rippling on the water, a bending in the grass. A sparkle through the leaves of a stand of birches. There was not enough of her to catch. She made less stir than Auld Syes did, and that was little.

But, childlike, she did not go straight along the way. It was halfway up a hill and down again, it was in and out a thicket. Silly child, Tristen thought, and did not follow the wanderings, only the general line she took.

And now he had Emwy village on his left. But of buildings that had once stood there – he saw thatchless ruin, gray walls stained with black.

462

Idrys was going to fire the haystacks, Idrys had said. But there had been worse, far worse than that, done against the village. He was troubled by the sight. He would have argued with Idrys – or whoever had done this.

– *Child*, he said. *Who burned the village?*

The faint presence hovered, like the movement of a dragon-fly, a quivering in the shadows.

And flitted on again, more present, and angry.

He took Petelly along ways that might once have been roads or paths, toward the south and east behind that fluttering in the leaves – which now was not the only such. Gusts flattened grasses in long streaks. Petelly, nonetheless, snatched up a thistle or two, and a gust blew his mane and twisted it in a tangle.

Saplings bowed and shook. Three such streaks in the grass combined and a sapling bent and cracked, splintered, showing white wood.

That was more ominous. He had had no fear for himself or for Uwen in his dealing with Auld Syes, but now he began to be concerned, and wished he had gained some word of safety from the old woman, not so much for him but for anyone following him.

Crack! went weed-stalks. *Crack!* went another sapling, and another and another, an entire stand of young birches broken halfway up their trunks.

– *Be still*, he said. *It was wanton destruction. It proved nothing but bad behavior. Be still*, he said, and wished the *young child to come back again. I have men behind me, good men. Don't trouble them. They mean you no harm. Be polite. Be good to them.*

It might have been a collection of old leaves that blew up then in the depth of a thicket, some distance away. It might have been, but he would have said it was the old woman herself. A single course of disturbance skipped toward it, a bent passage through the grass that tended this way and that way, that sported along a low spot and scuffed through the pebbles. And the ragged-skirted shape of leaves whisked

463

through the thicket and dissolved again, with the little one skipping on where it had been and beyond.

Still the streaks of flattened grass appeared on the hillside, intermittent and angry, and the sun declined in the sky, making the shadows long, his and Petelly's, on the grass.

But he had come into that vicinity where he had ridden with Cefwyn as they were coming away from the ambush someone had laid for them in the woods – he recognized the hills. They touched on shapes – not shapes arriving out of some unguessed recollection, as the servants said he remembered things, but out of the certainty that he had seen these hills, and he knew where he was. It was near Raven's Knob, where he had seen the tracks that led around the hill, the warning they had had of men hiding in the hills.

They were near Althalen – though nothing of that Name unfolded for him: just, it was Althalen, where he had been with Cefwyn. He thought that perhaps what guided him now was a kind of Shadow, though a simple and harmless one. He did not take her companions for simple and harmless, and did not want to deal with them after dark fell. But the guide he had sported this way and that with abandon through dry leaves and green grass, and the sun turned the greens darker and more sharp-edged with shadow as it inclined toward the hills.

– Do you know this place? he asked of Auld Syes, in the chance that she heard. Cefwyn thinks I should. But what should I know? Can you say?

There was no answer.

Still, there was nothing of the smothering fear he had felt when he had ridden through it before – the very dreadful presence he had felt that night, a Shadow of some kind, maybe many of them, that would keep to the deep places at the roots of wild hedges, and the depth of arches, and creep about at night, frightening and doing such harm as they could. Mauryl had not told him how to fight against Shadows, only how to avoid them, and that was by locks and doors. He had none such here – and perhaps he was foolish for letting Syes' child become his guide.

But he did not come now to disturb the Shadows. He came only for the truth, and rode among the old stones, following his wisp of a guide, thinking of the Name, Althalen, trying to coax more pieces of relevance to come to him. But the expectation that did come to him on the wings of that Name was an expectation of pleasant gardens – the thought of halls where elegant folk moved and laughed and met, and where children played at chasing hoops and hiding from each other, much as his guide went skipping through the stones.

He rode Petelly among the mazy foundations of what had been not a fortress like Ynefel but a community of buildings scarcely fortified at all. It had never had walls. That certainty came to him with the Name of Althalen: it had been a peaceful place, never considering its defense – trusting folk. Gentle folk, perhaps.

Or powerful.

But everywhere about him now, as he had seen at the village, fire had blackened the remnant of windows and doors. He smelled smoke, as where had he not? It might be the smoke of old Althalen; or of yesterday's Emwy; or perhaps the dreadful smoke of the Zeide courtyard had clung to him and Petelly even through last night's rain – he was not certain, but he felt a loosening of his ties to the rock and stone around him, a dispossession as if something, perhaps many such things, did not accept him here, as if – smothering fear met him and just scarcely avoided him.

The world became pearly gray. The walls stood, still burned, still broken, and Petelly and he moved all in that gray place, in a shifting succession of broken walls, less substance than shadow here. The burning and the smell of smoke was true in the gray world too. Only the Fear that Emuin had named to him . . . Hasufin . . . rolled through his attention, and seemed to have power here, power like that tingling of Mauryl's cures for skinned knees and bumped chins.

That tingle in the air might, he thought, be wizardry, and if it was, he reminded himself staunchly of things as they ought

465

*to be: he thought of Ynefel, and, feeling a sudden chill and a
sense of dreadful presence, drew back out of that gray light.*

Then a wind sported through the grass, an ominous, tree-
bending sort of wind which swept in a discrete line across the
ground.

– *Child! he called out in warning – because that gust made
him think of the wind in the courtyard, that had raised the
shape of dust and leaves, and he heard the faint wail of
a frightened voice, as a breeze skipped behind him, at
Petelly's tail. Be still, child, he said to it. Go back. Be safe.
I know my way now. Go back to your fountain. There's
danger here!*

– *Very noble, the Wind challenged him, blowing up a puff
of leaves. Elfwyn would have done that sort of thing. And see
what it won him.*

– *Hasufin? he challenged it. If that is your name, answer
me.*

– *Why? Are you lost? Could you be lost? Or confused? –
You're certainly in the wrong place, poor lost Shaping.*

The wind whirled through the brush, whipped leaves into
Petelly's face, and Petelly reared, not at all liking this presence.

*Neither did Petelly's rider. Begone! Tristen wished it, and
the wind raced away, making a crooked line along the
ground, raising little puffs of dust among the stones very
much as the child had done, but far, far more rapidly.*

It was no natural wind, no more than the other had been. It
retreated as far as an old foundation, and a heap of stones,
where it blew leaves off the brush.

*Then the line of disturbed dust swept back toward them.
This is Death, it said. All the Sihhë in this place died, even
the children, should you find that sad. Mauryl and Emuin
conspired to murder us. I was a child, did you know? I was a
child of Althalen. But it did not stop the Marhanen. They
murdered all the children in the presence of their mothers
and fathers. And Mauryl was one of them that did the
murder. Were you here?*

He expected wickedness of it. Now it lied to him. Mauryl would not have killed children.

But the gray place filled with halls lit with pale sunrise fire, and children and all the people were running from the flames. They did die. They burned. They ran like living torches, their clothes set ablaze with that faded light and arrows shot them down.

A young boy lay sleeping on a bed. A man came, one thought, to rescue that child. But the man stabbed the sleeping boy, and that man's face was Emuin's.

"No!"

It was wickedness. And a lie. He had pulled at Petelly's mouth by accident, making Petelly back and turn as he cleared his eyes of dream and wished the brush and the stones back into his sight. Petelly smelled something, or heard something still: even after he had resumed his even grip on the reins, Petelly kept bending his neck this way and that, trying to turn, backing a step at a time, showing the whites of his eyes and flaring his nostrils; but an even hold on the reins and a firm press of his knees steadied Petelly's heart and kept him moving.

That the enemy would lie and deceive – why should it not? What could a lie weigh against murder?

So he argued with himself, refusing to believe, having learned deception, and having used it himself.

The wind blew dust into his eyes, making him blink them shut on that gray space, but, tears running on his face, he doggedly watched the space between Petelly's ears, refusing to start at the Shadows that urged on the edges of his sight. He saw the taunting breeze skirl along the dust. It performed wild antics in his path, it danced in the brush, and turning, blasted him with chaff and grass.

– Tristen, it said to him. Tristen, you dare not blind yourself. These are not lies. I do not lie to you. You've believed the Guelenfolk, and Emuin. Very foolish of you, though you might not know it. Shall I tell you what Mauryl called Emuin?

467

He smelled the smoke still. It seemed stronger. He saw shadow-shapes flitting to the stones and through the brush, shapes which he might have believed, except they passed the most delicate thorn-boughs without disturbing them.

– Mauryl called him weak. Mauryl called him timid. Mauryl called him many names. And you rely on him. Not wise. Not wise at all. You surely died here.

– Go away! he cried. Begone!

– Oh, but you haven't Mauryl's force, have you? And you should indeed listen. Mauryl was my teacher. And Emuin's. Dear Mauryl. Do you remember how he served the Sihhë Kings? He betrayed them: they would not let him have his way – so he dealt with Guelenfolk, and conspired with the Marhanens, who were mere servants to the Sihhë. Do you know how I know? I – I was that murdered child, I was the great and fearsome enemy Mauryl dared not face alone, and all this ruin and all this death he made for me, for me, do you hear me? Because Mauryl feared me, he opened the gates to the Marhanen, he pent me in my room, and sent Emuin to do murder. Would you hear more?

– Heryn Aswydd seemed an honest man, he said, struggling to find resistance to the voice that now seemed so aggrieved, and so reasonable. Heryn twice tried to kill us all.

– Oh, seemed, seemed. The Marhanen seems. Did Mauryl ever bid you trust the Marhanen? I think not. I know Mauryl's advice. He sent you on the Road, but at Ynefel is your answer, Shaping. I have your answer. All you have to do is ask me.

The voice roared close and swept about him, a rush of wind along the ground. It blasted a growth of brushwood, and laid bare a slab of stone whereon something had burned.

– Oh, many of us, many of us, the Wind said. Hasufin . . . said. They burned the dead. They burned the living, did your precious Marhanen. They meant to leave no charred chip of bone to anchor us to the earth. But I have found that anchor. Ask! Come! Temporize with your fate. Ask me all your questions! Shall we search for your Grave, Sihhë soul?

Petelly fought the rein, turning and turning, pressed back by his knees. He saw the gray light, and the towers of Ynefel under shadow as the blackness arced across toward him.

– Then where and when was I born? he asked it, he knew not by what impulse, but it was his question, it was the question only Mauryl knew. Tell me that, or own you are ignorant and tell me nothing at all!

The Wind whipped away from him, breaking branches as it went. It poured across the sky in a scream of frustration and rage.

Then was quiet. Utter quiet. Foolish, he thought, striving to hold Petelly from a wild rush across the ruins. He was aware of another, subtle presence, so faint and so far he all but missed it. He had not driven away the danger alone. This presence had helped him. This presence had given him steadiness when he most needed it.

– Young man! it said, ever so faintly, now. Young man! Be aware. Be away . . .

– Master Emuin? he asked. It felt very much like Emuin's presence, but it was too elusive to see or to catch in this place. In that other world darkness had enclosed the area of silver gray where he and Petelly stood – all but that place and a patch of brightness ahead of him, and he saw it glow and falter like the guttering of a candle-flame.

– Emuin? he asked, again, not certain that it was, but not daring leave his ally weak and faltering as he seemed to be.

But it was a plump, kindly-seeming man who came toward him from that guttering light, a man he did not know in life – a man who called to him and held out hands in urgency – but the winds caught him away and their reaching fingers missed before ever he thought that there might have been a chance to catch him. He was gone. The encroaching Shadows flowed like water, broke like waves against the pearl-gray of the world.

He felt – afraid, then. Bereft of help. He shook himself and tried to come away from that gray place, fearing tricks.

He sat, trembling, on a shivering horse. Petelly stood with feet braced and head up, sniffing the wind.

He might have done the right thing, he said to himself. He had set the spirit aback. It was unable to answer that simple question, who he was, and what he was – and somehow that prevented it – Hasufin – from mischief. He thought that the child had gotten away from danger. He no longer saw the flitter in the leaves that betokened her presence.

But he thought, strangely, that he knew direction – amid the vast maze of lines of mostly-buried stones that was Althalen. There was presence at the heart of it: he thought so, from time to time, but it was a presence he did not think harmful. He thought rather the contrary, now, that the old man was someone he needed to find, another who had the right and the ability to travel in that gray space.

Petelly had not liked the Shadow that had come near them, but Petelly was not quite terrified, for he had the presence of mind to snatch a thistle-top, went, walking along through ripe grasses, along a line of stones that had been a wall.

Some distance he went, down a stream-course he thought might have been the same stream bent back again, perhaps tributary to the Lenúalim, who knew?

"Hold there!" someone cried.

He looked up atop a wall, at a man with a bent bow and an arrow ready to let fly at him. It was a man in gray and brown, and another, appearing in front of him.

Woolgathering, Mauryl had used to call it, when he let his wits go wandering,

"Sirs," he said, in the courtesy he hoped would prevent arrows flying. "Good day." Neither of these was the presence he had felt. He supposed they thought him quite foolish, being where he was, so unaware; or perhaps they thought him a danger.

The one man came closer. "Your sword," that man said.

"I have none," he said. "Nor any weapon. Have you a master, sir? I believe I've come to see him."

The man on the rocks relaxed his draw and leaned on his bow. "And whose man would you be?"

"Cefwyn's," he said. "And you, sir?"

"Men of Uleman," the archer said. "The lord Regent of Elwynor."

CHAPTER 26

Sullen, dejected men rose from their seats near the one tent of a fireless camp to lay hands on weapons and stare as, through the deep dusk, Tristen led Petelly in, with the archers walking behind him. Besides the tent, he saw the wagon to carry it, and some number of horses grazing within the ruined wall which surrounded the small camp, a ground with pavings here or there breaking surface amid the trampled grasses: it was some former room, or hall, and of men there were thirty or so, hardly more.

"What's this?" a man confronted them to ask.

"M'lord," the older of the archers said, "m'lord, he came unarmed. He claims to be Cefwyn's man."

"A bedraggled sort of emissary. And no attendant? No ring, no seal? A scout, far more likely. Where did you find him?"

The archers gave a quick and slightly muddled explanation, how he had come walking up to their post, how he had not argued with the request to go with them.

The man was not convinced. "And what do you have to say for yourself?"

"Sir," he said, "I am Cefwyn's friend, and I'm fully willing to carry messages to him." He did not add that they were strangers in Cefwyn's land, and that, absent the weapons, he should most properly be asking them the questions about their intentions and their right to be where they were. "But I came to speak to your lord."

The man said nothing to his offer, nothing at all, as he turned and went away into the only tent, a tent improbably pitched, its guy-ropes running to the ruined walls, and its pegs driven into earth where they had pried up paving-stones to accommodate them. The Elwynim had been at some great

472

pains to set their tent here, when there was far softer, deeper soil just across the ruined half wall. He found it curious and significant that they had been thus determined to have it inside rather than outside the walls. Lines on the earth, Tristen thought. Someone here knew.

And if the Regent of Elwynor was camped at Althalen, he might well be the one who had killed Cefwyn's father – and he might be the very lord of the Elwynim with whom Heryn Aswydd had conspired, which cast an even more unpleasant light on the situation.

Of all troubles he had gotten into and of all mistakes he had made, he said to himself, falling into the hands of the Elwynim might be the worst and the most costly to Cefwyn, although so far he could not complain of his treatment. By the archers' general behavior they were honest men, well-spoken, and not, at least, bandits who fired from hiding and without asking.

The men otherwise stared and talked among themselves and did not venture closer or threaten him. He was wearing Cefwyn's cloak, with the Marhanen Dragon plain to see: that was one cause of the talk; and he was equally aware of the coat beneath it, which had the Sihhë arms, not plain to see at the moment, but there was no hope of pretending to be other than what he was, and he did not intend to try, thinking it could only make matters worse if he seemed to deceive them.

Finally the man came back out of the tent and beckoned him to come inside, or for someone to bring him, he was by no means certain. He went of his own volition and the archers walked behind him, into an interior warm, lit by oil lamps and partitioned by curtains, one of which was folded back.

He had expected a vigorous and powerful lord – but the two lords present were attending an elderly man who lay on a cot against the back wall of the tent: two other men stood by, guards, or servants; and a dark-haired woman was kneeling by the old man's side, holding his hand.

"My lady," said the lord who had summoned him.

The woman glanced around and up. He saw painted ivory,

a cloud of dark hair, a crown of violet flowers – and in the selfsame moment he saw on the cot the round, kindly-looking man who had reached for his hand through the light and the advancing shadow.

This was not a wounded leader of soldiers. This was an old man who should be safe under a roof, not out in the elements, and on the wrong side of the river.

And he had not strayed amiss in his riding. He had found the object of his search after answers – he had by no means known what he was looking for, and least of all that he was looking for the Regent of Elwynor; but he had found him all the same, and on an impulse of the heart moved toward him in this world of substance and that of Shadows.

The men behind him pulled him roughly back. The clasp at his neck parted, and the hard-used cloak came off and fell.

"Marhanen," the young woman said angrily, and then looked up at him. "Oh, dear *gods!*"

It was his black coat, ruined as it was, with the Sihhë arms embroidered in silver thread.

"Sihhë," exclaimed the man on the cot. "I hoped, I did hope."

The old man's eyes had opened. The look on his face was the same he had had in the gray light, a man of such uncalculated kindness, such affable, cheerful goodness that Tristen wanted at once to take the old man's hand and draw him back from the dark brink that threatened him. On that thought, gray was suddenly all about them, but the soldiers moved to prevent their touching, although the old man, in this world and that other, reached out his hand.

The woman intervened, caught the old man's hand instead and pressed it to her. "Father. Father, do you hear me?"

"He –" the old man said, with the gray light of the other world streaming past his shoulders. Tristen could scarcely get his breath, the urgency of that request was so intense, and the shadows were forming patterns in the light, seeming like faces gathered about them, listening. "Lord of Ynefel. Who are you? *Who are you?*"

It was the very question Hasufin had asked him in seeking power over him. It was the central question about himself that he could not answer and that Hasufin could not answer. But he had had no fear of this man, on what evidence he did not know, but that his presence in the gray place was most like Emuin, and not at all like the enemy.

"My name is Tristen, sir. I was Mauryl's student. And lord of Ynefel, yes, sir, I am, so Cefwyn says."

"Cefwyn," the daughter said, and clenched her father's hand tightly, tightly, trying to compel his hearing. "Papa, no more. Send him away. It's too late for Marhanen tricks. This is no one. Look at him! He's all draggled and muddy from last night's rain. He's just a man, Father, just a man."

"Lord of Ynefel," the old man echoed him, seeming to hear nothing of his daughter's protest. "Are you? Are you in fact Mauryl's successor in the tower?"

"I suppose I am, sir. But Hasufin holds the tower, so far as I know."

"Hasufin." The old man struggled up on an elbow. "Look at me, young sir. *Look at me!*"

"Father." The young woman interposed her hands. "Tasien, he mustn't tire himself. Take this man away from him!"

"I am still Regent," the old man said, in a voice that trembled. "Lord of Ynefel, I know you, do I not? Did I not meet you just now?"

"He dreams," the daughter said, but Tristen said quietly, wary of the angers and the grief running wild in the close confines, "Yes, sir. You did. You helped me. Dare I try now to help you?"

"You cannot draw me from *this* brink," the man said faintly. "Far too dangerous to try. But I hoped for you. Oh, gods, I hoped – hoped you existed. I dared not believe it. I feared it gave the enemy purchase on us all."

"My father is ill!" the daughter said bitterly. "He is in no state for this. – Father, please, send him away. These are all dreams. They're only dreams. Cefwyn's scouts have found us, that is all this proves. We have to move from here as soon as we can."

"No. Not dreams. Not dreams, daughter. No more than it was dreams that brought us here. Hasufin's tomb. Hasufin's burial-place. So that I do battle with him – I must not leave here. I must never leave here!"

"Hasufin is dead!" the daughter cried. "He is *dead*, Father, Mauryl saw to that here in this very hall. You dream, you only dream. And the Marhanen dares send us this mockery. I will not marry him, Father! I shall never marry him!"

The Regent's white hand lifted, trembling, and smoothed back the hair that fell about her face. "Daughter, but you see, you see, I'm not mad. Is it not the Star and Tower?"

"Wrapped in the Marhanen Dragon. This man is nothing but Amefin – even black Guelen, for all we know –"

"No, the rumors – the rumors – are all true. And this is their evidence. Look at him, indeed." The Regent lay back on the pillows. "Mauryl's student. But not only Mauryl's heir. You are – Mauryl's. Are you not?"

"They say so, sir. Master Emuin said –"

"Emuin the traitor," Tasien said.

"Let him speak!" the Regent said. "Go on, my lord Sihhë. Where have you lived? Where have you hidden from us?"

"With Mauryl. Then Hasufin came and took the balconies down. He put Mauryl into the stones, sir."

"He knows," the Regent exclaimed. Breath was coming hard for him. His eyes wandered from one to the other face hovering near him. "You see, he does know. He was there, just now, in my dream, – were you not, Lord of Ynefel? You drove Hasufin away!"

"I think it was quite the other way, sir. He fled when you appeared."

"He fled *you*, young King! I dared tread further then, to find you. Oh, gods, I've found you, Majesty. I have found you!"

"Take him *out!*" the daughter cried, and men seized him by the arms to hasten him away, but the old man cried out, "No!" and motion ceased.

"I am Uleman Syrillas," the old man said. "I am Regent till I die. And I have waited – I have waited all my life for my King. Are you not that King, Lord Sihhë?"

"Mauryl never said I was a king. Mauryl said I was not all he wanted." He saw the dark closing about the man and tried to see only the gray light. He fought for it, desperately insisting to see it. "But when Hasufin came Mauryl knew I couldn't help him. He said I was to leave Ynefel and follow the Road. And the Road led me to Cefwyn. But I think it led me here, too."

"Mauryl called him," the old man said. It was scarcely a voice. "Ninévrisë, daughter, do you hear? Mauryl called him, and he has the Sihhë gift. I see him clearly in the light. I see him. He shines – look, look at him! He shines!"

"Father," the woman said. "Father? – Tasien, please, please, take him *out!* He's making him worse! He dreams. He doesn't know –"

He wished to take the old man's hand. He thought he could hold him. The old man was all in shadow now. He reached, and the guards held him by force.

"He's fading," the one man said, looking at the Regent's face; and the archer at Tristen's ear said in a low voice, "Just you come along, Lord Sihhë or whatever you are, sir. You come along gently, now. We'll find you somewhere to sit, something to drink, anything you like."

They were afraid of him, and of their lord's illness, and had no choice but to do what the lady said.

The lady. Ninévrisë. Cefwyn's offered bride.

"You granted her Amefel?"

It was very rare that one took Idrys entirely aback.

Cefwyn shook his head and started down the steps to the lower hall, Idrys in close accompaniment, with the other guards. "I see no other course. The lesser lords are all a tangle of Amefin allegiances we do not understand, of blood-relations, disputes of inheritance, jealousies and feuds, one district against another. Worse than a united Amefel is one fragmenting under us in civil strife, with this business on the border. The lady, of course, well knows that point."

"Why not add Amefel to the grant of Ynefel?" Idrys muttered as they went down the stairs, banquet-bound.

"I did consider that. But Tristen's off chasing moonbeams and Orien asked so prettily."

"You jest in both, I hope, Your Majesty."

"What? That she asked politely? – A basilisk, seeing that woman, would seek thicker cover. But I have a sure hold on her. When she weds, her title in Ylesuin passes to her husband, whatever the Amefin hold to be the case. I swear if she crosses me once, I'll give her one who'll cut her throat if she crosses me or him. Sovrag, perhaps. *There* would be a match."

"Take my advice and unsay this thing."

"I am looking for any excuse, I confess it."

They came down together into the lower corridor, and, by the back door, in among the lords gathering and milling about in the Ivory Hall. The herald required attention, the lords bowed and swept a path before him, a storm going through a field, more rapidly than recent habit – it was his dour countenance, Cefwyn thought, and, facing the lords, he tried to better that expression. He took his chair at table, in a room that smelled of food and ale waiting to be served. He still found his appetite lacking, not alone by reason of the Aswyddim: the leg was swelling again, and he looked askance at the food as pages and cooks' helpers carried in two of the four meat courses, braided breads, dark beer, southern wine, and strong ale. There would be six cheeses, favoring the southern provinces, summer cabbage and sausages, pickled apples, broad beans and buttered turnips, green herbs and peas and pickled eggs. He did not favor the delicate fare of the east and north. He had a peasant's taste for turnips and cabbage and inflicted it on the court – the King could decree such things. The Amefin lords held out for partridge stuffed with raisins and apricots – which he had ordered to please them and Umanon, who tended to such luxury; Cevulirn particularly favored the pickled apples, and figs from the southern Isles; Pelumer had a fondness for the famed partridge pies, and Sovrag for ham and sausages: cook had searched out their several weaknesses, and was under orders to keep them content.

While Efanor and his Quinalt priest dined by choice on Llymaryn beef and the locally disdained mutton; and Duke Sulriggan of Llymaryn – who had ridden in this afternoon with said priest, two cousins, six men-at-arms, twenty-nine stable-bred horses for which they had no stalls, and a useless handful of servants and grooms who had already antagonized master Haman's staff – claimed distempers gained of an excess of red meat and brought his own supplies, his own cook, his own pots. Doubtless Duke Sulriggan was surprised to find Efanor *not* in possession of the province, and Efanor's brother not in disfavor, but King.

The priest and Prince Efanor had closeted themselves in the Quinalt shrine for three hours of prayers and gods knew what excesses of mourning. Sulriggan had attached himself to the affair and there had been some sharp words between the priest and the local prelate over some niggling purchase of oil in unblessed jars.

Sulriggan's cook prepared separate fare for Sulriggan and his Llymarish attendants under a canvas in the courtyard: small wonder, that self-established exile, considering the ire of the spurned Amefin-bred cook. It was fear of poisons, he was certain, that underlay Sulriggan's pretensions of a delicate stomach, but murder all the southern lords at once? Annas was there, supervising all details, his defense in the kitchens, far more gracious than Sulriggan. Sulriggan perhaps suspected *him*. And did the offended Amefin aspire to poison Sulriggan *and* his supercilious cook and his high-handed servants – the King could willingly turn a blind eye if they only warned him of the dish involved.

The partridge pies and the bread and cheese found instant favor. So did the dark beer and the ale and two sorts of wine.

Another arrival – the King set his chin on fist, and stared with basilisk coldness of his own.

Late – and dramatic – came Her red-haired Grace, Lady Orien, *not* considered in the culinary selections, but, then, her tastes were wide. Her coming, with the first course served, startled the barons, who went from the pleasantry of ale and men deep in masculine converse, to stark silence, to a lower murmur in the hall, an assessment, an account-taking, even among the Amefin lords present and the servants about the edges of the hall.

She wore dark green velvet, the Amefin color, and had a bit of funereal black knotted about her right shoulder, like a man; more, she had cut her red hair shoulder-length, like a man's. That despoilment shocked him as nothing else Orien had done. And the mourning – which by tradition of Selwyn Marhanen no Marhanen King wore – was a direct and silent insult, worn into this hall, at this time, in Heryn's cause.

There were two empty places, Heryn's being one, and she went to it, an empty seat at Efanor's left, the place of the host province in council, court and feast-hall. Her eyes should have been downcast: they were not. She stared round at each of the lords in turn as if measuring them as she spread her skirts and took that place.

"Her Grace Orien Aswydd will swear fealty in her brother's place," Cefwyn said in a low voice. "She is my ward; her sister and her cousins will soon depart this court under my extreme displeasure. Amefel is under Crown protection, until Her Grace has a man by her. Or perhaps," he added, looking askance at her shorn hair, "she will take up the sword in her own defense."

"I rule," she said in a voice startlingly level, "until I also meet the Marhanen's displeasure."

"You are never far from it," he muttered, which was doubtless heard at the nearer seats, and he hoped that it was. "Your health, my lords. Discuss no policy; Lady Orien will retire after dinner, by my order, and then we may deal among ourselves."

There was, then, a marked scarcity of topics for conversation; it drifted, through the various courses, from a discussion of the relative merits of Amefin and Guelen wines, to the breeding of Cevulirn's horses versus Sulriggan's, and finally to the hunt, the latter discussion spirited and the gathering good-natured, until it came down to discussion of districts and game.

Then Orien's voice cut through, soft and high. "I wonder how the hunting might be in Lanfarnesse," Orien said, "since you border Marna, Lord Pelumer. Do you see odd things come from there? – Where *is* the lord of Ynefel this evening? I had rather looked to see him."

Cefwyn struck his cup sharply with his knife, choosing not to have the public scene Orien clearly wanted. "We have business to settle. Clear the tables. Lady Orien, your guards will conduct you. Your interests will be represented here for you."

She did not rise. "I am competent to represent my own, Your Majesty."

"Then I tell you bluntly that you are still under arrest, and your removal from this council now is for suspicion of your character, not your competence. Must my guards lay hands on you? They will."

"My lord King." She rose, pushed back her chair, dropped a deep curtsy, and strode off, her guards moving to overtake her, a long progress toward the farthest door.

Idrys closed the doors and returned to stand at Cefwyn's shoulder.

"My lords," Cefwyn said. "You have been patient to remain under hardship of absence from your own lands. Your grace and favor will be remembered throughout my reign. I am about to ask more of you . . . that you stay while the northern barons come in for their oath-giving – which means staying during harvest-season. I know the hardship. But for the stability of the realm, and in view of the foreign threat, – I ask you to stay."

"My lord King," murmured Umanon, "it is in our interests to remain, if that is the case."

"But," said Sulriggan, "will Your Majesty not return to the capital?"

"You've not been informed, then."

It was not the answer Sulriggan had wanted. It set him down. It gave him no ready point of argument.

"No, Your Majesty, I have not."

"My father was murdered. *Murdered*, sir. I am not done with investigations, and by the gods, no, I do *not* go to the capital when the evidence is here."

Sulriggan said, prudently, whatever the argument he had devised, "I beg Your Majesty's pardon."

"But what," Sovrag broke in, "is this Aswydd woman about? Going as a page?" Sovrag had made a joke. He elbowed his fellow Olmernman in the ribs. "I'd take 'er. And 'er sister."

"I decline to know what Lady Aswydd does, save she risks excessively. Our patience has its limits." He was conscious of the lesser Amefin lords at the lower table, their lord's head, lately removed from the south gate, rejoined to his body in the Bryalt shrine along with the remains of two earls and their relatives. Three of the remaining earls were in bitter dispute of the Aswydd kingship that went back into the aethelings of the years of Sihhë rule: he had already heard the stirrings of restless lords, and Annas, who kept careful watch over protocols, had noted new pretensions in three lately received expressions of loyalty to the Crown. Each was petitioning the Marhanen King for honors they claimed had been unjustly denied by the Aswyddim, and which Annas warned him might imply fitness to be Duke of Amefel. Granting any one of them would incite the people to believe such a move was pending. And now came this entrance into hall, a brave show from Orien Aswydd, a provocation that could not but set her brother's former vassals to thinking each that he might make good those claims and take Heryn's place if he proved a better man than Orien – as Orien evidently thought unlikely.

She *was* aetheling, meaning royal blood of the old Amefin line came through her. No matter the ancient claims of the earls, legitimacy came through her – for any Amefin earl who could marry her and get children; while the King of Ylesuin and all his horsemen dared not affront so sensitively poised a border province by humiliating the Amefin nobility, meaning that he dared not vent his frustration. Much as he wished to bestow Orien on Sovrag exactly as Sovrag said (and that had been a dangerous remark of Sovrag's which thank the *gods* had not carried to the lower tables) he could not do so. What was now a simmering pot of intrigue would boil over in an instant.

"So," he said, "regarding the matters we have to deal with, and the safety of lives and livestock on this border – no, I shall not return to the capital until I can bring my father home in good conscience. Prince Efanor will go to the capital if there is urgent need, but for now and until matters are settled I need him more as my right hand on this border. I shall not encourage all the court to assemble here. I shall come to the capital in good time, I hope before the winter. As for those of you remaining to defend the border, I realize your responsibilities elsewhere at this season, and wherein the Crown can assist you we shall most gladly consider your specific requests." He snapped his fingers and Idrys obtained the charts that he had brought down. He rose as Idrys spread them on a clear space on the high table and other lords rose with a scraping of chairs to gather around.

It all but covered the beginnings of a commotion, an altercation against the very doors of the hall. It shocked the company to silence, hands reaching for dinner knives.

And it had an Olmern accent.

"Bridges," one voice shouted, penetrating the doors. "M'lord sent to know, and they're deckin' bridges. We seen 'em up an' down the damn river."

The gray light came all laced with Shadows, now, fingers and threads of darkness weaving all about the horizon, coming near the old man, try as Tristen would to chase them. Tristen sat where the guards had bidden him sit, on the low wall that surrounded the camp. The horses were eating hay at the end of that wall, Petelly among them and, nearer the tent that sat spiderlike in its web of ropes at the heart of this strange and cheerless camp, men sat on stones that lay out across the old pavings. They sat, shoulders hunched, heads bowed together, speaking in voices he could not hear.

He was aware of the sinking of the sun and the gathering of the true night in the world. Now came the dangerous time, when Shadows were strong, but he was determined to hold them until the dawn. He had discovered a power in himself to dismiss certain Shadows, although he knew no Words to speak and he had nothing but his presence and his refusal to let the Shadows have the old man. One would creep close, and he would face it in that gray place, and challenge it merely with his presence – then it would retreat. But there were very many of them, whatever they were, and so long as he was wary and quick enough he could frighten them singly back before they could combine into a broad, fast-moving Shadow that could threaten the old man.

But he was slowly losing. He knew that he was. So was the old man. There were more and more threads. It would have been easier if he could have held him, clung to his hand, made one defense of the two of them. He was tiring. His efforts raised a sweat despite the cold of the world of substance. He hoped, though, that if he could last until the dawn, if the old man seemed better –

Then someone said, very close to him,

"Here! What's he doing?"

"He's been like that," one said, and someone drew a sword, a sound that rasped through his hearing with cold familiarity. Metal touched him, a shock like a burning fire, but when he blinked and saw it, the sword had done him no harm. The man had only laid its edge along his hand.

"M'lord, m'lord, be careful of 'im. The Regent said he might be Sihhë for real and all. That he might even be the King. We was only to watch 'im."

"The Regent says. And what says Tasien?"

"Don't know, m'lord. Some around the fire say as he's Lanfarnesse, but the Regent said as he is Sihhë for a fact, m'lord, and ordered us to keep 'im close, and we don't do 'im no disrespect 'ere, m'lord, please."

"Some damned Quinalt praying curses on the lord Regent," another man said. "That's what he is. A Sihhë come wrapped in a Dragon's cloak! Not likely, say I."

They were all shadows to him in the dark, discussing his provenance and his purpose here, which ought to concern him – but in that gray light from which they had called him the Shadows were multiplying so quickly he dared not spare his thoughts for them: he went back. The old man was losing ground quickly. The Shadows had combined into skeins and ropes: they had grown reckless – until he faced them. Then they rapidly unwove. They became threads again, and tried new tricks to get behind him.

But now the lord Regent turned toward the attack. The old man knew a Word, and spoke it, but he could not hear it, as he had never been able to hear Mauryl's Words when there was magic about them.

The old man was a wizard, he knew that here quite clearly, but no one else had seemed to know it. He liked the old man in that reasonless, trusting way he had liked Mauryl and Emuin. When the old man, exhausted now, beckoned him close, he longed to go – but it seemed to him that in this respite from the Shadows the old man had gained for them both, he would do better to stand and drive the Shadows back.

– Come closer, the old man said. Come closer, Majesty. Forget them. They're small threat to me now. Let me see you. Let me touch you.

– Sir, he said, I might win. Let me try, first.

– No. The old man had grown very weak, and caught his hand in a grip he might have broken. But it was not the strength of that hand that held him, it was the expression, the same gentle, kindly expression that had ensnared him when first they met.

485

– You are the one. You are what Mauryl promised. I doubted. Forgive my doubt.

– Sir, he said, I am not as wise as Mauryl wished, nor as strong as Mauryl wished. But I do learn. I am learning, sir.

The old man laughed through his tears, and pressed his hand, and laughed again. I warrant you are, that. And Hasufin trembles. I warrant he does. Learning! I had not expected a brave young man. I expected someone furtive, and hidden and wary. Even cruel. But, oh, there you are, there you are, my dear boy! Bright and brave as you are, whatever you will be, you are my King, you are what we've waited for – you are all of Mauryl's promise.

– But what shall I do, sir? Mauryl never told me what I was to do for him. Can you teach me?

– Teach you, my King? Oh, gods, what first? – First, first and always, beware Hasufin's tricks. He will use your hopes as well as your fears. He will trade you dreams for dreams. Let me tell you – he came to me in my dreams, oh, years and years ago. He promised me visions, and before I could break away I saw Ynefel, and Mauryl.

– You knew Mauryl, sir?

– Never in the flesh. And not before this. But I knew him, the way one knows things in dreams. I saw Mauryl old and alone, tired and powerless. It troubled me for days. I feared to go back, and I could not, in the end, forbear listening to Hasufin disparage my hopes, and warn me of my own lords, and tell me true things – mark you, true things about their plots – which I think now he engendered. I began to doubt the goodness of the men I ruled, and my doubts changed them. I asked myself whether there was any hope of a King and whether I should not take the crown for myself and forestall the plotters against the Regency. My doubts, my precautions, estranged the very people who should have stood by me. That was how Hasufin found purchase on my life. That was how he pried apart the allegiances that supported me. I became unjust in my own heart. Don't disbelieve your friends, young King. Never go dream-wandering with him.

You dare not. And I know that he will invite you.

– I hear you, sir. I do hear. But you withstood Hasufin. You fought him.

– Oh, yes. But came the time I would not follow down his trail of questions and doubts. I said to myself – no, I need no more visions: my foresters would go to Ynefel and see what was the truth. But my foresters lost themselves in Marna and never came back. So after all I had only my doubts to keep me company; and I bartered with Hasufin. I said – take a year of my life, I'd see Ynefel again – if he would let me ask Mauryl two questions. He showed me the tower. I thought I was so clever. I asked Mauryl in this dream: Lord Wizard, when will you keep your promise? And Mauryl was angry, because he knew at once how and with what help I had come there. He told me the price was far too dear. But I asked my question, all the same: I asked him when he'd keep his promise, and I asked him how I should recover my faith; and he said only, I shall keep it when I will, and when I must, no sooner. As for your faith, it matters not to me. After that the dream stopped. All the dreams stopped. But after all that, I was never sure even of that answer, you see, because it was Hasufin's magic that had taken me there, and Hasufin's voice that whispered ever afterward in my dreams. I lost all certainty, that was what it did to me. Mauryl was right, that my faith was my affair. My faith was that you would not come in my lifetime, no more than in my father's. My faith was that I should die sonless – and I shall; Hasufin foretold to me that Elwynor should be thrown into civil war when I die – and I had faith in that. So two of my lords have raised armies, and now a third bids to do so – all demanding my daughter so that they dare claim my place. In desperation I sent even to the Marhanen, as my last hope to secure my daughter's safety and to preserve the realm against a Marhanen conquest by arms. I hoped – I hoped – he would come here –

The Regent's voice faded. *– Sir?* Tristen called to him, and took a firmer grip on his hand, which became like gossamer

487

in his, and impossible to feel. Lord Regent, what will you? What shall I do for you?

– I must not become a bridge for Hasufin to any other place. I listened to him too long, you understand, and I fear – I fear he will lay hold on me. For that reason I came here. I must be buried here in Althalen, where Hasufin is buried. I came here to fight him – on ground sacred to him. Make them understand. Make my daughter understand –

– Sir! The old man slipped from his hold. He reached out, and the old man caught his hand again, but oh, so weakly.

Then it seemed to him he saw Althalen standing as it had once stood, and that years reeled past them, or that they spun together through the years.

– Listen now, the old man said, compelling his attention. *Listen. In my father's time, in the reign of the Last King's father, an infant died; and came alive again when they came to bury him. Do you know that story?*

– No, lord Regent. Shadow had wrapped close about them both and the old man seemed dimmed by it, sent into grays – but his own hands blazed bright.

– Hasufin could not do for himself what Mauryl did for you. Hasufin could only steal the helpless, infant dead, and grow as a child grows – but you – you are a marvelous piece of work, a theft from Death itself, flesh and bone long since gone to dust – Oh, gods! Oh, gods! – Oh, gods protect us! I know you! You are not that lost, dead prince – you are not. I do guess what Mauryl has called!

– What is my name, sir? Who was I? – Tell me! Don't leave!

But the old man broke free of his hold and the Shadows drew back in turmoil. The old man blazed bright, held his hand uplifted and said a Name he could not hear, a Name that went echoing out into echoes the sounds of which he could not untangle, and for an instant he feared the old man had deceived him about his strength: the old man was fearsome, and blinding bright.

– Most of all – the old man said, *do not fail in justice, lord*

King! Love as you can, forgive as you can, but justice and vision are a king's great duties! Never forget it!

The Shadows began to circle in like birds, alighting about them, thicker and thicker – bad behavior, he would chide his pigeons in the loft. He would chase them like pigeons – he would call on Owl and rescue the old man –

"You!" someone said, and seized his arm and shook him. "You! – This is wizardry! Stop him! Someone for the gods' sake stop him!"

He looked up, startled, exchanging the rush of Shadows for surrounding night and a murmur of angry voices about him. "Guard the old man!" he called out to anyone who would hear. "He's in danger! *Help him!*"

He could not tell if they understood at all. He heard voices declaring he had worked some harm on their lord, and some spoke for killing him.

Lines on the earth, Mauryl had said. Spirits had to respect them.

Windows, Mauryl had said to him, windows and doors were special places. Mauryl had spoken of secrets that masons knew. And masons had built these ruins. When he looked for other lines, those lines showed themselves, still bright in the gray space, clear as clear could be, glowing brighter and brighter to his searching for them. He saw one crossing beneath him as he began to follow the tracery they offered, lines far more potent than the hasty circle unskilled Men had made, lines of masons offering him a path along them, to doors and windows that masons had laid.

But search as he would through this maze, he could not find the old man. There were abundant Shadows, flitting about in confusion, and he could see nothing but the lines, nothing of company in his vicinity. He had never asked the old man what the Shadows were, and it seemed now a grievous omission. He called out again, **Lord Regent! Do you hear me?**

He heard a murmur then like the sound of voices. He looked back in the direction from which he had come and did not see the place he had left until he looked for it to be there.

489

And in the blink of an eye – he was overwhelmed and buffeted with voices, and tried to know where the old man was, here, as well as in the gray place.

– Where is the lord Regent? he asked, and there came to him, echoing like the axe blows off the walls, the answer: Dead, dead, dead.

"Wizard!" Voices came through the dark. "He killed him! He bewitched him!"

Then one shouted,

"Send Cefwyn's man with the lord Regent!"

"Hold!" someone cried then, and silence fell.

It was the man called Tasien, with two other lords.

"He killed the Regent!" a man said. "Ye didn't see 'is eyes, m'lord. He was sittin' and sittin' and starin' like to turn a man to stone. He's cursed him. Kill 'im before he kills us all!"

"The lord Regent is scant moments dead," Tasien said. "For the gods' good grace, do your lady the courtesy of awaiting her orders."

"Wrapped in Marhanen arms," one of the lords said. "A wizard, besides, and have we not suffered enough from wizards? Strike off his head! This is no king of ours. It's a Marhanen trick!"

It was clearly his head in question, and he knew he must do something desperate if it came to that, but Tasien – Tasien, who did not like him – said, "Wait for the lady's word. Keep this man safe, I say, or answer to me."

Tasien and two other men went away toward the tent, and left him in the care of the others in the starlight. He only knew individuals by the edges of their clothing and their gear. They had no faces to him. They spoke to him in quieter, more respectful terms: "Lord," they called him, and said, "You sit there, lord wizard," directing him to sit again on a section of the old wall, under their watch.

He saw no gain in arguing with them. He had had experience of guards who had orders, and he avoided looking at them – nor did he venture into the gray place: he only remained subtly aware of it.

But the Shadows had gotten their comeuppance, that was one of Uwen's words: he felt that the old man was safe in some unassailable way, and had crossed a threshold of some Line invisible to him and unreachable. The old man had not lost. And perhaps, he thought, this time with a tingle of his skin and an inrush of breath, perhaps Mauryl had not.

Perhaps he had come where he had to be, and perhaps *he* had not failed, either. He no more knew where to go from here, and how to persuade the Regent's men – nor dared he think that the Shadows of Althalen were powerless to do harm to him or to Mauryl's intentions. Hasufin marshaled and commanded the Shadows in this place – but it seemed to be the Regent's purpose to contest him. The old man had been fighting Mauryl's fight for years. And waiting for *him*. His King, the old man had called him. What was he to do with that? Clearly these men had no such notion.

More, there were dangers attached to this place, both in the gray place, and in the world of substance. Uwen he was certain was looking for him, and in the dark, and with their distress over the loss of the lord Regent, the archers might not restrain themselves for an ordinary-looking soldier and a band of Cefwyn's guard. The lady might prevent disaster, if she would listen, but she was refusing to see what the old man had seen – she had been refusing steadfastly, trying to hold him in life and to keep him with her, and, wrong though that had been, it was not as wrong as other things she might decide to do. Removing the lord Regent from this Place, if he understood what the lord Regent had tried to tell him, would free Hasufin to act as he pleased and work whatever harm he pleased without whatever hindrance the lord Regent might have been to him. These men must not listen to Hasufin. She must not.

Cefwyn's Ninévrisë. That was the other matter. Somehow and suddenly there were too many Kings.

He had ridden out to listen to the world and not the clamor of voices. He had ridden out hoping to understand answers – but another world opened under his feet, and purposes he had never guessed turned out to involve him.

I shall not harm Cefwyn, he had sworn to himself. I shall not harm Uwen.

And even that simple, desperate promise came back to him tangled and changed.

Bridges, for certain: with decking in one case hidden near them on the Elwynim side of the river, and with new timbers stained dark and with smith-work cleverly concealed along the stone of the old bridges, making a bed ready to receive decking. That meant the bridges which looked stripped of surface and unusable could become a highroad into Amefel within hours of the engineers setting to work, and *which* of several bridgeheads the Elwynim might use could be settled in strategy at the very last hour it was possible for them to move troops into position.

It settled the question of Elwynim preparation for war in Cefwyn's mind. It did not say where they might strike – perhaps, which the Olmernmen had not had time to investigate, not into Amefel at all, but to the north. The Elwynim had the flexibility to do anything, to challenge Ylesuin at its weakest point, or to feint and strike in several attacks.

Grim news. Arys-Emwy's bridge was definitely involved, and others, and very suspect was another bridgehead lying within the haunted bounds of Marna Wood, of which neither Olmernmen nor Elwynim were as cautious as other venturers – where, in fact, Olmernmen had lately had Mauryl's leave to be: it had been no surprise to him, certainly, Sovrag's admission of trade with Ynefel, and he would not be surprised at all to find Elwynim rangers and engineers venturing into Marna. If there were, it cast still a darker hint of Elwynor's allies in their actions – and on Tristen's flight. Cefwyn did not want to think ill in that regard – but the thought was there: he could not help it.

The extent and advanced progress of the matter advised him that he had been complacent in assuming his spies were loyal and well-paid enough; and in assuming they were receiving valid information. More – the concealment and the extent of the preparations indicated affairs some months in organization under a firm hand, at a time when he had been receiving marriage-offers and taking them as possibly sincere.

Fool, a small voice was saying to him, and urging that in some way he might have managed this province more wisely – that, if he had, his father might then not have died, though gods knew his father had not done wisely, either.

"We should have men up there and break those stoneworks down," was Efanor's conclusion, and Cefwyn did not agree, on several accounts; but he said only, "That is certainly one thing we might do," to avoid starting a public argument with Efanor before the wounds of the last unfortunately well-witnessed dispute had healed, and before his own thoughts were in order. Wine was involved. One could obtain consent of the lords on a matter not requiring debate under such conditions. He did not want to discuss this news until there were clear heads and straighter thinking.

But perhaps he should not even have hinted of contrary thoughts. Efanor went glum and stared at him, and spoke quietly with the priest. Clearly Efanor's pride was still getting before his reason – one certainly saw who stood high in Efanor's personal council, and it truly threatened to annoy him.

Cefwyn let the page refill his cup again, and ordered Sovrag's two scouts set at table and served with the rest: it had been a far trip for two exhausted travelers, and plague take the skittish Amefin diners lowermost at the tables, who were far enough in their cups to be fearful of piracy – at the tables, did they think? Two weary rivermen were going to make off with the Aswydds' gold dinner-plates?

They served enough ale and wine to make the company merry – except Efanor and his priest. The Olmern scouts fell asleep not quite in the gravy, and Sovrag sent men to carry the lads away, while the lordly Imorim were discussing gods-knew-what with Sulriggan. Cefwyn had yet one more cup, and vowed to himself he would go to bed forthwith, on half of it. Efanor was withdrawing, with his priest, doubtless to godly and sober contemplation.

But on a peal of thunder Idrys, who had been at the doors, came down the narrow aisle between the chairs and the wall, and bent beside Cefwyn's chair to say, in the quietest voice that would carry:

"Master grayfrock's at the gates, m'lord. It's a storm wind tonight, blowing in all manner of wrack and flotsam."

"Would it had blown Tristen in with him," he muttered in ill humor. He had drunk rather too much since the scouts had come in. He was not in a mood, in this collapse of things he had hoped were safe, to face his old tutor, the arbiter of his greener judgment, the rescuer of his less well-thought adventures – and to inform Emuin that, no, he had not outstandingly succeeded in his charge to keep Tristen out of difficulty.

But Emuin had been conspicuously absent in his advice as well as his presence, and had fled for clerkly shelter when he remotely comprehended the potential for hazard in the visitor Emuin counseled him keep – and love.

So he swore under his breath, and arose as he had already intended, to take his leave. There was a clap of thunder. Men looked for omen in such things. "Give you good night and good rest, gentlemen. It sounds as if heavy weather has moved in. A good night to be in a warm hall with friends. Drink at your pleasure and respect my guards *and* the premises, sirs. I shall hope for clear heads by midday, and good counsel. Good night, good night."

Cevulirn rose to excuse himself as well, early and sober, though his lieutenant would remain; Sovrag and his lieutenants would tax the staff's good humor, and Umanon and Pelumer were drinking in quiet consultation on the far side of the room with glances in Sovrag's direction, while Sulriggan and his man were likewise departing. They gathered themselves to order and rose and bowed, on their way to the door.

The King cared little. The King had his old tutor to deal with, and withdrew to a private door that led to a hall that led again to the main corridor, in the convolute way of this largest of the Zeide's halls of state. Idrys followed him; so did his guard – not to the stairway which led to his apartments, where he would have received most visitors, but down the corridor to the outer west doors, which, before they reached them, opened to the night and the rain, and a gray-frocked trio of rain-drenched religious.

One of them was Emuin, white beard and hair pouring water onto his shoulders, cloak sodden, standing like a common mendicant.

"M'lord," Emuin said, and to the doubtful servants, who arrived from their stations, began giving orders. "Find somewhere for the good brothers. Take them to the kitchen. Feed them. They're famished."

"High time you came," Cefwyn said, in the rumble of thunder aloft. Idrys said nothing at all.

"High time," Emuin echoed him, wiping dripping hair out of his eyes, and followed as Idrys led the way to the secluded passage. "I came," Emuin said, "as fast as old bones could bear, m'lord."

"Since which of my messages?" He was temperous and felt the wine impede his speech. Emuin had not yet acknowledged him as King: he did not miss that small point.

"With all speed, my lord. As it was I came without escort."

"Tristen *left* without escort. He took to the road. He eluded all my guards. He's gone toward the west."

"The lad's doing what he sees fit," Emuin said. "The lad is in deep and dangerous trouble. I could not prevent it, either."

"Did I call you here only to hear that, master grayfrock? We need more advice!"

"I gave my advice," Emuin said. "Did anyone regard it? Did he? I am not an oracle, young King. I never was."

Young King. There was, finally, the acknowledgment. With the *young,* setting them again in the old relationship: it vastly nettled him.

"And what shall we do now?" Idrys asked. "Is there advice, sir – or only lamentation?"

"Advice," Emuin said. "Advice. Everyone wants it once the string is loosed, not when the bow is bent. Advice I have, m'lord, advice for him if I can lay hands on him, gods send they find him before matters grow desperate."

"What, they? Who should find him?" Cefwyn asked, and Emuin:

"The men you sent. Who else? Who else should be looking for Mauryl's handiwork – besides an enemy he cannot deal with and men too desperate for better sense? The Regent is dead, m'lord King, and our Shaping is standing at this hour amid more than he knows how to cipher, by all I can determine."

"How, determine?"

"By slipping about the edges of the matter, by means I do not want to discuss and you, my lord King, do not want to know. Ask me again for *advice*, by the gods' good grace. No one yet has heeded the advice I have given, but I give it nonetheless – Mauryl's spell is still Summoning, still working, and gods know what more it may do. *I* cannot rule him."

"You came all the way here to tell me that?"

"Find him for me. Bring him here. *Then* I have hope to reason with him. But he is not what I first thought. He is –"

"What, master grayfrock? He is Sihhë? We have no doubt of that! That he is the King-to-Come of the Elwynim? We know it."

"More than that, m'lord King." Emuin's face was rain-chilled and pale. Perhaps it was only that. But the man seemed to have aged a dozen years in the time he had been gone. His mouth trembled. When had it ever done that? "I fear what else he is. So should we all – fear – what he is."

Men went into the tent, and Tristen watched their shadows on the canvas walls. He saw the lady's shadow, as she sat in a chair, and bowed her face momentarily into her hands before she sat back and dealt with the men who came to speak with her. He was sorry to eavesdrop on such a private moment;

but all who came and went became shadows against that wall, as the night had been full of Shadows, and was still full of them: the movements of men through the camp; the play of light and dark against the canvas; and, always, the prowling of the greater, more ominous Shadows beyond their encampment, of which he was constantly aware. So far, these had stayed at bay, perhaps weary from the struggle that had ended in the Regent's death, perhaps satisfied, or perhaps restricted from entering this place by the Lines that still, though glowing more and more faintly, defined the walls – he was not certain. He knew far less than he ought of the gray realm and things that had effect there – he chased his surmises, seeking them to unfold like a Word, but they eluded him. Hasufin had said he himself was buried here – curious thought, and yet, in the way of Words, he would have thought if that was so, he should at least be able to find that place – as *his* place. But perhaps he did not understand such things. Perhaps something very terrible would befall him if he did find it.

Yet through such a connection Hasufin claimed Althalen and through such a connection the old man intended to contest him for possession of it. So there *was* ownership he should have if that were the case and if he knew what to do. And had he not fought the Shadows? Had he not done well at that?

– *Emuin, he said, wishing to be both there and here. Emuin, I have found someone you should have known. Perhaps you did know him. I need you. I need to know things.*

But he found no echo of Emuin, either, only a small furtive presence in the grayness, a presence that deliberately eluded him.

And quite suddenly he met those ill-meaning Shadows that circled and circled the perimeter of the walls, like birds looking for a place to light. He retreated. He held his Place and tried to ignore them in theirs.

Silhouettes against the light within the tent, men filed out again, silent and grieving Men. He could see in the play of shadows against that canvas wall how each man bowed and took the hand of the old man's daughter, who sat beside the light, and that they then passed into a confusion of images where the old man lay. This momentary distinction and subsequent confusion was very much what he had met in the gray realm, and he feared unwitting connection, one with the other: he feared resolution of images here and in the gray place, that might carry something of danger.

Men outside the spider-tent gathered in small sad knots, angers subdued in uncertainty as cloud rolled in above the brush and the ruins, taking even the starlight. The night had turned cold. His cloak was in the tent. He worked chilled hands, and could not feel his own fingers; but the velvet-covered mail pressing the damp padding and shirt against his body were some protection, so long as the wind stayed still. He was as weary as if he had walked all the distance he had traveled in the gray space, and as if he had grappled with substance, not Shadow.

He did not know what to do, except to wait. And that had its own dangers.

Then, the cap on all their discomfort, a cold mist began to fall. Men shifted off the stones in the midst of camp and clustered by a taller section of the ruined wall, looking at him or toward the tent and talking together in words he could not quite hear. They had come ill-prepared for anyone's comfort but the old man's, he thought. There should have been more tents. He had the feeling, he knew not where he had gotten it – perhaps from the old man – that they had been encamped here for some time, and he wondered what had already befallen them, whether they had been escaping something as he had, in his own lack of preparation; he wondered how they had lived, and thought that Emwy village might have helped them with some things – but Emwy was burned, now.

Things had surely changed for the worse for them with that. He wondered whether the men who attacked the King had known they were here, or what it had meant to them; and he wondered whether the men Idrys had out had simply missed this place, being afraid of it as men were, or whether the Regent, himself a wizard, had sent searchers astray.

But there were no answers in chance things he overheard, only curses of the weather and from a few, talk of whether they might go home now.

No, one said shortly. It seemed they might die. Or something dire would happen.

At last two men came to say the lady had sent for him. He rose from his place on the wall and went with them, trailed by a draggle of unhappy and suspicious men as far as the door.

He ducked his head and went inside, where the lady sat. Ninévrisë wore a coat of mail which compressed her slender shape. She wore the Regent's crown, at least he supposed it was the same thin band holding her dark cloud of hair. Armed men stood beside her, among them, Lord Tasien.

At the other side of the tent, beyond a wall, the old man lay still and pale, with lamps at his head and his feet.

"They say you killed my father," Ninévrisë said. "They say you bewitched him."

"No, lady, no such thing. I tried to help him."

"Why? *Why* should you help him?"

"He seemed kind," he said, in all honesty, but it seemed not at all the answer that Ninévrisë had expected. Overcome, she clenched her fist and rested her mouth against it, her elbow on the chair arm and her face averted, while tears spilled down her face.

"I believe nothing that the Guelen prince sent," said the man beside Tasien. "We should go back across the river tomorrow and seek a peace with the rebels as best we can."

"I shall *die* before I go to Aséyneddin." Ninévrisë brought her arm down hard against the chair and hardened her face, tear-damp as it was, as she looked back to Tristen. "You, sir! Are you another prospective bridegroom? Why should my father listen to you? Why, except that *lie* the Marhanen bade you wear, should my father hail you King? The Sihhë arms, wrapped in a Marhanen cloak? Give me grace, the gods did not make me so gullible! Someone knows where our camp is. Someone told you."

"The cloak is Cefwyn's, my lady. I was cold. He lent it to me, that's all."

"Lent it to you. And sent you to my father? The Tower and Star are outlawed, sir, *by* the Marhanen. And how dare you?"

"Cefwyn didn't send me."

"Do not play the simpleton, sir. Whence the arms you wear? Is this Prince Cefwyn's joke? Does he think us fools? Or what does he wish?"

"Cefwyn said I should be lord of Ynefel, because it was in his grant to give."

"Ynefel? In the prince of Ylesuin's grant?"

"The King of Ylesuin, lady, since his father died. But he was prince when he gave it."

"Ináreddrin is dead?" The lady and her men alike seemed shaken.

"Near Emwy village." These were not the men that had attacked Cefwyn's father, he was certain of it. The Regent certainly would not have done it; and he grew convinced they would not have done it without the old man knowing. "A day ago. I think it was a day. The time is so muddled . . ."

"How did he die?"

"Men killed him before any of us could reach him. Cefwyn believes that they were Elwynim. But he killed Lord Heryn for it. Heryn sent the message that brought the King there."

He had not wanted to say the last: he thought that it might make trouble. But it seemed best to deal in the truth throughout, and not to have it come out later.

"Aséyneddin," one man said.

"Or Caswyddian," Tasien said, and Tristen, hearing that name, felt a coldness that might have been a breath of wind from the open vent. Ninévrisë seemed to feel it, too. She folded her arms and frowned.

"You may tell King Cefwyn, from me," Ninévrisë said, "granted we send you to him at all, that we had no knowledge of Caswyddian's act. The Earl of Lower Saissonnd has dealt with Lord Heryn in the past. Heryn conspired with him and with Aséyneddin alike – and they drove my father out of Elwynor."

That was not entirely so. The old man had said it otherwise; but he ignored that.

"I think you should go to Cefwyn," he said. "I think he would wish to speak with you at length."

"To speak with us? He killed our messengers!"

"No." He knew he had no perfect knowledge of doings in Henas'amef, but he did not believe that. "No. He did no such thing." He was not entirely clear on his reasons for believing so. And not everything fit in words, where it regarded the gray place, but something he did know, one certainty that the lady needed to know in regard to Cefwyn and the Regent: "Your father came here hoping to talk to him. But your father could not leave this place."

That also disturbed them.

"My father is *dead* of this place," Ninévrisë said. "He was in ill health. This ill-omened place – the running and the hiding . . . he was not able. I grant, it took no wizardry to kill him. I know that. But your being here – brought it sooner. And I have held dear every hour of his life. I will have you to know that. Do not try my patience."

"But it *was* wizardry that killed him, lady. He knew it would. Hasufin has Ynefel. He has this place. He tried to harm your father. He was Mauryl's enemy, he is mine and he is Cefwyn's, and he was your father's enemy all his life. That's why your father came here, to *be* here, to remain and hold Hasufin, not to escape any of your lords."

Ninévrisë was silent a moment. Her face had grown suddenly frightened and still. Then: "Tasien, leave me with him."

"No, my lady," Tasien said. "Not for any asking."

Ninévrisë bit her lip, defied by her own men. Her face showed as pale as that ivory portrait.

"Then, sir, what do you know of my father's dealings?" she asked. "Go on. Tell me more wonders my father told you."

"That he dealt with Hasufin – for which he was very sorry. – That he visited Mauryl in a dream."

"Leave me, I say!" Ninévrisë's fist struck the chair arm, and she cast a baleful look about her.

"My lady, –"

"I say go *out!* Go stand by the door. I have private questions to ask him."

"Such as we could hear, we have already heard," Tasien said. "Do we credit it, my lady, as the truth? Do you know anything of your lord father's dealings with Mauryl?"

"It is true," Ninévrisë said, and her voice trembled. "My father told his dream to me, but to none other, that I know, except my mother. And this Hasufin – where did you learn that name?"

"From before your father told me. Perhaps from Mauryl."

"And where and when did my father bestow such confidences on you?"

"In that gray place."

"My father's dreaming. My father's fond wishes. My father knew no magic!"

He felt a slippage of a sudden, toward that Place, but did not go. He did not know who or what might have called him, but something certainly had. The Place was troubled, rife with struggle.

"My father dreamed of Hasufin and Mauryl. He dreamed, I say! He never met them in his life! How can you know the things you claim? You've been here. My father never left his bed."

"Lady, your father wanted to be here. He fought Hasufin. He wishes –" In the unsettling of that Place, it became overwhelmingly important to say, "He wishes very much to be buried here. He said to me that Hasufin's grave was here, and his must be."

"I shall not bury him in this wretched place!" Ninévrisë cried. "I shall not!"

"I think – I think he means to oppose Hasufin, in this place. I think he is not done with fighting."

"He says what serves his master," one lord said harshly. "And the gods know who or what his master is."

"My master," Tristen said, "was Mauryl. He sent me to Cefwyn. And I think Mauryl also sent me here. – Your father is not gone, lady: I can't reach him where he is, but the Shadows did not defeat him. Only if you take him away – then he would have lost all he struggled for."

It was enough, only thinking about the old man. The gray place opened wide, and the light came around him. He could see faint stars, which hung in front of his face where the men stood – he could see the gray shape of Ninévrisë herself, growing brighter, and a cluster of stars around about, which he suddenly thought were men outside and near the tent. The darkness to dread was a vast, abrupt edge in one direction.

The walls, he thought then, made that abrupt edge, and he saw the lines on the earth glowing very dimly, one running right past the tent, which was the wall to which the ropes ran. Shadows leapt at that wall. Shadows prowled desperately, just the other side of that line, trying to gain entry.

– Gods!

It was Ninévrisë's voice, fearful and shaking.

– Lady. He reached out an offering of safety, amazed that Ninévrisë alone of all of them had followed him. She was overcome with fright as he caught her hand, a warm and solid touch, not the gossamer of her father's hand. Around them, just across the wall, was threat gathering: Shadows leapt at that barrier, seeking to get in. But the lady looked at him.

– This, she said, wide-eyed, this is what he saw!

He could not answer her: he did not know what she saw, but he knew she was afraid and he knew how to guide her back to safety. It was only a thought. It was that quick.

He found himself on his feet holding her hand, as startled as she. She drew back her hand in consternation and the men around her seemed not to know whether to lay hands on him or draw weapons. But she signaled them otherwise, unable, it seemed, to utter a word. "No," she said, belatedly, and caught a breath. "No. Oh, merciful gods." She pressed a fist against her lips and waved her other hand, as if seeking room to breathe. "Tasien, Father knew, Father knew! There *is* another place. I was just there, and he – *he* was there, too!"

"Wizardry," Tasien said. "Would our King come bringing Marhanen promises? Or bid us go to the Marhanen? Let him prove he comes from Mauryl – and not from this wizardous enemy he claims your father came here to fight."

It was, Tristen thought, a very wise question to ask, as Tasien seemed a wise man. He wished he knew how to prove himself.

"What *do* you say?" the lady challenged him.

"That you should do as your father asked." That was the wisest answer he could think of, and it seemed to strike home with the lady in particular.

"To bury him where he wished?"

"I don't know that it *will* stop Hasufin. But your father thought it would prevent him taking this place."

"So he says," Tasien echoed scornfully, as if it was as much as he could bear. "And what care if some dead wizard takes this heap of stones?"

"It's a dangerous place." Tasien's irreverence dismayed him. He saw things that had no Words, no breath, no outlet, and he couldn't warn them. "It's where Hasufin died."

"And can stay dead," Tasien said.

"But he hasn't, sir. He can reach here and perhaps not to other places, at least not so easily as this. The lord Regent knew that. He said that Hasufin could reach him wherever he was. He wished to *be* here."

"My lady," Tasien said, "I'd ask some better proof than this man's word."

"What can we prove? And what choice have I, my lord? Go back to Elwynor? To Aséyneddin?"

"The lords in Elwynor would many of them rally to the Regent's banner, my lady, – as they would have rallied to your lord father if he had stood fast and declared a rallying-point and not – not this war against ghosts, in hostile territory, without tents – without – hope. Lady, your lord father, whom

I bore in all reverence, for whom I would have laid down my life, would not hear me. All of us that left our lands came here to die with him, or at least to prevent him from falling into hostile hands, but if you'll only hear me, we can do more than that, by your will, and I *beg* you listen. Aséyneddin and his rebels do not have the other lords' trust or their acceptance. Caswyddian has already raised another rebellion, against him. Elwynor will tear itself in pieces and Ylesuin will pick the bones if you do not go back, now. You *are* his invested heir. You have a duty, m'lady."

"Two lords in rebellion. And what can we bring to counter it? Thirty-three men? Thirty-three men who followed my father however strange his folly? An investiture only you and these men witnessed? Answer me *this*, Tasien! How many of the lords will follow me without demanding marriage to themselves or their sons? And how will *that* sit with their brother lords? I divide the realm only by existing."

There was brief silence.

Then one said, "How many will follow you if you ally yourself with the Marhanen?"

"Will *you* desert me? Will you, Haurydd? Or you, Ysdan?"

"No," one and the other said.

"But," the lady said, "can you make me lord Regent, and raise the standard in Elwynor, and make men rally to me without each seeking to be my husband? Here are three of you, all driven from your lands, all with wives and children at great risk. Where is my choice, m'lords? Tasien, you carried me on your back when I was little. Where can you carry me now?"

"My gracious lady," Tasien said, and gave a shake of his head. "Wherever you wish. You are the Regent. I would take you to a safe place, in Elwynor. I would send to reliable men. I would not see you risk the Marhanen's land another day – let alone ask him for refuge. Choose a consort from among like-minded men, and we will go back into Elwynor and fight any rebels that come against you, to the last of us. Aséyneddin cannot hold his alliances together if we return."

"And if Aséyneddin found us? And if anyone betrayed our whereabouts? Men die, who supported my father. Houses burn. Sheep are poisoned. You may be too high-placed for that, so far, but act against him and he will move against you. That is what he can do. But – more than that. There is this man – this visitor of ours, my lords, –"

"You cannot believe him."

"No. No, Tasien, – I cannot deny my father's witness. I cannot deny what I've seen. I cannot deny that there is magic in this place. I cannot say now that I *should* be Regent . . . or that there should *be* a Regency any longer at all. If my regency denies the King we've waited for, then –"

"My lady, you cannot accept his claim. A man cannot ride up to us, rain-bedraggled, and *claim* to be the King."

"How else must he come, then?" Ninévrisë asked. "Ride out of Marna, with armies and trumpets? Rise out of the ground of Althalen? I don't know, I don't know! My father never told me how to know him. My father only told us in plain words that this is the King and he recognized him. I have just *been* to that magic place Father claimed. I have just seen this man look as he looked to me. What other sign am I supposed to expect? How am I supposed to decide? I need time – I need to know the truth! And if there is a chance in the Marhanen, I will try that chance before I leave this land."

"Are you," lord Tasien asked him bluntly, "the King we look for?"

"Sir, I never heard so from Mauryl," he said truthfully, and did not add to their confusion the fact that he did not want to be a king, nor that Cefwyn; who had given him title to Ynefel, knew a great deal more of kings and claims to kingship. But he did not think that Cefwyn's belief in him would allay their suspicions, rescue him, or move them all to a point of safety. An unbearable feeling of danger had begun to press on him, in their dispute, a smothering fear more acute than he had felt since Marna Wood, and he wanted their argument over, with whatever issue, and the old man settled safe under stone – under stone! – where he wished to be. He wanted them away, as soon as they might.

"We shall bury my father," Ninévrisë said, "as he wished. Then we shall go to the Marhanen and ask for a treaty – by marriage if need be. By oath, if we can secure it."

"His father has just died," Tasien cried, "at the hands of Elwynim!"

"So has *mine!*" Ninévrisë said sharply, "at the hands of gods know what, in this land of his, because of the same rebels who killed his father, and I will ride to the Marhanen and have a treaty or a fight of it! Does not the gods' law protect messengers? I am my father's messenger from his deathbed, and I shall have the answer to my suit or I shall have *war,* sirs!"

"Gods save us, then," Tasien said.

"The Marhanen will see me. He will deal fairly with me. My lord of Ynefel swears that he will. Does he not?"

"I shall ask him to," Tristen said. "He is my friend."

"And of course this is our King," Tasien said, "who cedes Ynefel to his master the King of Ylesuin and takes it back again in fief – gods have mercy, m'lady! A *friend* of the Marhanen? This is a man owing *homage* to the Marhanen! Ask him!"

"Are you?" Ninévrisë asked, looking at Tristen. "Have you sworn homage to him?"

"I swore to defend Cefwyn and to be his friend."

There was heavy silence in the tent. The men were not at all pleased, and did not intend to accept him, he was certain; but he would not lie to the lady, who would know the truth in that gray place – he at least had no skill to deceive her.

"Gentle lords," Ninévrisë said, "at least let us try. Shall we sit here until they find us?"

"This is madness," Tasien said.

"So you called my father mad," Ninévrisë said, "yet you loved him with all your hearts. You came here to die for him notwithstanding your own lands, your own wives, your own children. I shall not lead you all back to Elwynor only to die, m'lords. I *have* another choice. I can seek alliance . . . "

"With the *Marhanen!* Gods save us, my lady."

"I will not see your heads on Ilefínian's gates, sirs! Nor will I marry Aséyneddin! You cannot ask that of me!"

"Will you marry this wandering fool and *beg* the lords of Elwynor swear oaths to the Marhanen? That is what they seem to suggest!"

"Have respect!" Ninévrisë said. "Have respect for my father, Tasien, if not for me. Lower your voices! Is the whole camp to hear?"

"Lord Tasien," Tristen said quietly, overwhelmed with anxiety, though he feared that his suggesting anything at the moment was a cause for them to oppose it. "Sir, we are under threat, of wizardry if you call it that. This place feels worse and worse to me. – Lady, if your lord father can do anything, I think we should do exactly what he said, and soon."

"Do we speak of wizardry?" the lord called Haurydd asked. "Is that what we have to hope for?"

"Yes, sir. So did the lord Regent hope for it. And if we wait we may lose all the hope he had. We should bury him and leave here."

"My father," Ninévrisë said, "warned us against going outside these walls after dark."

"Yes, if there were safety to be had inside. But this place is losing its safety, as Ynefel became unsafe. I do feel so. We should go. Leave the wagon. There is no way to take it. There are men searching for me. There must be. We can find them on the road and they will protect us."

"Run like thieves, you mean. To Marhanen men."

"Sir, this is very serious. You should do what the Regent asked. There is danger."

"Read me no lessons in my lord's service. And we can afford the decency of daylight," Tasien said angrily, "for a man who, if you are our King, may have kept your throne safe, sir, little though you may love me for saying it and little though I think there is any likelihood."

"Tasien!" the lady said.

"My lady, I do not respect him. I do not respect a soft-handed man who bears every insult. He agrees to everything. He *has* no authority but his orders to bring us into ambush. Perhaps there *is* some sort of protection in this ruin. He certainly urges us away as hard as he can!"

"We must go, sir." Arguments could easily confuse him. Words betrayed him. And danger was coming closer, a threat that distracted him, a threat changing and growing by the moment, as if the venture of himself and the lady into that gray place had attracted unwelcome attention, and now it had turned toward them and come to do them harm. Besides the prowling of the Shadows, there had arisen a sound, a thumping in the earth that reminded him most of horses. "For all our sakes, Lord Tasien."

"Tasien," the lady said, "we shall go. We shall bury my father, and we shall go as he says, to speak to Cefwyn Marhanen."

"This man will not fight your enemies!" Tasien said. "Is this a king? Is this the King we have waited for?"

"Sir." Tristen looked Lord Tasien square in the face. "I am not afraid of you. I do fear *for* you."

Tasien stared back at him, and the anger seemed to desert him for a different expression – almost. "If we go, then we shall have you for a Hostage, lord of Ynefel. If Cefwyn does not respect a Truce, and attacks our lady, I will kill you myself."

The Words made sense, and offered a way out of this place, both practical and frightening. "If it pleases you, Lord Tasien, and if it please the lady, and if we can leave this place, I have no fear of giving you such a promise."

"I thought," Emuin said, his fist firmly about a cup of mulled wine. "I have thought about it and thought about it, m'lord King, and, though in my earliest youth I saw all the royal house of the Sihhë and knew their faces, and, more, knew them in ways a wizard knows – I had no impression I knew the lad. It worried me that night I first saw him and realized what he was: I told myself that of all the dead souls at Althalen Mauryl might have chosen, he could well have chosen Elfwyn's true brother Aswyn, who died at birth – as a natural restraint upon the one who had that body . . . "

"We know that story," Cefwyn said impatiently. They were upstairs in his apartments. Idrys stood with his shoulder against the door, making certain there were no eavesdroppers even among the trusted guards. "This is not Elfwyn. Nor any stillborn babe. He is skilled in the sword *and* horsemanship, which I do not think comes in the cradle. The *name,* old master. Favor me with the name, no other, no explanations, no long narrative."

"Plainly, – Barrakkêth, m'lord Prince. – M'lord King." Emuin was more disturbed than he had ever seen the old man. "The founder of his line. Or one of his cousins. I do believe so."

"A fair guess," Idrys said from across the room. "A name that can be written. You could have spared a messenger to say so before now."

"Peace, sirs." Cefwyn grew more than impatient. "We knew at Emwy he was no scholar-king. But whence this? Tristen is not cold hearted, nor self-seeking, nor a wanton killer. Barrakkêth was. Why Barrakkêth?"

"Mauryl did not *like* your grandfather."

It was like the turns of Tristen's speech: it startled him into laughter. "None of us *liked* my grandfather. My *grandmother* never *liked* my grandfather. Tell me something more dire than that, sir! Where is your proof? Prove to me your notion!"

"To Mauryl, the Marhanen as successors to the Sihhë were a choice of chance, at best. The Marhanen were there to take advantage of the situation, but your grandfather was very uneasy with Mauryl. Remember that Mauryl was not of this age, not of whatever blood men share. He had no loyalties even to the Galasieni, who were supposedly his people. Elfwyn's father had besought – call it the gods, the gods some Sihhë worshipped if they worshipped any at all – to raise his stillborn son. The blood had run very thin by that time, and

Elfwyn's father certainly couldn't have raised the dead. Except – he opened a door. As 't were. To a dead wizard."

"Hasufin Heltain," Idrys supplied, and Emuin cast him a troubled look.

"We have had to seek our own answers," Cefwyn said. His leg was paining him, acutely, he was peevish, and trying to be patient. "Many of which, it seems, are on the mark, master Emuin. Go *on,* sir, don't dole it out like alms. Give me your reasoning. Tell me what you fear happened at Althalen, and why this is Barrakkêth."

"Young King, Mauryl fought this wizard in Galasien. Mauryl chose in Barrakkêth and his cousins an agency of destruction so ruthless – so ruthless – there is a Galasite word for it . . . so lacking in attachment. Yet honest. Mauryl did call him honest. He contended with wizards by magic – magic, not wizardry, mark you – and with men with the sword. I don't know why. Mauryl said they were not Men as we understand Men to be. The true Sihhë had an innate, untaught power that would not be deterred. What the true Sihhë willed, so I understand, and am beginning to fear, wizardry does not easily prevent."

"A god," Idrys said dryly, arms folded, and walked back to stand at the tableside. "You describe a god, master grayfrock."

"Something very like." Emuin's voice was hoarse. He had a large gulp of the heated wine. "Something far too like, for my taste. And the Quinalt and its witch-hunting have been too thorough in their hunt for wizards. There *are* few wizards left worth the name, m'lord King. There is no one to contain either Hasufin or Barrakkêth."

"Oh, come now," Cefwyn said. He had until then been concerned, but drew a longer and easier breath, and massaged the fevered wound in his upper leg. "Our Tristen? A ravening monster? I think not."

"Ask Barrakkêth's enemies."

"Idrys tracked a Hasufin Heltain through generations of musty chronicles. And found a Hasufin *in* the royal family. So what *did* become of him? Is he still alive? Or haunting Althalen – or what?"

"My lord, I killed that child, I, myself, at Mauryl's behest. I killed Hasufin's last mortal shape." The old man rocked to and fro in discomfort and had another large drink, the last. "Do you suppose, m'lord King, there is anything left in the pot?"

Emuin – kill a child? "Idrys," Cefwyn said, feeling a chill himself, and Idrys looked, filled another goblet, poured more wine into the pot and swung it further out over the fire to warm.

Emuin took a sip, seeming as glad to warm his hands as his insides. He looked frail tonight. His skin was pale and thin, his lately drenched hair and beard were drying in wisps of white. His shoulders had grown very thin.

I dare not lose him, Cefwyn thought. I dare not. "And what," he asked Emuin, determined to unravel the matter, "what, precisely, was Mauryl's judgment on Elfwyn? Was it his father's sin? Was it retribution?"

"It was simple fear, my lord King. Fear not only of Hasufin, dreadful enough, but the union of Hasufin's very great wizardry and the innate Sihhë magic, dilute as it had grown by that day. No one could predict what would happen – with a wizard potent enough to bring himself back from death, joined to a Sihhë body. One simply didn't know."

"One thought you priests knew such things to a fare-thee-well," Idrys said.

"My lord King, I will not bear with his humor. I do not think I have deserved this. This is difficult enough to explain."

"You might have been here," Idrys said sharply.

Emuin clamped his lips tight. "Aye, that I might, and added *my* bit to the brew. You might have been very sorry, Lord Commander, if I had swayed to the left or the right the force that Mauryl had set on course. His spell was still Summoning, still *is,* sir. I warned you of it, and I would not to this day put my meager working in the path of *that* force, no more than I would tamper with a river in flood without knowing what lay downstream – which is the difference between myself and those that meddle with things they do not understand, sir, as is the habit of some people I could name!"

"Peace, peace, good *gods*, I had forgot the sound of you both under one roof." Cefwyn poured his own wine from a pitcher on the table, unmulled and untampered-with, and hoped for surcease of the ache in his leg that now beat in time with the ache in his skull. "So you don't know, in sum, what we are dealing with."

"I have had years to think on it."

"More years than most, as a matter of curiosity," Idrys said.

"Peace! Damn you, Idrys, let us *have* his account undiverted."

"Tristen is at Althalen," Emuin said.

"You are certain of that."

"I am certain. So, in a wizardly sense, is Hasufin. And something – let loose as a consequence of his dealing. I don't like to think of it. Quickly! Ask me another question!"

"The same question! What did Mauryl intend? What are we dealing with? Why Barrakkêth?"

"The same answer, my lord King: the Sihhë were Mauryl's choice to succeed the folk of Galasien, nine hundred years ago. Mauryl loosed Barrakkêth on the south, from what Mauryl claimed to be his origins up far in the Hafsandyr. No one knew more than that. Barrakkêth arrived well-versed in arms, he subdued what is now Amefel and Elwynor and Lanfarnesse with brutal thoroughness. He would not go among Men, but ruled as High King from Ynefel, which was in its present gruesome state: he ordered the building of Althalen and its pleasures, but he rarely stirred from Ynefel except for war, and, save once, he left the begetting of heirs to the handful of Sihhë that arrived with him – who amply attended that duty."

"He enchanted those faces into the walls?" Cefwyn asked. "I take it, then, that those rumors are true."

"They are true. They are most awfully true, and contribute to the strength of the place. All I know is what Mauryl said: that the walls of Ynefel became what they are during the battle between Barrakkêth and Hasufin Heltain."

"And Mauryl."

"And Mauryl." ·

"Who seems to have been a damned busy man. Why should he *care* what this Hasufin did? He was old. He was dying."

"My lord king. He is dead. I do not know that he was dying."

"Meaning?"

"He *lost*, m'lord. He lost to his enemy. Now *we* have Hasufin to deal with. But Mauryl was not a man to go down without revenge. We also have Tristen."

"Revenge on whom?"

"That is the question. What did Mauryl promise the Marhanen when he stopped Hasufin the second time? To rule forever? I think not. Mauryl promised the Elwynim a King. And was it for love of them – or for some sort of balance with the Sihhë themselves? Far less did he love your grandfather, or your father, or care to leave Ynefel long enough to inquire what manner of King you would be. Was this the man they called Mauryl the Kingmaker, who, surrendering all power to the Marhanen and a regency in Elwynor, locked himself away from worldly power and said *nothing* for eighty years? Was this the action of the man who ruled behind the thrones of two kingdoms? I don't believe he went down without arranging something to settle accounts."

There was no love wasted between Emuin and Mauryl. He saw that, too. And possibly it colored all Emuin said.

"He could have sent a plague on my grandfather. None of us would have cared. He sent us a gentle and reasonable young man."

"So I apprehended. Mauryl took no oath to your father, neither of homage nor even of fealty. Little it would have mattered to him."

"Tristen has. He swore to defend me. Knowledgeably. He did swear, Emuin."

"I am aware. Perhaps that is the test Mauryl set you: to deal with young Barrakkêth."

"Like lessons? Like *that*? Guess the reason? Guess the purpose?"

"My old student does remember."

"Damned right I remember, old master. But is that all your theory?"

"It's my most hopeful one. And direst magic may have an escape, however improbable. Therefore I said, Win his love. We wizards are cranky, impatient sorts. We live long – unless we abandon our practice – and we grow damned impatient with fools. That is the worst thing about living long. One sees so many mistakes repeated, over and over and over. It makes one a little mad and desperately angry. Mauryl – was a master wizard. A Man, I have always thought, in the sense that he was not Sihhë himself. But one never knew his loyalties."

"One never knew," Idrys echoed him. "And what master do you serve? 'Win his love, m'lord Prince.' 'Win his good will' – all the while telling us *nothing* of his nature. It is damned *late*, sir priest, to come to us with your advice!"

"Now you understand me. Not then. Now you've dealt with him. I see fear, sir, that may still destroy you; but I see respect for what is by no means like yourself. You are dealing with your greatest enemy. His good will is *still* your best hope."

"I *said* he was a wizard," Idrys muttered, and paced away again, rubbing the back of his neck.

"He is not a wizard," Emuin muttered under his breath.

"This *man*," Cefwyn said, "whatever he is, this man you advised me to win, this friend, this sworn friend of mine, is nothing evil – a plague on your suspicions, Emuin. I do not believe he is my enemy. I refuse to believe it."

"That might be best," Emuin said. "All along, that might be best."

"Don't read me such lessons! You think something else, sir. Out with it."

"That wizardry at its highest is not cattle-curses. That what the Sihhë *are*, wizards struggle to be. Hasufin was not a greater wizard than Mauryl. But prone to cheat. Too willing to work in the physical realm, that was what Mauryl said. An assassination here, a tweak of wizardry there – Mauryl despised him. He'd brought Hasufin very far along before Hasufin's nature became clear to him, is what I very much suspect. Wizardry requires a man search himself very deeply and face all his most secret faults – lest they work the spells, that was what Mauryl used to say: that there comes a point when one realizes one has power, and the faults work the wizard as the wizard works the spells."

"So with kings," Cefwyn said, feeling they had wandered far from the subject.

"So with Tristen, too. This is the trap Mauryl set you and me and the Elwynim all in one."

"You've lost me."

"To live life *without* him, my lord, or to bring back the reign of magic over the world of Men by our own choice. The Quinalt, with its holy abhorrence of wizardry, has left us all but unarmed against that boy's lightest wish, and hope to the powerless gods we find better help. Mauryl has left me the last, the *last* teacher of the higher wizardry that stands any chance of denying that young man what he wishes."

"To all I know," Cefwyn said, feeling a most unaccustomed and angry moisture in his eyes, "what Tristen most wishes is my happiness. What are we saying? Tristen named us an enemy! And yet we're speaking of *Tristen* as the danger!"

"All the same," Idrys said, "all the same, I hear what Emuin is saying, my lord King. And it disturbs me. What both of you say – disturbs me profoundly."

He cast a frowning look at Idrys, and knew that there was yet another danger that Emuin did not reckon of: Idrys' loyalty, and Idrys' perception. Idrys had taken oaths of homage to him. Of fealty to him. But in the challenge to the Marhanen that those oaths had never anticipated, he found himself without sure knowledge what Idrys' attachment was:

to him, as King; to the realm; to whatever man Idrys served –
or to his own unexpressed sense of honor. Idrys measured
things by some scheme that had never yet diverged from his
personal welfare.

He had, in that light, to ask himself what that welfare was,
or might become, and what Tristen's was, or might become.

Tristen was now at Althalen, Emuin said. With this
Hasufin.

How in hell did Emuin know? How did wizards know?

But Emuin said, Tristen was not a wizard; and presumably
did not use wizardry – whatever that fine mincing of words
meant. He was no longer certain he knew, and he was sitting
at table with a man slipping fast toward wine-drowsiness
who *was* the one and *did* the other.

In a small alcove of the ruin, a section of the wall with several
such arches still standing, the Elwynim made a grave for the
lord Regent, piling up loose stone from nearby rubble, in the
dark and the misting rain. They had brought out one of the
lamps from the tent. One man sheltered it with an upheld arm
and his cloak, while others labored by that scant light to
make their wall solid and to make the lord Regent a secure
resting place.

The lady stood beside Tasien and the other two lords, a
quiet, small figure in mail and a man's heavy, hooded cloak,
her father's, Tristen thought, as the crown was her father's
and the mail shirt was doubtless her father's, worn over her
gown and halfway to her knees.

She was not a tall woman: she would never tower over
anyone – but she wielded force of will and wit. She was very
young, and was accustomed but not acquiescent to Lord
Tasien making decisions, as Lord Tasien had grown accustomed to giving orders, probably, Tristen judged, in the lord
Regent's decline and sickness. And Tasien seemed a good and
faithful man, even if Tasien doubted his honesty and his
intentions. Tasien was trying to protect the lady, considering

that she was young, while taking as many of her opinions as he dared, because she was her father's successor.

And honestly seen, that Tasien wished to prevent the lady rushing off into the dark on a stranger's advice was only sensible – unless Tasien were aware of the threat piling up more and more urgently around the ruin.

Ninévrisë was aware. Tristen felt it. Having found that gray space – she kept worrying at it, and was too reckless, and very much in danger.

The old lines of the masons held against the Shadows thus far. The horses had begun to grow restive – *they* knew, and the men who had gone to saddle them and have them ready for departure were having difficulty with them.

There was no preparation to take the wagon: Tasien had sensibly agreed with him, saying they would be able to come back for it and all it contained if all went well, and that if things went badly, they would need nothing at all. But Tasien had ordered certain things taken from the tent, among them the banners, and various small boxes and at least some of the lady's personal goods, the latter packed onto the backs of the two horses that ordinarily pulled the wagon. All that was going on while the burial proceeded.

But if his help had been at all welcome, Tristen thought, he would have taken up stones and put them in place himself. The men were building at a frighteningly deliberate pace, each one a measured clink of stone on stone as they first formed an arch and then, after the Regent's body was laid inside, sealed up the opening – stone by stone, while in the awareness he snatched out of the dark around them the lines on the earth were weakening, disturbed by the breaking of an old pattern, and something – some presence coming up on them was pressing more and more insistently, searching, as he thought. It was not alone wizardry, but men, many men.

For such eyes, the lantern-light by which they worked was a beacon. The place was overgrown round about, concealing them, but it equally concealed danger that moved against them as well, at least in the world of substance.

He dared not reach too often, too far into the gray, lest he guide trouble to them more quickly than he knew it was coming. But it had direction, now. He stood as respectfully, as quietly as the others stood, but he felt his flesh crawling with apprehension, a threat very strong in the same direction as the men taking down the rubble of that other arch to build this one. Stone after stone they brought, and the threat shivered in the air, out of the north, very definitely now from the north. He thought of warning the lady – but his welcome with them was already scant: he feared giving them cause to do something less wise than they were doing.

And possibly she felt it for herself, though awareness of that gray place had not come to him all at once. Reaching far off came with knowing one could do it. She did reach out at times, but he thought that that was an accident: she wanted her father – and that was a danger. She was a burning light in that other Place. She was angry and she was loyal to the old man, and that came through very surely.

But out there in the rainy dark was more than one presence, he thought. He perceived two subtly different sources, now, one wide and diffuse with distance and one terrifyingly, stiflingly close. One, elusive and strong and clever, was pulling the diffuse one, which he could feel only faintly – and which he could only see as a haze in the gray place, defined against the gray place itself. The elusive one was very, very close to them, very difficult to see, a presence tingling in the air, clinging to the stones, as if it possessed all the walls that protected them, and he had not *felt* it before they began to work.

Wind gusted. Trees down a little removed from the wind sighed and roared with it. The feeling of harm was very strong. Wind pulled at cloaks, seized edges, whipped them free, and the owners struggled to hold them. He had Cefwyn's cloak about him again, and the wind pressed it against him and rocked him on his feet. A horse called out, a warning cutting through the dark and the spitting rain, and in a distant play of shadows men fought to hold it still.

But by now there remained only a small opening at the crest of the sealing wall they had built and the feeling was worse and worse. Tasien placed a large stone, and the lady came and placed one, and a second: the last. She pressed her brow against the rubble, then, speaking to her father, Tristen thought: he could *feel* that disturbance in the gray realm, as loud as the panicked horse a moment ago. He was thinking, too, **Hurry, oh, lady, hurry, and let us go. Can you not feel it?**

He thought she heard him. She turned with a frightened look. The sound of the trees down the slope from them, leaves blowing in the wind, all but overwhelmed the thunder.

But another sound had begun, not in the air, but in the earth, a thumping like horses running, louder and louder.

"Riders!" she exclaimed, and a man near them who had been pulling stones from the wall of the other arch leapt back as, with a rattle of stone and for no evident reason a section of wall crumbled.

Pale bones were in the rubble that fell out, bones sticking up among the tumbled stones. It was another burial they had disturbed, in their meddling with the stones. It had lain unguessed in the walls that protected them, and the feeling that came with that disturbance broke about them in a smothering fear.

The man protecting the lamp lost his battle to a watery gust of wind. The light failed. The wind sent something noisy skittering across the pavings, and in the gray world the lines of blue all faltered and began to fade.

"Lady!" he warned her.

"Let us go!" Ninévrisë cried, and Tasien seized her arm and hurried her toward the horses, the men running with panic just under their movements.

Tristen went, too, all but running among the others, biting his lip on pleas for haste for fear of another debate or anything to delay them. Petelly was in the number of mounts waiting, rolling his eyes so that the white showed. He took the reins from the man who was managing four of the horses at once, and in his ears and in his heart alike he heard the arrival of riders through the brush to their north.

"Caswyddian!" he heard a man say, and Tasien: "Hold them off, sergeant! Hold them long enough – and join us as you can! The Regent has to live!"

"Aye, m'lord!" a man said, and rattled off the names of others to stay behind as Ninévrisë protested the order.

"There is no choice, m'lady! Ride! Ride!"

The lords, the lady, and two of the men rode for safety, and Tristen turned Petelly's head and rode with them, to the south of the enclosure, where a doorway in the ruined hall provided them a way out. A number of the men overtook them, but not all: at least half the soldiers had stayed.

They had no hope, Tristen thought. It was impossible against what was coming. He might help them – but he had no weapon, they feared him as much as they feared their enemy, and the lady, Cefwyn's lady, had to be safe. *He* knew where the road was – *he* could see the lines glowing in the dark, marking obstacles for the horses, and Tasien could not. He abandoned care for the men behind and sent Petelly forward as fast as Petelly could run, shouldering horses around him until he reached the fore.

"I can see the path!" he called out and, Tasien willing or not, he took the lead and stayed there, leading them by a twisting path along old walls, through ruined doors, and sharply around an old cistern that gaped in their path. The wind was blasting into their faces. Rain spattered him, stung his eyes. He heard – in one realm or the other – the clash of weapons, horses running over stone – shouts and outcries of men fighting for their lives behind them while the earthly wind shrieked like a multitude of voices. He felt all his senses assaulted at once, and Petelly shied under him, trying to bolt, just when a wall loomed up ahead.

He did not know himself how he made the jump. They lost two men. The horses came past him riderless. But the rest were with him, and Petelly threw his head, fighting to see in the gusts that flared in their faces.

He rode continually south. He encouraged Petelly with his hands and his knees as he saw masons' lines ahead of them and turned instead down a brushy slope where there was only darkness – south again, as the wind wailed with voices in his ears, and Shadows streamed about them.

"Where is he?" he heard someone call out in fear.

"This way!" he called out, heard a man swear, and waited at the bottom of the slope, with Petelly trembling and panting for breath.

Tasien and the lady came down. Lightning flickers showed others coming down behind them as quickly as they could. He knew he had to do better. He had to keep their company together, not let them fall behind and not let the Shadows take them. He was certain that, of all who might pursue them, those in the gray world were the deadliest and the ones hardest to outrun.

Then came the sound of horsemen passing above the bank, and all of theirs were here. That was, he thought, pursuit narrowly missing them or their own riders trying to rejoin them. His companions reined in, their horses wild, panting for breath, and all of them alike looked up in fear, trying to find the source of that sound, but the brush and the storm hid whatever riders were up there, heading for the blind end he had led his company away from.

"Follow me!" he said to them. And they did.

Emuin had gone off to bed, in the numbness of the air that had followed such dread confidences. Limping, hurting this evening to the point of outrageous temper, Cefwyn paced the length of the room and back again, goading himself to an outburst he had no moral courage to make otherwise, and Idrys must sense it, since Idrys did not remind him he had warned him.

"So?" he challenged Idrys. "Tell me I was wrong."

"Lord Tristen saved your life," Idrys said. "I do not forget it, nor shall."

Twice over Idrys eluded him. And cheated him now of a fit he wanted to loose on someone able to defend himself.

"Emuin fears him," Idrys said, "perhaps too much. You, not enough."

"And you have it right, do you?"

"I make no such claim. I think Emuin was right and I was wrong, how to deal with him – at the first. Not now."

Three times eluded him. "Then what? What are you saying? Damn it, Idrys, I am unsubtle tonight. The wound aches like very hell. Be clear."

"I am saying, m'lord King, that I know precious little of wizardry, but if Emuin speaks half the truth, whether this Shaping lodged in Elwynor or in Ylesuin, he would have his own way. Am I mishearing? Your Majesty did study with Emuin."

"Emuin is full of contradictions. I am half of a mind to send him back to the monks. He's been too little with practical men. What in hell am I to do? Did you hear practical advice tonight? I did not. Nothing workable. Nothing that brings peace to this border. What Emuin promises seems rather other than that, did it seem so to you?"

"It has always been other than that, m'lord King. And I will not advise we sit idle, but –" Idrys had walked to the window and stared outward, a shadow against the glistening black glass. The window was spattered with rain. Lightning lit edges for a moment and thunder muttered to the west. "I do not trust the lord of Ynefel. But I trust Emuin's judgment far less."

"Do you think Emuin is deceiving himself?"

"Not that we have all the truth out of Emuin, nor shall ever have." Idrys' shoulders lifted, as if he had caught a chill, and he looked back. "I told Emuin before he left that he served you ill. He denied it. And I said to m'lord Tristen that if he harmed you I would be his enemy. He knows that. But I foresaw nothing of this bolt toward Althalen, I confess, and I find fault with myself for that – at least for not instructing the guards, who saw only his favor with you."

"I would I had seen it too. But maybe natural cautions had

nothing to do with it. Wizards. Seeing clear to Althalen. –
Emuin *never* told me he could do such things. I never read
that they could do such things. *Tristen* told us the truth. He
was feckless toward wizard-secrets, too – and were it not for
him I swear I would not believe Emuin now. I'd swear his
warnings came of some other source. – And damn him, he
ignored my messages."

"We believe now the dead do walk. Should we stick at
this? I greatly fear for our men up by Emwy, m'lord. None of
our evening's messengers have arrived, from any direction. It
may simply be the rain. But master Emuin did not want to
discuss Althalen. That doubly worries me."

Men would have gone in search of those missing reports by
now, up the road, to find the messengers if the causes were
the weather, or a horse gone lame. If they did not meet them
they would ride all the way to the borders to find out the
conditions and come back again, while a third set of messengers took to the roads outbound. It was a new arrangement
he had ordered, precisely to have nightly reports on that
uneasy border, and it was already in disarray. He hoped it
was initial confusion, some misunderstanding in the orders,
possibly the weather, indeed, bridges out, torrents between –
such common things, and nothing worse.

"Damn him," he said again. And meant Emuin.

"Master grayfrock is very worried," Idrys said. "And will
not discuss Tristen's actions. *Or* Althalen. He drank more
than I have ever seen him drink. He did not want to return
here. He sees a danger, and he may have named it very
honestly tonight."

"This Hasufin? This dead wizard at Althalen?"

"Lord King, he said it in this chamber tonight, and you
didn't hear him. When he rebuked me with his fears – they
regarded Tristen."

The way ahead was a maze of trees and overgrown walls,
forgotten foundations hidden in the dark and the rain, and
Tristen dared not set the company to running here. To his

eyes, perhaps to the lady's, the walls and the traces of foundations of this arm of the ruins showed still wanly glowing, the masons' long-ago defenses yet holding, however weakly, as he led along the old courses of the ruins.

He might have gone faster. It risked losing the men, especially the soldiers, who with their armor weighing on the horses were riding slower and slower, and who could not take another jump. It had become a curious kind of chase, keeping the horses to the fastest pace they could – for despite the misdirection at the height, they could not for an instant trust that their pursuers, Men or otherwise, were not following on guidance better than his and more familiar with these ruins. Hasufin could do such things, and the gray space seethed with Shadows.

Now, nightmare smell, came the faint stench of smoke, and then, between two blinks of rain-blinded eyes, the apparition of fire touching the brush, setting the shadows to leaping. "They've fired the brush!" a man said, and the lords drew rein in confusion, refusing to ride further, gathering their men about them.

Whether it was burning in the real world or not, it seemed to Tristen that the tops of real walls did reflect red, that the sky had lightened to gray beneath the spitting clouds, and that firelit stakes lifted figures above the tops of the walls, a ring like a dreadful forest, at which he did not wish to look twice.

With the lady and her men gathered about him – some swearing they smelled smoke and others denying they saw any fire – Lord Haurydd demanded of him in a frightened voice to know the way out, while Tasien called him a liar. "Find the path, sir," the lady demanded in a thin, high voice, cutting through their confusion. "These are haunts, specters. The place is known for them. Keep going."

He urged Petelly away, then, trusting they would follow. Petelly snorted, breathing hard, and of two ways clear he chose the right-hand way, at random in the first choice and then with a clear conviction that it was the *right* way, the way he had to lead them. A spatter of rain rode the wind into their faces. He blinked water from his eyes, feeling Petelly struggling for footing on wet leaves. A horse slid as they went downhill, and took down another, downed riders and horses struggling to untangle themselves from among the trees and get up. He delayed an instant for their sakes – saw the first horse and rider afoot and then rode, sensing safety so near them.

Uwen, he became sure: Uwen was out there. He didn't know how far ahead that was, but he tried to press more speed out of Petelly and the riders behind him, fearing they were bringing enemies to Uwen, and were out of strength themselves. Petelly was laboring as they cleared the edge of the ruins, and he flung a glance over his shoulder at the others still following as best they could.

"Hold there!" someone shouted from ahead of them.

He reined in, reaching fearfully into the dark and the gray to know who hailed them as the other riders came in around him.

"Who goes?" Tasien shouted.

"King's business!" a voice called out. "Who goes?"

His heart leapt. He knew that voice. "Uwen, don't harm them!" he called out on what breath he could gather, and on a second, shouted out loud and clear: "Beware men behind us, Uwen!"

"Hold, hold, hold there!" Uwen's voice called out. "All of ye, hold! Let 'em pass! This is m'lord Tristen. I don't know who them with 'im is – just brace up. We got others comin' we don't want!"

Tristen could scarcely see the riders on the hillside for the misting rain – the horses were blowing and panting around him, as he let Petelly move forward. The rain-laden gale blasted along the dell, blew up under the bellies of the horses and startled them, exhausted as they were.

Then a wayward breeze blew soft and warm all about Petelly, at Tristen's back, at his side, under Petelly's chin and around again.

The bad men, he heard wafting on the wind. The bad men is coming, the wicked, wicked men. Run, run, run! Mama, run!

It was a child's voice. Seddiwy's voice. **Child!** *he cried after her.*

But the shadow-shape of a child ran implike back through the company, waving her arms, startling the horses one after another.

After that, what came was dark and angry. The sapling at his right went *crack!* and broke. Others did, white wounds in the dark thicket.

From the hill and the ruin behind them also came the cracking of brush, then the screams of men overcome by fear. The Elwynim with him looked about them in alarm – but no more trees broke in their vicinity. The presence – a great many presences – had followed the child, back along their trail. Tristen tried to see them, but they were all darkness in the gray, darkness that walled off all Althalen.

In a moment more there was only the ordinary wind, and the rumble of thunder.

Then a rider was coming down the slope, braving all that was unnatural, and Tristen knew that manner and that posture even in the dark.

"Uwen!"

"M'lord, what is it back there?" Uwen was plainly ready to fight whatever threatened them; and the Elwynim had turned about to face that crashing of brush and the gusting of wind behind them, drawing swords and setting the lady to their backs.

But the enemy who should have overtaken them by now – was up on that hill, where now there was nothing to see but the night and the rain.

"We come chasin' all about this damn ruin," Uwen was saying, at his left, breathless, sword in hand as he looked uphill. "Sometimes we was on a path and then again we weren't, and then, damn! m'lord, but we was smellin' fire and being rained on at the same time – your pardon."

Ninévrisë and Tasien had drawn back close to them, Tasien with sword in hand.

"These are your men?" Tasien asked.

"Uwen is mine," Tristen said. "Who are they, Uwen?"

"Ivanim, m'lord," Uwen said, "looking for you. Blesset a long chase you run us. I'd draw back, m'lord. It don't feel good up there."

It seemed good advice. Even the Elwynim accepted it, and drew away with them up the hill, toward the waiting men.

"M'lord of Ynefel!" a voice came out of that dark, from among shadowy horsemen. "Who is that with you?"

"The lord Regent's daughter, sir, his heir, three of her lords and –" He looked back, unsure of numbers; there were only a handful of soldiers, no threat to anyone. And the valiant packhorse, that one man led, that had somehow stayed with them. "The lady Regent, her men, half a score of her guard. To see King Cefwyn, sir!"

Tasien shouted toward the hill: "We ask safe conduct for Her Most Honorable Grace, the Regent of Elwynor and her escort, sir: Tasien Earl of Cassissan, His Grace Haurydd Earl of Upper Saissonnd, and His Grace Ysdan of Ormadzaran. The lord of Ynefel has agreed to be our hostage against your King's safe conduct!"

"Lord Tristen of Ynefel," the shout came down to them. "What will you?"

The wind was still blowing back on the hill. A new sound had begun in the ruins up there. It sounded as if stones were falling and clattering, as if walls were coming down in the anger of the Shadows – Shadows, he thought, not of the dead of Althalen, but of Emwy – that was where the child had come from. And only the child had guarded them.

"I agree to what he wishes, sir. I think we should go to the road as soon as we can!"

"Gods hope." The Ivanim rode downhill and met them and Uwen in the dark. "Captain Geisleyn of Toj Embrel, at your service, Your Lordship. How many are there, asking safe conduct?"

"Scarcely fifteen," the lady said on her own behalf. Lightnings flickered, showing a sheen of wet leather, wet horse, wet metal about all of them. "Captain, please take us to His Majesty of Ylesuin, if he is in Henas'amef. And then we wish ourselves and our men given safe conduct back to the river."

"Brave lady," Geisleyn said. "His Majesty himself must say for your return – but on my life, you and yours will reach him without any difficulty."

"That is agreeable," Ninévrisë said.

"And if any of Your Lordships," Geisleyn said then, somewhat sheepishly, "has a notion where the road is, we might all be there the sooner."

"Follow me," Tristen said, for he had no doubt at all.

And perhaps, as Uwen said as they rode away in that direction, some wizardry had been acting on Uwen's side and on his to have gotten them this far and to have brought them together. "We was going one way," Uwen put it, "and then we was going another, and we had no idea how, but there you was, m'lord, and, gods! I was glad to see you."

"I was glad, too," Tristen said. "I wish I had done better by you, Uwen, I swear I wish so. I knew you would follow me. I didn't want you to. I've treated you very badly."

"Oh, I knew when ye didn't come upstairs," Uwen said, "that you was off somewheres. I just thank the good gods it weren't the tower."

"You were entirely right about the tower," he said with a feeling of cold. "It would have been very foolish to go there. I could not have matched him."

"Who, m'lord?" He had puzzled Uwen. But it was not an answer he wanted Uwen to deal with, ever.

Uwen said, after they had ridden a distance, "I wish I'd come downstairs sooner."

"It was very good you came when you did." He asked himself if he had said that, or thanked Uwen. He could not remember. "I am grateful. Petelly couldn't have run further. But, Uwen, be ever so careful when an idea comes into your head to do something you know really is not the safest thing to do. Ideas come to me sometimes, very strongly. I don't know if they do to you. But I think some ideas come from wizards. And some come from my enemy."

Uwen made a sign above his heart. It was rare that Uwen did that – or, at least, other men did so more frequently at moments when he discussed things in absolute honesty. "That's certainly a thought," Uwen said. "That is a thought to keep a man awake a' nights, m'lord."

"I think it's wiser not to think a great deal on the tower, at least, or on this place, either. I don't know if ordinary folk have a gray place they can go to when they think about it, but it's become very dangerous."

"A gray place."

"Do you?"

Uwen scratched his nose. "I guess summat of one if I just shut my eyes. But it fills up with dreams and such."

"Mine is shadows," he said, and Uwen made that sign a second time. He thought he should not say more to Uwen than he had, or make Uwen wonder about something maybe he never had wondered about before. And he could not himself answer all those questions – what Shadows were and why they were, except – except he might be one himself, and that was a thought he did not want to pursue.

The old man had wanted to be buried there because it gave him some special power: maybe their moving the stones had made new lines of which the old man was now part – but they had disturbed something else in doing so, and dislodged other bones. He did not know whose, but he hazarded a frightened guess.

– *Emuin*, he said, touching that grayness. *Master Emuin, I'm safe now. We are all safe. I met Uwen and some of Cevulirn's men. There's a lady whose picture Cefwyn has, and she will come to see him. I hope that's not a mistake. Advise me, sir. I do very much need advice.*

But no answer came to him, not even that fleeting sense of Emuin's presence he had had earlier in the day. Toward Althalen he did not wish to venture. Toward Ynefel he least of all wanted to inquire.

At least the Shadows stayed at distance, the ones that belonged to Althalen and the ones that belonged to Emwy, Shadows which, he suspected, down to the witch's child, had fought for them tonight, for whatever reason.

CHAPTER 27

❧

Emuin had hangover, abundantly, the natural and just result of a pious life returned suddenly to old habits. Emuin was, Idrys reported, suffering the prayers of two pious brothers above his bed, and they were brewing a noxious tea.

It served him right, Cefwyn thought. He had, right now, this morning, the departure of the Duke of Murandys to the capital: Murandys had come with his father's men, had fought at Emwy, and would go back to the capital full of news.

He had, on his desk, the disposition of the Lord Commander of the Dragon Guard. The Prince's Guard had to guard the heir. That was now Efanor. He *would* not cede Idrys from his own service, which meant replacing Gwywyn, but he had to consider the morale of the Dragon Guard, which had a strong attachment to its Lord Commander. Promoting Gwywyn to higher office was the apparent answer – but he had to find the right office.

Soon, atop his other worries, delegations from Guelemara were bound to come pouring in, condolences and good wishes from lords offering to give their oaths, as they were obliged to do, and this and that royal secretary with papers to sign – the inevitable flood of petitioners who thought a new reign might give new answers. He had seen his father face it with their grandfather's death, he braced himself for it, and meanwhile he had the local business to attend. He was already arranging to receive the oaths of the several barons, – counting Orien – who were within daily reach of him, a ceremony which had to be arranged in due formality, with all respect to the color and pageantry that bolstered the dignity of the courtiers as much as that of the King.

But, no, at the moment he did *not* want to consider the

menu for the attendant festivities, *or* his wardrobe – his Guelen tailor was beside himself, having discovered himself suddenly in charge of a King's oath-taking for a third of the provinces. Master Rosyn, at the height of his dreams, was obsessed with secrecy and cursing the necessity of dealing with what cloth two very rivalrous and doubtless gossip-prone merchants of Henas'amef had in hand.

He did not count his tailor's requirements for secrecy quite on a par with the reports that were not coming in from the border. He privately feared there would be no ceremony at all, and that the oath-taking would be on horseback and soon: the account-books on his table now weighed down a set of maps also far more secret than master Rosyn's forays to the drapers' shops. The books contained the Aswydds' reck-onings of the armories and the Amefin levies; and, on sepa-rate parchments, a small curling pile, were the voluntary but probably far more accurate accounts of the other southern barons detailing their resources. War at least on some scale was all but a foregone conclusion to the building of those bridges, and the death of the Regent (if Emuin's wizardly knowledge was accurate and Uleman Syrillas was in fact dead and not leading his forces across the river) did not mean peace: it would not affect the Elwynim rebels except to encourage more reckless moves inside and outside Elwynor.

But their fighting each other under such circumstances was a possibility, and he hoped such a war was long and very wearing on them before the victor turned any other direction.

If, in order to gain the advantage of surprise over the Elwynim before they spilled over the river, he went to war immediately, he might face an enemy divided and vulnerable. If he raised an army, however, it meant taking men from the harvest in his own lands, a harvest now in progress and already suffering from the rains – and he would have angry lords and hungry peasants on his hands, especially if later intelligence proved it unnecessary. He had also to consider that there would be no demonstrable gain of land or property from such a war, as he was certain there would not be: they could hold Elwynor out of Amefel, but never hope to take and hold Elwynim territory – while Elwynor could gain a province, if it could peel away Amefel.

The warring earls of Elwynor might unite if he attacked, uneasy and fragile union though it might be. And he himself was a new King, bolstered with the popular expectations of a new reign and vulnerable to those expectations turning very quickly to apprehensions: any early reverse could make the new King of Ylesuin look a fool, not even considering the reasonable anxiousness over Mauryl's demise, and the shifting of all balance of power in the region – which certainly his barons were considering. In any loss of confidence in him, the barons north and south would have their heads together in two opposing councils making plans to take certain decisions into their own hands, and to assure their own survival.

There was all that at risk in going to war. But if he wagered everything that the Elwynim would not move until spring, and if he acted too late, and could not hold the Elwynim out of his land, they could be defending Henas'amef from siege it was ill-prepared to sustain. The walls of his only walled town in the province were not modern. The inner citadel's defenses were the only ones up to modern standard, which said a great deal about where Heryn Aswydd regarded his real threats to be, but the outer town defenses were, he had seen from the first hour he rode up on the town, generally too low to protect against the engines he was certain Elwynim engineers were as capable of building as were his own engineers. Modern ballistae would send fire and stones of tremendous weight right over the wall which two generations of Marhanen kings had not seen fit to authorize raised, and which Heryn probably had never asked to raise, preferring to spend the money on his marble floors and his wardrobe.

Two generations of Marhanen kings, however, had not considered as urgent the possibility they would be the besieged inside Henas'amef and not the besiegers outside.

All of which argued to him that Efanor might be right, and that perhaps he should retreat to the capital immediately. But his leaving Amefel would virtually cede a rich and generally willing province to Elwynor: Amefel *had* no loyal lord, the earls were divided, and its fall was certain in the absence of a strong royal hand on the reins. If it did fall, in the stead of a deep and treacherous river, Elwynor's southern frontier with Ylesuin would be a wide land boundary defined by nothing more than a meandering brook – a vast, open approach with well-maintained roads leading right to the heart of Ylesuin and Guelessar itself.

Ceding Amefel, whether by policy or by defeat in war, was not a viable option: Amefel one summer, and an Elwynim army coming right down those well-maintained highroads by the next spring. The Elwynim need not spend any time consolidating their hold on a province the commons of which were of the same customs and religion as themselves, and considering they had both been the heart of the Sihhë holdings only eighty years ago.

He had never conducted a war. Skirmishes, yes; the wide-scale movement of fair-sized forces against bandit chiefs on the edges of Ylesuin . . . but no outright war between Ylesuin and another kingdom.

He had the dicta of his grandfather, helpful advice such as: Make the first strike and make the last one; Taking prisoners encourages surrender (this from the man who had butchered the Sihhë at Althalen); and, lastly, Never outmarch your baggage.

The latter seemed sensible advice. Tents and supper were a reasonable requisite for men who had to keep all Elwynor from pouring across the bridges – who might already, if the silence out of Emwy was an indication, have established themselves in fortified positions across the river. He had read about fortifications such as the Sihhë of the middle reigns, notably Tashânen, had built. One could see remnants of them in the ditches all about Amefel.

The earthworks Tashânen's *Art of War* described had been his despair in Emuin's hard tutelage. Even the copied Guelen version, in the modern alphabet, had not been easy going for a nine-year-old. But it had stayed with him. It was part of him. When he was twelve he and Efanor had dug a miniature of such earthworks in the middle of the herb garden, which had won them severe reprimand: cook's wife had turned an ankle and fallen very painfully in their siege of the thyme and the goldenseal.

He did not forget the old lessons. There had been no place to use them. Earthworks and rapidly advanced entrenchments ill-suited a bandit war in the stony terrain of the foothills eastward. But defending a valley of villages and farms and prosperous towns was another matter.

Tashânen had dug in along the Lenúalim's lower course in his war, combining mobility behind the fortifications with clever design, reshaping the land itself to make it more convenient for his enemy to do what he wanted his enemies to do. More, Tashânen, relying, as Sihhë would, only seldom on war engines, and far more on mobility, had still set outlying defenses to make their use against him impossible. He had had no hesitation to attack in winter, at planting or harvest, or any other time inconvenient for the enemy – possible, since the Sihhë of those days had had a large standing army that did not go home on the annual schedule of farmers: it had been hellish famine in the lands where that war was fought, but Tashânen had kept it out of his own territory, another lesson.

The warfare of the Marhanens had never been so elaborate or so deliberate: Grandfather had been one of Elfwyn's generals, but, again, King Tashânen had subdued the whole south when, consequent of a rift in the Sihhë royal house, a claimant to the throne had broken away and fortified himself, as he had thought, invincibly in what was now Imor Lenúalim. Grandfather in his day had faced no such advanced threat or tactical necessity: Grandfather in the wars he had undertaken for the Sihhë had faced nothing but what existed today, a matter of subduing isolated rebels and pacifying the perpetually troublesome Chomaggari border – skirmishes that required mobility over strength, and on which various lords of Men had gained fair reputations of generalship.

Entrenchments had not been the style, not for hundreds of years, not since Tashânen's dynasty had dwindled away in foolish grandsons, enabled by Tashânen's brilliance to be foolish and to base their court in luxurious, unwalled Althalen. The *Art of War* had existed in one known copy, which his grandfather had taken and had copied for his own use along with various other Sihhë works – fortunately *not* burned by the Quinalt like so much else. It was one of his grandfather's best acts, the saving of such Sihhë wisdom – granted Grandfather had burned the library at Althalen, not intending the fire, so he claimed.

And if a general taught by some other surviving copy of Tashânen's *Art of War* were ordering things on the Elwynim side, it was possible he could look not only for bridge-building across the river at several points, not one, and on the land border a series of incursions to establish fortifications at various points along the frontier, where the enemy would dig in behind steep wall-and-trench formations designed to funnel cavalry into brutal traps; that situation could last for several seasons, the enemy seeming to claim no more than a few hundred paces of territory.

But from those initial castellations, the enemy would extend wall-and-trenchworks to the left and right until they formed a formidable earthwork, increasingly difficult to take, and a screen behind which the enemy might shift forces about and arrange surprise excursions into the countryside: *then* try to dislodge them, or prevent their taking one set of villages, and the next, and the next.

Considering the Sihhë wars, which had been fought on this very land, before, there was indeed a way to attack and hold a territory the size of a kingdom. Barrakkêth had done it first, through wars rarely involving siege; and the halfling Tashânen, whether by his own genius or by relying on some other work now lost, had repeated Barrakkêth's feat and written down his tactics.

But Barrakkêth, one of the five true Sihhë, had relied on magic, wizardry, whatever Sihhë truly used, as well as arms, and come down from the Hafsandyr, where Men were, if anything, a distant rumor and where, one supposed, wizards' towers were common as haystacks – more common, granted there was, by other account, nothing but barren ice to live on, as far as the eye could see, and gods knew what sustained a people there *besides* magic.

What then, did one do, if one's opponents could work magic? He had seen in the last two days the efficacy of wizardry at getting messages passed – while his own couriers could not. The whole question was a matter Tashânen's book had scanted, though supposedly there had been Sihhë and magic on both sides. And Tashânen, mortally disappointing for the boy of nine who had expected magic as his reward for pressing on in a very demanding text, had not so much as mentioned it except in reference to Barrakkêth. He wondered why now. He wondered was it forbidden, or simply buried between the lines so matter of factly his eyes could not see it. Did the Sihhë put some sort of magical barriers about them? Did they curse their enemies? Was there simply some point of honor about war and wizardry?

There was Tristen. If they could find him, there was Tristen for advantage – if Tristen had any sense of what to do. He could lose abundant sleep on that score.

Worse, he was not in Tashânen's position, able to snap his fingers and move an army without destroying his own source of supply: he sat, instead, at the edge of harvest, with winter approaching, in a town vulnerable to siege, with no earthworks to defend it – although that was at least one thing he could change at Henas'amef, if he was willing to sacrifice the three-hundred-year-old orchards and pasture hedges.

But *that* fortification set him inside entrenchments that were a damned embarrassing trap to be in, a king of Ylesuin sitting still while the Elwynim hammered at him. They had gotten ahead of him with their bridges. He might try to take them down without their using them. But it was a long river, and action at one place might bring action at another – besides that he had limited numbers of men to take away from the fields to create such an elaborate defense.

They would more than lose their harvest for certain if Henas'amef fell.

And, with all disadvantages, the notion of making Henas'amef too tough a nut to crack *did* tie the Elwynim down to a siege in which they could be under attack from the other provinces, unless they wished to rush past an untaken town to attack Guelemara. That would be a mistake if they did it, exposing their supply lines to attack from Henas'amef.

Fortifying Henas'amef with earthworks would not please the peasantry, of course, nor the lords who derived income from those fertile, long-tilled fields, which in turn thrived on the sweepings of the lordly stables.

But fortifying that outer wall might be an answer to the town's other defensive faults.

He had the book with him. It was in his small chest of personal items. He was reading it again, had it under lock and key so as not to have it disappear to the Amefin, and hoped the Elwynim earls did not have a better book. They might. The Quinalt burning of the libraries had not gotten to their side of the river, and gods knew what they had, as gods knew what was sitting in Mauryl's tower, prey to the mice and Tristen's fancied enemy.

He wished he could see how magic worked into Tashânen's account. Emuin had professed not to know, except to say the Sihhë had used it – or wizardry, which distinction Emuin had drawn in Tashânen's case, and an angry nine-year-old had *not* paid strictest attention: gods, he'd deserved the stick, and not gotten it at the right times.

He also wished he could believe he had months to prepare. But the system of scouts and post riders he had instituted (lacking magic or a wizard reliably willing to inform him) had been supposed to shuttle back and forth with messages regularly from a watch on every bridgehead on the river, and settling King's men in way stations or villages, whichever happened to be feasible.

It was supposed to keep him constantly apprised of events on the river, and damn it, the system, like any new system, began with problems: the messengers from two of the three sites had come trailing in, one two hours late, complaining of heavy rain, and the other confessing that he had mistaken an intersection of roads in the dark and the bad weather and ridden an hour and more along a road that proved to lead to a sleeping and terrified village.

But the rider from Emwy-Arys never had made it in at all. He hoped it was for as silly a reason, but it was making him increasingly concerned – the man never had shown up, and now, at midafternoon, he reckoned he could begin looking for the return of the messenger who had to check on the messenger.

And if *that* man failed, they could assume that their entire scheme *had* worked and that something had gone very wrong on the section of border nearest Marna, the section where they had patrols out, the section where his father had been ambushed, and where they had a village of dubious loyalty.

If something had happened to that messenger, (and he was down to asking Emuin whether he could see *that* matter, once Emuin's headache subsided) it meant a siege of Henas'amef, he would wager, before snowfall, the Elwynim intending to disrupt the harvest and prevent Henas'amef from storing adequate food, as well as to rampage through the villages during a time when the roads did not make relief easy.

It meant, of course, that the Elwynim disrupted their own harvest by taking men away from the farms, but if in years previous they had had the foresight to hold reserves of their grain, they could bring it from Elwynor, managing the extended supply that Grandfather had declared was the most important item to have secured: Never rely on the farmers for food, was another of Grandfather's rules; it makes the farmers mad, gives your enemy willing reports, and it never amounts to what you think it will once you most need it.

Grandfather was silent on the problems of feeding the farmers of Amefel while the armies of five provinces and all the enemy camped on their fields and their sheep-meadows – when the Amefin were farmers and shepherds of the chanciest loyalty in all Ylesuin. As well the King *did* stand on their pastures; holding Amefel otherwise would not be possible.

And damn Efanor's Quinalt priest, who had been sniffing around the local market, and had this very morning, in these unsettled times, had the town guard arrest a simples-seller who happened to have the old Sihhë coinage for amulets in her stock. Efanor of course supported the priest. Efanor –

The door opened, a guard holding the door and a wind-blown, panting page unable to get out his message. "Your Majesty!" the boy said, turning a bow into a hands-on-knees gasp for wind. He had run the stairs, by the look of him. "Your Majesty. The Elwynim –"

It was a cursed bad word on which to run out of breath.

"– with banners and all, coming on the gates, Your Majesty!"

"The whole army?"

A wild shake of the head. "No, Your Majesty. No." Another space for breath. "With the Ivanim, down by their camp. They'll be coming in the gates and right through the town next! So the messenger said!"

"Will they?" Cefwyn did not think so. He pushed back from the table and levered himself to his feet. "Boy, run down to the stable, have horses saddled. Taywys, –" That for the guard who had brought the boy. "Advise the Lord Commander, and have men to ride down with me. Go!" The leg hurt and he did not look forward to the stairs. He had arranged his whole day so that he need not go down those steps today, and now the damned page had gone, the guard had gone, the servants were not at hand, and, needing to dress for outdoors, he was daunted by the prospect of doing it alone: he had begun to measure such small distances as that to the door and back as he had only a fortnight ago measured distances between provinces.

541

But the whole Elwynim troop could be riding through the gates and measuring his inadequate town walls if he delayed to call Annas and the pages and put on the prudent mail shirt or the elegant velvet coat with the royal crest. If he had to deal with some Elwynim demand for territory or a challenge to combat, he could cut a martial enough figure on horseback with a soldier's cloak slung about him, and damn what was beneath.

He took the cursed stick in hand, ordered the door guard as he passed to go back and fetch his cloak, and started down the hall without it: he declined to descend the stairs carrying its weight or having it swirling across his view of the steps when his footing was unsure as it was. The one guard hovered while he descended, and the Olmern lad, Denyn Kei's-son, who had gone back to fetch his cloak, overtook him before he reached the bottom, offering it to him as he went.

"I'll put it on outside," he said curtly to Denyn, and to the guard who had dogged him down the steps as if he could have rescued him from behind in a fall: "Don't flutter 'round me, damn it. If you'd be of use, get in front." He thought about descending the outside steps without the stick, but he considered the spectacle and, worse, the omen of the King of Ylesuin tumbling down them onto the courtyard, and let prudence rule.

The whole descent took long enough that a horse was saddled and ready for him at the bottom – not Danvy: Danvy was down in pasture, recuperating from his cuts and bruises, and Haman's chief assistant had given him that damned blaze-faced, showy black Efanor had ridden, when they had saddled everything in the stable to remount Efanor and his company: Synanna, – who was a good horse in most points, but tall; and facing that climb to the stirrup, in which he had to use the help of the guard, he thanked the gods it was his right, not his left, leg wounded.

He handed his stick down to the groom with an order to keep it for him, and took the cloak the guard handed up, steadying Synanna's foolery with his feet and his knees: his right leg hurt with the pains of hell as he slung the cloak about him and used his knee to steady Synanna from a compensatory shift sideways.

More, the horse was sore, having been ridden that break-neck course for Emwy the last time out of the stable. Consequently he had his ears back and was going to take every chance to have things his way on this outing. The horse was looking for excuses as he rode to the gate with five of the guard clattering after – and the King's standard-bearer riding to catch up, still unfurling the King's red banner, at which Synanna threw his head and acted the thorough fool under the gate arch.

Another horseman overtook them there and fell in beside him: Idrys, on black Drugyn, this time having heard the summons. The standard-bearer and the bearer of Idrys' personal banner made it to their position in the same general flurry of riders.

"I had the report," Idrys said.

"Gods know what this regards," he said. They passed through the town streets and on the cobbles Synanna wanted to drop into his worst gait, which took work to prevent; it hurt, and stopping it hurt, and he was in far less pleasant a mood as he reached the lower town and saw the town gate standing wide – to welcome the Elwynim, one supposed. He was not thoroughly gracious as first Cevulirn and a small number of riders, with the White Horse standard and pennons and all, rode up and joined them at that open gate.

Then Umanon and three of his lieutenants arrived, making a collection of banners enough to make a brave show for a King whose wounded leg and whose temper could not stand much more of Synanna's jolting trot.

But his two loyal lords might have shut the gates and met the damned Elwynim where they could not get a good look inside or a head count on all the camps down that lane.

"Pass the word to all the watches," he said to the gate-guards. "No foreign banner and no foreign courier is to pass

543

this gate until an officer of the Dragon Guard comes down *himself* and takes charge of them. Do you hear that?"

"Yes, Your Majesty," came the answer; "Yes, Your Majesty," came in awestruck tones at his back as he rode out westward with his growing company.

And there on the muddy road, plain as a horse in a henyard, were the Elwynim, with the banners of three earls behind the black and white and gold Tower banner of the Regent of Elwynor.

And with them, the pennons of six squads of the Ivanim light horse.

That was much better; Cevulirn's men were escorting the visitors in. There was Uwen Lewen's-son, up at the fore. And best of all, *Tristen*, thank the blessed gods: he had no idea how all three elements had gotten together, but he was both vastly relieved and disquieted anew, and for the same reason.

Synanna went into his bone-jarring trot in his momentary lapse. He corrected it, and in the abating of pain, and past the cracking satin of his own red banner, saw a black-haired woman in a mail shirt and a billow of mud-spattered blue skirt that blew back on white linen – a woman, his startled gaze informed him, who rode preceded only by the Regent's standard-bearer, ahead of the other banners; more, the Regent's crown flashed in that mass of dark hair – and he knew that hair, that heart-shaped face that had resided for months in a keepsake chest in his bedchamber.

"The Regent's daughter, in the flesh," Idrys said, coldest reason. "No sign of the lord Regent. And with Ynefel. What *have* we knocking on our gates, m'lord King?"

"I'll wait to see," he muttered, while his thoughts were flitting wildly to Tristen's safety, bridges spanning the Lenúalim, the missing messenger, the whereabouts of the lord Regent Uleman, the young lady's distractingly pretty and apparently unconscious display – *and* her reasons for approaching the gates of Henas'amef.

To pursue a royal marriage by passage of arms? He did not think it likely. But she was certainly far deeper into Amefel than any lordly delegation reasonably ought to come without his leave. It was an extravagant challenge of his good nature, which the Elwynim might guess was not good at all at the moment.

And Tristen showed up in this business?

Trust Tristen's naïve confidence. And damn Idrys if he dared remind him now he had predicted Tristen's blithe honesty could be his bane someday.

Their two parties reached a distance at which their banner-bearers mutually stopped for protocols, and he rode up even with his banner, with Idrys riding beside him and Cevulirn and Umanon and their standard-bearers staying behind him. The young woman similarly advanced to the Regent's standard, and one man rode to her side.

"We've come to speak with the King," that man called out.

"Stay back," he said to Idrys, and raised the wager by riding forward of Idrys. Only his banner-bearer advanced with him.

There was consternation on the opposing man's part, a frown on the lady's face as her captain put out a hand, clearly wishing her to make no reciprocal advance. But the young woman rode forward alone, and the Regent's standard-bearer advanced with her.

"I am King Cefwyn," he said as she stopped her horse within a lance's length of him. The portrait-painter had not lied, never mind the mud and the mail coat: the image that had haunted his more pensive evenings was facing him in life, a face pale and wind-stung and afraid, and a resolve not giving backward a step.

"The lord of Ynefel has made himself our hostage," she said, "against your grant of safe conduct for me and my men back across the border."

"I shall certainly grant that. I would be obliged, however, if you returned me the lord of Ynefel and accepted my simple word to that effect, gracious lady. Am I correct? Do I recognize you, or have you a sister?"

"I am the Regent." The voice quavered slightly. "My father

is dead, last evening, Your Majesty. I have come to ask your forbearance for our presence in your lands, and your permission to fortify a camp in your territory."

So Emuin was right. It was a sad event for the lady to report, a grief more recent than his own. It was, moreover, a very precise military term, doubtless her advisors' idea, which she had been told to ask in its precise wording. He wondered if she understood it.

"To *fortify* a camp," he echoed. His view of blowing skirts and white, mud-spattered linen was competing with the consideration of Elwynim in view of his very vulnerable town. "I give you my sincere condolences, and ask why fortified, Your Most Honorable Grace."

"I understand that Elwynim crossed the river against your father the King up in Emwy district."

"Yes," he said, not seeing how this answered his question. "They did. In collusion with the Aswyddim. We recovered shields from that field, and wounded now dead, three of them of Lower Saissonnd."

"Caswyddian," she declared without hesitation. "Lord Caswyddian of Saissonnd. A rebel against my father – a rival of Aséyneddin."

He had heard rumors, he knew that name and had marked it down as a man who would pay in Heryn's fashion, did he turn out to have been on that field at Emwy, or to have known of it – and did he ever fall into his hands; but he did not wish to tell her what he had heard or how much he knew. "So you bring Elwynor's troubles onto Amefin soil, and want to fortify a camp, making us, I suppose, your allies of a sort, certainly as Aséyneddin will see it. That could cause us trouble. And, forgive my suspicion, Your Grace, but of how many men do you propose to make this camp?"

"These men –" There was the least tremor in the lady's chin, the first thorough fracture in her composure. "– these fifteen men, sir. Thirty-three were camped with my father. A band we think was Caswyddian's attacked us last night and half my men stayed to guard our retreat, so that I might remain alive to make this request – in which regard, I would ask you, if you would, if you would be so gracious, should they chance into your hands – place them under the same safe conduct."

That last seemed both sincere and from a lady not used to asking abject favors of strangers.

"I shall," he said, "most gladly, and I shall advise my searchers to be careful. I must, however, advise you, Your Grace, that fifteen men hardly constitute a fortified camp, certainly none to strike fear into your enemies."

"Fifteen men is what I have, Your Majesty. But if we could make that camp as a secure point, and send into Elwynor –"

"You can gain more men for your camp?"

"I am confident, sir."

Confident, he believed not in the least. But it was a sensible plan, and a far better one than he had expected of a young woman in such a desperate situation. Whether or not it was her idea, she presented it with authority, used the right words – and did know why the camp should be fortified. It was the Sihhë entrenchment, plain and simple: dig deep and hold on, then spread out.

More, she had not once appealed him in terms of the marriage proposal lying just uphill in his bedchamber, not so much as acknowledged it existed, nor asked for troops, nor requested alliance with Ylesuin. The mischief the artist had put into the eyes was all iron and fire today – gray, was the answer to what the artist had made ambiguous.

They were still ambiguous. Gray as morning mist. Gray as new iron. The mouth had dimples at the corners, but they were part of the set of a determined jaw, which he would like to see in that other expression – gods, he knew this face. He had lived with this face. He was fascinated out of his good sense – so fascinated he had imagined beyond her proposed camp and her proposed recruitment of an unspecified number of Elwynim onto his side of the river to launch a war from his territory against her enemies – and not asking the number of men this Caswyddian and gods-knew-who-else might have across the river up there, and where his post rider might have disappeared to.

He needed to ask Tristen what he had seen. He needed to talk to the Ivanim captain about how what he had seen agreed with what the lady now Regent was saying. His leg was hurting and he was distracted by Synanna's restlessness.

But it was toward late afternoon, the lady herself was the potential source of a great deal he wanted to know about the intentions of Elwynor, and he could hardly ask the Regent of Elwynor to camp in the orchard next the lord of Lanfarnesse, in the mud and the midst of apple-harvest, with – he could see – no tents and a couple of horses with very scant baggage.

"Your Grace," he said, "I shall consider your proposition. May I ask an indelicate question? Are you aware of a proposal and a medallion that your father sent to me?"

Her cold-stung cheeks were already blushed. The pink reached the rest of her face, and the frown stayed. "Since our messengers did not return to us, Your Majesty, and since you mention it, I can only surmise it did reach you, and that your silence spoke for you."

"The messenger did not return to you."

"No, sir. As others did not. Do you say this was not to your knowledge? That there *are* no Elwynim heads above your gates?"

Heryn, he thought, and damned him to very hell. "Lady, on those terms your courage in dealing with me is amazing. Will you marry me?"

The color fled. The lips parted – and clamped tight. "Sir."

"Will you marry me?"

"You are mocking me."

"On my most solemn oath, Lady Regent. I by no means mock you. Your state cannot be more desperate. On the other hand, the bloody Marhanen does have troops at his disposal and wishes to assure peace on this frontier. What terms would you wish?"

The lips had relaxed, as if she were about to speak one word, and then another, and finally, on a deep breath: "I would agree to nothing, Your Majesty, without the advice of my own lords. They have given up their safety and risked their families to come here."

"Their advice, but not their consent?"

"Majesty, I am in my own right Regent of Elwynor. And if you ask my terms, sir, they are that I *be* Regent of Elwynor, in my own right, and not subject to any authority of yours."

"You have the most extravagant eyes."

The eyes in question widened and sparked fire. "I am not to be mocked, sir."

"I am a King more absolute, and can agree without my advisers, who will damn me to hell if I take such terms from you."

"I shall take my safe conduct and ride to the border!"

"I said I agreed."

The remarkable eyes blinked. Twice.

Cefwyn asked: "Did you talk to the lord of Ynefel? Do you find him pleasant, agreeable – somewhat mad?"

"You *are* mocking me, now."

"I mock myself, dear lady; I see war inevitable if your rebels have their way, and wizardry is already with us. Things will not be for us what they were for our fathers. Mauryl Gestaurien is dead, my friend yonder is beyond all doubt Sihhë, and possibly your King – some do think so – who may be bent on having his kingdom, if he does not tomorrow take a fancy to some other pursuit."

She took a large breath. "Sir! I –"

"But should you find yourself in that event without a realm to rule, I shall be glad to reconsider our pact of separate rule."

"You are the most outrageous man I ever met!"

"Since you've met Tristen, I take that for a sweeping statement. – Do you accept?"

"You are mad, sir!"

"And?" He had almost seen the dimples. The look was in her eyes.

"I – shall consider it, *with* my advisers."

"Your name *is* Ninévrisë. Am I right?"

She stared, in deep offense. Then she laughed. "You know that!"

"One should always be sure. – In the meantime, while you're considering –" He left all banter, and turned completely serious. "Will you and your advisers be my honored guests? I swear to your safety."

Her anxious glance traveled to the heights and back again. "I put you on your honor, sir." She gathered up the reins, began to turn her horse. And looked back. "– Cefwyn. Is *that* your name?"

With which she rode briskly back to her men.

He shut his mouth, and rode back to his – to Idrys, in the main, but Umanon and Cevulirn were moving in.

"I'm going to marry her," he said.

"My lord is not serious," Idrys said.

"Tristen's upstairs room for the lady – Tristen's belongings are all downstairs, are they not? The adjacent quarters for the lords, the men disposed with them or elsewhere at their wish. Send ahead of us and set reliable servants to work on the details. The betrothal within a day or two, I swear to you."

"My lord King," Idrys began, and, in the presence of witnesses, fell prudently quiet.

"Oh, I've thought about it, Idrys. I have most seriously thought about it. The woman demands sole title to the Regency of Elwynor. *I* have more imminent concerns." He cast a look at Umanon's frowning face – and Cevulirn's, but Cevulirn showed no more expression than usual. "I am not mad, sirs. This lady is an ally who has importunate suitors raiding our territory to have the better of each other. That will stop. I had far rather, if I must go to war, go to war to settle a permanent peace on this border, and if a marriage is the price of that peace, I shall."

"They are Elwynim!" Umanon said.

"Patently. That is their *use*, Your Grace. A pious Quinalt lady will not get me a peaceful border. This lady will."

Cevulirn had never batted an eye. As for Umanon, he knew

how to reason with him: make it a plot, a scheme, a strata-
gem. Then Umanon understood.

He had thought, however, that shadow in the wind and
sound of a horse moving quietly up beside him was Idrys'
standard-bearer. It was a different horse. It was Tristen on
him, Tristen unshaven, mud-flecked and shadow-eyed.

"Gods," Cefwyn said. "You startled me."

"You will marry her," Tristen echoed, as if assuring himself
of what he had heard. Tristen's eyes were unwontedly opaque
to him. Guarded. Gray as the lady's: he had never thought it
until that instant, and a chill went with that awareness.

"I shall indeed marry her. – Ride with me. Tell me later
what happened." Whatever Tristen had been up to, he did
not think it a story for Umanon's sensitive ears and gossip-
prone mouth. He wanted nothing of any of Tristen's doings
or the lady's until he had Tristen in private. "Are our
Elwynim going to ride with us, or not?"

There was apparent consternation among the Elwynim
bunched together on the road. He could guess that at least
one of the three lords was unconvinced of their safety and
argued for a camp outside the walls.

"Lord Tasien is anxious about coming here," Tristen said
with his accustomed bluntness. "But she will do what she
wishes to do."

"And what is that?" he asked, before he remembered he
wanted no news.

"To find men to fight the enemy, sir. Mauryl's enemy."

There was consternation on Umanon's face. Even Cevulirn
gave Tristen a troubled glance.

"A matter for council," Cefwyn said quickly. Religious
anxiety would be far more potent among the common
soldiers than among their lords, but their lords' response
forecast the commons'. A moment ago he had been half in
love. Cefwyn, the lady had said, as if their meeting were
chance and he were any would-be lover with not a thought in
his head but that pretty face.

The fact was she need not have been pretty. She needed to

be the Regent of Elwynor. Better yet if she were at least publicly Quinalt.

Best for his peace of mind if he had not found those eyes suddenly so familiar, and so disturbing. He could not imagine why he had not realized in their ambiguity even in the portrait, that they might be gray – or recalled, when he had fallen under their spell and offered himself in marriage, that they were reputed, like that mass of black, black hair, as a Sihhë trait.

It was nothing he need fear, but, gods! how the whispers would run, even in Amefel, even by this evening.

The Elwynim joined them, and names were named, Lord Tasien of Cassissan; Lord Haurydd of Upper Saissonnd; Lord Ysdan of Ormadzaran . . . names hitherto belonging to aged parchment and crooked trails of ink.

"My lords," Cefwyn said, and could not resist a bow, ironic mockery of their clear apprehensions. "The bloody Marhanen bids you all welcome and hopes for your good opinion. Bear the Regent's banner next to mine. Such are the terms the lady Regent requests, and Ylesuin will honor – whatever the lady requests. I cannot daunt her. I am resolved to please her."

The Elwynim bowed. The lady, to his astonishment, blushed.

But he said to Idrys, as Synanna, on his casual mistouch of the reins, brushed Drugyn's shoulder: "The west gate, for the gods' sake, not the south. Bid someone remove the heads tonight."

Cefwyn was completely occupied with the lords around him, and Tristen thought it a good time to keep silence. It was comfortable enough to ride with Uwen; and it was comfortable to be riding up a street he knew, among people who knew him.

But it was a long ride up that hill, with the townsfolk of Henas'amef turned out to stare and talk together, wide-eyed, at the display of Elwynim banners that he was sure they had never expected in their streets.

Then someone cried out, "Lord Sihhë!" and others took it up, crying "Lord Sihhë!"

They did not cry out that way for the other lords. He had had his fill of being conspicuous, last night. He was tired, he was aching and, as certain as he had been not so long ago that he could not possibly bear the confines of his rooms and the mundane chatter of Uwen and his servants, he thought now that nothing could be more dear or more welcome to him.

The rain had come down on them most of the night and again during the morning. Petelly was switching his ears and clearly had honeyed oats in mind, and Uwen's borrowed Ivanim mount had protested strenuously at the gate, knowing that he belonged down in the Ivanim camp, as all but a few of their Ivanim escort went aside to their well-earned rest. The Ivanim had come with provisions, as the Elwynim had, so they had not gone hungry; and they had rested on the journey – at least three times; but only once, toward dawn, had they stopped for enough time for men and horses alike to catch a little sleep.

It had not been enough – nor real rest. Tristen had feared sleep as he had not feared the ghosts that walked the earth of Althalen, and sat half-drowsing, content to watch Uwen's rest as Uwen had sworn himself willing to watch his – but Uwen had very quickly nodded off in the quiet and the stillness of the wind that, after the gale against their wet clothing, had seemed like warmth.

The lady had dreamed. The lady had dreamed of children's games, and children's songs, and the childish voices haunted him no less than the ghosts, rhymes about blackbirds and skipping steps, and memories of rain-puddles and gray stone.

They terrified him. He knew that they were her memories and not his. And in them she had *felt* small, which he never had. Their memories were so much the same, or hers had delved into his, and diverged again, into being she, and being he, and living in a bright hall and fearing the dark, and living in a keep that always ran and rippled with it.

Ynefel touched his drowsing thoughts with poignant

warmth, with longing to see his familiar loft and the stairs to his room, and to hear Mauryl's familiar step-and-tap; but the lady had waked from his dream with an outcry, afraid of the stone faces, and Tasien had asked her what was wrong.

A nightmare, she had answered Lord Tasien, and hugged her cloak about her and shivered.

That had more than stung: it wounded him; and he had sat watching her while she fell back to sleep, thinking, in his own fears, how very strange it was to have been so small as she had been, and to have weighed so little on the earth, and yet to have enjoyed the same pleasures as he treasured – except, except dodging around the stone walls, and looking at the faces, and thinking of them as familiar.

She had never known her father was a wizard . . . or whatever it was that gave her father the strength he had to travel that gray place. He had wondered once if everyone could go there. He had wondered whether it was a place Emuin had made for them alone – or that Emuin had let him into; and here at least was someone as surprised and dismayed by that place as he had been.

It made him feel . . . older, somehow. It made him wish he could give her in one instant all that he knew, and have someone then who would always understand the things he saw and how he saw them; it made him wish that he could leave all the others behind in camp and go somewhere alone and tell her and ask her . . . so many things, so many questions that stirred tonight in the grass, in the leaves, in the memories of Ynefel's creakings at night, the force of a gathering storm of Words and Names and so, so much about the world that he might almost understand if events and dangers had not swept him from one thing to the other. It was like the pigeons carried on the storm: they stayed aloft, they flew, but they rode the gusts, not choosing their own path so much as choosing the violence that went where they wished to go; they dived at the last into the safety of the loft on the blast of the rain, and a boy who was never truly a boy waited for them, with the wind blowing straws about and blasting the rain in through the broken boards – that boy called them home to the loft, waved his arms and called out Hurry! hurry! never knowing they were helpless to do more than they did.

He could not have been different than he had been. He could not have been the child that the lady had been. He could not remember the long ago that people kept attributing to him. He could find only dark before the light in Mauryl's keep.

The banners snapped and thumped in a wind that had never warmed with the sun. He saw, past their intersecting folds, that they were coming to the western gate, the stable gate. They passed beneath the arch, and into the stable-court by the shortest way, and to the western steps of the Zeide, where grooms ran to take the horses, Cefwyn's first, and the lady's, Cevulirn's and Umanon's, and the other lords'. A boy came running to take Petelly's reins.

Tristen dismounted quietly, and Uwen got down. He saw a boy hand Cefwyn a stick, which he did use, and seemed for a moment to be in pain, but Cefwyn was at hand as Ninévrisë slid down in a flurry of skirts: so was Tasien there to take the lady's arm. Cefwyn and Lord Tasien were polite to each other, and Lord Haurydd and Lord Ysdan were there, all of them being polite, all of them concerned about the lady.

He supposed it would be difficult to add himself to that crowd. He could speak to the lady in a way they could not. He could tell her things they could not: he would gladly, when his knees were not shaking from exhaustion, help her explain to Cefwyn what had happened, and why there was a danger up by Emwy, and what had happened to the old man and to the Elwynim rebels.

But he knew better now than to intrude on Cefwyn when Cefwyn was dealing with the lords – least of all, he supposed, when Cefwyn was dealing with the lady Regent.

Marry her?

Cefwyn had talked about marriage, before now.

Marriage was a Word of great importance to a man and a woman. Marriage entrained other Words so . . . numerous and so strange to him that he lost his awareness of where he was, and realized that he was walking across the courtyard, watching Cefwyn and Idrys and the lady and the lords climb the steps, Cefwyn using his stick and limping in pain and talking all the while.

It was one of those moments in which he felt shut out, unwelcome. And he supposed Cefwyn was angry with him for leaving – deservedly so. He wanted Cefwyn to be as glad to see him as he appeared to be to see the lady – as he wished the lady herself would speak well of him. He thought he had deserved it. He could show her things Cefwyn could not. But, no, they would settle things as they pleased, without him.

Uwen was with him as he walked up the steps. They had already gone inside. He heaved an aching sigh, found tears almost escaping him, and realized how tired he truly was. He was foolish to expect a welcome after he had stolen Petelly, lied to the guards, and sent six squads of Cevulirn's horsemen out looking for him. Well that Cefwyn had been as pleasant and glad to see him as he was. He had not at all deserved well of Cefwyn for what he had done.

He had not deserved, either, to have Uwen still faithful to him, and forgiving of a soaking and a long, long ride and a chase through very dangerous places. But Uwen did forgive him. He supposed that Cefwyn did; and the lady, after all, owed him nothing.

He followed the lords inside, and while they went down the corridor to one of the halls of state, he went upstairs, and down toward his apartments, where his guards, to his chagrin, were still patiently standing, as if he were still there.

Had they never left? he wondered. He saw their faces lighten as he came, and, "M'lord," one said, and *they* were glad to see him, which he did not at all deserve.

It made him ashamed.

"You go fetch His Lordship's servants," Uwen said to the youngest. "You tell them he's here and wanting to rest and they should be quick."

"Yes, sir," the guard said, and hurried to do that as the others let him in and wished him well.

Every detail of the rooms, the very fact of coming home, when he had not been sure he would ever see any of it again – filled up his senses to a dizzying fullness. He stood in the middle of the room just looking at the furniture and finding somewhere he had, wonderful to say, come back to and found again.

He heard a step behind him and thought it was the servants. But a brush of gray as soft as the footsteps told him a further amazing thing before he even turned around.

"Master Emuin!"

"Tristen." Emuin came and set his hands on his shoulders. "I wish I had foreseen more than I did."

He had done badly, Emuin meant, on his own. He found himself facing the judgment of the only teacher he had alive, and found it a hard judgment of his choices. "I did what I knew, sir," he said. "I tried to reach you."

"You have met so much. A great deal of changes. A great deal. You've had to find your own way, young lord. And not done so badly, perhaps. Tell me, tell me what you did, and saw, and how you found your way."

Emuin held out hope of approval, which he was all too ready to grasp: but Emuin began to draw him into the gray space – which he feared since last night, and with the Regent dying, and with Ninévrisë – and the Shadows, and their Enemy. He refused; and Emuin stepped back of a sudden, ceasing to touch him.

He had not remembered Emuin's face seeming so old, or so drawn, and Emuin, who had at first seemed so wise and calm, looked haggard and afraid. "I see," Emuin murmured faintly, "I *see*, young lord."

"Do you know all that's happened? Hasufin was reaching out of Ynefel. But the lord Regent said he shouldn't have Althalen, and wanted to be buried there –" Things made far better sense, telling them to Emuin, than they had to the lady, or than they would when he told them to Cefwyn. "He said he'd listened to Hasufin too long. He came to Althalen to be buried because he feared he would be a bridge for Hasufin if he was buried anywhere else. And I brought the lady here, sir: her father wanted to talk to Cefwyn, and Cefwyn says he wants to marry her."

"Merciful gods. Marry her."

"I think –" he said, because he had had all the ride home to reason it out, "I think that the people of Emwy village were hiding the lord Regent. I think they knew he was there all along, and they protected him. He was a good man. But now all the houses are burned and the people are Shadows. Idrys might have done it; he was going to burn the haystacks; but I think it was a man named Caswyddian, looking for the Regent. He found us – but the Shadows caught him. I don't think he followed us out of Althalen. I heard the trees breaking."

Emuin passed a hand over his face and went over to the table and sat down as if there were much more to hear. There was not. But Tristen went, too, and sat, feeling the weariness of what seemed now days in the saddle, Cefwyn's father's murder, and now this ride to and from the Regent's death – there was so, so much in turmoil around him, and too many dying, whatever it meant to die – he could not puzzle it out. And he wanted to have Emuin tell him he had not been mistaken, and that he had not brought Cefwyn worse trouble.

"I should have been there," Emuin said.

"Have I done wrong, sir?"

"It remains to see."

"I've killed people. I fought Cefwyn's enemies. But I – knew how, sir. It came to me – as other things do."

"Did you do unjustly?"

"No, sir. I don't think that I did." It was a question the like of which Mauryl would have asked. It showed him a path down which he could think. "But is this what I was meant to do? Is fighting Cefwyn's enemies what Mauryl wanted me to do? I thought by going on the Road I might find the answer, and I found the lady and the lord Regent. I think this was where I was supposed to go. But I can't tell if this was what Mauryl wanted. How am I to know such things?"

"Gods, lad, if I only knew, myself. But you did very bravely."

"Hasufin still has the tower, sir. He has that, and he might have Althalen, now. I don't know. The old man, the lord Regent, was fighting to stop him. – He was a wizard. *I* think he was, at least."

"The lord Regent?" Emuin sounded surprised. "Why so?"

"Because he went to the gray place. So did his daughter, but she didn't know she could do it. Can only wizards go there?"

"The daughter can?"

"Yes, sir."

Emuin drew a long, slow breath.

"Is it *wrong* to do?" Tristen asked, not understanding Emuin's troubled expression.

"No. Not wrong. But dangerous – especially in that place. I have always told you it was dangerous."

"Because of Hasufin."

"Because of him, yes."

"Could you have defeated him, if you were there?"

"Where Mauryl failed? I am not confident. I am far from confident. And you must stay out of that place! You and she both must."

"The lord Regent said –" He tried to follow the tangled reasoning that the lord Regent had told him, how it was easy to slip into Hasufin's trickery, but all thinking was becoming a maze for him, like the dazedness that came with too much, too fast. His tongue forgot the words. His eyes were open, but they were ceasing to see things clearly. He was all of a sudden profoundly, helplessly weary, and knew he was where he could trust, and that there was his own bed very near him, which he wanted more than he wanted anything in the world.

"Poor lad," Emuin said, as Mauryl would have said; or he dreamed, and rested his head on his hands. He heard the scrape of the chair as Mauryl rose, and he tried to wake. He felt the touch of a kindly hand on his back. He might have been in Ynefel again. He might have begun to dream.

"Poor m'lord," someone said, and he heard someone say, "Put him to bed. He needs that most of all."

He felt someone at his shoulder, heard Uwen's voice then, saying, "On your feet, m'lord."

"Emuin, –"

"Master Emuin's gone to his supper, lad." Uwen set an arm about him, and he waked enough to help Uwen, and to get his feet under him. "Servants has got hot towels, m'lord, and your own bed is waitin'."

He could walk for that. He let Uwen guide him to his own bedroom and set him down on a bench by the window. Uwen helped him off with the coat, and with the mail shirt, and with the boots, and then he sat and shivered in clothing that never had dried.

But the servants came with stacks of hot, wet towels, and he shed his clothing and let them comb his hair and shave him and warm him with the towels, until his eyes were shutting simply with the comfort, and he was near to falling asleep where he sat.

Uwen and one of the servants pulled him to his feet and took him across a cool floor to his bed. There was a fire going in the hearth, he could see that as he lay back and let Uwen throw the covers over him.

"Was Emuin angry? I don't remember."

"He wasn't angry, m'lord. He said you'd sleep a while. He said not to worry, he'd talk to the King."

"I am tired, Uwen, unspeakably tired. That's all, now." His eyes were shut already, and the mattress was bottomless. "I'll sleep through supper, I fear."

"'At's all right. 'At's just all right, lad. Ye've done very well."

"I wish I thought so."

"Ye've weathered more'n ye'll say, is clear." Uwen's gentle hand brushed the hair off his face. "Ye got to stay out of such places."

"They seem where I'm most fit."

"That ain't so, m'lord. Don't ye ever say so!"

"Uwen, forgive me for bringing you out in the rain."

"There's naught to forgive, lad. Only I hoped ye'd fled the blood and the killing and just took a ride in the country, is all. And ye found ghosts and worse."

"I found Hasufin. I found him and he still was too strong. But the old man drew me to the Elwynim. And I drew you to us, at least I think I did. I was wishing you away, but toward the last, there was nothing I wanted more to see than you coming down that hill."

"Nothing I wanted to see more than you, lad. But ye done right well, ye done right well. I heard you askin' master Emuin. It's a spooky business, I say. The Elwynim talking about fire and smoke, which we was smelling, with the rain coming down in buckets and tubsful. The Ivanim say that's the reputation of the place, that the haunt often goes with that smell about it. But what broke the trees, m'lord?"

"I think it was the folk of Emwy," Tristen said, and tried to open his eyes, but they immediately closed again. "Talk of something else. Talk about the village you came from. Talk about the town. Make me laugh. I would like to laugh."

Uwen talked, and talked, but it became a lazy sound to him, and dear and distant at once, telling him about his aunt and the priest and the pig, which was a funny story, and made him laugh, but he could not for two blinks of his eyes follow it, or consciously understand the joke, except the pig had found its way home again by sundown, and the priest had wanted to have it for dinner. So he was on the side of the pig.

CHAPTER 28

~

Gossip had run the halls all evening and it had had twins by morning, so Annas reported.

And mostly it was true what the gossip was saying, simply that there was rebellion in Elwynor, Emwy village was burned to the ground – and the King was marrying the Regent of Elwynor. Cefwyn looked at least to have an hour or two before he had to refute wilder elaborations on that report. He had had a late night of questioning Cevulirn's captain, and discussing matters with Cevulirn – a later night, with the pain in his leg keeping him awake. But he had not finished his morning cup of tea when Efanor came bursting past the confused guards in a high fit of temper.

"You cannot be serious," was Efanor's opening plaint. "You cannot do this. You dare not do this."

"I can, and I can and I dare," Cefwyn muttered over the rim of the tea cup. He felt a sort of triumph to have set Efanor so thoroughly aghast. It was good to have some forces of nature predictable. "Name me a disadvantage, brother, and do sit down, have a cup of tea. Shush! You know I hate uproars before I've waked."

Annas brought another cup, and Efanor settled. There were smiles. There were nods. The door shut.

"The woman is a heretic!" Efanor cried.

"I'll ask her whether she is. If she consents to my suit."

"The King cannot marry a heretic! He cannot blaspheme against the gods! He cannot make light of them!"

Do you really think they notice? he was almost tempted to say. His leg was hurting this morning and he was quick to temper. But he could be at least as crassly self-serving as Efanor's priests, and cold-bloodedly larded his own unreligious philosophy with priestly cant. "I believe the gods send us chances, Efanor, I do believe that chances to do great good are rare, perhaps one in a lifetime, and this is mine." Luck was the way he personally thought of it. But, inspired to one impiety, he proceeded to an outright fabrication: "I had a vision, night before last night, and I saw the sun shining on the far side of the Lenúalim. I think it's the gods' providence that Tristen came to us instead of across the river where Aséyneddin, who *is* truly faithless, would have seized on him and used him ill, and I think it's the gods' good providence that they have given me a chance to bring the realms together."

"They're heretics."

"Good loving *gods,* Efanor! Whom *else* can one rescue from sin? The pious? The gods already *have* them. It's the heretics the gods have to court! It's heresy to deny the gods' providence, – is it not? These are clearly providential events, absolutely unprecedented, tumbling one upon the other! And surely the good gods want converts and influence in Elwynor, which the lady can give to them, – if the gods' pious Guelen worshippers make a good impression and don't offend the lady by arresting doddering trinket-sellers in the market. Let us have a sense of proportion, here, brother, and give affairs their sensible importance! What matters more to the gods? Scaring some old woman? Or having peaceable relations with Elwynor and the chance to secure a border? Leave the gods to take care of the old women in their good time and let us do what they clearly have set before us, in the matter of this border, and the Regent, and a chance that has never ever come to any king, not for a hundred years. If we fail – if we fail, we shall stand accountable for thousands of lives. We shall lose all we hold dear and defeat the gods' own purpose. And I would not have that on my soul, Efanor, I would not!"

Efanor's mouth opened, and shut, and maybe Efanor's wits had begun, however belatedly, to work. Efanor had gone from sincere childhood fears of things going bump in the stairwell at night to a fierce belief that supernatural things had kept him from the good in life and could be cajoled into working better for him in the hereafter. Efanor had had his wits fairly well about him until his desertion of Emuin's easy-going Teranthines to the more rigid orthodoxy of the Quinalt, with their rules and abstinences – and their course of atonement for faults. Efanor's self-doubts and his demand for a solution he himself could apply had brought him to a sect that instilled doubts of the morality of his every thought, every thought of a thought Efanor had, and taught him then how to atone for those sinful thoughts and search for more fault in himself – which took an increasing amount of Efanor's attention from what was going on in the world.

Probably, Cefwyn guessed, it was the effect of growing up with a grandfather who knew he was damned to some unguessed hell and an uncle who'd said something prophetic about his demise the day before he died. Efanor was clutching at straws of salvation in a flood of the increasingly inexplicable.

But the brother he had loved had owned a keen wit once upon a time; and it seemed to him on an odd provocation that a surfeit of inexplicable ideas, complex beyond that damned priest's limited wit, might be his best chance to rescue his brother.

So he sipped tea and sat discussing the notions he had of matters military and matters involving Elwynor, and he saw that his brother was pleased – his brother, he saw in a vision at least as thunderous as the one he claimed to have had about the sunlight and the river, hated to be ranked down among the other lords, and hated to have his information when they received it.

So he would have to make time to see that Efanor was not surprised by matters of state. Efanor relaxed over that cup of tea and a second and a third, and, granted he must be very, very careful of the new-sprung and thorny hedges that defended Efanor's religion, Efanor positively expanded, and considered, and even advanced a rational thought or two.

Efanor had always liked to know things others did not – and once Efanor knew there was a complexity of reasons, rather like Umanon, but with more wit, Efanor was haring off down the ramifications and thinking up ideas – which could not be state secrets if he told his priest.

In that tactic, Cefwyn thought, he had his best chance to rescue his brother: get Efanor so deep in state intrigues, little ones at first, that Efanor would lean to him and keep his secrets rather than the Quinalt's.

Then beware the Quinalt, he thought, foreseeing trouble of a dangerous sort once the Quinalt saw Efanor slipping from their grasp.

He was rather pleased with the outcome of that conversation. His leg ached less. He felt he was on top of matters, at least starting the day, as he saw Efanor out the door.

But no sooner had he gone back to the table and his morning agenda, than Emuin was at the door, craving admittance of his guards.

And on two more cups of tea – Emuin spilled another web of less divine scheming, with secrets to tell *him*.

"Our young man," Emuin said, among other pleasantries, "is aware of Mauryl's enemy and in occasional communication with him."

"Here?" he was moved to ask.

"Occasionally. But Place is important. Magic clings to places, and places once built mark the earth for a long, long time. He and the late lord Regent sought to *take* Althalen from Hasufin. I believe he did at least give good account of himself. He has prevented absolute disaster in that precinct, and wizardry of some sort called him up there. But I do not know whose maneuver it was and I do not know whose maneuver the lady Regent may be in coming here. I am *not* confident it's Tristen's doing. He's young, he's sometimes unaware – I don't know but what the enemy could instill an idea in him. Certainly *I* can't. But I don't put it beyond Hasufin to do so."

"This is the dreadful Barrakkêth. This is the wizard capable of turning the Zeide into Ynefel! Now you're saying he's a feckless child open to malign and subtle influences!"

"He's not a wizard. And I am saying Mauryl did not Shape

him as he was at his height of power. Mauryl – the gods know what Mauryl did. Mauryl certainly didn't capture all of him."

"Glorious! Half a wizard."

"Don't make light of it! There is every chance he is simply – young, as I said from the very beginning."

"And getting older by the day, master grayfrock."

"Be careful of him. Only be careful. He may have done you a great and very wise service at Althalen. I think, perhaps, since things are quieter, that Hasufin may have gotten his fingers burned. – Did I mention the lord Regent had Sihhë blood? You distracted me with your questions, young King."

He swallowed the tea he had in his mouth. "No, you did not mention it. I've proposed to marry his daughter – Did I mention *that,* sir? And the lady has gray eyes."

"It was wizardry, however, that the lord Regent used. Wizardry, as I strongly had the impression. I don't say Sihhë can't *become* wizards, and I think the lord Regent was, if Your Majesty wishes, my considered opinion, both."

"Good blessed gods, old master, I am speaking of *marriage* with this woman. I have deliberated marriage with this woman for months. Do you just now report this small fact? Damn it!"

"First, I didn't know about the lord Regent until Tristen told me. There are wizards about. They do make rustlings in the world. Second, that blood is very thin, very thin, or the lord Regent himself could have fulfilled the prophecy. He could not. He was *nothing* to what Tristen is."

"Will Tristen inherit Elwynor?"

"I'm sure I don't know."

"Should I marry her?"

"If you fancy her, why not?"

"Why *not?* Good gods, spare me. Give me *advice,* sir."

"I confess I don't know. I could never select a wife for a man, being celibate, myself."

"Another reason not to trust wizards."

"It's not a requirement. It does seem to work out that way. But I have told you what I came to tell you."

"What shall I do, damn it, sir? Where is your advice?"

"Idrys knows far more of worldly things than I. You might ask him."

With which Emuin took his leave, off to, Emuin declared, his devotions.

"Hell!" he said to the four walls.

"My lord?" Annas asked, having arrived from the other room.

"Hell and damnation." He went and stared out the window, at the roof slates and the morning sky. The breakfast dishes were vanishing behind him. He heard the quiet clatter.

And a page slipped up, diffidently to hand him a note.

It was sealed with wax, with a seal of a Tower and quarterings.

Her seal. Of course her seal. They had carried the banners. Packhorses with bundles aboard. Certainly the Regent's seal – which he lifted with his thumbnail, and unfolded the note.

I accept your offer, it read. *I shall marry you.*

The sun was well up and the household about its day's business when Tristen waked – staring at the ceiling of his own room, lying in his own bed, in uneasy comfort.

He hardly wanted to face the day. He had far rather lie still and cause no one any more difficulty.

But he could not, lying there and staying quiet for fear the servants would rush in, keep his thoughts from wandering over where he had been and what had happened, and, worst of all, to Cefwyn, and Cefwyn's reasons for being angry at him.

He supposed it was a fault in himself that he could not leave it at that, that he needed desperately to make peace with Cefwyn. He was not even entirely certain Cefwyn was angry. But it seemed at least that Cefwyn had every right to be.

That was what finally drove him out of bed.

He had his breakfast, which pleased his servants; he dressed deliberately in clothing his servants somehow found for him – black – and, resolved to mend his behavior, talked pleasantly with Uwen, who had been able to sleep late, too, which Uwen almost never could. He took a little bread and opened the square of window that would open and set it out for the pigeons, which he would do every morning he had leisure – he wanted to have his life quiet and the same again, and he did all those things he would do when his life was at its most even.

But after breakfast he excused himself to Uwen and said he was going across the hall. "I promise, Uwen," he said. "I do most earnestly promise to go nowhere else without coming back for you. Rest. Do what you care to do."

"I don't distrust ye, m'lord," Uwen protested.

"I deserve your mistrust," he said. "And I am going to do better, Uwen. I promise I am."

"M'lord," Uwen said, seeming embarrassed. But there was little more he could say than that.

It was clear by the number of guards at Cefwyn's door that Cefwyn was in and most likely alone: at least no other lord's guards were standing about. He went across the corridor, trailing the two members of his guard that were obliged to go with him even this distance, and asked entry to Cefwyn's apartment, half-expecting that Cefwyn would not grant it, and dreading the meeting if he did.

But the guards passed him through on standing orders, it seemed, which had never been revoked, and he passed through Idrys' domain between the doors, finding that vacant, and so on into Cefwyn's rooms, where Cefwyn sat at the dining table which he had had pulled over to the light of the window.

"M'lord," he said faintly.

"Tristen." Cefwyn started to get up, and it cost him pain. Cefwyn settled again with a sigh, and beckoned him.

"I didn't know that you'd see me," Tristen said, and came and took the chair Cefwyn offered. "I'm truly sorry, sir."

Cefwyn reached out across the table and caught his wrist. "Tristen. I would have called you last night but they said you were abed."

"I was, sir. What did you want?"

Cefwyn laughed and shook his head, letting him go.

"Constant as the sunrise. 'What did you want?' I wanted you alive, you silly goose. I wanted you well."

"That's very kind, sir."

"Kind! Good gods. What's 'kind' to do with it? I might have known you'd turn up unscratched."

"I stole. I lied. I went where I knew danger was."

"That fairly well sums it up." Cefwyn shook his head and seemed amused instead of angry. "I knew every damn step of the way you'd taken. Uwen knew. I knew. Idrys knew, the moment you turned up missing, and you still got away from us."

"It took Uwen a while to get a horse."

"To get six squads of cavalry. *Uwen* had the sense not to go alone."

"Yes, sir."

"You should not have seen," Cefwyn said soberly then, "what you saw that night. You shouldn't have gone outside."

He had half-forgotten the start of the business, or what had prompted him to the meeting Cefwyn was holding.

"Yes, sir," he said, accepting Cefwyn's rebuke.

"Heryn," Cefwyn said, "was responsible for my father's death. It turns out – for Elwynim deaths as well. Heryn Aswydd was on every side of the business, and he was seeing that messages went through him. If the message didn't suit him – that messenger died. He was dealing with every Elwynim faction, dealing with me, informing my father with lies about my doings, informing my brother and informing any lord of any province who would listen to his poison. He was guilty, Tristen. And if there is war, as I fear there will be, he is in no small part responsible for that."

"I think that he listened to Hasufin."

"Your bogeyman in the tower. I don't know who he listened to, my friend. But his own greed – and his panic when I began going through his tax records – made him desperate. He was, I am almost certain, directly behind the attempts on my life. Certainly he indirectly instigated them and possibly secured safe passage of assassins to get near me. Certainly with his men on patrol up by Emwy, it was

569

easy for that bridge to be rebuilt and for any number of Elwynim to come across that route: his so-called guards passed them through like a sieve."

It certainly made sense of a great deal that had happened. "I believe you're right," he said.

"You do." Cefwyn seemed faintly amused, and then sober again as he leaned back in the chair and shoved it back a little to face him across the corner of the table. "Lucky for everyone you were able to get the lady Ninévrisë to come to Henas'amef. I dislike encouraging you to your folly, but I think there would have been a far worse issue without you. – Emuin did explain that you felt something was about to happen, and that you went for that reason."

"I couldn't defeat him."

"Who? This Hasufin?"

"Yes, sir."

"Forget the 'sir.' Forget 'm'lord' while we're talking in private. Tell me the absolute truth. Tell me every detail you know and I shan't interrupt."

He did try. He began with stealing Petelly, and ended with their coming to Henas'amef; and once a guard came in to say a councillor wanted to see Cefwyn and once to give Cefwyn a note, for which Cefwyn excused himself a moment and wrote a brief reply, but Cefwyn would not let him go on until he had seated himself again and heard everything. Cefwyn made him tell about the Regent and the gray place. He made him tell about Ninévrisë meeting him there, and about what he had told Ninévrisë about his having the portrait. It was the longest anyone had ever listened to him, except Mauryl, and he was less and less certain, when he came to the business on the road, that Cefwyn wanted to hear him in that detail, but Cefwyn said leave out nothing. He was not certain that his talking to the Elwynim about the portrait might not make Cefwyn angry; but Cefwyn gave no sign of it. Cefwyn kept all expression from his face.

And when he had finished, and said so, Cefwyn nodded and seemed to think for a moment.

"You dream of this Hasufin. But you say he's very real."

"Very real, sir."

"And can cause harm?"

"I think that he could. I think certainly that he moves the Shadows. And the wind. He made the door come in. He cracked the walls. He made the balconies fall."

"Certainly substantial enough," Cefwyn agreed. "But he can't come here."

"The lord Regent said he could come where he had something to come to. Someone who listened to him. I think Heryn listened to him. Not well. And not the way the lord Regent did, because I don't think Heryn was a wizard. I think it's most dangerous if wizards did it."

"But to some extent, Hasufin could come here."

"If we began to listen to him, he could, yes, sir, that's what I think."

"Very good reason not to do that, is it not?"

"I agree, sir. But he's much stronger. Much stronger. And we should go there."

"To Ynefel."

"Yes, sir. We should stop him."

"How?"

Tristen bit his lip. "I don't know. I tried." He felt the failure sharply. "If the lord Regent had been stronger, maybe the two of us could have driven him back. We did, for a time."

"Could you and Emuin do so?"

He did not want to say the truth. But Cefwyn had expected him to be honest, and Cefwyn was listening to him. "Emuin is afraid," he said. "Emuin is afraid of him. – And the lady can't help. She's only just able to hear me when I speak to her. She could be in great danger. She's not as strong as the lord Regent. Maybe she could learn – but I couldn't say."

Cefwyn seemed to think that over a time. "Tell no one else about the lady."

"Yes, sir."

"I have offered to marry her. She's accepted. I expect to meet with her – in not very long. Should this wizardry of hers prevent me?"

571

It was loss for him. But he could not mislead Cefwyn from what was good. "I don't think so, sir."

Again Cefwyn gazed at him a long time without speaking. "I don't think it should, either. You don't affright me. You dismay me at times, but you have no power to frighten me, not when I have you close at hand. It's when you're gone that I'm afraid."

"Of me, sir?"

"No, not of you. Of your not being here. No matter what, Tristen, always be my friend. And, damn it all, don't say 'sir' to me."

"I'm sorry."

"You mustn't steal horses, either. If I gave you a horse – which would you?"

"I don't wish you to give me a horse."

"Well, you can't be stealing them, either. How is that to look, the King's friend, a horse-thief? You have an excellent eye for horses. I should like a foal of that red mare, I do tell you. You may have Gery, if you like, though. Look over the horses I have. Take the one you want, except Danvy. You should have at least three or four."

"I should like Petelly," he said. It did not console him. But that Cefwyn wished to give him something said that Cefwyn wished to please him. That was something.

"Which is Petelly?" Cefwyn asked.

"The one I stole. I like him."

"That's not very ambitious. I have far finer."

"Petelly is a very good horse."

"Well, I'm sure. And if you picked him out I should have another look at him. But he's not enough for heavy armor. And I shall ask you to do several things for me."

"What are they?"

"First –" Cefwyn marked the item with a finger. "Go down to master Peygan. Do you know him? Uwen does."

"The master armorer."

"Exactly. These are chancy times, and if you ride off again into a fight, by the gods, you'll go wearing more than you wear about the halls. Choose anything you like. I'll give the armsmaster his orders. And you'll want a horse that can carry you wearing it. I have one in mind. One of mine, in fact, out of a mare I have."

"I would be very pleased," he began, and intended to say he hardly knew what to do with such an extravagant gift. From abandoned – he found himself smothered in gifts he supposed proved Cefwyn's forgiveness – perhaps even Cefwyn's determination not to abandon him. But Mauryl had given him things just before – just before the balconies fell down.

"Good!" Cefwyn said. "That's settled. You'll join me this evening. Will you?"

"I would be very glad to."

"Then –" Cefwyn gathered himself up, leaning on the table, and Tristen understood it was dismissal, perhaps business disposed of with that. But unaccountably Cefwyn embraced him, and held him at arms' length and looked him close in the face. "My friend. Whatever happens, whatever you hear of me, whatever I hear of you, no one will ever make us distrust one another. You'll take another oath, do you see, in a few days – but I shall not ask you this time to swear to obey me. Only tell me now you'll take me into your confidence. Kings should not be surprised. Kings should never be surprised. That's all I ask."

"I have promised Uwen, too. But I might have to go."

"Do you know that already? Damn it, *what* do you know?"

He didn't know how to answer. Cefwyn reached toward him, toward his collar, and pulled at the chain he wore, of that amulet Cefwyn had given him.

"Does this," Cefwyn asked, "– does this give you comfort?"

"That you gave it comforts me."

"Does it protect you?"

"I haven't felt so." He had never looked for it to do so. "But I've never looked at it in the gray place."

"The gray place."

"Where Shadows live."

573

"Tell me. You can tell me. What gods do you serve? Emuin's?"

Gods should, perhaps, be a Word. Men seemed to hold it so. But he found nothing to shape it for him. He reached for the chain and slid the amulet back within his collar. "I don't know. I don't know, Cefwyn."

"And, with you, not knowing . . . encompasses much, does it not? – Can you say what the Elwynim are doing, up by Emwy?"

He shook his head. "But they will know that the lady is here. Aséyneddin listens to Hasufin. I am sure he does. He will dream it. He most likely knows."

"Is he a wizard?"

"I don't know. I haven't met him."

"I heed you," Cefwyn said at last. "You are free. But I ask you, wait and ride with us. Will you? – We shall ride to Emwy and deal with the Elwynim rebels. If you learn anything, by whatever means, you will tell me. Promise me that."

"I promise it."

"And don't keep me wondering where you are, or what you think. I am fond of you, damn you. I need you. I shall be sad all my life if you leave me." Cefwyn shook at him a little. "I shall have to be a king. I'm obliged to. It's a damned boring thing to be. – Join me tonight. Will you?"

It was a dismissal. But Cefwyn embraced him a second time, and with a fierceness that said he was welcome, and wanted, and would not be abandoned, and he held tightly to that embrace, his heart beating hard even while he asked himself was it only kind, what Cefwyn did, and did it hide what Cefwyn knew he would do.

There had been a time he would have been sure that Cefwyn would know what to do. There had been a time he had been sure that Cefwyn would protect him.

Now, if nothing else, it seemed quite the other way about. In the lord Regent he had lost someone who might have stood with him against Hasufin, had his Road led him there instead of here – so certainly so he had to ask himself whether he had indeed mistaken his way in the world; for he knew now with

574

clearest sight that Emuin had the knowledge, but lacked the courage to begin a fight, and that Cefwyn, who did have all the courage anyone could ask, was helpless against this enemy as they all were helpless to stop Cefwyn's pain, or turn aside the danger that was coming against him.

Mauryl might have helped Cefwyn. Mauryl could have worked a healing on him, and Cefwyn would not be in such unremitting pain as was beginning to mark his face.

But none of them, not Uleman, not Emuin, not Cefwyn, were what Mauryl had been. He himself knew reading and writing and horsemanship; he knew the use of a sword. He knew things about buildings that no longer were, like what he now knew was an older state of the lower hall.

But he knew nothing of what he most wanted, which was to be what Mauryl had wished him to be, and to make Cefwyn happy and safe and free from his wound.

"Thank you," he said to Cefwyn in leaving, and wished to the bottom of his heart that he were better than he was, and stronger than he was, and wiser than he was; and he wished that there were indeed some wise old man to take care of him and tell him his fears were empty.

The fact was they were not empty. And would not be. He had to do something. He did not imagine what that was. But that was what Mauryl had left him to do – even if his worst fears were true, and he had been mistaken in coming to Cefwyn, he had to find a way to make things right; or, if he had been right, to turn things as they were . . . into what they had to be.

The stables had sent in their accounts – Haman did not write well, and the scribe who had taken them down from Haman's dictation had a florid hand clearly Bryalt in style, which he was trying to puzzle out, when Idrys came to say that the lady had answered his last missive, among missives they had been exchanging with increasing frequency since breakfast.

In fact, the lady was at the door.

"Damn!" Cefwyn cried, and looked for a place to bestow the border reports, the maps. "Here." He shoved maps at a passing page. "In the map-cabinet, for the good gods' sake. – Annas!" More pages were running. He handed them the maps and the sensitive documents. "Put them in the bedchamber."

"Where in the bedchamber, Your Majesty?"

"On the bed! Put them somewhere. – Idrys, let the lady in."

He did not want to use the stick. He set that in the corner. He had put on the cursed bezaint shirt under the russet velvet, as Idrys insisted, and carried a dagger, which was not his habit: he counted that precaution enough against murderous Elwynim intentions and subterfuges of marriage.

"Are you quite ready, m'lord?"

"Open the damned door, Idrys!" He forced the leg to bear his weight naturally. It would do so once the initial pain passed. He walked toward the door, and was prepared for an informal meeting such as he had requested in the last note he had sent upstairs.

Ninévrisë wore darkest blue velvet, with silver cord – was in mourning, by the quiet black sash she wore; she wore velvet sleeves, and wore the Regent's crown. Her hair was modestly braided now, with a black ribbon – and answering the provenance of it, Margolis was with her, Margolis, the armorer's wife, a matronly woman of a constitution undaunted by relocation to the least civil province in the realm; Margolis could bring order to any situation – and if that gown had not been in the packs the Elwynim had brought, he could well believe that Margolis had stitched it up on a moment's notice. He did not know who had enlisted her to Ninévrisë's aid, but he was grateful.

"Welcome," he said. "Your Grace of Elwynor." He took Ninévrisë's offered hand, and after it, Margolis' stout one. "Dear Margolis. Thank you. Gracious as always." The last was for Margolis; but his eyes were for Ninévrisë whose demeanor was reserved, and whose mourning sash was a reminder to sober propriety. "After a day of messages – thank you for coming. I would by no means press your attendance –"

"My father is not lost," Ninévrisë said firmly, and walked past him to look about the room. "Lord Tristen said so. So I do not mourn him for lost. Nor do I count my war lost before it begins. May we dismiss our guards, Your Majesty, and speak frankly?"

"Lady," he said to Margolis. "Lord Commander." The latter to Idrys, who offered the armsmaster's wife a gracious retreat, likely no farther than the outside room.

The lady of Elwynor was so beautiful, so – unreachable, so unattainable by any wile or grace he had ever used for any other infatuation he had had, offering herself to him – and yet not to be had, ever, if he made her despise him. He had felt as attracted to a lady, but never so unsure of the lady's reasons in accepting, and never so unsure of acceptance when he had committed himself this extravagantly.

"I was delighted by your acceptance," he said, "and now –" – devastated by your coldness, he could finish, in courtly fashion. But it would be a mistake to enter that ground with this woman, he thought, because she would not quickly abandon the manner he set between them. "Now," he said, with utter honesty, "I see that you have reservations that did not at all enter today's messages. Constraint upon you was never my wish, Your Grace. I swear I shall keep my word. I am sad if you think so badly of me. And I assure you I shall be your ally in war. Common sense constrains that. So – you are not obliged to accept my suit."

She was not a woman, he had thought, who would use tears. But she turned away in the best tragic style and wiped at her eyes furiously.

He was angry, then, seeing her set upon him with such common tactics.

She stayed with her back turned. Wiped at her eyes a second time. "Forgive me," she said. "I had not intended to do this."

"Please," he said coldly. It had not yet reached him, how

577

many of his plans were affected by her refusal of marriage, and how many more were threatened if he insulted her pride. He felt more than angry. He felt, rejected, the ground giving way under his feet; he was desperate for the peace that he might yet salvage, and he could not, like a man stung in his personal hopes, answer in temper. "If not your love, Your Grace, at least I hope to win your good regard. I never wished to imply a condition to my help. What do you ask of me?"

She looked slowly around at him, and turned and stared at him as if she by no means believed it.

"That you grant us the camp," she said. "That you aid my men to cross to Elwynor and gain what help they can."

"I grant that. Freely."

"Why?" she demanded of him.

"Your Grace, your enemies as well as your friends will cross the river to find you. They have killed my lord father as well as yours, and just as recently. If your men will hold them at the bridge and remove their legitimacy with their supporters, that would be a great service."

"And you would let me go."

"I promised safe-conduct. I give you alliance."

"I shall not support any claims of territory, Your Majesty of Ylesuin."

"Nor shall I make any. As I recall, you came to *me*. I did not seek this. I did not seek the war which you have graciously brought with you. But it is here, it would have been here eventually on any account, and I had rather support your legitimate claim and far more pleasant countenance than have my father's murderers as neighbors. So you see – my offer was well thought. I am sorry to have conveyed any other impression. I thought, yesterday, that we understood one another."

She heaved a small breath, and another, and the tears were still on her face, but her face was calmer.

"Yesterday we did. But –" Another perilous breath. "I thought all night – what your reasons might be."

"And then sent the message?"

"It seemed a way to be done with it." She ducked her head, bit her lip, and looked up. "I have no better suitor. And I find you not the devil I thought. With many worse waiting in Elwynor – who would also take arms against Aséyneddin."

"Pray don't consider me a last resort, m'lady. I do have some pride. You are free to go."

"I might like you. I think I do like you. – And I don't consider you a last resort. To save my people, I would marry Aséyneddin. And put a dagger in him. That is my last resort."

"Good gods, do you consider putting one in me? I hope not."

"No." She walked toward him, hands folded, and looked up at him. "I do think I like you far better than I thought I would."

"That's very gratifying."

"Perhaps a fair amount better."

"Still more so."

"But do you like me at all?"

"I find you –"

"If you say beautiful I shall like you much less, sir."

"I was about to say, remarkable. Outrageous. Amazing. Gentle. Gracious. Intelligent. A good match for my own outrageous qualities, not least among which they tell me are my looks, and my intellect."

"You *are* outrageous."

"So my accusers say."

There were the very ghosts of dimples at the corners of her mouth – an attempt at restraint.

"I am accounted," he said, unwilling to be defeated by a reputation, "a fellow of good humor. Not quarrelsome. Not meddlesome."

"My cousins say I'm forward. Moody. Given to pranks and flights of fancy."

"My grandfather was a lunatic."

Her eyes went wide.

"I am," she said, "faithful to my promises, chaste, – not modest, however."

"I could be faithful. I abhor chastity. I cannot manage modesty."

The dimples did appear.

"Gods, a smile. I have won a smile."

"You are reprehensible, m'lord."

"But adoring."

"Gods save me. I am a heretic to your Quinalt. I have heard so."

"I am a heretic to the Quinalt did they know the opinion I hold of them. I may desert them for the Bryalt faith if they annoy me."

"Six months of the year I shall reside and rule in Elwynor. On my own authority."

He took her hand and kissed it. "My lady, if I cannot make you wish to shorten that time, I shall account myself at fault."

Her face went an amazing pink. Her hand rested in his. He kissed three fingers before she rescued it. "I insist on six months."

"I shall at least make you regret them. Is that yes to my suit? Or shall we commit venial sin?"

"Sir, –"

"I said I was not chaste."

She escaped a few paces, around the edge of the table. "As regards the defense at Emwy –"

"Yes?"

"Caswyddian is dead, or most of his men are, by whatever means – I think so, at least."

"Your fortified camp is well thought. But undermanned."

"What else can I do?"

"Send more men. I'll lend them."

"Guelenfolk? Alongside Elwynim?"

"Amefin. A Bryalt priest, if I can pry one out of sanctuary – at least in hopes a priest is worth something. There's too much wizardry loose. He might be more use than a squad of cavalry. But you aren't going."

"I command my own troops!"

"Gods, it seems the fashion of late. Listen to me, m'lady. These are very brave men who came with your father, if I understand accounts, and I believe I do. These are men who had determined to stand by their oaths and give their lives for your father; who are prepared to give them for you – but best for them if the Regent stays safe and lets these good men do what they can, until my men are ready to carry an assault. If the bridge is decked, they will dismantle that decking. If they bring more timbers, the camp as we'll set it up will have a garrison sufficient to hold that bridge against any force attempting to cross out of Elwynor. We'll have watches on all the other crossings, including those that might be made by boat. And if we are to go to war, my gracious and wise lady, I command all the forces, unless you can tell me on what fields you have fought, and prove that one of your men has experience to order your forces without me. Otherwise, leave matters to me. I'll be accommodating of your command in civil matters. Not in this, and not where a novice's mistake can expose other forces to danger."

She did listen. He saw comprehension, however unwilling, in her eyes.

"Are we to be married?" she asked. "I would marry you."

"I am still willing."

"Willing?" Clearly that was not enough.

"I *said* yes, my lady. What more do you want?"

A faint, a diffident voice: "A nicer yes."

He saw that there was here no exact rationality – nor one called for. She was alone. She was uncertain at best. He came around the end of the table and took her hand.

"Yes," he said, and in lieu of kissing the hand, snatched her by it into his arms and kissed her, long and soundly, until with her fists she began to pound his shoulder.

She did not find words immediately. She was searching after breath. Finally: "You are a scandal, sir!"

"I would not have you in doubt, my lady. And would not marry a statue. I don't think you are a statue. You give no evidence of being. And I think you know that I am none."

She was breathing quite hard, still, and again put the table between them. "You must not do that," she said, "until there is ink, sir, abundant ink. And agreements sworn and written down."

"I don't think you could list the points of negotiation. I know I should miss a few."

"If we are to be married," she said, between breaths, "we should be betrothed immediately – before my folk go. I have no one here but them. And I would like them to be present."

"Shall we be betrothed, then?"

"Yes."

"Soon?"

"Yes, good gods. Give me peace." She set herself all the way around the table, for safety. "I have put on mourning. But my father would well understand what I do. I have no hesitation on that account. Have you, sir?"

"None. Our custom is against mourning."

"I shall try to love you. I think I would like you – if we met by chance. I do wish to love you. But do me the grace of courtship. I should like to be courted – a little, sir."

There were tears, at least a glistening in her eyes; it was not an extravagant request, nor, he thought, false: she was very young, and still possessed of romantic notions.

So, he admitted to himself, was he.

"My lady, marriage is my duty and yours. But a little court-ship – *that,* I have no difficulty to promise, an extravagantly scandalous courtship, which –" he said, "I do count on winning. But for now, my hand, my respectful attention." Wherewith he offered his hand, and she was about to take it, when:

"You have not," she said, "– not mentioned the lord of Ynefel."

"Tristen? What of Tristen?"

"The succession."

"Ah."

"And I insist we shall not merge our kingdoms! I shall be sovereign over Elwynor, and through me, there will be one child to inherit Ylesuin, one for Elwynor."

"Hardly something we can achieve holding hands, my lady."

"And if Tristen – if Tristen is our King –"

"Tristen is happiest as he is."

"He is your friend. Is he not your friend? You cannot dismiss his rights – you would not, would you? We should settle that question in the nuptials."

"Tristen would not wish it. Believe me." He walked around the table and took her not unwilling hand. "Ask him if you like. His concerns are elsewhere. But if he reaches a point that he wishes to declare himself, then I trust that he will do that and I shall free him from any oath that stands in his way. One does not prevent or protect Tristen from what he decides to do, gods save us all. You will discover that first of all things you know about him."

The tailor had entered collapse – the oath-taking for tomorrow and a royal betrothal this evening: to save his reason, the King promised him a coronation to come; and the coat, if not the cloak, was ready. And even a king did not need to outshine his bride – who had come with her jewels, he was informed by a distraught Margolis, but not a betrothal gown. The tailor had risen triumphantly to the occasion, declared he knew where was the very shade of velvet, and gods only knew how, in details the King decided were far beyond his competency, Margolis had turned up a score of petticoats and the jewels had turned up stitched, the tailor interrupted his work to say, to sleeves and bodice, as a veritable army of Amefin ladies had invaded and barricaded the lesser hall to stitch and stitch and stitch for the lady Regent.

Somehow, another miracle of the gods, or the Amefin ladies, the tailor personally turned up with the King's sleeves, beautiful work, Cefwyn had to admit, of Marhanen red, with the Dragon arms in stitchery at least on the right sleeve, and the King would accordingly set a fashion tomorrow, of a cloak skewed and draped down the left arm.

It was all too much. But there was arranged a set of trumpeters – gods hope they managed, for the honor of Ylesuin, to start together: Annas had his doubts. There was arranged – not such a banquet as Guelemara would put on, but at least a selection of meats and pies and breads, which, the King was given by the cook to understand, were being done in ovens all among the Amefin nobles about the hill and in two bakeries, *if* the captain at the gate would let the food be brought in from the town. Cook had arranged it, the plans were about to fall apart an hour before the event, and the King had to intervene with a written order on behalf of a cart full of cheeses, let alone the meat pies – "Good gods," he said, "if they're to poison us, they'll poison the whole court. Just bring mine and the bride's from this kitchen, and the hell with it!"

There were barrels of ale brought up to the courtyard, and tables set up for the commons in the lower town. That, the household managed on prior experience. There were musicians. There were entertainers for the courtyard. There was a man who offered to bring a trained bear, but in the crowded condition of the hall, Annas and Idrys alike thought this folly and the King agreed.

The King, nerving himself and trying to numb the leg with a prior cup of strong willow-tea chased with a cup of wine, was in the main trying to decide whether he should use the stick getting down the stairs or, if he must use it, exactly where he could abandon it, and how long he might have to stand during the ceremony.

Past the initial rounds of drink, and the bride-to-be's maidenly withdrawal from the hall, he supposed, the King could find similar excuse and go. He was advised that Amefin betrothals were rowdy and licentious, and rowdy and licentious seemed to mean even the King could be jostled, which he did not want to be, nor wish to have the King's presence in the hall if any fool did bring in a weapon – he gave Idrys stern orders that the guard was to be vastly lenient, that they should try to protect the Elwynim from drunken folly, and that the interpretation of death for weapons drawn under the

King's roof should find as wide a latitude as they could contrive, including bashing an inebriate offender over the head and depositing him outside the gatehouse. He had, he told Idrys severely, no wish to have the evening marred by a death sentence. He wished to celebrate, that was all, and to have no cases before him tomorrow when he waked with whatever of a hangover he could achieve. He wished to be happy. Devil take those who disagreed.

And with that, he did use the stick getting down the stairs, and took the back approach to the great hall, and all the lords there present, including Efanor and his bosom friend Sulriggan. Elwynim were there as well as Ylesuin, the greater and the lesser lords, thanes, ealdormen, whatever: Elwynor's titles were like Amefel's. Tristen had come, with Emuin. The ladies of the Amefin lords and of the Guelen captains and lieutenants were there, dressed for festive doings. Orien had arrived reasonably on the stated hour, decked in the green velvet of her house and outfitted with a waspish temper, which she used only against the servants, thus far.

The trumpets had managed tolerably well on the King's entry. Annas had sent upstairs for Ninévrisë the moment he was downstairs, and while the musicians played and the guests came wishing the King well, the King fidgeted and watched the faces of the guests, who were already at the wine and the ale.

A blast of trumpets – only slightly out of agreement, and Ninévrisë swept in from the front entry, in all the glory of the new-made gown, deep blue velvet with sleeves stitched with jewels of every color, with a cream silk pulled through and puffed, and a deep blue cloak with a rose silk lining. A black ribbon was wound around the glittering gold of the Regent's crown – that was the concession to mourning. There were ohs and ahs from the crowd as she passed, delight in the eyes of no few ladies, if only that she was beautiful, and there was a spontaneous applause as she reached the dais and reached for his hand.

He kissed her hand. He held it joined with his for all the

company to see, and said, in a loud voice the exact words they had hammered out to bridge the gulf of religion: "My lords and ladies, I declare before you one and all I shall hold myself faithful and true and marry this woman in the sight of gods and men, in the first month of winter!"

Ninévrisë said, "My lords and ladies, I vow before gods and men I shall hold myself faithful and true and marry this man in the first month of winter!"

The musicians struck up. There was more applause. He was watching Orien's face no less than Efanor's, and found it stark, pale, and in that flare of nostril – absolutely furious.

"Her Most Honorable Grace the lady Regent of Elwynor has agreed," he said, gathering up all he had to say to them, "that the Elwynim conflict has already cost lives precious to her. It has cost my father's life, the lives of men with him; attacks on my person; the burning and slaughter of Emwy village . . . and loyal men have died in defense of Ylesuin. It has cost the life of the lord Regent of Elwynor, who had come to treat peacefully with us; and those that killed him did so on our land. In defense of our right and our land over which the gods have granted us rule; and by the gods' great might and by their will we shall come to the aid of the Regency of Elwynor, which has in past been a neighbor not utterly agreed with us, but which has never invaded our territory.

"I do not aspire to rule Elwynor – as I believe Your Graces of Elwynim came here with no desire to rule Ylesuin. Let us declare, all, that we have no designs on each other's land or lives, and that our greatest resources are not gold; they are good will on the borders and farmers reaping harvests untroubled by brigandage or war.

"I will not have for a neighbor the man I believe conspired in my father's death and in my bride's father's death. By the gods and my oath I shall maintain the rights of Ninévrisë Syrillas as lawful Regent of Elwynor and agree that the realm of Elwynor does not come to me by marriage nor by any other oath. Her Most Honorable Grace will remain Regent of Elwynor in her own name and right, as I shall remain King of

Ylesuin, granting neither land nor honors save the estate of wife, and she shall bear her own titles and honors, granting none to me save the estate of husband. We shall both with the help of our loyal subjects assure a peaceful border open to trade and safe for those villages neighboring the roads."

The hall had grown very quiet. Men who had not expected an oath to follow at that point had fallen into a dead hush, realizing, suddenly, that their own lives and lands and those of their children were being accounted for then and there.

"My lady? What say you?"

"I wish that my lord father might have seen his daughter a bride. I wish that more of my lords were present and not in danger of their lives in Elwynor. But by your help, my loyal and honorable lords of Elwynor, and you gracious lords and ladies of Ylesuin, and by the gods who bless peace, I swear I will take back my land and become the just Regent of Elwynor, the friend of all peaceful and honest people of this land and a faithful wife to my husband. I swear I shall give justice and secure the rights and honors of my own faithful lords. That is what I most wish. That is what my father came to Ylesuin to urge. I ask you all, eat and drink together in peace and please may the good holy men here present pray safety for all men's houses, great and small."

That was a thorny question: which gods and which priests. A small, seemly applause attended, wildly enthusiastic from certain of the Amefin – but not from all: decidedly not from the Quinaltines and not from Orien Aswydd.

But Emuin leapt bravely into the gap, launched forth in a loud voice with the good Teranthine brothers on either hand and intoned a blessing on all present, mercifully brief, at which the crowd cheered; and, with the value of a small shrine in perpetuity in his purse, the local head of the Quinalt, not Efanor's priest, forestalled briefly by Emuin's quick action, began a state prayer clearly designed to have been first – he might, however, have elaborated it on the fly, seeing himself potentially outdone by the Teranthines; Cefwyn guessed so, at least, for it went on into blessings on the town and blessings on the company present, blessings on the peace and blessings on the King and blessings on the lords and ladies, on their houses and their hearths, their sons and their daughters, their cattle and their horses. He had paid, and by the gods, he was going to have his prayer at rivalrous and inspired length.

He stole a glance at Efanor's priest, who looked to have swallowed sour milk; and in the close of it, gods save them, not to be outdone, the Bryalt cleric stood forth in a long appeal for religious harmony. Then, with the Bryalt's signal disregard of cultic divisions, the good man threw in Quinalt blessings and Teranthine and several others the provenance of which Cefwyn was truly glad he did not know; but the Amefin minor nobility made assenting nods of their heads, called out approbations, and a few mopped at their eyes.

Then, then they were done and the crowd applauded. He was permitted to give the bride a kiss on the cheek and he made an exchange of rings – he had had Annas buy his from an Amefin goldsmith, a simple band, and she had brought hers among her jewels, her mother's troth ring.

He found himself missing her finger with it, or at least feeling weak in the knees, as it suddenly struck him that he was not making a political speech, he was well and truly sworn to a treaty with Elwynor and committing himself to a household and offspring and all of it. Somehow he managed to put the damned thing on the lovely finger, gave a second kiss on the other cheek, received one, and in a moment of dizziness, all was done. The trumpets blared out wildly, not at all together, and this time there were loud cheers: the Amefin town dignitaries and their ladies who were crowding the back of the hall for the festivities clearly loved kisses far better than they understood the treaties the lords were still thinking through with suspicion, and they saw that the speeches were over and that the wine was about to flow in earnest.

After that, thank the gods, the musicians struck up a merry country dance, and the crowd made for the tables where wine and bread and cheese were set, with mugs of ale and the little pies, a tower of which the guests rapidly demolished.

"You seem truly happy, my lady," Tasien came to say, taking Ninévrisë's hand, while Cefwyn was busy with a well-wisher from the town. "Are you? Dare you say?"

"I think I may well be," she said, and Cefwyn, overhearing, drew in a breath of very heady nature. "I do think I could become so. Only take care. Do take care at Emwy." She let him kiss her hands, then, and Tasien passed on to him.

"I am greatly taken with her, Your Grace," Cefwyn said quietly to Tasien. "I shall send troops to reinforce you. But I made help to you no part of our agreement. The early betrothal – *she* asked the haste, so that you might be here, to stand as her father would have."

"Your Majesty," Tasien said, only that, and bowed, clearly not taking it for the truth, and managed to preserve a stiff and misgiving demeanor. So he knew he had not won Tasien, nor, he thought, the rest of the Elwynim.

But eat and drink they would, and so with the common men with them, who had put on their best, and whom Ninévrisë had wished admitted to the hall and seated in honorable places, because, she had said before they came in, she had given every one of them a modest if currently landless title and promised them rewards from the Crown when they reached Ilefínian in Elwynor, they, or, if they fell, their next of kin.

So he congratulated each of them as they came to pay their lady their good wishes, and, a trick he had learned from Emuin, knew their names and their new titles, which won astonished looks and no small good will for himself, he hoped. So it was at least one half-score of Elwynim who were happily celebrating tonight, and, perhaps their natural wary bent, or perhaps some sense of new responsibility, they were more modest in their attack on the wine-bowl than some ladies of Amefel, to look on the scene – and not participant in the handing-out of the diverse cups, none of a set, which he had declared the guests might take away with them.

That Amefin betrothal tradition had proved imprudent. There was no little wine spilled in the encounter at the tables.

"We should send a score of *them* up to the riverside," he muttered to Ninévrisë. "Gods, such graces!"

Orien had somehow *not* come up to felicitate the marriage, but other Amefin lords and ladies were beaming. Tristen came up the step, and said in his own way, to Ninévrisë, "Cefwyn will do what he says. He is honest," and to him, "She thinks everything is beautiful and the people are kind and she likes you more than she trusts you."

Ninévrisë was appalled and distressed. He was appalled and amused. But Tristen went away then, as if, though able to know what he knew, he entirely failed to know the dismay he left in his wake.

"Do you?" he said.

"Which?" she asked. But an elderly Amefin lady was attempting to hand Ninévrisë a charm done up in ribbons. "Children and grandchildren," the lady said. "Hang it over your bed, Your Grace. It worked for me."

He saw that Tristen had gotten himself some cheese and bread from the table below the dais. It was all Tristen seemed likely to secure for himself without warfare in the crowd pressing close, but Uwen was there, and, old warrior that he was, even while he watched, snatched a pair of plain, less contested cups of wine.

Dancing began, a handful of couples and a number of young gentlemen who, in the refilling of cups, felt immediately inspired – and though he had left the cursed stick propped in a side hall and had steeled himself to walk and climb steps without it, he certainly was not fit for this part of the festivities. The bride had now stayed longer than a Guelen bride would stay – though the continued line of well-wishers was adequate excuse, and would afford no gossip.

But the line had run almost to its end now, and he was thinking of passing her the hint of leaving when Efanor came up finally under the cover of the music and the noise of voices to pay a word or two.

"Your Grace," Efanor said. "A gift, if you will." He offered her a little book with the Quinalt sigil in gold on the cover. "For your meditations. My priest gave it to me when I was first sworn, and I would be delighted if you would accept it."

"Thank you, Your Highness." Ninévrisë accepted it, and held Efanor's hands afterward, at which he saw Efanor go white and then blush and look quite strange – as if, he thought, he had expected Ninévrisë to go up in smoke at the taking of the holy book. "How kind. Thank you very much. I shall treasure it."

She let him go. Efanor went back to his priest, and excused himself along the wall and into the crowd, doubtless for fresh air. Dancers came between.

"That was very nice of him," Ninévrisë said. "Is it a magical book?"

"No," he said quickly. "Tuck it away. – Not there. Somewhere reverent. I'll explain later."

"Is it malicious?"

"Oh, no. I think actually very well-meant. Even a sacrifice. But you have to understand Efanor."

"I don't see him."

"He's rather shy. We'll see him in the morning. I fear he's had a cup or two. He's given away something dear to him."

"Then I should give it back!"

"No, no, keep it. He'll never retreat from his generosity. And now that he's *been* generous he'll not know how to change the rules. Be generous to him. Trust me in this. It will do him ever so much good."

An Elwynim lord was talking with Pelumer, gods bless the old man. An Elwynim this very evening made gentry, Palisan, an excruciatingly handsome lad, was the quarry of Lord Durell's plump daughter, and Lady Orien was nowhere in sight. Probably she had resented acutely the matter of the cups. But it seemed to him it was fair enough, the forgiving of a few taxes.

Probably she had resented most of all his inviting her – for which he was actually sorry, because he had not meant ill. But he plucked Ninévrisë's sleeve and said to her very quietly,

"Dear lady, the King, who is very tired, is about to withdraw upstairs. By proprieties the bride-to-be should precede him, since I'm told the party will grow so rowdy that only the Guard is safe. Will you do me the grace?"

She laid her hand on his and said, only for his ears, "Thank you, my lord." And squeezed his hand with a little glistening in the eyes. "Thank you."

He thought her very brave, seeing how things had been thrown together, and she had none of her friends, only Margolis and a couple of the Amefin ladies to attend her: very brave and very gracious, under the press of circumstances and ladies with fertility charms and his brother's prayer-book. He gave the word to Idrys, who sent to the musicians and the trumpeters, and the music stopped and the trumpets blared out. He let Ninévrisë leave the dais first, with Margolis and with her own guard, and watched Ninévrisë accept words from Tasien and Haurydd and Ysdan, words and an avuncular embrace of each, since she would not see them before their departure for the border – in Haurydd's case, tonight.

Haurydd would go with Sovrag's men, and cross the river into Elwynor, to some landing they swore was safe. Haurydd would try, so the plan was, to reach loyal lords who would attack Aséyneddin by whatever means they could.

It was a mission he did not at all envy Lord Haurydd.

Cefwyn and Ninévrisë were leaving. Tristen watched from over the heads of the crowd, evaded a young lady evading a young gentleman, and decided the wall was a far safer place. But a plump and rather pretty lady was talking to Uwen, who was looking at her with close attention.

He thought tonight he understood. He had touched the gray place or Ninévrisë had, he was unsure who had done it first; Emuin had stopped it quickly, but not before he had felt ever so strange a shiver go through him, and ever so good a feeling that he had never felt, so much excitement and a little edge of fear and heat and cold and a great deal of desire for what he could not put a Name to. He found himself disturbed, now, by the sight of Uwen and the plump lady dancing together, and by the sights and sounds of so many, many couples doing the same. It seemed that all the world was paired, male and female, and the whole room was full of warmth pressing in on him, a Word trying so hard to be heard —

Someone plucked his sleeve, and he looked down at Lady Orien. "Please," she said. "Come."

He no longer knew where right and wrong was with Orien Aswydd. She was Lord Heryn's sister, and once upon a time Cefwyn had said not to speak with her — but she went immediately out the door and into the outer hall, where there were many other people.

It seemed foolish to be afraid of such an invitation, and perhaps there was indeed something he should hear. He walked along the wall, weaving his way among those watching the dancing, and went out among three or four others, into the well-lighted hall.

Orien was waiting along the wall outside.

"Lord Tristen." At once her lips were a thin line and her chin showed an imminence of tears. "Thank you so much for coming."

"What do you wish, lady?" He was distressed by her distress. "What troubles you?"

"I must speak to you. I must. I can't speak here. I daren't. That man is watching. I have so few chances to see anyone. And I am not a traitor. I am not! I have proof. I know things — I know things I would say if only the King would hear me. But I cannot speak to him. You must do it for me!"

"I would carry a message to him, most gladly, lady. Tell it to me."

"Even my friends are afraid to speak to me. I have no allies left. They have all, all deserted me, and Cefwyn has sent my cousins and even my sister away out of Amefel to exile. I miss her so."

"I'm very sorry."

"No one – only a handful of my women – can pass my guards; and they can do nothing. Please come. I have proof I was innocent. I want you to see what I found in my brother's records. Please. I know that you will be fair."

"What do you wish to tell Cefwyn? I shall have no hesitation to tell him."

"No! I will not beg him, sir, I shall not beg him. I only ask you come and see and listen to me and see a letter I have. Will you listen? I am desperate. I think he means to kill me as he killed Heryn, and I am not guilty! I am so afraid, sir. You can pass my guards. The King's friend can walk through any door. And I trust you, but none of them. Please!"

He thought it was possible for Cefwyn to have made a mistake. The lady had smiled at him, from his earliest days in the Zeide. She had baffled him and puzzled him – though Emuin had said she was among the principal ones he should not speak to, in those days they had wished him not to speak to anyone. But he did not know that it was true now.

"Please," she whispered urgently, and gave a glance sidelong and back. "They are with me. My guards are always with me, do you see them?"

He did. They were standing where Orien glanced.

"Come with me. Come with me now. I'm afraid to go back to my rooms alone with them. They frighten me. They threaten me. Please come with me."

"I should tell Uwen."

"No!" she said fiercely, and pulled on his hand. "None of Cefwyn's men. I will not talk with Cefwyn's men. Only with you – please."

He gave a step and two, and he saw the guards move, too, following them: they were Cefwyn's guards, so there was very little trouble he could get into, and he followed the lady as she led him by the hand down the hall and up the stairs of the east wing, then down the corridor to a door where more of Cefwyn's guards waited.

By then she was not leading him by the hand: she walked

with her arm linked in his, as men and women walked together. It was pleasant to walk with a lady in that way – it made him like other men. It seemed right enough, and the guards without a word opened the door and let them in.

And when they were inside, in the foyer room where there was no one waiting, no light but a single candle, and very heavy perfume wafting from the inner rooms, Orien embraced him.

He was surprised, but he thought she was afraid, and embraced her gently in turn. But she put her arms about his neck and pulled his head down so their lips met. Then he realized what she intended, and they kissed, but not the way Cefwyn and Ninévrisë had kissed, on the cheek. Lips met, and mouths met, at her instigation, which was a very strange and dizzying sensation. She was trying to undo his clothing, he realized, and Words came to him which had hovered about his awareness, disturbing Words, which had all to do with men and women.

But it seemed to him – it seemed to him that he was being rushed headlong toward a familiarity he did not feel with Lady Orien, and he *had* been warned, and she had spoken of proofs and messages none of which he saw in this darkened foyer.

He attempted to step back and remove her hands gently. She would not, and he caught her elusive hands and brought them down perforce.

"Are you my enemy?" she asked, with the tears welling up again. "Are you my enemy, too?"

"Where is this proof you wished to show me?" he asked.

"In there," she said. He had her hands prisoned. She nodded her head toward the inner rooms. "I will show you."

He was surer and surer that this was not as she had presented things to him in the hall. And he had no wish to go further than he had already gone, with feelings running through him that confused him. "I think," he said, "that you have lied to me, Lady Orien."

"I have not lied!" she said. "How can you treat me this way? How can you be so cruel?"

"Lady." He found his breath short. "*Show* me your proof. Now."

Immediately she began unlacing her bodice, which showed him a softness and whiteness he found quite disturbing and quite fascinating – he wished and did not wish to see more, which provoked the same feelings her hands had provoked, and he thought that it was the same attempt to confuse him. So he said, however difficult words were, "No, Your Grace," and laid his hand on the latch and opened the outer door to leave.

"Damn you!" she cried, and other things besides, which he had only heard among the Guard.

The guards outside gave him a questioning look and, feeling somehow ashamed, he put his clothing to rights. "Her Grace said she had a message. But I don't think it was true."

"Lord Warden," one guard said, "we heard the message story before. We sent a man for the Lord Commander, begging your pardon, on account of we couldn't stop you."

"Thank you," he said. "It was very kind of you. It was what you should have done."

He walked down the hall, embarrassed and angry at himself. He met Idrys and Uwen both on the stairs coming up, and said to Idrys, glad at least that Idrys had not had to come in to rescue him:

"I excused myself, sir. I believe she was lying about a message."

"I believe that she was, yes, Your Lordship." Idrys was perfectly composed, perfectly sober. "Good evening, and good rest."

Idrys continued up the stairs. Uwen turned and went back down with him, saying not a word. Tristen still felt foolish, and deeply embarrassed, and could feel the touch of the woman's hands.

"You know," Uwen said, "that widow, the nice-looking one? She dances nice, but I do think she's in a mind to marry, and I damn well ain't, m'lord. So I 'scaped, meself."

"I shouldn't have believed her. I *knew* better, Uwen. I did know better, and I'd sworn I wouldn't go off like that, and there I did. I'm very sorry."

"Oh," Uwen said, "well, m'lord, I was worried, but ye had the rare good sense to come back. Remember me coming down the hill, a couple of nights back? I swear I was that glad to see ye coming down them stairs. I was sure me and the captain would have to go battering at the door, and gods know what all, and there ye was, bright as brass and onto her tricks." Uwen put an arm about his shoulders, however briefly, before they entered the trafficked area where the musicians were still playing and the crowd was busy and thick. "There's many a man wouldn't have had the good sense, lad."

He thought he should be pleased he had understood, but he felt disturbed all over, and wished in some sense that he had stayed and found out those mysteries, and was glad he had not, because he did not think he would have liked to have had such an experience with Orien.

"I think I shall go home, though," he said.

"Seems a fine idea," Uwen said. "I got me a flask of summat nice and warming, and we can sit by the fire, you and me, like the wise fellows we are, and have a drink and go to bed."

So the two of them sat by a very comfortable fire in his apartment and had the drink, and Uwen told him about courting girls and his village and where he met his wife.

It was a very enlightening story. He became sure there were nicer ladies than Orien, but it made him feel a little lonely.

"I think your wife was a very fine lady," he said, and Uwen grinned and said,

"A fine lady she weren't, oh, but a damn fine woman and a brave one, a brave, brave woman."

"I would wish to have met her," he said, and Uwen wiped his eyes and coughed and said he was for bed, now.

So was he. He lay down in the cool sheets and shut his eyes, seeing first Orien, and feeling only discomfort in the memory; but seeing Ninévrisë too, how she had sparkled in the candlelight – how her face was when she laughed, how her eyes were when she was grave and listening. There was nothing about Ninévrisë that was not wonderful, and nothing about her heart that was not good.

He knew. He had touched it, in that gray place this evening. And Emuin had quickly intervened, and told him it was dangerous, and he must not.

He went on feeling what he had felt with Orien, who had lied to him, who was not in the least like Ninévrisë; he went on thinking of Ninévrisë and thinking that marriage meant that Cefwyn and Ninévrisë would share a bed and share their lives, and love each other. Cefwyn gave him gifts and asked him to be his friend – and perhaps he would not lose Cefwyn. Perhaps he would have a chance to speak often with Ninévrisë as he wished, and things would work out.

There was a knot in his throat. It was a hurt, he thought, to which he told himself he had no right, since their being married was long since arranged.

Meanwhile they were going to war against the men that Hasufin brought against them – which, with the skill he had at arms, must be something Mauryl had intended, at least it seemed so now, in the evidence of things tumbling about him.

But Mauryl had been in a hurry, and had brought him for a purpose that mattered, and not thought much, he supposed, about anything else, such as things he might discover and things he might come to want for himself that had no place in Mauryl's purpose. He remembered in little things it had been that way: he might have been exploring the loft or discovering something he had never seen before – he might just have found the most wonderful thing in Ynefel; but if Mauryl wanted him, he had to leave it at once and answer when Mauryl called, that was what Mauryl had always insisted; and it mattered not that he was older and that both his distractions and his self-will were stronger – it was still true.

He would go where Mauryl had wished. He had gone to Althalen. He had come back again. He could see no one and nothing standing against Mauryl's purpose for him – not standing against it successfully, or scathelessly: such were his deepest fears for what he loved – and he dared not let them try to oppose what Mauryl had intended.

It was not Mauryl's fault, of course: he was brought into the world because of Mauryl's need, and that he inclined in other directions was not Mauryl's fault. He wished he could speak with someone who understood Mauryl. But he could not reach into the gray space after Emuin tonight: he feared he could not touch the gray space without troubling Ninévrisë's dreams, and he would not do that. Most of all, he dared not risk that tonight, and with the strange things he was feeling toward her.

He lay watching the fire-shadows dance around the edges of the walls, and once he heard a thump and rattle, as if the latch of the window were disturbed.

If that was Hasufin, he said to himself, well that Hasufin did not trouble him tonight, because he was suddenly very angry – and wished he had somewhere to put that anger.

But no one else he remotely knew deserved it, except Orien. And he had been close enough to wizards he was afraid to stay as angry as he was. He was afraid to dream, or to skim close to that gray place so long as he was in a state of hurt, and anger.

So he got up and tried to read, sitting on the hearth, long into the night, until he fell asleep over his Book, and waked with his neck stiff and his legs cramped and the fire long since gone to glowing ashes.

He waked – with a sense of apprehension. Not the window, he thought. There had been no sound. There had been no breath of wind.

But something had changed while he slept, he thought. Something – perhaps in the gray space he dared not visit, what other men called dreams – had become much more dangerous and much more urgent tonight, and that change seemed to have a sharp edge to it, a point at which it suddenly became true. He did not know whether it was because of his mistake with Orien, or perhaps something Emuin had done in his prayers, or something Ninévrisë herself might have done in the gray space, with him all unaware –

But he was increasingly afraid, and knew no one he dared tell. He thought of waking Emuin – and knew if he did, he might say and hear things that might make him more disturbed and more in danger of making a mistake than he was now. He sat there still in the dark with the embers aglow beside him and with the dry, blind parchment of Mauryl's Book in his hands, and he thought to himself with sudden realization: Orien wanted to harm Cefwyn.

It wasn't myself she wanted. It was Revenge.

I was very, very foolish to go there.

CHAPTER 29

In the press of time, as regarded what the King himself willed, the King would gladly have drawn the barons aside for a few moments last evening before the ceremony, and held moderately sober council in the other chamber, considering the situation on the borders, and considering that moderate drinking might even assure a certain harmony in his diverse council – he had worked that ploy before.

But it would have intruded on the dignity of the betrothal, it would have slighted the Elwynim *and* the lady's feelings, for whom he was surprised to realize he did have a tender consideration in the matter.

So he was further along the rose-strewn path than he had thought he would ever come for a lady he would for state reasons be obliged to marry. He was amazed to realize that he had spent an unaccountable amount of time today already thinking about the Regent's daughter and far too little time committing to memory details of the riverside fortifications, which did the Regent's daughter no practical service, and far too little memorizing the other matters on which he *must* not make a slip of the tongue, and, *gods* help him, he kept thinking about her face, her voice, her eyes. Which were gray. Again, gods help him – the Quinalt would not like that, and the Quinalt thought it had a right to be spiritual guides to the queens of Ylesuin – which his affianced bride refused to be, and *that* news was going to cause a clatter the like of which his father's approval of Emuin as his tutor had never remotely touched.

But they would not daunt him, not for the principle of the thing (he had sought ways to diminish their influence) and not for his personal choices. He knew his foolish faults, that he was easily infatuated, that it lasted a time, and vanished some unpredictable morning in total disillusion. He never wanted such affairs to end, but end they would, and yet, this morning after a commitment which should have been the most calculated and reasoned decision of his reign, he was appalled to find himself slipping closer and closer to that passionate mark with a woman who, first, was capable of launching war on his kingdom and who, second, had maddening and attractive personal qualities he had to admit his light-of-loves had never had.

He perceived himself in real danger, waking with Ninévrisë in his mind, and being entirely unable to recall the number of wagons he had already dispatched to the river – or to remember the third point he had to make in argument as, dressed in his regal best (except the crown) he walked with his guard and his household around him (except Idrys and Emuin) to meet Ninévrisë and her small household, with her sworn men, on *her* way down the stairs.

"My lady," he said to her.

"Your Majesty," she said. There were bows. There was pleasantness. Lord Tasien was glum as they continued down the stairs.

Gods, it was three months until the wedding – three months of hand-holding and chaste kisses on the cheek, such as he had had last night.

And he could not be thinking about a wedding. He had a ceremony to get through, a ceremony he had had to throw together, the next thing to a battlefield coronation on the day he was sending men to hold the Lenúalim against invaders – but he had seen increasingly even with Idrys that he could not continue as he was, not knowing clearly where the most loyal of his barons' loyalties were. As importantly, he had to swear *them* assurances of *his* behavior, in the shifting of all familiar points of reference, his father gone, the Elwynim marriage – and Tristen arriving.

What he had to do and say this morning, he was certain was going to provoke controversy. Men still in some points enemies to each other had politely reserved opinions behind their teeth last night, knowing they were drunk. Today, politics would out, most coldly sober, equally as dangerous, and Lord Tasien had come here with strong reservations about any alliance. He was a relative on Ninévrisë's mother's side, married himself, and sonless, so he had had no designs on Ninévrisë – Lord Tasien was decidedly to win.

So was his own brother. And Sulriggan of Llymaryn. There *was* Sulriggan. And that damned priest of Efanor's.

But given that Umanon and Sovrag might have severe headache, and so might Lord Ysdan, by the quantities he had seen them imbibe, this morning council at least would render them more docile and less inclined to loud argument and debate. There were no more alarms to report to them: the daily messengers from the riverside had come in with no change and no sighting of the enemy – no better news, either, meaning no hope that lightning had struck Aséyneddin in his bed.

The council of barons and the ceremony he had determined necessary – he had arranged it with Annas and Emuin in indecent haste. The situation on the border afforded little time for true deliberation: such as they could do that involved the lords – they had done the night of his father's assassination; and to open the matter again to debate only gave the dissenters, this time with Sulriggan instead of the lord of Murandys, a chance to delay preparation he dared not delay. Granted rumors were cavorting behind every door in the Zeide – precisely because of that, matters had to be settled, today.

Ninévrisë and her entourage entered the great hall by the main doors. He heard the herald announce them. He did not intend to give the Elwynim lords time to stand and converse in that uneasy company. Idrys clearly had the same notion, joined him from inside, by the small side entry, and prompted him with, "When Your Majesty wishes," while he was measuring the time that would carry Ninévrisë and her lords in decent order to their place at the fore of the great hall.

If he was lucky, he said to himself, he could deliver what he had to say while the barons were still numb, have the swearing done, and have them packed off to their own tasks before they had quite waked up to the fact they were being told that war with Elwynor was imminent and inevitable.

"Her Grace of Amefel is *not* here," Idrys said, as the doors were opening a second time.

Cefwyn drew a deep breath and walked in and down the aisle with Idrys at his back and his guard around him, in the echoing proclamation of His Majesty of Ylesuin. He walked to the first step, turned and acknowledged a head of state, not his bride, with a direct look, a hand outheld in invitation, and, "Your Most Honorable Grace."

Ninévrisë was there in her own right, as she insisted – composed, not a hair out of place, clear-headed and gracious. It *was* infatuation, Cefwyn feared, bestowing a kiss on her hand which, with the knowledge he could not place it elsewhere, served only to distract him. He led her from her escort to the last step of the dais where only his guard and Idrys joined him besides.

"Brother," he said, to Efanor, in the first row of standing nobles, and invited him to the same place, which his father had not done with his own brother, but he did.

Then, taking that one step higher, he turned and looked over the assembled barons and household.

Orien was, indeed, not there. One assumed that Lady Orien still claimed her lordship over Amefel, but as she had not answered the general summons, they need not have the protests when he barred her at the doors, as, damn it, he would do. She might have attended in good grace last night and possibly, by a gracious show, won a step toward a royal pardon. She might have done many things besides what Idrys had reported to him she had done, and his tolerance of Orien Aswydd and all her kin was balanced on a knife's edge this morning. He was very close to ordering her arrest before they left this hall.

Idrys had brought down the requisite, unmarked, maps. The servants had provided tables at the side of the hall, adequate to spread them out for general view. Everything was in its place. Everything was in order.

"My lords," he said, receiving the bleary-eyed silence and courteous attention of the company. "Lords of the Elwynim, your plan to fortify a camp at Emwy Bridge has our agreement, and as some of you are aware, I have already set men and wagons moving with supplies, counting that you can quickly overtake them on horseback, today, as I believe is my lady's wish."

Ninévrisë inclined her head. "Just so, my lords."

"Also," Cefwyn said, "I am requesting those forces of the Dragon Guard which came to this town in my late father's company stay with me, as well as the Prince's Guard; I require that official messages now return to the heart of Ylesuin with orders for the movement of supply and the disposition of forces all along our northern border with Elwynor, as a precaution against an incursion taking an unexpected route. Also, far from least of my concerns, I am issuing orders for the arrangement of civil matters in the capital. The news of my royal father's assassination has undoubtedly reached the city by now, and I do not wish the court convening here at this time, for reasons I shall make clear. I have had documents drawn up which provide for the transfer of authority in the capital, and I am maintaining all my father's appointed councillors and officers pending a review of records."

No one looked away from the King while he was speaking except the King's guard. He saw Efanor's face relatively complacent: a very lengthy missive had arrived at Efanor's door this morning – he had trod all around the edges of Efanor's religious sensibilities and superstitious fears, and wished him to stay at Henas'amef at least for two more months, until they could establish a sustained effort against Aséyneddin and secure the border. Leaving the capital without a head was one sort of risk. Leaving it to Efanor, with Efanor's weakness toward religious appeals, was another. Idrys had urged that such was the case, and while the realm would carry on very well and stably in the care of old Lord

Brysaulin, who though elderly and feeble was an iron-willed administrator, the realm would be in danger in the to-do surrounding a younger and obsessively religious prince unexpectedly turned up as caretaker of the realm, overturning Brysaulin's sensible decrees – which had never favored the Quinalt.

Disturb nothing that his father had set in place until it was time to take hold of it and shake it mightily, that was what he had determined: the roads to the capital were good enough – the winter would not greatly discommode them from travel to the capital once the wedding was a fact the Quinalt would have to live with, and by then –

By then he would have the border matter at least at a state he dared leave to Idrys and Cevulirn.

"Meanwhile," he continued, "the greatest change in my plans – precludes my waiting for the oath-taking of the northern barons before I pursue matters against this incursion on our frontiers. I had wished to have the winter to prepare. We are not to have that grace, I much fear, and while I had asked you, sirs, to remain here at disadvantage to your domestic affairs, I must now prepare differently. I took the crown on the field without ceremony. I have entered into agreements with the Regent of Elwynor. I have done many things –" For a moment he lost his thoughts and his breath at once. But the next breath brought the next line back. "– many things unanticipated. As King holding power from the gods I swear to them due observance and reverence, and am prepared to swear so. So I shall swear to you. So I ask you to give oaths of homage, first of all the provinces, and of fealty for yourselves as I am prepared to swear, without ceremony such as the capital could provide, so that when you part from this company of brothers and friends you will have the assurance of me, as I require of you."

There were looks, shaking of heads in amazement, a little muttering from Sovrag's lieutenants, who, with war pressing on the border, and – which they did not necessarily know – with Ynefel increasingly perilous, could not get their boats safely home. He could not permit the attempt. He had other use for those boats.

Emuin came, in his immaculate gray: his personal – Teranthine – priest, well-known to the court, now counselor to the King, bearing the battle-crown, and presenting it.

Then he could let go his careful grip on the things he had to say: then it was for Emuin to remember, and Emuin to deal with while he answered yes and I swear, and had the crown in his hand and in Emuin's.

The hall was very quiet. No one so much as coughed, the lords surely wondering by now why they had not been advised and where the trap might lie. There were the solemn bows and the oaths the Teranthine rite required. There was the setting of the crown on his head, the religiously valid coronation, which would hold valid against all claims until his death, and which settled any remote challenge to his kingship.

He called his brother first; Efanor knelt and swore the simple oath as he swore his to Efanor, confirming him as heir, in terms he had advised Efanor, against the getting of an heir of his own body. Then the officers of his household, the Marhanen custom; and third the barons, in the order their houses had sworn to his grandfather, first Pelumer, and then Cevulirn, in their true sequence. Third of ducal houses present was Umanon's, then Sulriggan's, and, far down the ordinary precedence of history, Sovrag, who, after swearing to defend the King and to be his friend, to preserve the life, the person and the honor of his sovereign, and receiving the customary vow of his sovereign to defend his life, his person, and his honor, asked if he could add the decks of his boats to his domains.

He could all but see Duke Umanon, with a port Sovrag used, gathering wind for a storm of protest: he knew the dispute on which the old pirate based his request, and the King did *not* grant it. "No," he said pleasantly, and gave Sovrag his hand to kiss.

"Don't hurt to try," Sovrag said.

"I need a brave man, riverlord. I hold you are that."

"Then we talk?" Sovrag asked.

"Swear and give me your hands, riverlord. I'll repair your boats. Or build you new ones. And hold you dear as a friend."

Sovrag gave him a look as sober as any he had had of Sovrag. He might have touched the man. "Aye," Sovrag said in a husky voice, "aye, Majesty." And kissed his hand with a grip fit to break it.

"Tristen Lord Warden of Ynefel," the next proclamation was, as Sovrag went down the steps. "Lord High Marshal of Althalen."

There was a murmur then. And he could feel the anxiousness arising among the Elwynim. But of Tristen he asked and gave only the oath of fealty, and set its term from harvest-time to harvest-time. "Annually to be renewed, an oath of friends, to save each other's life, limbs, rights and honor, before the blessed gods and by their favor." He lifted Tristen up and, embracing him, said against his ear, "Say, Before the blessed gods, and say it so they hear."

"Before the blessed gods, Your Majesty," Tristen said, and added, in his own way but with a straightforward look as clear and as knowing as ever he had heard from Tristen, "I *am* your friend."

Thank the aforesaid gods he said nothing else. Cefwyn could see the clenched jaw of Efanor's priest, and Efanor's hand tightly clenched on a prayer-book.

No one knew what oath had existed between Mauryl and his grandfather. There had been no witnesses, no priest, nothing holy. The barons were surely asking themselves where Tristen ranked in relation to lords grown old in service to Ylesuin: the Warden of Ynefel had never *been* at court, nor ever fit within the protocols.

Cefwyn embraced him a second time. "Thank you," he said into Tristen's ear, and released him.

After that, Ninévrisë in brief and in her own as Regent: "Before the gods, to bear true friendship to the land and people and the Crown of Ylesuin."

Then he dared breathe. No one had refused their oath, no one had protested, and Lord Tasien through Ninévrisë was bound. "My faithful friends," he said, and added, "truly first, as your houses were to the first of my line. I shall *not* forget who stood here, and who swore."

"No one is here to swear for Amefel," Cevulirn pointed out, "Your Majesty."

"For Amefel we do as we can," Cefwyn said under his breath. And more loudly: "Gentle lords, I shall swear for Amefel, under Ylesuin's law. Under my wardship Her Grace Duchess Orien holds the province. For one thing, we shall fortify all the bridgeheads leading to Amefel, since I take Amefel for Aséyneddin's immediate desire, rather than to attack the northern border, which would be exceedingly fool-hardy. Aséyneddin, on my best information, believes that he can peel away Amefel easily and present Ylesuin a land-bound border directly fronting Guelessar. He thinks that Amefel will defect to him as lord. I think not. He thinks we dare not arm the Amefin. I think not. We shall fortify all along the river to protect Amefin villages from Aséyneddin's threats. Her Most Honorable Grace the lady Regent will herself send to those villages jointly with me, urging them to stand fast against Aséyneddin. Those messengers go today." The politics of that joint appeal were an embarrassing fact Ylesuin was not wont to admit, one that brought mouths open and lords ready to speak, but he plunged ahead.

"We have already sent men and supplies for the fortifications; and Lord Haurydd has, by now, in company with Lord Sovrag's nephews, entered Elwynor, to reach forces loyal to the lady Ninévrisë and defeat the rebel Aséyneddin, so that the lady Regent's loyal men may set her in authority at Ilefínian."

That was a careful treading through a maze of prickly jeal-ousies: he carefully skirted any statement that credited or rewarded Ylesuin in saving the Elwynim Regency, as if fifteen men with no more than their horses and their swords were going to accomplish that. There was a murmur of dismay,

609

even indignation, among his own barons, but he refused to acknowledge it. "Lord Tasien will command the Elwynim fortification at Emwy, which we will supply. I ask that you delegate captains, my lords of Ylesuin, to command the extension of fortifications along the river, which these captains will build according to a design I shall give you." Part of those instructions involved the last-moment destruction of the bridge decks on two bridges north of Emwy. But he reserved that for Sovrag, personally.

"And instead of holding you here idle, I dismiss you now to attend matters of need in your own provinces, to return on the next full of the moon prepared to launch war against Aséyneddin. If there is an incursion sooner than that, I shall notify you to move on the instant, so you must have men ready to muster to a forced march to reach us. Leave all your baggage here, wagons, teams and drivers. We will bring them in our train. If I must call you before the appointed time, you will need all the speed you can make. I do not doubt that Lord Aséyneddin will take very hard my betrothal to the Regent of Elwynor when he hears it. We should be ready to defend all along the frontier. I do not think his attack will wait until spring. But I do not think it will be immediate: he has yet to subdue Elwynor's loyal men. He cannot move against us until he assembles sufficient force from various points in Elwynor where he is holding districts who would otherwise be loyal to the Regency. If he moves those troops out of those regions they now hold by such force and terror, they may attack at his rear. It is my earnest hope – though one on which I do not heavily rely – that a strong enough presence threatening that important bridge may distract his forces from regions of Elwynor uneasily in his grip, and encourage the loyal men of Elwynor to remove him. But if he crosses this border – as he may – at whatever point he crosses – he will face an army prepared to fight him in any season, and he will face the justice of our ally the lawful Regent."

There was silence. Even Sovrag, who had his nephews off

with Haurydd, and who had no water-route home but through Marna, had not been advised in advance of the full scope of what that night mission meant; and for the first time in recent memory it seemed not even the whisper had gotten out to the staff of exactly what he would ask. The barons were surprised, they were taking it with sober faces and likely a clear realization that they were, indeed, counting the inclusion of the Elwynim Regent against Aséyneddin, facing all-out war – costly, dangerous, and without a conquest of Elwynim towns and fields at the end of it.

"No," said Tristen suddenly. "Please. I *have* to speak, my lord King."

"Lord Tristen," Cefwyn said, feeling the whole matter lurch perilously sideways. He sought to catch Tristen's eye, and failed. "We have another matter before us. Wait. I will hear you later."

"My lord King, I know I –"

"*Wait*, I say." His voice came out harshly. He took a step and the leg shot fire. "Privately, Tristen."

"I cannot!" Tristen said. "You said I should tell you what I know. And I do know, sir." Tristen crossed the hall, reached out his hand to the map centermost on the table and laid his forefinger on what, to Cefwyn's distant observation, appeared to be the district of Arys-Emwy. "This is what must be stopped. There is the danger. He will not go to the east, not to these other two bridges, because he wants to draw you west and north, near Marna." Tristen's face was pale and glistening with sweat, and Cefwyn found fear closing like a fist about his heart, fear that Tristen was, Emuin had said it, hearing things ordinary men did not.

"And he will come," Tristen said. "He will not wait until spring – because you *are* threatening him, and he will not let you grow stronger."

He, Tristen said. And they must all think he spoke of Aséyneddin – all who did not know better. But he did know, and felt everything, all the affairs of his kingdom and his reign, slipping into ruin on a wizard's purpose.

"The plan is made," Efanor said, "and you should leave this to military men, lord of Ynefel."

Tristen's gray eyes went vague for a moment, and he turned his head and stared at the other lords, one by one as if acquainting himself with them deeply. Lastly his gaze fell on Efanor, Cefwyn could see it, with that naked quality that made it hard to endure.

"How can I tell you?" The voice was scarcely louder than a breath. "I *see* it. Here, here by Marna Wood is a narrow place. Spread this Shadow wide over the land and there are no more places where you may hold it." His hand moved over the wide frontiers of Amefel. "You must make this fortification so he will go past and straight onto the plain here. There will be no more chances to stop it. If he turns you back, you will fall as Ynefel fell. Everyone will die."

"He *is* Sihhë," Pelumer said at last. "I no longer doubt it. But let me ask, aside from the oaths we have all sworn, how *he* is disposed to us."

Tristen looked about at all of them. "I know all your lands but Olmern," he said in that hushed, strange voice. And indeed, Cefwyn realized with a chill, Olmern alone of all districts of Ylesuin was younger than a hundred years. Most had been independent kingdoms. "Yet I don't know how I am disposed toward any of you," Tristen said. "I have knowledge of the devices you wear. I know names, but – they are not your names. I only know that you must stop him here, by Emwy."

"One asks," said Lord Sulriggan's cutting voice, "where your loyalties *are* disposed, sir. With these Elwynim? Or with Ylesuin?"

"At Emwy it will not matter how I am disposed to you. Cefwyn says that I am Sihhë, but Mauryl is all my memory. Cefwyn says that the Marhanen murdered me, but I know nothing of that, since I am clearly alive. I am Cefwyn's friend. If you are his friends, you are mine. If you wish otherwise, still I wish that you were my friends. And *that* is not important, either. Your going to the river, here, is. There is an enemy all your plans are forgetting. And he is *my* enemy, and

Aséyneddin listens to him. The lord Regent knew. I think the Elwynim know. I am certain that Aséyneddin knows."

Efanor said not a thing, only made a sign against evil. As did his priest.

But Tasien: "It is at Althalen. It killed, there. It killed our lord."

"Halfwit he may be," muttered Cevulirn, "or mad, – or unnatural as the rumor is . . . but the further it spreads, and bordering Marna, the worse it is. We of Ivanor know whereof he speaks. As does Lanfarnesse. A wide battle is worse than a narrow one, if our task is to hold anything of *that* sort."

"We may move the army to that quarter," said Umanon, "and find no enemy; and then we shall have twice the difficulty. There is a certain danger in moving too soon – or committing force to one area. I agree with His Majesty. If we commit up there, Aséyneddin will immediately strike where we have no presence."

"More danger in acting too late, where they do have one," said Sovrag. "I've got cousins on boats, holding the river near them bridges, with Marna twixt them and home, and I don't see no Imormen in danger. I don't trust may be and might wi' my men, m'lord King, they're damn poor whores, might and maybe. I'm for putting an army up there, damn fast. Hell with the harvest."

"*You* may wish to hell with the harvest," Umanon said. "Those of us who obtain our honest revenues from the *land* think otherwise, sir. As happens, I should be concerned, did the general council defer action; but we all have concern for that border – as well as for what flows out of Marna. But if units from Ivanor come in with that dust and to-do, and the Amefin on the riverside are roused, what enemy there is may melt away and strike gods know where and when. There are clearly Elwynim on this side, of ill intent."

"Caswyddian of Saissonnd," said Lord Tasien, "is no longer to fear. He is dead."

"There are Elwynim rangers," said Ninévrisë, "who doubtless are on this side of the river. But most do not serve him and none of them fight in the field. They know where your forces are, I am sure, Your Majesty. But if Ynefel says the attack will come to the north, I do indeed believe him."

There were frowns. The lords were uneasy and thinking each of their own interests. Cefwyn cast a surreptitious glance at Emuin, who, damn him, had not said a thing, not to Tristen's ill-timed declaration, not to this supposition of disaster.

"Particularly difficult," said Umanon, "if we drag this out. Each man returning to his village will bear tales and discontent. A smaller, more flexible force might do more."

It was possibly good advice; and still Cefwyn had that fear, that Tristen knew what he was saying, and that Tristen – and Emuin, standing there silent as a stone – had sources beyond any of them.

"Your own counsel, lord of Ynefel," Efanor asked sharply, "or a wizard's sorcery? Where is Emuin's advice?"

Cefwyn glared at him, wordless for the instant under the witness of the others.

"Your Majesty's pardon," Efanor said, "but you are my brother, and I ask you again before these lords – abjure sorcery altogether. I have serious doubt whether it be friendly to you or to us. Stay by the plan. Do not listen to this."

"No," Ninévrisë said in that perilous silence. "I would believe Tristen. I *saw* this thing, lords of Ylesuin. I saw it. Every man with me saw it. Ask Lord Cevulirn what his captain saw. We were all witnesses. There were Shadows behind the walls, and trees broke with no one touching them, and men died."

"Your Majesty," Idrys said from behind Cefwyn's shoulder, and Cefwyn found his heart pounding. For a moment he could not answer, and then caught his breath and made his voice level and calm.

"Your concern is appreciated, brother. But Tristen's urging is *not* to use sorcery; his warning is that unholy sorcery may be aimed at *us*."

That sent more than one misgiving glance toward Tristen,

and toward Emuin, who stared, arms folded in his sleeves, at the floor of the dais.

"You and I are old friends, Lanfarnesse," Cefwyn said, feeling the whole alliance, the whole kingdom tottering. "How do you say?"

Pelumer drew a deep breath. "I have already come here on faith, my lord King. My house and the Marhanen were first to rise against the Sihhë kings. You became kings; we, your most loyal subjects on Marna's very border. I have a great respect for wizards. I've lived too near 'em, too long. I like less committing my men into any pitched battle. Lanfarnesse *will* support you with archers, the best of my men. But I much prefer the notion of fortifications."

"No," said Tristen. "They will not hold. There will no man be alive, sir. There will be substance and Shadows to fight. Enough men, *enough* men can deter even my enemy, because he has no substance without moving men to act for him, and if *his men* can be frightened, it may daunt *him*. At very least it would remove some of his strength. If the men can be stopped, it will stop him – at least in the world of substance. But you cannot replace numbers of men with walls."

"I like this not at all," Sulriggan said. "This is folly, Your Majesty. One cannot fight unholy magic with swords. Our war is against Aséyneddin. We should root out the influences – all godless influences – we should purify our land of taint and accept no advice from those who carry that vile taint into our land."

"Tristen's is advice worth listening to," Cefwyn said sharply, because, now it was launched, he had to keep his hand on its scruff and not have the Elwynim war and Tristen's war become the same thing in the lords' minds. "I suggest, sir, that we do so."

"Wizardry and Elwynim," Sulriggan muttered. "On our very souls, Your Majesty, – we –"

"A *warning* of wizardry; and these are allies opposed to intrusion into this border!"

"Heretics, Your Majesty! We cannot swear with heretics!"

"By the blessed gods whose anointing *I* bear, sir, hold allegiance to me, or count yourself forsworn. Bear faith to this kingdom's allies, or, if not, wait at your fireside for the issue, and deal with me later. And I warn you, if you fail my summons when attack does come on this province, if I go only with what Guelen and southern forces I can muster, then pray for our enemies across the river, because if I prevail, I shall be next at your gates, sir, with questions to which I shall want answers. I've *no* doubt of Lord Tristen's good will to us, and if his advice runs counter to my plans I shall still heed it and take precautions of both sorts. I will support the Elwynim who are fighting with us: it is unconscionable and *foolish* to turn away from them, and I will not! Olmern is already in a predicament: he cannot withdraw; and I think that Ivanor may stand with us. I think that Lord Cevulirn understands me."

"Aye," said Sovrag. "You do got us, m'lord King."

"You will have cavalry, Your Majesty," Cevulirn said, his thin lips taut.

"Cavalry and foot," said Umanon, "as soon as we can muster, Your Majesty."

"I shall be with you," said Pelumer heavily. "If so many fall, we have no safety, else. But I greatly fear for us, Your Majesty."

Cefwyn found himself almost trembling, angry at Pelumer, angry at Sulriggan, angry at Efanor, and tried to disguise it by leaning on the table. "Brother?"

"*Aye,* my lord King."

Gods, that infuriating, punctilious manner.

"Will you hold Henas'amef for me? Will you be my right hand here, my viceroy, to serve here and gather forces, and advise yourself what action should be taken should anything go amiss? At any time you find it wise to withdraw to the capital, do so, but I would have you here, at my back, close enough to be of help."

"As the northern lords come in, Your Majesty?"

"Yes. If needed. – My lords of Ylesuin, prepare to meet on Lewen plain in Arys-Emwy at the full moon. Sooner if we must. Give me the tallies you anticipate before you depart. Establish signal fires along the way through Amefel – we shall do the same for outlying villages – and set those men by fives, under canvas, and well supplied. The weather may turn any day and it will be a difficult, long watch for them."

Heads nodded, Pelumer's reluctantly, Sulriggan's last of all and but slightly.

The trembling did not leave his hands. Gods, gods, he thought, first thinking it was rage, and then knowing it for fear. Why am I in such haste, he asked himself, to start this menace from cover? It might bide longer and give us more time, time to bring in the northern lords. Efanor could be right . . . sometimes he is right.

Northern lords of Sulriggan's ilk, or at least men solidly Quinalt, and Sulriggan's natural allies. That arrant fool Sulriggan will politic with any situation. And dares front me, in this hall, and in peril of the realm? *He* has to fall – and soon.

"Brother," said Efanor, "by your leave I'll dispatch a messenger of our own, summoning half the Guelen levies. They can be in reserve in Henas'amef against Your Majesty's need."

He looked at Efanor's frowning face, suspecting his motives, suspecting that Efanor, with the help of such as Sulriggan, wished to protect himself and keep himself isolated from the Amefin as much as he meant to have those men in reserve for his rescue. Did he send for them in some hour of need, there even was a chance Efanor would not send them: in his worst fears, Efanor, realizing Henas'amef's defensive deficiencies and besieged by his priest, would feel constrained to secure a peace with Aséyneddin, abandon Ninévrisë, and cede heretic Amefel to the Elwynim for peace in *his* reign over provinces solidly orthodox.

But that was only supposition. And it gave too little credit to the clever little brother he had once – loved – when the enemy was their grandfather.

Efanor gave him nothing – *nothing* – of what he thought,

or agreed to, or purposed. Efanor had not ventured an opinion – except to bring in the Guelen regulars in force, which, with their officers, gave the new heir of Ylesuin a Quinalt force under his hand.

"Call them," he said to Efanor. "And call Lord Maudyn with them." That was, next Idrys, the most experienced of Ylesuin's commanders. "We dare not risk both of us. I know you would rush in if I needed you. But I forbid it. I *forbid* it, do you hear me? Send Maudyn."

Something like guilt, or was it bitter shame? touched Efanor's face and Efanor ducked his head. He clapped Efanor on the shoulder in walking down from the dais, closed his hand on Efanor's arm and pressed it. Emuin had always counseled him that if he would have the best from a man it was needful to expect that best. And (his own sullen thought) to do so as publicly as possible.

Then he walked on down the steps, taking a chance, desperately willing the leg to work – to convince the lords it would. It didn't hurt so much. He could ride in two days, he thought, with sufficient bandaging – it would heal by the next full moon.

Meanwhile Efanor's precious Quinaltines were not doing outstandingly well at praying calamity away from their borders. Call it fate, call it the actions of wizards more than one in number – he had his heart in his throat when he thought about entering battle with a very demonstrable wizardry as one of the weapons, far more demonstrable than the gods' presence on the field; and when Tristen admitted that *he* was afraid – he began to worry indeed.

Change the plans? Rely on Tristen's untutored skill? Tristen's guesses which were no guesses?

Somehow, in the push and pull of wizardry that seemed to be a condition outside plain Guelen sensibilities, Tristen might prove their worst ally or the best defense they had. The wound that kept him sleepless with pain had only happened when he sent Tristen away. His father had not died until he sent Tristen away. In constant pain, he was exhausted of mind and body and becoming outright childishly superstitious about Tristen's presence, as superstitious, he feared, as Efanor had become about his gods: he wanted to know where Tristen was. He began to feel safe only when Tristen was in his vicinity. Tristen had brought the Elwynim to him, which was more than good fortune; Tristen had brought him Ninévrisë when malign force had meant otherwise. He had never ignored Tristen's warnings except to his peril and now he took the most emphatic one entirely to heart.

He knew what Idrys must think, and he sensed Idrys' worry, when he had begun improvising on their already deliberated plans that suddenly, on as little sleep as he had had – Idrys would warn him. Idrys would have very strong things to say to him for this morning's work, though Idrys had renewed his oath without demur or question.

Meanwhile the lords must be scratching their heads, trying to figure had they witnessed a real change of plans or a maneuver cleverly devised to sweep their objections sidelong into an agreement with the Elwynim and wizardry that they would not have otherwise taken.

But he took Ninévrisë's hand, and left the hall the private way, by which they could reach the stairs, Ninévrisë to her guarded apartment, himself to his own, in search of privacy and rest. The leg, although it would stay under him, hurt so much, walking and standing on it this morning, that the pain had begun to cloud his thoughts. He was scarcely past the door when a page came running to bring him the stick, all concerned – was his misery that evident? he asked himself, and in relative private, he followed Ninévrisë and her guards up the stairs, seeking his own floor and his own apartment where he could limp and hurt and worry about whether he *could* in fact sit a horse in the requisite time. He could not send a leaderless army into a battle on the scale this required. The King had to be on a horse and on that field.

"My lord," Ninévrisë said, delaying on the steps, in her ascent to the floor above. "My lord?"

The air was cold on his face. Ninévrisë was concerned, as if he should not be trusted to carry himself down the hall. Ninévrisë – whose plans – whose life and welfare – relied on him, as everyone's did.

"Climbing steps," he said, out of breath. "Not the easiest."

"You changed what you said you would do," Ninévrisë said. It might accuse him. It might be a question. It was uncertain. He took it in the most charitable light.

"I believe Tristen," he said, leaning on the stick. "I have not entirely changed what I plan. We will still deal with the whole riverside. But if Tristen is certain enough to insist – I believe him. He knows things." It sounded foolish. He did not know how to explain.

"I think he does know," Ninévrisë said, and added, in a quiet, diffident voice: "And he *is* truly your friend. I see that. I have no doubt of you, now."

Upon which saying, she was up the stairs in a quick patter of steps, with her guards hurrying to catch up.

He was staring. He knew that his own guards were waiting, Idrys among them witnessing his drift of thought, and he bit his lip and limped off the stairs and on toward his own door.

And toward his ill-assorted guard, the disposition of whom had entered his mind this morning, but he had not wanted to give warning of his intentions.

Now he stopped and looked at the two in question, the Ivanim Erion Netha and the Olmern lad, Denyn Kei's-son. "You were given to my service," he said in a low voice. "You've paid for your trespass. I've given your lords orders to prepare for war. Ivanor is bound for a brief sojourn at home and Olmern has its boats to see to. If you will rejoin your lords, go and do so. Or remain in my service and take the field with the Dragon Guard or the Prince's Guard, at your will. I give pardon. It is without condition. Commission I also grant."

And he passed into his apartment, walked to his own fireside . . . not alone, never quite alone; he heard Idrys behind him.

I have loosed everything, he thought. I have let go all the power I gathered. Gods hope they think of no excuses and I get them back, or I am no King, and this kingdom will fall.

He looked around into Idrys' disapproving frown.

"What, Idrys? Speechless? Have I finally amazed you?"

"Leaving yourself only a few Guelen, the Olmernmen and the Amefin to guard you? I find nothing left against which to warn my lord King. You have done it all."

That angered him, so that for a moment he did not speak. Then reason came back to him and he nodded. "As you say. But occasionally I do as pleases me, Idrys."

"I am well aware."

"It is good, is it not – for a king to be generous . . . while he has a good man to watch the recipients of his generosity?"

"You have given me many causes to watch, my lord King, and in too many places for your safety or the realm's."

"I shall mend my ways hereafter. Will you leave me? You may, without prejudice. I could well use your talents in the capital."

"My lord." Idrys shook his head, with contrition in his dark eyes. "Leave you in this – I will not. Did I not swear?"

"I need you. Gods help me, you are my other nature, Idrys. What would you advise me, granted I am committed to war and have done what I have done – for very good reasons?"

"That you be very thorough in your dealing with your enemies, lord, domestic and foreign. That if you pursue this war, you leave *no* half-measures to haunt you, however prettily your bride asks. That you beware of your brother's priest and beware most of Orien Aswydd and her sister."

"And Sovrag?"

"Cannot safely negotiate Marna now. He will take orders."

"Pelumer?"

"Has never committed himself to a quarrel; smiles on all; fights for none; in the wars against the Sihhë his father sat snug in Lanfarnesse and fought by withholding forces from a Sihhë ally. Pelumer has a poor memory, m'lord."

"I did mark that."

"Otherwise, take it that Lanfarnesse is loyal as a rock is solid, – and, like a rock, will prefer to sit. Lanfarnesse rangers are another matter. They are not for battle in the field: Pelumer objects very wisely there, and did you ask him to lend you *those* men even to venture Marna, you might obtain a fair number of them. But Pelumer says this time he will commit archers in a pitched battle. I have found no reason to doubt his given word, m'lord King, and they will be well drilled."

"You confess there is one honest man in council? You confess that Tristen is telling the truth?"

"As he knows it," Idrys said, as if the irony of that were wasted on him. Likely it was not. Cefwyn waved a dismissal, sank wearily into a chair.

He had left himself nothing but war, from the time he had accepted the lady Regent's hand.

The Elwynim lords and their men were saddling up in the stableyard, the afternoon of Cefwyn's charge to them, and there were horses waiting for Cevulirn at the west door. Sovrag was off to the river, he said, to see to his boats; he had left at noon with two ox-carts loaded with cordage and pitch and another with seasoned wood. The lords of the south were all breaking camp and leaving with the same suddenness with which they had arrived, and Uwen said if one didn't want to wait forever while master Peygan the armorer took care of the other business that His Majesty had set underway, it was a very good idea to get master Peygan started as soon as possible, the proper outfitting of a young lord for war taking a fair long time.

Uwen had known Peygan for years: Peygan had come from the capital with Cefwyn and had taken over an armory in disarray – so Uwen said on their walk across the yard. "The place was full of rats what ate the leathers, and the old armorer was drunk by day and night, with accounts all in a muddle, gods, ye'd be amazed."

"What happened to him?" Tristen said.

"Oh, he took out the day we arrived and nobody's seen 'im since. The old fellow wouldn't complain, that's what I guess. That rascal Heryn was making of them books what he liked, and the old armorer knew he should have taken the business to the King, but he drank, instead, being afraid to report the state things was in. The armorers, ye may know, m'lord, is all Crown men, master and 'prentices, alike, so's ye ain't dealin' with anyone of Heryn's lot, here."

"They belong to the King?"

"Same as all the arms stored here, m'lord, in name, at least. The lords is to manage it all, and the King's armorers is to keep accounts. And accounts gets kept, now. They don't put nothing over on master Peygan. If something's broke it don't go on the rolls."

They walked up the steps, and into a place which had fascinated him and frightened him from the first day he had seen it, a place with Words echoing of War, and Iron, and Blood, a place with rows and rows of orderly weapons, displayed on the walls and in the racks, banners hanging in still array.

He wished to turn on the step now and rush out of the place, and not to take anything it offered. He disliked the mail shirt he was bidden wear, although it had saved his life. He had no desire to have any armor heavier or more extensive than he did – and most of all he dreaded the dark and metal feeling of this place.

But Uwen was to draw armor of a guard issue better than he had ever worn, which pleased Uwen mightily; Uwen was carrying a paper to that effect, which Idrys himself had given him, commissioning him into the Dragon Guard: and Uwen's enthusiasm made him think differently from moment to moment, that it was not the armor that threatened to smother him, but the constraints of purpose it imposed – and that it was not the weapons that frightened him, but the skill in his own hands.

"Heavy armor," Uwen said. "Plate and chain. If happen somebody bashes ye square down on the shoulder, m'lord, as do happen in a close tangle, or if ye catch a lance-point, a lot

623

better you should have plate. The King," Uwen added, "wouldn't be limping about now if he'd had a good Cuisse in that melee, 'stead of them damn light-horse breeches."

It was a language of its own. The names of the pieces and of the weapons did come to him, and he knew that Uwen was right, for a man who did not look to ride hard or fast.

"But," he said, while they waited for attendants in the darksome and echoing hall, "are *you* happier with it, Uwen?"

Uwen laughed. "M'lord, I'm a Guelen man. We was always the center of the line, heavy horse and foot. It ain't but since I turned gray they sent me to protect young lords who fly off in the dark wi' naught but a mail shirt and a stolen horse."

He did not think Uwen should joke about that. He knew he had been rash and he wished that Uwen would not follow him if another such moment came on him – that was the consideration Cefwyn had laid on him, by giving him Uwen.

Peygan came, welcomed them, looked at Uwen's paper and gave it to a boy who gave it to a clerk who was setting up in the entry. Master Peygan looked him in particular up and down, muttered, "Tall, sir," and with a well-used piece of cord took various rapid measurements of his limbs and across the back of his shoulders.

"I've little that *will* serve," Peygan said, then. "At least – that I'd have confidence in. His Majesty gave strict orders, and I must say, it will not be gold or gilt, Lord Warden, nor pretty nor even matched. I cannot swear to that. But quality and a right fit I do swear to."

"I've no objection, sir," he said. "As best you can, sir – light. I wish to see." He rarely objected to others' choices. But this frightened him, despite Uwen's assurances.

"A challenge, Lord Ynefel."

"Yes, sir. If you please. And whatever Uwen wants – I'd have him safe."

Peygan rubbed his chin, scratched his unruly hair – it was liberally grayed, like Uwen's; and Tristen stood watching while Peygan measured Uwen, too.

"Hmm," Peygan said, and walked off.

So he sat down to wait with Uwen for most of the next two hours, while the master armorer, clearly working on a number of requests at once, fussed and marked this and that strap his assistants would bring him, and a man Uwen said was Peygan's son sat at a bench using an array of curious implements and mallets on the fittings Peygan had marked.

In time, Peygan came back bringing an armload of pieces, and cast them on a nearby bench.

"It's old," Peygan said, of a fine piece of brigandine. "Still solid, though they say –" Peygan seemed hesitant. "They say it's Sihhë work, Lord Warden."

His fingers did not tingle when he touched it. It was black, and showed wear, and was not like what the Guelenfolk wore. But it felt right.

"M'lord," Uwen said dubiously. "She's pretty, but a lot's come and changed. She ain't modern."

"Neither am I," Tristen said. "Isn't that what they say?" He liked weapons no better, but this was the only piece that made him feel safer.

"Mostly," said master Peygan, "there's no such silk these days. They say it came from oversea. There's some as is afraid of the piece, truth to tell."

He did look, in that gray place, but it showed not at all.

"There is no harm in it," he said. "Though such things seem to come and go." It felt comfortable to the touch. He could not say the same of the mail shirt he wore. "I'd try it."

Uwen was less pleased. But he said, "I am very sure, Uwen."

Uwen gave a tilt and a shake of his head. "Might be, then, m'lord."

The straps and laces of the silk-woven brigandine were worn, and wanted work. And Uwen was still to fit out. So they waited. The armory was echoing with the comings and goings of Peygan's boys, who were, by now, with the afternoon's work in full clatter and bustle about them, counting out to Guelen and Amefin sergeants and attendants the equipment they requested, and counting in what tents and wagons and other such things the departing lords were leaving behind.

At a table near the door, master Peygan's clerks kept careful account of what went out and what went in. Carts pulled up at the door and bundles of pikes went in, long arrows by the score, as well as buckles, girths, bits, harness, pennons and odder items of equipage: all of it came in from the armory storage, and from the armory's outlying storage, and the whole flowed in past the clerk, who kept a painstaking and amazingly rapid account in various codices stacked on the table by him, while stacks of requests accumulated beside him, and a junior clerk, reading the requests, sent a score of stout armorer's boys running with apprentice clerks to read the orders.

It was a tangle, lords' pages demanding their equipment be taken to shelter immediately, since there were clouds overhead, threatening a shower, and master Peygan's clerk informing said pages that nothing would go into or out of storage without it being written fair and wide in request, which went on the stack.

Meanwhile Amefin companies were being equipped for weapons-drill, and someone was complaining about a box of buckles that had gotten set down and swept up with someone's equipment.

A clerkish young man came out lugging an armful of odd plate up to them, then, and said they were to have bards for two horses, and would he approve what he had found so he could put it with their gear.

Tristen had no idea. He had never handled horse armor, but Uwen said that it was very fine, he was sure, but they were mistaken in the number of horses unless they wanted a spare.

Meanwhile another boy came with a tablet and said he had to draw the arms for the man who was going to paint the shield, and was the device correctly displayed?

That, Tristen could answer, and had the Star set a little

larger and the Tower a little smaller above it; so the youth went off busily to inform the painter. Uwen said that likely they would stitch up a caparison for his horse and all – the horse Cefwyn had given him being still on his way in from the country, from what they knew. But the standard he would have carried before him would be the one they had unfurled in hall.

It was an amazing amount of activity, and they were often crowded upon, where they sat, so Tristen took the notion to tell the clerks where they were, and go out to the smithy which stood next door.

So they went out into the cool air and in again to the heat and smoke. He liked to watch the smiths work: he was always entranced by the sparks and most of all by the metal when it was hot and all but transparent. He hung about as long as he had an excuse, but the smiths and the wheelwrights were as harried as the armorer, since several of the lords, independently, it seemed, had been postponing work on various transport in the thought it would last until they got home. Now they were leaving the wagons here in the care of the drivers and the Crown would not count them in unless they were received in good order, so the drivers were frustrated, and felt they were put upon by someone.

It was the most amazing lot of racket, not alone the hammering, but the shouting and the arguing. And things growing hot there, and the wind shifting and carrying smoke into their eyes, they went back to the relative quiet of the armory, to sit and wait again on the bench against the wall, where at least they would not be impeding the traffic coming in and out the door.

It was a lot of standing and sitting and waiting, it was now toward supper, and he had hoped to have it over and done long since. He thought of asking Uwen to go for a book – but watching him read was dull for Uwen, so he sighed and thought otherwise.

"I've seen a lot of odd doings," someone near them was saying, "but I never thought I'd see the Elwynim for allies."

"In the winter." He knew that voice. It was Lord Pelumer. He had, Tristen thought, come in while they were gone. Pelumer was talking to someone behind a rack of equipment. "I make no secret I don't like it at all," Pelumer said.

"Wizardry, is what it is – grave-dust and cobwebs for an ally. Give me a man that has somewhat more natural in his veins, to my preferences. Ghosts and now this Elwynim bride? You have the King's ear. Urge him against this folly."

"Oh, this is the man that has the King's ear. I'm certain I don't, nowadays, sad to say."

Uwen had started to get up. Tristen prevented him with a touch on his arm. And he recognized the first voice, now, as Sulriggan's.

"If we deal with the old man of the tower, even dead, what can we look for?" Sulriggan was asking. "This Tristen is Sihhë. There's Sihhë blood all through Elwynor. Gods know what they'll do. Did you mark the bride's eyes, Lanfarnesse? Gray. Gray as I stand here."

"I confess I mislike the turn things are taking," said Pelumer. "We were neighbors to Althalen, we in Lanfarnesse. Marna Wood covers a great deal that the east has forgotten. But we remember. Some things there are that cannot be made friendly, even by their own will. I count the new lord of Ynefel as one of them."

It stung. He knew not what to do or say. Clearly they did not know he was present. Clearly they had said things they would not have said to his face and could not be comfortable with if they knew he had heard them.

Then someone said, a whisper that sounded like one of the boys that ran errands, "He's *here,* m'lords. Be careful what you say."

"Here?" He imagined them looking around, and he knew nothing now that would help matters, except to indicate to them that, indeed, he did know. So he rose from the bench, which was along a rack of axes, and confronted them with, he hoped, a mild if not friendly expression.

"Sirs," he said. "Good day."

"Spying on a body," Pelumer said indignantly.

"Hardly by intent, sir."

"I make no secret I don't like the plan you advanced, sir. I'll say that in polite discourse. I don't like assuming it will be Emwy and I don't like to start a campaign in this season."

"It will be by the new moon, sir. I might be wrong. But I believe that will be the time."

"He believes that will be the time," Sulriggan said. "Do you hunt?" Sulriggan asked. "Do you gamble? D' ye have any common pleasures, lord of the cobwebby tower? Or do you spend all your time chasing up and down the roads and making mysterious predictions?"

"I read, sir. I feed the pigeons. Such things as that." He knew that he was being baited. He saw no reason to hunt or to gamble or to be like Lord Sulriggan, which seemed to be all that Sulriggan approved.

But for some reason Sulriggan failed to seize up what he said and mock him in those terms as he expected Sulriggan to do. Sulriggan's face went quite angry and red.

And abruptly Lord Sulriggan stalked out of the armory.

"Ynefel," Pelumer said, "he had that for his due. Accept my apology, if for nothing else than indiscretion. I am sure we may differ on a question of tactics without anger."

"I am not angry, sir. I am sorry he is."

"Ynefel, you will not win that man. I listened because for His Majesty's sake I would know what he is about. Believe it or not, as you have learned me to be."

"Sir, I find no reason to doubt what you say."

The old man bit his lip and gnawed at his white mustaches, seeming unhappy, but thinking, too.

"Well, well," Pelumer said then. "He would have been mistaken to attack you at arms. I think he thought you an easier mark than that. I think he had expected to entrap you into a challenge – which is not lawful, under the King's roof, as you may recall. You possess the field, sir. I congratulate you."

Pelumer went away then, out the door, pausing to pick up some paper of the clerk at the door.

"I fail to understand," Tristen said.

"I think Lord Pelumer meant you scairt His Grace who left," Uwen said. "Meanin' Sulriggan ain't the fool altogether. That 'un wasn't on the field at Emwy. That 'un come in after all was done, and settled in wi' Prince Efanor. He ain't seen you fight, m'lord. But I think he knows now he was in deep waters."

He wished he understood, all the same. That the man did not like him hardly surprised him. But that the man wanted to fight him did not make sense. That the man wanted to entrap him and to discourage Cefwyn from friendship with him – that, he did see. He didn't know if it was fair to warn Cefwyn. It seemed to him that there were intricate Rules to govern men's behavior, and to govern what they told authority about and what they did not and settled unto themselves.

He did not know those Rules. He only saw they existed. He was quite, quite stunned by Sulriggan's kind of malevolence. But Hasufin's sort of harm and this man's seemed to have tactics in common, and he found it worrisome this was the man who stood closest to Efanor, except only Efanor's priest.

Efanor did not, over all, like him, and at least this one man, possibly with Efanor's knowledge, possibly without it, was going about quietly trying to turn Pelumer to their side, too.

He was not certain where Fairness lay, in this – whether it was Fair for him to tell Emuin, who would surely tell Cefwyn, and that would make trouble with Efanor, which would make Cefwyn unhappy, when Cefwyn had enough pain.

It seemed something he could deal with. It seemed at least the man had gone in retreat.

So it was not something he chose to tell Cefwyn, in the meeting they had. And Cefwyn was not angry with him. Tristen was very glad of that. He had gone to Cefwyn's door specifically to apologize for interrupting him in council, but Cefwyn took his hand and said it was very well, he had been right to speak out under the circumstances. And Cefwyn had asked him in and shared a cup of tea with him, and directly asked him about the armor, which he said was very fine.

Then Cefwyn told him he had ordered Haman to make a choice of horses for Uwen as well, since, as Cefwyn said, for the King's pride he could not have the chief of personal guard of a lord of Ylesuin drawing his mounts at random from the stables. He gave Uwen the horses and their upkeep, the written order said, as long as Ynefel stabled horses at Henas'amef.

It was a very handsome gift, Tristen had no difficulty in recognizing that. It was another in the succession of gifts Cefwyn had poured out on him in the context of his betrothal to the lady, and he did not know altogether what it meant. "If I had any means," he said to Cefwyn, troubled and embarrassed, "I would provide for him. I understand what I should do, and I cannot, and I am very grateful."

"If I had any desire to weigh you down with the administration of a province," Cefwyn said, "I swear I would bestow Amefel on you and send Orien Aswydd packing. As it is, I find it a very modest upkeep for an entire province of Ylesuin. The horses have come in, Haman advises me. You will need, of course, grooms, standard-bearers, *their* horses and upkeep. And upkeep for your servants."

He could scarcely conceive of it – or understand what Cefwyn was doing to him: pushing him out on his own, perhaps, which was not unkind, and perhaps even timely; but he still had the suspicion that gifts and generosity came before bad news and parting.

"I am not a lord in any useful sense. I hardly need more than Uwen."

"Oh, you are *far* more useful and far less expensive than, say, Amefel. How did you find Orien? Civil? Or otherwise?"

"Idrys told you."

"Oh, my dear friend, Idrys indeed told me. And I wish to know if you have any complaint against her."

"I know that I shouldn't have gone there. I was there before I knew that. But her guards were wiser than I was: they told Idrys and he came for me."

"Idrys says you made it out on your own," Cefwyn said. "Which is far more sense than I had."

That was a joke, but Cefwyn did not laugh, and Tristen did not. He did not think of anything to report that Cefwyn did not know, but he did not think he could as freely forgive Orien the way he had forgiven the gate-guards and Idrys and all the people who had done him harm of one kind and another. Orien's action seemed somehow more mindful and of a purpose he did not wholly guess, nor wish to. But he tried to guess.

"I have no idea what she wanted," Tristen said, and Cefwyn looked at him oddly.

"I believe *I* know," Cefwyn said, as if he were being a little foolish, even for him. But beyond the evident conclusion, he thought it far more than a ploy to lure him to – what he only dimly visualized. Still, he did not wish to launch into that discussion tonight, for Cefwyn seemed very tired, certainly in pain, and should go to bed. "I'll deal with Orien," Cefwyn promised him. "I am very aware of her displeasure."

"You should rest," Tristen said.

"I fully intend to," Cefwyn said, and declared his intent to go to bed like a good betrothed husband, after which Tristen made his excuses and withdrew across the hall to his own apartment.

Cefwyn had seemed in increasing pain since last night, and that was hard to watch as well as disheartening for their preparations. He could not imagine of his own experience how acute the pain of such a deep wound was, but Cefwyn's face had been quite pale, at the last, and damp with sweat. Tristen wished – desperately wished – that he had Mauryl's ability to take the pain away and to heal the hurt; but he did not.

And worry over Cefwyn might have put him out of the mood to have supper, except Uwen was so entirely delighted and overcome when he heard about the horses and the King taking a personal interest in him, it was hard to remain glum.

So he took supper in his sitting room with Uwen and the four servants, who were, since he had come back from Althalen, very willing to linger by the table and gossip. He learned, this evening, for one thing, that Lord Sulriggan's personal cook had had a dish turn up very, very salty at the betrothal feast, and Lord Sulriggan called it witches, but the servants thought it likelier the scullery-lads.

Tristen found himself laughing, in far better humor than he had begun. He felt a little guilt, because it was a misbehavior, but not harmful; and by now the servants and Uwen probably had traded stories, so Lord Sulriggan's discomfiture in the armory would probably make the rounds, too – and find especial appreciation in the kitchens.

Opinions about Ninévrisë were also making the rounds of the staff: there was a deep curiosity about a woman who would be, if not queen, still, the next thing to it. The general opinion the servants gave – far more cautiously – was that she was a very kind, a very gracious lady, who, moreover, politely had not complained of a wool coverlet, though her skin could not bear anything but lambswool: it came of being a princess, the staff said, and the servants had had to send after more linens to case all the blankets until they could find proper ones.

Tristen was duly appalled that such information was a matter of common gossip, but Uwen reminded him what he had said to him from the beginning, that a lord's reputation among the servants was just as important as that he achieved among his peers – because it rapidly *was* among his peers. So Ninévrisë was well begun, at least with the staff, who thought her very proper and very accepting of the staff's good intentions.

There was a muttering of thunder as they finished supper. The clouds today had gone over with no more than a spit of rain, and would shed their burden on Guelessar. The farmers of the south and west were doubtless happy, and so, doubtless, would be the lords and their men who, leaving their tents with the baggage, had started home to their own lands.

Tristen for his part thought it a good night to sit by the fire, and in that comfort, still thinking of Cefwyn's misery, he took it in mind to try just a little magic, foolish as the attempt might be, to see if it worked for him at all. Cefwyn's well-being was something he wanted very much – and that might help. Mauryl had said it was easiest to make things what they wanted to be.

So he lit the candles in his room – he always thought of his bedchamber that way, *his* room, as opposed to the outer room where the servants came and went and where Uwen sat and talked with them, or talked with the off-duty guards. Usually the doors stayed open between the rooms, but he shut his tonight, saying that he would retire early and manage for himself, so the servants and Uwen could play dice or what-ever they pleased.

He took his Book from the shelf and sat down to read by firelight, the page canted toward the warm glow, and after a little, he looked into the fire as sometimes Mauryl had done, and made pictures to himself in the fire as he had used to do. He saw mostly faces, that suddenly seemed to him like the faces of Ynefel, which was not at all what he wanted to conjure.

He tried to think of Cefwyn, instead, and of Cefwyn's wound being well. Mauryl had done it so effortlessly, and he wanted so much, just, for a beginning, for Cefwyn to be able to rest without pain, and to walk without pain.

A wind gusted up, and came down the chimney, fluttering the fire. He did not like that.

Then he heard a rattle at the window-latch.

He liked that far less.

He shut the Book. Then came a tapping at the glass, which he had never heard, and could not imagine what it was in the middle of the night, on the upper floors, until he thought, as he had not thought in some number of nights, about Owl.

He rose from the fireside, Book in hand, and went over to

the window. The tapping kept up, in a curious pattern, and in the light coming from inside the room, he could see a pigeon on the narrow, slanted window-ledge.

He had left the bread out earlier. But it was an odd time for pigeons to be after it. He could not think that it was natural behavior, and the bread was, he saw in that same outflow of light, gone from the ledge.

Tap. The bird pecked the windowpane, perhaps attracted by the light. Tap-tap. It lost its balance on the narrow ledge and used its wings to recover.

Tap. Tap-tap.

It sounded more frantic. Tap-tap-tap. Tap-tap. It wanted in. It was a bird he knew. Perhaps for some strange reason it had decided to take his offerings of food from his hand and wanted him to feed it. But he would have to open the little windowpane, and he hesitated to do that.

He tapped the glass with his fingernail to see if that would deter it. Silly bird, he thought. But it hammered the glass with its beak, more and more frantically, beating with its wings. Then it dived away into the dark.

That was very odd, he was thinking; and of a sudden the bird came flying out of the dark and hit the window so hard it left feathers stuck to the glass. It was gone. It had fallen into the dark – broken. He could see in the light from the window a smear on the glass and its soft down stuck there.

He was shaken.

More, he knew who was responsible, and that it was a prank, nothing but a wretched, cruel prank, using a creature he had taught to trust that window for good things.

He was angry. He was very angry.

– *Hasufin,* he challenged the dark and the Wind. *That was not brave. It showed me nothing new about you. I have met a man like you, vain, and sneaking, and a liar.*

– *It was only a bird,* the Wind said. *You should worry about other things.*

Hasufin was trying to scare him. The latch rattled and the pane rocked back and forth.

– You have much more to lose than this, the Wind said, and with a thump at the windowpane, it was gone.

Then it began to rain, a brief spatter that showed drops against the pane, and washed away the feathers and the blood.

CHAPTER 30

❧

The next was one of those silken satin mornings, the sort with puddles in the yard, the air smelling fresh, and clouds of pink and silver trying to be gold – it was impossible, in Uwen's cheerfulness, to be down-hearted; and Uwen was right: it was a good morning to nip down the back stairs and through the warm and noisy kitchens, to beg their breakfast still warm from the ovens, bread too hot to hold, with abundant butter, and mugs of tea the kitchen girls brought them on the steps. The bread and the tea alike sent up steam in the nippish morning air and the warm air from the kitchens carried smells almost as good as tasting them.

He decided not to worry Uwen about the bird. Uwen wanted to talk about horses, excited and trying to contain it. So was he looking forward to the trip down to the pastures, and once the mugs went back to the kitchen, they headed out to the stables in the morning chill.

He rode out on Petelly, and Uwen on a bay, Gia, that was his favorite – but today Gia was Uwen's horse, for good, as Petelly was his; and the pleasure Uwen had in the fine-looking bay was that of a man who, Uwen said, had never owned his own horse, and never looked to own one at all, let alone one so fine as this.

"So ye brought me luck, m'lord," Uwen said. "Tell His Majesty, because he don't share converse much wi' me, of course, that I'm glad, I'm very, very glad, and I won't for the life of me make him sorry he was so generous."

"I shall tell him so," Tristen said. They rode down through the gate and down the main street, among the first abroad on this all but eerily quiet morning. The Zeide court had been cluttered with business yesterday, but now they rode all the way to the main gate seeing nothing but a handful of early wagons and the craftsmen opening their shops.

They rode out the gates and there was nothing but trampled ground and a small camp of wagons and horses where
the camps of the lords had stood. The mud was deeply
tracked, showing the tracks of all the horses taking out in
their various directions home, some south, some east.

But strangest of all, the trees – the trees had gone overnight
to red and brown, as the grasses had already gone to gold and
pale browns.

"The border lords are all leaving," Tristen said as they rode
along the wall eastward, toward the pastures. "It looks so
bare. It frightens me, Uwen. The leaves – the leaves are all
dying."

"Why, lad, of course they die. It's autumn."

"Autumn?" It was a word of brown and falling leaves.
Like Winter. Like snows white and deep.

"Aye, lad. Of course."

"But they come back."

"In Spring? Of course they do."

Uwen laughed and he felt foolish. Of course they did. He
suddenly apprehended that they did. It was far rarer nowadays that a Word that vast came leaping up at him out of
something constantly underfoot and never, till then, comprehended. But of course it was autumn, and the nip that had
been in the air was part of those changes, and Snow might
come. He was fascinated by the thought.

And there, in a set of stallion paddocks insulated from each
other by tall hedges and strong fences, they had brought in
the heavy horses, huge creatures with platter-sized feet and
heads the size of apple baskets – wonderful, powerful creatures he had seen hitherto only in scant numbers: Cefwyn's
big black, Kanwy, and Umanon's gray, both of which the
grooms had exercised in the practice yard.

They dismounted at the stables that lay alongside the
paddocks and some distance down the lane, leaving Petelly
and Uwen's bay in the care of one of Haman's boys, and
walked down the high-hedged lane in the direction the boy

told them, deep into this maze of paddocks separated by old hedges. In the paddocks they passed, boys with buckets were grooming and clipping and braiding the manes of several of the horses; and in one, a farrier and a number of apprentices and grooms were tending feet and seeing to the immense shoes the heavy horses wore – not an easy job, as it looked: the horse in question was not wanting to put his foot up.

They were watching that, when an old man on a pony rode up behind them to say the horses they wanted were right along next, and to come with him.

The next hedged paddock, that at a crossing of lanes, held a horse so like Kanwy that Tristen at first thought that was the horse he was seeing – a huge black fellow with abundant feather over vast feet. The horse looked up, and there were no eyes, just a nose under a huge fall of hair, with ears coming through it. He had to laugh.

"He wants clipping," the man said, having slid down beside them. "His name is Dys . . . Dysarys, but we call him Dys. His Majesty's Kanwy is his full brother, and their sister, Aryny, she's staying up in the hills: His Majesty don't risk her, no, Lord Warden. I'll hail up his trainer."

The old man led the pony down a side lane on that errand. Tristen put out his hand, and Dys came over to smell his fingers and look him over from the secrecy of his fall of bangs.

"Gods, he's fine," Uwen said reverently. "Pretty, pretty lad."

He knew Uwen most wanted to see what they had for him. He reached out his hand further, and Dys went off with a flip of a thick tail, kicking up immense heels.

The trainer came walking up from the paddock next, a middle-aged man who introduced himself faintly as, "Aswys, m'lord. I come with 'im, and hopin' to stay with 'im a while, courtesy of His Majesty. I'm trainer to Dys, here, and to Cassam, next over, who's to be your man's horse."

"I would be very pleased, sir," Tristen said. "Thank you." The horse had come over again, clearly accustomed to the trainer, who patted the huge neck that extended across the rail at this gate-end of the paddock. He did not think, regarding taking Aswys along with the horses, that he needed doubt Aswys' skill: Cefwyn would not have a man who was not competent, and he saw nothing in the way the man looked at the horse that told him otherwise.

"He's hard mouthed," Aswys said, "if ye have a hard hand, m'lord, but if ye go a little easy, he'll heed ye far better." The trainer was worried, Tristen heard that, and saw it on his face. "Should I saddle him up, m'lord, by your leave?"

The trainer wished him to ride and not wait until later. The trainer hoped he would like the horse and appreciate him. The man was, if anything, very proud and fond of this horse that he could never own, and Cefwyn had given Dys away to a lord with no land and – Sulriggan had said it yesterday – no good reputation.

"Do, please," he said, and the trainer looked at least moderately encouraged, and ordered the boys to fit Dys up with his tack while he showed them the other horse in his charge.

That pen held a blue roan gelding that Cefwyn had bestowed on Uwen, a bow-nosed fellow with a beautiful satin coat; Cassam was, their guide and now trainer said, also of the King's stable, not related to Kanwy or Aryny, but out of a Marisal mare and a Guelen stallion.

"Can we have 'im under saddle, too, sir?" Uwen asked hopefully, and while they arranged that, Tristen went back to the other paddock, where at that very moment the thump of large feet hitting the mud beyond the hedge told him Dys was not accepting saddling quietly.

As he came back in view, Dys was snuffing the air, then came across the pen at a run, appearing to move slowly, by the very size of him, but carrying himself lightly all the same.

And the boys went over the fence.

Then the trainer came back and whistled at him, ducked through the fence and whistled again. Dys came trotting up and let himself be caught. The trainer buckled a chain to his halter, jerked it as Dys snapped peevishly at the boys that brought the tack through the fence, not intending to strike them, Tristen marked that as he leaned on the top rail. Dys did not like strangers in his paddock; and Dys was a fretful horse even while the saddling went on in the hands of a man he trusted. Dys observed everything about every movement around him, and wanted to keep all strangers including the one at the fence where he could see them: his skin shivered up his forelegs, his nostrils were wide, and even from where Tristen was standing he could see that Dys had begun to sweat.

And the trainer had known it when he sent the boys in – arranging to *show* m'lord what a young and stubborn lord might not heed in the way of warnings.

This lord heeded. The trainer called him over. Tristen ducked through the fence, keeping clearly in Dys' sight, and Dys, snorting and snuffling as he walked up, lowered his head and stretched out his neck to smell him over. Dys was interested in his fingers and his coat as they brought up the mounting block.

He did not believe the calm for a moment. "Give me the brush," he said, and took it from the trainer and went over Dys' shoulder and neck and patted him. He ran his hands over Dys' legs and, trustful at least of the mail shirt he had on under his coat, let Dys smell his back and around his face.

Then he quietly took the reins and with a quick use of the block, rose into the saddle.

Dys moved out a few paces and turned a quiet circle, wanting more rein, maneuvering to have his way. And did not get it.

It was different than riding Gery's light, quick motions. But a Name almost came to him, a Name, not a Word; and as they picked up speed around the enclosure, Dys answered his call for this lead and that, shaking his neck when the pressure went off the reins. The boys opened the paddock gate and they went off down the lane between the pens, the boys and a stray, yapping dog chasing after.

Trees passed in a screen on either hand. They went as far as the sheep-meadow beyond, and he asked turns of the horse, while the foolish dog, outdistancing the boys, nearly came to grief: Dys kicked out unasked, clipped the hound, and turned, and the dog after that kept his distance as Dys made long passes and turns across the meadow.

Then Tristen gave him a free run, which happened to be to the west, toward Ynefel, and the thought came simply to run and run and run, and somehow to escape, and to take Dys, too, where he need not do what all his existence aimed at doing – to be safe, and free, and doing no harm. He began to like this horse – but not what his training had made him; and what they both were created to do.

But they reached the end of the meadow, and a fence; and when he rode back again, Uwen was out with the roan gelding.

Dys accepted his stablemate quite reasonably. There was a little to-do, a little fighting the rein; but they rode out together for some little distance, and Dys began taking the rein very well, changing leads with ease, making nothing of rough ground, quite willing to have the roan behind him or beside him on either hand.

They were out for long enough for the horses to work up a good sweat, and, mindful that the horses had been moved in yesterday, and on the road for days, they rode back again, the horses breathing easily, shaking themselves and seeming to have enjoyed the turn outside.

The trainer did not doubt either of them now, Tristen thought, when he turned Dys back to him at the paddock gate. And one of the boys said, not intending to be overheard, Tristen was sure, that the Sihhë were known to bewitch horses, and he had bewitched that one.

After that, for, in anticipation of dealing with horses and mud, neither of them had worn their best, they took a hand in the unsaddling and the brushing-down, to the amazement of the boys who usually did such things for lords and their men.

But by then Aswys was talking to them both, going on at

length about how Dys had been foaled late in the season and how Cass, for so they called the blue roan, had been one of those horses into everything – had gotten himself up to his neck in a bog when he was a yearling and fallen in a storm-swollen stream the next year: "Keep 'im away from water," was Aswys' advice on Cass. "He'll drown, but he's too stub-born to die."

Tristen liked Aswys. Aswys had gone from guarded, worried, and unhappy to a man, as Uwen put it, they'd drink with: a Guelen man, moreover, Uwen said. Not that the Amefin lads hadn't the knack with the horses, but, Uwen said, Guelenfolk and the heavy horses talked a special language.

And Uwen was very pleased with Cass, as he himself was with Dys, though he was still taken with Petelly, and made it clear to Petelly, as they rode up to the gates again, that he was still in good favor. Uwen said, regarding Cass, that he was the best horse he'd ever had under him.

"I do like the big 'uns," Uwen remarked as they rode through the streets. "There ain't no foolery about 'em. But if you ever get one hard-mouthed, gods, I rode one once in my foolish youth, the grooms was tryin' to saddle and he took down a shed with both heels and dragged me an' four boys through the fence. Gods, I hated that horse. I rode him four years, till a damn Chomaggari ran him through the heart. And I cried me eyes out."

It was, Tristen believed, all the truth. And they went up to the hill for baths and a change of clothes, and talked horses for hours.

Uwen was the happiest he had ever known him. And Tristen sat down while Uwen watched and wrote a note to Cefwyn, saying how pleased they were, and how fine the horses were. The door guards when Uwen delivered it said that Cefwyn was sleeping, which was good, and that Emuin had given him a sleeping-potion to achieve it – which was not good.

But Tristen thought that Cefwyn would be glad to have the note, or any other expression of cheer, and for what it was worth, he sat down by the fire and wished Cefwyn well, as hard as he could.

That evening he shut his inner doors again, wanting quiet – and leaving Uwen the chance to come and go on his own business. He had saved a little bread from yesterday, and set it out for the pigeons that frequented his window – but they were shyer than usual, and perhaps afraid. There might be the smell of blood about the window, for all he knew. He waited a little while, then gave up and in the fading sunlight laid out both his Book and Mauryl's little kit on the table.

It had occurred to him that Mauryl had given him both gifts, and that more than the Book might be magical – or, a new thought, it might take both gifts together.

But the mirror was only a mirror, silver polished bright; and it reflected only himself, Tristen no-one's son, and not any dreadful Sihhë lord, and certainly no potent magician.

He mused over perhaps going to Emuin with Book and mirror in hand and asking him – if he knew precisely what he would ask, or in what way the two might be connected. He had been foolish once today, although Uwen had laughed at him very gently about the falling leaves. Certainly he couldn't take for granted that he understood things as ordinary folk did.

But no understanding came to him – and the mirror, reflecting the evening sun, made no sense. He stared at the Book, and he leafed through it, and all it did was call back, in its aged parchment and battered, worn leather, memories of Ynefel, which he told himself were dangerous in the extreme.

He caught then what he thought was Emuin's presence, although Emuin had been very strict and at him instantly if he transgressed into the gray space. He had an impression of many candles, and of pain in the joints, and thought that Emuin might be at his prayers, somewhere nearby, perhaps just a slippage.

But underlying that, he caught the touch of some other

presence, and guessed that it was Ninévrisë thinking on what he was not sure, but he feared she was thinking of Althalen, which was dangerous.

– *Be careful,* he wished her.

And the presence went away, either afraid or guilty.

She was very beautiful. She was very sensible, for as young as she was, and she was brave. He wanted to see her. He wanted to talk with her, even to tell her about the horses, and – to talk to her about the gray place, and about discovering the hazards there, because he knew that she had good sense, and he wanted the opinion of someone else who had something in common with him. He found her his safe doorway to the mysteries women posed him – he wanted just to sit and look at her very closely, as he had begun, today, to look at the autumn; he wanted to listen to her, and let unfold to him, in what seemed a far kinder, more truthful person than Orien Aswydd, all the things she was.

But he could not go visit her. Propriety did not allow that: he was a man, and she was the King's betrothed; and that was the way things would be – men could not, apparently, be alone with the lady. Even Cefwyn could not be, until they were married; and after that, he was not certain. She would always be Cefwyn's: that was the way of men and women getting together – *natural* men, he said to himself with a wounded feeling of which he could not rid himself. Natural men – not, as Sulriggan had said, grave-dust and cobwebs.

And what could Ninévrisë or anyone really see in him but that? What could anyone see, who did not, for reasons of what he knew, like Cefwyn, or for reasons of being ordered to attend him, like Uwen, forgive what he was first off? Those who knew him long enough seemed to get over their fear; but all men were afraid of him. Ninévrisë had been afraid at first.

And once she was with Cefwyn – Cefwyn had so little time, he would surely give a great deal of it to her. So possibly he *would* lose both of them – or at least they would have very little time to spare. So Cefwyn was giving him gifts and making it possible for him to be on his own.

It was good that he would have Uwen. But did everybody go away, always, in an abundance of gifts, just when things seemed most settled and happy?

Maybe it was the morose and distracting character of that thought, maybe it was just general distraction, but something was nagging at him as he tried to read, and he could not make up his mind what it was.

It did not feel quite like Ninévrisë. He feared it was something much more to do with Ynefel and Althalen, and he tried on that account to ignore it – although – if he could judge at all, it came from the east rather than the west, where Althalen was: it felt easterly the way Emuin had always seemed to have direction in his thoughts.

Then – quite a sharp hurt pierced his skull, right at the base of his neck, and he clapped a hand there, jolted forward against the table-edge by what became a sickening pain. He had never felt anything quite the like. He felt ill, and smelled candle-wax, as if candles had spilled over. He felt hazed, and scarcely able to breathe.

There was stone. Gray stone. A silver eight-pointed star.

– Master Emuin, he asked, daring the gray space, for it was not ordinary, what was happening to him, and it involved candles. He seemed to hear voices echoing. He saw blue lights fixed at intervals. He saw the Sihhë star blaze with a white, ominous light, and he heard footsteps echoing in some stairwell.

He caught breath enough to stand, steadied himself against the table, and went out to the other room, past the startled servants, and to the foyer. Uwen had gone down to the kitchens, the guards said, when he went outside and inquired.

"Is something wrong, m'lord?" one asked.

"I don't know. Do you know where master Emuin is?"

"He hain't been by here, m'lord. The brothers was about, but they went back downstairs and he wasn't with 'em."

Emuin had no constant guard, such as he and Cefwyn did. Emuin's rooms were just down the hall, under at least the watch of the guards at his and Cefwyn's doors, and he went and rattled the latch, hoping the old man was all right, perhaps only having a bad dream. But no one came to the door, and he opened it, his own guard quickly getting before him to make a quick search of the premises.

"Ain't no sign of 'im, m'lord," the guard said.

By then he was very concerned. "I think we should set the downstairs staff to looking."

"Is summat wrong, m'lord?"

"A pain. A hurt. – A place with candles, many candles."

"A shrine," one said, which was perfectly reasonable. "We can send down to the Teranthines, m'lord."

"Do," he said. "Ask the brothers. They might know."

The brothers did not know. The Teranthines in the courtyard shrine didn't know. By the time the guards had come back with that upsetting report he had long since asked the guards at Cefwyn's door what they had seen, and, none of them wishing to rouse Cefwyn from his scant rest, one of them had gone to Lord Captain Kerdin, who set a more general search underway, and who came to ask questions of him as to what he had seen or heard or what reason he had to fear for Emuin's well-being.

The pain in his head was constant, and disturbing. So was the smell of candles and damp, where it was not the surroundings about him.

Then Idrys came upstairs, and heard what was happening.

"The Bryalt shrine," Idrys said the instant he heard the word candles, and sent one of Cefwyn's guards, Denyn, running downstairs and out in that direction.

Idrys went down the stairs more deliberately, and Tristen tagged him, his skull aching with that stabbing pain. He was beginning to be very afraid, in a way he could not explain to Idrys, who had never been over-patient with vagueness and bad dreams; but Idrys was at least heeding him, and led the way down the east main stairs, and down again to a door he had not found in all his early explorations. It led down two turns and outside to a little courtyard that must be almost within the shadow of the – he had been told – unused East Gate. Inside that courtyard was a very old building, modest and plain: the granary and warehouses he had once visited towered over its courtyard wall.

They entered a cool, dank interior, with voices echoing in just such a tone as he had heard. "This is the place," Tristen said, "this is where," as a handful of Bryaltine monks came hurrying along a columned aisle that disappeared down a narrow, dimly lit stairs.

"You!" Idrys said sharply, and the monks flinched and bowed, their faces largely hidden by their hoods.

"Lord Commander," one such shadow-faced monk said, opening hands in entreaty. "Master Emuin – he's slipped and hurt his head. Please. One of your men –"

Idrys was past them before the man finished. Tristen followed him, down and down the stone steps, where the smell of damp and candles matched exactly what he had been smelling. The pain in his head was acute, all but debilitating, so that he had to follow the wall with his hand to know where he was. He could scarcely see, at the bottom of the steps, where Emuin lay in the arms of a Bryaltine monk – awake, he thought, but there was a great deal of blood about, and blood down the shoulder of Emuin's robe, blood all over the monk and the guard – the guard Idrys had sent was there, trying to help.

"Master Emuin." Tristen dropped to his knees and touched Emuin's hand, saying, in both worlds at once, *"Sir. Do you hear me?"*

The Shadows were close about, dangerous and wicked. Emuin was trying very hard to tell him something. He gripped Emuin's hand, and it seemed very cold in the world of substance, hard to feel in that of Shadows.

"Tristen," Emuin said faintly. *"The Shadows. A wicked – wicked – thing –"*

Idrys knelt, seized Emuin's shoulder and turned him to see the back of his head, moving the bloody hair and a wad of blood-soaked cloth out of the way. What he saw made him grimace. "Get the surgeon. Damn it, fool – run!"

The guard ran. There was so much blood. There was so very much blood.

– We have sent for help, Tristen said, holding to Emuin in the gray place. Master Emuin, be brave. Stay with me. Stay. I shall not let you go.

In that place Emuin was listening to him. Emuin said, I saw it coming. I was trying to find a way – trying to find what his attachment is – he has a Place. He's found his open door. Be careful, be careful.

He would not let Emuin die. He had lost the lord Regent. This time he recognized that black brink and the threads of darkness for death itself, and he fought with all that was in him.

Men came and men went, and finally Uwen shook at him, saying he had to let go of master Emuin because the surgeon had come and had to sew the wound.

He let go. He had difficulty even yet seeing through the murk. The little chamber with all its candles seemed unnaturally darkened. Candle flames burned with all ordinary vigor and yet did not shed light onto the stone around him. When they went outside Uwen kept hold of his arm. When they took Emuin into the Zeide and upstairs he walked behind. When the surgeon worked, he sat outside and tried to think of Emuin being well, that being all that he could do.

Emuin never quite lost awareness, but it was very low. When the surgeon let them all come in, Emuin looked so very pale, so very weak. He had a bandage around his head. The surgeon talked to Idrys in quiet tones and said the bone was broken and most such did not heal.

But Emuin was listening, lying in his bed, and looked very weak, and very pale. Tristen paid no attention to the surgeon and Idrys. He went to the bedside. Emuin was distraught – afraid, he was aware of that, and kept reciting poetry, or some such thing.

– *Prayers*, Emuin gave him to understand, then, and there was something bitter and something frightened about him at the same time. *I gave up wizardry. I gave it up to find another way. And I've grown old in the world. I let myself grow old to find some sort of holiness, and I'm not what I was. I can't fight your enemy. Forgive me, boy. All that's left now is to step off that brink and hope there's something there.*

– *No!* he said angrily. *No, master Emuin. I need you.*

– *You've no damned right to need me! To hell with it, to hell with it. I grow so weary – so very tired –*

"Ask him," a cold voice said – Idrys, he thought – "ask him if he fell, or if it was an accident."

– *Was it an accident, master Emuin?* he asked faithfully, and:

– *Hell if I know. That's just like the man. Master crow, always picking bones, looking for trouble. Cefwyn and Efanor. Clever boys. Both – very clever lads . . . damned brats. Did you know they loosed three sheep in the great hall?*

"He doesn't know what happened," Tristen said quietly to Idrys, unable to see him, but knowing he was there. He grew afraid, and squeezed Emuin's hand until he feared it hurt, but the brink seemed nearer to both of them. *You're too close, sir. Please come back.*

– *It's my peace, damn you! I've earned it. Let me go.*

– *No, sir. No! Cefwyn needs you. Listen to me.*

– *I am, I confess it, are you satisfied? a very bad wizard. I'm old, I'm out of practice, out of patience, I can't do these things any more, that is my dreadful secret. No, the worse one is, I never was any good. Mauryl knew it. Don't look to me. I've one chance – one chance, that the gods do exist, that salvation is there, and it's my only hope, boy, it's the only hope I have left. You heard them. By nature, I shan't get well from this. If I heal myself, I can only do it by wizardry – and I should be damned. I've done murder, and I'm old. I shall be damned.*

He knew nothing of damnation. He saw Death coming, a

650

black edge Emuin was willfully seeking, and he would not have it. You will get well, sir. You are the only one. I tried to help Cefwyn. I could do nothing! I could never –

There was a tumult somewhere outside. He could not tell what it was. He ignored it until he saw, in the world of substance, Emuin look toward the door or attempt to. "Fire," someone was crying, and Idrys was on his feet. "Fire, captain, there's smoke all through the hall!"

"Damn," he heard from Emuin, an exhalation of breath as much as a word. The next was stronger. "Cefwyn?"

There *was* a smell of smoke, however faint, that he had taken for a draft from the fireplace. He heard doors open and close. He saw Idrys leave in haste. He felt disturbance from master Emuin and even through the closed doors heard Idrys shouting at someone in the hall. Emuin was afraid. Emuin was aware, through him, if no other way.

He left Emuin's side and went out through the several doors to the hall, where Uwen was. Servants were standing up and down the hall, all looking anxiously toward the endmost, servants' stairs, where smoke was billowing up. The kitchens, it might be: that was where most chance of fire was, down below and on that face of the building.

"M'lord," Uwen said, looking, it seemed, for orders, but he had no idea what to do. It was too much disaster at once. They perhaps should move Emuin and Cefwyn to safety – but Emuin could scarcely bear more jostling about; and he had no idea which direction was safe.

"Where is it?" he asked, and no one seemed to know. He headed for the main stairs, which were still free of smoke. Uwen wanted to come with him, but he said, "Stay above. Don't let the servants leave. We may have to carry Emuin and Cefwyn downstairs. I'll find out."

He hurried alone for the central stairs, those past Cefwyn's room, supposed Cefwyn's guards, absent from their posts, were inside with him, perhaps preparing to take him to safety, and he was halfway down the steps when he heard Cefwyn call out to him from above.

651

"Tristen! What's burning?"

Cefwyn, without his guards, was standing in a dressing-robe, holding to the newel at the landing. He began to answer, but all of a sudden Cefwyn just – fell down, and his hand slipped on the steps, and he kept falling.

Tristen raced up the steps and stopped Cefwyn in his arms, but there was blood on the steps and blood on him, and Cefwyn had fainted.

Booted feet came running down the steps from above him. "M'lord, –" Uwen began, bending to offer help.

"Where are his guards?"

"I don't know, m'lord, Idrys –"

"Find Idrys!" Too much was going wrong. He feared to take Cefwyn downstairs, exposed to a confusion without guards, without the protections that hourly surrounded him. "Wherever the fire is – Idrys will be there. Find where it's burning. I can carry him. *Hurry!*"

"Aye, m'lord!" Uwen said, and ran past him down the stairs.

He tried to pick Cefwyn up. He almost could manage it, though Cefwyn was utterly limp, and the wrong way about on the stairs. But by then Cefwyn's guards had come running down the steps from above, and helped shift Cefwyn head-upward so he could get his knee and his arms under him and rise on the steps.

He carried Cefwyn up the steps as the guards attempted to help, white-faced and trying to express their contrition, to him, since Cefwyn heard nothing, but he turned his shoulder and went past them, fearing that his carrying Cefwyn might hurt the leg further. Cefwyn was a still, loose weight, hard to keep safe as he maneuvered through the doors of Cefwyn's apartment. His boot slipped a little on the floor and he real-ized it was blood that made his foot skid. He maintained his hold on Cefwyn's yielding weight, the air hazing dark about him, maneuvered him through more doors, into his bedroom and with a last, difficult balance and rending effort, laid Cefwyn down carefully on the bed.

At that moment Annas appeared, took one look and began calling out rapid orders to pages to bring water and linens, while the guards attempted to explain to Annas they had been trying to assess the danger from the smoke coming up the other stairs, that they had believed Cefwyn asleep, that they never otherwise would have left.

Pages came running with towels. Then Idrys arrived on the run, smelling of smoke, his face streaked with soot. He had a quick look at Cefwyn's leg, and ordered tight bandages.

"The physician is on his way," Idrys said.

"He fell on the stairs," Tristen said, still out of breath. "He heard the alarm –"

"Where in hell were the guards?" Idrys demanded, pressing a linen wad against the wound, and the guards again attempted to explain – but Efanor came through the doors, cursing the guards and demanding to know what was happening.

"The kitchen's afire," Idrys said shortly.

"– Happening to my *brother*, sir!"

"Stupidity!" Idrys said. "Damn it, where is the man? Annas! I need linens! – He fell on the stairs, my lord Prince. We've sent for the surgeon. If you would help His Majesty, Your Highness, see if you can stir the surgeon out of hiding. He only lately attended master Emuin, of another fall on the stairs – he's probably in his residence. He wasn't at the fire."

Efanor, without another word, turned and left.

"We'll have the damned priest in here next," Idrys said. He had a pad of linen pressed to Cefwyn's wound. Blood soaked the sheets. The endmost stitches had burst. It was not all red blood that came out. "Damn it! Lord Tristen! Go out into the hall, set a guard over Emuin, Prince Efanor, and the lady Regent – gods know, it may rain frogs next."

"Yes, sir," Tristen said, and went out and caught one and another servant of his own and had them find out what was happening downstairs. He sent one of Cefwyn's distraught guards upstairs to order the guards watching over the lady to be alert and to make no such mistakes – he thought that the guard might be especially passionate in urging the point. He had one of his guards to fill out the number at Cefwyn's door and sent another to put extra guards with Efanor, who was searching, he hoped, for the physician.

Rain frogs. Idrys meant ills of every improbable sort. It was too much calamity. He tried to reach Emuin. He called to him, in that gray place, from where he stood; but Emuin was waging his own struggle – and when he would have joined it, Uwen came up to him in midhall. "His Majesty's come awake," Uwen said. "But he's not well, m'lord, he's not real well. The captain said you might ought to come quick."

He all but ran to Cefwyn's apartment, and Idrys was still at Cefwyn's bedside. Cefwyn was absolutely white, but his eyes were open. The physician had arrived, the same that had stitched up Emuin.

"Tristen." Cefwyn reached out his hand and Tristen took it, wishing the pain to stop and for the wound to be well, but clearly it did no good. Cefwyn's mouth made a thin line and sweat broke out on Cefwyn's white face.

"I can't do what Mauryl did," he said in a low voice, only for Cefwyn. "I wish I could. Mauryl could make the pain go away. And I've tried."

"Emuin says you're not a wizard," Cefwyn said. His grip was painfully hard. "I don't call on you to be. Is the fire out?"

"Kitchen grease, Your Majesty," Idrys said.

"I'd at least expect something more exciting," Cefwyn said. Cefwyn all but fainted, caught a breath and several more, before he asked: "Emuin. Where is Emuin?"

"Stairs have lately turned hostile," Idrys said. "Master Emuin fell, m'lord King. He will mend, but he's in no better case than you."

Cefwyn seemed to have fallen asleep, then, but he was so pale, so waxen-looking.

"It's as well His Majesty should sleep," the physician said. "Close the curtains. All of you. Out. Away, m'lords." He set out a jar on the bedside, full of something noxious and something white and moving.

"You," Idrys said, "take that from this room, sir."

"The wound is suppurating, Lord Commander. The flesh is corrupt. The maggots will keep it clean."

"There will be no damned maggots, sir. Out!"

"The flesh is corrupt. I tell you that you are trifling with his life!"

"Get him out of here!" Idrys said. "Get master Haman."

"I shall go to the prince."

"Go to the devil!" Idrys said. "I'll not have your hands on him! He'd have been well by now if you'd the talent of your damned maggots. Out!"

Tristen drew a long breath as the man gathered his bottles and left.

"His Majesty don't like the Lord Physician, m'lord Commander," Uwen ventured, head ducked. "He wouldn't let 'im near Lord Tristen again, he swore not."

"With good cause," Idrys said, and adjusted pillows under Cefwyn's knee. "Go! Out! The lot of you! Annas has business here. The rest of you – out!"

They had gotten the fire in the kitchen out, so Uwen said, by flinging sand on it, which had been Cook's notion. Cook's hair had caught fire and three of the boys were badly burned: there was sand all over, brought in buckets from the smithy, and every pot and wall was blackened with soot. The fire had broken out, the report was, while the night-cook was asleep.

"Wasn't nothing going on," Uwen said, "except the morning bread risin', and then by what they say, the grease-pot was overset and it run down into the coals. After that, it was merry hell, m'lord. They don't know if it was some dog got in, that knocked it over, or what, but Cook's just damn lucky. It's sausages from the courtyard, campfires and kettles for us tomorrow. It's a rare mess."

Tristen paced the floor, with nothing better to do – there was nothing he *could* do. Emuin was holding out on his own and cursed at him for a distraction, saying there were untoward influences. *The ether is upset,* Emuin insisted, which he did not understand, but he remembered the pigeon and the latch rattling, and with the dark outside the window-panes, he paced and he looked for the intervention of the enemy in all that was going on – he feared to attract Hasufin's notice, but feared Hasufin was laughing at all of them this moment. If a window-latch could rattle, he said to himself, a pot might rock and go over.

He had not prevented calamity, he with his little attempt at magic. He felt his failure keenly, and wondered whether he was not in fact responsible for the calamity. And from time to time he went across the hall and asked the guards how Cefwyn fared, but there was no news, except that master Haman had come and looked and said he could bring up a poultice they used on the horses, and he could stitch it up, but that was all that lay in his competency.

According to the guards and the gossip in the hall, Idrys had then said, "Do the horses generally live?" and Haman had said, "Yes, sir," and Idrys had had Haman bring what he had.

It did not please Prince Efanor, who sent the physician back with two of his guard and ordered Idrys to accept his treatment. Idrys had told the guards and the physician they were in danger of their lives if they meddled further.

So they had gone back to Prince Efanor to report that.

A long time went by, in Haman's comings and goings, in the drift of smoke from the downstairs – many rooms had their windowpanes ajar, letting it flow out, but the smell of smoke clung to everything, and the servants were bundling fine clothes into linen wrappers and sealing the doors of chests and such with wadding. Emuin seemed better, at least so his servants reported, and had called for tea, but had headache and did not want to be moved, cursing his servants and telling the good Teranthine brothers that he wanted them to go light candles in the sanctuary.

What good would that do? Tristen wondered when he heard it, and wondered whether Emuin was in his right mind, or hoping for this salvation of his. He went down the hall to see Emuin, and Emuin was indeed better in color, but seemed to have lost substance, if that were possible.

"Sir," he said. "Did you want more candles in here, or what can I do?"

"I want the brothers to light the candles," Emuin said, and confided to him then so faintly he could hardly hear: "to get them out of here before I go mad. Is it dawn?"

"Not yet."

"Do you feel it – no! don't look there. Stay out of that Place. Something's prowling about. It's here. Gods, it's *here.*"

"I feel something dreadfully wrong. The air is *wrong*, sir." He went down to his knees and caught Emuin's cold hand in his – but Emuin did not move his head at all from where it rested, and seemed in great pain, perhaps not hearing him, as no one else ever had heard him when he tried to say the most desperate dangers. "It doesn't ever stop, sir. It's getting worse. I had my window rattling. And one of my birds killed itself."

"He's reaching out," Emuin whispered, so faintly he might not have heard if he had not had his ear close. "He wants *me.* He wants me to die, apostate from the order – he wants me very badly. He wants me to die *here,* in this place – and damned to hell. Useful to him. Another stepping-stone."

"Mauryl used to speak Words, and the tower would feel safer, at least. Do you know any of those Words, sir?"

"I haven't the strength right now to think of them. Let me rest awhile. Let me rest. My head hurts so."

He brushed his fingers across Emuin's brow, ever so gently, wishing the pain to stop. But it was impudent even to try with a wizard such as Emuin was. "If my wishes help at all, sir, you have them."

"They are potent," the whisper came, but Emuin's head did not move, nor his eyes open. "They are more potent than you know, young lord. Potent enough I could not die. Damn you!"

"Yes, sir," he said, and took it for an old man at the edge of sleep, and in pain.

"Cefwyn," Emuin said then, seeming agitated. "Watch Cefwyn. Young fool."

He did not know which of them Emuin thought the fool, but he said, "Yes, sir," and got up and left for Cefwyn's room.

But the guards, very quiet and very correct since Idrys had had private words with them, said only that the King was in some pain, and that Idrys had said he might come in whenever he wanted.

He thought that he might visit Cefwyn, but there was a sense of ill everywhere alike, that same sense that he had had before, and he seemed to bring it with him.

There was a commotion on the stairs then, a number of men – Dragon Guard – came up the steps and kept going, to the next floor, as Cefwyn's guards and everyone else looked anxiously in that direction.

But not just men of the Guard. Efanor. The priest, all with very determined mien. Lord Commander Gwywyn. Why to that floor? was Tristen's first thought, and then: Ninévrisë.

Efanor had objected to her presence. The priest disliked Elwynim. Gwywyn had begun with his loyalty to Ináreddrin. "Uwen!" Tristen called out, and to the guards:

"Tell Idrys. Efanor is going against the lady. With Gwywyn. Quickly." He ran for the stairs, following the guards, who reached Ninévrisë's floor just ahead of him. He hurried along behind them, overtaking Efanor and the priest, who were among the last, along with other priests, some carrying candles and some silver and gold vessels.

"Lord Prince," Tristen said. "What is the matter?"

"Sorcery," Efanor said, and a disturbed look came over him. "But you would know."

"Yes, m'lord, I would. And there is no need to disturb the lady." He saw the Dragon Guardsmen, with Gwywyn, sweep the mere sergeant of the Prince's Guard aside from Ninévrisë's door, along with the rest of the guards. They were going inside, and Tristen went to prevent harm to the lady, as, past the invaded foyer, a handful of frightened Amefin servants were trying to stand between Ninévrisë and a Guelen prince, armed soldiery and a priest of the Quinalt.

"There she is!" the priest called out from among the hindmost. "There is the evil! There is the sorceress!"

"No, sir!" Tristen said, and pushed his way past the soldiers and the Lord Commander. "This is wrong, sir!" he said to Lord Gwywyn. "No. I've called Idrys. He's coming. Wait for him."

"Idrys is bewitched the same as the King!" the priest cried, "and this is a Sihhë – don't look him in the eyes! Arrest him! Arrest the lot of them!"

Gwywyn's face betrayed deep doubt. Tristen looked straight at him, but the priest was pressing forward and flung ashes at him, which stung his eyes, and the guards went past him, as the servants cried out in alarm.

"What *is* this?" That was Idrys' voice, and of a sudden something thumped heavily against the wall and clattered down it – a guard in Idrys' path. "You! Out! The rest of you get out of here! Good loving *gods,* have you lost your senses?"

"You have clearly lost yours, Lord Commander!" Efanor shouted at him. "I hold you accountable – I hold you accountable for my brother's life!"

Idrys shouted back. "The King is not dead – damn it, put those weapons away!"

"No!" the priest said. "You have brought the King under unholy influences, Lord Commander, among them this man's! Arrest them, and the women!"

Idrys moved, spun about and set his back to the wall and his side to Tristen, and that quickly a dagger was in his hand. Tristen did not want to draw. It seemed to him once that happened there was no reason, and he only moved to prevent the guardsmen getting past him, men who showed no disposition to want to lay hands on him. The men of the Prince's Guard that Idrys had brought were pushing and shoving those of the Dragon Guard who had come with Efanor and

659

Gwywyn. On Idrys' side was Uwen, who shoved his way through and stood with a drawn sword facing Gwywyn and his men, followed in rapid succession by Erion Netha and Denyn Kei's-son – armorless, wild-haired, with shirts unfastened, both carrying swords unsheathed. They and men behind them, all of the Prince's Guard, looked as if they had just waked and seized up weapons as they could.

"Hold, all!" Idrys said. "Damned fools! Your Highness, His Majesty is well enough. And he will have you to ask, sir, whence you made this ill-advised assault. This is utter foolishness! Put the swords away, I say! Put them away!"

"I do not take your orders, sir!" Efanor said. "Until I hear the King's word and see his eyes, I do not believe you – and I will have the physician, not a horse-surgeon, attend His Majesty, and other matters I shall set right, beginning with the inquiry into why an accident in the Bryalt shrine, and why the fire, and why His Majesty my brother is lying in peril of his life within hours after a betrothal that gave away far too much to an Elwynim witch!"

"Accuse me of sorcery?" Ninévrisë cried. "Oh, very well, dear sir!" She snatched up a small book from off the sideboard and held it aloft. "I have your gift, my lord brother-in-law, I am reading your gift in search of *your* truth and *your* faith! I had not known it came with such other behavior!"

"Don't listen to her!" the priest was shouting, and Ninévrisë:

"Oh, well, and am I so dangerous? I have dismissed all my men! I have trusted you! I have His Majesty's sworn word for my safety and his personal grant of these premises for my privacy!"

"This is enough!" Gwywyn was saying, appealing for reason and truth, but the words were starting to echo, with the priest shouting, and Ninévrisë shouting, and of a sudden men were shoving one another again, and steel rang on steel, as came a stabbing pain at the base of his skull, Emuin's presence . . . drawing him in, warning him . . . such as he could hear . . .

Small and angry, something in the east . . . close at hand.
Deadly dangerous. A step in the dark, a burning of candles,
candleflames, not orange of fire, not blue of amulets, but
smoldering black, with a thin halo of burning white, smoke
going up in thin plumes above them . . . above a fluttering of
wings . . . shadows and wings . . .

– *The east, he heard Emuin say. Harm . . . against the*
King. The stairs. The east stairs by the grand hall . . .

He could not get breath to speak, he could not think past
the pain, except that he could not desert the lady, he needed
help, and he snatched Ninévrisë by the wrist past Uwen and
Erion, with the outcries of the servants in his ears, with
Efanor bidding them stop him, and men attempting to do
that, but Uwen and Erion were there with drawn swords,
holding off a number who backed away from them, as he
whisked Ninévrisë past the priest, past Efanor and Lord
Gwywyn and in an instant in among the Prince's Guard.

But that was not where he was going, blinded by headache
and so afflicted by Emuin's pain it all but pitched him to his
knees. He reached the stairs. Ninévrisë was crying out questions. He realized he was holding her too tightly, and let her
go, wishing her to come with him. Hearing Idrys and
Gwywyn shouting at each other above, he ran, and she ran
with him, down and down the steps –

He was aware of alarm in the lower hall, then, people
staring in fright as they passed, people trying to intervene
with questions. He saw the east stairs in front of him, and he
did not need Emuin now. He knew. He felt it, a small tingling
in the air, but a presence, nonetheless, that had taken alarm.

"What is it?" Ninévrisë breathed, hiking her skirts, trying
to overtake him on the steps as he reached the floor above.
Orien's guards looked at them in startlement as they came.

"Sirs," he said as calmly and reasonably as he could, and
hoping pursuit did not overtake them. "Open this door.
Now."

The guards did as he ordered. He had never been past the
foyer of lady Orien's rooms. Now he went past those inner

doors, with Ninévrisë and the guards, as women inside cried out in alarm. In the opening of both inner and outer doors, cold wind gusted through a window-panel wide open to the night, and carried on it a stinging, perfumed smoke. Candle flames wavered in the gale, and flung shadows about a group of black-clad women with astonished faces, horrified looks.

In front of them were candles on a table, a basin of something dark, severed red braids and a sprig of thorns. Among those women he *felt* presence, and chief of them he sensed was Orien Aswydd, who faced him with her face stark and hard, in the flaring light of a single candle. All the other candles had gone out.

"*Damn you!*" *Orien said, and indeed there was a flash of gray and a tingle in the air.*

"*Is this Orien Aswydd?*" *Ninévrisë demanded.* "*Is this Orien Aswydd, who killed my messengers?*"

"*Get out!*" *Orien cried at her, then, in fear,* "*Keep away from me!*" *for Ninévrisë brought anger into the gray world – Ninévrisë started for her and women scattered, and Shadows scattered around them. It was not good to feel. It shivered through the air, it set all the gray to rippling like curtains, fluttering like wings. It welcomed anger.*

"No!" Tristen cried, and seized the table edge, overturning it in the way of the women, and the candles and the basin and all went over in the light from the door. Fire flared in the spilled wax on a woman's skirts, and shrieking, the woman tried to smother it.

In that firelight metal had flashed in Orien's hand. He saw it, spun Ninévrisë back as Orien came past the end of the table, and evaded her as another woman drove a blade past him. She did not aim well, he thought, and in the slowness of such moments and without difficulty he caught the woman's wrist – in near darkness: one of the guards had smothered the burning cloth and the other stopped the women from fleeing. He took the knife and let the woman who had attacked him go, at least to the keeping of the guards.

But Orien also had gone down in a pile of dark skirts and

Ninévrisë was standing on Orien's hand with one slippered foot. There was another knife, as the guards were finding the women in general so armed; and Ninévrisë trod hard on the hand when Orien tried to claw her ankle and tried to overthrow her by dragging at a handful of her skirts.

Tristen bent and took the knife from crushed fingers, then took Orien by the wrist, pulling her not entirely gently to her feet.

"Damn you!" Orien's eyes burned with rage and with fear. She fought to be free and he let her go. "Damn you!" She spoke Words, but no sound came. Wind blasted into the room.

"Good bloody gods," one guard said.

"I think you should take her away from here," Tristen said. They were Names she had spoken. He did not know what they attached to. He found no image of them but dark. The air felt far less dangerous after that gust, but a cold wind was still breathing through the open panel. "Shut the window, sir. I think it's far better shut."

"On my soul we had no idea, m'lord," the chief of the guards said unsteadily, while the others held the women – there were five of them – at bay in a corner backed by shadowy dark drapes and gilt cord. The light all came from the hall, the doors open straight through, but that itself was dim. Came then another touch at the gray – but that was Emuin, glad despite the headache, glad to know what was happening, though Tristen felt a fine sweat on his skin and felt the room go around only in that instant of awareness.

"Content to be the Marhanen's chattel," Orien said, nursing a sore wrist. Her face was lit strangely by the remaining candles. It seemed no longer beautiful, but ominous and terrible, the countenance she turned to Ninévrisë. "You above all others should be ashamed."

"Your Grace of Amefel," Ninévrisë said with utmost coldness, "you have made a very grave mistake." And to the guards: "I would call the Bryalt. I have no intimate knowledge of this sort of thing. But I think they should see this room, these women, and these objects before they are removed. There are some of these things very surely of harm. I know what things like this mean. They are banned in Elwynor. I assure you, sirs, I have done none of this, nor ever did my father."

The four guards were not the only ones present now. There was Lord Captain Kerdin, and Prince Efanor who came in clutching an amulet and trailing a number of Quinalt priests.

"It *was* sorcery," Efanor said. "It *was* black sorcery. Arrest them."

"I trust this time you don't mean me, Your Highness," Ninévrisë said. "Or Lord Tristen."

"No, Your Grace of Elwynor." Efanor's expression was strained. "I fear we did mistake the source. But if you knew where to go – I ask why you waited so long."

"Your Highness," Ninévrisë began in exasperation.

"My lord Prince," Tristen said. "*I* could not find the source, and I am Sihhë; master Emuin scarcely did, and *he* is a wizard."

"He is a *priest*," Efanor said harshly. Tristen recalled how Idrys had said never argue about priests with Prince Efanor, and did not argue the point.

"I think your priest should make prayers in this room," he said, not seeing how it could do good or ill, but that it might please Efanor. "But first I think they should close this room and let wise men and Emuin decide what to do with these things."

"This is a nest of evil," Efanor's priest muttered, "and these women should be burned."

The women some of them began weeping. Orien did not. "No, sir," Tristen said respectfully, and added, knowing he posed them a quandary of authority, "I think His Majesty the King should decide what to do with them."

That silenced them.

"Take them to the guard-house," Efanor said. "Set a guard on them and light candles all around. Your Grace of Elwynor, my apologies."

"I do accept them, Your Gracious Highness," Ninévrisë said, and offered her hand, which Efanor hesitated to take, then kissed gingerly. "Thank you, Your Highness. If you would take me to His Majesty, please, I should much be obliged. I've had a fright."

"Lady," Efanor said, and, which Tristen would have thought very improbable upstairs, he watched Efanor with the lady on his arm walk out past the priests and the guards, in all good and fair grace.

He looked then to the Lord Captain for wisdom in the matter. Kerdin looked quite dubious himself. But Tristen thought Ninévrisë had acted very wisely, since she had put Efanor on his best manners. More, she had not embarrassed Efanor when she might have. And Efanor knew it.

He knew when he had seen something wise. He could admire it, at least. And he saw the guard gathering the women to take them to the guard-house, for which he was very sorry: he had been there himself, and Orien would not like it.

She stared back at him with no apology. And he supposed she was angry about Lord Heryn. He thought she was very brave to have attacked Cefwyn where there was at least one wizard to have seen it, and he did not think that sorcery had broken master Emuin's skull.

"I think," he told Uwen and Captain Kerdin in that thought, "that there is someone in the Bryaltine shrine who attacked master Emuin. It might not be one of the brothers, but I don't think master Emuin slipped on the stairs. I think there was someone helping Lady Orien, someone there and in the kitchens."

"If master Emuin gets well," Captain Kerdin said, "I don't think I would like to have been that person, Lord Warden, and I fear he's the most likely besides yourself to find out who. But I'll ask the abbot and the kitchen staff who came and went."

He cast an uneasy glance about him, at the room, at the women. Orien's glance still smoldered. There was still harm in her. There was still the anger. He felt it as, finding nothing for himself to do, he thought he would also like to be sure Cefwyn and Emuin were safe, and went out into the hall and down the stairs. Uwen stayed with him, saying something about how Prince Efanor had been willing to listen to Idrys, finally, and how Gwywyn and Idrys had gone together to see Cefwyn, whether he was well.

But as he came into the lower hall he had that same feeling, that dread feeling he had had when of a sudden he had known direction to Orien's ill-working – and it was the same direction.

"M'lord?" Uwen asked, as he stopped. Uwen's voice came from far away. The sense he had was overwhelming, that it was *there,* down that hall, on the *lower* floor.

"My lord?" Uwen said again.

It was that end of the hall that had distressed him when he had first come, that place where the paving changed from marble to older stone.

Lines. Masons' lines.

"Stay here," he said to Uwen, and when Uwen protested regarding his safety: "Stay here!" he said, and went, alone down that hall, past other people, past servants. "Get away," he said to them, and servants, looking frightened, moved quickly.

He walked all the way down the hall, to that place where the pavings changed. He saw the hall hung with old banners, and looked for the lines, such as he had seen at Althalen, at his very feet.

The lines were scarcely there, scarcely a pale glow. He looked up, up at the bannered hall, and heard the rustling of wings, hundreds of wings. He saw the stirring of Shadows hanging like old curtains, perching on beams, spreading wings like vast birds, and the whole hall shifting and stirring with the darkness that nested in every recess. Wings began to spread, Shadows bated and threatened him, and he stepped back behind the fading safety of the line, wishing for a Word such as Mauryl had used, a spell, whatever it was that Mauryl worked.

– Tristen, came Emuin's voice. Tristen! Stay back. Hold on to me. . . Do not let me fall. Hold me!

– Yes, sir, he said, and was aware of Emuin near him in the gray space, and was aware of Emuin growing stronger and stronger and that blue line at his feet growing brighter and brighter, until it blazed, until it turned white, and the Shadows were only banners, and the place fluttering with wings had gone away. . .

"M'lord!" Uwen said, having disobeyed him, having come, with his sword bare in his hand, to stand by him looking at a hall full of faded banners. "Is summat here, me lord? Is it somebody hiding here?"

Master Emuin was alive. Emuin had retreated until he could only dimly feel his presence, but something had changed in that presence. It was far, far warmer, far more vivid, of far more substance, if one could say that in the gray realm.

He had never seen Mauryl. He had never heard Mauryl in the way Emuin had shown him to do – and he thought that Mauryl might have been fearsome in this place. Emuin was not – at least, not toward him.

"It's gone," he said to Uwen. He drew an easier breath. "There's no one. We should go upstairs, now."

There were a great many people gathered around his bed when Cefwyn waked next. There was sunlight coming through the window, so he had certainly slept a while; and he blinked in slow amazement to see Idrys, and Tristen, and Ninévrisë, and Efanor, all sitting or standing around him.

He could not remember what he had been doing when he went to bed, but he shifted the leg that had been giving him misery, to find it was sore, but no longer acutely painful.

"Is there some occasion?" he asked, embarrassed to be the object of such anxious attention. "My lady." He did not at all look his best. His hair would be in tangles. He ran his hand through it, and felt his arm quite inexplicably weak.

Annas arrived with a bowl of soup, saying that the kitchen was limited at the moment until they could wash all the pots, whatever that meant, and while he was trying to think of a question, a page came and stuffed cushions behind his back and another held the bowl and spoon for him – prepared to spoon the soup into his mouth in front of all these witnesses.

"No," he said sharply, and waved away soup, spoon, and boy. "What is this?"

"It was witchcraft," said Efanor, who sat on a reversed chair, arm along its back.

He was not prepared to make judgments on Efanor and witches.

"Orien Aswydd," Ninévrisë said. "Master Emuin broke his skull but he says he will be better soon."

"I feel fine," he said. "I keep telling you I feel fine. What are all of you doing here?"

"You should fare much better now," Idrys said.

"I shall, if I have fewer people staring at me." He was unaccountably weak. He had no desire for the soup. He most wanted to sleep. He decided he would shut his eyes for a moment, and said, "Did you see the horse, Tristen? What do you think?"

"I think he's very fine, sir."

"Good," Cefwyn said, remembered his betrothed bride was in the company – with his brother, which he found unlikely, and made the effort a second time to lift his eyelids to be certain it was true. "Forgive me. I don't mean to fall asleep."

The eyes shut. He was aware of them moving about, and discussing him quietly, and Annas saying they would put the soup back in the pot and it could go on waiting. He had as lief escape it. But Annas was very hard to escape. He had learned that, at Annas' knee.

Was it porridge he should eat? He thought of the sunlight coming in a window of his childhood.

But that was silly. Or magical. On this particular morning, when he was about six or seven, he could hear all the voices of most of the people who would be important to him in his life. So it was a very important dream, although he didn't know their names, now; but he knew that he would, some-day, and he should remember it when he grew up.

CHAPTER 31

In two days a Frost had come, and rimed the black slates of the Zeide roof outside Tristen's window. He opened it to test the strangeness of the white coating, and found the air very cold, and the Rime slick and cold and quite remarkable. People went about morning chores in his narrow view of the courtyard below and their breath made white steam. So did his own against the glass. "Look!" he said to Uwen, quite foolishly, entranced by this miracle, and Uwen looked.

"Why does it do that?" he asked Uwen, and Uwen scratched his morning-stubbled chin.

"Because it's cold."

"But why?" Tristen asked.

"I can't say as I can answer," Uwen said. "I can't say as I ever asked anybody as would know. That's a wizard-question. Breath's warm. Horses do that when they're hot."

"Give off steam?"

"They can."

"That's very odd," Tristen said, and blew more steam at the glass and watched the magic instead of dressing in time for breakfast. He would have liked to ask master Emuin further about the ice and the steam, but Emuin did not wake much, except to eat, even yet, and then he had so fierce a headache Tristen wanted not to be near him. Emuin was angry at him, and upset, and would not see anyone. The priests kept praying in the shrine and called Emuin's getting well a miracle of the gods, but Emuin called himself damned now and said it was his own fault for coming near him again.

That stung. But he told himself Emuin didn't mean it that strongly, and that once Emuin was well, which Emuin would be, Emuin would be in a much better frame of mind. Meanwhile Emuin had confided in him that he was mending himself, far more slowly than he might – and that such strength as he had to spare at all, he gave to the King.

And Cefwyn was on his feet. Cefwyn was inquiring, Annas said, about the kitchens, the boys that were burned, and the whereabouts of Orien Aswydd, Idrys having told him that troubling matter and the reason of his wound not healing. Cefwyn came down the hall to visit master Emuin, using the hated stick the way Emuin peevishly said, lifting one blackened eyelid, that His Majesty should have done in the first place and not fallen down the stairs like a damned fool.

More kindly spoken, Ninévrisë came downstairs, made Cefwyn tea and fussed over him, Idrys fussed over him, Annas fussed over him – Tristen did the same, such as the others left him room: he brought Cefwyn reports from the pastures and the armory; he had done that yesterday. And he thought, in his collecting of cheerful things to tell Cefwyn, about telling him about people's breaths steaming and the air turning cold, but he thought that it was probably much too commonplace a miracle to entertain Cefwyn.

Annas and Idrys gave orders and kept the household in order; servants were lugging water up the stairs and washing everything the smoke had smudged, and it turned out to have coated even walls that looked clean. Cook had the courtyard full of tubs and fires going, while servants brought out the blackened pots and tables to scrub, and a master builder had taken a look at the timbers and masonry of the kitchen and given orders to a number of workmen. A pile of charcoaled pieces from the kitchen timbers fed the fires in the courtyard, and the smell of cooking vied with the lingering smell of smoke.

Wind bore down on the citadel that night, a noisy, cold wind, that had every fire lit and that rattled doors and windowpanes, but it seemed innocent. Cefwyn invited him, among others, and sat in front of the fireplace, in a comfortable chair, with his leg propped up, a quilt about him, a cup of wine in his hand, and his friends, as he said, around him: Ninévrisë and Margolis came down, and he and Idrys and Annas were there. Efanor, more quiet than Tristen had ever seen him, came in while Ninévrisë was reading poetry aloud, and sat and listened, before he came and rested his hand on Cefwyn's arm and in a quiet voice asked him how he fared and wished him and his lady well. The harper entertained them. No one argued. No one mentioned Orien Aswydd. Efanor did not seem comfortable the entire evening, but he was there, and he was resolutely gracious to the lady, who, when he took his leave, early, seized his hands, looked at him and said quite gravely, and in everyone's hearing, "Thank you."

Efanor did not seem to know how to answer. He turned very red, and held the lady's hands a moment looking at the floor as if he were trying to say something and could not decide what.

Then he said, "My lady," and left.

Idrys cocked his head with a look at Cefwyn. Cefwyn was looking toward the door – or at Ninévrisë who was looking at the door. Tristen wondered what Efanor had thought of saying, and realized he had held his breath.

On the next day leaves lay thick about the land. Tristen rode Dys out and about the meadows, through an orchard bare-branched and piled with leaves that scattered under Dys' huge feet. He on Dys and Uwen on Cass had chased a hare through the meadow and into the brush, and came back with the horses blowing steam into the chilly afternoon air.

And to his surprise and the guards' distress, Cefwyn had come down to the pasture stables. He had ridden Danvy down, followed by a mounted guard. The chill had stung his face, and he was pale, but red-cheeked, and cheerful. "There you are," he said, and rubbed his leg, if lightly. "Danvy does the walking, fairly sedately, thank you, but far, far less difficult than a sennight ago. I waked this morning feeling very little pain. I won't attempt Kanwy – but I'd take a turn out and back with you."

"Gladly," Tristen said, and Cefwyn and he and Uwen and the guard rode out a good distance across the sheep-meadow.

"How do you find the young lad?" Cefwyn asked, and Tristen perceived he meant the horse under him.

"Very fine." He slapped Dys on the neck, and, in truth, if one had asked which was which horse, he could have told Dys from Kanwy, but most could not, he thought. "I do like him. And I do thank you."

Cefwyn talked to him then about Dys' breeding and his line, and how Dys had been foaled on a bitter cold morning. Their breath made clouds. Cefwyn tired quickly, but it seemed to him that Cefwyn was very much better very quickly.

"His Majesty looked good," Uwen said later, "almost so's you'd say he didn't need that stick."

He was glad of it. But not glad when he visited Emuin directly on his return to the Zeide, and found Emuin scarcely able to wake. He took Emuin's hand, and knelt down by him, and said, into Emuin's ear, so the good brothers who tended him should not hear: "I know what you did, master Emuin. Cefwyn is mending ever so fast. But you must do something for yourself now. Do you hear me, sir?"

Emuin gave no sign of hearing him. He was very frightened. He thought he ought to be able to do more. He wanted both of them, Cefwyn and Emuin, to be well. Emuin had grown so thin, and his hair was all white now, so that he looked very much like Mauryl. The faces were different, but there was something in him that touched those memories and said, though it was not exactly, every-day true, that there had always been something about Mauryl that shone, and that Emuin had that quality, now.

"Master Emuin," he said. Emuin's hand was very frail, very smooth in his, as if it were becoming like fine silk, like dust on old boards, the way home had felt under his hands, in Ynefel. "Master Emuin. I am here. If there is anything in me that you can use, if there's anything I can give or you can take, and it won't prevent me from what Mauryl sent me to

673

do – I am here. Do you hear me, sir? I want you to mend yourself."

– *Easier said than done, the answer came to him. But it seemed to him then that things grew dimmer, and the lines of the Zeide showed around them, blue, and faint, and brighter, then. He still wants in.*

– *Inside? he asked. Why inside, sir? Why not do harm to us outside? It was so reasonable a question he wondered he had never asked Mauryl. And why, he wondered, at evening? And why indoors?*

– *Curious question, Emuin said. What is there about buildings? About houses? Dwellings?*

– *That people live in them. It was like sitting with Mauryl, the question, the answer. Foolish boy, Mauryl would say. But perhaps his questions had gotten wiser, if not his answers.*

– *That people live in them, Emuin said ever so faintly, and the lines glowed bright. That we invest something here. That it becomes a Place for us. And we cannot be harmed . . . in certain ways . . . while that Place exists for us, even in our dreams. We must violate our own sanctuary, to be harmed . . . in those ways. But your Place is also his. And his is also yours.*

– *At Ynefel, you mean, sir.*

– *At Ynefel, Emuin said. He felt Emuin's fingers move, and tighten. I shall hold fast. I have done what I can. I fear what you are. But I shall not cripple you by asking anything or by restraining you. Do what you were Summoned and Shaped to do.*

– *You fear what I am, sir, . . . Do you know what I am? Can you at least answer that? Can you warn me what I might do wrong?*

– *No, Emuin said. I don't think I can. I can't think of those things. I can't foresee. . .*

I cannot begin to foresee the things you invent to do, Mauryl said. Rain in puddles. Rain on the parapets. Flash of lightning. Can you not think of consequences, Tristen? And he had said . . . I try.

– You have never admitted the enemy to your heart,
Emuin said. *You have never compromised with him. Never
do it. Never do it, boy. Now go away. Don't bother me. I
have enough to do.*

He was in the room again. His foot had gone to sleep.
Emuin rested, no worse, no better than he had been. He
thought he had heard Mauryl's voice. Or that he touched
what Mauryl was. Or had been.

He rose quietly. The brothers bowed to him in their dutiful
way. He bowed to them, and felt the amulet beneath his shirt,
the circle that Cefwyn had given him, that Emuin had given
Cefwyn. It never showed in the other world. He was only
conscious of it now because it had been Emuin's, and was a
wish for protection.

But he was Emuin's protection. He had become Cefwyn's.

I cannot begin to foresee, Mauryl had said, *the things you
invent to do.*

Think of consequences, Tristen.

The next day likewise dawned with frosting breath and a
slick spot in the courtyard where one of the servants slipped
and fetched himself a crack on the head that master Haman
had to attend, since the lord physician had left in angry
disgrace – in attendance on Lord Sulriggan, the rumor was,
who had left for his capital, and good riddance, most said.

Cefwyn called a war council for noon, in his apartments.
Tristen was hesitant, but Idrys said he should be there, so he
came. So did Efanor. And Ninévrisë and Lord Captain
Kerdin, and Lord Commander Gwywyn, but none of the
Amefin lords, many of whom were at harvest, and no one
from Sovrag's men, who were all over on the river, Cefwyn
said, in opening, but they were sending messages by way of
the daily couriers from several points, and that he had sent
dispatches to the villages and the lords of Amefel.

The dining board bore a stack of small maps, which Idrys
said had just arrived last night, which recorded every large

rock, every hillock, everything Ninévrisë's few men had explored in the area of Lewen plain, north and west of Emwy's ruin. Lord Tasien had sent a message to Ninévrisë by way of the Guelen messengers: Lord Tasien said that he had met with rivermen from Lord Sovrag, who had brought supplies downriver, and who had reported a quiet shore: that was the same as Sovrag's messages had said.

Lord Tasien had also reported in his letter to Ninévrisë that they had made a wall and trench camp that was well begun, with the help of the Amefin peasants who had come up with the wagons. Tasien reported his men under canvas, digging their fortification, and awaiting word from inside Elwynor, and said they had seen no sign of hostile forces on this side of the river.

Efanor shook his head only slightly, perhaps in amazement that they were receiving such a report from the Earl of Cassissan – less charitably estimated, in personal disbelief that Lord Tasien's word could be relied upon. But Efanor said nothing, only remarked later and very mildly, for Efanor, that it was very odd, very odd to have a woman in a council of war, but that the Elwynim were very efficient, and seemed to be experienced men – which made Tristen ask himself where the Elwynim had been fighting; but he kept that question to himself.

Efanor in general was on very good behavior. Gwywyn was very proper and made no allusion at all to the doings the night of the fire. He only seemed apprehensive, and increasingly relieved as the meeting went on and his counsel was taken with equal weight with others'.

"There's a lot that's ashamed of themselves," Uwen said when he spoke of the meeting later. "What I hear, that night all that business got started there was a gathering over in the Quinaltine, praying and the like, and the lord physician having a tantrum and saying His Majesty was going to die. *I* think," Uwen had added, "that the Prince thought His Majesty might have died, on account of the lord physician being sent out. I don't doubt the lord physician was a lot of the cause there. And there was priests out talking to the staff, saying that the King was bewitched. Which I'd put to nothing, m'lord, but I don't like much that gathers around that priest."

Then Uwen added another thing that troubled him. "I'm Guelen," Uwen said. "And I seen just a touch too much of Quinalt priests and their politicking. Ain't nothing to do with praying. They don't like wizards."

"Why?" Tristen asked.

"On account of the Quinalt says the gods laid down the world the way things are, and wizards meddled with it. They don't like 'em. Meanin' they killt no few. I'd be just a little careful, m'lord, and stay clear of 'em."

It seemed to him Idrys had warned him much the same. So he told Idrys in private that evening what Uwen had said. And Idrys nodded and said, "His Majesty's Guard is well aware of the priest, Lord Warden. Believe me." Then, unusual for Idrys, Idrys had stopped him for a second word. "It was very well done, Lord Ynefel, that night."

"Catching Orien, sir?"

"Among other things. I must tell you my mind that evening was on one of Lord Heryn's partisans. Sorcerous action does not naturally occur to me as a cause."

"I don't think anyone used sorcery against Emuin, sir. I think they had to keep Emuin from seeing them."

"Seeing them."

"So to speak, sir. Wizardry might make someone fall on the steps, but I don't think Orien could have done it. And certainly sorcery wouldn't break someone's skull."

"Certainly," Idrys echoed him, and Idrys' lean, mustached face was both earnest and troubled. "I fear wizardry encompasses few certainties with me, Lord Warden. What is the likelihood Emuin will be on his feet and with us come the full of the moon?"

"I fear it's very little likely, sir. I think he's helping Cefwyn most."

"You are not to say that."

677

"Yes, sir."

"So the Aswydd lady had someone attack Emuin."

"As I think someone moved Orien to do it. Mauryl said it was easy to make things do what they want."

Idrys was silent a moment. "Is wizardry a consideration, then?"

"Hasufin's, yes, sir."

"Hasufin Heltain?"

"I don't know all his name, sir, but he made a bird fly at my window. It killed itself. And in the lower hall, in the banner hall – the lines were almost gone, that protect this place. Emuin brought them back."

It was deliberate, that confidence, a test he made of Idrys and how far Idrys did see; and Idrys did not exclaim in exasperation or walk away. Idrys only gazed at him steadily. "So has Orien Aswydd flown at the glass, – has she not? What do you recommend we do with her?"

Idrys turned back his test, he thought, whether he had the resolve Idrys thought a lord needed. Cefwyn had not condemned her. Cefwyn had not gotten to that matter. Or Cefwyn shrank from it.

He did. It was one thing on the field. It was another in reasoned thought – to kill. And a lord, he thought, ought to be able to do such things – as Owl had to eat mice.

"Come, sir," Idrys said. "Do I trouble you? I had thought you unmoved by the lady's charms."

"At least," Tristen said, and found his hands shaking, "she should not die as Heryn did." He nerved himself to say that Idrys was right, and that Orien should die, but then he thought of the lord Regent, who was also a wizard. "But where she is buried, where she dies, she will be like Hasufin. She might ally with him. She would be bound to this place. I think that would be dangerous."

He had not given Idrys, he thought, what Idrys looked to have. "Persistent, you mean."

"Sir, as best I understand – she is less a wizard than Auld Syes up at Emwy. Very much less. I think she did very little

678

but let Hasufin in, and perhaps helped him a little. I think she hates us. But I would not let those women together. I would send them all apart, and send them all away from here."

"Does it run in families?" Idrys asked. "Heryn is buried here."

It was a disturbing thought. "I have no idea, sir. He'd always have a Place here, if I understand it. But I would move him. Bury him among good men. Holy men."

"Holy men."

"I think so, sir. That is my advice."

"Digging up corpses," Idrys muttered. "Holy men. This is not to my liking, young sir. Not at all. – So wizard me who did this. Who set the fire? Who cracked master Emuin's head?"

"I'm not a wizard, sir."

"Just like Emuin. Never the hard questions." Idrys began to walk away.

"Sir," Tristen said as an odd recollection came to him. He had spoken. He had Idrys' attention. He hesitated, then said: "Lord Sulriggan's dish was salty, at the dinner. He was furious at his cook."

"Was he, now?"

"Cook's boys played a prank." It seemed incredible to him that so small a thing – could do so much harm. "He would have been very angry. And Sulriggan was leaving."

Idrys drew a long breath. "An angry cook. Well. Well. Sulriggan. – And what of the other, lord of Ynefel? Who struck master Emuin?"

"I don't know, sir. That, I truly don't know."

"An Amefin shrine," Idrys said. "Lord Heryn had his connections. So has Orien. Of various sorts. You've given me enough, lord of Ynefel. Quite enough to serve."

"But –" A terrible thought came to him. And he had not thought. Idrys had started a third time to leave, and stopped again. "Sir. Orien knows about the lords leaving. She knows about Lewen plain and the full moon – she must have found out."

679

"Sulriggan's cook, carrying lady Aswydd's messages?" Idrys asked. "Hardly likely. And in the wrong direction. A Bryalt priest, now, – or someone connected to him –"

"No, sir. That's not the point. Lady Aswydd doesn't *need* a messenger. Hasufin needs none. She could have told Hasufin. Hasufin *will* have told Aséyneddin, across the river. Aséyneddin knows the place. He knows the day. He will move before that, sir. He will cross at Emwy and take Lord Tasien's camp. I *said* it would be the new moon."

Idrys' face had gone very still, expressionless. "Say nothing of this. – However you wizard-folk say such things, keep it to yourself."

"Sir," Tristen said, thinking of the bird, and the cook, and how very small things could move, even against their will. "Sir, it's as well the lord physician went with Sulriggan."

"Another damn witch?"

"No, sir. An angry man. Things do what they want to do. But the bird didn't want to fly into the glass. If it had wanted to, it would have been easier."

Idrys did go away, then, quickly, to Cefwyn, he was sure.

He thought that they had very little time, now. For no particular reason he had thought of the new moon.

He remembered Mauryl's cipherings. The moon-plottings. He had never understood them. But no more did he under-stand the work of masons or wizards than he ever had. He only knew that something very dire was coming at Amefel, and at Cefwyn, and, now, purposefully, he realized, – at him.

"He said – it would be sooner," Cefwyn said, and sat down. "Damn. *Damn* the woman."

"That would have been my inclination," Idrys said.

"It would not have prevented this," Cefwyn said, with all they had been talking about in council – all the figures and estimates of supply and logistics – tumbling through his head. "Why did *Emuin* not perceive this going on, if Tristen didn't?"

"I could not possibly guess," Idrys said, "save that master

grayfrock showed no enthusiasm for wizarding. Perhaps he didn't – whatever wizards do. Perhaps lady Orien didn't – whatever m'lord Tristen thinks she did: whatever Tristen does: talk to passing birds, or hear it from the frogs, or whatever. This is far beyond my competency, m'lord King, but Tristen's chancy warnings have in the past been of some weight."

"I should have heard this one," Cefwyn said. "I told him not to speak. I tried to silence him in council, thinking him –"

"Feckless?"

"Innocent." The room seemed stifling. He rubbed the leg, which was both sore and itched devilishly with healing, asking himself whether he was remotely fit, and distractedly adding in the back of his mind the same figures they had added in council, and wondering if three days was enough to see him more fit than he was – and the baggage train delivered to Lewenside. Fear crept in – the sensible sort, that said there were additional troubles, of the sort he could have expected.

"Did I not say –" Idrys began.

"Oh, you often said, master crow. And I listened too little."

"He *is* still the mooncalf. But on the field he seems to have a very clear understanding. He comprehends in council. He says Orien alive or dead should not remain here. That her *brother* should not be buried here. Nor anyone of great animosity. He seems to imply – though I was already past my understanding – that anyone of animosity, wizard or not, could be moved by a wizard to act against us."

"Good loving gods, there *are* grudges. There will be grudges."

"That was my impression. It may be incorrect. But he was definite about two things: first, that, through Orien, Aséyneddin knows our plans, which may include, I would surmise, lord Haurydd's mission into Elwynor, and that fortification at Emwy, and the day on which we plan to move. And second, that Orien Aswydd and Heryn must move – Heryn to holy ground."

"Holy ground. Heryn!"

Idrys held up a languid hand. "I assure my lord, it is not my fancy."

"He said the lord Regent had to remain at Althalen. That he came there to die."

"We are contending with the dead, m'lord King. I'd take the advice of one who should know."

Cefwyn drew a deep breath and shook his head. And had a chilling thought. "The skulls from over the gates. Send those with Heryn Aswydd – to the same interment. Tonight."

"What a wagonload," Idrys said. "The Aswydds – and their victims."

"It seems due. Light the signal fires and pass the word. I'll have written messages – for my brother, for Tristen, for my lady, – for Sovrag, on the river. They should go out together. But meanwhile, light the fires."

Tristen sat by the window in the early night, with the Book shut in his hands and saw the fires – one after the other, on the hills. A single glance at the writing had shown him he knew no more than before. Then the fires had begun to go. And Uwen came in, his face aglow with the cold wind, cheerful – until Uwen looked at him.

"M'lord?" Uwen asked.

"We are moving," Tristen said. "It's come."

Uwen caught a breath, shrugged off his cloak, and tucked it over his arm. "Has His Majesty said?"

"The fires. Do you see them?"

Uwen came near the window and looked out into the dark. "Seems as if the lords is hardly had time to take their boots off," Uwen said, and went and put his cloak on the bench. "So there ain't no putting that away."

"I told Cefwyn what I should have realized sooner – when I knew about Orien Aswydd – that they would know. I should have seen it. I should have understood."

"They. They – the Elwynim."

682

"Aséyneddin."

"Ye're saying Aséyneddin knows."

"The day. The place. Lord Tasien is in very great danger."

"Can ye – warn him, wizardlike?"

"I don't think even Emuin could. And he – far more likely. I should have known, Uwen. I should have seen it."

"Ye've had summat to occupy your thoughts, m'lord."

It was Uwen's duty to cheer him. It was his to take Uwen into more danger than Uwen knew how to reckon, and it was his not to upset Uwen, or to spread fear around him to his staff and the army. He tried to gather his wits, and his composure.

But that he *did* not know, and *had* not known in a timely way indicated more than the reason Uwen gave; wizardry had *not* provided him the answer in a timely way, and Words had *not* unfolded to him. The blind, trusting way in which he had ridden off to Althalen, expecting things to become clear, had not worked, with devastating implication that they might not work in future. He felt betrayed, in some measure, betrayed and not knowing what else might fall out from under him.

But, moved to fling the Book with violence onto the table – he did not. He laid it down carefully. "I must take this. Above all, Uwen. Don't let me leave it behind. I give nothing for my ability to remember anything." His hands were trembling. He rested the one on the table, hoping Uwen failed to notice. "I have let slip very important things. Or important things have escaped me."

"Fact is," Uwen said, "we're mostly ready, m'lord. I don't deny I'm a little surprised. I expected a few more days, perhaps, but not beyond. And you watch: we'll get up there and we'll sit and wait. I've seen the like of *this* before. – Ye could do with a cup of tea, maybe."

"I might," he said, and Uwen went over, poked up the embers, and swung the kettle over.

But while he was doing it, the servants let in one of Cefwyn's young pages, a grave-faced boy with a sealed note for him.

It said, in a hasty hand, *My dear friend, we are going. Wagons move tonight. The signal fires are lit, on your advisement. Do not hesitate to give me further thoughts you may have. I should have heeded your warning in council. Do not think that I shall fail to heed another one. Advise your household. In the second watch, be prepared to bring baggage down to the wagon at the west doors.*

My Household, he thought – like a Word showing itself in all its shapes. His Household was Uwen, and the servants, all of whom had declared they would go into the field with him; and the guards of several watches, that were assigned to him. There were the horses and their accoutrements, and the staff that managed all that. Master Peygan's boys had brought his armor and shield and Uwen's to the apartment a day ago as they had brought all the lords' gear to have it handled by the lords' own staffs; and they were supposed to have sent all horse-gear down to Aswys this afternoon, to store in the pasture-stables' armory, where there was more room than up on the citadel; but the citadel armory kept the lances and other such in its adjacent buildings. There had to be one wagon, he had discovered, only to carry his servants, his tent, his equipment, and there had to be drivers, which Uwen had added only yesterday, whose names he did not even know; and besides all that, besides the horses they would ride, and their gear, and Dys and Cass, that Aswys cared for – there were water-buckets and grain for the horses, including the horses to pull the wagon, and everything sufficient for the number of days it took to send and resupply them from Henas'amef – the whole tally was enormous. He knew all the pieces of it.

Except finding a standard-bearer. And the standard was important, even if he had only seventeen soldiers, counting Uwen, in all his company, who needed to find it on the field. He knew Cefwyn intended it be carried conspicuously, because of what it was – and someone had to carry it, which was not far different from a death sentence. Aséyneddin would want to bring it down early.

"The standard," he said on a deep breath. And Uwen said, with his ordinary calm, "Not your trouble, m'lord. We'll find somebody. Is that the order?"

"We *are* going, my lord?" Tassand asked – the servants had come into the bedchamber doorway, following the page, and stood there, four solemn faces, as gentle, as modest, as kind-hearted a set of men as he had ever dealt with. "Is it now?"

"Yes," he said. It seemed that the floor dropped away from under him, as, with that one word – he ordered everything into motion, and every choice that he had, or imagined he had had – was gone.

Or begun. He was not certain.

"No sleep for us tonight," Uwen said cheerfully. "Doze in the wagon, we will, or ahorse, or wherever, tomorrow. I'll tell Lusin he can go down in the cold and the wind and rouse out the drivers. This damn little courtyard, we'll have wagons atop each other if we don't move fast. Tassand, let's get it moving. – Lad," he said to the page, who still waited, "I don't think m'lord has a reply, except he's ready and we're going."

The fires are lit, the note had said, because Idrys had told Cefwyn his fears regarding Orien – and on that surmise the message to summon the lords and the villages was flaring across the land not as quickly as wizards could warn one another, but still as fast as men could light fires, and as fast as the lords could turn around and come back again, only scarcely arrived and with no time to prepare – but this time traveling without wagons.

At least, he said to himself, at least and in spite of his tardiness even to think what assumptions must change once he knew what Orien had done – Cefwyn had implicitly believed him. But wizardry had failed him, or he had failed, perhaps because of failing with the Book, perhaps simply that the wizardry working against them was stronger, he had no idea.

CHAPTER 32

It was a night impossible to sleep, the courtyard rumbling with heavy wheels – and on a short and fitful rest, Tristen rose well before daylight, with the whole Zeide awake at that unaccustomed hour. He took a cold breakfast while the servants gathered up the leather bag of armor, which he would not have to wear until things were more dangerous than Henas'amef's streets. A wagon was supposedly in the courtyard, at the west stairs, and it and three others made such trips with whatever of the lords' baggage had to be gotten down the hill in the dark. His servants and his guards took turn about carrying items down the stairs: one of the guards already on horseback and Tassand, who did read, at least as far as lists, would ride the wagon down and check everything against the tally-tablet, being sure the men helping loaded it off into the right wagon in the line.

It was their last load, his personal equipment and Uwen's. He put on his mail, and a padded black coat, new, since the night at Althalen – gathered up his Book with the mirror tucked into it, put it where he reckoned it most safe, next his belt, and laced up the coat. He took the sword from beside the fireplace, where it had rested since he had brought it home, except Uwen had taken its measure and the armory had sent a sheath for it, with a good leather belt, which he buckled on.

Last of all he slung a heavy cloak about his shoulders, and put on his riding-gloves, of which Uwen had said he would be very glad in the chill air.

There was nothing to do, then, but to watch the servants put out all the candles and put out the fire, and for all of them to take a last look at a home no one knew if they would see again, in a gathering that might never come together again.

Then it was down the stairs amongst the servants with Uwen and Lusin, one of the guards who had been with him longest, to the courtyard, where they were bringing horses up, by precedence.

Outside the town walls, on the lords' former campground, was where their personal wagon and their drivers would be waiting, also in their order of precedence – a long line, since the Guelen guard and the Amefin contingent had not only their own baggage, but also the baggage train of the absent lords and their armies under their escort.

Their wagon was already loaded with the gear and trappings from the pasture-stable, which Aswys himself had accounted for, and seen loaded – at least that was the prearrangement, if Aswys had been able to get to the wagon.

"He'll be there," Uwen said. "He's a King's man. They'll let him through. Hain't no trouble at all, m'lord, compared with the ranks tryin' to find their gear in a thunderstorm."

Heavy-axled wagons had been rolling for half the night, as anyone trying to sleep could attest, the most of them loading once, at the granary, as they understood, and not to unload again until they reached their final encampment: a certain number would distribute grain to the individual wagons at the first camp, and immediately turn back to Henas'amef, to reload and go out again. Supply for that many horses when the hazard of attack precluded letting the horses out to graze was a very great difficulty; and feeding that number of men over the same number of days, plus the supply of firewood when foraging might be dangerous made necessary another number of wagons – and heavy wagons traveled at the same speed as a man could leisurely walk, no faster, often slower. That meant that the ground a man on a light horse could cover in a day was three to five times the rate at which loaded wagons would travel, and if an experienced rider on a well-conditioned horse needed make the distance only once rather than three or four days' sustained effort, the rider might push it to six times the distance a wagon might cover over a number of days, granted the day-after-day wear on the wagon teams, the wheels, and the axles did not create further delays.

The supply had to be there: it was no good for scattered units of horse to arrive and run into battle without the infantry, or for the infantry without their weapons or food to eat or shelter from the chilling rains. It was, Cefwyn had said it, and the words had made absolute sense, not a skirmish, but full-scale war: and that was right, in his own thinking.

So the Guelen and the Amefin went necessarily at the speed of the baggage train and the Amefin foot. With the signal fires flaring out across the land, they counted on Amefin villages coming to the muster, and all of them counted for their very lives on the southern light horse in particular being able to use their speed – counting that each lighthorseman had two horses. Umanon, with the other heavy horse contingent, would not make Cevulirn's speed overland, but the Imorim heavy horse had good roads, and Lanfarnesse, which had primarily infantry and longbowmen, had the shortest distance to come.

That, at least, was the reckoning they had made in their session with Cefwyn as late as yesterday, with a detailed list of every wagon, with the wagon-bed measured and the wagons and their teams rated as heavy or light, horse or ox. They had hoped for dry roads. They did not have them – but the rains had been light.

But if he was right, *if* he was right, the faster they could reach the river, the greater were Lord Tasien's chances of survival and of their holding the bridge. They had already reinforced Tasien's garrison; and if they could hold the bridge, as Lady Ninévrisë had said in council, the greater were the chances her partisans across the river might rise against Aséyneddin and make it a civil war, not a war between Elwynor and Ylesuin: that was their best hope, the one that shed the least blood on either side and ended the war before winter set in. Those were Cefwyn's hopes, at least, and Ninévrisë's.

But Tristen did not, himself, believe that they had that

chance – not with the likelihood that Hasufin had found more than Aséyneddin to listen to him; one did not know that there were no wizards in Elwynor – there very likely were.

Orien would have told their enemy everything, by means he should have days ago accounted of. And that meant there could be far worse happening: Sovrag's nephew had escorted lord Haurydd into Elwynor – and possibly Aséyneddin had discovered that indirectly from Orien. Aséyneddin could locate Haurydd and discover the names of those people Haurydd had relied on meeting.

In that event, there would be no chance of Ninévrisë's friends inside Elwynor laying any sort of plans before Aséyneddin came against them. And there might be no help for Cefwyn from that quarter, if ever there might have been.

The wagons rumbled on iron-shod wheels over the cobbles, and dogs yapped and men shouted at each other.

Uwen was in his own. He was able to sort out the horses for Lady Ninévrisë's borrowed staff, two young Amefin ladies of good reputation and their fathers, very minor nobles, who had been given good horses of the King's stable, to bear the four of them – the King's servants managed the lady's tents, baggage, and provisions, and the ladies and their fathers, who would, with Ninévrisë's four guards, take charge of her establishment in the camp, had no staff to manage and very little to do but find the horses – with which none of the four, town gentry, had any skill whatsoever, the ladies being there for Ninévrisë's reputation and the ladies' fathers being there to set the seal of noble propriety on the household.

Banners were being uncased and unfurled, with the least hint of light in the sky. The grooms began to lead the horses out. Uwen went off with one of the servants and came back with his horse and Petelly, ahead of a scar-faced man who, bearing a furled banner, also led a horse up. That man said, in a voice low and somewhat shy, "I'm Andas Andas'-son, m'lord. I'm to bear your standard, His Majesty said. I served eleven years in His Majesty's Dragons. The sergeant there knows me."

"He's a good man," Uwen said under his breath. "A fine man. I know 'im those eleven years. He'll keep matters straight."

"Then thank you," he said, "Andas Andas'-son." He knew – he all but knew that this man would not leave the field; and did the man not know it?

No more would Uwen leave him. No more would his servants. Or the others. He did not understand. Least of all could he understand the determination it took to take that post, for a lord who was not his own. He made up his mind if Andas'-son lived and ever he could do good for him, he would do it. But it was no favor Andas'-son had been granted.

The groom brought Petelly and he rubbed Petelly's nose and patted his neck as Petelly cast a white-rimmed eye about the proceedings and cocked ears toward the racket. The steam of their breaths commingled in the light of a lantern a man carried past. He felt calmer himself with Petelly under his hands. He climbed up and from that higher vantage, out of the shadows of wagons and horses and men and the flare of lanterns, saw the dawn well begun, a faint glow about the peaked roofs of the Zeide, and above the high walls.

At that moment a shout went up. Cefwyn and Efanor had appeared in the doorway, held up joined hands in the lantern-light, embraced with more than formal warmth, then parted at the steps. Efanor was staying as defender of the town, taking command of the Guard that stayed, and Cefwyn was moving to take horse, as Idrys rode close to the base of the steps.

Then Ninévrisë and her ladies came down, and grooms brought those horses up; Cefwyn mounted up on bay Danvy, and Idrys joined him as Ninévrisë and her ladies were assisted into the saddles. The Dragon banner unfurled, red and shadow and gold, transparent where it crossed the lantern-light. Cheers went up all about. The Tower of the Regent billowed out, and cheers went up at that, too.

Petelly was growing excited, working the bit and looking about at this and that movement. Tristen kept him as close to his place in line as he could manage until Uwen had mounted up; the grooms, Aswys' lads, handed them up their shields, which they would carry through the town.

Then the two of them rode over to the place he was assigned, with the King. He could not see Cefwyn, but he saw Ninévrisë, and saw Cefwyn's personal guard. Erion Netha and Denyn Kei's-son were with them, Erion carrying the short lance the Ivanim favored; and Denyn with the curved sword and small buckler common among Sovrag's rivermen. The several Guelen guard with them were armored as they were, as light cavalry, but bearing heavy horsemen's shields.

Of a sudden another cheer went up. He had no idea why, until he saw the Tower and Star billow out, eerily pale in the light that broke above the walls – his own banner had unfurled.

A horn brayed across the din, and the three standard-bearers began to move out the gates, down through the town, no mad haste in this ride, but solemn deliberation. The bells of the town began to peal, ringing from every town gate and from the citadel, a clangor that started every bird still drowsing in the towers.

Townsfolk that gathered along the street waved and shouted. Boys broke from the crowd as the banners passed, and ran along beside them – boys too young to have been mustered to the Amefin lords, boys clutching bows and carrying old swords, boys some of them with no weapons at all. The young lads coursed their route and stayed with them, though he saw mothers and fathers shout at them to come back. Tristen saw a band of them break from the crowd as the banners passed, and as they rode under the gate and turned to the right, along the long, long line of wagons, the boys burst forth from outside the gates and ran alongside the foremost riders.

Dogs joined the chase. Several stray sheep wandered through, among the wagons, right across the path of the horses, and, with the dogs behind, jogged back through the line in front of them.

Outside the town gates, the nearby rural and town levies mustered in the dark, and there came a flood of Amefin infantry behind a few horsed lords. The Eagle standard of the Amefin swept in just behind their rank, with the several earls and their separate standards, and behind those the pennons of the various sections with their lieutenants and sergeants in command.

They passed their wagon in line near the head of the column: Dys and Cass were with it, along with Aswys and two of his boys on horseback, and Tassand and the other servants. Lusin and the other fifteen Guelen guards, the four shifts that had stood at his door, all on horseback, rode in to their assigned place behind the King's guard, the King's Dragon Guard being under Gwywyn, who rode behind the leaders. But Lusin and the rest were directly under Uwen's command, since Uwen's armoring and commission as a Guelen officer and, at least by honor, as Tristen now understood, a captain over the almost nonexistent forces of Ynefel and Althalen.

Uwen had said when Cefwyn had given him the horses that he could not figure how he had gotten to such a station, being a man of the villages, not of the court, and seemed quite overwhelmed by it. Now he had a command.

But Tristen thought most of any honor he simply wanted Uwen and all his folk to come through alive – and Uwen's rise to fortune occasioned him a guilt he himself did not understand, not because the wish to have Uwen safe was wrong, he decided, but because he had so much he should be thinking about and understanding rather than worry, as he could not help but do, about a household and the men who depended on him.

He was not the same as the lords of the south, he told himself, as he rode beside Cefwyn and Ninévrisë in the rank of Kings, with their three banners snapping and cracking in the dawn wind ahead of them. He was not the same as Cefwyn, who was born to be a king; he had no attachments for good or for ill the same as they. He had stolen them, he had borrowed them, he had put up the pretense of being a Man, even though he had had but one thing to do from the hour that Mauryl had called him into the world, a dangerous thing, and he had no justification for allowing Men to form such attachments to him, where their dangers were more than they could know. Uwen – had been so confident, had known so well where things ought to be, and what had to be done to move men and horses: he was a calming presence this morning for all the household, and yet Uwen with all his common sense was only giving orders that someone once had given to him, and that the soldiers knew how to obey, anyway.

But, he thought, Uwen more clearly than any of them had an inkling he was facing some danger very different from anything they knew, and Uwen was not spreading fear around him: Uwen had calmed *him* when he had faltered this morning, when the attachments he had made had suddenly added up and overwhelmed him; and Uwen did all that he did with a kind of courage he did not know if he possessed.

He had said it as clearly as he saw it himself, that if they could defeat Hasufin's allies on the field, they might deprive Hasufin of agencies to do his bidding – but the cost of that, he saw all around him, this morning: men who were not at harvest, boys who had no notion what they were facing – Ninévrisë and Cefwyn who were arguing about her presence on the field. Ninévrisë had suddenly said she would not stay in camp when it came to a battle, and Cefwyn had relied on her to do exactly that, "Which is why," Cefwyn said with asperity, as they rode nearby, "I gave four damned fine horses to get you an escort."

"We should not be thinking of defeat," Ninévrisë said, "my lord."

"I am not thinking of defeat! I am thinking of men who may die satisfying your whim, my lady, to view a battle."

"I have men at risk at Emwy, – my lord! I owe it to them to come as far as I can!"

"As far as you can come is the camp, woman, without

693

diverting precious reliable men to guard you! You will not give an order on the field! Leave it to men of experience!"

It went on, several exchanges more, but nothing was resolved. Tristen agreed with Cefwyn: he wanted Ninévrisë safe in camp, too, and would have told her so, but resort to the gray space was dangerous, and he did not wish to do it – or to intervene between Ninévrisë and Cefwyn. It was another attachment he could not spare the thought to maintain now. Ninévrisë was one more life to fling at the lives Hasufin flung at them. But she was not Emuin, and whatever her father had been, Ninévrisë had nothing of his ability.

Nor had he. He had not had the strength to reinforce the old man at Althalen, and he was responsible for far more than just the fires being lit days earlier than Cefwyn had expected. He had swept up Cefwyn and all his men into Mauryl's struggle and carried them from Ninévrisë's war into her father's, and into Emuin's, and into Mauryl's.

He did not know, in fact, if Mauryl's struggle would end on Lewen plain – and did not know, in fact, whether he himself would. It seemed he had little use to Mauryl after that was done, and for all that he knew the magic Mauryl had used to bring him here would be finished, too, win or lose, as Uwen would say.

He had had time to think of very many terrible things during the hours of preparation. Now he watched the road above Petelly's ears and past the moving barrier of blowing silk – black, white, red and gold. And, Ninévrisë and Cefwyn being largely occupied in argument, he found it needful to say little at all, except to Uwen.

He won the dispute. Cefwyn thought so at least, since Ninévrisë conceded it might not be the wisest thing to advance with the line, but that she might take up an observation point, and be ready to send messengers to advise the officers immersed in battle of any unanticipated flanking movement: she did know whereof she spoke. She had studied, she said. She had read the same writers on the topic. She had read Tashânen.

"I considered," she said, "that it behooved me to know what I do and what I ask when I send men in certain numbers to certain tasks, my lord King."

"You constantly amaze me," he said.

"I trust you will never be amazed by my competency, my lord."

What did a man do with such a woman? His lady mother had not answered his father in such terms. "I see I have years of discovery ahead." Clearly a man dared not let Ninévrisë gain an ell. "— And I commend your zeal to know, my lady, but were you any man of my association, and you had not commanded in the field, you would stand on that hill with no men but your personal guard."

He expected a spark. He received a calm nod. "Very well."

"I am adamant," he said.

"Justly so, my lord. Do you take advice?"

"From my captains, my armorer, my grooms, my servants and my pages, my lady, where warranted."

"And your wife?"

"Oh, I do. I do. See — that's Sagany Road ahead, Sagany and Pacewys villages, their standards." He waved as a peasant contingent joined them — he reached down from Danvy's back and waved to the men, nodded to acknowledge their bows, and, a custom which had appalled the Guelen Guard early on in his tenure, offered his hand to a bright-eyed young man on horseback, their local gentry, the Thane of Sagany, the only horseman in their company. Fingers touched, and horses drifted apart again. "Lord Ardwys. Fall in behind Lysalin's pennon."

"Your Majesty," Ardwys said, said, "Your Grace," to Ninévrisë and, "M'lord," to Tristen; and drew off to join his men in waiting.

At every major side-road, now and again at mere sheep-paths, boys and men had been joining their march. Behind the men of Sagany Road, a handful of women and grandfathers wept and waved handkerchiefs – and, Cefwyn thought, things which afforded the pious less comfort. Countryfolk pointed at the banners and waved. A clutch of old men with their dogs and their sheep stood by the ditch along the road and doffed their hats and stood respectfully.

"We are outnumbered," Idrys said under his breath.

"Hush, crow," Cefwyn said in thickest Guelen accent. "Manners."

"Gods, I would you were safe in the capital."

"I would I had more Guelen. But the countryside had no special love of the Aswydds and their taxes. They cheer us, do you hear, Idrys?"

"So far, my lord," Idrys said. "Well that the page has your shield, I say. I wish you would not do that."

"Pish," he said, and grimaced and rubbed his leg, which had ached in that reach after the young thane's hand.

"Shall we rest?" Ninévrisë asked.

He shook his head. "Not yet." He had the marked places in his head as he had learned the village lords' names, each and all. He had come to know this cursed road in his sleep and in his bad dreams. "Tristen."

"My lord King."

"How do we fare?"

"My lord?"

"In time?"

"I see nothing worse, my lord. I *see* nothing. I would not look. It would tell him where we are."

"Aséyneddin," Cefwyn said.

"Through him, yes, Aséyneddin."

Tristen had said very little; and wished not to, he thought. He could not escape the notion that Tristen was listening, if not – doing – whatever wizards did. Uwen dozed in the saddle at times. The King, unfortunately, could not.

Nor would Tristen, it seemed. But cheerful converse with him was impossible – and if wizardry of some kind was going on, either with his gray-eyed bride, who kept rolling a set of beads and silver amulets through her fingers, or with Tristen, who simply rode scanning the horizons of this world or some other, he had no wish to disturb them.

Their column lengthened constantly with such arrivals. By noon, so Tristen heard, the hindmost must finally be clear of the town walls, but they would be obliged to stop in midafternoon, only to assure that the hindmost wagons made it in before full dark, the hindmost being the grain-transports that would go all the way to Emwy. The lords' equipment, the warhorses, and the weapons were interspersed into the infantry marching order in the entirely unlikely event of an attack while they were well within their own territory: the tents for each unit came in wagons not far removed from those units.

It was a fair day, a light wind, by afternoon, and by midafternoon, as the plan was, they made camp on a high spot beside the road – Massitbrook, the map showed running along the road, a ford that might be, the drivers said, a hard pull for the heavy wagons that came hindmost: the order went out after the first of them had crossed it and the first wagons had come up the far side, for arriving contingents to take shovels and move rock and ease the slope on both sides. Men grumbled, but the assigned units set to work, while sergeants paced off the aisles of the camp and men drove spears into the ground to mark the lanes.

It was all, all like a Word, Tristen thought. Everything that was done found place and fitness in his mind: the King's pavilion went up; and the Regent's; and his wagon turned up with two Amefin boys, who, casting themselves at his feet, swore they would wash pots and fetch and carry, as they said, for the great lord.

"We want to be soldiers, m'lord," one said. "I'm fifteen. Me cousin's the same."

"They seem very small," he said to Uwen.

"Aye," said Uwen. And gruffly, "If you steal a damn thing, you little fools, I'll feed you to the fishes. Haul that tent

697

down! Spread the canvas out! – Thirteen summers. At very most. And they'd not go home if we sent them."

"Do you know them?"

"Oh, gods, I know them," Uwen said with a shake of his head. "I sees 'em in the mirror 'a mornin's. And like enough they'll come home if any of us do. – Look sharp, there. Stand back and watch how the tent is folded. If ye'd be soldiers ye'll do it just the same in the dark of the mornin' or a sergeant'll take 'is boot to ye and ye'll carry it on your bleedin' backs a day's march. – Ye need 'em, m'lord. Your servants has got too many to provide for to be heftin' the canvas or the water-pots."

I cannot bear two more lives, he thought with a rising sense of panic. But he said nothing. He went to see to Petelly and Dys, but Aswys and his boys had Petelly unsaddled and already led away to the edge of the camp, so he strayed back again to watch the spectacle of the tent being raised, with the two boys now joined by two others, hammering at stakes and pulling at guy-ropes and poles.

Uwen and the guards had the business of the tent in hand, and needed no advice from someone who had never seen a tent raised. So he stood with arms folded, as more wagons rolled in and disgorged canvas in a measured cascade of bundles down the row between two spears. Amefin guardsmen cheered and catcalled, and seized their tents and began at once to unfold them, with a marvelous economy of effort.

He was not the only lord to have importunate help: boys of the town and the villages had come with the wagons, and even a stray dog that refused all attempts to drive it off – it belonged to a boy and it would not go.

Another wagon deposited firewood at the intersections of lanes in the camp. Men and boys ran and seized up armfuls, as if there would not be enough.

His two boys came back with sufficient, and began to make a fire. So in the newly raised tent he sat in a folding chair from his own apartment, and had a leisurely cup of tea while the wagons came in.

The camp grew very soon in directions he could not see, as if the pace of the order of march had translated directly to the pace of the distribution and raising of tents. The outer edge and the horse-camp would continue growing as the supply wagons rolled in, but they would have the most of the men in camp and those who had walked farthest with the army camping earliest, and those who had joined them latest camping last. The camp had taken shape first around the spears marking the rows, then in a division established next by standards, those of the lords set by quarter, and those of villages set as they came in proper intervals, so that men would know where tents were to be set. Campfires were lit, men were having tea, preparing their own meals by units, a block of tents together.

So were the lords in command: there was one mess for the combined guard, the King's Dragon Guard with a tent of their own adjacent to the three lords' tents, with Lord Commander Gwywyn, and Lord Captain Kerdin directly in charge not only of the regulars but of such of the Prince's Guard as had come with them. By Annas' direction his servants took themselves in with the King's staff and the high command to prepare supper.

By the time the sun approached the horizon it was only the heavy wagons coming in, and the first of the distributions of grain was being made, sacks dumped off a wagon beginning not with the King's tent, but from the established edge of the camp and on, as the wagon rolled and the men aboard heaved grain sacks off into the waiting arms of men belonging to those tents, and a youthful scribe sat atop the stacks at the front of the wagon ticking off the sacks on a tablet.

It was all quite remarkable to watch. It went very quickly, considering the number of men involved, many of whom had not had drill; but there were enough soldiers who did know, who yelled instructions or imprecations as appropriate.

Cefwyn offered supper to them in his own tent, and Uwen and Idrys, and the lady and her two ladies all came, which was a fair number for a tent to accommodate. They brought their own folding chairs, and the dining table was the map-case set on two chests, adequate only to hold the cooking-pots from which they served: the young ladies were very tentative, and had no idea at all how to manage, but Ninévrisë was well at home, and laid a slice of hard bread into a bowl and had Annas put the stew on it. Then the ladies thought that it was proper to do that, too.

They were, Tristen thought, as young as he had been when he arrived among the folk of Amefel.

It was a simple, hasty stew; but it came very welcome after no sleep and a day of leave-takings and moderate confusion. So did a cup or two of wine. Tristen marked how Cefwyn's face was drawn and how his hand would steal surreptitiously to his leg. But after a little wine the pain seemed to ease.

Idrys came in, and had his supper; from outside came the smell of fires and cookery. Someone in the distance had a pipe, and played it quietly and well. They sat in warmth and pleas-ant company and discussed the day and the weather and their situation, while now and again reports came in – Gwywyn and Kerdin managed that, and Idrys, on whose shoulders a good deal of the effort of ordering the march had rested, stretched out his long legs in front of him, drank two cups of wine and relaxed. Gwywyn came in once to report that the outriders had met the returning messenger from the outpost at Emwy ruin, nearest Tasien's camp: and, their intelligence consequently extending all the way to the river, they could state with assur-ance that the field beyond Emwy was clear and their line of march toward Emwy and Lewen plain was secure: Aséyneddin had not crossed the river – and that was very good news.

That brought a third cup of wine, and there were far lighter expressions. The lady said then she was for bed, and so they all said.

"We shall break camp before light," Cefwyn reminded them, and they were beginning to take their leave of him, and went out into the dark, Ninévrisë to the north and himself to the south.

But just then came a rider thundering down the road and,

by the sound of it, to their very door. The guards shouted angrily outside, and the rider kept going past the tent, hoof-beats fading in the distance.

Cefwyn had started from his chair. Idrys had been quicker; and at the door of the tent a Guelen guardsman was on his way in.

"Your Majesty," that man said, distraught and angry.

But in just that small interval – came another such rider thundering past, and another angry outcry from the guards, as the rider passed.

Cefwyn cursed and walked past Idrys' questions and the guard's attempt at explanation – and stopped still in the door-way of the tent.

Tristen came and stood at Cefwyn's shoulder. The only oddity he could discover was his own banner, which had stood alone a short distance from the Marhanen Dragon and the Eagle of the Amefin of Henas'amef.

Two poles now stood imbedded in the earth, bearing village standards of the Amefin, at angles crossing his own black banner.

Another rider came speeding through the camp, village standard flying from the spear he held.

"Damn," said Idrys, and would have gone out.

"No," said Cefwyn sharply; and to his guards, "No alter-cation."

That man came by and flung his spear – and another standard joined the Sihhë banner.

Came a body of men afoot, right behind him, and four more of the Amefin standards went into place about the Tower and Star. Without seeming to notice the guards or them watching, they planted their standards, troubling them-selves to straighten and make firm the standards hastily set. Then they turned and walked away.

"Plague on them!" Idrys muttered; and Tristen felt cold and isolate – somehow at fault for what he understood as a shifting of allegiances of the Amefin – to his banner, which he neither wanted, nor knew what to do with. He thought that he ought to say something, to protest that he was against it, but he did not know what had caused it, and the words stuck in his throat.

"Orien," Cefwyn said. "Damn her!" There was another rider coming.

"We should stop this," Idrys said, and by now Gwywyn and Kerdin and a number of the Guelen guard were near the door, from their tent at the rear. But Cefwyn said, "No, damn it, let them do as they will. Do *nothing!* I'll not break what unity we have!"

Cefwyn thrust past them back into the tent, and before Annas could intervene, Cefwyn poured himself more wine and flung himself down into his chair. A frown was on his face in the candle-light, and Tristen came back to stand uncertainly facing him.

"What shall I do?" Tristen asked. There was such anger and resentment in the look that Cefwyn gave him, a gnawing sort of anger, hurt and small and frightening to him. "Can *I* stop it? I will. I shall go and talk to them."

A moment Cefwyn seemed unable even to speak to him, but sat with his hand clenched on his chair-arm. Then Cefwyn gave a great sigh and shook his head. "No."

"I would go with Idrys."

"No," Cefwyn said again, and looked up at him with a wry expression, made strained, Tristen hoped, by the lantern-light. "This is a fact. I am Marhanen. I am not loved. And Orien Aswydd has chosen her proxy. Quite clearly she has gotten a message out somehow, to arrange this."

"They are Amefin, all," Idrys said from the door. "And my lord King will recall, the bond between the Amefin and Althalen. Well that they *have* allegiances they will follow."

"And may follow on the field. If they will – if they will, then well enough. I said I would as lief have you lord of Amefel."

"There are good men of Amefel," Tristen said tentatively, "and if the Aswyddim are gone, still – one of them would expect, would he not – ?"

"Then let the Amefin *lords* exert authority to prevent it," Cefwyn said shortly, and with a glance at the two pale-faced Amefin ladies who attended Ninévrisë: "I see none of them doing so. The earls fear their own commons. – And what matter, as long as they attach themselves to a loyal man? Orien wished a rift between us, but it will work against her wishes, because I shall not be jealous and Tristen is my friend. Go, take your chairs, peaceful sleep. I shall sleep soundly, I assure you. They have answered my question, and if no Amefin earl durst step in, I shall appoint you over them. You should regard that as a threat, my friend, not a benefice. First I advise you appoint a taxman who is *not* a moneylender."

"I know nothing of such things," Tristen protested.

"So appoint men who do. You could do no worse than the Aswyddim."

"I want no more men following me," Tristen said. "I have *enough,* my lord King. I need no more."

"Go to bed, I say." Cefwyn moved his injured leg, and crossed his ankles before him. "I want my rest. – My gracious lady, forgive me. I am not a gentle host tonight."

"We should go to our tents," Ninévrisë said, and they went to the doors. Uwen gathered up their two chairs, the Amefin ladies took the others, in which Annas intervened and called a page to help them.

"Idrys," Tristen said with trepidation, seeing Cefwyn had said he would not deal with the matter, "Idrys, how shall I deal with this?"

The man looked at him with all his usual coldness – and yet with a little change in his regard. "Make it clear to them that you are the King's friend."

It seemed sound advice. Tristen nodded and went outside, giving place at the door to Ninévrisë.

Ninévrisë looked at him, a half-shadowed look in the fire-light, near the standards, and said urgently, "Lord Tristen."

"My lady."

Ninévrisë seemed to have changed her mind about speaking, then changed it again and came carefully closer. "Our enemy," she began, then said, "Your enemy. Is he there tonight?"

He did not so much fear the gray space, as distrust it. And he did not look. "Doubtless he is," he said. "He always is."

"And at Althalen?"

"I cannot say, m'lady." He thought then that that was what she feared: she had said not a word when they chose one of their camps as a site near Althalen, but he had seen her face in the council where they had worked out such details, seen the small nip of her lips together, clamped on an anxiousness about the notion. "But I have no sense of trouble there – or I would have said. Cefwyn did ask me." It had not been a question aloud, but at least a look, when they had measured the distances. "I would have spoken if I thought so."

She looked reassured, then. And it came to him that, perhaps worse than being able to see to Ynefel, if he chose, was the inability to see far at all, only to feel the threats in the gray world. She was not a strong wizard – yet, or perhaps ever. She perhaps had only enough of the sight to frighten her.

"You," he said, "will at least feel danger if it comes. As you felt it that night. Then is the time to advise Cefwyn. And me. But I will very likely know."

She looked at him, and put out her hand and touched his arm. "Be my friend, too," she said. "I *have* this sight. I don't know when it will come or where, and I don't know what it will show me. I fear to sleep here – but Althalen may be worse, and I did not sleep last night –"

Tears were very close. Her lips trembled, and he touched her hand and let it fall.

A shadow had come in the doorway of the tent.

Idrys.

Tristen looked in his direction. "Sir," Tristen said, feeling as caught in wrongdoing as ever he had with the man.

But Uwen was there, and Ninévrisë's ladies, and Tristen made a little bow and went away into his tent, where the servants had the lantern lit, and where Uwen helped him shed the wearying mail and the servants helped him with the boots and the clothing. Uwen lay down to rest then, on the cot in his division of the tent, and soon Uwen was snoring, in honest, hard-won exhaustion; and the servants became quieter and quieter.

Tristen sat a time and tried by lantern-light and until his eyes swam, to read anything in the Book, on page after page after page, seeking any letter that offered him anything understandable.

But now and again through the night his peace was broken, with men passing the tent.

And it was plain, after he had blown out the lantern and lay abed in his tent, what was continuing to happen outside. The guards were doing nothing to prevent it, on Cefwyn's order – because Cefwyn did not want a quarrel within the army. They had already had a nearly disastrous encounter between the two Guelen guard forces in the affair of Orien Aswydd, a confrontation which had left uneasiness between the two units that Idrys and Gwywyn had only scarcely patched. They could least of all afford a second one between Guelenmen and Amefin.

He did not know what he should do. It seemed he had not done what he should have, on any account. It was well possible that the enemy was already reaching out to push and pull things – just little things – to make them fail; and he did not know how to stop the desertions that threatened Cefwyn . . . or the constant accumulation of followers of his own, that terrified and distracted him on every side.

In the morning as the first light touched the camp, forty or more of the village banners made a tight cluster about the Sihhë standard.

But the Dragon of the Marhanen did not stand alone either, for the unit pennons of the Guelen guard had been moved by their own men, and stood ranged about Cefwyn's red and gold banner, defiance and challenge of the Amefin. Tristen knew what he saw, coming out of his tent at the first stirring about; and, "Well," Cefwyn muttered, seeing that sight from the doorway of his own tent, and seemed greatly touched.

"Break camp!" Idrys ordered, and tents began, in that area, to come down, as they had already come down in the row next to them, in that dim light. Very quickly their guy-ropes and pegs formed a bundle on their several tents which became a bundle, and they were among the first laid out along the lane the wagons would travel picking them up. Cefwyn stood in the chill morning wind, and Tristen stood beside him. The grooms brought their horses to them, but Cefwyn did not offer to mount yet, so no one else did.

Eventually there were only men and horses standing where there had been tents, as far as the eye could see. They were behind their scheduled departure. They stood, and went on standing, and as it became evident to everyone that they were standing there on the King's will, and waiting for the King's order, there fell an unnatural quiet, on their personal guards first, and at last over all the camp.

"Guelen!" Idrys shouted, then, and there was a movement forward, the Guelen camped around the command tents, who massed toward their standards all in confusion. Idrys shouted angry orders; the standard-bearers took their standards to their respective units, and the Guelen fell into order.

Then, unbidden, but in rivalry, perhaps, not to be left behind, came a tide of Amefin surging forward, who noisily possessed their own standards, but they did not take any orderly form. There was shouting, there was pushing, and a fight broke out as men surged forward and began trying to rescue their standards, and as the Guelen shoved them and made space for the King and his company.

Tristen stared helplessly for that instant, then – understanding the symbol of what these men were struggling for – he knew the only thing the Amefin and Guelen in that press might all see. He seized the Sihhë banner from Andas, who had moved to protect it, and carried it himself to the front of Cefwyn's tent. The pole had a sharp end; and with a great thrust he planted it in the earth beside Cefwyn's Dragon, aslant, as it settled the poles touching.

A murmur went up, and the fighting stopped. He was not capable of speech. He went to Cefwyn and they embraced before the army. A cheer went up around them, and Cefwyn laughed and grinned broadly, and embraced him again.

There was a cleaner feeling in the air. Tristen hugged Cefwyn a third time for gladness of that feeling, and Cefwyn's eyes sparkled with tears, his lips drawn tight.

"To horse!" Idrys shouted, waving his sword. "Districts by order! *Move!* We are *late,* sirs! Move, move, *move!*"

It seemed to mean everyone. Cefwyn went toward his horse, and he went quickly to the groom that held Petelly, took the reins and swung up. The wagon had not been able to get through. Now it was coming, as men ran for their appropriate places, and Andas reclaimed the Sihhë standard, as the standard-bearers of the Dragon and the Regent's Tower took up their own.

A breeze lifted them. The morning sun streamed gold through light cloud. The King moved out and Ninévrisë joined him as their standard-bearers got to horse and moved out ahead. Tristen rode to join them and Andas took the Sihhë banner out to the left, where it belonged. Their guards mounted up, the Amefin lords came next, and before they had left the camp grounds, the Guelen Guard, both rival regiments and the regulars, had started up the same marching-song, shouting it out and going along at a brisk pace.

In no little time there was another song from the Amefin ranks behind, and that was the way the troops contended with each other.

He felt quite cheered. He had won something, he saw that, things seemed mended that had been broken, and Cefwyn laughed and joked with him and with Idrys and the lady. The morning lay like a sheen over the road, making their shadows long as they marched toward the west, casting that early-morning glamor on things that made ordinary colors seem different, and more magical. This morning they could do nothing wrong.

But then his eyes lifted to the horizon, toward the north

and east, and the morning seemed not so bright there – he was tempted to look with the vision he did have, terribly tempted; but he thought it was exactly what he should not do.

They rode in that direction on a road that could not lose sight of that shadow, and it was impossible to forget it. It distracted him from the light mood the others set, and his distraction seemed at times to make them anxious. But they asked no questions, perhaps fearing the answer he might give.

"Do you see any shadowing on that horizon?" he asked of Uwen when they stopped for rest. He hoped that it might be some natural thing. If autumn could surprise him, then other things still might, and Words might arise he had never met.

But Uwen looked where he looked and said only that he saw a hint of cloud, but that it was not all that black.

He went to Ninévrisë while they were paused, and said, looking at the grass at their feet, "M'lady, if it comes to you today to have a look into that other place, resist it. Resist it with all your might."

"Why?" Ninévrisë asked in alarm. "What do you see?"

"Nothing imminent," he said. "Only be prudent."

Natural men could not see it; and Cefwyn could not; and even Ninévrisë failed. So he rode with the knowledge to himself, alone, as slowly, subtly, to his eyes, a line of shadow began to reach along the horizon, like a smudge of smoke, a presentiment of night.

It seemed, to his eye, closer, and wider.

They met the contingents of four more villages. They were, Cefwyn said, approaching an end of Amefel where villages had been once, but where now were far fewer – where forest rimmed the horizon and where roads ran more scarcely.

By Cefwyn's reckonings they should have begun to pick up the southern lords this morning. And they had not; the levity with which they had begun diminished through the day, and when they saw the sun pass mid-afternoon and they were neither at their campsite nor seeing any sign of their allies either ahead of them or to the south or behind them, concern began to work among them, and Cefwyn and Idrys cast frequent, anxious looks toward the south as he did to the west.

"We might wait a day for them," Idrys said. "We might well, m'lord King."

But Ninévrisë said, "Lord Tasien cannot wait," and Tristen added, "We dare not," because that was the truth he could not doubt.

CHAPTER 33

All about them now were meadows and forest-crowned hills, low rolls of the land that rose toward Althalen – treacherous land, which, like that around Raven's Knob, could mask an entire army. They had had that message last night that their way was clear – but that condition could have changed ahead at any hour an Elwynim army appeared on the riverside.

Cefwyn shifted his weight in Danvy's saddle both to ease the throb of his healing wound, and to see whether, by standing a handspan higher, he could see significantly more. They were behind their schedule. He did not want to order the column stopped prematurely, short of their planned camp; but he was beginning to ask himself was it wise not to stop sooner, and whether they had not overestimated their rate of march altogether, which would affect their ability to meet their other contingents and which might turn very serious indeed, if their army was going to move more slowly than their plan all along the march. The heavy horsemen rode today with their shields and weapons, but not in their full battle armor, and the heavy horses all traveled under saddle, in the hands of their grooms, though they as yet carried no riders and did not carry their full armor or caparison. That had been the plan they had made, that once they passed beyond the first encampment and especially as they rode in the vicinity of Althalen, they would count themselves in hostile if not imminently threatening territory. The light horse had carried riders all day, the destriers at least a slight weight all day; the infantry had marched with shields and spears since noon rest instead of having them transported in the baggage – and they might have to revise that plan to make the speed they needed. But going without defense was increasingly a risk, in territory uneasy in more than the sense of Althalen's haunted precinct. In the rolling land not only was the rear of the train out of sight in the distance, hours behind the front ranks, simply because of the length of the column, but even nearer ranks were often lost to view in the rolls and windings of the road. The wagons for baggage and supply had a small rear guard and the whole line of march, foot as well, was interspersed with horsemen who could ride for help in the event of attack, which could otherwise have cut off the tail of the army without the head even aware an attack was in progress.

If the enemy could cut them off from their equipment, their tents, their supply – they would be in a very grave situation, in which many of them would never survive retreat and regrouping near Henas'amef. It was not a risk to run lightly, to have the men lighter-armed, because there had been incursions such as Caswyddian's, and the Regent had camped at Althalen completely unknown to men searching the hills. It was rough land out there. Tristen warned that Aséyneddin did know their intent and their schedule, and they were racing with all the skill and strength they had against an enemy doing the same with the help of Tristen's mysterious enemy, an enemy capable of killing Mauryl Gestaurien, chilling thought.

They had to start earlier tomorrow morning. They had to reach Lord Tasien's encampment at Emwy Bridge in order to hold Aséyneddin in Elwynor; at very least, if they were too late, they had to do something to keep from meeting Aséyneddin on ground Aséyneddin or his wizardly ally chose.

Wizardry. *Sorcery,* rather. It was the first time he had ever used that word advisedly; if it ever applied, that dark art which Emuin had named in the necessary lessons of a prince of a land with such a history, it should apply to this ghost, this – whatever it was that Tristen feared.

But they faced mortal enemies too, and it would be fatal to panic, to tire his forces, or wear down either the horses the heavy horsemen used for travel, or the warhorses who would, over much shorter distance and under all the weight of their armor, carry them into battle. Nor dared he have wagons and draft teams broken down under rushed and imprudent handling: that would be as fatal as losing them to the enemy.

He looked across at Tristen to ask what he thought . . . and saw that Tristen gazed as often he did toward the west, toward Marna.

Toward Ynefel, Cefwyn thought. Now the nature of Tristen's lapses seemed transparent, which they had never been to this degree before, with walls to mask their direction.

"If it will satisfy you," Cefwyn said to him, fearing that attention of his to the west, "once we have settled with the Elwynim matter, next spring, I shall agree we must concern ourselves with Ynefel. So I plead with you, my friend, as you swore to *be* my friend, delay what you can delay. Sovrag's boats can provide you and what forces you need a safe way to Ynefel, if go you must. No walking that end of Marna. You may have done it once under Mauryl's protection, but never think of going there alone. Never think of leaving us. I shall stand by you at your need – but now I have need of you. You are my eyes toward that enemy. If you fail me I am blind. Do you understand that?"

Tristen looked at him, lifted his hand to the northwest, between forest edge and plains. "He will meet us *before* Emwy."

It was possible Tristen had heard nothing of what he said. "Are you certain?" he asked Tristen.

"Yes," Tristen said distantly. Then: "Yes. I have feared so all day. Now I know. I wish not."

It meant Tasien's annihilation, almost certainly. Cefwyn's heart sank, and he glanced aside to see who rode in hearing of them. Idrys was. Ninévrisë was speaking with one of the Guelen guards he had assigned to guard her, and could not have heard. "More of Mauryl's visions?"

Tristen shook his head. "Mine, sir."

"Is Lord Tasien fallen, then?"

"I think he is, sir. I feel it certain. I have feared it for hours."

The news was maddening. He did not want to believe it.

"Then Aséyneddin has crossed the river. That is what you are saying."

"Yes, sir."

"Don't say it to Her Grace, and don't say it to anyone yet. Even Uwen. Not until I say so."

"Yes, sir."

"Across the river. – Then, *damn* it. –" He looked where the scouts had ridden over the hills to the south. "Where is Lord Cevulirn? – And when will we find him?" he asked, with his father's irreverence for visions and, still, a hope that wizardry would fail or find exception. "Vision me that vision and save my scouts the hazard."

Tristen gave a visible shiver, a drawing in of the shoulders. "No. I would not venture to say, lord King. I don't see them. But I do see a shadow on the land . . . westward and north, that is not good. That is not at all good."

"A shadow. Wizardry, you mean."

"It is, sir. But it's all the same a Shadow."

Cefwyn scanned the western horizon and saw nothing. "You can see bad news but not good? Is that it? Or what *do* you see?"

"Things that a wizard touches. My enemy is *with* Aséyneddin. He is *at* Ynefel."

"One's at the bridge, one's in the heart of Marna! How can he be two places at once?"

"I don't think he's at Althalen. I hope, sir, I do hope for Althalen to be safe. If it isn't –"

"If it isn't, we're destined to camp there tonight. We rely on camping there and passing that place without being engaged. If there was a possibility of this, you might have told me before now!"

"I would have told you, sir, if I thought he was there. I don't think so. And going overland is far slower. – But where Lord Cevulirn is, I don't know."

Wizards. It was enough to give a man pause. And when Tristen was rapt in thought he forgot all instructions of protocols, all agreements, all that was between them – he simply told what he believed; and increasingly he did believe it. He had a sudden vision of himself, a man of practical Marhanen blood, pursuing Tristen's will-o'-the-wisp enemies across two provinces of ancient superstitions, elder gods, and demonstrable wizardry.

Scratch an Amefin and wizard blood bled forth. And if he fought for Amefel against what tried to claim its ancient soil – it was most reasonably a war of wizards. By his own choice, a Sihhë standard, black and ominous, fluttered beside the Marhanen Dragon. By his own choices the Amefin rural folk, emboldened by the fall of the Aswydds and the impotence of their own lords, had flocked to Tristen's standard. He could bear with that.

But in Guelessar and the northern provinces were honest and good and loyal men who would shrink in horror from what their King had allied with, even if their King won.

If their King lost a province – and retreated into the heartland of Ylesuin, with sorcery let loose in Amefel and the Elwynim in its employ – he would have failed his oath to his own people. The wailing of slain children had haunted his grandfather to his dying hour. In the gods' good name – what might haunt him hereafter?

"A rider," Tristen said, and he saw it at the same moment: a scout coming back full tilt down the hills toward them.

More bad news? he asked himself. He braced himself for it. Idrys swung closer, clearly seeing it. Gwywyn and Ninévrisë came near.

The man – of the Prince's Guard, as all their scouts were of that regiment – slid to a walk alongside them. "Your Majesty," the scout breathed, while his horse panted and blew. "Your Majesty, – dust on the south – all *along* the south, m'lord. My companion rode ahead to see."

"Fall back and find Qwyll's-son. Have him inform the ranks. Pass it back by rider."

"Yes, m'lord." The man drew rein and fell back in the line.

"It may be Cevulirn," Cefwyn said. "That would be *very* good news."

"Certainly better than such sightings on our north," Idrys muttered. Idrys had been close on Tristen's other side, close enough to have heard his exchange with Tristen. And Idrys believed bad news before good. Always.

"Coming from the south, they must be ours," Ninévrisë said.

Tristen said, solemnly, "They *are* ours, my lady. But *we* are to their north. Best they be certain who *we* are."

Tristen said such a thing. Something else had clearly unfolded to him, in only so few days.

Possibilities unfolded to the Marhanen King, too.

What if it were the writer of the *Art of War* Mauryl had brought back? His mentor of that long-ago text, riding unguessed beside him?

It was too cursed poetic. And, no, Tashânen was an engineer and a strategist.

He recalled their last council before the barons had left. He said to himself as they rode side by side looking for that encounter, Tristen knows strategy – Certainly he knows the sword. Uwen says he knows the lance, that he *will* ride Dys, and that he has no doubts of him. The Sihhë *brought* the heavy horses with them to the land: how should he not know them?

Tristen counseled us no earthen walls. He spoke out *against* fortifications. Everyone will die, Tristen said, and we didn't heed him – when he was counseling us, damn it, on the one answer I could never find in Tashânen's book, the one question I most wanted to know, and I didn't *hear* what he was saying.

Tashânen didn't write it in his book because the Sihhë of his age *knew* that answer. It was the art of siege Tashânen invented – against enemies who used other Sihhë tactics as a matter of course. Tashânen had all prior lore – books *burned* at Althalen – and why should he write down the use of magic innate in his kind? Other texts would have held that – whatever a man's born with, there's always a cleverer way to use it: *that* would have been his object in writing: what he wrote

715

down was the new thing, not the old. Why should we expect a Sihhë or any man to write down the obvious?

What held me from hearing Tristen?

Are we all so blind? Or is it another blow his enemy has struck us, through Orien Aswydd?

What *did* one do, he went on asking himself, without that knowledge innate (Emuin had said it) in Tristen's kind?

Strike at flesh and blood? That he could do. The other possibilities – he did not even see. And in his blindly following a Sihhë text, he had not regarded Tristen's warning – he had seen only the dangers of Tristen confronting him in council; and in his infatuation with Sihhë skill in war, he had sent men to an untenable, fatal position against wizardry.

He had let his bride's kinsman make a deadly mistake. Tasien had acted the best he knew against his enemy, in the absence of any trust of Guelen kings. But as King, he certainly could have argued with Tasien with more force, rather than accept Tasien's plan as he had done and (gods forgive him) embroider it with his own boyhood fancies.

Trenches in the herb garden. Good blessed gods, why had he not used his wits?

But without sending Emuin, or Tristen, neither of which was possible – what *could* he have done against a wizardous attack? What could he do against the one he knew was coming at them all?

And how did he break the news of Tasien to Ninévrisë?

In a plume of sunlit dust the remaining scout from the south came riding up over the swell of land. *"The Ivanim!"* that man called out as he came near. "I saw their banners, and the sun on their helms!"

Even as that rider came, the sun was picking up color in the west, and they all could see a second plume of dust on that horizon, farther away, behind the first.

"That is Umanon," Cefwyn speculated aloud, his heart lifting.

Idrys, quick as his own thought, pulled back in the column and gave orders, and two more scouts immediately rode away from the column and overland in that direction, this time to welcome the lostlings in.

"Thank the gods," Cefwyn breathed, certain now that they had found at least two of their missing contingents.

Within the hour the riders from the south had crested the rise along the road, a rolling tide of the swift-moving Ivanim light horse, and behind them, their slower-moving allies of Imor, a dark mass of riders and warhorses at lead. The banners were plain in the sunset, and Tristen drew a deep, glad breath when he saw it.

"Two of them," Cefwyn said in Tristen's hearing. "Now, gods save us, if now Pelumer will come in . . ."

Olmern had perhaps succeeded, Tristen thought when Cefwyn made that wish. He could in no wise tell for certain, but he felt none of the hostile influence to the northeast, and that said to him that their enemy had not gone that way. The way they *had* left open to Aséyneddin had cost them dearly, those two bridges eastward of Emwy district, which Cefwyn had hoped would make an incursion from the forest-edged west the only answer if Aséyneddin wished to cross quickly into Amefel. Tasien was gone. The Elwynim *had* crossed and committed themselves. No second rebel force could threaten Henas'amef without coming by way of Emwy, and without passing them.

That portion of the plan was, he hoped, working. Cefwyn had designated reciprocal messengers that daily came to Henas'amef from the east reach of the river, upstream, and one would have reached Henas'amef last night. After that, Efanor should have sent the regular relay out north to the river and sent another courier west after them, bringing Cefwyn word of the riverside and Sovrag.

Cefwyn's system of messengers, Tristen thought, was very well done; it had freed him personally of the necessity to try to reach Emuin, which was the most dangerous thing he could do short of speaking to Hasufin himself. Cefwyn's couriers had gone out from the army directly north this morning, to reach Sovrag directly and to bear Ninévrisë's second messages of reassurance and encouragement to the Amefin riverside villages, jointly with Cefwyn's, to assure them they were not abandoned, that Sovrag was not a threat to them, and to urge the villages to report to them directly overland in the now remote chance Lord Aséyneddin should cross somehow – on that matter, the defense of the province might have turned.

But now the bonfires they had lit on the hills had brought them Cevulirn and Umanon, and that was another wonder of Cefwyn's forethought: the simultaneous muster of the barons and their being able to join Cefwyn's column on the move had all relied on measuring distances, which Cefwyn had done in advance, and knowing very accurately how fast the various forces could move, granted they saw the signal fires and moved at all.

If one had no way into the gray space, it was a very clever way of doing things. It was a way of getting around wizards – and it was important to know how that could be done. He marked it always to remember, and never to become complacent in what he saw.

And the gray place was constantly urging at him. It was full of shadows and lights and whispers. Now with the sun taking the light from the land and making the hills gold, and with their allies riding toward them, he felt that the missing pieces that had to exist had now come together.

But he did not have that feeling of inevitability about Pelumer that he had had all along about Cevulirn's coming and Umanon's. Marna's dark edge was Pelumer's route – and he had no wish to look deeply or long in that direction.

Cevulirn came riding up in the sunset with the White Horse flying, leading his own warhorse with him, as every man in his company had a remount with him and his lance and shield and a small amount of provisions packed on the warhorse's saddle.

That was the way the southern horsemen had done forever,

constantly changing from mount to mount. So Cefwyn advised him as the riders came, and it unfolded in Tristen's thoughts that it had indeed been that way, that on their longest marches they had two and even three horses in their string. He saw it so vividly that a Name almost came to him, and he felt comfortable with the Ivanim, and knew their thinking, for reasons he did not clearly know.

Cefwyn told Cevulirn his place in line and his place in camp from memory – a precedence in line behind the Amefin, whose province it was, and ahead of Umanon, whom he had beaten in – Cefwyn told Cevulirn where his warhorses should be, and where his wagon was and where his tents would be, which they had brought for him.

"Your Majesty leaves no work for the scribes," Cevulirn said with the mild lifting of a brow. It had seemed a point of amazement among the barons in all the preparations that Cefwyn did remember such things in very certain detail.

"Join us this evening!" Cefwyn wished him in sending him off. "We'll take a cup of wine together – and explain this haste!"

Umanon also came riding up, his men traveling in the same style as the Ivanim, leading a contingent of heavy horse. "Majesty!" Umanon called out. "A short stay at home. I'd scarcely built a fire in the hearth!"

"I shall explain tonight!" Cefwyn said. "But things are as well as they can be. Thank the gods for your meeting us. We're in good order, with you here, Your Grace! See me when first you've set your tents!" And Cefwyn told Umanon the numbers and place of his camp as well, after which Umanon rode off to his assigned place in the order, and to claim his personal baggage.

The day had worn hard on Cefwyn. He had started the day as he had started yesterday, riding strongly, but now despite the good news of a moment ago, he seemed to Tristen to be clinging to his courage and to his composure even at Danvy's sedate walk. Danvy had given a couple of quick steps as horses came up to him, and Cefwyn had corrected that, but at a price.

"Not far," Tristen said to him, the only encouragement he could offer, for if there was one road in the world he knew it was this one and if there was one thing he could now sense like his own bonfire in this night, it was Althalen.

It was deepest dusk when they came to their projected camp, in that area of the road respecting Althalen's perimeter and across the road from any accidental encroachment on what Cefwyn called the cursed precinct. Tristen was very glad, himself, to get down. The wagons were yet to come and the least essential ones, with the units of horse that guarded them, would be arriving long into the night.

"Set the unit standards with their units," Cefwyn called out, pointed warning against any such carryings-on as yesterday night. "Bid everyone keep their standards in good order. From this place on, there is danger of the enemy at any hour!"

Ninévrisë had not gotten off her horse, and Tristen walked over to see if she needed help; so did Cefwyn, at the same time.

"My lady?" Cefwyn said.

"My father's grave is here," she said. "I wish to ride just to the edge of the ruin, my lord, to stay only for a moment, if I can do it without endangering the camp. But I feel – I wish to, my lord."

Tristen stood by, having been ready to offer Ninévrisë a hand down. He knew that Cefwyn did not want to grant such a request, and that Cefwyn out of his willingness to please Ninévrisë would get back on Danvy and take a guard and go, though he was in pain. He would not send Ninévrisë only with an escort.

"I shall go with you," Cefwyn said, with never a protest.

"My lord," Tristen said. "My lord King, this is a place where I can see things others may not, and defend against things others cannot. I can take Uwen and my guards."

Cefwyn looked at him, seemed to consider, and let weariness and gratitude touch his face. "Half yours," he said. "Six of the Dragon Guard. We've tents to raise. – And be careful. In this matter, I trust *you* as no other, but for the gods' own sake, for the *gods'* sake and on your oath to me, be careful."

"Yes, sir." He went to get Petelly and gave orders to Uwen, glad that Cefwyn had been reasonable – but most of all feeling now in his heart, as clearly as he saw the sun sinking, that Ninévrisë's request was both urgent and advised.

He mounted up and by that time Uwen had collected the men Cefwyn lent him. They crossed the road, on which a seemingly endless line of riders and men afoot stretched on out of sight, and they entered the meadow on the other side, riding up through a screen of trees to another grassy stretch, farther and farther then, out of sight of their camp, and up into the area where they had met Uwen that dreadful night, in the rain, and with Caswyddian's forces behind them.

Uwen grew anxious. So did the men with them. And perhaps, Tristen thought, he should be apprehensive himself, as he saw streaks of wind run through the grass, and one little one, following a thinner, very erratic course. He knew the child, saw her frolic without seeing her at all.

Ninévrisë said, "Something is there."

"It is," he said. "But don't look too closely. She doesn't like to be caught. – Uwen, it's the witch of Emwy's child. She's a little girl. I'm glad to see her. Her name is Seddiwy."

"That old woman?"

"I don't think the child died when Emwy burned. I think she might have died a long time ago. I don't know why I think so, except the Emwy villagers are here, too, and they're not so friendly, or so happy as she is. – But they won't harm us. She's stronger than she seems."

"Gods," Uwen muttered, as four distinct marks flattened the grass ahead of them, leading where they had to go. "Is it those streaks in the grass?"

"Yes, those."

"M'lord, I do hope you know where we're going."

The light was leaving them very fast, now, and none of the men looked confident – they were very tired, they had been two days now on the road, and they might, except for this venture, be sitting at the fires and drinking wine with their friends and waiting for their suppers; but on Cefwyn's orders they came, and fingered amulets more than weapons.

Petelly snorted and twitched his head up as the little spirit darted beneath him – and then right under a guardsman's horse. It shied straight up, and the man, most anxious of their company, fought hard to hold it from bolting.

"Behave!" Tristen said sternly, and that stopped.

They were coming among saplings that had been all broken off halfway up their trunks. Rocks lay shattered in the grass.

Then one of the Dragon Guards reined aside from something lying in the grass, and said, not quite steadily, "Here's a dead man, Lord Warden."

"Caswyddian's men," Ninévrisë said calmly enough, though her voice was higher than its wont. "Are we in danger, Lord Tristen? Might *their* spirits harm us?"

It was to ask. But –"No, I don't think so. The Emwy folk seem to hold this place to themselves."

They came up that long, difficult ridge, where two men had fallen. The rains had not quite washed away the scars they had made on that climb.

They reached that place that overlooked the ruin, and it stretched very far under the cover of trees and brush and meadows. Despite the chill of the winds below, the air on this exposed ridge was quite still, even comfortable. There was a sense of peace here that had not existed before, tempting one who had the power to look in that different way – to stop and cast a look in this fading last moment of the light.

Ninévrisë said, in a shaken voice, "Father? Father, is that you?"

Then a change in that other Place caught Tristen's attention, as certainly a presence would: and in that instant's glance he saw pale blue, and soft gold. He risked a second look and saw the Lines of the ruin, the lines on the earth that had grown fainter and fainter in the hour of the Regent's

722

death now spreading out brightly far and wide. Brighter and brighter they shone in the dusk as the world's light faded, until they blazed brightly into inner vision. Other lines glowed where those lines touched, and those touched other lines in their turn, like fire through tinder, blue and pale gold, each form in interlocking order, as far as the eye could make out, one square overlaying the other – all through the grass, and the thickets.

It was the old man's handiwork, he thought, astonished and reassured. Late as it was, the earth was still pouring out light. Shadows flowed along the walls, but respected the lines of those walls now. The men about him glowed like so many stars to his eyes; and then his worldly vision said it was not the men, but the amulets they wore, the blessed things, the things invested with their protection against harm – as Emuin's amulet glowed on his own chest, in the midst of the light that was himself.

That glow seemed the old man's doing, too – yet none of the men with them, not even Uwen, seemed to see all that had happened. Only Lady Ninévrisë gazed astonished over the land.

"Your father's work!" he said. "Do you see, my lady? He is not lost!"

"I see it," she said, holding her hands clasped at her lips. "I do see!"

"What, Lord Warden?" a guardsman asked; but Uwen said, quietly, "What m'lord sees ain't bad, whatever it is. Just wait. He's workin'."

"No," Tristen said, for the men's comfort. "It's not bad. It's safe. It's very safe here."

The Lines, as they had that night, showed him what Althalen had been, bright as a beacon, now, advising him here had been a street, here had stood walls, here was a way through the maze, though brush had grown up and choked the open ground.

And when he thought of that, a Name the old man had not been able to tell him seemed to sound in the air, unheard, that Question to which the old man had known the answer resounded through the grayness, and Lines on the earth rose into ghostly walls and arches, halls full of people who walked in beautiful garments, and ate delicate food, and laughed and moved in gardens and a river ran near that had boats sailing on it, boats with colored sails and with the figures of beasts and birds on their bows. He did not know whether he could say it as the old man did – but he had almost heard it ringing through the world.

Not Althalen, he thought, then, aware he was slipping very rapidly toward the gray space – but not – suddenly – at Althalen.

There was a murky river. He knew where that river ran – he was in sudden danger. He had risen into the gray space – and gone badly astray, trapped, by an enemy old and clever, and *still* able to have his way.

He met the attack. He set himself to the fore of Ninévrisë, approaching the enemy on his own, but not taking the enemy's vision –

When he thought that, immediately he found a vantage he knew, outside, on the parapet of Ynefel, in the sunset. He knew his loft, the high point of a vast hall across the court-yard, highest point in the keep.

He could see his own window, with the horn panes glowing with light in the twilight, as if he were there himself, reading by candlelight – but with the shutters inside open. That was wrong, and dangerous.

It was his window, and it was his home, and he knew the study below, in which he kept his books, many, many of them – not Mauryl's books, but his own books. He was puzzled, and thought, That was never true.

The height of Ynefel rang with a Word, then, which he could hear, but not hear, in the curious barriers of this dream; and at that Word, all of this glorious building trembled and fell quiet.

He stood on the very parapet, where he had gone – or would go – naked in the rain.

He watched all the buildings from there – the illusion of a living city widespread about Ynefel's skirts, streets busy as the streets of Henas'amef.

But it had not been Ynefel on that day. It had had another Name. So had he. And he had come there with Mauryl's help to cast all that citadel down.

He was angry, he knew not why or at what. That anger grew in him, and as it reached the point that he must loose it or die, he let it loose.

In that loosing, a wind swept the halls, swept up the men in their elegant clothing, and the women in their bright gowns, and the children, alike, with their toys, and whirled them all about the towers, tumbling one over the other, out of the bright world and into that gray space where they hurtled, lost and afraid.

Some, more determined and more powerful, found their way back to their former home, and peered out of its walls, frozen in the stone.

Some became Shadows, angry ones, or fearful ones, or simply lost ones, wailing on the winds that carried them through that gray light, until darker Shadows hunted them down, one by one, and ate their dreams and their hopes and their substance.

But all such shadows as came to him for refuge he breathed in and breathed them out again with his will, and by them he mastered the anger that threatened his reason. By them he learned . . . better things.

A young man in gray had stood by him, but that man was gone. He possessed securely the walls, the woods, the river, in all the vacancy he had made.

He had done this. All the City was gone. He remained. The Tower of Ynefel remained.

The faces watched from the walls, and the lives flowed through him with a heat like too much wine. He was trembling now. He wanted to know – who had done such a thing, and could it possibly be himself who had begun it?

But of his own countenance and his own reasons he could discern nothing.

He had lived – or would live – in that small room with the horn-paned window. He had come at Mauryl's asking, and he knew at once his enemy was the man who had stood beside him, the young man in gray, against whom he had fought with all the resources at his disposal – even binding the lives of the people of Ynefel to his effort.

He wanted to know who he was. He wanted to see the face of the one who would have drunk up all the world only to cast out the man in gray.

He had asked Mauryl – or would ask one day – whether Mauryl could see his own face. He thought it clever of himself to wonder that in this dream, a trick by which he could make the dream reveal itself – and him.

But in this dream he had no mirror, nor were there any such, until, still in this dream, suddenly standing within his own room – or what would be his room – he found on the bedside table a small silver mirror. Threads of shadow formed about it, resisting, strands clung to it as he picked it up, and shriveled when he would not be deterred.

He had been clever. He had gained in this dream the mirror Mauryl had given him; but once he had found it, he was back in the courtyard by the kitchen door and the rain-barrel. Daylight was behind him and even with the mirror he could see no more than he had seen in the rain-barrel that day, only his own outline, an outline with a shadowed face.

So the dream had tricked him, and would not at any trick he could play unfold more than he had seen.

He was sitting on Petelly's back again. He had his hands locked before his lips. He was aware of the men watching him. He had come all that distance through the past, alone of those living, and alone of the dead – but he knew nothing. Nothing.

He had found reason to fear – and out of his fear, and in revulsion at Hasufin's cruelty, he thought now, had flowed his terrible anger.

And when his anger broke loose – at least in the dream – he had used lives for the stones and anger for the mortar of his fortress.

It might be illusion. Mauryl had said not to fear dreams, that there was not always truth in them. He thought that Mauryl had had a part in what had happened.

The old man had said – Hasufin would use even his dreams.

The old man had proposed to hold Althalen, and everywhere around him, now that he had broken with Ynefel, was the evidence of the old man's power. *Surely* Hasufin could not make something seem so fair – more – *feel* so fair, and so safe, and so familiar.

But the faces of Ynefel lately in his memory were a truth he could not deny.

They moved on certain nights – or seemed to, when the wind blew, the balconies creaked, and candleflame wavered in the drafts.

Ynefel, which held always a warm, homelike feeling for him – was a terrible place, where he – he! – had done something unthinkable and destructive.

"M'lord," Uwen said, moving his horse close. "M'lord?"

He could not move. He could not look aside from that structure of glowing lines, feeling always less than he needed to be, less wise, less kind, less – able to create something like this, so fair and so bright in the gray world.

His handiwork – was other than this.

Men feared him. All men did well to fear him.

Uwen took the reins somehow, and turned Petelly about, and once they were faced the other way he realized that Ninévrisë was close beside him on one hand, and the guardsmen had gathered about them, hands on weapons and yet with no enemy against which they could defend him.

He put his hands on Petelly's neck, and patted his neck. "I can manage, Uwen," he said as steadily as he could.

"M'lord," Ninévrisë said – frightened, too, he thought. He had taken her into danger. "I saw nothing – nothing amiss here."

"Then the harm, if there is harm, is in me."

"No such thing, m'lord," Uwen said firmly, and, leaning

727

from his saddle, managed to pass the reins over Petelly's head again, which required his help to straighten out. Petelly lifted his head, making the maneuver more difficult; but he secured the reins, settled Petelly's anxious starts in one direction and the other, and as their small party began to ride home, went quietly, reasonably back the way they had come, among the hills, shadowing with night, and finally across the road, down the busy center lane of the camp, where wagons and men continued to come in.

He said, to the men, when they crossed the road, "What I saw – what I saw boded no harm to you." He knew that he had acted in such a way that might spread fear through the army. "I beg you not mention it. I shall tell His Majesty when I know the answer."

The leg ached, ached so that a cup of wine was Cefwyn's chief wish, far more than a supper, no matter the servants' efforts. It was past dark, there was no sign of Tristen and Ninévrisë, and he had debated with himself whether to offend Ninévrisë by sending men out – or whether to sit and worry.

But the mere sight of Cevulirn and Umanon was reassuring, and persuaded him he had so many men in the vicinity that no enemy scouts would be too daring, and that the Elwynim rebel that tried Tristen's mettle would find that small band no easy mark at all. Sit still, he told himself. Let them learn what they can learn in their own way. Sending someone into wizardous doings was not wise.

Sending two most valuable persons to seek out wizardry worried him intensely.

But he had trusted Tristen too little so far. He could *not* rule by hampering his best counselors, whatever the frightening nature of their investigations.

Outside the royal pavilion, the White Horse of the Ivanim and the Wheel of Imor Lenúalim were snapping in a stiff wind alongside the Dragon and beside them, the Tower and Star, the Regent's Tower and the Amefin Eagle. The wagons belonging to the Guelen regulars were disgorging their supplies. The Duke of Ivanor and the Duke of Imor had pitched their tents alongside his, with Tristen's on the other side, next Gwywyn's tent, which was the command post for the Dragon and the Prince's Guard. They made no individual fires tonight, in the tents of the common men, so as to give any spies that did venture onto surrounding hilltops no convenient way to count their number. But fires were starting outside, and cooks were hard at work with the big kettles, boiling up soup and unpacking hard bread they had brought from town. The common men would not fare at all badly tonight, mutton stew and enough ale to wash it down, very good ale, he had ordered that personally. But it would not be enough to become drunk.

There was a grimmer and very businesslike feel to this camp, from which they would set out on their final march either to fight or to establish a camp in the face of the enemy, from which they would launch a more deliberate war.

There was more and quicker order, for one thing, so Idrys had reported from his latest tour about. Untaught peasants, accepted into Amefel's line, followed lords' and officers' orders and soldiers' examples tonight in the not unreasonable confidence that their lives very soon would hang upon what they learned. So from a slovenly behavior at the outset, things were done remarkably well this evening among the Amefin, and two of the Amefin village units, of Hawwy vale, were at drill even in the dark and by lantern-light, an excess of zeal, Idrys said, and he agreed: they dared not have the men exhausted.

Meanwhile, Kerdin Qwyll's-son said, the Guelen regulars moved among the Amefin, impeccable and meticulous in their procedures, instructing those who would listen. A few officers had gone about near the fires and had eager and worshipful entourages of wise Amefin lads who wanted to live long lives.

Among them, too, in the attraction of the bonfires, were Cevulirn's riders, drilled from boyhood to ride the land and teach the young village lads what time they were outside the

729

service of Cevulirn's court. They had set the small Amefin section of the horse-camp in good order very quickly, and joined the tale-telling around the fires. So did Imor's men, mostly townsmen, well-ordered and well-drilled; merchants' and tradesmen's sons, they drilled on every ninth day, and of those merchants' sons every one that afforded his horse and attendants was proud and careful in his equipment – a haughty lot, more so than Cevulirn's riders, who, if the ale did start flowing, might grow less reserved than their gray, pale lord.

But they had not heard from Pelumer and they had not received Olmern's messenger.

He had made his third venture to the door, and to the fire at which his own cook was preparing the lords' fare, when horses came down the main aisle of the camp, and he saw Ninévrisë and Tristen and their escort coming in safe and sound.

Then he could let go his anxiousness, particularly when firelight lit the arriving party's faces, and Ninévrisë leapt down and ran to him saying that things were very well at Althalen.

"It was beautiful," she said, accepting his hands. "It was *beautiful*. I wish you had seen –"

"I doubt that I could," he said, conscious of Guelenfolk about and wondering what she might have said or seen out there that might find its way to orthodox ears; but he had not meant to make it a complaint.

"The lord Regent protects us here," Tristen said. "I was right. He *has* won Althalen. He's held. Men loyal to the Regent died there, and so did his enemies – but most of all is Emwy village. They've sided with the lord Regent. I think they have, all along."

"They fed us when we were camped there," Ninévrisë said. "They kept us secret from Caswyddian's men. They were good people, in Emwy village."

"Then the gods give them rest," Cefwyn said, though he thought perhaps the wish was ill considered. They were uneasy dead, by what Tristen claimed, and would always be.

But Tristen was looking downcast as he turned Petelly off to the groom. He stood gazing off into the distance at the moment, and comprehension seemed to flicker in those pale eyes, cold and clear in the firelight, as if he had heard from some distant voice.

"What is it?" Cefwyn steeled himself to ask – as he should have asked in council before. He had determined to mend his faults. And to tell Ninévrisë what he did know.

"Trouble," Tristen said, "trouble. My lord, I very danger-ously misstepped tonight. He carried me to Ynefel. I was very foolish. I almost lost everything."

"What did he gain?" He did not need to ask who it was Tristen meant; and he had no room for charity. "Tristen?"

"Little, I hope. Perhaps knowledge of me. I – do not think lord Pelumer will join us. My enemy is moving. He is well ahead of us."

"Tasien?" Ninévrisë asked in alarm, and looked at Tristen. Tristen had spilled it. Gods knew what else he had let loose. "We fear Lord Tasien may have fallen," Cefwyn said, gently. "My lady, – Tristen only *fears* so. At this point –"

"It is certain," Tristen said; and anger touched Cefwyn's heart – he bore with all Tristen's manners, but he could *not* accustom himself to interruptions especially on important points.

And something happened, something clearly happened, then. Tristen had looked at Ninévrisë and Ninévrisë looked at Tristen, her clenched fists against chin an instant, and then – then something else was there – all he himself could have done, the knowledge, the comfort – all that passed in changes *he* saw, and could not touch, and could not feel.

Anger welled up in him.

And yet – yet how could they do otherwise, and how could Tristen not *be* the gentle creature he had always been, with all his impossible questions and his impossible ways.

He could not rebuke Tristen. He turned and began to limp into the tent, and Ninévrisë came hurrying after, to walk beside him, to offer a gentle, almost touching hand, respectful of his royal person, at least, when his friend would have had no such good sense.

Tristen said, from behind him, "Sir, I know now. *He* has Tasien and all his men, my lord King. If we defeat him – there might be help for the men."

He turned. "And what will you do? Raise them from the dead?" He was angrier than he had known. He wished it unsaid an instant after. He *feared* what he had said.

But Tristen said, quietly, as if anger could never touch him, "No, my lord King."

"The leg pains me," he muttered, and turned and went inside the tent, with Ninévrisë. He looked back at Tristen standing by the fire. "Come. Come. Sit with me. Share a cup. Bear with my humors. I was in desperate fear for you."

"Yes, sir," Tristen said mildly, and came into the tent, in its shortage of chairs – but before they had gotten to that difficulty, from one of those arcane signals that provided such things, two boys of Tristen's service had come in with his chair for him.

So, close on that, came Umanon, with his page, and bearing a chair, a cup, such necessities as even the King's pavilion did not manage to provide all comers.

Came Cevulirn, and Annas had the royal pages hurrying about, harried lads, pouring wine into any outheld cup – Tristen lacked one, but Annas provided it.

"My lords," Cefwyn said, sat down with a sigh and extended the aching leg. "Supper will be coming. In the meanwhile, sit, ask any comfort – I would you had had your season at home, but we had treachery in Henas'amef, plans were betrayed, and tonight the enemy's overrun Lord Tasien, gods preserve his unhappy soul, so Tristen informs us, by sources – I don't think dismay you gentlemen."

"Treachery," Cevulirn said. "Of the Aswyddim?"

He gave a rueful nod. "Clearer-sighted than your King, sir, and hence I limp, gentle sirs. Which does not hamper my riding. Nor will it keep me from answering this incursion.

Thus the summons. Which you answered in excellent order. Tristen says that Althalen is made safer than it was."

"It's safe to leave the tents here," Tristen said. "And we must move, before light."

"Our men have ridden hard," Umanon protested. "If they're across, they'll loot the camp. And we've Pelumer to find."

"Pelumer will not reach us," Tristen said, "and the enemy will not delay. They are closer. They've camped, I do think, but not – not longer than they must."

There was an uncomfortable silence in the tent. The servants had begun to bring the food in, and stopped where they stood.

"A disciplined army," Umanon said, frowning in clear dis-belief, "that can move on its forces past a chance for loot even at a fallen camp. This is not what I've heard of Aséyneddin. The Lord Warden is venturing a prediction – or has he certain knowledge? And whence the news of Lanfarnesse?"

"Late," Tristen said. "We dare not wait for him. We *must* not, sir."

"Sorcery," Cefwyn said, and said to himself he had no knowledge. "If he's met ambush of some kind – Lord Tristen might say."

"I cannot see through it," Tristen said.

"What," asked Umanon. "Through Marna?"

"I dare not," Tristen said, "reach toward it. But Aséyneddin will face us. Tomorrow. And all Hasufin's wizardry aims at that. These men will move because Hasufin wills them to move. They will not do as men might do other-wise."

"We," Cefwyn said quickly, before Tristen could say more to terrify sane men, "we found treason, sirs. And sorcery. Orien Aswydd betrayed our plans, so we made new ones."

Suddenly Tristen stood up, staring elsewhere, toward the northeast, though the blank walls of the tent were all anyone could see.

"For the gods' sake," Umanon said, and even Cevulirn

looked alarmed. Cefwyn quickly rose and took Tristen's arm.

"Tristen. Sit down. Is something amiss? Is there something you should say?"

"No," Tristen said shortly. And without leave or courtesy he drew aside and left the tent.

Uwen looked distressed, gathered up his sword and Tristen's, and rushed after him. The servants stood confused, with dishes in hand.

Cefwyn rose, and went to the door of the tent.

"My lord King." Idrys met him outside, and was in clear disapproval of such mad behavior, but he had done nothing to prevent him. Tristen was beside the fire, calling for his horse, in the aisle of the camp, then running past the tents, toward the northern end. Uwen had overtaken him – trying to press weapons on him, to no avail.

"The man's quite mad," Umanon said, behind Cefwyn's shoulder.

"Idrys," Cefwyn said, "for the gods' sake stop him." But then he knew in what bloody fashion Idrys might prevent an act that endangered him or the army, and caught Idrys' arm before he could move. "No. Get my horse and the guard."

"No, my lord King. You should not!"

"I said fetch my horse, damn it!"

He went back inside, limping, swearing as he struggled back into his armor while the guard and the horses were on their way; Erion Netha helped him, doing Idrys' ordinary service, for Idrys was ordering the guard, and Cefwyn endured the mistakes of unfamiliarity with impatience; but Umanon and Cevulirn, who had not entirely disarmed before arriving for supper, were on their way after Tristen. Ninévrisë was directing the anxious pages to take sensible action to save the supper – practical, in a descent into chaos: whatever fell out, men who had run off to what might be another hard ride would come back wanting something in their bellies.

He is *not* mad, Cefwyn said to himself, sick at heart. He is *not* mad, and all that he does has our interests at heart. He could break Amefel out of the army if he wished. He could be king of Elwynor tomorrow if he wished. But sometimes his wits go muddled. Damn him!

But he had no sooner come out the door of the tent than a Guelen man came running up, saying, "My lord King!"

At the same moment he saw riders coming down the dark aisle of the camp, and Tristen returning with them – "My lord," said Erion, but Cefwyn could see from where he stood that there was no use chasing out into the dark, now, as sore as he was, after all the trouble of arming. Tristen, and Uwen, Cevulirn and Umanon all were riding back with several other men in accompaniment.

"What is it?" Ninévrisë asked, peering past him into the dark. Then: "Oh, merciful gods," she said, and went past him, running, while, in a sore-legged and kingly dignity, he could only watch and ask himself what in the good gods' name they had found.

But Ninévrisë's recognition of someone in the company could tell him something, if it was not some wizardly notion of hers to do with Tristen or her father's grave – and he thought not, for her concern was for one rider in the company, a man whose horse was walking, head hanging, coughing. A crowd had started about the rider and the company, men rising from their campfires and gathering in the aisle. In the next moment it was a matter not only of escorting a stranger in, but of clearing the man's and Ninévrisë's path. Tristen led them through – a messenger, it seemed certain now, and a leaden foreboding had settled into Cefwyn's heart even before they brought the procession to a halt in front of his tent.

The rider slid down, but his legs would not bear him. Guards, Uwen among them, caught him and carried him, and Ninévrisë came with him, trying to help, and finding no means.

"Lord Tasien," the man began his account, straining to see Ninévrisë. "My lady, – Lord Tasien is dead – they are all dead – the winds – the dark – came over the river –"

735

Uwen slung off his own cloak and put it about the man, who shivered and could scarcely, but for his and other help, stand on his feet.

"The rebels," the man said, shaking as if in the grip of fever. "My lady, my lady, I was to ride – ride for help – for m'lord – when it began – the winds –"

"Inside. *Inside*," Cefwyn said, conscious of the men gathered about, common soldiers who had heard enough to send fear into the army. Gossip was inevitable. The men had to know and it was going to run through the camp on the fastest legs. "Deal with the matter!" he said to Gwywyn. "We know the message already. We are marching early to meet it. – Damn it!"

They had borne the young man into the tent, into light and warmth, and set him at Tristen's bidding into Tristen's own chair. Annas gave the man a cup of wine to drink, and Tristen steadied the man's hands, while Ninévrisë, all dignity aside, knelt down and had her hand on the man's knee. "Palisan," Ninévrisë said. "Are they across? Have they crossed the river? Have *any* lived?"

"They –" The man lifted his head and stared in fear into Tristen's eyes, and went on gazing, Tristen's hands holding both his hands on the cup. He had a gulp of wine at Tristen's urging, and only then seemed to catch his breath.

"Sorcery," he said. "I saw this camp – I was not certain – I was not sure it was friendly."

"What did you see?" Cefwyn asked. "Speak it plain, man. Your lady is listening."

"I – grew lost. I didn't know which way about on the road I was. I couldn't tell east from west, though the sun was up. – I lost the sun, my lady. It changed." The man struggled to speak amid his shivering, and he took a third gulp. "It was noon. And the sun was dark. And they were coming across. And the winds were blowing. M'lord can't have held them. They were so many –"

"When did you leave the battle?" Idrys asked coldly.

The Elwynim turned a frightened glance on him, and began

736

to shiver so his teeth chattered, and Tristen set his hand on his shoulders.

"Where did you ride?" Tristen asked him.

"My lady." The Elwynim looked to Ninévrisë. And she drew back. "My lady –"

"You could not have come so far so fast," Ninévrisë said, "without help."

"He had help," Tristen said.

"What help?" Cefwyn asked. A King should not be caught between. His men ought to inform him. "Damn it, what do you know? – Tristen. What more?"

Tristen walked away from him and stood looking at the canvas side of the tent.

"Answer the King," Idrys said, "lord of the Sihhë. You swear yourself his friend. What are you talking about?"

"A Shadow."

"It's another of his fits," Uwen said in anguish. "M'lords, it's another one. He had one out there, and they pass."

The messenger cried out, and the wine cup left his hand, sending a red trail across the carpets that floored the tent. He fell, sprawled on the stain. And he had wounds – many wounds.

"Gods!" a page whimpered. "Oh, blessed gods."

"Sorcery," Umanon muttered, and others present, even servants, were making signs against evil. Ninévrisë's face was white.

"Tristen," Cefwyn said. "What's happening? Tell me what you see! What is this Shadow?"

"Evil," said Cevulirn.

"Tristen." Cefwyn seized his arm, hard, compelling his attention.

"Aséyneddin provided a Place," Tristen said, "and it must have a Place. Shadows are coward things. But this one . . . this one . . . is very . . ."

"Tristen!"

"The lord Regent denied it a Place here. But . . . it can find others – even here. It's trying. Men in camp mustn't listen to it. Hasufin *sent* this man. He helped him through the gray place, to see us. To *see* us, and know our numbers."

"Tristen!" Cefwyn shook at him, aware of the fear of the lords near him, and the priest-fed superstition and the palpable terror this messenger had already engendered.

"It shifts," Tristen said faintly. "It moves. The trees of Marna are its Place. The stones of the river are its Place. The Road changes and moves. The things that are – change from moment to moment. It's advancing. But it much prefers the trees."

"What is he talking about?" Umanon asked. "– My lord King, do you understand him?"

"I should take him to his bed, Your Majesty," Uwen said.

"No!" Tristen said. "No, Cefwyn. Hear me. We must ride and stop them."

"Now? At night? Men are exhausted, Tristen. We have mortal limits."

That seemed to make sense to Tristen, at least. But he made none to anyone else.

"We will have panic in the camp," Cevulirn said, and cast a fierce look about him, lingering on the servants. "Say nothing of this death, do you hear, you!" It was a voice very loud and sharp for Cevulirn, and it sent cold fingers down the backbone. "Sire, we must send men through the camp, to quiet rumors. Very many saw this man come in."

"We must advance," Tristen said with a shake of his head, and in a voice hardly more than a whisper. "Nothing can help Tasien. The enemy is advancing. There's a Place we must meet it. But that Place could become closer, and worse for us. We must go."

"Now?" Umanon asked sharply, and Tristen left that hazy-eyed look long enough to say,

"Emwy would help us."

Cevulirn was frowning, Umanon no less than he; and pressing exhausted men on this advice, in the chance of catching the Elwynim at some sorcerous disadvantage – it might be their only hope. It might be their damnation. Tristen *knew* no common sense at such moments. What Tristen might do – other men might not.

"No," Cefwyn said, then, deciding. "Weary as we are, we cannot. In the morning, before dawn, we will move, with horse and foot, as fast as we can, and still arrive fit to fight. Lady Ninévrisë will command the camp. – Tristen?"

But without a by-your-leave, Your Majesty, Tristen had simply – left, with Uwen close with him.

That Distance came on him, and he could not breathe. He went to his tent past startled guards and servants.

He had not reckoned that Uwen had followed him; but when he reached the shelter of his own tent, he caught his breath and wiped his eyes, and turned to find Uwen staring at him.

Trembling, he shrugged as if it had been nothing.

Then the shadow came on him again, so that he caught for the tent pole and leaned there, half-feeling Uwen's hands on him. Uwen gripped his shoulder hard and shook at him; and he saw the two boys had somehow retrieved the chair from Cefwyn's tent.

"Uwen. Ask them to go. Please."

Silently Uwen braced an arm about him, and said to the servants what he wished him to say, in kinder terms than he could manage, and steered him for his chair. He sat down. He saw that, clever as his servants were, by whatever means they knew such things, they had his armor laid out ready for him – the suit of aged brigandine, of all that the armory had had, the one that best pleased him, because of its ease of movement. That was as it should be. And he already wore the sword he would use.

He took the sword from his belt, and sat with it in his arms.

"M'lord," said Uwen, and knelt by him, hand on his knee.

"Uwen," he whispered. "Go away."

"M'lord, ye listen to me, ye listen. What am I to do wi' ye? Out wi' the army and one of your fits come on ye – what am I to do? What am I to do when some Elwynim aims for your

739

head and ye stand there starin' at him? Nothin' ye done has scairt me, m'lord, but this – this does scare me. I don't like ye doin' that on the field. If we go to fight tomorrow – ye can't do this."

"It will not happen."

"I didn't like goin' out to them ruins. I had bad feelings."

"It will not happen. – Uwen!" Uwen had started to rise and Tristen gripped his shoulder hard enough Uwen winced. "Uwen, you will not go to Cefwyn. You will not."

"Aye, m'lord," Uwen muttered reluctantly, and Tristen let him go.

"Please," he said carefully. It was so great an effort to deal with love . . . that, more than anything, distracted him, and caused him pain. "Please, Uwen. Believe me. Trust me that I know what I do."

"Ye tell me what to do, m'lord, and I'll do it."

He held the sheathed sword against him, rocking slightly, gazing into the fire as he had done at Mauryl's fireside. "When the time comes, tomorrow, I shall know very well what I must do. Never fear that."

"And I'll take care of ye, whatever, gods help me. But, m'lord, give me the sword."

"No."

"M'lord, I don't like ye sittin' like that when ye hain't your right wits about ye."

"Please," he said, for the grayness was back and he could not deal with here and there together any longer. "Please, Uwen!"

Uwen tried all the same to take the sword from his hands, but he clenched it to him, and Uwen abandoned the effort.

Then he felt a manner of peace, a time in which his thoughts were white dreams, neither past nor future, only a sense of warmth, with, now, the consciousness of Emuin hovering near him in the grayness, a presence as safe as the shadow of Mauryl's robes, anxious as he had become about venturing into that gray space.

Puddles and raindrops, circle-patterns, and the scudding

clouds . . . Pigeons and straw and the rustle of a hundred
wings . . . Candle-light and warmth and the clatter of pottery
at suppertime . . .

The dusty creak of stairs and balconies, gargoyle-faces,
and, seen through the horn window, golden sun . . .

"Silver," he murmured, coming back from that Place,
remembering the black threads and the silver mirror. He
wondered where he should find silver other than that – then
put a hand to his chest, where the chain and the amulet lay,
which Emuin had worn, before he gave it to Cefwyn and
Cefwyn had given it to him.

He took it off, silver and belonging to two people who had
wished him well, one of them not unskilled in wishing. He
eased the sword from its sheath.

"My lord," Uwen said in a hushed and anxious voice, and
stirred from his chair. "What in the gods' good name are ye
doin', there?"

He could not spare the thought to explain. He took the
Teranthine circlet on its chain and held it in his hand while he
passed the blade of the sword through it. He saw no way to
anchor it but to bend it, and he bent the circlet until it met on
either side of the hilt – with all the strength of his fingers he
bent it, and shaped it, and bound the chain around it.

When he looked up at Uwen then, Uwen was watching in
mingled curiosity and fear. "Silver. And what beast would be
ye hunting wi' such a thing, m'lord?"

He had no idea *why* silver should have effect – only that in
that Place the dark threads evaded it.

And it shone. It soothed. It felt right. Mauryl had done
such odd things. The pigeons had known. The old mice in the
walls had known. He had known. Could living things not
feel, smell, breathe, sense such things when they were right?
He would ask Emuin how that was, but Emuin had faded
away into distance, having, perhaps, prompted him: the
touch had been that slight.

He fingered the worn leather hilt, the iron pommel. It was
an old hilt, but a new and strong blade, so the armorer had

declared; and so he felt with his hands and his sense of what should be: it was a blade forged in fire for honor, carried in stealth for murder and taken for defense of a dead king and a living one, by a man himself neither dead nor alive. There was enough improbable about it to satisfy whatever oddness he could think of, and whatever demand there was in attacking a Shadow without substance.

"Uwen. You have that little harness knife."

"Aye, m'lord," Uwen said, and pulled it from his belt and gave it to him, a very small blade. And with that sharp point, as if it were a pen on parchment, he began to work on the surface of the blade while Uwen watched over his shoulder.

Designs: letters. On one side he scratched laboriously the flowing letters of Stellyrhas, that was Illusion; and on the other face he wrote, in severe characters, Merhas, that was Truth. What speech it was, he did not immediately know, but in one world or the other it had meaning. It was hard to make any scoring on the metal. The knife grew blunted. His fingers ached. But he persisted, while sweat started on his face.

Then he began to work, slowly, painstakingly, to widen those letters, though scarcely could the eye see them.

Uwen watched in silence, perhaps fearing to interrupt him, although he would not have objected to interruption now: it was only a task; his thoughts were at peace. Sweat ran on his face and he wiped at it with the back of his hand and worked on what had now become elaboration in the design, for beauty's sake, because he did nothing haphazardly, on what became determination, because he would not abandon the small idea he had of what he faced, in substance and in insubstance.

Perhaps Uwen expected some magic. After a long time Uwen gave up and sat down on his cot.

"You should go to sleep," he said to Uwen. "You should rest."

"Are you going to do something, m'lord?"

"Not tonight," he said. He rubbed the design with his hand. Marks on the metal wove in and out, and it at last seemed right to him.

– *Finished?* Emuin asked him, at cost, and from two days away. He had known Emuin was there – or at least knew Emuin had come close for the last several moments. The letters shone under his fingers, bridging here and there, as though he could thread one within the other.

– *Am I right?* he asked Emuin. *Or am I foolish?* – I was afraid today, master Emuin. I saw Ynefel. I was almost there. I fell into his trap, and I had no weapon – I could not take it there.

– *The edge too has a name,* Emuin whispered to him, ignoring his question. Emuin's presence in the grayness very quickly became drawn thin, scarcely palpable, and desperate. *He will know. An old Galasieni conundrum. The edge is the answer. I cannot help you further. You are Galasien's last illusion, Man of the Edge, and, it may be, its noblest. I hope for what Mauryl did. I hope – Boy, – boy. Did he show you – did he show you – ?*

– *What, sir? What should he have shown me?*

Emuin began to say. He thought so, at least. But the presence had gone. Deeply, finally, the weak threads of communion with Henas'amef were pulling apart, the fabric unweaving in little rips and gaps. He could not reach it now. He tried, and was back at that lattice-work of Lines and light that was Althalen. It answered to him. But Emuin did not.

Not dead, he thought. But at the end of what strength Emuin had mustered for himself. He feared for the old man, who, not brave, had found courage to fight not for his own health, but for Cefwyn's. He feared for all of them – and he did not know what Emuin meant – or even how he had come here, except that Henas'amef still stood untroubled, and that Althalen had become safe, sheltering all of them within its reach –

It was Althalen that gave him respite from the Shadow and rest from his struggle.

It was Althalen that would keep Ninévrisë safe tomorrow. It was Althalen that had taken the messenger to its rest.

But he himself could not hide in it. Resting here was not why Mauryl had Summoned him into the world.

He drew a deep breath. He plunged his face into his hands and wiped his eyes, then flung his head back, exhausted, not knowing, save from Althalen, where he was to get the strength – not the courage, for tomorrow, but simply the strength to get on a horse and go, knowing that Cefwyn relied on him, that Emuin relied on him, that the lady relied on him – and that, in a different and far more personal way, Uwen did.

Uwen was sleeping – Uwen dropped off so easily, and slept so innocently: he envied that ability, only to sleep, and not to find the night another journey, to worse and stranger places than the day, and another struggle, that did not give him rest.

But he had hours to spend before the dawn, and if he could do more than he had done, he had to try. He *had* Althalen, if he knew how to use it, if he dared another vision such as he had had on the brink of the ruin.

He knew of himself that he was not good – or had not been, once and long ago.

He knew of himself that such as Ynefel was, he was responsible for it being.

He knew of himself that he had more than killed his enemy, he had used the innocent.

Or – he thought that he knew these things. He had no map to lead him through the gray place. He had no Words written there to say, this is Truth, and this is Illusion.

Here he had made a sword to divide them. Here he had Mauryl's Book, and Mauryl's mirror – though only the sword seemed of use to him, he did not think it was Mauryl's intention. It was not, it occurred to him, Mauryl's gift.

He had a few hours yet. He had not failed until those hours were gone. So while Uwen slept, while the servants slept, and even his guards drowsed, he moved his chair closer to the tent-pole, where the lamp shed its light.

He sat down with his Book, then, and opened it to the place the little mirror held – blinked at the flash of bright, reflected light, and moved the mirror so that it did not reflect the lamp above him, but the opposing page.

The letters were backward in the reflection – no better seen in that direction than the other, though it seemed to him a small magic in itself. He wondered if all letters did that in all mirrors, or whether it was a special mirror, or whether, after all, just to reflect his face.

It was a changed face the mirror cast back to him. A worried face. A leaner face, not so pale as before. His hair he never had cut, and it fell past his shoulders, now. He had not realized it had grown so long. He had not known his face showed such expressions. He knew all the shifts of Uwen's expression – while his own were strange to him. That seemed – like inspecting his elbow – an inconvenient arrangement.

Silly boy, Mauryl would say. There's so little time. Don't wool-gather.

Reflection in the rain-barrel. Light coming past his shoulders. Reflection of sky. The shadow of a boy who was not a boy. He had not known how to see himself, then. He had not had the power.

He wondered what he was in the gray space. And as quick as thinking it, he saw – he saw –

Light.

He shut his eyes and came back, his heart pounding in his chest. It was so bright, so bright it burned, and burned his hand.

It was hard to hold the mirror. But he could call the light into it. He could see his own face, blinding-bright, and frightening in its brightness. He could take the silver mirror into that Place.

He wondered if he could take the Book – or reflect it there – and when he wondered, a light from the mirror fell, a patch of brilliance, like sun off metal, onto the page of the Book.

Moving the mirror into the gray place, and calling the light back onto the page was the first magic he had ever worked that succeeded, just to move light and the reflection of light from place to place.

*So he did know something now that he had not known
before; and he tried, though it was hard, to manage both
Places at once, the one hand with the Book, the other with
the mirror, until, out of the gray world the mirror drew into
the world of substance, and looking only at the mirror, and
reaching into the gray place, he saw the Book appear in the
reflection the mirror held.*

*But the mirror's image of the Book was blurred to him,
until he could manage the mirror with one hand in the gray
place, and angle it just so, and the Book in the hand that was
in the other world, so that he could see the reflection of the
page in that gray world.*

*Then he could see the letters. Then he knew what they
were:*

*It is a notion of Men, it said, that Time should be divided:
this they do in order to remember and order their lives. But
this is an invention of Men, and Time is not, itself, divided
in any fashion. So one can say of Place. That there is more
than one Place is a notion of Men: this they . . .*

*. . . this they believe; but Place is not itself divided in any
fashion. Who understands these things knows that Time and
Place are very large indeed, and compass more than Men
have divided and named . . .*

He was no longer reading. He was *thinking* the Words and
they echoed ahead of his reading them. He thought ahead,
further and further into the pages, and *knew* the things the
Book contained. He had written them. Or *would* write them.

That was what it meant – to one who could move *things*
between the gray space and the world of substance.

He let down the Book and folded it on the mirror, and took
up the sword again, not for a sword, but only for something
to lean on while he thought.

That was how he waked, bowed over the sword, Uwen's
hands on his; he lifted his head and Uwen took the sword
from his fingers and laid it carefully aside.

"It's time, m'lord," Uwen said. "The lamps is lit next door.
His Majesty is arming and he's ordered out the heavy horses.

We're leaving the camp standing and going on. The lady's seein' to that. Scouts ain't seen nothing, though that ain't necessarily what we want to hear, may be. I hate like everything t' wake ye, but there just ain't no more time."

In the sense Uwen spoke – there was no more time. But things he knew rattled through his thoughts. He bent and took off his ordinary boots. And stood up.

CHAPTER 34

～

He held out his arms patiently as Uwen assisted him into his armor, still by lamplight, with great care for the fittings. He stepped one after the other into the boots that belonged to the armor, and Tassand buckled them snugly at the holes that were marked. Uwen belted his weapons about him, sword and dagger, and slipped the small boot knife into the sheath that held it.

There was only the lightest of breakfasts, a crust of bread, a swallow of wine, which took no fire-making, and put no stress on the body. So Uwen said. And he knew Uwen was right.

Mauryl's Book – *his* Book, held no comfort at all in the sense that he understood now what Hasufin had understood all along and that he knew what Hasufin wanted.

Most of all he knew what Hasufin wanted to do, which was to unmake Mauryl's work: him, for a beginning, but, oh, more than that.

Hasufin wanted Galasien back, for a second part.

Hasufin wanted substance enough to use what was in that Book, for a third. Those desires were enough to account for all that was and might be. But that was not all Hasufin wanted. Beyond that – he could also imagine. That was what put him out of the notion of breakfast, and made him certain that, whatever defense the armor was, Hasufin would be determined to turn every weapon on the field toward him – for Hasufin, he was sure, cared very little about Aséyneddin, only to maneuver to his own advantage. All, all that would be out there was nothing other than what Hasufin willed, substantial so long as Men were willing or able to contend; and in so many places.

He even guessed what had brushed past him that night

while he slept on the Road in Marna, and why he had dreaded it so. It was, in a strange sense – himself.

But this time he must go toward that sensible fear from which he had once fled – and what there was to meet, he must meet, and go wherever he must.

He was glad that Uwen saw nothing of what he saw. He would not wish that understanding on him for any price, not on Idrys, or Cevulirn or Umanon; nor on Pelumer, in whatever nightmare the Lanfarnesse forces might be struggling next the woods.

And not on Sovrag, who, if things went well, might yet arrive to strike at the Elwynim from the river, but he much doubted it: the Olmernmen had Marna to traverse to reach this far past Emwy, if they would go by water, and Marna of all places would not aid them.

But now with all the fear, came an impatience for this meeting. Something in him longed in a human way for encounter with Ninévrisë's enemies, to feel the wicked certainty of himself he had felt before, with the sword in his hand, and such certainty what had to come next. Nowhere else and at no other time did he have that.

And for no reason, tears flooded his eyes and spilled. He wiped them unconsciously.

"M'lord?"

Uwen thought he wept for dread. But he wept for Mauryl's gentleness, which only he had seen; he wept for Cefwyn's, for Uwen's kindness, which he did not have – not in their terms. He knew what he could do. He knew what he had done, and knew that he could not, by the nature of what Hasufin had loosed in the land, wholly win.

If there was disaster about to fall on those he loved, it was of his attraction, and he –

He had one thing to do. Beyond it – he could not see anything for himself, but he wanted it: he could no longer temporize with it, or delay it, or understand any more than he did, and he could not bear the increasing burden of his own household, his own following – men who looked to him for reason and right, men who wanted to pour out their devotion on him, never knowing him as he was, not seeing into his heart, and not knowing – not knowing he enjoyed that dreadful time when the sword flew in his hand like a living thing and he *had* no questions.

"Well, I done what I can," Uwen said, testing the motion of his arm. Uwen looked him in the face. "M'lord, take care of yourself today."

"Take care for yourself," Tristen said. "Promise to care for yourself, that is what you can do for me. You will know the time, Uwen, and you must take no shame in turning back: I know this is the most difficult order I could give you; but do not follow me too far."

"Ain't retreating before I get there, m'lord."

Uwen had made up his mind not to listen. With curious abstraction, then, Tristen reached back into that place of white dreams and snared something of that blinding, peaceful light. It took form in his hand, bluish-white, and he passed it to the other hand, tossing it back and forth, back and forth, a little illusion that whitened the floor and the canvas.

That was, he thought, illusion enough to frighten any Man, the simultaneity of Here and There which men did not ordinarily see.

For a moment the faint letters on the sword blazed bright.

He let the illusion go.

"Gods," Uwen said.

"Uwen, believe me that I am capable of going where you dare not. Where you *must* not."

"I'd still try, m'lord."

"I know you would. I ask you not to. You could endanger me. I would have to defend both of us."

"Then I ask ye to come *back,* m'lord. Ye swear to me ye're comin' back or I'll swear I'm goin' behind ye, and I don't break my given word."

Yesterday he would have had no hesitation to swear what Uwen asked. But now every binding of him to one realm or the other seemed full of dangers. The small illusion he had wielded to scare Uwen was no weapon potent against a wizard who had the skill of Shaping – and thereby of unShaping.

"Uwen, – no. I shall not swear that. I swear I shall try. But there may be frightening things, Uwen. There may be reasons you should retreat – believe them when you see them."

"Horses is waiting, m'lord," Uwen said. "I heard 'em come up."

So Uwen chose to look past illusion as well – in his own way, the Edge that moved between.

"Uwen. I swear – I swear that you may call me, and also send me away. That power I give you, and I know that I have no safer guardian."

It took a great deal to make Uwen show fear. Now he did. "I ain't no priest, m'lord."

"You're a good man. You understand right and wrong so easily. I don't. Mauryl always *said* I was a fool."

"Of course ye understand," Uwen said with an uncertain laugh. "And ye're the least like a fool that I know, m'lord."

"But I swear I *don't* understand such things. I haven't lived in this world long enough to be wise. So I trust you with my going and coming. Call me only if you truly want me. Then I shall know at least one man wishes me alive. Then I might come back to the world. But think twice before you call me."

"Now ye're being foolish. And His Majesty would never send ye away."

"Cefwyn has no knowledge what I might do. Nor does he have pure reasons. Yours I trust. Do not beg off, Uwen. I give you the calling of me. You cannot refuse. And if you should die, Uwen, – there would be no one to call me, would there? So you mustn't die."

"M'lord, –" Uwen opened and shut his mouth. "That were a clever, wicked trick."

"Cefwyn taught me," he said, and gathered up his Book and walked outside. The horses had indeed arrived, wearing their war-gear, Dys and Cass in black caparison that made them part of the dark.

"M'lord," said Aswys, their trainer.

"I'm ready," he said, and tossed the Book into the heart of the fire.

"My lord!" Uwen exclaimed.

The pages glowed along the edges and began to turn brown, the ink still showing. And that, too, began to go.

"He shall not have it," he said, "neither Book nor mirror." He went to Dys, who was working at the bit and fretting in dangerous boredom. Dys' face was masked in the metal chamfron, and nothing showed but the gloss of his eye, scarcely a hint of his nose. Tristen patted him under the neck, put his gauntlets on, and waited until he saw Cefwyn come out of his tent, with Idrys. They had Kanwy waiting; and Idrys' heavy horse, Kandyn. Cefwyn rose to the saddle, and Tristen took the reins from Aswys, then, and was not too proud to use the mounting-block as Cefwyn had, not wishing to have the girth skewing. He cleared the high cantle and settled, moving his leg to let Aswys recheck the girth, while Uwen got up on Cass.

Tassand brought his helm and other servants handed up his shield, while Lusin, who used a mace by preference, would ride in the second line and carry the lance for him, in their lack of mounted aides, as Syllan would carry Uwen's. One of the boys they had acquired came bringing Uwen his gauntlets, with worship on his face – and ducked back in awed haste when Cass took a casual snap at him.

Dys usually whipped his tail about. Today it was braided and tucked for safety, and Dys moved with a flexing and rattle of the bards that protected his neck, the straps of the armor passing through the caparison. The white Star and Tower blazoned central on his black shield and barred on Uwen's, floated in the dark, while, beyond them, Cefwyn's Dragon banner writhed and rippled against the firelight. Further away, the Wheel and the White Horse shone out of the dark, as Umanon and Cevulirn appeared.

Ninévrisë came out of her tent, wearing her father's mail shirt and with her father's sword belted on; after her came her ladies, her standard-bearer, and the two Amefin lords who guarded them. "Come back safely," she said, and sent her standard-bearer to his horse.

Then she said to Cefwyn, "I would rather be on the hill. I would *rather* be closer."

"If it comes this far," Cefwyn said, "as it may, you do not fight, m'lady. You ride. My brother has excellent qualities – among them a walled town. The whole northern army will rally to him if the war goes that far."

"You do not pass me on like a gauntlet! I shall marry *you*, m'lord, or ride after you!"

"The gods," Cefwyn said, "see us all safe, m'lady." He turned Kanwy, then, and established an easy pace down the aisle toward the edge of the camp.

"Be well," Ninévrisë called to them as they passed. "Gods keep you! My lord of Ynefel, be safe!"

The standard-bearers, ahorse, caught up the standards, and the order established itself as the Guelen heavy horse and the Amefin fell into line, creaking of saddles, a slow, quiet thump of hooves on the trampled ground of the aisle, more and more of them as they passed their own sentries, and reached the Emwy road.

The dawn was beginning in the east; and in the west . . .

Even by night, that shadow was on the horizon; Tristen could see it without looking toward it in the gray world. He rode side by side with Cefwyn, westward, with only the standard-bearers in front.

With open road and a cool night, Dys wanted to move; but they had the Amefin foot to follow them – and not so far, in terms of the horses, before they should look for the Elwynim force that had crossed the bridge and rolled over Tasien's defense.

"Aséyneddin will stay to the road," he said to Cefwyn, when Cefwyn was about to send scouts out. "They have reason to fear Althalen – and even for Hasufin's urging, I doubt he will risk Caswyddian's fate. Or if he does – he will not fall on the camp without Ninévrisë knowing. Send no men by that ruin."

"Dare I trust all our lives on your advice? She has no defense. Should she have no warning?"

"The camp is very well defended. The scouts you send into the ruin will not come back, m'lord. They will die if you send them. I beg you, don't. They have no defense. We were safe. They won't be. The sentries are enough. Her father will protect her."

Cefwyn drew a deep breath, started to argue, then shook his head, and sent the scouts only to the fore, down the road. Idrys was not pleased with it. But Cefwyn did as he asked.

The next was a long ride, Dys and Kanwy walking along quietly, but Kandyn and Umanon's horse took such exception to each other that Umanon drew off well to the side of the road.

Cass had no such animosities: he and Idrys' horse alike were stablemates of Kanwy and Dys, and trained together. He was amiable, of his kind; but Dys, young, in his first campaign, made a constant demand for attention: he snapped and pulled at the reins, seeking to move ahead of Kanwy, which Tristen did not allow, or to the side, where he could annoy Cass. Tristen kept ahead of his intentions and refused to let him work himself into exhaustion: Dys, very much of a mind with him, seemed to sense the reason he was born was coming closer and closer, as yet unmet, untried. Dys wanted this day, too, not knowing entirely what he wanted, and keeping Dys in check kept his hands busy and his fears from having precedence: in that regard Tristen was glad of Dys' antics, and only half-heard the converse of the other lords.

But he knew from what he did hear that, behind them, at all the speed they could safely manage, the Amefin troops were marching behind the Amefin Eagle, footsoldiers fewer in numbers than they had planned and lacking the support of archers they had planned to have, both by reason of Pelumer's absence. And they could not go more quickly than they did for the sake of the Amefin.

The wagons would not follow today: Ninévrisë, in command of the camp since their change in plans, would stand ready to strike the tents and advance to Lewenside, just the other side of Emwy, if they drove Aséyneddin in retreat – or to order the baggage burned, the horses and oxen driven off, and save herself and the men in camp if the battle went the other way and it looked as if Aséyneddin might take it. Messengers were already designated from their army to make the ride back to her, once they knew the situation that developed at the army's approach to Emwy.

The sun was well into the sky, all the same, a gray sky, when they came near that series of ridges that preceded the turn toward Emwy-Arys.

Then in the distance a saddled horse turned up, grazing beside the road, no one in evidence. It looked up as they came, still chewing its mouthful of grass.

"One of ours," Idrys said. "Pelanny's horse."

Of the rider, one of their Guelen scouts, there was no sign.

"Dead or taken," Uwen said quietly. The horse, its master fallen, had run for its pastures, but running out its first fear, had stopped, and would wander home, Tristen thought, perhaps over days. One of their outriders, light-armed, rode over and caught the horse, freed it of the reins that might entangle it, and sent it on to their rear.

Past the next ridge, the wind picked up out of the west, into the horses' faces. The woods came into view, lying across that small series of hills that he so well remembered. That was the woods where he had met Auld Syes. The woods of the fountain. And the Shadow was there, plain to his eyes.

"That," Tristen said with a chill. "That place. That's where."

"A place fit for ambush," Idrys said. "I'd thought of it. If we don't go overland, we're bound to go through it. That's what they plan. And overland is a maze, forest and hills. I rode through it."

There was discussion back and forth. Umanon and Cevulirn moved their horses closer. No one wanted to venture that green shadow without sending scouts. Some argued to go overland, toward Emwy, but Idrys said no, it was too rugged and made for ambush by lesser forces.

"Of which they may have several," Cefwyn said. "Earl Aséyneddin is well served by the Sâendel."

"Bandits," Umanon said. "Bandits and thieves."

"Well-armed ones," Idrys said.

But, Tristen thought, fighting Dys' attempt to move forward – but there was no sense in debate. There was no question, none, that it was hostile. It was fatal, if they sent a man into that. It was a risk to venture that gray place, but look he did, and it was eerie to know it vacant, very, very vacant. They had now to go forward. The lords debated other ways, but they had no choice but fight or go back to Althalen, where they were far safer for a camp under attack.

And something masked itself in that gray vacancy – as it masked something else in that distant woods. Something in the gray place was both shadow – and gray like mist, moving about where it would. Mauryl had not stopped it. Emuin had not. It was insubstance. It manifested as the wind.

That which waited in the woods – was substance, and thick beneath the leaves.

"Tristen?" he heard Cefwyn ask. But it was not a voice in the gray place, it was here, and Cefwyn's voice held concern. "Tristen, do you hear me?"

Something shadowy leapt at him in his distraction. Not a small something. Something that wanted to hold him, seize him, weaponless, and carry him off to Ynefel. He jumped back from it, heart pounding against his ribs, and in the world of substance, Dys kicked and pulled to be free.

All trespass into illusion had peril now. The Shadow had advanced this close, and that said to him that they would find their enemies in this world closer, too: Aséyneddin was there.

"It's another of his fits," said Uwen.

"No," Tristen said, trying to shut out what was still trying to take him, holding to this place, the solid mass of horse under him. He kept his eyes open, burning the light of the world's sky and the shadow-shapes of hills and woods into

756

his vision. Cefwyn and Uwen and Idrys were close at hand. They willed no harm to him.

The other thing would unmake him – if it could not use him against those he least wanted to harm. Against all Mauryl's work in the world. It wanted that undone, the barriers to its will all removed.

"Tristen."

"No, my lord, forgive me." It was hard to speak against the weight that crushed him, and he must hold Dys, for the horse felt the tension trembling in his legs and in his hands, and was fighting him continuously to move. Do not leave us, Cefwyn had begged him. Do not leave us. And he tried not to. He did try to keep his wits about him in this world.

"Aséyneddin is there, m'lord King. In the woods. I have no doubt."

A shiver came over him then. He slipped into that risky place, and felt thunder in the air, like storm.

He twitched as he escaped there to *here* in a shock that rang through the world, but the two lords by him had never felt it: they talked on of strategy and ambush while he felt ambush in the very roots of the hills. He felt the Shadows all stir beneath the leaves of Marna Wood, but the lords talked of whether his warning meant mortal enemies, and whether they could draw attack out to them and not risk the woods.

"If they stay in that woods," Idrys said, "they risk having it fired around them. Your grandfather would not have stuck at it."

"These are my lady's people," Cefwyn said, rejecting that. "Not all of them may even be here by choice. We carry her banner with our own, master crow. No fire."

"They are rebels," Idrys said.

"No fire, master crow. I'll not make war after that fashion."

"Against wizardry, m'lord? What will our enemy stick at? We'll not venture in there. We'll have them out, if they are there."

"They are there," Cefwyn said.

"Tristen is here," Idrys said. "That indeed is our certainty, m'lord King. And I do believe his warnings. It's the advice I doubt. This haste to go blind into that."

"He is not blind," Cefwyn said.

Came a rush of air just above their heads. A shadow swooped over them. The horses snorted and threw their heads in startlement. But Tristen knew it with a leap of his heart.

"Owl!" he called to the wide sky. "Owl, *where are you?*"

"Gods!" Uwen gasped, and men about them swore.

"Devils," some said.

But Tristen lifted his hand to the sky and Owl settled on his fist, bated his great blunt wings a moment and flew again, a Shadow indeed, by broad daylight.

"Gods save us," Cefwyn said, and Idrys muttered in his hearing. "Gods save us indeed, my lord King, but – this *is* our ally."

"Well he were our ally," Cefwyn said. "It harmed you none at all. Did it? *Did* it, master crow? Did it, any of us?"

"Follow Owl!" Tristen said, for Owl's path was clear to him, as Owl's warning was clear as a blaze across the sky: as, discovered in its ambush, a darkness of men and horses began to stream out of that line of woods ahead of them. It spread out, moving first to fill the road, and then to spread out wings beyond it, like some vast creature taking to flight.

"Aséyneddin has sprung his trap!" Umanon shouted out. "Attend the flanks, Your Majesty! He'll want the hills!"

Likewise they needed room to spread wide – needed the flat and the hills on either side in front of that stretch of woods, and they did not yet, by reason of the trees, know how many that army was.

Kanwy struggled to be loosed. Dys pulled at the bit. All about, there was a shifting in their own ranks as a wind out of the west ripped at the standards. The standard-bearers, Cefwyn's, his, Ninévrisë's, all three in the center, and Umanon and Cevulirn on either hand, were advancing; but the hills had taken on an unnatural quality in the pearl-skyed noon, distinct in their edges, seeming cut from velvet, the trees still breathing with secrets.

"My lord!" Tristen said, reining Dys back with difficulty. "They are already in the hills, my lord – they're there, left and right of us, where we must pass!"

Cefwyn did not question. "Cevulirn!" he said, and waved the lord of the Ivanim and his light horse toward the hills on their left. "Umanon!" Him he sent to the right flank; and dispatched a messenger to the Amefin lords at their backs. "Follow my banner," his word to the Amefin was; and to messengers dispatched on the heels of Umanon and Cevulirn: "Sweep them east, away from the woods! We shall break their center! Do not let them close behind us!"

Dys was pulling at the rein, breathing noisily and chafing at the bit, and given rein – but of a sudden Elwynim light horse were pouring off the hills toward them and sweeping in to try to envelop them, downhill against Umanon and Cevulirn on either hand. The heavy center, still coming out of the woods, lay beyond those two rapid-moving wings that attempted to fold in on them.

They were in danger of the same swift envelopment they had broken around Cefwyn's father. Dys was working at the bit, shaking his neck so the barding rattled, traveling sideways, nudging Cass, who likewise worked to be free.

"Lances!" Cefwyn called out, and the trumpets blew. "Lances!"

They were going. None of it he had ever done, save only with Uwen, in the practice field by Henas'amef – but like a Word, it had been with him then and it had always been with him. He ducked his head to brush his visor down, settled his reins in his shield-hand and looked up within the narrow frame of that visor as he reached out for his lance. It arrived in his hand, Lusin coming up at his side, horse bumping horse and falling back again. He took a solid grip, tucked the length of ash-wood high for a hard ride as he brought the shield up. Dys was pulling at the reins, a warfare occupying all his attention else.

Cevulirn's men and then Umanon's engaged with the Elwynim wings, two almost simultaneous hammer blows. "Ride for their heart!" Cefwyn was saying to the standard-bearers and the riders that would pass the word. "Let them see the standards! Break their line and go around them again! Unit standards – keep spread, in the gods' name! Pass through them, behind, and around! *In the good gods' name!*"

Cefwyn loosed Kanwy. Tristen let the reins fall, settling all his grip on the shield and all his mastery of Dys on his knees –

Dys broke into his run – like chasing rabbits through the meadow, like chasing the leaves and the wind down the road, with Uwen by him, likewise shielded, likewise helmed, likewise with lance braced. A thunder was growing in the earth, the strike of hundreds of plate-sized hooves, whuffs of breath entering a vast unison, like a blacksmith's bellows. There was nothing in the world but that moving vision of shielded line and forest that the visor-slit held.

– *Sihhë prince,* said the Wind, *above that rolling thunder. Remember the Galasieni. How many of these foolish Men will you kill? Turn back now. Your friends will be alive. You can win them that. You can save them all. Didn't you learn, the last time? I know the outcome of this. But you don't, – do you?*

The Shadow grew above the woods, above the opposing line, that was a forest of lances. Something throbbed in the air, faint and far in the dark West, like the beat of a great heart to his ears. Or perhaps it was still the horses gathering speed. On either hand came a clash of metal, as if a cartload of pots were being shaken, on the hillsides. But the thunder throbbed and beat like his heart in his ears.

Owl flew past his vision and flew on past the banners, that were dimming in the shadow.

Let them see the banners, Cefwyn had said. And Men could not see them in the dark – Men would lose their way on the field, and grow confused.

Tristen pulled white light out of that gray place and sent it around himself, around Uwen and Cefwyn and Idrys. It spread to the standard-bearers, and snaked up the poles and spread about the edges of the standards and across their surface, white and red and gold blazing bright against the dimmed world.

– *Ah,* the Wind said. *The Dragon with the Sihhë Star – there was once a sight, when the Marhanen and the Sihhë king went to war. And here we are again.* The voice filled his ears. Dust, coming past the visor, stung his eyes to tears, and he could not reach them to clear them. He could only blink. *Where is vengeance for Elfwyn, Sihhë prince? Mauryl never called you to save the Marhanen. Mauryl never called you, my prince, to kiss the hand of traitors. They should tremble at the sight of you!*

Closer and closer. He saw the shields of opposing riders – saw, through the gloom, the forest of lances lower, and lowered his own against them.

– *Sihhë king,* the Wind wailed, *you are of the west. I shall serve you, as Mauryl should have served you. Stay, do you want them? I shall make these creatures of yours lords of the earth. I shall make each of them a king, and they will live a thousand years. I can do that for you. Only keep riding. Keep doing as you are! You are doing my bidding, in all you do and have ever done. You're mine, now. Mauryl's lost you. Keep coming! – Keep coming. . .*

The light had dimmed so they scarcely showed the shields ahead of them – but the banners were still there, still shining.

"Tristen!" he heard Cefwyn shout at him, and he caught breath into a body grown stiff in a cold instant, sense into wits gone wandering in the wail of the wind.

"Its name is Hasufin!" he shouted, stripping it of all mystery. "It is a liar, Cefwyn! It is still telling me lies!"

"The banner of the King of Elwynor!" Cefwyn exclaimed suddenly, and indeed there was the glimmer of a shadowy white Star on a black field waving against the center of the lines. "*That* banner does not belong to them!" Cefwyn cried. "There is Aséyneddin! Let us go and take it from him!"

– *Aséyneddin,* the Wind said, *would welcome his true*

King, the Sihhë king he and his fathers before him have awaited. This man would fall on his knees at your feet. I can assure that will happen. Be that King. You can stop this. No one need die.

Then do so! he thought of saying; but he recalled the lord Regent's warning never to begin to listen, and never to begin to answer.

– I do not want to fight you, the Wind said, *I do not, my mistaught lord of the Sihhë. So I shall not. Come to me when you're done with him.* – *I'll wait.*

Aséyneddin's banner too blazed with a pale, unnatural glimmering in the dark, Illusion of light, no more, no less than he could do: that was Hasufin's working in the world.

But at the same moment a new presence impinged on his awareness, distant, desperate, and mortal, against which Hasufin strove – a distraction to him it was possible to feel as he felt the outlines of Hasufin's power unfurl within the woods, a trap for any Man who rode too far.

Pelumer, he thought. It was Pelumer, fighting for escape, in the edge of Marna.

An enemy shield was coming toward him, a Griffin blazing white. He centered his lance. A howl went up from the oncoming ranks of the Elwynim, metal lit by the illusory glamor he had sent over them. Dys' hindquarters bunched and drove with all his force. Uwen was on his left. Cefwyn was on his right as a lance raked off his shield and line met line with a thunder-crack and a shock that went up his arm.

His lance bent and exploded in splinters, a lance grated off his shield, and the riderless horse passed him as he cast the stump aside. He shielded off a blow from the following rank and ripped his sword from its leather bindings.

Guelen blades, Guelen maces hammered about him as lighter horses and lighter-armed riders and foot now struck behind the heavy cavalry, Elwynim riders that had not carried through attempted retreat and became involved in a dark mass of their own Elwynim infantry bristling with weapons and trying to defend against the Guelen horse.

He sent Dys into the midst of footsoldiers, drew the light of illusion about him and all the riders near him, harmless show – but it terrified men before him, and ranks broke.

Riders followed him . . . he was aware of it as he knew the whereabouts of Lanfarnesse so far lost and of the Amefin troops entering the fray behind them. Dys trampled men trying to bring pikes to bear, and never stopped, his breath coming hard, his huge shod hooves making nothing of living or dead, brush or uneven ground. Tristen laid about him with the sword, cut down men as he found them, making a path, sending Dys this way and that, to right or to left of oncoming enemies and threatening steel. His sword burned with white fire as it swung. Dys shone as if a white light were on them. The silver wrap glittered on the sword and left ghosts before his eyes.

Then they reached an astonishing vacancy in the noontime dark, confronting nothing but forest: they had come through the Elwynim's lines, and he reined Dys about to ride at the faces of men trying to flee – Aséyneddin's center had split in two, and riderless horses were bolting through the confusion, trampling light-armed men running for the woods in an unthinkable hammering of swords and axes. The wall of Amefin foot gnawed its way forward and heavy horse continued to wear at the outsides of Aséyneddin's split forces.

Wind skirled against their flank, blasting up dust. The banners of the Dragon were gouts of bright blood across a fatally bunched knot of black and white Elwynim standards, with the banner of Aséyneddin in the midst of it.

But a shadow swept over all of it as he watched, with nightmarish swiftness darkening the ground and the air itself. Cefwyn's men and the surrounded enemy alike were in danger, and the approach of the Shadow to that place was like a nightmare he was doomed to watch and not reach, across a screen of terrified enemies whose very defeat and panic made them a barrier to his advance.

He laid about him with the sword, blind to all but that patch of threatened red within his visor. Cefwyn could not by any human means realize what menaced him – it might seem the passage of a cloud in the sky, salt sweat in the eyes, a blurring of vision in exertion. It was nothing Cefwyn could see, or understand.

But it was there, in this world and the other, an unnatural twilight that roused chill winds to lash at cloaks and the manes of horses. Tristen heard it taunting him. Men at last realizing their impending danger looked up, distracted from the battle. A few lifted swords or lances to challenge the cold and the dark, and the threatened Elwynim themselves looked up, afraid. The battle between Men began to dissolve in a stinging cloud of dust, the very air suddenly aboil with pieces of leaves, twigs, grass, bits of cloth, whole branches, flying banners.

– *Hasufin! he shouted at the Wind. Here I am! Let them be! If you have no hostages – you cannot hope to govern me! I am listening to you! I shall listen so long as you can hold my attention! Talk to me, Hasufin! I am here!*

Came the hollow rush of winds and the thin shriek of men and horses caught in its path as that blurring in the world turned toward him. Some Men stood to fight, and it rolled over them. Some Men fled, and it rolled over them the same.

In the shadow now was a white light behind which were only the trees of the forest and the black shapes of the fallen. In its path were still living Men – Cefwyn's men; and to turn it from Cefwyn he could only taunt it, call it ahead, to roll over men he knew, men who had laughed with him, shared their provisions with him. Brogi was one, trying valiantly to reach his King. Kerdin Qwyll's-son was another, and his man with him.

– *Come ahead! he called to the Wind, making himself heartless. Dys shivered under him and tried to turn from the blast as he had turned from no mortal enemy, but Tristen pressed him with heels and knees, making him face it, drawing the presence down on him – for now he could feel it – as willingly, as unresistingly, as he drew the light to his hands.*

From behind him his own black banner flashed past him and to the fore of him. Andas Andas'-son was riding for the very heart of the Shadow, the Sihhë banner braced in his left hand, sword in his right. But he could not reach it. The black standard skewed back and aside on a blast of the wind, all but carrying Andas'-son from the saddle, and Andas'-son fought to hold it. His horse went down. The Shadow hesitated above him, and Andas'-son, rising, struck with his sword at empty air.

– Keep coming! Tristen shouted at it, taunted it, pleaded with it. Coward! Come to me!

Andas'-son, his horse and all went into a glare of white as if the world had torn like fabric and white nothingness shone through, pervisible, through a rip grown wider and closer. Numbing cold howled out of it as it grew. Horses reared up at the edge of it and fled in panic, trampling the dying and the dead as they escaped. Men left afoot cast down shields and weapons and ran until it passed over them and they lay dead.

"M'lord!" Uwen cried close behind him, and knowing Uwen was in its path, Tristen's heart went cold – for he was staring now directly into the rippling light-through-water burning at the very center of the rift. He was deafened by the roar of the winds. Dys, refusing to go, came up on his hind legs.

He gripped his sword and for the first time truly used the spurs, sending Dys forward as Dys himself seemed then to take his madness and go with a will, into the burning heart of the light.

It was like passing through water. Things beyond that limit were distorted, but in perfect clarity within the compass of it, he saw the bodies of men and horses lying on the ground. Debris of the forest buffeted him, flying in the wind, but he clung to the silver-wrapped sword, and the light, no illusion here, blazed from the silver until his glove smoked. The letters on the blade shone with white light: Truth, and Illusion.

Around him were ragged shapes that whirled like torn rags, that shrieked with terrified voices, and whipped away on the winds. He and Dys were the only creatures alive within the compass of the light.

Then – then the wind stopped. Then a silence. A stillness. A hush, as if hearing failed. A loneliness, a white light, with no other living creatures.

– Why, there you are, the Shadow said to him in that quiet, and the tones embraced, caressed, as the wind slid around him and beneath Dys, caressing and gentle. There you are, my prince. And here I am. Take my allegiance. I give it. I ask nothing else of you. I can show you your heart's desire. Ask me any favor and I am yours.

Time stopped, and slipped sidelong. All the world seemed extended about him, and he struggled out of that burning light into grayness again, clinging to the illusion that was himself, on the truth that was a field near Emwy.

But that place fell away from him in dizzy depth. He was elsewhere.

Came a distant sibilance like the whispering of leaves before a storm. Ynefel loomed up through a veil of mist and he stood on a promontory facing it, though he knew the fortress stood alone.

Came a rumbling in the earth, and the rock under him began to crumble in a rushing of winds and water. He had a sword – but it was useless against his enemy in this place.

Came a wind through woods, as, on the white stones of the Road, he saw himself asleep among the trees, against a stream-bank. And the Book was there.

– Tristen of Ynefel. Came a whisper through the dark and came a light through the leaves. Tristen, I do not in any fashion oppose you. I never did. Leave this intention against me, and go through the light. Be with Mauryl. You can find him again. You have that power.

He remembered leaves in the courtyard, leaves that whirled and rose up with the dust of the ground into the shape of a man. He remembered that Time was one time, and that Place was one place.

He sat, still on Dys, in the paved courtyard. He saw a young man sitting on the step, trying to read a Book. He saw Mauryl's face looking down from the wall, the youth all unseeing of his danger. And the Book was there, on the young man's knees, perilously within Hasufin's reach.

Rapidly the shadow of the walls joined the shadow of the tower, and grew long across the courtyard stones. It touched the walls, complete across the courtyard, now, and he knew that on any ordinary day he should be inside and off the parapets and out of the courtyard. . .

But he was thinking as that young man. The enemy was waiting for him. And for the Book the young man held.

– Take it up, the Wind said to him. Or shall I?

The wind suddenly picked up, skirled up the dead leaves from a corner of the wall, and those leaves rose higher and higher, dancing down the paving stones toward the tower – toward the youth, who shivered, with the Book folded in his hands, his hands between his knees as the wind danced back again. The faces set in the walls looked down in apprehension, in desperation, saying, with a voice as great as the winds, Look up, look up, young fool, and run!

The youth looked up then at the walls above his head – and recoiled from off the step. Mauryl's face loomed above him, stone like the others, wide-mouthed and angry.

The youth stumbled off the middle step, fell on the bottom one and picked himself up, staring at the face – retreated farther and farther across the stones, carrying the Book as he fled.

Came a strangely human sound, that began like the wind and ended in the choked sobs of someone in grief, but distant, as if cast up and echoed from some deep. It might have been in the real world. It might have been the youth making that sound. It might have been himself.

– Tristen, the Wind said to him, Ynefel is your proper place, this is your home, Sihhë soul, and I am your own kind – well, let us be honest: at least more hospitable than Men. The world outside offers nothing worth the having – not for the likes of us. Be reasonable. Save this young man the bother – and the grief. Would you look ahead? Ahead might persuade you.

– I am not your kind, Tristen returned angrily – and yet

the niggling doubt was there, the doubt that wondered – But what else am I? And what shall I be?

– A weapon. That's all. That's all you ever were, my prince. Mauryl used you. Men use you, – and unwisely, at that. You always had questions. Ask me. I'll answer. – Or change things. With the Book, if you take it up, you can do that. You can be anywhere you've ever been. Only the future changes. Would you free Mauryl? You can. I'm certain I don't care, if he'll mend his manners. But you can change that. I'm sure you can.

He saw light . . . light as he had seen at the beginning of everything. The other side of that light was Mauryl's fireside. He could step right through the firelight. He would be there, that first of the safest nights, most kindly nights of his life, welcomed by Mauryl's voice and warmed by Mauryl's cloak.

He would be there. Mauryl would be alive again, Summoning him out of the fire.

He could think of the library, the warm colors of faded tapestry, the many wooden balconies and the scaffolding. He could think of Mauryl's wrinkled face and white beard.

He could think of Mauryl at his ciphering, the tip of the quill working and the dry scratch of Mauryl's pen on parchment, as real as if he stood there at Mauryl's shoulder. He could step through. He could stand in the study. He could be at that very moment Mauryl Called him. He saw the firelight like a curtain before him. He could all but hear Mauryl's voice. It was that moment. He could have it all again.

Forever.

– You see? said the Wind. Seemings are all alterable. Restore what was? You are of the West, not the East. Never fear what you were. Glory in it. Look to the dawn of reason. Look to the dawn of our kind. Your name –

"My name," he shouted at it, –

– "is Tristen, Tristen, *Tristen!*"

Wings – he was certain it was Owl – clove the air in front of him. And he – *he* moved them all through Time, following Owl, chasing Owl back to where Owl belonged.

He heard his horse's hoofbeats. He felt Dys striding under him. He saw Owl flying ahead of him, black against the heart of that white luminance in the very moment it came down on him. There was no feeling-out, no conative attack this time. The Wind enveloped him with cold and sound.

– *Barrakkêth! it wailed. Barrakkêth, Kingbreaker, listen to me, only listen – I know you now! Deathmaker, you are far too great to be Mauryl's toy – listen to me!*

He fought to hold the sword, but he gripped its mortal weight, swung it into the heart of the light – the sword met insubstance, clove it, echoing, shrieking into dark as the silver burned and seared his hand.

The cold poured over him as Dys and Owl and he lost each other then. He spun through dark, nowhere, formless and cold. He had no will to move, to think, even to dream, nor wanted any.

"M'lord. Tristen, lad. Tristen!"

A horse gave a snort. He was aware of dark huge feet near his head. Of something trailing across his face, a horse's breath in his eyes. Of the world from an unaccustomed angle.

Of silence.

"M'lord." Another snort. A thump and clatter of armor nearing him. He saw a shadow, felt the touch of a hand on his face, a hand that burned his cheek, it was so very warm.

Then strong arms seized him and tried to lift him. "M'lord, help me here. Come on, ye said ye'll heed me. Come on. Come back to me, m'lord. Don't lie to me."

It was Uwen's distant voice, Uwen wanted help for something, and, obliged to try, he drew a deep breath and tried to do what Uwen wanted, which required listening, and moving, and hurting.

He saw Uwen's face, grimed and bloody, with trails of moisture down his cheeks, shadowed against a pearl gray sky. The air about them was so quiet, so very, very quiet he could hear Dys and Cass as they moved.

He could hear the wind in the leaves. The world . . . had such a wealth of textures, of colors, sights, shapes, sounds, substance . . . it all came pouring in, and the breath hurt his chest as he tried to drink it all.

"Oh, m'lord," Uwen said. "I was sure ye was dead. I looked and I looked." He stripped the wreckage of the shield from his left arm; he moved the fingers of his right hand and realized that he still held his sword. The blade was scored and bright along one edge as if some fire had burned it away. The silver circlet was fused to the quillons and the hilt, the leather wrappings hung loose and silver writing was burned bright along its center. He tried to loose his fingers and much of the gauntlet came away as if rotten with age. The skin there peeled away, leaving new, raw flesh.

He struggled to rise, with the other hand using the sword to lean on, and Uwen took it from him and helped him to stand.

All the field was leveled where they stood. There were only bodies of men and horses, and themselves.

"We won," Uwen said. "Gods know how, – we won, m'lord. Umanon and Cevulirn took the hills and kept the ambush off our backs. Then the Amefin foot come in, Lanfarnesse showed up late, and the lady's coming with the baggage. It was you we couldn't find."

"Is Cefwyn safe?"

"Aye, m'lord." Uwen lifted the hand that held his sword. "See, His Majesty's banner, bright as day, there by the center."

Tristen let go his breath, stumbled as he tried to walk toward that place shining in sunlight – the gray clouds were over them, but it was brilliant color, that banner, brilliant, hard-edged and truer than the world had ever seemed. A piece of his armor had come loose, and rattled against his leg, another against his arm.

"Don't you try," Uwen said, pulling at him as he tried to walk. "Easy, m'lord. Easy. Ye daren't walk this field, m'lord. Let me get you up on your horse. I can do it."

He nodded numbly, and let Uwen turn him toward Dys, who, exhausted, gave little difficulty about being caught.

Uwen made a stirrup of his hands and gave him a lift enough to drag himself to the saddle. Then Uwen managed to climb onto Cass with a grunt and a groan, and landed across the saddle until he could sort himself into it: Tristen waited, and Dys started to move, on his own, as Cass did, slowly.

Around them, from that vantage, the field showed littered with dead – until it reached the place where he had lain; and after that the ground was almost clear.

"It stopped?" he asked Uwen. "The Wind stopped here?"

"Aye, m'lord, the instant it veered off and took you, it stopped. Just one great shriek and it were gone, taking some of its own wi' it. And some of ours, gods help 'em. Andas is gone. So's Lusin. I thought you was gone for good, m'lord. I thought I was goin'. I thought that thing was coming right over us. But Cass was off like a fool, and I come back again and searched, and I guess I just mistook the ground, 'cause there ye was, this time, plain as plain, and Dys-lad standing over ye, having a bite of grass."

He looked up at the pallid, clouded, ordinary sky.

"What *were* that thing, m'lord?"

He shook his head slowly. For what it was, he had no Word, nor would Uwen. He turned Dys toward the place where Cefwyn's red banner flew, and saw that Ninévrisë's had just joined it.

The land along the forest-edge and across the hills had become a place of horror, riven armor and flesh tangled in clots and heaps, wherever the fighting had been thick. Someone moaned and cried for water, another for help they were not able, themselves, to give. Men moved among them in the distance, bringing both, he hoped.

They came on a little knoll, a tree, and a dead horse. One man sat with another in his arms. They wore the red of the Guelenfolk.

Erion and Denyn. The Ivanim, wounded himself, held the boy, rocking to and fro, and looked up at them as they stopped.

"Come with us," Tristen said gently. "We shall take you to the King."

"I will go there soon," Erion said faintly and bent his head against the boy's, with nothing more to say.

Tristen lingered, wishing there were magic to work, a miracle he dared do; but there was none: the boy was dead – and he would not.

He rode on with Uwen. He saw the Heron banner of Lanfarnesse and the Amefin Eagle planted on the nearer hill, the White Horse and the Wheel on the slope of the farther. They rode to the tattered red banner of the Marhanen Dragon, and the knot of weary men gathered about it.

They rode up among the Guelenfolk. He saw the faces of those about Cefwyn turn toward him. He saw hands laid on weapons. He thought that they did not know him, and lifted his free hand to show it empty . . . he saw Cefwyn's face, that was likewise stricken with fear.

"Cefwyn," he said, and dismounted.

Idrys was there, and caught at Cefwyn's arm when Cefwyn moved toward him, but Cefwyn shook him off and came and took his hand as if he feared he would break.

"I lost my shield," Tristen said, only then feeling his heart come back to him. "– And my helm. I don't know where, my lord."

"Gods." Cefwyn embraced him with a grate of metal. He shuddered and held to Cefwyn's arms when he let go. "You fool," Cefwyn said gently. "You great fool – he's gone. Aséyneddin is dead, his whole damned army has fled the field, or surrendered under m'lady's banner! Come. Come. The rest of us are coming in. Pelumer is found . . . lost himself in the woods, to his great disgust . . ."

"It is no fault of his."

"Holy gods, – Wizards. No, I knew it. Ninévrisë's had word of Sovrag; his cousin was wiped out, lost, and Sovrag couldn't pass upriver. A blackness hung over the river, and the boats lost themselves while it lasted . . . even so, they've taken down the Emwy bridge. The rebels that did escape us won't cross. – Gods, are you all right, Tristen?"

He flexed his hand, wiped at his eyes. "I'm very well."

He walked away then. Uwen led Dys and Cass behind him.

He had no idea where to go, now. He thought he would sleep a while. True sleep had been very long absent from him.

– *Emuin*, he said, but he had no answer – a sense of presence, but nothing close. Possibly Emuin was asleep himself.

"Where are ye goin', m'lord?" Uwen asked. "Sounds as if they'll be bringin' the wagons in, if ye please. We'll have canvas 'twixt us and the weather. She's clouded up, looking like rain tonight."

He looked at the sky, at common, gray-bottomed clouds. He looked about him at the woods. Owl had gone, Shadow that he was, into the trees, where he was more comfortable. But he knew where Owl was. Owl had gone to the river, where the small creatures had not been startled into hiding. Owl would wait for night. That was the kind of creature Owl was, as kings were kings and lords were lords and the likes of Uwen Lewen's-son would always stay faithful.

He saw no shadow in the sky. None on the horizon. He did not know how to answer Uwen's question, but he thought that he would sit down on the rocks near the road, and wait, and see what the world of Men was about to be.

Sideshow
Sheri S. Tepper

Barbaric customs and bizarre human cults are preserved on the planet Elsewhere. The rest of the universe has been taken over by the Hobbs Land Gods, which means that everyone alive, except the people on Elsewhere, lives in perfect harmony with nature and with each other.

But Elsewhere is ruled by computer-encrypted professors who have been dead for a thousand years. The professors were dedicated to maintaining human diversity. Their ancient analogs are dedicated to something infinitely more sinister.

The time has come to consider whether enslavement by the Hobbs Land Gods is not preferable to the depravity being cultivated on Elsewhere. The time has come to ask the Big Question, What is the Destiny of Man? And answer it.

'Tepper has developed into one of the best novelists in the field . . . she is magnificently skilled' *Locus*

'*Sideshow* deserves to be on the same shelf as any classic you care to name. Sheri Tepper is one of the greats of human literature' *Analog Science Fiction and Fact*

ISBN 0 00 648004 7